FOURPENNY FLYER

The Easter Empire Trilogy

BERYL KINGSTON

AGORA BOOKS

ABOUT THE AUTHOR

Beryl Kingston is the author of 30 novels with over a million copies sold. She has been a writer since she was 7 when she started producing poetry. She was evacuated to Felpham at the start of WWII, igniting an interest in one-time resident poet William Blake which later inspired her novel *The Gates of Paradise*. She was an English teacher from 1952 until 1985 when she became a full-time writer after her debut novel, *Hearts and Farthings*, became a bestseller. Kingston continued writing bestsellers for the next 14 years with titles ranging from family sagas to modern stories and historical novels. She currently lives in West Sussex and has three children, five grandchildren, and ten great-grandchild.

ALSO BY BERYL KINGSTON

HISTORICAL FICTION

Hearts and Farthings

Kisses and Ha'pennies

A Time to Love

London Pride

War Baby

Two Silver Crosses

A Stitch in Time

Avalanche of Daisies

Suki

Gates of Paradise

Hearts of Oak

Off the Rails

THE EASTER EMPIRE TRILOGY

Tuppenny Times

Fourpenny Flyer

Sixpenny Stalls

THE OCTAVIA TRILOGY

Octavia

Octavia's War

The Internet Revolutionary

THE JACKSON FAMILY SAGA

Everybody's Somebody

Citizen Army

FICTION

Maggie's Boy

Laura's Way

Gemma's Journey

Neptune's Daughter

Francesca and the Mermaid

NON-FICTION

Lifting the Curse

A Family at War

FOURPENNY FLYER

BERYL KINGSTON

This edition published in 2020 by Agora Books

First published in Great Britain in 1990 by Sphere

Agora Books is a division of Peters Fraser + Dunlop Ltd

55 New Oxford Street, London WC1A 1BS

To Mary

CHAPTER 1

It is a shattering thing to have your dreams suddenly come true. Exciting certainly, but the excitement brings apprehension nudging along behind it, and to experience two such contrary emotions at one and the same time is uplifting but daunting, as Harriet Sowerby was beginning to understand.

Ever since she'd first seen the gentry arriving for the hunt ball at the Athenaeum, stepping down so elegantly from their grand carriages and dressed so splendidly in all their finery, she'd longed to attend a ball. She'd always known it wasn't possible, of course, because her father wasn't even on the fringes of Bury St Edmund's society. He worked as a junior clerk for Mr Alfred Cole, the bookseller in the Buttermarket, and although he and his wife were very proud of his position, he certainly wasn't gentry and neither was she. But that didn't stop her dreaming.

And now, despite everything, here she was, Harriet Sowerby, in the summer of her sixteenth year, actually dressing for her very first ball. She could hardly believe her good fortune.

She stood on her own in her little narrow bedroom, trembling with excitement, her fingers fumbling the tiny pearl buttons on her white ball gown, and her heart jumping like a wild thing caged. Her movements were so quick and her breathing so erratic that she made the candle gutter and spit wax. She withdrew from it at once, of course, pulling the long straight skirt of the gown away from harm, for it would never have done to get it burnt or spattered with candle grease, not after all the money Miss Pettie must have lavished on hiring it. Dear Miss Pettie. This was all her doing. She was like a fairy godmother, arriving one afternoon with the ticket, 'as a little reward for my Thursday helpmate, who has been so kind to me, coming to my house week after week to assist with the sewing'. And then, when Mr Sowerby had pulled a sour face and protested that, much though he appreciated Miss Pettie's undoubted kindness he could not afford the extravagance of a ball gown, she had hired a gown and long gloves and a dear little pair of embroidered dancing pumps, and even looked out a tortoiseshell comb of her own 'to finish off your hair, my dear'.

Harriet had long straight fair hair which her mother always insisted should be worn in a modest plait behind her back or tucked away underneath her white day-cap. So it was a pleasure to be able to display it for once, especially as she knew that neither of her parents really approved but couldn't say so for fear of annoying Miss Pettie. They were rather in awe of Miss Pettie, for although they all attended the same Unitarian church, Miss Pettie was rich and lived in one of the grand houses on Angel Hill and had a fine carriage to drive her about the town, and the Sowerbys were really rather poor.

Harriet brushed her long hair and combed it until there wasn't a single tangle left, and then she set about the complicated process of coaxing it into a fashionable topknot, holding the pins between her teeth, and smoothing and patting until she was quite sure there wasn't a hair out of place. It would have been a great deal easier if she'd had a looking glass so that she could see what she was doing, but she wasn't even allowed a little hand mirror. Her mother, who was very religious and horribly strict, maintained that mirrors were an encouragement to vanity in young girls and wouldn't permit one in her daughter's room — although she had a cheval glass in her own bedroom, and checked her appearance in it every single morning. As Harriet knew, because she'd watched her doing it. But perhaps, she thought wryly, fixing the tortoiseshell comb in place, it was only young girls who grew vain if they looked at themselves in a glass.

However, there were ways round most things if you used your wits. When her hair was dressed to her satisfaction, she put the candle on the edge of her wooden chair and knelt down on the floor beside it so that her face was level with the low window. Her mother might have forbidden mirrors, and of course her mother had to be obeyed because that was one of the Commandments, but there was nothing anyone could do to prevent a reflection in a window.

The Sowerbys lived in a cramped four-roomed cottage, next to a laundry at the unfashionable end of Churchgate Street in Bury St Edmunds. One of a terraced pair, it had been built at the time of the great Elizabeth for a local butter merchant who had money to spare, and, in its day, it had been quite a desirable residence. Now it was dark and damp and old-fashioned, and the fact that it was the best that Mr Sowerby could afford was a source of constant irritation to his wife, who did daily battle with mice and cockroaches and weekly battle with bugs and fleas, so that all four rooms always smelt of camphor and turpentine.

There were two rooms upstairs, just as there were two rooms down, and in both cases the back room, which was small and narrow, led directly out of the front room, which occupied the meagre eight-foot width of the house. Harriet's bedroom was above the kitchen and its one low window gave out to an inner courtyard where the laundry hurled its daily suds and the privies oozed filth onto the cobbles in winter and attracted a buzzing cloud of flies in the summer. What little light that managed to filter in through the window was smeared and grubby, as though it too had been dunked in the dirty suds with the washing. But at night and with a candle to encourage it, it would sometimes give you back your reflection. As it was doing now.

There was her face, ghostly white in the smudgy glass, but looking very grown-up beneath those unfamiliar folds of twisted hair. Do I look right? she wondered, peering at the image. It was so important to look right when you went to a ball. Balls were where you met important people. Balls were where young ladies of quality met the young men who were going to marry them and make them happy ever after. She knew that because she'd just finished reading Miss Austen's new book *Pride and Prejudice*.

For Harriet Sowerby had a dream. Nourished by all the successful matchmaking in Miss Austen's novels and encouraged by Miss Pettie's highly romantic view of the world, she felt sure that one day a young man would fall in love with her and take her away from the home where she wasn't wanted into a new life where she would be happy and cherished. She was good and quiet and obedient, except in her thoughts, and surely, surely there must be a reward somewhere, sometime, for all the effort that took her.

It was going to be such a splendid occasion, a 'Grand Subscription Ball' to celebrate the defeat of that awful Napoleon and the end of the French war, which had been going on for years and years. It had started in 1792, so Miss Pettie said. Imagine that! Seven years before she was even born. And now it was over at last. Everybody who was anybody in Bury society would be certain to be at the ball — Miss Pettie said so. The mayor and Mr Cole the bookseller, and the Honeywoods who were very, very rich and owned all the land from Bury to

Rattlesden, and the great Easter family who were newsagents and owned newspaper shops all over England and were even richer than the Honeywoods and lived next door to Miss Pettie. And tonight she would be dancing among them. She, Harriet Sowerby. Was it any wonder she was trembling? Oh it was a very great honour. But the nicest thing about it was the fact that her mother hadn't been invited.

Harriet was always extremely careful to obey her mother in every particular, and when she sat in church of a Sunday, she accepted that it was a child's duty to 'honour' her parents, which as far as she could see meant doing everything they said. That was what the Commandments required, so that was what she did. But secretly she knew that she didn't really like either of her parents. They made her too unhappy and they frightened her too much.

Her life might have been easier if she'd had brothers and sisters, but she was an only child, born in the first month of the last year of the old century, when her mother was past forty-four and her father nearly forty, and as an only child she had to carry the full weight of her mother's rigid upbringing.

'An imp of Satan,' Mrs Sowerby had said, looking down at the peaceful face of her newborn infant. 'An imp of Satan, like all newborn creatures. Full of original sin. We must tame her, Mr Sowerby. It is our plain Christian duty.'

'Indeed we must,' Mr Sowerby agreed.

They set about their God-given task immediately.

So Harriet was taught to control her appetites from the first bewildered day of her life. When she cried to be fed, her mother made her wait, listening to her screams and telling herself complacently that it was necessary to fight sin from the very outset. When she was a little toddling creature, no more than a twelve-month-old, her curiosity was curbed with a stick. When she was three and able to express a preference for pretty clothes and pretty toys, they were instantly removed from her and never returned so as to inculcate a proper sense of modesty and decorum. By the time she was seven, she was quiet and withdrawn and fearful, a perfect child according to Mrs Sowerby's religious cronies, all of whom were convinced that children should be seen and not heard and that the best children obeyed without question whatever their parents saw fit to command.

But although Harriet obeyed any order meekly and immediately, rebellion bubbled inside her sleek little head. As it was doing now.

'I am going to the ball,' she said to her reflection, 'and Mama cannot stop me.' What a lovely private pleasure it was to be able to say such things!

In Angel Hill, a mere three hundred yards away from the Sowerby cottage, Miss Pettie was just beginning to dress for the ball, and next door to Miss Pettie, the Easter family were still at dinner.

It was a very grand occasion, for the great Nan Easter had invited all her family, and her lover, Mr Calverley Leigh, and her closest business associates, in order to make an important announcement. The firm she had founded, when her children were little more than babies and the French war had just begun, had grown from a simple newspaper round to a huge empire with shops all over London, and in most of the important towns in the south of England too. Now it was time to expand even further, and to do that she would need to delegate some of her responsibilities.

'I been a-giving the matter the most careful thought,' she said to her guests, 'and it do seem to me that changes will need to be made. There are some have urged me to marry and share the burden with a husband, and there was a time when I agreed to it, under duress mark you. But I have to tell 'ee I en't the marrying kind and that's the truth of it. I been a widow too long and I like my independence. So what I propose to do is this. I propose to take my two sons into the firm as managers, Billy to take charge of warehousing, Johnnie to be responsible for sales throughout the country, with salaries commensurate, as you would expect. That being so, the firm will henceforth be known as A Easter and Sons. I have given orders for the London signs to be altered as from today.'

Her elder son, Billy, was delighted by the news, but John Easter was shattered. So shattered he couldn't speak. He knew that his eyes were staring and that his mouth had fallen open and that he probably looked as much of a fool as he felt, but there was nothing he could do about it. He couldn't even assume a more acceptable expression. And that annoyed him because it was extremely important to him to appear calm and controlled, no matter what he might be feeling. In fact, the more powerful the emotions that racked him, the more necessary it was to keep them hidden. But really this was too extraordinary for words or control. For years and years he'd been planning what he would do if he were in charge of the firm and now, suddenly, when he was least expecting it, she'd given him the power to do it. It was a dream come true.

The faces round the table were turning in his direction, smiling congratulations. His sister Annie was looking up at him to mouth, 'Well done!' But he hadn't done anything. Except dream. And try to tell his mother the truth sometimes, without upsetting her, which was horribly difficult because she was the most determined and powerful woman.

Billy was looking very pleased with himself, leaning back in his chair so that their old nurse Bessie could kiss him and stroke the fair hair back from his forehead the way she always did when she was comforting or approving. But Billy had always known he would have a place in the firm, being the elder son. Everyone had known. It had been talked about at his twenty-first birthday party two years ago. 'When Billy goes into the firm...' While *his* twenty-first, last summer, had passed without comment of any kind. And now this!

'You won't regret it, Mama,' Billy said, smiling at his mother.

She smiled back at him, so warmly that her look could have been an embrace.

It was always the same, John thought, as his heart gave its familiar yearning tug at the sight. Whenever she looked at his brother or his sister, there was this easy warmth between them, this accepting, tolerant affection. It was something he had ached for all his life, and yet, whatever he'd done to earn it, it had never been given to him. But now, perhaps, it would all be different, for now she had given him a place in the firm. An important place, the sort of place he'd always dreamed of. I suppose I ought to say something to thank her, he thought, for the faces had turned his way again expectantly.

'In two years, Mama,' he said, 'I will double your profits. I give you my word.'

And at that she smiled at him too. 'I don't doubt it,' she said.

Then she was speaking again, detailing company arrangements, praising old Bessie's husband, Thiss, for the way he'd been running the East Anglian branch of the business, appointing Cosmo Teshmaker as head of the London branch. Another surprise, because Mr Teshmaker was the company lawyer, but a surprise they should have been prepared for because his loyalty to the company was peerless.

The talk about the table buzzed on, but John didn't hear any of it. He was too busy with his thoughts. Now he could put all his carefully written plans into operation. Even when his mother signified that the meal was over and everybody else went rushing upstairs to get ready for the ball he was still absorbed.

He walked across to the window, and stood there, looking down at the sloping square of Angel Hill below him. It was full of stalls and crowded with people, for a fair was being held to celebrate the peace. Now that Wellington had finally defeated the French army and Napoleon had been sent into exile in Elba there was reason to celebrate.

Dusk had gathered while they had eaten their meal, and now rush lights were being lit beside the stalls and sideshows. Two huge lights were beginning to flare at the top of the swings, and he noticed that the moment they were lit the swings disappeared in a total and obliterating darkness. It was a curious phenomenon, and one he'd often observed, that the sudden arrival of light actually restricted one's vision, which was the very thing it was designed to assist.

There were so many puzzles, so many hazards. Life was beset with them. And the human hazards were the most difficult of all.

People were hard enough for him to contend with one at a time because he was terribly shy. In the mass they were impossible, constantly on the move, shifting and turning and avoiding, leaving sentences half finished, walking about or away, changing their direction, their appearance, their minds. Was it any wonder he preferred the company of his family and the splendid dependability of mathematics? Left to his own devices he would have avoided the fairground, which was very definitely not to his taste, and the victory ball, which he was going to attend because his mother expected it of him, and hidden himself away in his bedroom to continue work on his coach timetables.

His mother was snuffing out the candles, moving briskly about the room, and working at speed as she always did so that she left cotton trails of smoke prickling in the air behind her. She was so quick. It was one of the many disconcerting things about her.

Now her skirts swished behind him and he could see her hand pale in the half-light, reaching forward towards the curtain. So he stood aside politely, thinking she wanted to draw them. But no, as he realised with the slight contraction of his heart that such knowledge always brought, she was going to talk to him.

'Could you truly double our profits in two years?' she asked abruptly.

'I believe so,' he answered. This was better. This was business. This was the thing he was best at.

'Tell me how,' she said.

'First,' he said happily, 'we could extend our trade along all Mr Chaplin's coach routes. The Portsmouth route is well established now.' What a satisfaction to be able to make such a claim, for *he* had established it, and single-handedly what was more. 'That being so...'

'We should use the same method upon other routes. A sound enough argument in all conscience. Howsomever we en't the only newsagents nowadays. We may have the monopoly in London, Johnnie, but in the provinces there's competition a-plenty. How do 'ee propose to deal with that, eh?'

'By timing,' he said. 'That is how it could be done. Sometimes the local shops are first with the news and sometimes we are. If we could make certain that we were *always* first, then we would be the first shop that local people would visit, come what may.'

She cocked her head towards him, alert and listening and dark-eyed like a robin. 'A matter we en't like to control, surely?'

'Ah but we could, Mama. It is simply a question of how we use the coaches. That is all. At present we do what everyone else does. We despatch our papers as though they were passengers. Those for York travel on the York stage, those for Norwich on the Norwich stage, and so on.'

'How else?'

'Why from stage to stage Mama, without rest. Passengers must pause for rest and refreshment, but why should our papers wait with them? They have no need of either.'

'Twould take a deal of organisation,' his mother said thoughtfully.

It was a moment of such pride. Such triumph. 'It is already done, Mama!'

Her dark eyes gleamed. 'For York and Norwich?' she teased.

'For every town we serve.' He was grinning like an idiot, his pleasure was so intense.

'Indeed?' Still teasing, for she knew it was likely. Whatever else she might think of this brooding son of hers, his intelligence had never been in question.

'I have been working upon such a scheme for — for rather a long time.' It was actually more than three years, and he'd enjoyed every minute of it, for mathematical calculations were the only solace when he was lonely. And being so shy he was often very lonely.

'I would like to see your conclusions.'

'My notebooks are upstairs,' he offered hopefully. 'You could see them now if you had a mind to.'

But Billy was already leaping down the stairs two at a time, the way he always did when he was excited. He was spruced and ready for the rest of the evening. Delay was impossible.

The rhythm of his descent ended with the thud and scuffle of landing, and presently his disembodied face peered at them through the half-light and the half-open door. The bottle green of his coat merged with the bottle green shadows of the room, but the white linen of his neckcloth was clearly visible, arranged in such thick folds underneath his chin that it looked as though it was propping up his head. His bulbous forehead was noticeable, too, gleaming like mother-of-pearl in the light of the last two candles his mother had left burning in the sconces beside the door.

'Oh come on, Johnnie,' he reproached. 'Ain't you ready yet? We shall be late if you don't look sharp. It's the opening quadrille in less than ten minutes, you know. Can't miss that.'

John would have been more than happy to miss the entire ball but, as always, his mother gave him no chance to demur or even comment.

'Quite right, Billy,' she said, dusting the palms of her hands against each other, swish, swish, the way she always did. Conversation over, ball begun in an instant: swish, swish. 'I will see your notebooks first thing tomorrow morning, Johnnie.'

And so the ball had to be faced. There was nothing else for it. Now I shall be trodden into the ground, he thought, wryly, as he followed his family across the square. The ladies of Bury all had such enormous feet, and wine seemed to deprive them of their sense of direction. Still, at least it was in the Athenaeum.

John Easter liked the Athenaeum. It was such a proper building, designed according to strict classical principles in two neat storeys, its tall windows perfectly balanced, three on either side of the entrance and three on either side of the balcony, a dependable, pristine building, painted white and maintaining perfect poise despite the slope of the hillside on which it stood. If only they weren't holding a ball there, he could have enjoyed it very much.

I shall stay beside Cosmo Teshmaker all evening, he decided, for Mr Teshmaker had a club foot and although he walked extremely well, with an odd gliding grace, he would hardly be able to dance. Yes, yes, that is what I will do. And he followed the lawyer into the ballroom and the sudden dazzle of the chandeliers.

The room was already buzzing with people, all dressed in their very best, the gentlemen red-faced with drink and gallantry, the ladies powdered and perfumed and twittering. John's heart contracted with alarm at the sound of them, for they were already gossiping, or fishing for compliments — which they manifestly didn't deserve — or hitting people with their fans or giggling about nothing. How could he possibly make conversation if he were introduced to any of them?

There were three in the far corner tossing their heads about like trees in a storm. And what heads! The coiffeurs must have been working all day to produce such complications. The tallest of the three had ringlets dangling beside her cheeks, plaits circling her ears and two stiff plumes of hair standing up above her forehead as though they'd been stuck there with glue. And her dress was almost as complicated as her hair, with a lace collar about her neck and at least three different kinds of sleeve, worn one on top of the next, and so many frills and flounces about the hem of her skirt that she looked like a wooden spinning top, particularly as she was moving with a similar speed and motion. Her two companions were similar creatures, and they were all making such a noise, like a flock of starlings. How could he manage conversation with ladies like that?

He was just wondering whether he could lead Mr Teshmaker into a quiet corner to discuss business when he saw his brother Billy approaching the shortest of the ladies and bowing and grinning at her for all the world as if he were asking her to dance. Oh surely not! Passing the necessary pleasantries, that was what he'd be doing. But no, the shortest one was handing him her card, ringlets bobbing. And he was writing in it. Oh my goodness! Now I shall have to endure an introduction. I don't see how I can avoid it. I'll wager their feet are gargantuan.

'An uncommon pretty trio,' Mr Teshmaker said. 'Are they known to you?'

'Why no,' John said. 'Although I fear they soon will be. Billy seems to know 'em.'

'Then perhaps I may prevail upon your brother for an introduction,' Mr Teshmaker said.

'Do you intend to dance, sir?'

'Why yes, indeed,' Mr Teshmaker said. 'As often as I may and as there are young ladies who will agree to partner me.'

It was a blow. Really quite a severe blow, for what excuse for not dancing could he now find?

'I had hoped to talk business to 'ee,' he said.

'And so you shall, Mr John,' the lawyer said as he began to glide away, 'so you shall, there being plenty to talk about.' And he was gone into the vociferous crowd, heading towards Billy and the spinning top.

Not for the first time in his life, John wished that he had the power to shrink away to nothing. He felt so conspicuous left alone among so many people. He looked for his mother, but she was dancing with the mayor, for his sister, but she was dancing with her husband, James, for Billy, but he was leaping round the spinning top. He was just beginning to hope that he could creep out while nobody was looking when he saw his mother's next-door neighbour bearing down upon him, old eyes glinting. Miss Amelia Pettie, who was so ancient she creaked when she moved and wore the most dreadful false curls made of yellow horsehair and, what was even worse, would insist on matchmaking all the time. He and Billy looked upon her as a joke, and now here she was, seizing him by the arm with her tatty old fan raised ready to whack him.

'La, you bad boy, John Easter,' she said, 'hiding yourself away I do declare. What would your dear mother say?'

'No, no, Miss Pettie,' he stuttered. 'I do assure you...'

'You should be dancing, my dear, with all the other young things,' the old lady insisted, tugging at her curls. 'Where's the point in a victory ball, eh, if the young don't enjoy it? That's what I should like to know. Where's the point?'

'Oh I do enjoy it,' he said. 'I've a score of dances booked already.'

'Oh you bad wicked boy!' she chortled. 'Let me see your card, do, for I long to know who they are.' And, before he could stop her, she had taken his card from his pocket and opened it wide.

Its emptiness fairly screamed up at them.

'Why John, what is this?' the old lady said, and she gave both sets of curls another tug in her agitation. 'You must not be shy,

18

my dear. Oh indeed, you must not. We can't have our dear John a wallflower. 'Twon't do at all. Now come, look around you and tell me which of these delightful young ladies you would like to meet. I will arrange an introduction. You have only to say the word.'

Caught! Trapped! How could he escape? He looked around him frantically at the tumult in the hall, at gloved hands gesticulating and dancing pumps bounding, at muslins flowing like gossip and gauzes drifting like dreams, at scores of fans fluttering and tapping, at hundreds of curls bobbing like coiled springs, at eyes unnaturally bright and cheeks flushed by wine and rouge, and his heart beat more painfully because he'd been caught out in a lie, and she was putting pressure on him that he couldn't resist, and he couldn't see a single lady he could bear to talk to, let alone dance with.

'You are very kind, Miss Pettie,' he murmured, swallowing with difficulty because his mouth had suddenly grown dry. 'Howsomever, I do not...'

'Tush!' Miss Pettie said, thwacking him on the forearm with her fan. 'Now look 'ee there. Ain't that a pretty creature?' And she actually used her awful fan to point at some poor young lady, as though she were buying a sheep at the market.

He was so embarrassed he didn't know where to put himself, but the old lady insisted, shaking his arm and bouncing those awful false curls. 'Look my dear, look there.' And, in the end, he had to obey her, because people were beginning to look at *them*.

There was a slender girl standing perfectly still beside the staircase, her hands clasped before her, her features composed, as pale and motionless as a candle. She was dressed entirely in white, in a simple gown made of some soft material which was probably lawn, he thought, for it swathed the gentle curves of her bosom so modestly, and its long skirt hung in soft folds in the best classical tradition. Her skin was as pale as alabaster, her eyes deep blue, and her hair was so very fair it looked silver in the candlelight, straight, neat, light hair, parted in the centre and drawn back into a modest topknot on the crown of her head. Her simplicity and stillness were quite dramatic in the hubbub around her, among the frills and furbelows and the ringlets and braids. 'Yes,' he said. 'She is uncommon pretty.'

'Such good fortune,' Miss Pettie was saying. 'She belongs to my church, you know. I brought her to the ball myself, along with little Miss Turnkey and the two Miss Browns. You must meet her, my dear.'

She was dragging him by the arm, trotting through the crowd towards the girl. 'Miss Pettie,' he begged, 'pray do walk a little more slowly. I cannot keep pace with you.' It was intolerable to be dragged about like a sack of washing and he really didn't want to meet any of these young ladies at all, not even a nice, quiet, pretty one.

But he was wasting his breath. Miss Pettie had caught the scent of a match and nothing and no one could deflect her now.

So that was how Mr John Henry Easter found himself dancing the minuet with Miss Harriet Sowerby and, although he would never have admitted it to Miss Pettie, it was really quite a pleasant experience. She was so light on her feet and so very slender that to dance with her was like dancing with a shadow. And she was extremely shy, even worse than he was, ducking her head whenever he spoke to her and blushing. But faintly, of course, for like everything else about her, even her blush was subdued, being the faintest trace of apricot pink that spread across her pale cheeks and rose from the warm folds of her gown into the translucent skin of her throat. He had never seen another young lady quite like her, and at the end of the minuet he asked if he might be allowed to dance with her again, adding, 'If you have any to spare, that is,' in case he seemed too eager.

She took her card from the reticule dangling on her arm and fumbled with it nervously. Her gloves were too large and clumsy for her hands, so he bent forward as if to help her and saw with a pang of pity and fellow feeling underneath its fine gilt heading, 'Grand Subscription Ball, Saturday May 18th, 1814', the card was almost unmarked.

'I — it is — I mean —' she stuttered, folding both hands across the card as if to protect it. And there was that blush again and that soft lower lip was held down by two charmingly crooked white teeth.

He rushed to reassure her, opening his own card and holding it up for her to see. 'I have always found these occasions impossible,' he confided. 'I never know what to say, you see, and most of the young ladies here are such teases. They rag me all the time.' And then he realised that he might have gone too far and that what he was saying could easily be misconstrued as criticism. 'I do not find fault, you understand,' he said.

'I do not like being teased either, Mr Easter,' she confessed. 'It makes me blush.' And she blushed to confess it.

'If you will allow me the honour of the next dance,' he said, feeling marvellously gallant, 'I promise I will not tease you.'

So she allowed him the honour of the next dance, and the next and as many more as Miss Pettie and propriety permitted. And they told one another how splendid it was that the long war was over at last, and she confessed that she had always been afraid of the dark in case the French had invaded and were lurking just around the corner, and he told her that dark nights could be uncommon beautiful, 'all by yourself with only the stars for company'. And for a brief moment he wondered whether he might ask her to take a turn about the square in the darkness of this particular night and thought better of it because it would have seemed presumptuous, and in any case the square was full of stalls.

But it was time for the first interval and refreshments, so the offer wasn't made and they went in to supper together instead.

'This is my very first ball,' Harriet confessed.

'Then may it be the first of many.'

'I never ever thought I would dance in the Athenaeum,' she said, as they walked up the grand staircase together. 'I've dreamed of it often enough, but I never thought my dream would come true.'

'This is a night for dreams to come true,' he said. 'One of mine came true at dinner.'

'Did it really,' she said, all eyes and interest.

So he told her about it, how he'd planned to extend the business, how the plans were written 'down to the last little detail', how they'd all expected his mother to marry and hand over control of the firm to her new husband, and how she'd changed her mind and given it to him and Billy instead. 'I still can't believe it,' he said. 'It's too good to be true. But I mean to make a great success of it, you may depend on that.'

'I know exactly how you feel,' she said, smiling happily at him. 'And I'm sure you will.'

'Capital ball, eh?' Billy said as he breezed past them with four glasses of fruit punch balanced on a tray.

And for the first time in his life John wasn't prevaricating when he agreed.

CHAPTER 2

When the final gallop of the Grand Subscription Ball shrieked to a boisterous finish, it was well after two o'clock in the morning and Harriet Sowerby was beginning to feel anxious. She had never sat up later than a quarter past ten in all her life, and at midnight she'd been drenched with fatigue. Now, glancing fearfully at the clock like a pale Cinderella, she was wondering what sort of reception she would receive when she finally got home to Churchgate Street.

Mr Easter returned her to her table, where Aggie Turnkey and the two Miss Browns were waiting with old Miss Pettie, and after a flurry of leave-taking and a confusion of movement and departure, she climbed into Miss Pettie's chaise for the second time that evening for the return trot about the town. But where she had been quivering with excitement on the way out, she was rigid with apprehension on the way back. And the nearer she got to her home, the more afraid she was. Church-gate Street was a mere hundred yards from the Athenaeum so she could have walked home if Miss Pettie had allowed it, and perhaps got back a little earlier, but the old lady had insisted on delivering each of her charges 'to the door, my dears', and that meant taking a round trip all about the town, for Aggie lived in Pump Lane in the easternmost corner and the two Miss Browns had a modest house beside the Risby Gate, and of course Miss Pettie delivered them to their doors first, because they were considerably higher in society than Harriet Sowerby, and whatever else might be said about Miss Pettie, she was acutely aware of the niceties of social etiquette.

So it was nearly three o'clock before the chaise finally trundled to a halt in the narrow roadway outside the Sowerbys' cottage. Harriet climbed out and stood beside her uncompromising front door, shivering in the chill air. There was a single candle burning in the front room and she could see the huddled shape of her father sitting disagreeably before the fire and her mother's shadowy figure walking stiffly towards the door. The air of disapproval in the room was unmistakable, even at that distance, and yet when Mrs Sowerby opened the door, she was unctuous with charm and polite gratitude.

'How can I *ever* thank you, my *dear* Miss Pettie, for the honour you do my humble family? You are too, too kind.'

'Not at all, Mrs Sowerby,' Miss Pettie said, happily. 'The child was excellent company. Oh, quite excellent. Drive on, Mullins. Straight home, if you please.'

Mrs Sowerby's tone changed the moment the front door closed. 'I cannot imagine what sort of hour you call this!' she said sternly to her shivering daughter. 'Your father and I have sat up *four and a half hours* after we should have been in bed and asleep. I hope you realise what an *inconvenience* you have caused.'

Harriet tried to deflect her mother's wrath by an apology. 'I am very sorry, Mama,' she murmured, looking down meekly at the flagstones.

It didn't work. 'After all the money we've spent on your education,' Mrs Sowerby ranted, 'all the trials and tribulations, all the scrimping and saving, I should have thought the very *least* we could expect was to be allowed to sleep sound in our beds at night. But no, you see how it is, Mr Sowerby, we give her an *inch* and this is how she repays us, *forcing* us to sit up all hours.' She was well into her harangue by now and swollen with the pleasure of it, her small grey eyes glaring, her long face flushed with righteous indignation. 'Well let me tell you this, my girl, you needn't think we shall be so quick to allow you such a treat the next time you come a-begging for it. You'll ask in vain if this is the way you intend to go on.'

'Unnecessary luxuries,' her father said sternly from his seat before the fire, 'invariably provoke selfishness in the young.' His chin was covered in grizzly stubble and his cheeks were lined by fatigue, but Harriet felt no sympathy for him.

It was horribly unfair, she thought, and quite untrue. She hadn't begged to be allowed to go to the ball. She never begged her parents for anything. It was a point of honour with her. But she said nothing for fear of provoking a beating. She knew how easy it was to provoke punishment and her mother's chastening rod was hanging beside the mantelpiece, ready for use and glistening blood red in the firelight. Meekness and stillness were the only defence she knew, so she stood quite still before her mother's renewed assault, listening to the click and rustle of the coals and watching the flickering pattern of the firelight on the flagstones, and taking great care not to let the slightest tremor of an expression appear on her face, as if she had been frozen to the spot. Only her thoughts moved, and although her mother couldn't know it, her thoughts were boiling.

'What have you got to say for yourself, eh, girl?' her father growled when Mrs Sowerby finally paused for breath.

'I am truly sorry, Papa,' she said obediently, 'to have been the cause of your distress. 'Twas not intended.' But she didn't look up at him.

'Let us pray!' her mother ordered, slapping the family Bible onto the table with a crash that made Harriet flinch visibly, despite her self-control.

The little involuntary shiver gave her mother an exquisite sense of satisfaction. 'Our Father,' she said happily.

So for the next twenty minutes Harriet was prayed over and prayed for. Her selfishness was deplored, and her tardiness, and the fact that she had forgotten the fifth Commandment, and finally Jesus himself was asked to forgive her sins through the power of His blessed blood, and she was allowed to take the candle and precede her parents up their narrow wooden staircase in the corner of the room and creep away to bed.

At the top of the staircase there was a dark space which the Sowerbys glorified with the title 'the landing', but which was actually little bigger than a doormat and served only to provide somewhere to stand while you opened the bedroom door. Here, Harriet set the candle in its niche and dutifully opened the door for her parents, standing aside while they entered, waiting while they lit their own candles, and then walking subserviently past them into the darkness of her own room.

It looked more like a cell than ever after the splendour and colour of the Athenaeum with its whitewashed walls and its sparse furniture and that formidable black crucifix suspended above her uncomfortable truckle bed, like an unforgiving eye of God. She snuffed out the candle, undressed quickly and got into bed, ready for sleep to blot out the unpleasant vision. Somewhere on the other side of the town she knew that a huge white moon was flooding the houses with clean light, but here the only hint of its presence was the silver edging that glowed along the ridge of rooftops immediately above her. The ball was over and Cinderella was back among the ashes, with her hired gown hanging on a hook on the door and her dancing pumps waiting to be cleaned in the morning.

But she *had* been to the ball and she'd danced with one of the princes of the town — Mr Easter, no less. Wouldn't Mama be cross if she knew that!

She folded her hands neatly together above the coverlet and

began to say her own silent prayers, inside her head where only God could hear them: Thank you for letting me go to the Ball, Lord, and letting me dance with Mr Easter. Could you possibly put it into his head to dance with me again? I would be very grateful. Of course, if you cannot do this, I shall accept my lot with cheerfulness... She knew that was the right sort of thing to tell her Maker, because He was an extreme power and as such, of course, He had to be propitiated... For Thine is the Kingdom, the Power and the Glory. Amen.

ON ANGEL HILL the revellers were still thronging the cobbled square, away from the deserted stalls and the debris of the fair, and the object of Harriet's prayers was climbing over the high flint wall into the shadowy darkness of the abbey gardens. He climbed under protest, because even in his pleasantly befuddled state he knew it was hardly a proper thing for an Easter to be doing, but Billy and his friends were already on the other side and hooting at him to join them and Billy was so drunk he would have to be looked after, so he really had little choice.

He had come drifting out of the Athenaeum with a head full of tender dreams, remembering the softness of that quiet girl, and the delicacy of her apricot blush and the way her long, light eyelashes shadowed her pale cheeks. Indeed, if it hadn't been for the fact that he was an eminently sensible young man, he might almost have fancied he was falling in love. But then Billy had erupted from the hall and gone staggering off towards the abbey gardens, and there was nothing for it but to cease dreaming and follow him.

The lawns below him were velvety black in the moonlight and there was still a faint trace of the woodbine and musk roses that had perfumed the place at dusk, and further down the hill, where the river Lark was gurgling towards the fishponds, a nightingale was singing its passionate throbbing song. For a few seconds, as he scrabbled precariously astride the rough flints, grabbing at the clumps of yellow stonecrop that grew along the top of the wall and gathering what little balance he had left before he jumped, John thought how very much more pleasant it would have been if he could have been walking in these quiet gardens with that nice quiet Miss Sowerby instead of chasing after his brother. Then the chirruping and hallooing began again. 'Chuck! Chuck! Johnnie Easter, who's afraid to jump?' And the moment passed as he plunged into the darkness.

Billy was already charging through the rose garden, slashing at the new buds with his cane, his rowdy friends close behind him loud with admiration and drunkenly falling about, either into one another or into the bushes. 'Ho, Billy Easter! Ain't he just a card?' They galloped and chortled downhill until they came to the swampy field where the ruins of the old abbey still stood haphazardly among the grasses like the broken teeth and jagged bones of some long-buried giant.

Billy took a running leap at the nearest remnant, which was a low broken wall from which two sides of an ancient tower still stood miraculously upright. He clung to the gnarled stones for a second, searching for a toehold among the lichens, then he began to climb, singing and chirruping as he went. 'I'm in love! I'm in love! With a heigh nonny no and a heigh nonny — oops — ne!'

John was appalled.

'Come down!' he said, standing at the foot of the tower and looking up at his brother's flailing legs. 'Come down before you fall!' He was aware that he sounded just like old Bessie Thistlethwaite scolding a child, and the knowledge irritated him and increased his anger. 'Have done, for pity's sake! You are making a spectacle of yourself.'

The rebuke made Billy worse. 'Ho, ho!' he chortled, clutching the tower with one hand and swinging his body carelessly out into the void. ''T ain't the way for an Easter to behave, eh Johnnoh?' His friends were cheering him on and throwing their kerchiefs into the air to twist and flutter and fall like huge ungainly moths, so he contrived a jack-knife bow to them in mid-air and began to blow kisses to them and the moon. 'Wheeee!' he shouted. 'I'm in love! In love! In love! With the prettiest girl in the world, what's more. Rollicking head over rollicking heels! Wheeeeee!'

'Who is she, Billy?' his friends called. 'Who's the lucky lady?'

'Miss Matilda Honeywood,' he shouted down to them. 'Miss Matilda Honeywood, the prettiest girl in the world, damn me if she ain't. Wheee! I'm in love!'

'You're always in love,' John said flatly, his own thoughts of love quite spoilt by all this silly talk. 'Come down, do, or you'll pretty soon be in the cemetery.'

But that only brought a barrage of mockery. 'Who's your friend, Billy? Who's Mr Killjoy, eh? Oh go home, Johnnie Easter, you wet blanket.'

Billy took no notice of any of it, being drunkenly and cheerfully self-centred. 'Look at me!' he yelled, unnecessarily, and he flung both arms in the air and fell backwards out of the tower.

For a few seconds they all watched in stunned silence as his legs disappeared behind the arch, then there was a thud as he hit the ground and they all ran to find him.

He'll have done himself an injury as sure as fate, John thought anxiously, as he scrambled over the wreckage of the wall, craning his neck to see where his brother had fallen. And sure enough there he was, lying on his back among the grasses like a dead thing, with one arm flung behind his head and his legs spread-eagled.

'Oh,' he said, as he ran towards the corpse, 'why wouldn't you listen to me?'

'He ain't dead!' Ebenezer Millhouse said, lugging Billy's body about like a floppy doll. 'He can sit up like ninepence, can't ye, Billy?'

'In love, Eb,' Billy said, with his eyes shut. 'Tha's what 'tis.' Then he slid back onto the grass again.

'We must carry him home,' John said, taking command, 'and put him to bed and call the surgeon. I can't think what Mama will say.'

'Sleep here,' Billy suggested happily.

'There's no blood,' Ebenezer reported. He'd been feeling the back of his friend's head. 'Not even damp. See?' And he held up his fingers towards the moonlight so that John could see the absence of gore for himself.

Between them they hauled Billy home, and very difficult it was, for he was very heavy and manhandling him over the wall was like shifting a hundred weight sack of coal. But eventually they were all panting on the doorstep of his mother's fine house and John could hear Bessie's slippered feet slopping towards the door.

'Lawks a mercy!' she said, when she saw her young master slumped against the pillar. 'What you been an' gone an' done to poor Mr Billy?' She was in her nightgown and her frilled nightcap was tied under her little round chin in an elaborate starched bow. Above its smoothness her face was crinkled with concern. 'Poor Mr Billy!'

'He's drunk, Bessie,' John explained quickly before Ebenezer could tell her anything else. 'That's all. We'll carry him to bed, if you will kindly light the way.'

So the groaning lover was brought to bed, and undressed and bundled under the covers, and while Bessie saw out his helpful friends, John took a good look at the back of his head in the light of one of his triple-headed candlesticks. He was relieved to discover that although his brother's hair was matted with leaf mould and there was a lump on the back of his skull, there were no abrasions and no other signs of injury.

'Easy on, Johnnoh!' Billy complained. 'Got a head fit to beat the band, dontcher know.'

'You're jolly lucky you didn't kill yourself,' John said, putting the tousled head back upon the pillow, none too gently.

'You ain't goin' are you, Johnnoh?'

'No,' John said wearily. 'I'll stay here. Don't worry. I'll look after you.'

Which he did, and very exhausting it was, for despite his careful examination of Billy's head, he was still worried that his brother might have hurt himself more seriously than he realised. So he slept lightly, waking at every sound and every movement, just in case it was the first sign of a seizure or a fever or some other medical emergency so dire he couldn't even name it.

When the chambermaid brought up their tea at eight the next morning, Billy was sleeping like a baby and seemed perfectly recovered from his night's adventure, but John crept down to breakfast dark-eyed with fatigue.

Their mother was already at table consuming a vast quantity of devilled kidneys, sliced bacon, eggs and potatoes, washed down by strong beer. 'Ho!' she said when she saw the fragile state her younger son was in. 'You had a night on the tiles and no mistake.'

He bristled with annoyance that she should have misjudged him so. 'Not at all, Mama,' he said, stiffly. 'Billy went climbing the ruins and fell from the tower. I've been sitting up all night with him.'

'Was he hurt?' she said carelessly, and as she spoke Billy ambled into the room, yawning and dishevelled but obviously healthy. 'What have you been up to, you rogue?' she said lovingly as he kissed her.

'Took a bit too much to drink, Ma,' he admitted ruefully, holding the top of his head firmly in a useless attempt to press his headache down and away. 'That's the size of it. Got a bit squiffy. Johnnie was a good scout —' grinning his gratitude at his brother. 'He brought me home in one piece. More or less.'

'More fool you,' she said, but affectionately and without the least hint of criticism. 'Is Annie up?'

'They are following me down.' Billy looked at the table where the usual two places had been set for his sister and her husband. The movement of his head made his brother look too, so that both of them noticed the same thing at the same time. There was no place set for Calverley Leigh. The seat he usually occupied facing his mother was standing against the wall and the table had been smoothly set just for the five of them. Was he gone already? John wondered. Then the love affair must be over. How very surprising.

'Left at first light this morning,' his mother said, answering his thoughts. 'Should be halfway to Wales by now.' Then, spearing another kidney, she changed the subject with her customary abruptness. 'Now. I've twenty minutes after break-fast to see your notebooks, Johnnie, and then I've booked a seat on the morning coach to take me back to London. There's work to be done what won't wait. And might I suggest to 'ee, Johnnie, that you do likewise.'

'I had every intention,' he said, stiff-necked, because she'd read his mind so accurately and because she'd wrong-footed him again, ordering him to do the very thing he was going to do anyway. 'I mean to start at Scole and follow all the roads leading out from there — after checking the arrivals, of course, for that is crucial to the whole operation.'

'Good!' she approved, munching the kidney. 'And what shall you do, Billy?'

Billy gave her his most mischievous grin. 'Well as to that, Mama,' he said, 'I shall stay here and start a-courting.'

'Shall you indeed?' she laughed at him. 'And what gives 'ee leave to presume I shall agree to it, eh?'

'Because she's a beauty, and she's a wit, and she's a darling, and she dances divinely, and I love her dearly.' There was some-thing else about her too, something that made him feel easy in her company, but that was too vague and too private to be confessed to his mother. 'And besides all that, her father is Mr Horatio Honeywood.'

'Is he now?' Nan Easter said, grimacing her approval, dark eyes glinting. 'Well she'll not lack for dowry in all conscience.' For Mr Honeywood was a considerable landowner and reputed to be worth a fortune. 'You're a scamp, Billy Easter, but you've an eye for a pretty girl, I'll say that for 'ee. Just don't 'ee go a-rushing things, that's all.'

'Depend on it, Ma,' Billy promised, and settled to his bacon.

Watching him as he ate, John felt aggrieved. I've done all the right things, he thought, bringing him home and staying awake half the night, and she doesn't even thank me for it. What if *I'd* said I wanted to start courting? What would she have said to that? And he had a horrid suspicion that she would have laughed at him or mocked him for it. And he chewed a mouthful of eggs and bacon slowly, remembering the quiet girl.

'We've a picnic planned for this afternoon,' Billy was saying. 'Will the weather hold, think 'ee?'

'With your luck,' John said, 'it's bound to.'

CHAPTER 3

The stagecoach to Scole and Norwich was late arriving in Bury St Edmunds that morning, and as a consequence the coachman was ill-tempered and inapproachable, which was a considerable disappointment to John Easter. It was a bad start, both to the day and to his new position as manager of the firm. And it was made worse by the memory of the words his mother had spoken as she left for London.

'I shall watch to see how you get along, Johnnie,' she'd promised briskly. 'Plans on paper are all very well, my dear, howsomever 'tis how you put 'em into practice that counts.'

'I will do my utmost,' he'd promised, bowing to her formally and keeping his feelings completely hidden.

But now, as he scrambled aboard the dusty vehicle and took his seat outside, he was inwardly wincing at the enormity of the task he'd set himself. The organisation of rapid and competent newspaper deliveries throughout the country depended almost entirely on the cooperation of the coachmen, and he wasn't at all sure how any of them would react to his proposals. He *had* to be able to talk to this one on the road, but such an attempt would be most unwise now they were late.

He wrapped his travelling cloak neatly about his legs, comforting himself with the thought that there were several miles to travel yet, and that the coach was scheduled to stop for breakfast at the White Hart Inn in Scole where such talk might actually be more opportune. Meantime he would sit tight and say nothing and enjoy the journey; which was easy enough because sitting tight and saying nothing was almost second nature to him.

If he could have chosen his own appearance and position in life, John Easter would have been a coachman. They had such style, these young, strong, ruddy-faced men, so marvellously broad of shoulder in their huge greatcoats with triple capes swathing them to the waist, wearing their flat beaver hats so rakishly, brims curled, and with such fine leather boots on their determined feet. Once he had contrived to borrow a greatcoat from a coachman affably in his cups and had tried it on before a pier glass, tremulously hoping that it would give him some of its owner's style. But it was a miserable disappointment. It made him look more feeble than ever, and a great deal younger, accentuating his narrow shoulders and his skinny frame and his pale, withdrawn features. He knew that he looked like a child in adult's clothing and he never repeated the experiment.

Now, sitting beside this particular coachman as their vehicle, the 'Phenomena', clattered across the cobbles of Angel Hill, he was quietly enjoying himself. There was something peculiarly rewarding about a coach journey, something contained and safe. And besides, it was such a marvellous combination of sights and smells and sounds, people far below them waving goodbye or watching with admiration, the green hillside rising so peacefully before them as they turned out of the square towards Eastgate Street, the pungent scent that rose from the horses as their flanks began to steam, the clock, clock, clip of all those iron-shod hooves on the cobbles, the pole chains clinking between the wheelers, the bars of the two leaders clattering, and the great wheels grinding, and then whirring and then, when they'd finally picked up speed, humming and purring like some great satisfied cat. And all without the need to say a word.

There was plenty of cheerful conversation among the other passengers on the coach that morning. Two young gentlemen who had travelled from Norwich to join their cousins at the Victory Ball were happily reliving every dance, their feet swinging in the air in time to the remembered rhythms and their flushed faces nodding, and a gentleman in a stovepipe hat was equally happy in his opinion that 'the war being over, we shall see some wonders now, you mark my words!' And none of them was in the least discommoded by John Easter's shyness, providing he smiled and nodded at them from time to time.

But at the first turnpike a farmer and his wife climbed heavily aboard with four creaking hampers and such an assortment of boxes and bundles there was barely room for them all in the boot. And they brought quite another flavour to the journey, because the farmer was the proud possessor of a Jew's harp which he thrust into his jaw as soon as the coach began to move.

'He onny know the two tunes, don't 'ee, my love?' the farmer's wife explained, wafting a strong smell of farmyard muck upon her fellow passengers. 'But you harken you shall see, I promise 'ee gent'men, he play 'em so moosical 'twould charm the birds from the trees.'

'Bravo!' Stovepipe Hat encouraged. 'Just the style for a fine spring morning.'

'It might discommode the horses,' John pointed out, but speaking softly because he didn't want to appear critical.

'Lord love yer!' the farmer's wife beamed. 'No chance a' that, sir, when he plays so moosical. What's your opinion, Mr Coachman?'

'Don't make no odds to me,' the coachman said, watching the lead horses carefully as they negotiated a bend in the road. 'Play all you like an' welcome. 'Tis a good team, well used to music.

Ho! Not *that* way, my beauty' — flicking the horse's flank with his long whip. 'We ain't a-dancin' in no ditches this morning, *if* you please.'

So the farmer's wife assumed a rapturous expression and the farmer began to twang his little harp, most unmelodiously, just as John had feared. From then on, he played to his travelling companions affably and tunelessly all the way to Scole and breakfast. And although the horses pricked up their ears and twitched their flanks, the birds stayed where they were and paid no attention to him at all.

THE WHITE HART Inn at Scole stood at a place where five roads met, and as all five were coaching roads, and from such busy places as Bury, Thetford, Norwich, Yarmouth and Ipswich, there was barely an hour in the day when it wasn't busy feeding travellers or changing teams of horses. The landlord kept a good table and employed more cooks and chambermaids, waiters and potboys, grooms and ostlers than he ever bothered to count. It was the sort of place where a hero could claim an instant audience and a recluse dine unnoticed, and even the most determined musician could be persuaded to put something more palatable between his jaws than a twanging Jew's harp.

It was an imposing building, John thought, even though it was extremely old-fashioned, having been built in the days of the old Queen Elizabeth, with serpentine gables and old leaded windows set in the narrow red bricks of the time. All three wings gave out to the cobbled coachyard and the stables and pastures where more than twenty teams of coach horses could be housed and fed at any one time. It was a wide space but it looked smaller than it was because it was always so crowded: with travellers creaking in and out of the coaches and ostlers manoeuvring the new teams into position, an assortment of dogs barking in every arrival and scores of brown fowls picking among the fallen straw, flurrying away from the great wheels just in time and with considerable loss of feather and returning to peck again as soon as the teams had been led away. And above it all, the painted sign of the white hart itself hung suspended above the central archway, an extremely placid, domesticated creature, lying nonchalantly within its oval frame like a lightly cooked rabbit on a plate.

Now, John told himself, you must talk to the coachman. He had been appointed manager and he had given his word. Worse than that, he had even had the gall to boast that he would double the firm's profits in two years. He took a deep breath to steady himself and walked across to the entrance to the coffee room where the coachmen had gathered.

They looked at him idly as he approached, estimating whether or not they should stand aside to make way for him.

'God give 'ee good day, gentlemen,' he said, using the old-fashioned greeting in an excess of politeness. 'Would you do me the honour of taking breakfast with me?'

Mr Wiggins, the driver of the 'Phenomena', answered for them all, 'Werry obliging of 'ee, sir,' he said. 'Thank 'ee kindly. We could use a little sustenance, couldn't we, boys?'

And they followed their host into the coffee room.

Breakfast was being served, and the long room was a bustle of movement and munching. Waiters skidded from table to table like skaters, with heaped plates held precariously above their heads and trailing steam; tankards were clinked for replenishment; knives and forks flashed and clattered.

But the arrival of seven coachmen in a massive and talkative phalanx was enough to stop even the heartiest eater, especially as the landlord himself came out to supervise the setting of a table large enough to accommodate them all. Soon necks were being craned to discover who the heroes were honouring with their company.

'Pray order whatever you require,' John said, when they'd taken their places about the table.

'Steaks and ale, sir,' Mr Wiggins said with happy authority.

So steaks and ale it duly was, and because it would never have done to sit apart while his guests were eating, John ate his portion too, despite the fact that, after an early breakfast at Bury, he had little appetite.

They talked of travel, of course, of temperamental horses and peculiar passengers and the deplorable state of the roads. And they greeted everything that John managed to say with a mocking good humour and the steaks were nearly devoured before he could manoeuvre the conversation to the matter of timekeeping.

'Powerful good timekeepers, us gentlemen of the road,' the oldest coachman said, wiping his mouth after a deep draught of ale.

'With so many hazards,' John said, nodding his head to signify admiration. 'It amazes me that you always manage to keep such good time.'

'Matter of honour, sir,' Mr Wiggins said, 'bein' as our watch-word is dependability. Dependability, sir. You may depend upon it.' And was cheered for his wit.

'I can believe it, sir,' John said. 'For 'tis my estimation that most journeys are completed within five minutes of the appointed time.'

It was generally and happily agreed that they were. 'Dependability sir. That's the ticket!'

Now was the time to dare, surely.

'That being so, gentlemen,' he said, staying calm with a considerable effort, 'there is a little matter of business I should like to discuss with you, if you would be so kind.'

Instant caution, a withdrawing of bodies, guarded expressions. Had he spoken too soon, or with too much eagerness?

'What manner of business did 'ee have in mind, sir?' Mr Wiggins asked carefully.

'I will be plain with you,' John said. 'It is my intention to dispatch newspapers daily from the printers in London to newsagent shops in all the towns in this region. I am here to buy shops for that purpose. Howsomever, for those papers to arrive in my shops in the shortest possible time, I must ask for your cooperation. Your *paid* cooperation, of course, since this is a matter of business.'

The seven men looked at one another quickly, assessing the offer and their reactions to it.

'The usual fare in these parts is fourpence or fivepence a mile,' John said, 'with a shilling remuneration for the coachman, of course. So what I propose to you, gentlemen, is half fare for the goods at tuppence ha'penny paid to the company plus the usual remuneration for your labours, since I would require the papers to be transferred from coach to coach according to my instructions in order to facilitate the swiftest possible journey.'

'And each of us to be paid according?' Mr Wiggins asked.

'Of course.'

'What sort a' quantities was we talkin' about?'

'Two reams per journey, possibly more.'

The matter was considered in half sentences tossed from one to the other between mouthfuls of steak and meaning looks gleamed from eye to eye across the tops of tilted tankards, and slow pondering nods while food and information were digested. Finally Mr Wiggins said that as far as he could see a shilling fee might be reasonable, 'bein' your papers got to be transported same as any other traveller. Howsomever, more than two reams and 'twould have to be negotiated again, if you takes my meaning, sir'.

John agreed with him, adding that the fee would of course depend upon the papers arriving in time to be put straight aboard the very next coach for the next stage of their journey.

'A' course!' the coachman said sagely, 'that stands ter reason, don't it? I tell you what though, sir, if you means ter make a business of it, if you takes my meanin', the man you oughter see is Mr Chaplin, him what owns jest about every blessed coach on these 'ere roads nowadays. A good bloke, Mr Chaplin.'

'I'm sure of it,' John said.

'So what you ought ter do, young man, is ter get your boss to go down to the Cross Keys in Wood Street and do business with Mr Chaplin direct.'

It was an excellent suggestion, which he would certainly act upon. 'Actually,' he said, with modest pride, 'I am the boss of the firm.'

'Should a' know'd, Mr Easter sir,' the coachman said, adjusting his tone immediately and touching the curled brim of his beaver hat with instant respect, just to make doubly sure. 'Well, there you are then.'

And there, apparently, he was. For once they'd realised that they were talking to the boss, the rest of the coachmen were quick to agree that his plan was not only interesting but workable and acceptable. And John had assured them all that he would see Mr Chaplin at the very first opportunity.

'Tell him Joseph Wiggins is agreeable,' Mr Wiggins said, as he put down his empty tankard. 'Joseph Wiggins is agreeable. That should swing it.'

But then the Ipswich coach drove through the great archway into the courtyard, coach horn blaring, and that was the signal for the meal to end and the coffee room to empty. By the time John and his guests had strolled out into the courtyard, the post-boys were running from the inn like a tumble of autumn leaves in their long yellow coats with their brown leg pads, and there was a commotion of boarding and departing.

The 'Phenomena' was the last to leave, which pleased John because it gave him the chance to treat his coachman to one last brandy. And this time he bought one for himself, too, because he felt he'd earned it.

As the coach trundled off towards the Norwich road, he remembered his brother Billy, and wondered how well his new courtship was progressing. It was just like Billy to be off courting while *he* was doing all the work, and for a few seconds he felt quite jealous of his idle brother. But then he comforted himself with the thought that he, John Easter, no less, was the one who was furthering the fortunes of the firm. He would rent the necessary shops, hire men to run them and establish deliveries. That was something he had done before and he knew he could do it well. Then he would go to London and meet Mr Chaplin. By the time he saw his mother again the deal would be concluded, and she could hardly fail to be impressed. As the coach picked up speed and the wheels began to purr, he was smiling to himself with satisfaction.

BILLY EASTER WASN'T DOING QUITE AS well on his envied picnic as his younger brother imagined. It had begun cheerfully enough, with their two fine vehicles bowling along between the May leaves under a warm blue sky. Billy rode in the Easter chaise with his sister Annie and dear old James, her husband, and their two little boys, baby Beau peacefully asleep across his mother's knees and three-year-old Jimmy sitting quietly beside his nursemaid. And the delectable Matilda rode in the Honeywood chaise with her younger brother Claude sitting beside her looking superior and her two cousins, Sophie and Maria, with their backs to the box seat, giggling.

They had travelled north to the little village of Fornham St Mary where the vicarage slept behind a thickset hedge of hawthorn and yew trees, and a row of untidily thatched cottages faced the green. As they trotted by, a gaggle of dishevelled children ran from the cottages to cluster about the village well and watch them as they passed. They waved and smiled, feeling grand and young and idle, and the children grinned back, their faces brown as earth between pale straw bonnets and unbleached pinafores.

But then the party reached the foot of the hill that would lead them up through the woods to the little hamlet of St Genevieve and the grounds of the manor house where they were to have their picnic. By now the day had grown quite warm and their horses were beginning to blow so, except for baby Beau and his nursemaid, they all came tumbling out of their carriages ready to climb the hill, Annie and James swinging little Jimmy between them, Claude escorting his cousins and Billy gallantly offering his arm to Matilda.

Unfortunately their arrival attracted a swarm of flies which until then had been occupied on a fresh muck heap piled beside a gateway. With the unwavering instinct of their kind, they homed in on the mouths and eyes of a new and moving host. They were death to romantic conversation, as Billy discovered almost at once.

'My dear Miss Honeywood!' he began. 'Pray do permit me to say how perfectly charming you look this afternoon. A Parisian bonnet is... Ugh! Ugh!' A fly had flown straight into his mouth.

'Why Mr Easter! Are you unwell?' Matilda said, peering at him through the buzzing.

'Fly!' he gasped, red in the face and pulling air into his lungs with a noise like a cock crowing. 'Swallowed a fly, dammit!' Oh what a stupid thing to have done! And just when he wanted to be suave and gentlemanly.

'Oh dear!' she said and began to giggle. She knew she shouldn't but she really couldn't help it because he looked so funny with his round face red and that sandy hair standing on end and the buttons on his shirt popping open with the exertion of all that leaping and spluttering.

'What is it?' Annie called back over her shoulder. She was

swatting the files away from little Jimmy with the palm of her hand. 'Oh shoo! Shoo! You beastly creatures.'

'Your brother has swallowed a fly.'

'All right now,' Billy gulped. 'No need to fuss, Sis. Only a fly.'

But his sister was already beside him and striking him firmly between the shoulder blades. 'Cough it up, Billy.'

'Imagine where the little blighter's been,' Claude said, enjoying the sight of someone else's discomfiture. 'Climbing over all that muck, damnit, and then straight down Billy's throat.'

And at that Billy discovered that he wasn't all right after all and he had to go stumbling off to the hedgerow to be sick. And by the time he'd parted company with the fly and most of his breakfast, his new beloved was several hundred yards up the hill and flanked on either side by her two giggling cousins. He trailed after them disconsolately, cursing his luck. And his tormentors followed him every buzzing inch of the way, pinging against his cheeks and dancing before his eyes.

It wasn't the way he'd planned this picnic at all.

Outside the manor house door they were met by young Mr Jeremiah Ottenshaw who, being the only son of the house, was a gentleman of considerable style and importance, and dressed in the height of fashion from the fine white stock neatly folded beneath his fine blue chin to the immaculate doeskin trousers on his long, aristocratic legs. For all his rather imposing appearance, he was an amiable young man and enjoyed being hospitable, especially when he could number the Honeywood cousins among his guests.

'Come in, Mr Honeywood, pray do,' he said as they rounded the last bend and toiled towards him trailing their unwanted companions. 'Miss Honeywood, how pleasant to see you. And the Reverend Mr Hopkins and Mrs Hopkins, I do declare... Miss Maria, Miss Sophie, pray walk this way. You must be fatigued after your climb. We have iced champagne and syllabub and water ices a-plenty all waiting for you. Ah now, you're never going to tell me that our young Jimmy walked all this way, all by himself up the hill because I'll never believe it. What a deuced fine thing!' And he bustled them on to where footmen were waiting to carry the picnic hampers to his chosen spot, and grooms to lead the horses to the stables, and maids to fetch and carry. And somehow or other in the general confusion of welcome and greeting and catching breath and cheerful gesticu-lating talk, the flies lost heart and drifted away to torment someone else.

So it was a good picnic after all and Billy perked up and began to enjoy himself. Even though Sophie and Maria spent the first ten minutes of the meal mimicking his behaviour when he'd swallowed the fly, with every splutter and retch most vividly recreated.

'Fell into the hedge, so he did,' Maria giggled. 'Positively fell in. The poor thing was spattered all over. Claude told us. Ugh! *I* couldn't bear to look.'

'Oh I say,' Billy protested weakly as the laughter continued. 'Steady on! It wasn't *that* bad.'

'Done a deal o' tumbling just lately, so I hear,' Jeremiah said. 'Fell out of a tower after the ball last night. Ain't that so, Billy?'

'Oh Mr Easter!' Matilda reproached him. 'How did you come to do such a thing?'

'Calling a certain young lady's name, so I'm told,' Jeremiah teased. 'Ain't that the size of it, eh? Plunged from the tower with her name on his lips, so he did. All good romantic stuff.'

'And which young lady was that, pray?' Matilda asked, magnificently innocent, her grey eyes opened wide between those swaying curls.

'Deuce take it,' Billy complained to his friend. 'Ain't a man to have any secrets?'

'Not when he screams 'em from the top of the tallest tower, old thing.'

'Oh do tell,' Matilda begged. 'Who is she? I long to know.'

'When we have finished our picnic, we will take a turn through the rose garden,' Billy suggested, 'on our own, and then I will tell you. I promise.'

'I could not walk with you alone, Mr Easter,' Matilda said, thrilled by the idea. ''T would not be proper.'

'Perfectly proper, Miss Honeywood,' Jeremiah said, winking at Billy with the eye Matilda couldn't see. 'I assure you. There are plenty here to see you and chaperone you. You may walk where you will. I mean to take Miss Maria and Miss Sophie to see the fishponds, if they will do me the honour.'

'I very much hope you will, sir,' their cousin Claude said, 'else I cannot ride your roan, as you promised.'

'We must sit here with our children, I suppose,' the Reverend Hopkins teased his Annie. 'Like the old married couple we are.'

'And what could be better, my love?' she said. So it was arranged.

It was very quiet in the rose garden, down in the dell between the house and the hazel copse, and if Billy and his new beloved *were* being chaperoned, they were quite unaware of it. They walked side by side, Billy holding out his right arm gallantly and rather stiffly so that she could rest the tips of three of her gloved fingers very delicately upon it.

'Now do pray tell me, Mr Easter,' she said, flirting her grey eyes at him. 'What was the name you called upon as you fell from the tower? Was it truly the name of a young lady?'

'It was indeed,' he said earnestly. Should he tell her? Or was it too soon?

'What prevailed upon you to do such a thing? I declare, you gave me to believe that you were a gentleman of the most serious intentions.'

'Did I?' he said, amazed to hear it. 'Oh I say, I don't know how I did *that*, upon me word.'

'Dear me,' she teased. 'Are your intentions less than serious, Mr Easter?'

'No — I mean — well yes — I ain't the most serious feller alive, Miss Honeywood, and that's the truth of it.' How bewitching her eyes were, gleaming at him in the pale sunlight. I could be serious with you, my beautiful Matilda.

'Dear me,' she said again, and this time she smiled at him, looking straight into his eyes. 'Do you trifle then, sir?'

'Oh no, indeed,' he vowed, quite overcome by such directness. 'I could never trifle with you, Miss Honeywood. Not when you are so — when you have — when I —'

'We have reached the end of the arbour, Mr Easter,' she said, still gazing into his eyes, 'and if we continue to walk in this direction, I fear you may fall into another hedge.'

'I have fallen in love,' he said truthfully.

'Have you indeed?' she teased. 'And who with, pray?'

'Why with you, Miss Honeywood.'

'Have you indeed?' she said again. And she began to laugh, chortling with delight at his declaration, beaming at him as if she were applauding.

It was such an infectious sound it set him laughing too. He seized both her hands and began to skip about, dancing with her between the roses.

The noise they were making echoed all over the grounds, from the open heath where her brother Claude was happily riding the roan, to the shade of the picnic oak where his sister Annie was half asleep with her head in her husband's lap.

'Oh James,' she said. 'I do believe our Billy has made a match.'

'If you could prevail upon him to refrain from swallowing flies,' her husband said, smiling at her, 'I do believe you could be right.'

CHAPTER 4

N an Easter, the formidable head of the formidable firm of A Easter and Sons was negotiating the purchase of a new London home. Never one to waste time in unnecessary searches or pointless preliminaries, she had discovered the property she wanted within three days of commencing her search for it, a first-grade house in fashionable Bedford Square, double-fronted and built in the Palladian style, with a huge pediment and engaged columns. Just the right sort of house for a woman in her position in society. Now she was bullying the vendor's solicitor to get the deal completed as quickly as possible.

He had come to her office in the Strand, cheerfully enough and according to her instructions, ready to undertake the sale in his usual leisurely way, but now, after a mere half-hour in the lady's demanding presence, he was already finding the transaction more difficult that he could ever have imagined.

She was so impatient and so domineering, quite unlike any other woman he'd ever had to deal with. The force of her character had been a considerable surprise to him, for she was such a little woman, barely five feet tall and slender as a reed in her straight green coat and her little button-boots, but the face above the green velveteen should have given him pause despite her lack of inches. It was such an open, confident, expressive face, framed by thick dark hair that sprang from her temples in forceful curls, wide of brow, with shrewd brown eyes and a wide mouth and the most determined chin he'd ever seen on a woman. An honest face, he thought, but with far too many marks of passion upon it; laughter lines fanning beside those eyes and two deep lines of temper between eyebrows as thick and dark as any man's. It was, as he now realised rather belatedly, the face of a person used to getting her own way.

He had opened the proceedings with his usual caution, stressing that it might well take some little time before a suitable price could be agreed upon but assuring her of his best endeavours in the matter. And she'd fairly brushed him aside.

'Tosh, Mr Randall,' she said, 'I'm a woman of business. I en't got all day to haggle, so I'll tell 'ee straight what we'll do. I will offer a fair price, you will inform the vendor, and if 'tis agreeable I'll buy and if it en't I'll look elsewhere. There are squares a-plenty in this city and one is much the same as any other.'

He was much put out, although he did his best not to let her see it. 'How if the vendor would prefer to bargain, ma'am?' he suggested. 'The asking price is often, if I may make so bold as to point out, merely offered by way of preliminary. Lengthy negotiations are customary.'

'Maybe they are,' she said, grinning at him, 'but I en't. Come now, the vendor wants to return to the Barbados and is to stay there, which I know for a fact. He'll be glad of a sale at the price I'm offering, depend upon it.'

Such bluntness took his breath away. 'This is all — um — rather unorthodox, ma'am, if you will forgive me for saying so,' he protested.

She put back her head and roared with laughter at him. 'So I should hope,' she said forcefully. 'Leave orthodoxy to the timid,

Mr Randall. 'T en't for the likes of us, I tell 'ee plain. Come now, is it a deal or no?'

So with considerable trepidation he had to agree to put her offer to the vendor. She seemed to have no qualms about the matter at all and no further time to spend upon it. He gathered his papers and bade her good morrow politely, but he noticed as he left her that she was already busy studying the close-packed figures in an account book. An extraordinary woman, he thought, to have so little care where she lives. One square as good as any other! Dear me! What an opinion! They'd have something to say about that in Berkeley Square or St James's. And he went down the stairs towards the midsummer heat of the Strand shaking his head with amazement.

Actually he was quite wrong about her, although it would probably have made his position even more difficult had he known the true state of her intentions. For Nan Easter meant to own the house she'd chosen, and neither he nor the Barbadian vendor, nor anyone else for that matter, was going to be allowed to stand in her way.

It was the right time for a change. She'd altered the management of her firm, increased her sales tenfold in the last five years and refused to marry her lover after an affair that had gone on for the best part of fifteen, and now, at the energetic age of two-and-forty, she was embarking on a new life of her own.

She read the accounts rapidly, making swift notes in the margins and glancing at the clock from time to time, for she had allowed herself twenty minutes for the task and then she and Mr Teshmaker would be meeting to discuss the London trade. And Cosmo Teshmaker was always scrupulously punctual.

Sure enough he came knocking on her door just as the clock began to strike midday. They smiled at one another like the old friends they were.

'Did all go well, ma'am?' he asked.

''Course,' she said. 'I shall be in residence by September, depend upon it.'

It didn't surprise him. When had the resourceful Nan Easter ever been baulked of anything she wanted? The idea of anyone opposing her was quite unthinkable.

'Sales are still poor, I see,' she said, waving her quill at the account book.

'Except in Mayfair and Bloomsbury.'

'Um,' she said. 'Peace may be preferable to war, but it sells fewer newspapers. Should we venture that second shop in Piccadilly, think 'ee?'

'On balance,' he said gravely, 'it is my opinion it would be a justified risk.'

'Then we will risk it,' she said, brushing the palms of her hands against each other, swish swish, the way she always did when she'd made a decision.

'What news of Mr John?' the lawyer asked.

'Still in Cambridge,' his mother said. 'I had a letter from him this morning. He means to come home to us via Ely, so he says, which seems an uncommon circuitous route to me, but all done to give him two days to inspect his new shop there.'

'He is thorough,' Mr Teshmaker said. 'That you cannot deny.'

'Unlike my harum-scarum Billy,' his mother said, grinning at the thought of her elder son. 'He spends every spare moment in Bury these days a-courting Miss Honeywood. I tell him I'm beginning to forget what he looks like.'

'Indeed, yes,' the lawyer said. 'He does seem much enamoured of the lady.' And he wondered whether a wedding might not just be possible but forbore to speak of it in case he upset his old friend's feelings, which must be tender, in all conscience, considering how recently she'd parted from her lover. He had the greatest respect for Mrs Easter and would never willingly do anything to cause her pain.

''Twould be a good match,' she said, grinning again. 'Mr

Honeywood is almost as rich as I am and Matilda quite as fond and foolish as my Billy.'

'So it is rumoured.'

'Well we shall see,' Nan said, opening her account book as a signal that their business meeting was about to begin. 'Billy is a loving creature, in all conscience, but he lacks seriousness. 'Twas Johnnie took a double portion of *that* commodity.'

'And makes good use of it, you will allow,' Mr Teshmaker smiled, gathering his accounts together in a neat pile.

''Twon't win him a wife,' his mother said, grimacing. 'Nor a lover I'm thinking. And that do seem a pity to me. Now that he's a manager of this firm a wife would be timely. Howsomever, I en't seen the slightest sign of any interest in that direction.'

'Still waters, Mrs Easter?' Mr Teshmaker suggested diplomatically.

'Lack of inclination, Cosmo. Now as to last week's sales…'

IT WAS an opinion she shared with Miss Harriet Sowerby, although of course neither of them knew it. All through that summer Harriet had been reminding her Maker of the possibility that He might help her to see Mr Easter again. She said regular and heartfelt prayers about it, tentatively suggesting possible lines of action: that the gentleman might drive up Churchgate Street as she and her family were walking to church, perhaps, or arrive by stagecoach at a time when she'd been sent on an errand that would take her through Angel Square, or meet her when she'd been sent to escort Miss Pettie on her weekly trip to market. But there was no answer. Mr Easter remained elsewhere.

His brother Billy came rollicking into town every Saturday night as regular as clockwork, as Miss Pettie reported to Mr and Mrs Sowerby equally regularly every Sunday after the service.

'Visiting again, my dears,' she would say. ''Twill be a match.

Depend on't. Mrs Thistlethwaite tells me they went riding this morning. Down to Rattlesden to visit with his sister, Mrs Hopkins, I shouldn't wonder. The romance of it, my dears!' And Harriet listened to the conversation, hoping that this time he'd brought his brother with him. And was constantly disappointed.

Finally when ten weeks had passed and twenty-one earnest prayers had been ignored, and the wheat was golden-brown in the fields, she decided that she would have to take matters in hand herself.

The next Thursday afternoon, when she was helping Miss Pettie with her sewing, she asked whether *other* members of the Easter family did not visit their house in Bury during the summer.

'Mrs Easter is uncommon busy this year,' the old lady said, squinting at her tacking and then happily setting it aside for the greater pleasure of a little gentle gossip. 'We have seen her but rarely, more's the pity of it, for she is a fine woman, my dear, and highly thought of in the town. Howsomever if Mr Billy and Miss Honeywood make a match then I am sure we shall see a great deal more of her. He is invited to her twentieth birthday party next month, which I *do* consider most significant. *I* introduced them, you know my dear, at the Victory Ball, little *dreaming* what might come of it. There was romance in the very air that night, my dear.'

And she was off into a happy reminiscence that lasted fully fifteen minutes. Harriet endured it quietly and smiled agreement when she thought it appropriate, but it seemed an age before she could rephrase her question and ask it again.

'And what of Mr John, Miss Pettie? Does he not visit with his brother from time to time.' Even as she heard the words, she knew she was being too direct. She sounded forward and unladylike and she knew she was blushing for shame at her presumption and ducked her head towards the chemise she was sewing, hoping that Miss Pettie wouldn't notice. Oh dear, oh dear.

Miss Pettie ignored the blush, for she was always the soul of discretion where the comfort of her guests was concerned. But although she said nothing she thought much and happily. For had she not introduced this quiet child to young Mr John that very summer? How if she were to further another match in the Easter family? What a triumph that would be!

'Well now, my dear,' she said, 'Mr John is busier than his mother, so they do say. He is a *manager* now, you see, with a deal of responsibility. Mr Orton tells me he has opened six new shops just hereabouts and each and every one quite as grand as the shop in the Buttermarket, with fine curtains in the windows and armchairs in the reading room and the signs all new painted and everything in order. But no more than we should expect, I do assure you. He was always such a diligent young man, even as a child. A scholar.'

This was better, for it sounded more like gossip than unseemly interest. 'You have known him for a long time, I dare-say,' Harriet said, prompting further information in the accepted way.

'Indeed I have, my dear. A very long time. Why, we've been neighbours for — let me see — it must be eight years at the very least. Mr Billy and Mr John were mere stripling boys when they first came to my door. Billy was just fifteen, I recall, the same age as you, my dear, and so handsome. Such a fine figure and *so* tall. He could reach any shelf in the house without even stretching his arms. Imagine that! "Pray allow me, Miss Pettie," he would say to me. So politely. And now he's courting Miss Honeywood. Who'd a' thought it? They went riding again last Sunday. And to think I introduced 'em. Oh there was romance in the air that night...'

Oh, Harriet thought, concentrating on the next buttonhole, if only some of it had touched my Mr Easter. And while Miss

Pettie rambled happily and garrulously on, she allowed herself the luxury of a little romantic daydream, and went riding with Mr John down the leafy lanes towards his sister's house in Rattlesden, where she was lifted, oh so tenderly, from her horse and led through bright sunshine into the welcoming house where Mrs Hopkins came tripping forward to kiss her welcome and to say…

'I am thinking of taking a little trip to Ipswich in a day or two,' Miss Pettie said. 'Do you think I could prevail upon your parents to permit you to accompany me, my dear? We could stay overnight at the Crown and Anchor, which is the most respectable establishment and served me a quite excellent dinner the last time I was there. Yes, indeed. Quite excellent. You would like that, would you not?'

'Yes, Miss Pettie,' Harriet agreed, setting her daydreams aside and reaching for the scissors. A trip to Ipswich would be very pleasant if her parents would allow it.

'And then if all goes well,' Miss Pettie promised, 'we could go further afield the next time, to Norwich, perhaps, or Cambridge, which is a trifle old-fashioned, but worth a visit. I should like to go to Bath and take the waters which they say are quite excellent for the rheumatics, howsomever that would have to wait until the spring for I can't abide that city in wintertime.'

Harriet said she would be happy to accompany Miss Pettie to any or all of these places, but secretly she would have traded every single one for a chance to see Mr Easter when he came to Bury to attend the Honeywood party.

UNFORTUNATELY THE HONEYWOODS, being the most hospitable of parents and mindful of their position in society, had decided that their daughter's twentieth birthday should be celebrated by a rout, a night-long, fashionable party with dancing and gaming and entertainments of every kind. Their country seat was good enough for a garden party, but there was only one place for the sort of reception they had in mind, and that was their town house in Cavendish Square. So on that warm September evening when the Easter brothers arrived to assist in the celebrations, Harriet was a long way away from their sight and their thoughts.

Billy was in a state of muddled intoxication, which was partly due to the half bottle of British Hollands he'd consumed before he left home and partly to the prospect of an evening being teased and tormented by his bewitching beloved. He was dressed in the very latest style, as befitted a manager of the great firm of A Easter and Sons, in a pink frock coat, white silk waistcoat and an exuberant purple cravat that wouldn't have looked amiss on the wild Lord Byron himself. His face was already flushed, and his forehead moist and his blue eyes watery, and he was saying secret prayers that this time he would comport himself with style and avoid the usual clumsy accidents that had dogged him all through the summer.

For wherever he went with the delectable Miss Honeywood, and however hard he tried to be adroit and suave in order to impress her, he always ended up making a fool of himself. When they rode together, his horse bucked him off, when they danced, he trod on her feet, and when he took tea with her parents, he smashed her mother's precious porcelain and, on one fearful occasion, broke the leg of a chair, which turned out to have been made by Mr Chippendale.

In the warehouse his broad shoulders and sturdy legs were useful and admired. He could shift the heavy batches of newspapers as deftly as any of his workmen, and besides that his knowledge of the trade and his ability to make decisions quickly had given him a reputation for dependability and common sense. But in salons and theatres, at parties and dances and routs, it was as if he'd reverted to his childhood again. Some part of his anatomy always seemed to be in somebody's way.

People fell over his feet or removed chairs just as he was about to sit on them. Or he would be rapt in some ardent conversation and wave an arm and demolish an entire tray of champagne glasses. And the more deeply he fell in love with his dear Matilda, the more clumsy and foolish he appeared before her. It was getting so bad it was beginning to upset him. If only he could be cool and contained like Johnnie. Not all the time, of course, because being cool and contained all the time was really rather a bore, but now and then, when he needed to be. Like this evening, for example, when his nervousness and fussing had made them terribly late.

He glanced at his brother as he stepped delicately down from their carriage, brushing an imaginary fleck from the cloth of his blue coat and surveying the road in his calm contained way.

But in fact John was not as calm as he looked. He had accepted this invitation because he couldn't find any credible reason for refusing it, and he too had dressed with care, but soberly, of course, in his new blue cloth jacket and his new buff trousers, and a cravat of plain white linen heavily starched and tied with such precision it looked as though it had been ironed to his neck, but despite all his efforts and his quite admirable composure, he was feeling terribly shy.

But the rout was shriekingly under way and there was nothing for it but to follow Billy into the house where a footman resplendent in green livery and gold braid dazzled them into the ballroom. It was an overpowering place, being decorated in red and green and hung about with bunting, and it was already uncomfortably full of guests, all taking up more room than usual because they were in their best clothes and making a great deal of noise since that was what was expected of them at a rout. Four great chandeliers blazed like burning bushes above the embroidered muslins and shimmering silks and extraordinary coiffures of the ladies. There was a band on a raised dais playing discordantly but very loudly, and everybody seemed to be rushing from place to place, glass in hand, spilling wine as they ran.

'Mr Easter, you wretched creature,' Matilda Honeywood said, scampering towards them with both hands outstretched to catch Billy's hands and twirl him about. 'I declare we all thought you had reneged upon us. How late you are! Mr Ottenshaw has been here an age, you bad, bad creature, and moping for lack of you.' And she smiled at him with her eyes and tossed her curls at him and beat him with her fan, which spun him into a state of such happy confusion that he trod backwards onto the feet of an unobtrusive dowager who had the misfortune to be sitting behind him.

'Oh!' he said, 'I am so sorry. I didn't mean…'

'Of no consequence,' the poor lady murmured, trying not to wince. 'I do assure you.'

'This is Mr William Easter, Aunt,' Matilda explained, waving one airy hand by way of introduction. 'He treads on everybody.'

'Oh steady on!' Billy protested. 'Not everybody, Miss Honeywood.'

'You've trod on me enough times,' she said dragging him off through the throng. 'I declare I'm black and blue all over.'

'Steady on!' he begged again. 'I ain't said how d'ee do to your parents. And anyway how do I know you're black and blue all over, eh? Tell me that. I don't see any bruises, upon me soul I don't.'

She turned to give him the full benefit of her fine grey eyes, standing so close to him that he could see the little pulse beating at her throat and feel the warmth of her body almost as if he were holding her in his arms. 'Shame upon you, Mr Easter,' she teased. 'Have I to strip to my chemise to show you the harm you do?' It pleased her to wonder what it would be like to strip to her chemise in front of Billy Easter, for he really was extremely handsome.

The thought of it made him weak at the knees. 'Miss Honeywood!' he said. 'Matilda!' But then a gaggle of her friends came bearing down upon them, all talking at once, and the image and the opportunity were lost.

'This is Miss Lizzie Moffat,' she said, seizing a tall, skinny girl by the hand and pulling her forward. 'My dearest, dearest friend. Allow me to present Mr William Easter, Lizzie my darling, and his brother Mr John.'

'How d'ee do,' the skinny girl said, proffering two limp fingers to each of the brothers in turn. 'Womantic wout, ain't it? Weally womantic. They've got woses everywhere. Positively miles and miles of wed woses. It's incwedible.'

She was a peculiarly unattractive girl, John thought, and her lack of charm was accentuated by that deliberate drawling lisp. She was far too tall for a start, and bony and gawky, her fair hair tortured into lank ringlets, and her faced so blotched with freckles that at first sight he thought she was suffering from some sort of skin disease. A bean pole with a skin disease he thought, wryly. But he was not to be allowed to avoid her.

'You are to dance with my dear Lizzie,' Matilda whispered, leaning towards Billy's chest until she was touching his waist-coat with the tips of her fingers. 'Both of you. Because she is my very dearest friend. And you are to dance with her first, Mr William Easter, or I vow I shan't tread a single measure with you myself. No, not so much as one single measure. So you've been warned you bad, bad boy.'

So of course Lizzie's card had to be marked there and then, and two dances booked with each of them, which she pronounced, 'Perfectly thwilling!' in tones of unalloyed boredom.

As he put his dance card back into his pocket John knew that it was going to be a perfectly dreadful evening. And for a fleeting second before Matilda rushed them off to pay their respects to her parents, he remembered the quiet girl he'd danced with in Bury St Edmunds and wished she could be here to rescue him.

But no rescue was at hand, and the impossible Lizzie was pushed before him at every turn, almost as if Miss Honeywood was going out of her way to fling them together, which heaven forefend. She was produced at supper time, to tempt him with a plateful of vol-au-vents as limp as her curls; she was propelled flat-footed into the centre of the Schottische to partner him; and even when he fled from her company to a quiet seat in the darkest corner of the long library, somehow or other she appeared on the very next seat before three minutes of precious privacy had passed. It was like being pursued by a broomstick. By the time midnight struck and he was endeavouring to waltz with her while keeping her at arm's length he was heartily sick of her. It was quite a relief to hear his mother's bold laugh and to realise that she had joined the company. Now at last he had a perfectly proper reason to desert the dance floor and leave his unwanted companion.

'My heart alive!' Nan Easter said, when the dance was done and he was able to join her. '*Who* was that apparition a-hanging onto your arm?'

He gave her a little grimace of agreement and explained. 'Her name is Lizzie Something-or-other, and she is Miss Honeywood's best friend, according to Miss Honeywood.'

'Ah!' his mother said, understanding at once. ''Tis the habit of pretty young girls nowadays to choose some great gawk to befriend. 'Tis uncharitable, in all conscience, but a neat ruse, for it renders their beauty inescapable.'

John grimaced again. 'It has been my experience tonight, Mama,' he said, 'that it is the great gawk who is inescapable.'

'Fetch me a rum punch,' she said, grinning at him, 'and we will go into the library and talk business.'

William Easter had been sent for rum punch too, and was equally glad to go, although for very different reasons. It was always a pleasure to wait on his dear Matilda and, besides, dancing had given him a thirst.

'D'you see my Matilda?' he asked his brother as they stood side by side at the serving table. 'Ain't she just a corker? Come and join us, why don't you?'

'Because this rum punch is for Mama.'

'Ah!' his brother said. 'Duty before pleasure, eh?' And was surprised when John laughed at him, for he'd really imagined that his brother was enjoying the rout as much as he was.

'If only you knew,' John said. 'I will tell you about her later.' And he followed his mother into the library.

'I've arranged to see Mr Chaplin at six o'clock tomorrow morning at the Cross Keys,' he said as soon as they had both sat down. And was pleased by the immediate approval on her face.

'Good,' she said briskly. 'He's an outspoken man, but you'll find him fair.'

'I have given much thought to this meeting, Mama,' he said. 'I do not think you will find me wanting.'

'No more do I,' she said cheerfully. 'For much depends upon this deal, which you and I know well. I mean to travel to York within the week, to open a shop or two there, and a reading room too, I daresay. I suggest you start work upon the Bath road when you've seen Mr Chaplin. 'Twould be as well to get negotiations underway before the winter puts paid to travel. What think 'ee?'

'I believe you have read my notebooks, Mama,' he said, 'since you suggest my own plans, entirely.'

'You understand this business as well as I do,' she said grinning at him.

'Not quite, Mama,' he said, gallantly but truthfully. 'But I mean to one day, you may depend on it.'

CHAPTER 5

Mr William Chaplin, the famous coach proprietor, and Mrs Nan Easter the famous newsagent, had a lot in common. Both were outstanding personalities, showily dressed, fond of their pleasures, quick witted, outspoken, ambitious and energetic. So naturally enough they got on well together, even when they were striking bargains, which they'd done with increasing frequency over the last five years. For A Easter and Sons, Newsagents, put plenty of business Mr Chaplin's way, carrying newspapers to more and more provincial towns, and the two firms had grown at a similar rate.

Mr Chaplin was an excellent judge of horseflesh and a superlative judge of men. Now, standing among the bustle in the coachyard of the Cross Keys, with his boots squelching in the early morning mud and his face reddening in the early morning drizzle, as the six o'clock peal echoed from the steeple of nearby St Edmund's church, and *the* first coaches of the day prepared to depart, he was giving half his sharp attention to the punctuality of his fleet, and at the same time he was rapidly assessing the character of Nan's younger son.

He knew him by repute, of course, as a 'pretty dull dog', and had seen him once or twice, boarding a coach or walking along the Strand, quiet as a shadow beside his mother's exuberance or his brother's high spirits. But now the young man stood before him, come to 'do business', and Mr Chaplin had no intention of making it easy for him. The business world was tough and uncompromising and if this withdrawn young personage wanted to make his way in it, the sooner he knew its true character the better.

A diffident young man, Mr Chaplin thought, looking straight into John's dark eyes through the thin mist of that pervasive rain, and noticing how quickly they were lowered. Not a strapping fellow like his brother. His shoulders were too narrow and his neck too slight for physical strength. But he stood well, making the most of his height, with his spine straight and his hands at his sides like a guardsman, ignoring the drizzle even though the rain was dripping off the brim of his black beaver hat and beading along the shoulders of his blue jacket. He had plainly taken great care over his appearance for this interview, for his linen was spotless and, what was more, he'd shaved his chin, which was rare at such an hour in the morning. 'Well sir?' Mr Chaplin said, flicking ash from the end of his cigar. ''Tis six o'clock, sir, and time for business.'

John had been taking stock, too, in his own quiet way, and knew that this business would have to be done quickly, because that was Mr Chaplin's way.

He came to the point at once. 'You currently carry our freight, I believe Mr Chaplin, at the going rate of threepence a mile, is that not so?'

Mr Chaplin signalled with his eyebrows that the Ipswich coach should depart at once and agreed that it was.

'That being so,' John said, 'perhaps we could discuss terms for a proposition which I have in mind and which I have already taken the liberty of discussing with some of your coachmen…'

One of Mr Chaplin's coachmen was rattling one of his fine

red and black coaches out of the yard with such a spraying of mud and such a braying of horns and such a cacophony of leaping mongrels that further conversation was impossible.

'Not that this was done in any spirit of presumption, you understand...' John felt compelled to explain.

The Ipswich coach was now being followed in its turn by the 'Phenomena', with Mr Joseph Wiggins magnificently in command and winking at him as he passed, and behind the 'Phenomena' two more trundling giants were preparing to leave. The noise was thunderous.

'I thought it best to sound their opinions, Mr Chaplin, sir...' How impossible it was to conduct business in all this noise. The great man wasn't listening. How could he hear?

The last coach swayed and tumbled through the misty entrance with a pancake of damp straw and dirty paper squashed beneath its rear wheels and the accompanying dogs fell into paroxysms of mud-spattered excitement. The post-boys adjusted their leg pads and wiped their damp foreheads with their wet caps and sighed with relief at a job well done. And Mr Chaplin turned his full attention to John Easter.

'Well then, sir,' he said.

John pulled a neat file of papers from the inside pocket of his jacket and handed it across. 'I have made certain calculations, sir,' he said, 'which should explain the proposition.'

But Mr Chaplin had no intention of letting him off the hook. 'In brief sir,' he said. 'Tell me in brief, for I'm a busy man.'

'In brief, sir,' John said, 'what I am asking of you is that your coachmen should carry our papers in a different manner. Delivery would be a great deal quicker if they were to be transferred from coach to coach at every lengthy halting place. At Scole, for example, Mr Joseph Wiggins — who said I was to tell you he was agreeable — would transfer from the 'Phenomena' to the Cambridge coach, which leaves the White Hart three minutes after his arrival. It is all explained in those papers.'

'Is it so?' the great man said, puffing his cigar. 'Is it indeed?' And he took the papers, thrust them roughly into the front of his jacket, and strode off towards the booking office.

Have we made a bargain or not? John wondered. It was impossible to tell. He made one last effort. 'If there are any points which require elucidation,' he called, 'a note sent to Easter house in the Strand will find me at any time. I should be most happy to...'

But Mr Chaplin was already halfway through the booking office door. He waved his cigar by way of acknowledgement and was gone.

Now John Easter was aware that he was cold and that his feet were soaking wet and that the rain was dripping down his neck in a chilly steady stream from the brim of his beaver hat. He removed the offending article and shook it angrily, scattering fat drops of water onto a black and white mongrel that was sitting hopefully in front of him in case he was going into the coffee room for something edible.

'I think I have failed this time,' he told the animal. 'I wasn't quick enough. I'm a pretty dull dog, and that's the truth of it.' But the animal perked up his ears and cocked his head on one side and gazed at him with admiration. 'And I can't see what you've got to look so pleased about, either. We're both pretty dull dogs.'

The mongrel was mightily pleased by such praise and sat up straight so that he could beg with one paw, for he was a cute animal and knew a soft touch when he saw one.

Why couldn't I be born like Mr Chaplin? John asked himself, envying the great man's splendid self-assurance. Or Billy?

The mongrel tried whining hopefully and wagging his tail.

'Oh come along, then,' John said, resigning himself to charity, which was at least something he *was* capable of. 'You shall have a mutton chop, I suppose. There's no point in both of us being miserable.'

So the mongrel had his chop and two days later John Easter had his reward.

It was a brief note and business-like, written in a bold flowing hand and signed with a flourish.

I have perused the proposition of A Easter & Sons and wish to make the following remarks upon it, viz:

1) that should it be agreed upon, Mr Easter would undertake to ascertain whether the coachmen are agreeable to it.

2) that Mr Easter should consider the offer of a bonus to the coachmen and the company to be payable on such occasions when punctuality was particularly essential.

3) that Mr Easter should entirely understand that no coach would ever delay departure for the arrival of his newspapers. Which being so it would be entirely Mr Easter's responsibility to ensure that the papers should arrive at their point of departure from London in adequate time.

I have the honour to be Mr Easter's obedt servt,
William Chaplin.

John read it through at once and very quickly, his heart swelling with excitement and hope. But the answer he was looking for seemed to have eluded him. Had Mr Chaplin agreed or not? He read it again, this time very slowly and with great attention. But he was still baffled. Paper in hand he set off along the long corridor to consult Cosmo Teshmaker.

'Do we have a bargain, think 'ee?' he asked, as the lawyer began to read the letter.

Mr Teshmaker read on studiously, paused to consider, and then gave his cautious approximation to an affirmative reply. 'Given that you are able to satisfy the gentleman upon all three of his conditions, I should venture to say it would be likely,' he said, handing back the paper.

'In that case, I shall put my mind to it at once,' John said. And did.

By a piece of singular good fortune, Nan Easter had left London that very morning to travel to York, where she was negotiating for two new shops and a reading room, and she'd told her sons, very firmly, before her departure, that she intended to stay there until all three deals were satisfactorily completed. So this time John had the chance to complete his own deal without her.

First, he wrote a carefully phrased letter to Mr Chaplin commending his 'admirable suggestion that a bonus be paid for necessary punctuality' and suggesting that they should meet, 'as soon as is mutually possible' to discuss terms. As to the coachmen, he said it had always been his intention to deal directly with all those 'involved in our enterprise' (a neat touch, that 'our'), as he had already done, 'with some success' on the East Anglian routes. (Oh, the pride of that modest understatement!) Then he assured his 'esteemed friend and colleague' that no coach would ever be kept waiting on account of any delivery from A Easter and Sons and signed the letter in the usual way but with a splendid sense of a job well done.

Then he went out into the Strand, where the cobbles were already unpleasantly crowded in the September sunshine, determined to solve the problem of getting his papers from the printing houses to Mr Chaplin's coaching inns in the shortest possible time. And discovered the fourpenny flyers.

They were everywhere he looked: small, dapper, two-horse carriages, carrying a single passenger at breakneck speed, and positively darting along beside the cumbersome progress of hansoms and cabriolets and all those heavy town chaises that were clogging the road. He watched with delight as one of them sleeked through the little space between two trundling carts and set off at a gallop towards Temple Bar. Fourpenny flyers! Of course. Why hadn't he thought of them before? He could have teams of them standing ready outside the post office, to take the papers the moment they were stamped. At fourpence a time they would be expensive, that was undeniable, but they would be trustworthy, and that was what would count when he was short of time.

He stood by the side of the road and waited until the next flyer appeared and was delighted when the driver agreed to his proposal almost at once.

'Ain't a deal a' work available that time a' mornin',' the man said. "Ow many was yer wantin', sir, if I may make so bold?'

Rapid calculations. 'Ten to start with. More later.'

'Leave it ter me, guv,' the driver said. 'You shall 'ave 'em by termorrer.'

And he was as good as his word. Rather better, in fact, for he arrived in the post office yard at five-thirty the next morning with a dozen of his friends. They made an impressive cavalcade and dispatched the news with all speed and considerable noise. It was rather exciting, John thought, feeling proud of his achievement. The only disappointment was that there was so little news for them to carry and, what was worse, the demand for it was diminishing by the day.

Nevertheless, by the time his mother returned from York, well pleased with her endeavours there, the machinery had been set in operation, the punctuality bonus negotiated with Mr Chaplin to the satisfaction of both parties, and A Easter and Sons were all set to be first with the news, the minute there was any news to be first with.

It was a disappointment to John that she didn't seem to understand what good work he'd done.

'My heart alive!' she roared at him when he presented the weekly accounts to her. 'What's this? Four shillings a day for flyers! Do you mean to beggar us, Johnnie? Or en't you in your right senses? What do we want with flyers?'

'We need them for their speed, Mama,' he said. 'To be first with the news, you know. They are standing ready to take the latest news the moment it arrives.'

'Our own vans do that.'

'But they couldn't do it so quickly. If news broke suddenly, we need to distribute it as quickly as we can.'

'And how often does news break like that?' she demanded. 'Once a month, if that.'

'It could be more often now.'

'Or less. No, Johnnie, our trade is down, and thanks to you our expenses are up. You will cancel all these unnecessary flyers this very afternoon, so you will.'

He was appalled. What a thing to ask him to do, after all the effort he'd put into collecting them and organising them. 'I understood that I was to be a manager of this firm,' he said coldly.

'Aye, so you are.'

'Then pray allow me to manage, Mama.'

'You may manage the sales for the firm,' his mother said, 'but *I* own it, don't 'ee forget. And if we're to make a profit overall, which I fully intend to see we do, then those flyers must be cancelled. We en't paying them to stand around doing nothing.'

'What if news were to break all on a sudden?' he said, pale with the effort it was taking to control himself.

'Why then 'twould break and we would profit by it.'

'But if we miss the coaches...' he tried, trembling with the injustice of it. Couldn't she see what a terrible thing she was asking him to do?

But she wouldn't hear him. 'The flyers go,' she ordered. 'And you'd best be off to the York road tomorrow to find shops. At least that's a thing you can do with some semblance of economy. You en't within the bounds of understanding, and that's a fact. Four shillings a day for flyers to stand about doing nothing. 'Tis rank exorbitance, so 'tis!'

'He can't go tomorrow, Mama,' Billy said mildly, helping himself to more wine. 'We travel to Bury tonight for the Otten-shaws' party.'

'And Miss Honeywood will be there, I daresay,' Nan grinned at him, humour restored. 'Oh very well, but you'd best make an early start on Monday, Johnnie.'

'I would go tonight should you wish it,' he told her, wanting nothing more than to get away as quickly as he could from her injustice. Besides, he had no desire to attend a party. What if that dreadful Lizzie had been invited too? Even the thought of it was insupportable.

But his mother was no help to him in this matter either. 'No, no,' she said. 'Go to Bury. Enjoy yourself. 'Twill improve your humour. All work and no play, you know. Now then, Mr Tesh-maker, show me the London accounts.'

He caught the first coach to York the very next morning. His mother could say what she pleased he would live his own life. If he wasn't allowed to hire the flyers he would open up new routes. It would keep him away from the dreadful Lizzie and his mother's authority, and besides this was the part of his job that he did best. And he was so cross that he was full of energy.

By Christmas he had opened shops in Tadcaster, Ferry-bridge, Doncaster and Selby, as he was happy to report when he returned to Bedford Square to join the family celebrations. And after Christmas he set off again, this time for St Albans to open another shop there. And after St Albans, Reading and Maiden-head and Newbury, and so on along the road to Bath.

The weather was excessively cold and travel excessively difficult, but he was determined. By the end of January he had moved on to Marlborough, and in the middle of February he arrived in the little market town of Chippenham. By then his solitary existence had become habitual. He was used to eating lonely suppers before scorching fires in wayside inns, to sleeping — or not sleeping — in damp beds in damper rooms, to travelling stiff with cold despite being swathed in shawls and mufflers and sustained by frequent flasks of brandy and hot water. His rewards were newly opened shops and increased profits and his mother's occasional praise.

But the Angel in Chippenham turned out to be the most comfortable of all the inns he'd sampled on his long, cold journey. It was a large inn, built to accommodate the ever-growing number of coaches that passed through the town on their way from London to Bath, and to provide meat and drink to the local traders who gathered there on market days, high days and holidays, but at this time of year few people stayed more than an hour or two, and coaches only ran twice a week, so John had the place virtually to himself, which was extremely agreeable. So he decided to stay there and make the place his headquarters while he worked through all the towns in the area. The food was wholesome to eat, the beds were warm, for once, and he had Mr Wordsworth's poetry for company.

He had bought a copy of Mr Wordsworth's newly published poem, 'The Excursion', just before he left London and was finding it very much to his taste in this self-imposed exile of his. It was a long poem, in ten books, and was the story of a travelling poet, with a great admiration for nature and the countryside, of course, who met up with a philosopher called the Wanderer and had now, in the second book, encountered a marvellously pessimistic character called the Solitary, who could have been modelled on John Easter himself, for he was described as having 'a pale face' and being 'a tall and meagre person' and was given to wondering 'wherefore was I born?' and to expressing sad, noble sentiments. It gave John a frisson of the most exquisitely miserable pleasure to read such things, and when he discovered that his hero wore 'a faint sarcastic smile' he decided that he too would acquire the same accomplishment and use it the next time his mother criticised the flyers. He spent several minutes at the end of every day practising sarcastic smiles by candlelight in his dressing table mirror.

In fact, in a perverse way, he was enjoying his stay in Chippenham. As far as he was concerned the winter and the work and the peace and quiet of Chippenham could go on for ever and ever. So he was rather put out when he was woken early one morning by a terrible hullabaloo outside his window. He was well-used to the clop and snort of a passing horse or the occasional voice raised in greeting, but now there were carts and horses by the score, grinding the cobbles to thunder, and people hammering and shouting, and children squabbling, and babies crying, and cocks crowing, and pigs squealing, and the noise was enough to split skulls.

'What is it?' he asked the chambermaid, when she brought up his early morning tea.

'Why 'tis the fair,' she told him happily, gazing at it from the window. 'First fair of the year, sir. First week in March. There's stalls from all over, an' a shambles jest across the way, d'ye see, fer the freshest o' meat. What a piece o' good fortune for you, sir, to be here for the fair.'

He was up, washed, shaved, dressed and packed within twenty minutes. There was a stagecoach running to Bath early that morning and he intended to catch it. Under no circumstances could he share his peaceful retreat with a fair. Whatever it was like, Bath was bound to be more congenial than that.

But, as it turned out, he was wrong.

THEY REACHED the top of Kingsdown Hill at a little after nine o'clock that morning and stopped to give the horses a breather before their long descent into the city. It was one of those dank miserable days, when the world is drained of colour and lungs are suffused with moisture. The newly grown catkins were quite sodden and hung from their black branches like small clothes pegged to dry. The sky was like a damp sheet, heavy and dirty-white and massively wrinkled. Even the sun looked apologetic, pale as the moon and shrunk to half its size.

The passengers stood about coughing dismally and taking the occasional swig from their hip flasks in a vain attempt to garner a little warmth. And below them the city of Bath lay in a hollow between the damp hills, almost entirely obscured by swirling clouds of greeny-white vapour. To John's travel-jaundiced eyes it looked like some huge steaming cistern where small black figures bobbed into view, as though they were being boiled, to swim and struggle for a second before being sucked into the muck again. Here and there through the mists he caught a glimpse of a pale yellow wall, or the honeycombed mullions of an abbey or the corner of some grand parade where miniature sedan chairs jogged and bounced and dark coaches rolled in and out of the mist, but it was a dispiriting view.

'What a ghastly place!' he said to his companion, a cheerful middle-aged man who had introduced himself as Mr Bourne.

''Tis the mist makes it so,' Mr Bourne observed, rearranging his muffler about his nose and mouth. 'In fair weather 'tis a fine fair city and uncommon good for one's health.'

John found that very hard to believe and was beginning to have quite serious doubts about the advisability of this visit. But it was too late to change his mind. The horses were rested and it was time to descend into the cauldron. Perhaps, he thought, trying to cheer himself as the drags were adjusted, it will improve upon closer acquaintance.

It got worse. As the mist gradually enveloped them, the outside passengers were chilled to the bone, and soon they were all coughing and spluttering and wiping their eyes and blowing their noses and wishing themselves anywhere but where they were.

But at last they reached the city and came to a steaming halt in Stall Street outside the White Hart Inn, and opposite an imposing colonnade which, so his new friend told him, led to the entrance to the Baths themselves. And John got his first appalled view of the inhabitants.

They were all old, all deformed, all cripples! And as noisy as crows. Either being carried into the place in bath chairs, swathed in bandages, pale-faced and complaining, and clinging like grim death to the greasy thongs that swung beside their ears, or being wheeled out of it, still swathed in bandages, but this time boiled red as lobsters and limp with heat exhaustion. He'd never seen such a hideous collection in his life.

I will have breakfast, he vowed, and then I will buy a map of the town, decide upon the most suitable site for our shop, rent it with all speed, and travel on to Bristol on the very first coach out.

The breakfast was surprisingly good, the map was informative, the choice of sites obvious, but the renting office was closed, and according to a neat notice hung on its clammy door would not be open until eight of the clock the following morning. He would have to stay a day in the city after all.

His fellow passengers were still in the coffee room of the White Hart when he came dripping back to join them.

'Ah!' Mr Bourne said, 'there you are. We waited for you, d'ye see. We're all off to take the waters, since it seems that everybody takes the waters or bathes at this hour. They say the Pump Room is splendid. Just the place to be, what?'

'If I take any more water I shall turn into a sponge,' John said. But at least it was one way of passing the time. So he went.

The Pump Room was really rather a handsome place. It was a long room, decorated in the best fashion in duck-egg blue, white and gold, and beautifully proportioned, with five long windows on either side divided from each other by Corinthian columns painted white and gilded gold. It was full of people and there were invalid chairs and their impatient patients pushing and shoving in every direction, but there were two good fires to warm them and a fine band to play to them.

'Have a glass of Spa water, my dear friend,' Mr Bourne said, pressing one into John's hand. 'There's a seat for us by the inner windows. I've sent my man to secure it. Just the place, what?' And although John had no desire to take the waters, he took the glass and followed his new friend's broad shoulders towards the inner windows.

'Your very good health, sir,' he said to Mr Bourne. And he sipped his metallic water, found it extremely disagreeable and turned his head to look through the window so as to avoid drinking any more of it.

And he found he was gazing straight down into one of the baths, an ancient stone pit filled with water as thick and green as pea soup, and steaming. And bobbing about in it were scores of people, some young and slender, others old and extraordinary: bald-headed men without teeth and billowing women without stays, tumbling together in the steam, wearing sulphur-yellow nightcaps above steam-red faces and sulphur-yellow nightgowns below. He had never seen anything so gross. But the fascination of the sight was so intense that he watched on, intrigued.

And one of the fat women suddenly rolled over in the water and turned up her eyes and gave a roar, flailing so wildly that she knocked several of her nearest companions into the water. Then, still roaring, she began to sink, her yellow gown slowly filling with air like a balloon. He watched with passing interest as two attendants arrived and dragged her rather unceremoniously to the water's edge. Then he looked back idly at the other bathers who were still struggling and floundering in the water. One of them appeared to be fainting, for she was drooping over the arms of her slender companion and her cap was drifting away from her on the scummy water. A rather odd-looking cap, he thought, watching it, for there were bunches of false curls attached to it on either side. False yellow curls, rather like old Miss Pettie's.

And the slender young women looked up, calling for help. And she was Miss Harriet Sowerby.

CHAPTER 6

Harriet Sowerby was never so glad of anything in her life as she was at the sight of her own dear Mr Easter looking down at her from the Pump Room on that dreadful, dreadful afternoon.

When the fat lady made that unearthly groaning noise and fell backwards into the water, Harriet was alarmed and upset, but when those awful flailing arms knocked poor Miss Pettie off her balance, she was so frightened she hardly knew what she ought to do.

She called for help but everybody was attending to the fat lady and nobody heard her, and in the meantime, Miss Pettie was sinking. She knew that the imperative thing was to keep a drowning person's head out of the water. But Miss Pettie's head was quite extraordinarily heavy and her body was drifting of its own accord. Oh! Oh! What should she do? What if Miss Pettie were to die? What would her mother say when she heard of it? She hung on, trying to push the air out of that awful swelling gown with one hand and supporting Miss Pettie's white wet head with the other and all the time she was praying frantically. Dear Lord, please don't let her die! Oh, please don't.

And there he was. Like a miracle. The answer to her prayer. Looking at her with so many expressions following one another so rapidly on his remembered face, surprise, recognition, alarm, and then the most tender concern. He was saying something to her through the glass, but she couldn't hear what it was. And the next second, he was gone. She was weak with relief, the strength ebbing out of her arms, but she hung on, and presently she could hear his voice echoing round the bath, giving orders. 'Attendant! Attendant! Quickly! This way! Follow me!' How wonderfully commanding he was.

And then he was standing beside her in the water, stripped to his shirt, and there were two bath attendants with him who lifted Miss Pettie out of her hands and carried her to the steps, dangling her body between them like some huge wet sail. And Miss Pettie wasn't dead after all, praise he! She was fluttering her hands and begging to be forgiven for being such a nuisance. 'I am so sorry, so very sorry. Oh John, my dear boy, how can you forgive me? What a dreadful thing!'

He was wading beside her, soothing her, his fine shirt stained by the water. 'It is no trouble, Miss Pettie. You are not to think it. We will soon have you better. Lift her gently, if you please, sir.'

They were lowering her into a chair which had been brought down to the water's edge by a third attendant, and now a small crowd was gathering around her, avid with interest, and what with their saffron-yellow backs and the steam rising from the bath, Harriet couldn't see any more of Miss Pettie except for her poor old head with its thin cap of scant white hair. And she remembered how sensitive the lady was about her appearance and how much she must be suffering to be seen in public without her cap, and she went wading off to find it.

By the time it was retrieved and Harriet had pushed her way back through the heavy water to the steps and finally climbed out, the fat lady had been carried away and the crowd around

Miss Pettie was consequently a great deal bigger. It now contained two physicians, who were both red in the face and shouting at one another for the privilege of attending poor Miss Pettie, who had been bundled in towels and blankets and seemed to be recovering. She was certainly a much better colour, although her mouth was trembling and she looked as though she would burst into tears at the slightest provocation. Mr Easter was wrapped in a towel too, but he wore his with a romantic air, swathed about his shoulders like a poet or a wild Scottish chieftain or a...

'Where do you stay?' he asked, walking to the edge of the bath and holding out his hand to assist her.

What a comforting thing to be supported so! And what a warm, firm hand it was. 'In the White Hart,' she said. 'Thank 'ee kindly.'

The attendants were wrapping her in a towel too. 'What good fortune.' Mr Easter said, smiling at her, 'for that is where I am staying too. I will escort you to your rooms. Does Miss Pettie have a maidservant with her?'

'Jane is here,' she said, handing Miss Pettie her bedraggled cap. 'We sent her to Milsom Street to make a few little purchases.'

'Then she may return for your clothes,' he said, and Harriet noticed that he was careful not to look at Miss Pettie while she draped her head. 'We need not delay here a moment longer.' And he turned to the physicians. 'I am sure we are all grateful to you for your concern, gentlemen, howsomever we have no need of your services at present.'

'You will take my card, sir,' the smaller of the two said instantly, handing one damply across. 'Recommended by Persons of Quality as you see, sir.'

'And mine, sir,' the other bristled. 'Recommended by a marquis, sir.'

'Your servant, gentlemen,' John said coolly and he turned his body away from them to give orders to the attendants. 'A chair for the young lady, if you please.'

'Oh no,' Harriet demurred, embarrassed to be put in the same social position as Miss Pettie. 'I can walk, Mr Easter. Indeed I can.'

But he wouldn't hear of it. 'After such a to-do and in such a state? The very idea! A chair for the young lady, *if* you please.'

It was really quite thrilling to be carried from the baths, even if the chairs *were* horribly damp and even if they *did* smell of mildew and even if she *did* feel she had no right to be in one. Mr Easter walked between her chair and Miss Pettie's, giving them both the most careful attention as if they really were equals. He had picked up his coat and hat, and carried them across his arm, but it was the arm nearest Miss Pettie and so Harriet had nothing to obstruct her view of him. And how handsome he was. A true knight, in his wet shirt and his wet breeches with that straight dark hair ruffled by his exertions. A true knight come to her rescue, just at the very moment when she needed him most. Even in her most daring dreams she'd never imagined anything remotely like this. It was like a fairy tale.

Miss Pettie began to weep the moment they emerged into the crowded street. Her false hair was so sodden that it hung on either side of her poor old wrinkled face in long, straw-coloured rats' tails.

'Oh John, John,' she sobbed, clutching at it. 'What a disgrace to be seen so. I cannot abide it. Indeed I can't. We must go home at once, Harriet. At once. I have brought shame to us both. And to you too, I fear, John. Oh what recompense for all your goodness.' She was awash with distress. Pea-green water dripped from the rats' tails, and tears rolled down her nose and the chair dropped puddles at every step. 'Oh John, John, I want to go home.'

He remembered his timetables even in the rush of rescue. 'And so you shall, Miss Pettie,' he promised. 'There is a coach leaves the White Hart for London at half past five this very afternoon. It would mean travelling by night, but if that is what you wish, I will take seats upon it this very minute as ever is.'

'Oh,' she said, as they dripped through the colonnade, 'it is. It is.'

And then they were being carried over the threshold into the White Hart and there was such a rush of activity that Harriet could barely catch her breath. Porters lifting Miss Pettie from her wet chair to a dry one and trotting away with her in a warm noisy procession, a stream of maids bearing brass bed warmers and potboys balancing brandy and hot water, Miss Pettie's old servant Jane arriving, rabbit-eyed with anxiety, bundled about with parcels, her bonnet askew and her grey hair disordered, patting her mistress's hand as well as she could as she ran beside the chair. And Mr Easter still coolly in command, requiring more blankets, giving Jane instructions, tipping the maids and the potboys, dismissing yet another unwanted physician and finally unlocking Miss Pettie's door and smiling at Harriet as she walked past him into the room.

'Should Miss Pettie require a physician,' he said, 'tell her I will arrange one for her. This town is full of quacks. If she were left to her own devices, she would pay a great deal to very little purpose. I do not think she has taken any real harm from the blow. She is upset, that is all, and overcome by the heat of the baths. Get her to bed and keep her warm. I will return.'

And so he did, with the news that he had managed to acquire four seats on the evening coach, 'two inside for Miss Pettie and Jane, and two outside for Miss Sowerby and myself.'

He was delighted to see that pretty apricot blush on Miss Sowerby's pale cheeks again, and those little crooked teeth biting her lip so charmingly.

'We dine at the Angel Inn at Chippenham,' he said. 'A comfortable place, which will serve us well, I assure you. I was there myself only this morning.'

'They will be surprised to see you back so soon, my dear,' Miss Pettie said.

But if they were, they didn't show it. They served a passable meal of chitterlings and roast pork and provided them all with quantities of hot water and the best brandy to sustain them on the next leg of their journey. And off they went again.

While they were dining, the rain finally stopped, and now the night was clear and cold, bright with moonlight and studded with white stars. Harriet, perched aloft in the biting air beside her hero, suddenly felt exposed and vulnerable, for the three other outside passengers were staying at Chippenham overnight and now they had the whole of the outside of the coach to themselves, quite unchaperoned. It was really rather romantic.

As they settled into the two best seats, side by side, and tucked their greatcoats about their knees and their mufflers about their necks, she was overpoweringly aware of him, of the warmth of his body, and the white breath streaming from his mouth as he spoke, and his eyes so dark and limpid as he glanced towards her.

And then the coach began to roll, swaying so suddenly and so violently that she was flung against his side, and he had to put out an arm to steady her. And that was very romantic. They were so close to one another she could see the reflection of the lantern in the pupils of his eyes.

How handsome he is, she thought, and how kind, looking after us all like this. And she felt secure and cherished.

As well she might, for he was feeling most concerned about her. Her face looked excessively pale in the darkness. He had hoped there would be a seat inside for her after Chippenham, but all the passengers were travelling to London.

'Were you long in Bath, Miss Sowerby?' he said to make conversation.

'Three days, Mr Easter,' she said. 'We were to have stayed a month.'

'Did you have a chance to see something of the city? It is very beautiful in fair weather, I'm told.'

So she told him about the fine shops in Milsom Street and the Assembly Rooms 'at the top of such a hill, but very grand and well worth the climb, so Miss Pettie said'.

'Did you dance there?' he asked remembering the Victory Ball.

'Well,' she confessed, 'not a great deal. The major domo was rather...' He'd been an overpowering snob and had spent no time on her at all once he'd discovered that she was an old lady's companion, but she didn't think she could say that.

'They are not a pleasant breed,' he said. 'They live to match money to money, and greed to ambition. I have never liked them.'

'And yet a ball can be such an agreeable occasion,' she said, remembering the Victory Ball.

'Given the right company,' he said, feeling extremely daring, because he was almost offering her a compliment.

'Yes indeed,' she said. And the coach threw her into his arms again like the obliging vehicle it was.

And so they talked all the way to the Pelican Inn at Newbury, where they spent twenty minutes toasting themselves before a blazing fire while their supplies of brandy and hot water were replenished. Jane stayed in the coach with Miss Pettie, who was fast asleep and snoring, and the two other inside passengers who were so well wrapped in rugs they said they didn't want to budge for anything. But Harriet was glad of the fire for it had been very cold on top of the coach. When she had to leave the inn, the air about her felt icy and before they'd gone more than a mile or two, she began to shiver.

'You are cold?' John asked, rather concerned.

'No, no,' she tried to assure him, shivering more than ever.

He untied the shawl that he wore wound about his shoulders and handed it across to her. 'Wear this,' he said, and when she opened her mouth to protest. 'I shall not take "no" for an answer, so wear it, pray do.' And because they were alone again in the swaying darkness, and he was still feeling extraordinarily gallant, and because it was very nearly the truth, 'I would not have you take cold for the world.'

Being cared for so openly and kindly suddenly made her tearful. She took the shawl and folded it about her. It was warm to the touch, and to her tremulous imagination it seemed that he was holding her in his arms.

'When we get to Reading, we have a ten-minute stop,' he said. 'I will unpack my green jacket and you shall wear that. I cannot have you shivering all the way to London.'

'I am sorry to shiver,' she apologised. 'I do try not to.'

'You cannot shiver or not shiver to order,' he said. 'That is an impossibility. When you are warmer you will not shiver, I guarantee.'

She felt she owed it to him to try and explain. 'It is not just the cold, Mr Easter.'

'Then what?' he asked, intrigued.

She dropped her head so that her face was obscured by the brim of her bonnet. 'It is because I am rather afraid.'

'Not of me, I trust.'

'Oh no, no,' she said hurriedly. 'Never of you.'

'Then what do you fear? Coaches are a deal safer these days, I assure you, particularly on a night like this. Look how full the moon is. Why it is almost as bright as day. And besides, this is the best road of them all since Mr Macadam took charge of it. You have nothing to fear on this journey. Nothing at all.'

'Well perhaps not afraid,' she said. 'A little concerned, perhaps.'

He considered her new words with splendid gravity. 'Then what concerns you, Miss Sowerby? If it is anything within my power to allay, I will do so at once, you have my word.'

He was so kind. But his kindness made her shiver more than

ever. 'It is nothing,' she whispered, her head still bowed. 'I am being foolish.'

'Tell me,' he urged. 'There is no one here to overhear us.' Which was true enough, for the coachman was singing to himself and in any case the noise of hooves and wheels would certainly cover their quiet conversation.

'It is just,' she said, deciding to confide in him, 'that I fear my parents will be angry with me.'

'Angry?' he said, very surprised to hear it. 'Whatever for? What could you possibly have done to make them angry with you?'

'They will say that I have failed in my duty,' she said miserably, breaking into a partial confession at his kindness. She could tell him *that* at least. 'I should have cared for Miss Pettie, you see, and if you had not been there she could have drowned. I was allowed to travel with her so that she would be looked after, and they will say I failed in my allotted task. I know they will.'

'But they will not be angry,' he said. Who could possibly be angry with her when she looked so pale and frail and charming?

'They will,' she said, and the tears welled out of her eyes and dropped upon her cheeks, glistening like silver in the moonlight. 'They will say I am a sinner.'

'You are not a sinner,' he said passionately. 'You are kind and gentle. I never saw anyone less capable of sin.'

His passion dried her tears.

'They won't be angry,' he said firmly, taking command of her.

'No,' she said, 'perhaps not.' Oh how much she would like to believe him.

The coach swayed on and he began to tell her about Mr Wordsworth's latest poem because he thought it would help her if he changed the subject, and she tried to listen, but by now, what with the lateness of the hour and the steady rhythm of the vehicle and the soporific warmth of all the brandy she'd drunk, she was finding it difficult to keep her eyes open. Presently her head began to nod.

John was surprising himself by the way he was describing Mr Wordsworth's poem. Little more than twenty-four hours ago he'd been in complete sympathy with the pessimistic views of the Solitary, now he was stressing the opinions of the travelling poet. 'It is a good world, Miss Sowerby. A good and beautiful world,' he said.

The coach gave a violent jolt that threw them together again, but this time, instead of recovering quickly and drawing apart, she stayed where she was, leaning against his chest with her head on his shoulder and, looking down, he saw that she was fast asleep. The poor dear girl, he thought. She is worn out. And he put his arm tentatively around her narrow shoulders so as to support her and hold her steady. It was a marvellous moment, intensely pleasurable and yet private. He had never known another quite like it.

When the coach stopped at Reading and Maidenhead, she was still asleep, so he stayed where he was, even though his feet were so cold he couldn't feel them and he was beginning to get pins and needles in his arm. But what of that, when this dear, quiet, patient girl needed his support? He was still holding her in his arms when they rattled over the cobbles into the Swan with Two Necks at three o'clock in the morning.

Then she woke with a start and apologised for being a nuisance, covering those delightful uneven teeth of hers with her gloved hand. But fortunately he had so much to attend to that there wasn't time for either of them to be embarrassed. The luggage had to be unpacked and put aboard a cabriolet, and Miss Pettie woken and eased from one vehicle to the other, blinking and clutching her curls, and fares negotiated and orders given.

And then when they were all arrived at Bedford Square, the

servants had to be woken and set to work to rekindle the kitchen fire and warm the beds and provide what hot water they could. And by this time they were all bone weary and Harriet was asleep on her feet.

She made one last effort in order to undress and fold her clothes neatly, then she fell into the mattress, briefly aware that it was made of feathers and quite miraculously soft and was asleep before she could think another thought.

In his own quiet room on the other side of the house, John was too excited to sleep at all. He took out his copy of 'The Excursion', lit two more candles and settled down to read himself sober. He had spent the better part, and it *was* the better part, of an entire night in the company of a young woman, and he'd looked after her, and cared for her, and reassured her, and held her in his arms. *He* had. *He,* John Henry Easter. Shy John Henry Easter. What an amazing thing.

He was still dozing and reading and still feeling amazed at his behaviour when the hall clock struck six and a servant came to call him with a jug of hot water and the news that his breakfast would be ready in half an hour. It was a new day and another journey. What a splendid prospect!

But this journey was in his closed carriage, and there, as was only proper, he sat beside Miss Pettie, with Jane and Miss Sowerby in the servants' seats facing them, keeping their place and only speaking when they were spoken to.

Miss Pettie was fully recovered and declared that she would be quite herself again if only her legs wouldn't totter so. She chattered all the way to Bury, almost without pausing for breath. Nobody else could get a word in edgeways, so the journey was interminable.

By mid-afternoon, when they finally arrived in Angel Square, John was heartily sick of her. 'Look out of the window, Miss Pettie,' he urged, 'and you will see a sight worth seeing.' Oh how glad he was of it!

Miss Pettie jammed her false curls against the carriage window and recognised where she was.

'Home at last!' she said rapturously, clapping her hands together. 'The Good Lord be praised for it, and you too, Mr Easter, of course. What a blessing it is to have such a good neighbour. And what a perfectly delightful journey this has been! I cannot thank you enough. And you, my dear,' she added, turning to Harriet. 'You were indeed a kindly nurse, and I was uncommon glad of your company.'

Their arrival put both households in an uproar. Bessie Thistlethwaite came out onto the Easter doorstep at once to commiserate with Miss Pettie and to offer to help her 'with any little thing', and Miss Pettie's servants gathered in their hall open-mouthed with surprise, and Miss Pettie wept, and Jane told everybody who was listening what a trial they'd all been through, and Harriet stood on the cobbles with her battered carpetbag in her hand and waited for the excitement to subside so that she could say goodbye.

'Have you far to go, Miss Sowerby?' John asked, touched by the sight of her, so slight and quiet and patient.

'Oh no,' she said. 'It is no distance. Churchgate Street. A step away.'

'I will escort you,' he said, taking the carpetbag. And did.

They walked together, and as slowly as they could, because their adventure was so nearly over. 'I must thank you for all your care, Mr Easter,' Harriet said as they climbed the hill of Churchgate Street and her house came into view. 'You have been so kind.'

'It was nothing,' he said, knowing how very much it was.

She stopped outside a little low cottage and knocked at the door once and gently. 'This is where I live, sir,' she said.

He looked at the cottage and the carpetbag and the thin cloth of her coat and realised, for the first time, that she was poor. Then he didn't know what to say to her. He wanted to see her again and had been wondering if he could suggest that she might like to accompany him to the theatre or the next ball at the Athenaeum. But what if he were suggesting something she couldn't afford? Ball gowns cost a deal of money, as he knew from the dresses his mother wore, and it occurred to him that she had probably hired the white gown she wore at the Victory Ball, and that she might not be able to afford to hire again. Even a visit to the theatre seemed unlikely for she might feel embarrassed to appear in a theatre crowd wearing such a shabby coat. Oh dear, oh dear!

They had been standing in silence for quite a long time waiting for the door to be opened. She looked at him hesitantly and knocked again. But there was still no answer.

'Could they be out, do you think?' he said.

'My father will be at his work at this hour,' she said, her brow puckering at the puzzle of it. 'Howsomever my mother should be at home.'

'Look through the window,' he suggested.

It took her a long time to obey, he noticed, and then she only peeped. Both the downstairs rooms were empty.

'I cannot understand it,' she said. 'Wherever can she be?'

'Ask next door,' he said, leading her up the hill. 'There is no sense standing here knocking at the door of an empty house, now is there?'

Next door turned out to be a laundry, where five dishevelled laundry maids toiled amid the steam, ironing sheets and small-clothes. They were all very surprised to see Harriet.

'Why Rosie, look 'ee here, tha's our Harriet,' the oldest said.

Rosie was a plump woman, who wore a sacking apron and a vacant expression and had a disconcerting habit of repeating the last words that had been said to her, like an affable parrot. 'Our Harriet,' she agreed, 'yes, Mrs Kirby, tha's our Harriet sure 'nough.' And she patted Harriet's arm affectionately.

'We thought you was in Bath for another three weeks,' Mrs Kirby said, tackling a sleeve, with professional speed.

"Nother three weeks,' the parrot emphasised.

'Do you know where my mother is?' Harriet asked.

'Mother is,' the parrot nodded.

'Why my dear, they've gone away,' Mrs Kirby said. 'Gone a-visitin' so Mrs Sowerby a-told us. Your aunt, or some such, down Ipswich way.'

Harriet's face fell visibly. 'When will they be back, Mrs Kirby?'

'Wednesday, my dear. First thing. Mr Cole gave your father four days off, didn't he Rosie?'

'Four days off,' Rosie confirmed.

'Thank 'ee,' Harriet said, but she looked stricken.

'I will see you settled in,' John said as they emerged into the cold air again. 'You could dine at my house this evening, if there is no food in your larder.'

'I cannot get into the house,' she said forlornly. 'I do not have a key. Oh Mr Easter, what shall I do?'

He was in charge of her again. What an amazing piece of luck. 'You shall dine with me, and then I will take you to Rattlesden,' he said. 'You shall stay with my sister.'

CHAPTER 7

The Reverend James Hopkins was sitting at his desk beside the parlour window in the rectory at Rattlesden, composing his sermon for the following day. Or, to be more accurate, trying to think of a text that would comfort his parishioners and give them a sense of worth. The Corn Laws kept the price of corn artificially high, so the landowners' profits remained steady, but since the peace their labourers' pay had fallen even lower than ever. Most of his neighbours eked out an existence so bare it was often little better than that of the beasts they tended. So it was difficult to find a good text for them.

When he heard the sound of a carriage grinding round the corner into the drive, he was quite glad to put down his bitten pen and call to Annie that they had company.

Annie Hopkins was sitting in the dining room of their rambling house making the most of the last of the light to mend a tear in her son's little blue trouser suit. Baby Beau was fourteen months old now and on his feet, staggering into everything, but determined to walk everywhere. Yesterday he'd tumbled into the mud beside the pond on the village green, and that afternoon he'd torn his trousers on a blackthorn.

She finished her work as quickly as she could, calling to James as she sewed, 'Is it Billy, do you think?' for she'd recognised the sound of her mother's pony cart.

She and James met one another in the panelled hall, just as their guests were climbing out of the cart, and by now it was necessary to light the candles before they opened the front door. In the sudden darkness before their little light, neither of them was able to see who was walking up the path.

'Is that you, Billy?' Annie asked, holding her candle aloft.

And John's voice answered, 'No, Annie. It's me. I have come to beg a favour.'

'Come in, come in,' the Reverend Hopkins said, stooping towards them to urge them into the house. 'If it is within our competence you have only to ask.'

And, of course, when the pony had been stabled and Harriet introduced and the story told, it was within their competence.

'What a misfortune to travel all that way and then to find no one home to welcome you!' Annie said to Harriet. 'I will have a room prepared for you this instant. You must be worn out.'

'I am a great nuisance, I fear,' Harriet said.

'Not at all,' Annie said, hastening to reassure her. 'You are most welcome and no trouble at all. Johnnie was entirely correct to bring you here. Come with me, my dear, and allow me to introduce you to Pollyanna and the boys.'

'Have you heard the news?' the Reverend Hopkins said to John when the two women had left the room. There was a copy of *The Times* open on his desk, and they both looked towards it as he spoke.

'No,' John said. 'We've been travelling all day.' He'd forgotten all about news and newspapers. How very remiss.

'Bonaparte has gone back on his word and left Elba with an army of a thousand men.'

It was shattering news, the kind that sold papers in their

thousands, and he'd been out of London when it arrived. 'When did it happen?' he asked.

'On 26th February apparently,' his brother-in-law said, 'but only reported this morning, it seems.'

'Is this this morning's paper?' John asked, picking it up.

'It is. I bought it in Bury this afternoon, when I was visiting the Canon.'

'From Easter's?'

'No, I'm, afraid not,' James admitted. 'It was on sale in Mr Cole's bookshop, arrived on the afternoon stage. Easter's had it too, I'm sure.'

But they should have had it first, John thought. It was the sort of news he ought to have sent out by flyer. His very first opportunity to show how his new system would work, and he'd missed it.

'May I?' he asked, unfolding the paper.

'Pray do. But it makes sober reading, I fear.'

It did.

We have hitherto delayed accounts of Bonaparte's landing on the coast of Provence,' the paper said, 'because the telegraphic dispatches which first made it known still communicate no details.

Bonaparte left Porto Ferrajo on the 26th February, at nine o'clock in the evening, in extremely calm weather, which lasted until 1st March. He embarked in a brig, and was followed by four other vessels, such as pinks and feluccas, having on board from 1,000 to 1,100 men at most, of whom a few were French, and the rest Poles, Corsicans, Neapolitans, and natives of Elba.

The vessels anchored in the road of the Gulf of Juan, near Cannes, on the 1st March, and the troops landed.

'He's been in France for nearly a fortnight,' John said.

'He has indeed.'

'And this is the first we hear of it.'

'It is.'

'Then he has not been repulsed or captured, you may depend upon it. If the news was suppressed, it was suppressed for a purpose. They would have waited for him to be rejected. And if he had been, they would have known of it by now.'

'You fear, as I do, that the French people have made him welcome and joined his cause?'

'I must return to London,' John said. 'More news will follow and I must be there to dispatch it.'

'Tonight?' James demurred.

'Tonight,' John said firmly. His adventure with Miss Sowerby was over. At least for the time being. Now he must return to work.

'But will your mother not…'

'My mother was not in town this morning. There was no sign of her at breakfast. Nor when we arrived last night. In fact I have no idea where my mother is.' He'd been so busy looking after Miss Pettie and Miss Sowerby he hadn't even bothered to inquire. If she was there, she'd be furious at his careless behaviour, and he'd best go back at once to face her and work with her; if she wasn't, it was an opportunity not to be missed. 'I will go back to town tonight.'

'Must you, Johnnie?' Annie said, when she and Harriet heard what he intended.

But his mind was made up. He was full of energy and wanting to be off at once. 'I will send the pony cart for you, Miss Sowerby, early on Wednesday morning. You are in good hands I do assure you.'

'You will stay for a hot punch?' James suggested. But even that was impossible.

Within twenty minutes, the pony was back in harness and none too pleased about it, and John Easter was on his way back to Bury.

'I will write to you,' he called, as he manoeuvred the cart into the darkening lane.

And Harriet, watching him go, wondered which of them he was talking to, and felt that she had no cause to hope it would be her. And hoped just the same.

LONDON WAS BRISTLING WITH RUMOURS, even in the small hours of Sunday morning; people said that the French were flocking to join Napoleon's army, that the British army was on the move, and there had been a skirmish, but no one knew where, that Wellington was on his way home to England to receive orders. If the country was not already at war with Napoleon, as everybody surmised, it certainly felt as though it was.

The Sunday papers had repeated yesterday's news and speculated upon it, but there were no further dispatches from France and nothing more was known, according to Mr Walter of *The Times* who was one of the most reliable newspaper owners in London. And no news from Vienna either, which Mr Walter said he would certainly have expected by now. Most of the 'Allied Sovereigns' had been meeting in 'Congress' in Vienna ever since the first of November. With Napoleon safe out of the way in Elba, they were supposed to be redesigning the map of Europe, but they'd made very little progress in the last five months and now of course, any work they might have done would be rendered quite useless by the dictator's return. The British army was still in Brussels, Mr Walter reported, but there was no news of them either. 'We must bear our souls with patience,' he said, 'and wait for what tomorrow brings.'

So John supervised the stamping, dispatched his papers in the usual way and went home to Bedford Square to find his brother. If there was no news yet, so much the better. It gave him the time to prepare for it.

Nan was out of town, so Mrs Pennyfield the housekeeper

said. 'Gone to stay in Hertfordshire, sir, and like to be there a week. We're to expect her back a' Friday.'

'Did she leave an address?' John asked.

'Holly Hall, St Albans, sir.'

'Thank 'ee, Mrs Pennyfield. Is Mr William up?'

'Rousing sir.'

'Then I will rouse him further. Would you prepare breakfast and send me up some tea?'

'To Mr William's room, sir?'

'To Mr William's room.'

For a gentleman who was supposed to be rousing himself Billy was singularly supine.

'Get up, you lazy dog!' his brother said amiably, pulling all the covers from the bed.

'That you Johnnoh?' Billy said, sitting up slowly and giving his hair a thorough scratching. One side of his face was still marked by creases and he hadn't opened his eyes.

'Put a breeze on!' John said, examining his own unshaven face in the dressing table mirror. 'We've got work to do.'

Billy swung his legs out, off the mattress, and eased them onto the floor. 'Wha'zza time?' he yawned.

'Time you were up. Napoleon's landed in France.'

'That's old news,' Billy said, unimpressed by it. 'Yesterday's news. Where did you go haring off to with old Miss Pettie?'

'Took her home. I'll tell 'ee about it later. Come on, Billy. Look alive. We've got a dozen flyers to hire before the afternoon.'

'You're never going to take on flyers again,' Billy said, opening his eyes at the very idea. 'What'll Ma say?'

But his brother ignored that. 'This time,' he promised, 'Easter's are going to be the first with the news, good or bad. I've ordered tea and breakfast.' He fingered the thick stubble on his chin. 'I must shave, then we're off.

'I've got enough to do without hiring flyers,' Billy said. 'I've got a warehouse to run, in case you hadn't noticed.'

'Come off it, Billy,' John grinned. 'You never go down to the warehouse until after breakfast. Sometimes not even then, if Miss Honeywood wants your company for a ride in the park.'

'Which she very well might this morning, for all you know.'

'Then you must send her a note pleading pressure of work.'

'I can't do that. She'd never forgive me. We're getting along like a house a' fire, I'd have you know.'

'Then if that's the case she'll understand. If we can get the next piece of news out to the provincial towns before anyone else, we shall outsell all our rivals and establish a precedent. Don't you see? It's the chance of a lifetime.'

Billy groaned. 'It beats me where you get your energy from,' he said.

It beat John too when he thought about it. He'd been awake since six the previous morning and had slept very little the night before that, and yet he was charged with energy, fairly bristling with it.

Fatigue caught up with him later that afternoon, when his brother had sent a note to Matilda, after much sighing and protesting, and the necessary flyers had been found and hired and were pledged to be outside the post office at half past five the following morning, and he'd written detailed instructions ready to be attached to each and every ream of newspapers. He took a cab home to Bedford Square, aching with exhaustion, gave orders that, no matter what, he was to be woken at half past four the following morning, crept up the stairs like an old man and fell into bed more asleep than awake.

The next morning was rather a disappointment. The flyers were there and ready, the instructions were tied in position, but there was no further news of Napoleon, and no news from Vienna or Brussels either, so although he and Billy got all the Easter papers to Mr Chaplin's coaches at dazzling speed, it was rather a wasted exercise. Billy said he might as well have stayed in bed as usual.

But on Tuesday there was a new dispatch, and *The Times* was held up for nearly an hour while it was printed. It came from France and was printed in full by *The Times*.

The unpleasant apprehensions which were pretty universally excited on Friday by the intelligence of Bonaparte's landing in France, had begun to subside in the course of Saturday and Sunday, but the news of yesterday has revived the first impressions of alarm. It has been asserted on high authority that he entered Lyons on Saturday evening, and was there welcomed by the general populace, many of whom have joined his army, which is now said to number several thousands.

'He'll have been welcomed elsewhere too by this time,' John said sourly, watching the printers at work.

'You may depend upon it,' Mr Walter said, 'or we should have heard otherwise.'

It was very bad news indeed, John thought, but it would certainly sell, if he could get it to the coaches in time. 'I will take the first batch with me, now,' he said, 'and send for the rest later.' If only he didn't have to waste time with all that damned stamping.

It was a frantic morning. John worked harder than he'd ever done in his life, and usually on the run, collecting papers from the printers with the ink still wet and smudging and smearing under his fingers, supervising the stamping, which was abominably slow, loading the flyers in a half-light that showed only too clearly that dawn was under way and that the first of Mr Chaplin's coaches would be leaving within minutes, and on one panicking occasion running the length of the Strand in search of another flyer because all the ones he'd hired were out on the roads and two more batches of papers were ready to dispatch.

But by breakfast time the papers were gone, the coaches caught, the first dispatch completed.

'We have made a start,' he said, as he and Billy and the rest of their team sat down at last in Galloway's Coffee House to eat a well-earned breakfast.

'Never mind about a start,' Billy said, laughing. 'It's damn nearly finished me. To say nothing of what it's done to my courtship.'

'It will be easier tomorrow,' John said. And in the meantime, he would keep his promise and write to Annie and tell her all about it.

He took time off that afternoon to write at length to Annie and to James, and when their letters were completed, he took up his pen again to write another even longer. And this one was to Miss Harriet Sowerby.

BACK IN RATTLESDEN HARRIET had settled into the Hopkins' household as easily as if she'd been designed for it. Little Jimmy had insisted on sitting beside her at the breakfast table that Sunday morning and talking to her all through the meal, and, what was more, he'd been allowed to do it, which was a great surprise to her because meals at home were always taken in complete silence.

Here at Rattlesden the breakfast table was a-babble with conversation.

'Did you sleep warmly?' Annie wanted to know. 'This old place is a proper rabbit warren. The wind blows in through the walls quite terribly sometimes.' But her tone was mild. She didn't seem to be complaining about it.

Harriet assured them that she'd slept very well indeed and added that she thought the rectory was a beautiful house. 'So old!'

'It has stood here for three hundred years,' the Reverend

Hopkins told her, 'but never so happily occupied as it is now, I think. Is that not so, my love?'

But at that point Mrs Chiddum, their cook, came bustling in with a dish of bread and milk for baby Beau, who was bouncing in his highchair with excitement at the smell of it. And that brought another amazing revelation.

'If he don't have his bread and milk first,' Annie Hopkins confided, spooning the soggy mixture into her baby's eager mouth, 'he won't eat a thing, will you my chicken? Not his nice coddled egg, nor his nice flaked fish, not a thing.'

And they see no sin in it, Harriet thought, looking from Annie's smiling face to her husband's approving one. They don't force the child. They let him eat what he likes. And the baby crowed and held the spoon and called for more.

'Will he eat his fish now?' she asked, intrigued, when the little bowl was scraped clean.

'Why bless us, of course he will,' Annie said. 'Won't you, my lambkin?'

'I eatin' my fish,' Jimmy said proudly, holding up his plate to show her the progress he was making.

'And a fine good boy you'll grow in consequence,' his father told him. 'I must walk across to church now, Annie my love, or I shall not be ready for the service.'

They are the gentlest, kindest people Harriet had ever met. She watched as the clergyman stooped to kiss his wife and little Jimmy and to submit, oh so patiently and lovingly, to having his face patted by Beau's sticky hands.

And she was touched to feel that she was allowed to be one of them, as she and Annie and the two children stood beside the draughty window to watch him as he went stooping along the garden path towards the holm oak and the wicket gate that led to the churchyard. He was so gentle and so diffident, and such a contrast to the unforgiving asperity of her own father.

'Oh! Oh!' Annie said suddenly, putting her hand to her

mouth. 'He's forgotten his muffler again, the dear man, and his chest is in no fit state to do without it. Look after the little ones, my dear. I shan't be a minute.'

She was off out of the room in a second, her feet skimming across the uneven flagstones as though they were winged. There was no doubt of her affection or her concern. Harriet watched with a lump rising in her throat while her hostess ran down the garden path in the sunshine to catch her absent-minded husband in her arms and wind the muffler he'd forgotten about his neck and send him on his way to church with another kiss. To love so and be so loved, she thought. What a blissful thing it must be.

And, as she discovered later that morning, his church was just like he was, gentle and welcoming and unassuming. She sat between Annie and the nursemaid, Pollyanna, in the third box pew, at a respectful distance from the grand party from the Manor House, with Jimmy cuddled on her knee, and listened to the first Sunday service she'd ever heard outside her own fierce chapel and was amazed at it.

For a start the Reverend Hopkins didn't boom a text at his congregation, he read them a story, the tale of the Good Samaritan, and he read it simply and quietly, pausing from time to time to smile at his poor parishioners or to give them a chance to cough or to settle more comfortably in their wooden pews. And then he set his great Bible aside and began a most extraordinary sermon.

Harriet was used to sermons and she didn't enjoy them, although of course she would never have admitted it, and especially not to her mother or the preacher who were the two people who lectured her most frequently. But she paid as little attention to them as she could, for they were always the same, telling her that she was a grievous sinner and would be punished for her sins with torture and hellfire as sure as night followed day. And even if she didn't believe them it was upsetting to hear such things.

But the Reverend Hopkins was a preacher of quite another persuasion. He talked to his congregation, and the God he spoke about was a gentle deity, a God who forgave sins and answered honest prayers, just as He'd answered hers in the King's Bath, a God who actually seemed to want his creation to be kind to one another.

Jimmy was sucking his thumb, lulled by his father's voice and baby Beau was asleep in his mother's arms. It is all so simple and easy and loving here, Harriet thought, looking at the communion table with its plain green cloth and the wooden crucifix set so simply upon it, flanked by its two glowing candles. You sleep when you are tired and you wake with the daylight, you feed your babies with the food they like to eat, you welcome strangers into your home when they have nowhere else to go, and you do not preach. For this man wasn't telling anybody what to do, he was simply talking about the need for 'mutual help and comfort' and the unsought rewards of kindness.

She looked up at the three bright rows of assembled saints, glowing red and blue and purple and gold in the great east window beyond the communion table and saw that in the space above them a figure of Christ was depicted in solitary glory, His hands upraised in blessing. And the face of the Christ made her heart leap in her chest. It was such a tender face, such a sad, tolerant, compassionate, understanding face. And she wondered whether she and her parents had been worshipping a different God all these years, and felt that it was very likely, and knew, beyond any doubt, that if she were given a choice it would be this living Christ she would prefer to follow.

The next two days passed in the same quiet mood of contentment. She helped to feed the boys, and took them for walks about the village and was allowed to tuck them into bed at night, and, in the afternoons, she helped Annie with her sewing until dinner, and when the meal was done and the candles were lit, she and Annie and her 'dear James' played cards beside the fire. It was a blessed existence, and when Mrs Easter's pony cart arrived to fetch her on Wednesday morning she couldn't hide her disappointment that her visit was over.

'You must come again, my dear,' Annie said, kissing her goodbye most lovingly. 'Drive her carefully, young Tom.'

Young Tom was recognisably Mr Thistlethwaite's son. He had the same untidy hair and the same brown eyes and the same wide mouth. But he wasn't as quick witted as his father. 'Lawks a mercy,' he said. 'I got letters for to give to 'ee an' I clean forgot all about 'em.' He was fishing three letters out of his trouser pocket, bending them considerably in the process. 'Come by the night mail, Mrs 'Opkins, mum,' he said, handing them across. 'Pa said to deliver 'em.'

'One for each of us, my dear,' Annie said, putting Harriet's into her lap. 'Dear John. He kept his word, you see. Now promise me that you will come again.'

'I will. I will. Indeed I will,' Harriet said, breathless with surprise and pleasure. To think that he had written to her too!

But she waited until the pony cart was out in the lane and had ambled downhill through the village before she opened her letter. She needed to be as private as possible before she read what he had to say to her.

It was a polite letter and very formal, hoping that she had taken no harm from her long journey and that her stay at Rattlesden would prove happy and comfortable. He was sorry, he said, that he had not been able to stay at Rattlesden himself, howsomever it was just as well that he returned to London when he did, for the news from France was very grave.

Then he spent two paragraphs telling her all about it but assuring her that Wellington would soon defeat the upstart and that she was not to worry that the French would be lurking in dark corners again to afright her. 'I do not forget what you told me at the Victory Ball, you see.'

Then, at the very foot of the page, he wrote something that brought a blush to her cheeks even in the cold air blowing past her on that early morning ride.

'I trust I may take an opportunity to call upon you, when I return to Bury, and that I may consider myself your respectful friend, John Henry Easter.'

She read it through three times before she could convince herself that she wasn't imagining it. Then she folded the letter carefully and, after a moment's hesitation, tucked it inside the bodice of her gown. If she put it in her carpetbag, her mother would see it and insist on reading it, and for the first time in her life she had a secret she wanted to hide. A secret she had every right to hide, for Mr Easter had written to *her*, not to her mother. The paper scratched her skin, as prickly as a conscience. But it was *her* letter and hers it would remain.

BACK IN CHURCHGATE Street her mother had been home for nearly half an hour and was already furiously at work with broom and duster.

'Mercy on us!' she said crossly when Harriet knocked at the door. 'What brings you back so soon?'

'Miss Pettie took a faint in the baths, Mama,' Harriet said, 'and wanted to come home.'

Mrs Sowerby was instantly and happily scathing. 'So you made a poor job of it, after all,' she sneered. 'I can't say I'm surprised. I never imagined you would be the slightest use to the poor lady. What must she be thinking of us now!'

'She said she was uncommon glad of my company,' Harriet said, defending herself. 'She called me a kindly nurse.' The remembered compliment was warming even in the chill of her mother's parlour.

Mrs Sowerby put aside her broom and turned to direct the full force of her disapproval upon her daughter. 'Hoity-toity!' she said. 'More to the point, what were you doing, pray, to *allow* her to be taken ill in the first place? Tell me that!'

'Nothing, Mama. Truly,' Harriet stammered, thrown into confusion by the vehemence of the attack.

'Come now,' her mother said implacably. 'Do not lie to me, miss, for I know when you lie. You were *careless* were you not? You have a careless disposition. I have often had cause to chastise you for it. Admit!' And she glanced at the chastening rod hanging beside the unlit fire.

'No, no indeed, Mama,' Harriet said, fear fluttering in her chest. 'I did my very best endeavour, truly. I do not believe I was careless. It was not my intention.'

'Then how did Miss Pettie come to take a faint? Answer me that.'

''Twas the heat of the bath, Mama. Mr Easter said so.'

'Mr Easter?' her mother said, quite stopped in her tracks by the mention of the name. 'Mr Easter the newsagent?' But he was the wealthiest young man in town. 'So you're on speaking terms with the Easters now, is that it?' She was confused by this information, torn between pride in the acquaintance, and aggravation that her daughter should have been given importance by it.

'We met at the Victory Ball, Mama,' Harriet explained, keeping her face very still and as expressionless as she could. 'He chanced to be in Bath. Miss Pettie said his presence was the greatest good fortune.'

'Aye, so it may have been. For *her*,' Mrs Sowerby said grimly. 'For a young girl with absolutely *no* prospects, *absolutely no prospects,* mark me, 'tis quite another matter, let me tell 'ee. I suppose he paid you pretty compliments to turn your silly head.'

'No indeed, Mama. He joined us so as to care for Miss Pettie.'

'Joined you?' Mrs Sowerby asked, and her tone was horrible.

'He escorted us home, Mama,' Harriet faltered, feeling impelled to explain.

'Ho, did he?' her mother said, rigid with righteous indignation. 'Well of course he did, you silly girl. We all know about rich young men like him. That's just the sort of thing he would do. You keep well out of his way, my girl. Men like Mr Easter are *dangerous,* let me tell 'ee. They *ruin* poor girls. *Ruin* them as soon as look at 'em. It is always the way. Have nothing more to do with him, do you hear?'

It was horribly unfair. 'He was uncommon kind to — to Miss Pettie,' Harriet said, defending him, but as meekly as she could. This was too cruel. Was she really not to see him again?

Her mother raised her voice and her eyebrows immediately. 'Do you *argue* with me, child? Do you pretend to know better than your *own* mother?'

Harriet retreated at once. 'No, no Mama,' she said. 'Of course not.' Cruel or not her mother had to be obeyed.

'And so I should think,' Mrs Sowerby said, mollified by the ease and speed of her victory. 'Then you will do as you are told, will you not?'

'Yes, Mama.' What else could she say? Perhaps she could find a way round it?

'Very well,' Mrs Sowerby said, using her broom again with renewed vigour. 'Let us return to our duties and hear no more about it. You are back now so you'd best get to work. There's a fire needs lighting and then you can scour that doorstep. I've never seen it in such a filthy state. From the look of it, half the world has been treading upon it during these last few days. I turn my back for five minutes and this is what I get, you see. I'm sure *I* never trod on anybody else's doorstep in all my born days. Oh there's no justice in the world. Well, don't just stand there. What are you waiting for?'

As Harriet went wearily off to fetch the bucket and rake out the fire, Mr Easter's letter shifted and scratched inside her bodice. And for a fleeting second, she was comforted because she had such a secret.

Mr Easter himself was as hard at work as she was. Early on Thursday morning news came through from France that the French army had deserted their new King Louis XVIII *en masse* and gone over to their old emperor. This time *The Times* printed twice its usual number of papers and John used twice his usual number of fourpenny flyers, and the energy expended at the post office that morning was enough, according to Billy, 'to haul a thousand coaches'.

'Mama will be home tomorrow,' he said. 'She'll be surprised at all this. I can't imagine what she'll say.'

But John didn't care what she said. He already knew that he had made his point. He'd had two letters that very morning from his shopkeepers in Ipswich and Reading. Their sales had nearly doubled, they said, 'thanks to the prompt arrival of the papers, some hours ahead of all other shops in the area'. Now they were suggesting that their daily orders should be doubled to keep pace, 'whilst the bad news lasts'.

'What d'you think she'll say when she knows what you've been doing?' Billy insisted.

But she knew already.

CHAPTER 8

'First with the news again I see,' Sir Joshua Barnesworthy called, striding across the terrace at Holly Hall and waving a copy of *The Times* at Mrs Easter.

'Bad is it, Josh?' his cousin Peter drawled, holding out his hand to receive the paper.

'Uncommon bad,' Sir Joshua said. 'See here. Dratted Frenchies gone over to the enemy, so they have.'

'Do I not recall that Mr Bonaparte was once crowned the Emperor of the French?' Lady Barnesworthy teased. 'Or am I mistaken, my love?'

'Damned foreigners, the lot of 'em,' her husband said cheerfully. 'Still we beat the beggars once, so I daresay we shall do it again.'

'How do you manage to get the papers here to us so quickly?' Lady Barnesworthy asked, turning to Nan as the three men studied the news. ''Tis an impressive achievement. Do you not think so, Mr Brougham?'

'Most impressive,' Mr Brougham said, smiling at the two women as they stood before him in the pale sunshine of that March afternoon. 'And intriguing, too. You must tell us how 'tis done, Mrs Easter.' A handsome woman, he was thinking, admiring her, for the long straight cut of her fashionable blue coat set off her figure to advantage, and the white fur with which it was trimmed at her throat and her wrists certainly enhanced her colouring. Ruddy cheeks and brown eyes had always appealed to Mr Brougham. It was what had attracted him to his first wife, poor creature.

'Well as to that,' Nan said, grinning at him, 'that's my son's doing, so 'tis. I can only guess at the workings of it, especially from this distance.' She had no intention of revealing such a valuable trade secret at a country house party. Not even at a country house party as aristocratic as this, and to a gentleman as polite and proper as Mr Brougham.

Mr Brougham smiled at her again, offering his arm as they continued their promenade around the garden. 'You give him full credit for it, I see,' he observed.

'Of course,' she said. 'Fair's fair, Mr Brougham. Johnnie did the work, so Johnnie gets the glory.'

'There are many would disagree with such sentiments,' he said.

'Then they would be foolish,' she said firmly. 'There's a deal more to a business than knowing what and when to sell.'

'I have a friend in the coaching trade who maintains much the same thing,' he told her. 'According to him, knowing how and when to reward, and how and when to rebuke, is the great art of running a business. Name of Chaplin. They call him the coach king.'

'I know him well,' she said. 'A man of sense.' But she was thinking, if you know Mr Chaplin then 'tis likely you will know of my affair with Calverley Leigh. And the thought annoyed her, because she would rather her new aristocratic friends knew as little as possible about her liaison with that gentleman. For Calverley Leigh, despite his charming personality and the undeniable pleasure of his company, had been a gambler and a wastrel too, and now that they had finally parted, she was rather annoyed with herself for having spent so much of her time on him.

Since she'd taken up residence in her prestigious house in Bedford Square, Nan Easter had been moving up in society. It was no surprise to her, nor to her friends, nor to those of her new neighbours who had enjoyed her lively hospitality. Some people frowned upon her, of course, because they knew her history and spoke of it in scathing terms whenever her success was mentioned.

'She was nothing more than a servant girl, my dear. Heaven knows what Mr Easter ever saw in her! His family cut him off, you know, for marrying her. What else could they do? And they do say Sir Osmond Easter refuses to receive her to this day. And then, of course, she took up with a lieutenant in the cavalry who was no better than he should have been. It was quite a scandal. And now she drives about town in a closed carriage, if you please, for all the world as if she were one of the gentry. Really, the presumption of the nouveau riche!'

And so she did and a very fine closed carriage it was, with the company sign painted boldly on its sides and a fine pair of greys to draw it. And although she knew that people gossiped about her, she was too busy and too sensible to comment on it. She was extending her trade and growing steadily more and more wealthy and secure, and that was what mattered to her. But this invitation to Holly Hall had been a great surprise. And a surprise made doubly sweet because she knew how much it would infuriate her enemies.

For Holly Hall was the country seat of Sir Joshua Barnesworthy. And Sir Joshua Barnesworthy was a friend of the Earl of Harrowby, no less, who was a British envoy to the Congress of Vienna, a man who negotiated with Wellington and Talleyrand. And if the Earl of Harrowby were to take her up, as the gentry noted at once, the rest of them would have to respect her. It was scandalous. Fancy inviting a woman like her to a house like that!

Actually the invitation had been sent because Mr Brougham suggested it, for Lady Barnesworthy was a secret and most successful matchmaker. From time to time she included among her dinner guests two people who wished to be introduced to each other, or one, as was rather more often the case, who wished to make himself known to a person as yet admired from afar. It was done with great discretion and absolutely no comment at all and had resulted in several extremely useful marriages. And it was being done again on this particular occasion.

She was a little surprised when her dear Frederick first asked her to invite Mrs Easter to her next house party, for she wouldn't have thought that the two of them would have had anything in common. After all he was related to the great Brougham family of Westmoreland, and had stern aristocratic features, being roman-nosed and grey-eyed and really quite tall although with an impressive embonpoint, as you would expect, while she was a commoner, and looked it. In addition to that, of course, he'd been quietly and successfully married to her own well-born cousin until the poor lady died of the smallpox, while Mrs Easter had been gallivanting about the town with her very common lover.

Nevertheless she did as he asked and was surprised to see how much the two of them seemed to be enjoying each other's company, comforting herself that it would be unlikely to go any further, given the lady's circumstances.

She would have been a little piqued if she could have overheard their conversation after dinner that night.

The rest of the company had adjourned to the drawing room, where two great fires were blazing and the tables had been set ready for cards. But Nan had walked quietly off in the opposite direction towards the library and, after a discreet pause, ostensibly to smoke a cigar with his old friend Sir Joshua, Frederick Brougham had followed her.

She was sitting at the writing desk beside the fireplace, with candles lit to right and left of her, busily composing a letter. He could see the energetic quivering of the ostrich plumes in her headdress and hear the purposeful scratching of her pen from where he stood in the doorway.

She had removed her long gloves, tossing them carelessly across the back of her chair, and her bare arms were as white as pearl in the candlelight. The sight of them gave him an unexpected frisson of surprise and pleasure. They looked so deliciously naked and there was something primitive about them, too, an honest, untrammelled urgency that roused his admiration and stirred desire in him for the first time since his wife's death nearly sixteen months ago.

He walked towards her, casting about in his mind for some light, quizzy remark that he could use to open a conversation and ease his emotions.

'You keep in touch with your company, I see,' he said. 'Even from this distance.'

She didn't look up. 'Aye,' she said, 'I do. War makes work for news sellers, Mr Brougham. And, besides, my son has done well this week, and 'tis only proper that I write and tell him so.'

Her hands were small and rough and short-fingered, a worker's hand's, and the complete opposite of the narrow long-fingered languid pallor that women of his class aspired to. He admired her more than ever.

'It is a sadness to me that I return to London tomorrow,' he said. 'I have enjoyed my stay here immeasurably, Mrs Easter.'

'And so have I,' she said, looking up at him at last, brown eyes laughing.

'I have disturbed your work,' he said, inclining his body apologetically towards the desk and the letter. 'That was most remiss of me. Pray do not allow me to disturb you further.'

''Tis done,' she said, folding the paper. 'Now it only needs to be taken to the mail coach. There is a servant comes to the library every evening for that very purpose.' And she dusted the palms of her hands against each other, swish, swish, dismissing her work and his apology.

'I f that is the case,' he said, 'we might converse.'

She was putting on her gloves again. 'We might indeed.'

So they sat in two armchairs before the fire with her timely newspaper on a little low table between them and they talked; about the house party, about their fellow guests, about the house and its grounds; and, finally, about themselves.

'I must confess,' he said gallantly, 'that one of the reasons I prevailed upon my cousin to invite me to this party was the hope that I would be introduced to you.'

Her answer was very surprising. 'Aye,' she said. 'I thought as much. We've been thrown into each other's company a deal too often for mere coincidence.'

'You must blame our hostess for that,' he said rather uneasily. 'I merely requested her invitation, not that any further action be taken by it. I trust you have not been too greatly incommoded.'

'I been amused,' she said, 'seeing I en't never been victim to a matchmaker before.'

'Oh come now, Mrs Easter,' he said, 'that is rather strong, is it not? A victim? Surely not. Whatever their faults matchmakers are well-meaning.' His own marriage had come about as the result of the efforts of two matchmaking aunts and he had never had cause to regret it.

'A victim,' she said firmly. 'I never use a word unless I mean it. To choose a partner is the most delicate decision. That you'll allow, I dare swear.' And, as he signalled his agreement with a smile, 'Well then, that being so, 'tis plain folly, to my way of thinking, to allow an outsider to make the choice for you.'

Put like that, what could he do but agree with her? 'You are a woman of independent spirit, I see,' he told her, 'which is wholly admirable. Although I must admit it puts me into something of a quandary.'

'How so, sir?' He had a pleasant-looking face when he was teasing.

'I had hoped to ask you if you would accompany me to the Theatre Royal in Covent Garden on Tuesday evening to see a performance of *Richard II*. The management have installed the new gas lighting which is reputed to be very fine. But now I live in such terror of a negative reply, I declare my spirit quite fails me.'

How clever he is, she thought, admiring his tact. I may accept or refuse him with equal grace. And she smiled ready to give him her answer.

And at that moment the door at the far end of the room was flung open to reveal Sir Joshua's cousin Arabella. 'Why there you are!' she said, flouncing into the room. 'Fie upon you Nan, you gave me your word of honour, so you did, that you would partner me at faro, and now you skulk away in here and leave me to the mercy of Mr Farquhar, who is playing quite vilely. How could you be so cruel?'

'Six o' the clock I promised 'ee,' Nan said, 'and it wants a quarter hour before that time, but you shall be rescued notwithstanding, for I en't so hard hearted as to leave any woman at the mercy of Mr Farquhar.' And she stood up ready to leave the room.

Mr Brougham stood too. 'You have promised to give me your opinion of *Richard II*, don't forget, Mrs Easter,' he said, bowing slightly as she walked away from him.

'I do not forget,' she said. 'I believe I am to visit the Theatre Royal on Tuesday.'

'Then may I wish you a pleasant evening?'

'You may,' she said, grinning at him as she followed Arabella from the room. 'You may indeed, Mr Brougham.'

. . .

JOHN EASTER WAS RATHER ALARMED to receive a letter from his mother, particularly as it arrived on the very day she intended to return. Had she heard about the flyers. Was that it? He broke the seal with some trepidation.

Easter's was first with the news in St Albans all this week, she had written. *We are much commended hereabouts for our speed and efficiency which, I have been happy to boast, was all your doing. If this war continues, which I can see no reason to doubt, I do believe you will make good your promise to me. I shall be more than interested to read the sales reports for this month.*

    Yr ever loving mother,
    Nan.

He put the letter to one side without comment and returned to his calculations, quiet and contained as always, but inside his head he was purring with gratification. Who would ever have thought that his mother would write to praise him? 'Wonders never cease,' he said to the inkpot.

But the letter he had hoped for and looked for ever since Tuesday, the letter from Miss Sowerby, had still not arrived. And although he tried to be sanguine about it, it was a disappointment and a puzzle, and it swamped his gratification with anxiety because Miss Sowerby had seemed to be the sort of person who would answer any letter by return of post. Something must have prevented her. What if she had taken a chill on that long, cold journey? What if she were ill? Perhaps he shouldn't have left her so precipitately. Oh, if only she would write and tell him how she was! Or if only he weren't quite so busy here in London and could drive to Bury for a day or two and see her. 'If wishes were horses...' he told the inkpot. But of course they weren't and he had work to do.

❧

HARRIET HERSELF WAS AS MUCH CONCERNED over her lack of reply as he was. Late at night, when all her work was done, she would take his letter from its secret hiding place under the floorboards in her bedroom and read and re-read it, and it was a marvellous comfort to her and a great worry. She knew that according to the rules of etiquette she ought to have answered it directly, but how could such a thing be done when her mother had forbidden her to have anything to do with him? She knew that it was imperative to obey one's parents. The preacher insisted upon it, every single Sunday. And yet obedience in this respect meant unkindness in another. And it upset her very much to think that she was being impolite to Mr Easter, especially when he'd done nothing to deserve it and he'd been so very kind to her.

A week passed and her mother was still disparaging and her father was in a most sarcastic humour and the dilemma was still unsolved. But at least it was Thursday, and she could take time away from her disapproving household and spend the afternoon with Miss Pettie, which was blessedly peaceful even though there was a great deal of mending to get through.

They worked together until it was so dark that Harriet could barely see to thread the needles. But when the candles were lit, Miss Pettie said all work was to stop until next Thursday.

'You are to dine with me, my dear,' she said, her faded eyes quite moist with excitement at the thought. 'I have ordered a goose. Your mother is quite agreeable.'

It was an unlooked-for pleasure and therefore doubly enjoyable. The goose was actually rather tough but they dined together very happily, chewing what they could and garnishing every dish with memories of their recent adventures. And when the cloth had finally been removed, Miss Pettie told her guest that she had received a letter that morning and asked her if she would be so kind as to keep her company while she wrote a reply.

''Tis from Mr Easter,' she said, patting the letter, 'so you can see it must be answered directly. 'Twould be a grievous fault to dally when he was so uncommon courteous.'

'Oh it would,' Harriet agreed with feeling, 'an uncommon grievous fault.' And she sighed so sadly that Miss Pettie looked up at her at once.

'Why what is it, my child? What's amiss?'

'Oh Miss Pettie,' Harriet confessed, 'Mr Easter wrote to me, when I was staying with Mrs Hopkins at Rattlesden, and I have not answered his letter yet. To tell 'ee true, I do not know how I may answer him at all.'

She looked so miserable that Miss Pettie leant across at once to pat her on the arm. 'But you can write, child, can you not? They taught you a fair hand at Mrs Crabtree's Academy.'

'Oh yes, Miss Pettie, I can write well enough. That is not the difficulty. Not the difficulty at all. Oh dear, oh dear, I fear I may offend my mother if I speak further.'

By now Miss Pettie's curiosity was fully aroused. 'You may speak to me quite freely, my dear,' she said, 'for I am an old woman and used to confidences of every sort. Nothing you say would go further than these four walls, you have my word on't.'

So Harriet described her dilemma, haltingly at first and rather shamefacedly.

'What am I to do, Miss Pettie?' she finished. 'I'm to have nothing to do with him. If I obey my mother, as I surely must unless I am to break the fifth Commandment, I must be discourteous to Mr Easter, which grieves me very greatly. What am I to do?'

Miss Pettie gave the matter the most careful thought, patting her young friend's hand in a comforting absent-minded way. And after thirty lip-chewing seconds she came up with a quite excellent solution.

'I will write my letter to Mr Easter directly,' she said, 'which is only right and proper, and when 'tis done, you shall add a postscript to it. A postscript is a trivial matter, is't not? Oh indeed yes. I am sure there are none who could think otherwise. It could hardly be considered an act of disobedience, could it?'

It is the way round, Harriet thought with delight. Hadn't she known there would be a way round?

And so it was written, neatly and politely on the end of Miss Pettie's rambling epistle. And after the carriage had been ordered and Harriet had been sent safely home, the old lady wrote a second postscript all round the edge of the letter, suggesting that should Mr Easter care to write again to Miss Sowerby it might be more practical for him to send his missive to Angel Hill where Miss Pettie would consider it an honour to deliver it, on account of the great affection she felt towards them both.

Then she went to bed, well pleased with her diplomacy.

AND SO MR EASTER received his first message from Miss Sowerby at last, and if he were surprised at Miss Pettie's post-script, he was too much of a gentleman to say so. It occurred to him briefly that she was probably matchmaking again, but the knowledge was harmless. The important thing was that Miss Sowerby was well and had written to him, however briefly. And if she wished him to write to her at Miss Pettie's house, than that was what he would do. Gladly. For although intrigues were foreign to his nature, the need for privacy was something he understood entirely.

That Tuesday evening, when Billy was dining with the Honeywoods and his mother was at the theatre with Mr Brougham, he wrote a very long letter indeed, telling Miss Sowerby all about Napoleon's progress through France, and about the splendid increase in the number of newspapers that were now selling in London every day, and about how much he was enjoying the third and fourth books of Mr Wordsworth's poem. And because he felt sure that she too would appreciate the philosophy of the Laureate, he copied out three of his favourite lines for her.

We live by admiration, hope and love;
And even as these are well and wisely fixed,
In dignity of being we ascend.

Isn't that splendid! These are sentiments I have often felt myself without being truly aware of it, if you can understand such a thing. To see them expressed with such clarity and in such true words is an ineffable pleasure, which I trust you will share, since I am,

Your true friend,
  John Henry Easter.

CHAPTER 9

All through the spring and early summer of that year the Allied armies prepared to do battle with Napoleon, and the London papers were hot with the latest news. Dispatches arrived in the city nearly every day with the latest information from Paris and Brussels and Vienna, except, of course, when the weather in the Channel was too bad for the packet ships to sail. And rumours were as thick as flies in high summer. Prices on the commodity markets rose and fell precipitously, for England was the paymaster to the great armies that were currently being mustered over in Belgium, and there were plenty of adventurers in London who were prepared to speculate upon the outcome. And the London gossips had a splendidly garrulous time.

On the night Nan went to the Theatre Royal with Mr Brougham, there were scores of them about, buzzing in the boxes and strolling in the pit, carrying off titbits with the assiduity of carrion crows.

'How we do love bad news,' Nan observed, looking down at the seething mass below her, where fans were already fluttering like frantic moths. The men were loud with excitement, baying their opinions and barking with laughter and the women were warm with their exertions, their bare necks flushed and their eyes gleaming.

But he had little interest in gossip or gossips. 'What do you think of the new gas lighting?' he asked.

''Twill take a bit of getting used to,' she said, looking at the new glass globes that were shedding yellow light from the front of every box, 'but 'tis a fine clear light, in all conscience.'

'And cost a fine clear fortune,' he said.

'How is it lit, think 'ee?'

'With a taper, I believe. And if you think this a clear light, wait until you see the stage.'

The scarlet curtains were looping upwards, gathering into scalloped folds as they rose, and behind them the stage was suddenly and dazzlingly revealed. Painted trees to right and left, a medieval castle with a portcullis and a drawbridge, storm clouds in an impossibly blue sky and all of it ablaze with light, throbbing with light, so bright and unexpected it quite hurt the eyes. The audience burst into spontaneous applause at the sight of it. And somebody in the next box squealed with surprise.

Nan knew who it was at once. No other woman in London squealed quite like that.

'Sophie!' she called, turning her head as the applause continued. 'Sophie Fuseli!'

'Nan, my dear!' Sophie said. 'Have you ever seen the like?' She looked very plump and very pretty, the heart-shape of her face echoed by the heart-shape of her headdress, her dark hair falling in heavy curls on either side of those fine blue eyes.

But there was no time to answer, for all about the theatre footmen were turning down the new lights by pulling upon slender chains attached to the globes, and Richard II and John of Gaunt were striking attitudes on stage and the audience was beginning to settle. 'I will see you in the interval,' Nan mouthed.

Which she did and a great pleasure it was to introduce 'my oldest friend' to 'my newest acquaintance', especially as her newest acquaintance instantly invited Sophie and her companion to join him in his box for supper. Sophie's companion, whom she introduced rather carelessly as Mr Macintosh, was a young man with a large appetite and nothing to say for himself, but as Sophie didn't seem to mind that he was being left out of the conversation, and she and Nan and Mr Brougham had such a lot to say to one another, they made a cheerful party, talking of the war and Napoleon and of the various artists of their acquaintance, including Sophie's husband, Mr Fuseli, whose great paintings were, so she said, 'little considered these days, I fear, although Mr Constable, who was once his pupil, you know, does uncommon well'.

'Which must, I am sure, be partly attributed to the excellence of your husband's tuition,' Mr Brougham said courteously.

But Sophie wasn't really very interested in her husband or his tuition.

'I used to call on Mrs Easter every week,' she said, changing the subject, 'or she on me, and now I declare I ain't seen her at home for above two months. Where have you been, you dratted creature?'

'Hard at work,' Nan said ruefully. 'There's been a deal to do.'

'You must save her from herself, Mr Brougham,' Sophie said, 'or she will work twenty-four hours a day and fade away to nothing. Are you to eat *all* those oysters, Mr Macintosh, or do you mean to leave some for Mrs Easter?'

Her companion handed the plate across to Nan without a word, but excitement had taken away her appetite. 'Oh it is good to see you,' she said to Sophie. 'You're right, I confess it. I've let work take me away from my old friends.'

'Then you must allow me to bring old friends together again and invite you both to dinner on Saturday,' Frederick Brougham said, smiling first at Sophie and then at Nan. The footmen had reappeared and were walking purposefully towards the gas lights again. 'And Mr Macintosh too?' he suggested, but so quietly that the young man could not hear him above the noise of his own jaws.

Sophie shook her head and grimaced. 'I think not, thank 'ee,' she whispered, as she stood up. 'Come now, Mr Macintosh, we must return to our seats.'

Mr Macintosh took the last pasty and crammed it into his mouth, spattering crumbs and thanks in the direction of his host as he followed her out of the box. Westminster Hall was being revealed on stage, with the Lords Spiritual and Temporal splendidly robed and the four actors who represented the Commons huddled together in sackcloth, looking gormless.

'Have 'ee heard the news of Calverley Leigh?' Sophie said from the doorway. 'Married an heiress over in County Kerry, so they say, twice his age, with three grown daughters and an idiot son.'

Nan was startled, but she recovered quickly. 'I'm glad to hear it,' she said. It was just what they ought to have expected.

'Call forth Bagot!' Bolinbroke commanded, striding into Westminster Hall with such vigour that he made the gas lights pop like balloons.

'IT HAS BEEN A MOST enjoyable evening, I think,' Mr Brougham said as he and Nan drove through the quiet streets towards Bedford Square when the play was over.

'Very,' she said. 'I'm beholden to 'ee, sir. 'Twas good of 'ee to invite Mrs Fuseli to supper.'

'A pleasure,' he said, smiling at her in the darkness. And thinking, but not an unmitigated pleasure for you, I do believe. For he had noticed her start of surprise when Calverley Leigh's name was mentioned and, knowing how long they had been lovers, had been concerned that she might have been upset by Mrs Fuseli's news. 'You promised to give me your opinion of the play, don't forget,' he said.

'Aye, so I did.'

'What did you think of it, pray?'

'Plays are all the same,' she said briskly, 'painted trees what don't rustle, and painted clouds what don't move and a man stabbed through the heart without a drop of blood spilt. I liked the new gas lights, though.'

He roared with laughter at her, delighted because she was so outspoken and relieved that she didn't seem upset at all, for she was laughing and teasing.

'How now, Mrs Philistine,' he said, responding to her mood, 'did the drama not move you at all?'

''Tis all play-acting when all's said and done,' she said. 'A chance to wear fine clothes and pretend to noble passions, but of no real consequence. However fine the play, it don't change the world.'

'True,' he said. 'And pithily expressed, as I have come to expect of 'ee. Well then, as you have such a poor opinion of players, I'd best not invite you to Covent Garden again next Wednesday.'

'Ah!' she teased, 'but then I should miss the oysters.'

The carriage was turning into Bedford Square, wheels crunching on the cobbles, grinding to a halt outside her imposing door.

He got out before her and offered his forearm for her to lean upon as she stepped down after him. It was such a gentlemanly gesture she was quite touched by it. Then he walked her to the door and waited with her until it was opened.

'I have taken much pleasure from your company tonight, Mrs Easter,' he said, smiling down at her, his long face gilded by the light from the hall.

'And I from yours, Mr Brougham.'

· · ·

AFTER SUCH A REWARDING evening it was no surprise to her that she should sleep sound and wake energetic. She packed her bags as soon as she got up, and at breakfast she told her sons that she was off to Bath, 'Seeing there's business there to be finished and you en't the ones to do it now.'

'True enough, Mama,' John said. 'We've enough to do here in all conscience.' The stamping that morning had been even more troublesome than usual and there were rumours that the government intended to put up the stamp duty yet again, which seemed highly likely given the enormous expense of the present campaign. 'If 'tis to be fourpence, as Mr Walter suspects, then the price of a quality newspaper will go up to seven pence,' he said, helping himself to more devilled kidneys, 'and that will have an adverse effect upon trade. I do not see how it may be avoided.'

'No 'twon't,' his mother said cheerfully, 'not with a war and battles to look forward to. There en't nothing sells newspapers so well as a war. You stay here and look after the shop, my dears, and I'll open another for us in the West Country. I shall be back by Saturday, you may depend upon it, for I've promised to dine with Mr Brougham, and Sophie Fuseli is to be there.'

It was quite a compliment to be left to 'mind the shop' but Billy said he was a 'bit miffed with all this war stuff'. The number of newspapers that had to be stamped and sorted every day had doubled since Napoleon escaped from his wretched island, and now that Mama and John had extended their trade to so many country towns, half their daily purchase had to be dispatched on the first available coaches out of London, and that meant that he had to be in the sorting rooms at the ungodly hour of five in the morning. And all this just at a time when he was courting seriously and needed his energy to keep up with Matilda at all the balls and routs and suppers they attended.

'As far as I'm concerned, Johnnoh,' he said to his brother after one particularly hectic night when the two of them were drinking tea in the chilly dining room at half past four in the morning, 'they can string old Boney up by his heels next time they catch him. Then perhaps we shall all have a bit of peace and quiet to get on with our lives.' He'd had no sleep at all that night, for the ball he'd been to hadn't ended until nearly three o'clock so he was in rather a sour mood.

But John enjoyed the pressure and worked well in the chill hours of early morning. He kept careful accounts of all their sales and watched their profits grow with all the satisfaction of a parent observing the health of a well-loved child. Routs and balls that went racketing on into the small hours had never been to his taste, although Mama and Billy loved them and were always out gallivanting somewhere. He was happy to dine at home and be in bed by ten o'clock. Especially as the last thing he did before he blew out the candle was to write a letter to Harriet Sowerby.

Thanks to his diligence, Harriet was probably the best-informed young lady in the whole of England during that nervous time. At the end of March he wrote that Napoleon had entered Paris, 'walking up the steps of the Tuileries, so it is said, with his eyes closed and his hands outstretched as though he were a blind man'. In April he gave her all the details of the Emperor's new legislation: 'He has abolished the slave trade, which is a thing I feel sure we should applaud had it been done by anyone other than Boney, and given a free pardon to all those who worked for the Bourbons while he was in Elba, saying, so it is rumoured, that they were under duress and could do no other. It is quite foolishly generous, but will ensure their silence now, if nothing else.' At the end of May he reported with some agitation that the Emperor's army now numbered more than a quarter of a million men, and that the Saxon troops, 'who are supposed to be on our side', had mutinied and been sent away, but that the Duke of Wellington was ready and waiting in Brussels with an allied army of a comparable size, 'for which we must be profoundly thankful' and that the battle when it came would be 'the clashing of Titans'.

In Miss Pettie's brown parlour Harriet read every word, and passed on the news to her hostess, like the dutiful child she was. But when she was alone in the dark cell of her little back bedroom, it was the beginning and end of his letters that she re-read and cherished. 'My dear Miss Sowerby… I have the honour to be your devoted friend, John Henry Easter.' and they were the hope of her dreams. 'Your devoted friend.' 'My dear.'

She had got into the habit of calling upon Miss Pettie nearly every day on one pretext or another and staying in her parlour long enough to read his latest letter and answer it by postscript. But the fifth was so long and so full of questions that she and Miss Pettie both thought it was only right and proper that it should be answered at equal length. A postscript that was longer than the original letter seemed a trifle foolish, so Miss Pettie provided her with a sheet of writing paper all of her own and left her in peace for half a discreet hour to write as she pleased.

'I have so much to do that I simply cannot stay with you, my dear,' she said, patting her curls, 'but if you will fold your letter and seal it before you leave, I will see that it gets to the post.' And she went tottering off to find something to occupy the time, chuckling to herself at how successful this match was becoming.

AT THE BEGINNING OF JUNE, the Honeywoods moved back to Bury for the summer, and Billy followed them whenever his work and his mother would allow. His presence in Angel Hill on that first Saturday afternoon cast Harriet Sowerby into a state of such tremulous anticipation that she chipped two of her mother's precious coffee cups after dinner that night and had to be prayed over for her clumsiness for more than an hour.

And this time, although she appeared to be listening meekly to her mother's hectoring voice, she was actually paying no attention at all, being busy inside her head with problems of quite another kind. What would happen when Mr Easter came to Bury with his brother, as he surely must sooner or later? He might even spend the summer in town as his mother did, and what then? If they were to meet — in the street somewhere or in Miss Pettie's parlour, perhaps — he would be bound to greet her and then what would happen? It would be most improper to ignore him, especially after all the letters that had passed between them. And he might invite her to join him at some ball or other. How could she contrive to accept him if he did? It was all rather complicated. But there was bound to be a way round it, if she thought hard enough.

'For Thy Name's sake, Amen,' her mother said with fierce satisfaction. 'Now see if you can mend your ways, my girl.'

Back in Bedford Square Nan had decided to go to Liverpool and open a branch of A Easter and Sons there, 'since Mr Brougham travels in that direction to assist his cousin Henry, who is hoping to be elected a member of Parliament for the town. 'Twill be pleasant to have company on the journey. 'Tis a growing town, with a deal of custom a-waiting us, if I'm any judge.'

But John was more interested in the coaches that were now running with dependable regularity from another growing town. 'The inland mails from Birmingham could take our papers out to the better part of the North West,' he said. 'To Liverpool and Chester and Manchester, which is growing apace so Mr Walter tells me with so many army uniforms and blankets and such being made. Why not start with a shop in Birmingham, Mama?'

But Liverpool had far greater attractions. 'No,' she said, dusting her hands together. ''Twill be Liverpool first. 'Tis all arranged. And if all goes well there, we will open up the North West between us. Liverpool today, Birmingham tomorrow, eh.'

'Birmingham will be far more use to us,' he persisted. It annoyed him that she would insist on doing his work for him. Having given him the job of extending their trade to the provincial towns she really ought to allow him to do it, and in his own way what's more. Particularly as his way was methodical and trustworthy and hers was somewhat haphazard.

But there was no gainsaying her. 'That's settled then,' she said, dusting her hands together.

However, they were both reckoning without Napoleon.

ON THE 13TH JUNE, while she and the Broughams were still busy in Liverpool, a dispatch arrived reporting that the Emperor had begun to move his army towards the Belgium frontier. Billy was recalled from his courtship in Bury, and Nan came back to London immediately, leaving Mr Brougham with his cousin, and her newly opened shop in Liverpool to fend for itself.

"Twill be a battle now as sure as fate,' she said. 'Have everything in readiness, Johnnie, for when this news breaks 'twill make us a fortune.'

It broke nine days later, and was printed in the London *Gazette* Extraordinary, headed *Downing Street, Thursday June 22nd 1815*.

Major the Honourable H Percy arrived late last night with a dispatch from Field Marshall the Duke of Wellington, KG, to Earl Bathurst, his Majesty's principal secretary of state for the War Department, of which the following is a copy...

It was headed *Waterloo June 1815* and was a laconic account of a great battle, written without emotion but detailing every attack and repulse until the final moments which came at...

about seven in the evening when the French army made a desperate effort with the cavalry and infantry supported by the fire of artillery to force our left centre back to Haye Sainte, and, after a severe contest, was defeated. Having observed that the troops retired from this attack in great confusion, and that the march of General Bulow's corps upon La Belle Alliance had begun to take effect, I determined to attack the enemy, and immediately advanced the whole line of infantry, supported by the cavalry and artillery.

The attack succeeded in every point. The enemy was forced from his position on the heights and fled in the utmost confusion leaving behind him as far as I could judge one hundred and fifty pieces of cannon with their ammunition which fell into our hands. I continued the pursuit until long after dark, and then discontinued only on account of the fatigue of our troops, who had been engaged during twelve days, and because I found myself in the same road with Marshal Blucher who assured me of his intention to follow the enemy throughout the night. He has sent me word this morning that he had taken sixty pieces of cannon belonging to the Imperial Guard and several carriages, baggage, etc belonging to Bonaparte.

Then followed the casualty lists. At a cost of more than 62,000 men dead and wounded, 15,000 of whom were from Wellington's army, the battle was over and Boney defeated.

Within minutes of the appearance of the first copy of the *Gazette,* all the spires in the city were clamorous with bells as the news spread from house to house and church to church, and soon people were waving and cheering from every window, and the streets were full of jostling crowds and carriages barely able to inch through the hubbub, and men on horseback waving their caps in the air. ''Tis a triumph!' people said to one another. 'Such a great victory in such a short time! Have 'ee seen the papers?' And the Easter family worked until they were dizzy with fatigue.

Fifteen days later Paris capitulated to the Allies, and six days after that Napoleon wrote a letter surrendering himself to the mercy of the Prince Regent, whom he called 'the most powerful, the most constant and the most generous of my enemies'. But flattery got him nowhere. This time there was to be no escape for him. It was announced that he was to be exiled to 'a lonely island in the midst of the South Atlantic Seas, from which his villainy would never again emerge to torment his fellow men'. France was to pay an indemnity of 700 million francs and submit to military occupation by Wellington's army. The war of a hundred days was over.

The Prince Regent, as was only to be expected from a man of such extravagant and flamboyant taste, immediately announced elaborate plans for victory parades in the capital that summer, with reviews, and masques, and firework displays and all manner of lavish entertainments. And not to be outdone, small towns and municipalities all over the kingdom planned their festivities too. The month of August, as Billy was happy to point out, was going to be one long, unbroken round of pleasure.

'I shall stay here in London to attend the review,' he said, 'and then I'm off to Bury for the Victory Ball. Shall you join me, Johnnoh?'

'Only if you give me your word that Lizzie ain't to be there,' John said. 'I've been lisped over quite enough for one lifetime.' But he knew he would certainly go. There was no pressure of work now, and it would be a chance to see Harriet again.

'We will all attend the Victory Ball at Bury,' Nan told them firmly. ''Twill be expected of us. As to the rest, you may go wherever you please. Billy will follow Miss Honeywood, I daresay.'

'Oh I say!' Billy protested, grinning sheepishly, and then

trying to explain: 'She's a deuced pretty creature, Ma. I might even marry her.'

'Don't torment your brother with that Lizzie, that's all,' Nan said.

'I shall make certain to keep well out of her way,' John assured them, making up his mind that he would spend all his time dancing with Harriet. How pleasant it would be.

So preparations went cheerfully ahead and Billy bought three tickets for the Victory Ball the next time he went down to Bury, and the citizens of that rejoicing town brought out their best clothes ready for the Grand Parade that would precede it during the afternoon.

Mrs Sowerby did not approve of the extravagance of new clothes for such an occasion and said so unequivocally, maintaining that her Sunday-go-to-meeting-clothes were quite good enough for any celebration and that Harriet had more than enough clothes already without swelling her pride by offering her more. But Mr Sowerby felt he owed it to his position in Mr Cole's establishment to look as well as he could.

'A new cravat, my dear,' he said, 'and new revers to my best jacket and perhaps a new beaver hat?'

'A cravat I will allow,' Mrs Sowerby said, 'for nothing looks worse than crumpled linen about the neck, and a small piece of velvet would be sufficient for new revers without putting us to unnecessary expense. I will steam your hat. That is all it requires.'

So the day before the Grand Parade a fine piece of cream linen for the new cravat was purchased at Mr William Pickering's drapery in Abbeygate Street, and after work that evening, while Mrs Sowerby was occupied darning her black stockings and Harriet was busy kneading bread for the following morning, Mr Sowerby retired to his bedroom to try it on.

He looked exceedingly fine. In fact, if he hadn't been acutely aware that he had to avoid the sin of pride, he would have felt quite pleased with himself. All that is needed now, he thought, was his gold-plated tiepin fixed right in the centre of the centremost fold. And as the tiepin was kept neatly in the trinket box beside the candlestick, it was the simplest matter to stretch out his hand for it.

The reason for what happened next was never entirely clear to him, because he was usually so careful with the candles, being mindful of their power to start fires or burn fingers or, even worse, drop hot wax on his wife's well-polished furniture. It occurred to him much later that it could have been an act of God deliberately designed to reveal the perfidious nature of his daughter. But whatever the reason, as he opened the lid of the box that evening, he passed his hand straight into the searing heat of his own two-headed candlestick. The unexpected pain made him jump, so that he dropped the box onto the floor, and as he rubbed the side of his hand and spat on it to ease the pain, the contents of the box scattered about the room. And his tiepin skidded through the connecting door into Harriet's little cold cell.

He got down on his knees irritably and began to gather the trinkets, his wife's jet beads and her agate brooch, fortunately undamaged. Then he stooped through the door and bent to retrieve his tiepin.

It was lying at a curious angle against a very loose floorboard. I shall need to mend that, he thought, and lifted it idly to test how far it had become disconnected. And what he saw underneath it stopped his breath with delighted horror. There was a positive cache of letters there. Thirty-six of them. He counted as he drew them out. Trembling with outrage, he took them through into his bedroom to read them by the light of his treacherous candle.

Then, enlarged by an overpowering and entirely righteous indignation, he took them downstairs to show to his wife.

CHAPTER 10

'Explain yourself,' Mrs Sowerby said terribly.

Harriet was so frightened she could hardly breathe. When her mother called her from the kitchen, she'd wiped her hands on her apron and obeyed readily enough, even though she knew from the peremptory tone of the call that she must have done something wrong. But she didn't think it could be anything particularly bad because she'd been working very hard and very carefully all that day. And besides, she'd been in the middle of such a happy daydream, looking forward to tomorrow when she would dance at the Victory Ball with Mr Easter.

She'd found a way round, just as she'd hoped. Or to be more accurate Miss Pettie had provided one, inviting her to this Victory Ball just as she'd invited her to the last, and even giving her one of her ball gowns, which they'd altered and trimmed and made over into quite a new garment — and such a pretty one, with a new waistband of pale blue velvet and the dearest little puff sleeves trimmed with pale blue ribbons to match. And now she only had twenty-four hours to wait before the ball began and she would see her dear Mr Easter again. The sight of his letters, spread out before her on the dining table, looking so white and vulnerable and naked against the unforgiving wood, gave her such a shock that she couldn't move another step.

'Well?' her mother said, standing beside the offending documents straight-spined and fierce-faced and black as thunder. The chastening rod lay on the table beside the letters, ready for use, its red leather most horrible in the firelight.

'I found — these —' her father said, speaking slowly and precisely as though every word were so distasteful that he had to spit it from his mouth, 'these — articles — hidden under the floorboards in your bedroom, my gel. What have you to say for yourself?' His face was so pinched with anger that his lips had virtually disappeared and his little narrow nose was as grey as dry putty. 'What? Eh? What?'

Harriet was too shaken to be able to answer. Yet. She stared at them mutely, her knees trembling.

'You don't deny they were sent to you I suppose?' her mother said.

'No.'

'Nor that they are from Mr Easter, with whom you were most *expressly* forbidden to communicate?'

'No —' her chest constricting most painfully.

'Nor that you have *disobeyed your parents* in the most flagrant and disgusting manner?'

Oh no, Harriet thought, there was nothing disgusting about my letters, nor about Mr Easter's. I can't agree with that. I was wrong to receive them but not disgusting.

'I disobeyed you, Mama,' she said, 'because you told me to do something that wasn't polite.' It frightened her to be making such a stand but it had to be done.

Mrs Sowerby was so surprised she couldn't believe her ears. 'What's this? What's this?' she snorted. 'Do you *defy* me, girl?'

'No, Mama,' Harriet said. She was calmer now that she'd made her stand.

'Then how dare you say such things to your Mama?' Mr Sowerby said.

'I say them, Papa, because they are true. Mr Easter is a fine gentleman. He wrote to me and I replied. 'Twas only common courtesy.'

Her mother picked up the chastening rod and jabbed the wooden end under Harriet's chin. Her eyes were blazing with hatred.

'I have never known such flagrant disobedience in all my born days,' she said. 'After all we've done for you. All the care we've taken of you. All the money we've spent on you! Only think of the money we paid to have you educated, and a fine waste that's turned out to be. Oh yes! We teach you to read and that is the sort of rubbish you spend your time on. "We live by admiration, hope and love." What wicked, wicked trash to write to a young girl. Admiration hope and love indeed! There is nothing in *you* to admire, let me tell you, nor to love, if this is the way you go on. Wicked, wicked trash! And if you don't know yet what evil will come of reading such vile words then I despair of you. Oh what a waste of your education! We teach you to write and you spend your time writing foolish letters to young rakes who will ruin you. And after all our efforts to protect you, to raise you up in the right way, to inculcate obedience and sobriety and self-control and gentleness and all the good Christian virtues, after all our efforts, this is how you turn out. Oh Mr Sowerby, words fail me!'

But words didn't fail Mr Sowerby. He knew exactly what to say and exactly what to do.

'There is nothing for it, Mother,' he said happily. 'She will have to be whipped.'

With her chin still held up by the rod Harriet had no way of avoiding the expression on her father's face. His mouth was twisted sideways with the force of his anger and his little eyes shone. 'She will have to be whipped, Mother,' he repeated with satisfaction. 'Whipped within an inch of her life. The evil will have to be whipped out of her.' And each time he said the word whipped he licked his lips as if he were already savouring the action.

I won't beg for mercy, Harriet thought, because this time I am right and they are wrong. I won't beg for mercy, no matter what they do. Her hands were still sticky with dough and she tried to rub them clean on one corner of her apron, acting instinctively as if clean hands might deflect their wrath. But she didn't flinch and for the first time in her life she didn't drop her eyes.

'You will take your punishment,' her mother promised grimly, thrusting a chair into the centre of the little room. 'Take off your dress and bend over that chair if you please.'

Harriet didn't resist because she knew from bitter experience that resistance only prolonged a beating. If they were going to beat her let them do it quickly and get it over with. She took off her shoes and her apron and unbuttoned her dress and stepped out of it without a word. She even folded her clothes and put them neatly on the table, because neatness was habitual to her and because it gave her a few more moments to compose herself before the pain began. Her heart was beating so fast it was making her chemise shake and her chest felt as though it was being squeezed by some giant vice. But she would endure it. She always had.

But this time, although her mother watched her prepare with her usual narrow-eyed anticipation, her father was infuriated by her slowness. He seized her roughly by the hair and pulled her down across the chair. 'Lay on!' ordered his wife. 'She has dallied long enough. Now do not spare her!'

Harriet lay across the chair, afraid but still determined not to plead and not to say another word. But she cried aloud at every blow. She couldn't help herself. They hurt so much and came stinging down upon her back and her legs and her shoulders so quickly and brutally and unpredictably, and with such force.

It was the worst beating she'd ever endured. Usually her mother hit her either six times or twelve, counting the strokes as they fell, her voice as sharp as the rod, and Harriet hung on to the edge of the chair silently counting the blows too because each one brought her nearer to the moment of release. But this time her mother beat without counting and without mercy, flailing at her daughter's body until her arms ached and she could barely see what she was doing. 'Repent your sins!' she shouted. 'Repent! Repent!'

And Mr Sowerby echoed, 'Repent, you grievous sinner! Beat her, Mother! Beat her! Repent! Repent! Repent!'

After the thirteenth blow Harriet began to scream, hanging on to the edge of the chair because her mind had stopped functioning and she couldn't think of anything else to do. But after the twentieth, reason and revulsion returned together and she struggled to her feet and stumbled away, dodging the next blow, and the next, pinned against the wall and swaying out of range, and still screaming a long, high-pitched, eerie wail of desperation and terror. Her unexpected resistance drove both her parents into a frenzy.

Her father grabbed at her, trying to pull her down on the chair again, tugging at her hair and shrieking at her to be still, and her mother beat her as though she was demented, terrible blows that cut her arms and her face until her whole body was slippery with terrified sweat, and she couldn't run any longer, and she couldn't stand either because there was no strength in her legs, and she fell sideways onto the flagstones, wrenching her hair from her father's grasp so violently that clumps of it came away in his fingers.

For a few seconds they were all quite still, looking at each other, while the Sowerbys blew like horses and the fire spat and hissed, and two drops of blood fell from Harriet's forefinger into two neat red circles on the flagstones. Then she began to cry, in long, drawn-out, forlorn sobs that hurt her throat and frightened her parents.

'Get to bed,' Mr Sowerby said abruptly. 'We don't want to see your ugly face again tonight.' The sooner she was out of sight the better.

Harriet crawled up the stairs on her hands and knees, sobbing and groaning, and stumbled through her parents' room, barking her shins against furniture that she could barely see, and fell onto her truckle bed in a state of total exhaustion. But even then, with the beating over and alone in the dark cell of her room, she couldn't stop crying. She wept on and on until the ache in her chest was sobbed away and she had no more energy left to cry with and no more tears to shed. Then she lifted herself wearily from the mattress, covered herself with her blanket and lay shivering in the dark.

And her thoughts went round and round in an endless, useless circle all night long. She had disobeyed her parents, which was certainly a sin. And she'd fought against them and she was glad she'd done it. For she wasn't sinful. Not this time. Writing a letter to a gentleman as proper and kind as Mr Easter couldn't possibly be a sin. She knew it. And as she lay stiffly under her blanket, she also knew, in that private innermost core of her mind and emotions, that she hated her mother and father and that she always would.

She was still cold and still wide awake when the dawn began to trawl a faint grey light across the little space of her window. She got up very stiffly and limped to the door to see if it was possible to get out quietly and go downstairs for a drink of water, because she was desperately thirsty. But the door was locked. And there was no water in the ewer either, because, as she remembered now, she'd been sent upstairs before she had a chance to fill it. Her mouth was so terribly dry it was an effort to swallow. But then it was an effort to do anything, she felt so sore.

She looked at her arms in the faint half-light, examining them quietly and dispassionately almost as though they belonged to someone else. They were both blotched with dark bruises and there were two long cuts on her right forearm that were still oozing blood. She examined her chemise, which was torn and bloodstained and very dirty. And she touched her face very delicately with her fingertips, because it was extremely tender and very swollen. Then she knelt down beside her narrow window and peered at the faint image of her head and shoulders in the darker corner of the glass. Her face was so disfigured she couldn't recognise it. One eye was half closed by two dark mounds of bruised flesh that puffed out beside and beneath it, there was a lump on her temple and both her lips were cut and swollen. I look like a monster, she thought.

But she didn't cry. She'd gone beyond tears now. She was quite calm. She knew that there was nothing she could do except wrap herself up in her blanket again and endure until one or other of her parents unlocked the door. They had done their worst, just as she had always feared they would. Now it was simply a matter of waiting.

Miss Pettie was rather upset when Mr Sowerby arrived on her doorstep that afternoon to tell her that Harriet would not be accepting her kind invitation to the Victory Ball after all.

'She is being kept to her room,' he said, 'as a punishment for a most grievous sin.' And the expression on his face implied that it was too shameful to be talked about.

'I am uncommon sorry to hear it,' Miss Pettie said. And a most uncomfortable suspicion came winging into her mind. What if the sin were something to do with Mr Easter and the letters? Oh surely not! Harriet was always most discreet and, besides, there was no harm in a letter or two. Surely not. But it worried her just the same. 'I shall look forward to seeing her on Sunday,' she said, 'when I trust she will be quite restored to obedience.'

But it was a great disappointment that Harriet would miss the Victory Ball especially as all the Easters were due to attend. It quite took the gilt off the gingerbread, which was a pity for this second Victory Ball was even more lavish than the first.

Mrs Easter was in splendid form in a blue and green silk gown cut in the very latest style and very much envied by all the ladies, who were either complimentary or scathing about it according to their natures, and Billy was dancing quite rapturously with his beloved Matilda, but John was very quiet and barely danced at all. He made no mention of the absent Harriet and that upset Miss Pettie too.

'I shall look out for her most particularly on Sunday,' she said to Jane, when the ball was over and she was home at last and her old servant was patiently unhooking her ball gown. 'She will be forgiven by then, surely to goodness, whatever the sin. And I can't believe it was as bad as Mr Sowerby made out for our Harriet is too kindly a creature, wouldn't you say so, Jane?'

'She's pleasant enough in all conscience ma'am,' Jane agreed, 'but if she don't obey the fifth Commandment, there en't a deal of hope for her, nor no Victory Balls neither.' She approved of stern discipline, did Jane. And when you've been sitting up until two in the morning waiting for your mistress to come home, it is hard to be full of Christian charity.

'I shall look out for her notwithstanding,' Miss Pettie said.

And she looked out.

But there was no sign of Harriet in chapel that Sunday, and when Miss Pettie made discreet enquiries, she discovered that nobody had seen her at all since Tuesday. Which was five whole days. By now Miss Pettie's hesitant suspicion was beginning to turn into alarm. She spent the rest of the Sabbath worrying and praying and all of Monday and Tuesday hoping in vain that Harriet would visit, and finally, early on Wednesday morning, she trotted next door to confide in Bessie Thistlethwaite.

'The family's all gone back ter London, Miss Pettie,' Bessie said, coming into the hall to welcome her visitor when the parlour maid had admitted her. 'Mr John went Thursday in such a rush you'd never believe, and Mrs Easter was off Sat'day, and now Mr Billy's gone too by the first coach yesterday morning. We're all on our ownsome, as yer might say.'

'Yes,' Miss Pettie said, clutching at her curls in her anxiety. 'I rather imagined that is how it would be. But 'tis no matter, Mrs Thistlethwaite, for 'twas you and Mr Thistlethwaite I came to see.'

'In that case, Miss Pettie,' Bessie said, 'would you care ter come into my parlour? You've just caught us in. Thiss is off ter Norwich in 'alf an hour.'

So Miss Pettie went into the parlour and Thiss and Bessie listened to her most seriously while she told her tale.

'You think they've locked 'er in fer writin' to our Mr John then, Miss Pettie?' Thiss asked.

'I fear so,' Miss Pettie confessed. 'And 'tis all on my account. What shall I do?'

'Never you mind, Miss Pettie,' Bessie commiserated. 'Don't you go a-frettin' yourself. Thiss'll think a' somethink. Wontcher, Thiss?'

Thiss stood up and took his pipe from the rack in the chimney corner and, after filling it slowly and thoughtfully, and then lighting it with Vesuvian clouds of smoke and much puffing, he sat down on the settle again and delivered his verdict.

'If Mrs Easter was 'ere, I should say we oughter tell Mrs Easter,' he said. 'Being she's the most forceful lady I knows. But she ain't 'ere. She's off in Hertfordshire somewhere, an' a fair ol' journey away. That bein' so, my opinion of it is this. They was Mr John's letters what caused the shindig so you sez, Miss

Pettie, which do seem a queer thing ter me when we considers what a fine gentleman 'e is. But no accountin' fer taste as the butler said when 'is master spread jam on the bloaters. So bein' they was his letters, I reckon 'e should know the outcome a' the correspondence, so ter speak. One of us should write an' tell 'im. What I'm quite willin' ter do, if you're agreeable to it, Miss Pettie.'

'Oh what a relief 'twould be to me,' Miss Pettie said. 'When could it be done?'

'If it ain't like ter take more'n twenty minutes,' Thiss said, 'I could do it fer you now. I got me pipe lit.'

So the letter was sent and arrived in Bedford Square the following morning while Billy and John were eating their breakfast.

It reduced John to prowling agitation. 'Read it, Billoh,' he said tossing the letter onto his brother's plate.

'Steady on!' Billy said. 'Now it's all over butter. Sit down, do, it can't be as bad as all that.' But when he'd read the letter too, he grew serious at once. 'We must go down and see about this directly,' he said. 'We can't have young ladies punished for writing to us Easters, dammit. Indeed, we can't. What's the world coming to?'

'Do you think it's true?' John said, drumming on the table with his fingers in his agitation.

'We'll take the first coach up on Saturday morning,' Billy said. 'That gives you today and tomorrow to find somebody else to do the stamping for you. Mr Lowther might be just the man. He's sharp enough. Then we'll see.'

'But what will we do when we see — whatever we see?'

'Time enough for that,' Billy said practically, 'when we see it. Come on!'

CHAPTER 11

It was a difficult journey up to Bury. They travelled on the 'Phenomena' with a rapid change of horses every ten miles, so at least it took as little time as possible, and the weather was fine and the roads dry. But in his present state of indecision and confusion, John found every minute unbearable. It was so necessary for him to be in control of his life or at least to know what he was going to do, and now he was being carried along with about as much volition as a leaf in the wind, feeling concerned about Harriet and guilt about his own part in the affair, and horribly powerless. To make matters worse, Mr Wiggins the coachman would insist on engaging him in cheerful conversation and cracking jokes with Billy, 'being we're partners in the same way a' business, if you takes me meanin'. It was all very difficult.

But once they'd arrived in Angel Hill and Thiss had been sent for and Bessie had bustled them into the dining room and served them breakfast and told them everything she knew about 'that poor Miss Sowerby', everything changed.

'They beat the poor soul sommink cruel, Mr John,' Bessie said. 'Hours it was, 'cordin' ter what Mrs Kirby said when I went down ter the laundry, and the poor thing cryin' and beggin' fer mercy all the time. 'Tain't nat'rul Mr John, now is it? And since then, she been locked indoors. Never out of 'er room a minute, 'cordin' ter Mrs Kirby. Always up at the windy a-lookin' out, an' so pale an' ill an' unhappy, poor soul. Which ain't ter be wondered at, now is it, Mr John, all things considerin'?'

John listened to her with growing distress and anger. By the time she'd finished her tale, certainty had solidified inside him like a column of ice. Now he knew exactly what he was going to do.

'She must be taken away from such cruelty,' he said. 'I will rescue her.'

'Bravo!' Billy said, chortling with delight and Bessie clapped her hands together like a child, relieved to hear it and thrilled by the romance of it.

But Thiss was cautious. 'That 'ud take a deal a' doin', Mr John,' he said. 'How d'yer propose ter go about it, if I may make so bold as to ask?'

John had very little idea. He simply knew it would be done. 'I shall go to Churchgate Street,' he said, deciding as he spoke, 'and see Mr and Mrs Sowerby and persuade them that it was polite and proper for Miss Sowerby to write to me and that they ought to let her out of the house. She shan't be locked in a minute longer, not if I can help it.'

'They'll be a mortal tricky couple ter persuade,' Thiss warned. ''Ard as nails the pair of 'em. She's got a face like a flat iron, an' 'e's swallered a Bible. What if it don't work?'

'Then I shall think of something else.' There was no deterring him now.

'I shall stay here and drink another cup of your excellent tea, Bessie, and wait the outcome,' Billy decided.

'I shall be at the stables should yer need anythink,' Thiss said. 'Take young Tom along with yer, Mr John. Keep it in the fam'ly like. Ain't no need fer the rest a' the servants ter know what's afoot. 'E's a useful lad, though I sez so who shouldn't. 'E could nip back 'ere sharpish and let us know if there was anythink you was wantin'.'

So Tom was sent for and his cap straightened and his blue jacket dusted down by his mother and was given instructions by his father. 'You're ter stick by Mr John 'ere, an' do anythink 'e says.'

'Right you are, Guvner,' Tom said, nodding and grinning until his jaw was in danger of dislocation. 'Always wanted ter be a gentleman's gentleman, I 'ave. Right you are!'

'Gentleman's gentleman, my eye!' his father mocked. 'Errand boy you are, and mind you looks sharp about it.'

'Sharp as a razor, Pa,' Tom promised, still grinning.

And off they went.

Churchgate Street was crowded with people and clogged with carts and carriages that morning as the daily shoppers took their empty baskets up the hill to the markets and returned with them laden. There was so much noise in the street that John wasn't really surprised when his first knock at Mrs Sowerby's low door brought no response.

He knocked again, this time with a double rap and considerably louder.

No answer.

He knocked a third time, rat-tat-tat.

And was still ignored.

'Look through the window and see if there is anyone at home,' John said to his gentleman's gentleman.

'The missus is in,' Tom reported. 'Out the back, in the kitchen. I can see 'er plain as plain, sir.'

As she has seen me, John thought, hooking Tom away from the window. Thiss was right. This was going to be difficult. 'Go back to your father,' he instructed, 'and tell him I have tried and failed with Mrs Sowerby and now I mean to visit the laundry and see Mrs Kirby.'

'Right you are sir,' Tom said happily, and sped off down the hill.

John waited until the next group of people was walking past Mrs Sowerby's window and then, suitable hidden among them, strolled to the laundry. Despite his outward calm he was beginning to feel as excited as young Tom, for he knew now that Mrs Sowerby meant to oppose him so this had all the makings of an adventure.

Mrs Kirby answered the door to him at once. 'Pray do step in, Mr Easter sir,' she said, standing humbly aside so as to give him plenty of room to walk into her laundry. 'How may we serve 'ee, sir?'

The door led into a narrow passageway where the dirty washing was received and the clean dispatched. There was a counter to the right of the entrance piled with clean bundles, all carefully docketed and neatly stacked, waiting collection.

'I have come to make enquiries about Miss Harriet Sowerby,' John said, breathing in the scent of starch and clean linen. 'I have heard from Mrs Thistlethwaite of the manner in which she has been treated. Now I wish to know exactly where she is. I believe you said she was locked in a room. Is the whereabouts of the room known to you, Mrs Kirby?'

'Come you through to the back yard, Mr Easter sir,' Mrs Kirby said, leading the way down the passageway at once. 'Downright cruelty in a Christian country, so 'tis. That oughtn't to be allowed.'

'Allowed,' Rosie echoed, stepping forward out of the laundry room to join them. 'Come you through, Mr Easter. Poor Harriet!'

He followed the two women past the piles of washing and the door to the laundry room where four dishevelled laundry maids stopped their work to gaze at him with starch-eyed interest, and along the passage to the back door where they stopped.

'Best to take a quick peek from here, sir,' Mrs Kirby said.

'Wouldn't do to let Mrs Sowerby see us, now would it? Bein' she got a tongue in 'er 'ead sharp enough to cut coal. Harriet is up behind the windy, look. She been a-shut in there eleven days, poor soul.' And she stood aside so that he could hide his body behind the door frame and look out into the yard. It reminded him of the way Harriet had hidden herself from view when she'd peeped into her own house on the day they came back from Bath. He had thought it merely curious then, now he realised that it had been a sign of fear.

It was a very small yard and very muddy and the smell from the two privies that stood side by side in the middle of it was so concentrated and noxious it made him gag. He looked where Mrs Kirby was pointing.

The Sowerby's house formed the fourth wall to the yard and from where he lurked John could see through the kitchen window into the narrow kitchen where pots and pans hung above the fireplace and the hearth was heaped with grey ash. Mrs Sowerby was standing straight and black beside the kitchen table mixing something in an earthenware pot. Directly above the kitchen window was another, a good deal smaller, with three panes of rough glass and behind the glass he fancied he could see a white-clad figure pacing to and fro.

There was a coal shed built against the wall to the left of the kitchen window and almost directly underneath Harriet's room, and although it was a rickety construction it gave John Easter an idea.

'You would know when the Sowerbys are out I daresay, Mrs Kirby,' he said. 'Gone to church or to market or suchlike.'

'You could set clocks by 'em,' the laundry woman said, sniffing derisively. 'Critturs of powerful strong habits the Sowerbys.'

'Then the next time you would expect them to leave the house would be...'

'Seven o'clock tonight, sir. Saturday meetin'. Never miss.'

'Would you happen to know how long the Saturday meeting continues?'

'Hour an' a half, Mr Easter sir. Hour an' a half, reg'lar as clockwork.'

'I'm much obliged to 'ee, Mrs Kirby,' John said, putting sixpence into her rough palm. Why, the plan was almost complete. 'If I were to return to your house at five minutes past seven tonight, you would be able to let me into the yard I daresay.'

'Well as to that, sir,' the laundry woman said, smiling at him, 'I should be at my supper with Mr Kirby and my cousin, an' not like to see anyone comin' or goin'. Howsomever, if all the washing en't collected, I leaves the latch up on consideration of my clients, if you takes my meanin'.'

He took her meaning very well and with the expenditure of another sixpence.

'I shall be there to 'elp 'er, sir,' Rosie said, nodding her great head. 'My poor Harriet!'

'Thank 'ee,' he said. He was so hot with sympathy for poor Harriet he didn't stop to think about the consequences.

Then he ran back to Angel Hill.

Billy was in the front parlour playing cards with Claude Honeywood and Ebenezer Millhouse. 'We're off to Fornham,' he said, 'to join the ladies. Tilda will be there for dinner with her cousins and Lizzie. They've quite a party planned. Why don't you join us, Johnnoh?' He seemed to have forgotten all about the rescue.

'I shall need a ladder,' John said urgently, 'and two people to hold it steady up against the coal shed, and a hammer to break a window with, and a blanket to cover up the jagged glass, and the pony cart to carry everything and get us all clear afterwards. Mrs Sowerby refuses to open her door to me, so I mean to steal Miss Harriet away.'

'Oh I say! Bravo!' Ebenezer said. 'Bags I to be one pair of hands on the ladder. What 'ee say, Claude?'

'I'm game for anything,' Claude said, tossing his un-played hand all over the table and jumping to his feet. 'What a lark, Billy!'

'My eye!' Billy said, looking up at his brother with admiration. 'You do mean business and no mistake.'

'Now I'm off to the stables,' John said, 'to tell Thiss and see about the pony. Young Tom shall come with us tonight and keep cave.'

'What a lark!' Claude said again, grabbing the jacket he'd flung across the back of a chair. 'Wait for me, Johnnie!'

'When is it to be?' Billy said, standing up at last and following his friends.

'I will tell you on the way,' his brother said. 'Come on!'

BEFORE THEY WENT to the Saturday meeting Mr and Mrs Sowerby made one more effort to persuade their daughter to change her ways. It was beginning to worry Mrs Sowerby that the girl was so thin and looked so ill. Even though, of course, the unremitting diet of bread and water on which she had existed for the last eleven days had been entirely her own fault and could be altered the moment she saw sense and agreed to obedience. But she wouldn't agree. That was the trouble. Some terrible evil had entered into her soul. There was no question of it. Mrs Sowerby had suspected it from the first. Now she and her husband could both see it quite clearly.

They had come to Harriet's room on the morning after her punishment prepared to forgive her. They were both aware that she would have to be kept within doors until her bruises healed, since not all their neighbours saw the necessity of training up a child in the way it should go, and some had idle, vicious tongues, but they foresaw no difficulties that could not be over-come by a few days' prayer and solitude.

'You will obey us now, I know,' Mrs Sowerby began, pleased because Harriet had risen as soon as they unlocked the door and now stood meekly beside her bed with her eyes lowered.

But the answer was an uncharacteristic question. 'What have I to do, Mama?'

'Why, promise me that you will not write to that dreadful man again, nor speak to him nor see him. That is all.'

Harriet lifted her bruised face and looked at her mother. One eye was closed by blackened, puffy flesh and her bottom lip was split by a scarlet fissure. But even before Mrs Sowerby could feel any pity for her she spoilt her chances.

'No, Mama,' she said, 'I will not promise.' Enough was enough. She would not allow them to bully her any further.

She quite took Mrs Sowerby's breath away. After such a thor-ough whipping, she expected abject obedience, not effrontery.

'You will promise,' Mr Sowerby said, angered by this foolish attempt at argument. 'That is all there is to it. We have not brought you up to be disobedient.'

'I will not promise,' Harriet said thickly. Her mouth was painfully dry and she was finding it difficult to talk but there was no going back. This had to be said. She had made up her mind to it. 'Mr Easter is a good man. I did no wrong in answering his letters, nor in speaking to him. I will not promise.'

'Men are *not* good,' Mrs Sowerby said. 'Particularly men like him. Men like him ruin girls like you. Is that what you want, eh? Do you want to be ruined? Do you want to end up with some wretched bastard child? Do you *want* to bring disgrace upon us, eh? Is that what you want?'

'No, Mama. But Mr Easter wouldn't ruin anybody.'

'He would! He would! Do as you are told.'

But the refusal was given again. 'No, Mama, I will not.'

'Have a care, child,' Mr Sowerby warned, 'that we do not beat you again.'

'If you do,' Harriet said flatly, 'I shall die.' She spoke so oddly, without any emotion at all, as if she were talking about someone else.

Mrs Sowerby felt quite chilled. What had got into the child? This was most unlike her. 'Then be a good girl and give us your promise,' she said, trying to cajole, and was annoyed that her own voice sounded false.

'No, Mama,' Harriet said again. 'I will obey you in all other matters but I will not be unkind to Mr Easter.'

'We will beat you,' her mother warned.

But there was no response. No fear, no pleading, no emotion at all.

'As you please, Mama,' Harriet said. ''Tis all one to me.'

'What is to be done with her?' Mrs Sowerby said, turning to her husband in exasperation. 'I begin to believe she is possessed.'

'If that is how things stand,' Mr Sowerby said, 'then we must try what the bread of adversity and the waters of affliction will do. She is to receive nothing else, Mrs Sowerby, until she comes to her senses, which we must pray will be soon. 'Tis a sad, sad thing to see one's child so stubborn, Harriet. You grieve me sorely. You grieve your mother sorely. Intransigence is a sign of the devil. Bread and water, Mrs Sowerby.'

'A day or two should see her more amenable,' he promised his wife when they were back in the kitchen and eating Yarmouth bloaters for their breakfast. 'Let the smell of good food waft upon her and we shall see a difference, you mark my words.'

But the smell of good food didn't appear to have any effect upon their daughter at all. Her answer was always the same. She would be obedient in all other particulars but she would not promise the very thing that was required of her. She was quiet and withdrawn, speaking only when she was spoken to and making no fuss or complaint, but they could not change her mind.

'I have made a broth of chicken bones,' her mother said on the seventh day. 'Would you not care to taste some?'

But the answer was the same lethargic, 'No, Mama.'

'I cannot understand it,' Mrs Sowerby said to her husband at dinner that evening. 'She must be hungry by now. She certainly looks it.'

But the gnawing pains in her stomach that made Harriet sit bent double like a jack-knife, and the cramps that locked her feet in a vice and pulled the muscles of her calves into tangible knots, and the scars and bruises on her face and arms that were taking so long to heal were silently endured and never spoken of. As the days passed, she grew weaker, it was sometimes hard for her to remember why she was locked up and what she was doing, but the sight of her mother's insisting face renewed her opposition, morning after morning. Whatever she had to endure she could not give way. Not now.

'No,' she said that Saturday evening. 'No Mama, I will not promise.' Her wrists were so thin she could circle them easily between finger and thumb, and she was so cold it was all she could do to stop herself shivering. As soon as they are gone, she thought, I will wrap myself in the blanket and sit by the window. There was little enough to look at in the yard but it was better than staring at the wall.

IT WAS GROWING dark when the rescue party escorted the pony cart across Angel Square and into Churchgate Street, with a sizeable ladder clattering in the back of the cart among a collection of saws and hammers that Billy had considered indispensable to the adventure, Ebenezer had provided a lantern and a tinder box, and Claude had insisted upon bringing a jar of treacle and an old sheet, maintaining that the easiest way to break glass without fuss was to cover it with a sticky cloth before you hit it. Young Tom was swollen-chested with importance because he'd been assigned to drive the cart, and they were all in a high state of excitement.

At the corner of Churchgate Street they stopped the pony and sent Tom off to peer through the Sowerby's window and see if the house was empty, which, as he soon came scampering back to tell them, it was. The laundry door was on the latch, as promised, there was a bundle of rather crumpled, exculpatory washing on the counter, and the back yard was empty.

They left Tom sitting in the street and gave him strict instructions that he was to watch the road and whistle a warning if he saw anyone coming downhill from the direction of the chapel. Then Billy took the hammers and the blanket and the sheet and the lantern and the tinder box, complaining that he'd only got two hands, and Claude bore the treacle before him like a sacrificial offering, explaining that it took a deal of caution to carry treacle damnit, and Eb and John struggled the ladder through into the yard.

It was dark out there between the houses for there was no light from any of the surrounding windows. The Sowerby house was black and deserted and Mrs Kirby had closed the shutters on her dining room above the laundry. John lit the lantern and hung it on a nail that was sticking out of the coal shed. Then he and Eb manoeuvred the ladder into position against the shed and under the window, hissing instructions at one another in hoarse stage whispers.

He was so charged with excitement and nervous energy that he didn't think to look up at the window until his foot was on the bottom rung of the ladder and he was starting to climb. And then what he saw made him catch his breath with pain and revelation. Such a little white face gazing at him mutely through the narrow pane, a little white ghostly face, hollow-eyed and disfigured by blue and green bruises, its thin cheeks lined with long eerie shadows from the flickering light of the lantern.

And in the single second, before he began to climb, a second without words or reasoning or even conscious thought, he knew that he loved her and that he would always love her, that he couldn't bear her to be hurt, that he would do anything to protect her, that he wanted to stay with her for the rest of his life. 'Hold up the lantern!' he whispered to Billy. 'Is that treacle spread?' And he began to climb.

As he drew level with the window, he saw that she was sitting on the floor wrapped in a blanket, and he signalled to her that she should move away from the glass and was pained to see how slowly she did it. But then he was too busy to look at her, as the sticky cloth was passed up to him and he spread it messily across the central pane and tapped it with Billy's hammer. It broke with a subdued cracking sound, falling into the room, sticky sheet and all, and he pushed in the jagged edges that remained with the palm of his gloved hand and Billy climbed up the ladder after him and stood on the coal shed to hold up the lantern so that he could see what he was doing.

'It is safe now,' he whispered to her as the last chunk of glass fell. 'You won't cut yourself; I promise.'

She was sitting on the edge of a low truckle bed, crouching with the blanket pulled tightly about her like an Indian squaw.

'What have I to do?' she said dully.

'Climb out of the window,' he whispered. 'You won't fall. I will hold you.'

But she didn't get up. 'Where is the good in it?' she said in the same dull tones. 'They will not let me see you. I might as well stay here and die.'

'You are seeing me now,' he said, speaking more loudly with the urgent need to persuade her. They were wasting time. Her parents could be back at any moment. Oh, how could he get her to act? He could feel strength flowing through his veins, down his arms, into his hands. His fingers were tingling with it. He stood at the top of the ladder, wishing he could touch her and send it coursing into her veins too. 'They cannot prevent us,' he said. 'It is beyond their power. Come out of here, my dear love. Just give me your hand. That is all you have to do.'

But she stayed where she was, looking at the floor.

'What's amiss?' Billy hissed from below.

'I can't persuade her,' John replied. 'She don't move. What is to be done?'

'Weakness,' Billy said, practically. 'That's what it is. Well if she can't stand, Johnnoh, she must be carried, that's all. Hold the ladder steady boys. That's the ticket! Now Johnnie. In you go!'

Afterwards John couldn't remember what he'd done or how he'd done it. He had a confused impression that he had caught his dear Harriet in his arms, horrified at how light she was, and that he'd half lifted, half dragged her to the window, and that Billy's hands had reached out of the flickering darkness to guide her feet onto the rungs. He knew that she'd clung to his shoulders for a long time, whispering, 'I can't! I can't!' and that Claude had whispered up from the yard. 'Hush! Is that the whistle?' But how they finally managed to ease her down the ladder to the ground he couldn't recall.

Once there it was a simple matter to pick her up in his arms and run. She was hardly any weight at all and in any case love and panic had given him quite amazing speed and strength. He bundled her into the cart as the others followed him out of the house, and Billy flung the hammer and the tinder box down beside her slippered feet, Claude hung the lantern on the cart, Eb jammed the ladder into the remaining space, young Tom scrambled aboard and took up the reins, and they were off, trotting downhill in the September dusk, smelling the smoke from the coal fires all about them, listening to the whinny of horses in Mr Kent's stables, the droning of prayers from the distant chapel, running and running until they erupted into the lovely open space of Angel Square, and Billy threw his cap into the air, chortling, 'Wheee! We've done it! Wheee!'

Bessie was waiting for them at the front door, with Rosie from the laundry standing beside her, with a black cloak over her arm and her odd round face as yellow as the moon in the light from their little lantern. And then there was another scramble as the cart was unloaded and Bessie handed up the cloak and Rosie trotted off to get a hot brick wrapped in a cloth which she put beside Harriet's feet, and the pony snorted and scraped his hooves on the cobbles with impatience.

And then the door was shut and Billy and his friends were gone and John and Harriet were alone in the cart and heading east along the narrow tracks towards Beyton and Drinkstone and Rattlesden. By now it was quite dark and the moon had risen, a milk-white crescent in a sky scattered with hard-edged stars. They drove in silence between the tangled hedgerows as a little owl shrieked in the woods above them.

It puzzled John that she was so quiet. During the rush and excitement of the rescue there had been no time for anyone to say anything, but now, out here, in the rustling peace of this empty lane, ambling between hilly fields washed silver by the moon, surely, surely, they should talk. Yet she sat beside him as still as a statue, saying nothing.

'You are safe now, Miss Sowerby,' he said, trying to encourage her.

But she was still silent, the hood of the cloak hiding her face.

'We are going to Rattlesden,' he said, trying again. 'You will be safe there with Annie and Mr Hopkins and the children, will you not?'

'Safe?' she whispered. 'Safe?' She turned to face him then, and he saw to his astonishment that her eyes were blazing with a hard-edged frantic intensity about them, like an animal caught in a trap. 'You will not send me back to them, will you, Mr Easter?' she begged. 'Oh promise me! Please promise me! I should die if you sent me back.'

'You have my word,' he said, answering passion with passion. 'You shall never go back. I swear it!'

'They will beat me if you send me back,' she said wildly, 'and oh, Mr Easter, I could not bear to be beaten again, indeed I couldn't.' Then she tried to regain control of herself and spoke more calmly. 'Forgive me. I should not talk like this. I have eaten nothing but bread and water for such a long time, I scarcely know what I am saying.'

'They starved you?' he said, struggling to control the rage and pity that the news had aroused in him. 'Why? Oh Harriet, my dear, why?'

'Because I would not promise never to write to you or see you again,' she said and now she spoke with pride, lifting her battered face and looking at him with calmer eyes. Now that she was sitting beside him again, she knew beyond any doubt that he was a dear kind man, just as she'd remembered him, and that her mother was wrong; he would never ruin anybody, only rescue them. But these were thoughts that couldn't be expressed. That would be improper. And she looked away from him, once more hiding her face and her emotions behind the black cloth of her hood, afraid that weakness would betray her into saying too much.

He, too, was far more moved than he appeared to be. He looked fixedly at the pony's ears to prevent the tears starting into his eyes. To have suffered so and all on his account.

'You shall never be beaten again,' he promised huskily. It was too soon to tell her how much he loved her. Better to wait until she was recovered. She must be treated tenderly after such an ordeal, that was clear. But he wanted to speak. Oh, how he wanted to speak.

With their thoughts in turmoil, he concentrated on guiding the pony through the dark lanes and she remained hidden in her hood, and neither of them said another word until they reached the pair of wattle and daub cottages that stood at the edge of Rattlesden village. They could hear the stream splashing beside the track and see the great dark shape of St Nicholas's church rising above them on its hillock like the ark on Mount Ararat. And there was the dark, stooping figure of dear old James waiting at the lychgate with a lantern.

He called to them as John turned the pony's head towards the rectory. 'Welcome! Welcome! We have stayed dinner for you. Pray let me assist you, Harriet my dear.'

And then Annie came tripping out of the door and flung her arms about Harriet's neck with such violent affection that they both burst into tears. Annie helped Harriet into the house, which gave John a chance to talk to his brother-in-law while they led the pony to the stables and removed the harness.

'She will be safe here with us, you may depend on't,' James said, as they walked back towards the house, 'for we are quite hidden away in this valley.'

And that was true enough, John thought, for the hills rose on either side of the village like protective walls and the rectory was hidden behind a holm gate and a screen of yews and hawthorns.

'Howsomever,' James said, smiling his slow, teasing smile as they reached the front door, 'you do seem to be making a habit of delivering your Miss Sowerby to our door, if you will allow me to say so.'

'Yes,' John confessed. 'I do.' It was warm in the panelled hall and the light from the candles was quite bright after the darkness of the journey.

'If this continues,' James said, opening the door to his study, 'I shall begin to wonder as to your intentions towards the lady. For' — still teasing — 'I am bound to say that stealing her away from her parents' home could easily be misinterpreted.'

'I mean to marry her,' John said.

'I'm uncommon pleased to hear it. Does she know of your plans?'

They could hear the two women coming downstairs. 'No,' John said hurriedly. 'Not yet. Say nothing I beg you. I will speak when she is well, you have my word.'

'And you my blessing,' James said, wondering how his mother-in-law would take the news. 'And now to dinner. We must feed our poor Harriet well, must we not, and, God willing, restore her to health as quickly as may be. And what could be better for such a task than a little dish of boiled beef and peas pudding?'

CHAPTER 12

Mr and Mrs Sowerby came back from the Saturday meeting in a state of rapturous elation. The chosen readings had been so apposite to their present difficulties with Harriet that they were plainly providential, and the preacher's conclusion had filled them with the most gratifying righteousness. 'We must fight against evil,' he had said, 'throughout our lives, my brethren, not once, not twice, not ten times ten times, but constantly and forever.'

They discussed the readings at length once they were in bed, speaking loudly so that Harriet could hear every word and understand that they had heavenly approval for their actions.

"Twould be a poor thing, wife,' Mr Sowerby said unctuously, 'if we were to allow this evil to possess our own dear child, whom the good Lord has given to us for guidance and protection. No, hard though it is for us, we must continue to mortify her flesh until her rebellious spirit is tamed. That is our plain Christian duty.'

It was a blessing to sleep so sound. And another to wake knowing that it was the Sabbath.

'I will speak to her directly,' Mrs Sowerby said as she opened the shutters on to the Sunday emptiness of the street. 'This time I do not doubt she will see sense.' And she unlocked Harriet's door.

The shock made her gasp. 'She's gone, Father,' she said. 'The wicked, wicked girl!'

'Gone?' Mr Sowerby said, jumping from the bed to join her. 'Impossible! You locked the door did you not? How could she be gone?'

But the cold wind was blowing its answer through the empty windowpane and the chill of it made them feel afraid, for the same thought was occurring to them both. By now people would have seen her bruises and noticed how thin she was. Tongues could be wagging about their affairs at that very minute.

'This is not to be endured,' Mr Sowerby said. 'We must find her and bring her back at once.'

'*Somebody* broke in,' Mrs Sowerby said, looking at the sticky sheet and the fragments of glass. '*Somebody* came here in the dead of night and stole her away.'

''Twill be that Mr Easter as sure as Fate,' Mr Sowerby said. 'She'll be ruined, Mrs Sowerby. Ruined!'

'Oh, how I'll whip her when we get her back!' his wife said grimly.

They went next door to enquire of Mrs Kirby as soon as they were dressed, but that lady was no help to them at all. She had heard nothing, seen nothing, locked her door as always 'the very minute our supper was done, ma'am'.

Mrs Sowerby was enraged by the duplicity of it. 'And don't 'ee tell *me*,' she said to her spouse when they were safely back in their own parlour. 'Don't 'ee tell *me* he could have dragged a great ladder through that passageway — and he *must* have had a ladder, Mr Sowerby — and she none the wiser.'

But it was time for chapel, so they had to compose themselves and leave their anger to stew.

'We will see what Miss Pettie has to say,' Mr Sowerby decided. 'She lives next door to the Easters, don't 'ee forget, and the woman is a powerful gossip.'

So they waylaid Miss Pettie after the service, and after exchanging religious pleasantries Mr Sowerby asked her, as casually as he could, if she had chanced to hear anything out of the ordinary in Angel Hill the previous evening.

She was effusively friendly and no help at all. She had been prostrated with the most acute attack of the vapours, she said. 'The sky could have fallen, Mr Sowerby, and I would not have heard a thing. *Did* something unusual happen? You intrigue me, I declare.'

'Nothing of any consequence,' Mr Sowerby said hurriedly but as smoothly as he could. 'We heard that there was a carriage being driven away at great speed. A rumour, I daresay.'

'Ah!' Miss Pettie said happily and with perfect truth, since a pony cart was not a carriage. 'No, I did not hear a carriage, Mr Sowerby, you may depend on't.'

'We will go to the Easters' house this afternoon,' Mr Sowerby said when Miss Pettie's own carriage had trotted away, 'and we will beard the lion in his den.'

But the only lion in the Easter house that afternoon was Bessie Thistlethwaite, mild, gentle, puzzled Bessie Thistlethwaite.

'Well now, sir,' she said. 'I'm sure you could see the master direct if onny 'e was 'ere ter see yer. Which a' the young gentlemen was you wantin'?'

'Mr John Easter, if you please,' Mr Sowerby said heavily.

'Well now, sir,' Bessie said imperturbably. 'Mr John is in London. Would Mr William be of any use to yer?'

'Very well then,' Mr Sowerby said, trying to keep his temper which was being sorely tried by her bland expression, 'we will see Mr William.'

'Onny the trouble is,' Bessie said, happily, 'Mr William ain't 'ere neither. 'E's off a-visitin' Mr Honeywood is Mr William and means to travel on ter London from there.'

'Oh come!' Mr Sowerby growled, 'enough of this shillyshallying. I would have you know, woman, that your precious master has stolen our child, and child-stealing is contrary to the law of the land.'

'Dear me!' Bessie said mildly. 'Then you'd better see Mrs Easter, if that's the size of it.'

'At last,' Mrs Sowerby snorted. 'Inform your mistress, my good woman, inform your mistress.'

'Mrs Easter is in Hertfordshire,' Bessie said with splendid aplomb.

'We will write to Mrs Easter,' Mr Sowerby said, his narrow face pinched with displeasure. 'You have her London address, I presume.'

So Bessie had to hand over one of Nan's business cards as she couldn't think of any way to avoid it. But the moment her visitors were gone she wrote her mistress a letter of her own:

Thort you shd no Mrs Easter dear, Mr & Mrs Sowerby is on the rampage after Mr John and meens for to rite to ee. Pray give my fond love to Mr Billy and Mr John. I hopes the young lady took no arm from her jurnee.

Yr obedt sert Bessie Thiss.

And Thiss delivered it on Monday afternoon just as Nan was about to go into the boardroom to chair the quarterly meeting of her regional managers.

'From Bessie?' she said surprised. 'My heart alive! What's amiss?'

'Not a great deal,' Thiss tried to explain. 'It's by way a' bein' a warnin', as the surgeon said when 'e dropped 'is leeches in the salt.'

But she was already reading it.

'I can't make head nor tail of it, Thiss,' she said. 'What young lady? Do 'ee know who 'tis? Where is Johnnie?'

But her managers were filing into the boardroom and as sales had been falling for the third month in succession and they were all plainly anxious about it, she could hardly keep them waiting while she solved the enigma. However while Cosmo was introducing the newest recruit, who was to be in charge of their West Country shops and reading rooms, she passed the letter across to John, signalling a query with her eyes and eyebrows. And she was pleased to see that he took it calmly, mouthing, 'I will explain.'

When the meeting was over and the regional managers better inspired, she asked her two sons and Mr Teshmaker to stay behind in the boardroom.

'Now then, Johnnie,' she said, briskly, holding out her hand for the letter. 'What's all this?'

He was pale with apprehension, but he looked her in the eye and told her without hesitation. If she were going to be angry with him, the sooner he faced it the better.

'The young lady is Miss Harriet Sowerby,' he said, 'who is a friend of Miss Pettie's. She has been whipped and starved by her parents because she answered some letters which I wrote to her. They locked her in her room and wouldn't let her out of the house. I have rescued her and taken her to stay with Annie.'

To his surprise and relief, she threw back her head and crowed with delight. 'Oh Johnnie, Johnnie, you dear boy!' she said. 'If you en't just like your father. He rescued me, so he did, the dear crittur, on the very day we met. What a fine good man you've grown up to be.'

Billy had been reading the letter too. Now he was rather worried. During the excitement of the rescue and the cheerful party at Mr Honeywood's afterwards it hadn't occurred to him to think of possible consequences. 'It ain't against the law is it, Ma?' he said.

'Cosmo must be the judge of that,' his mother said. '"Licit or not, 'twas well done, Johnnie.'

'How old is the young lady?' Mr Teshmaker asked. 'If she is over sixteen, she may live and work away from home with some impunity, and consequently a charge of child-stealing may be difficult for the parents to prove; if, however, she is younger than sixteen then child-stealing may well be a charge we have to face.'

John had to admit he didn't know how old she was. 'I intend to go to Rattlesden and visit her on Saturday,' he said, glancing at his mother to see if she would approve of that too. 'I will ask her then, if you think it sensible.'

Mr Teshmaker was as cautious as ever. 'It would be helpful to know,' he said. 'However, I would not advise you to alarm her with much questioning. Let us reserve judgement until the parents have written. Then we will see what may be done.'

'I have given Miss Sowerby my word that she need never to return to her parents' house,' John said. 'I do not intend to go back on my promise.'

'What *do* 'ee intend?' Nan asked. 'Do 'ee mean to marry the girl?' Her tone was half mocking so that he could deny it if he wished, but she already knew what he would say.

He answered her most seriously. 'Yes, Mama. I do.'

How exactly like his father, Nan thought. He don't stop to think whether she'd suit the family. He rescues her, he loves her, he'll marry her. And she made up her mind at once not to oppose him but to support him in every way she could, dear loving crittur that he was.

'I'm glad to hear it,' she said. 'He'll be beating you to the altar, Billy, if 'ee don't look sharp.' Billy thought it very likely because Matilda was still keeping him at arm's length with her teasing, and he was no nearer to the point when he could propose than he'd been on the day they met. 'Have you asked her, John?' Nan said, turning to her other son.

His eyes were very dark in his pale face. 'No,' he said. 'Not yet. She should recover a little first, don't you think? She was most unwell when I took her to Annie's. And this matter should be settled.'

'It should,' his mother agreed, admiring his sensitivity, 'Is she like to agree, think 'ee?'

'I hope so,' he said fervently, 'with all my heart.'

'Then you must also hope that she is at least sixteen years old,' Cosmo Teshmaker said, 'and that her parents will consent to it. Which I must confess don't look particularly likely at this juncture.'

'They'd be blamed fools to turn down such a match,' Nan said, 'Bein' they en't monied folk or gentry. Leastways none I've heard of.'

'Her father works in Mr Cole's bookshop,' Billy said.

'Well, there you are then.'

'They may be aggrieved,' John pointed out soberly, 'and refuse their consent by way of revenge.' This business was becoming more fraught with difficulty the more he thought about it.

'Fortunately,' Cosmo Teshmaker said, 'the law is designed to serve the rich, and there are many ways round trouble, Mr John, if you have the wherewithal to open the routes.'

The Sowerbys' letter arrived two days later. It was a furious epistle, signed by both of them and written at great length and with extreme venom. The gist of it was an accusation of child-stealing, for which crime they said they intended to take the Easter family to court. 'No matter what this may cost,' they wrote, 'we mean to have our dear daughter returned to our care before she is utterly ruined.'

'Much of this is mere bluster,' Cosmo said. 'Howsomever 'tis my opinion we should avoid coming to court if that is at all possible. I suggest we meet these people and endeavour to find some compromise.'

'She is not to go back,' John said. 'I have written to her assuring her of that.' And had such a charming letter back, thanking him so touchingly 'for all your care and concern'.

'No more she shall,' Nan assured him. 'Arrange the meeting, Cosmo. Write and tell 'em their daughter is safe and well and has found herself a good position with the family of a man of the cloth. That should quieten 'em. Then suggest a time and a place when we may all meet.'

'Let us suggest that it take place here in London at the end of September,' Cosmo said. 'It will put them at a disadvantage to have to travel and delay of a few weeks will do no harm. It might do positive good. Waiting often cools tempers.'

So it was agreed. And John left the boardroom buoyed up by the marvellous feeling that he was a loved member of a powerful, supportive family. It was a new experience for him and one that filled him with importance. Who would have thought it? Especially as his actions in this matter seemed to have verged upon the criminal.

He would have felt even more important and cared for had he known that his mother went straight from her work later that afternoon to discuss the whole matter with her friend Mr Frederick Brougham, the lawyer, and that Mr Frederick Brougham, the lawyer, had agreed to act on his behalf, although 'with an ulterior motive, since I mean to ask a favour, now that I have some hope of a positive reply'.

Nan was intrigued and amused. 'Ask away,' she said.

'I plan to hold a little dinner party here on Thursday evening for some of the more discerning of my friends,' Mr Brougham said. 'And a good dinner party needs a fine hostess if it is to be truly successful. Since my wife died, mine have been rather lacking in that capacity, as you will understand. Would you do me the honour of joining me as my hostess for the evening?'

''Twould be a pleasure,' she said, grinning at him, 'but 'twill link us together in uncommon public fashion. En't you afraid of gossip?'

'In this city?' he observed drily, 'tongues wag at the slightest provocation. You and I must be above such nonsense. So what say you? Your company at my table would be much appreciated.'

And so it was, for besides having considerable style, she was a witty creature and, being at the centre of the newspaper world, singularly well-informed, a highly suitable hostess for Frederick's highly civilised home in Bedford Row. And to her great pleasure, the first of his guests to arrive was an old friend of hers, Mr Francis Place, who had once been a breeches-maker but now sold books from his shop in Charing Cross Road and wrote extremely radical pamphlets urging reform. And the second was another. And the fifth and sixth were Sir Francis Burdett, the Member of Parliament for Westminster, and his elegant wife, both of whom she already knew and liked. This was going to be a very good evening.

It was certainly a heavily political one for, in all, the guests included four Members of Parliament and their wives, and all eight were Whigs and highly radical. They were criticising the Corn Laws before the first course had been served, declaring they were laws made 'by the landowners to benefit the landowners' and were now, according to one gentleman, 'making the rich richer and the poor poorer'.

'But not without opposition,' Frederick Brougham pointed out, smiling across the table at Sir Francis and Mr Place.

'Opposition is of little interest,' Mr Place said seriously, 'while those who are oppressed have no representation. Until we have achieved full adult suffrage, an annual parliament and voting by ballot, we shall achieve no change. The poor will continue to starve.'

'Oh come,' one of the ladies protested. 'There is relief for the poor, is there not? They may go upon the parish.'

'When there were a mere handful of destitute families,' Frederick said, 'the parish could sustain them with relative ease. But now, I fear, those who are unemployed are numbered in their thousands. Mechanical threshers put whole families out of work, the parish cannot possibly afford to feed them and the government does not consider it any part of its business to enquire what is to become of them.'

Sir Francis Burdett nodded his head in agreement. 'The growing number of the poor constitutes a real threat to the stability of our economy,' he said. 'We should not forget what happened in France a mere twenty-seven years ago. It could easily happen here.'

'Let us hope that reason will prevail,' Frederick said.

'That's a thing I shall see later this evening,' Sir Francis told them, 'for delegates from all the Hampden Clubs are come to London to press for reform and I am to chair the meeting.'

'I trust you will urge moderation,' Frederick said.

BUT THE DELEGATES were in no mood for moderation.

By the time Sir Francis joined them in the long dark hall behind the Crown and Anchor in the Strand, the place was so full it took him more than five minutes to struggle through to the rostrum. Every seat at every table was taken, and men stood crammed together in every other available space, leaning against the walls or crouching on their haunches beside their seated companions, or standing together in a close-packed phalanx of broad back and passionate argument. Potboys squirmed themselves between the tables taking orders and carrying heavy trays loaded with tankards, and sweating in the heat, for what little air there was in the hall was much-breathed and clouded with wood-smoke and the blue fumes of tobacco. It was high time to call the meeting to order and begin.

The first speaker that evening was Thomas Cleary, the secretary of the London Hampden Club, a slightly built, eager young man, who welcomed the delegates most warmly but spoke too quickly and too softly to command their attention for very long. The second was Joseph Mitchell, a delegate from Liverpool, who spoke so passionately of the need for reform that he lost the thread of what he was saying and had to step down, to vociferous applause, but in the middle of a sentence so muddled as to be completely incomprehensible. The third was a cotton weaver from Salford.

At first sight he looked ordinary enough, a thickset, stocky man in his late twenties, with a shock of dark hair, and a broad squat face. But the way he leapt up onto the platform showed an uncommon energy and when he began to speak it was as if he'd sent an electrical current pulsing out into the audience. Heads were raised at once, spines straightened, eyes gleamed in the candlelight. Soon all conversation had petered out and even the tankards were being ignored.

'Friends,' he said, 'I've come here tonight, to ask three questions. Pertinent questions tha might say.' It was a strong voice and melodious, used with deliberate artistry, the changing expressions on his face endorsing his meaning. There was powerful irony in the next thing he said. 'Pertinent questions. Aye, tha might well say that.' And a cheerful sense of conspiracy in the next. 'Happen tha'll know the answers.'

By now the entire hall was listening to him, concentrating so intently that the click of the burning logs could be heard quite clearly in every pause. And a gentleman with fair hair and rather splendid ginger whiskers, who had been sitting quietly just below the rostrum, took a black notebook out of his pocket and wrote down every word.

'I don't need to tell thee again of th' hardships we suffer,' Mr

Rawson went on. 'Mr Mitchell's done that for us, and done it right well, and we only need reminding the once. We know all about bad masters, so we do, wi' poor wages and being laid off and children wi'out boots to their feet, and children in fever houses, and children dying for lack of food. What we need to know, friends, what we need to know, is what's to do about it. That's what we need to know. Now some may say, let us sign a petition and send it to Parliament and see if our masters there'll tek pity on us and gi' us what we want. And I say, aye, let's do it. 'Tis a first step, 'tis common politeness, it should be done. But dunna forget 'tis t' masters we deal with, and t' masters hold on to their own. They're renowned for it. We know that. Who better? Of course, they *might* see t' sense in it and gi' us what we ask. It's wi'in t' bounds o' possibility. Pigs might fly. Happen.' And he waited while his audience laughed and growled their agreement. But when he continued, he'd changed his light, mocking tone and now spoke to them most seriously.

'I tell thee, friends, they'll not open t' door until we threaten to batter it down. They'll not gi' us what we want until we stand in t' streets in our thousands and demand it. Very well, then, we send our petition, we ask 'em politely, but we *prepare* to show our strength. For mek no mistake about it, there'll be bloodshed afore we win t' vote, and heads broke and men jailed, I don't doubt. But we will win it in the end, mek no mistake about that either. We will win it in the end. And why will we win it in the end? I'll tell thee why. We'll win it in the end because there's no moral argument that any right-thinking man can use against it. We'll win it in the end because it's right.'

He was cheered until the low rafters rang with sound as though they were glass goblets. Hats were tossed into the air and kerchiefs waved like flags, and as he left the platform he was seized by the hand and thumped in the back, so that his journey through the crowd back to his table was like a triumphal procession.

'My eye!' one of the platform party said to Mr Cleary. 'Who did ye say yon feller was?'

'Caleb Rawson,' Mr Cleary told him. 'Cotton weaver from Salford.'

'Caleb Rawson, eh?' the man said. 'We shall hear more of him; you mark my words.'

And the gentleman with the ginger whiskers certainly did, for he wrote down everything they were saying too.

CHAPTER 13

Harriet and Annie were playing blind man's bluff with Jimmy and Beau and Pollyanna in the hall of the rectory. It was a riotous game which took them scampering all over the ground floor of the house, squealing and giggling and calling to one another, for they played according to new rules of their own. Any child who was 'caught' had to be hugged and tossed in the air for several minutes before the blindfold could be used again. Harriet enjoyed it more than any other game they played, because it was really just a marvellous excuse to tumble about together and cuddle one another, and to have the baby's warm arms holding her so lovingly about the neck was pure joy. So when she first heard the knock at the side door, she took no notice of it but went on calling Beau so that he could catch her and be kissed.

But the knocker was persistent and tried again while the tumbling was in progress and again and louder when she was tying the bandage round her eyes and the rest of the players were squealing off into the parlour. She took the bandage off and passed it to Jimmy, calling, 'I'll go!' Then she went to attend to it.

There was a man standing subserviently on the doorstep, looking down at the strips of sacking that were tied around his feet. He was covered in mud-grey grime from his matted hair to the blackened toes exposed through the sacking, and he was dressed, if that really was the word, in several layers of mud-coloured rags, so old and torn and evil-smelling that at first, she took him for a beggar. There was a slatternly woman standing behind him wearing a soldier's red coat that looked as though it had come straight from the wars, for it was horribly stained and had a jagged bullet hole in one shoulder. She had a filthy baby tucked inside the coat and two equally filthy little boys clinging to her muddy skirts and she looked at Harriet sullenly, her eyes very blue and very young under the tousled bush of her hair.

'Yes?' Harriet said, feeling a sudden and yearning sympathy at the sight of them. How terrible to be so poor and dirty? 'Who did you wish to see?'

'The Reverend 'Opkins,' the man said, 'if 'ee'd be so good, miss.'

And the woman said, 'Tha's right Jack, you tell un.'

'He is not here just at present,' Harriet said. 'He is out visiting the sick.'

But she was wrong. He was in the garden, striding towards them with hands outstretched in greeting. 'Why Mr Abbott!' he called. 'How good to see you home and safe.'

'No work, Mr 'Opkins, tha's the size on it,' the man said mournfully. 'Mr Morgan, 'e's a-layin' off so 'e say. Got a new machine fer threshin' an' such, so 'e don' need the men so 'e say. I told un I was willin'. 'E's a-layin' off so 'e say.' And his face crumpled and he began to weep, strange tears that Harriet found most upsetting.

And the two little boys began to cry in sympathy and the woman repeated, 'You tell un, Jack,' in the same belligerent tones.

'Come into my study,' the Reverend Hopkins said, and the filthy family followed him into the hall.

The cloying, sour smell of them was so strong once they were inside the house that Annie was alerted by it and came out of the parlour to see what was going on. She took one look and whisked her children out of harm's way at once, signalling with her eyes to Pollyanna and Harriet that they were to follow her.

'Who are they?' she asked Harriet when the parlour door was closed behind them. 'Did you catch the name?'

'Mr Hopkins called the — gentleman — Mr Abbott.'

'Jack Abbott, I'll be bound,' Annie said, sitting down beside the fire with baby Beau on her lap. 'Went for a soldier years ago, just after we were married. That'll be Jack Abbott. Well I only hope they don't stay too long, that's all, for they smell worse than old Hannah's pig.' Which was strong criticism, for old Hannah kept her livestock in such filthy conditions that they could be smelt all over the village.

'I think they've come to Mr Hopkins for help,' Harriet said, quite surprised by Annie's sharpness.

'I don't doubt it,' Annie said. 'Let's have some more coal on the fire.'

They waited while the voices in the parlour mumbled and grumbled on, punctuated now and then by an occasional stab of aggression from the woman. Then they heard the study door open and shut and the Reverend Hopkins came stooping mildly into the room.

'Mr Abbott has nowhere to stay, my love,' he said to Annie, 'so I have invited him here. It will mean five more to dinner. Do you think Mrs Chiddum can manage?'

'I daresay she can,' Annie said, and it was plain that she was none too pleased at the news, 'but she won't like it.'

'You will explain to her, will you not, my love?' he said. 'They have been on the road for the last ten days, hoping for work once they got home, so poor Jack tells me, and now of course there is no work for them and no room in the cottage either, since his brothers came back from Gedding. And he fought at Waterloo. It is uncommon sad. We must help them all we can.'

'Are they to stay here, James?' There was an edge to her voice, but he answered her as mildly as ever.

'We can hardly turn them away, my love. They have nowhere to go.'

'Those children are crawling with vermin, James,' she said, and there was no mistaking how she felt. 'I could see the lice in their hair as plain as I see you. Do you truly wish to put our boys at risk of *that*?'

'There is always turpentine,' he said gently. 'I am sure you will do all you can to help them, will you not, my love?'

'I shall use turpentine most certainly,' she said, and now she sounded quite brusque. 'But I tell 'ee 'twould be better to send them all elsewhere.'

'Come now, Annie,' he said, 'there is nowhere else for them to go.' And now there was a harsher note to his voice too. 'You would not have me cast them out into the wilderness.'

Watching them, Harriet realised to her surprise that they were arguing. They were quite calm, they didn't shout or turn red or stamp about the room, but they were arguing, nevertheless. It was amazing.

'Rattlesden is not a wilderness,' Annie said, shifting little Beau on her knee.

'It is a wilderness to Mr Abbott, there being no work and no shelter in it. Come Annie my dear, consider the Good Samaritan.'

They gazed at one another for a long while without saying a word, while Jimmy looked from one to the other, and Beau fell asleep and Pollyanna looked at Harriet, warning her not to move or speak.

Finally Annie broke the silence. 'I will do as you say,' she said, 'on one condition.'

He answered her most lovingly. 'Name it, my dear.'

'They sleep in the east wing, well away from the rest of us.'

'Agreed,' he said. 'And now you will have a room prepared for them, will you not?'

'Pray take the baby, Pollyanna dear,' Annie said, lifting him gently. 'And Jimmy too, if you will. Go along with Pollyanna, there's a good boy Jimmy, and then you shall have a sugar stick the next time we're in town.' Now that the argument was over, she was her busy, practical self again as she called her maids and led the way to the narrow east stairs.

Once inside the little east room, she had all the linen stripped from the bed and thrown on the floor. 'You can take that off to the linen cupboard presently,' she said to the maids. 'Don't 'ee bother to fold it just yet awhile. Come and help me with this mattress Molly. They ain't having my nice clean mattress,' she added to Harriet, 'them and their bugs, and he needn't think it, dear though he is.'

She had the maids working at furious speed. The mattress was already rolled and ready to carry away. 'Charity is all very well,' she said, as Molly helped her to lift it from the bed, 'but I draw the line at lice and bugs. There is a mattress cover at the bottom of the cupboard, which will do well enough, once 'tis stuffed with straw. But we must make haste or he will bring them up here before we are ready.'

The maid was sent to collect old sheets and blankets while Harriet and Annie ran from the rectory to the barn like conspirators and returned bouncing the now bulky mattress between them. The Abbotts were still in the study as they could hear from the murmured voices behind the door.

'And a fine old job we shall have getting *that* clean again,' Annie said crossly, as they dragged the mattress towards the east stairs. 'First thing tomorrow I shall ride into Bury and buy turpentine and camphor and as many cakes of soap as my money will run to.'

Mention of Bury worried Harriet. 'You will not want me to accompany you...' she hoped.

'No, my dear, of course not,' Annie said. 'You must stay here and help Pollyanna with Jimmy and Beau. And watch that Mrs Abbott gives those children of hers a good scrub down. Under the pump mind, not inside the house. I will buy them some clothes at the slop-shop otherwise James will order new ones to be made for them, which we certainly cannot afford, and then we will make a bonfire of all their old rags and with luck we may burn their livestock too.'

She was full of energy. The new bed was prepared in minutes and covered with an old sheet and two even older blankets, and the chest of drawers was locked and the new wash set replaced by an old one. It was as if she were preparing for a siege. Which in many ways she was.

Her unwanted guests ate in the kitchen that evening quietly enough, and retired to their straw pallet afterwards, telling 'the Reverend' how grateful they were. But the next morning, when Annie tried to wake them, since it was seven o'clock and the rest of the house had been up and about for more than an hour, Mr Abbott growled to her to, 'Go 'way an' leave us be'. And that was the signal for action.

She tied her protective mop cap more tightly under her chin, checked to see that all her hair was safely tucked away inside it, and went into the room.

'I am leaving this house in five minutes, Mr Abbott,' she said, glaring down at the five verminous heads that now lay tangle to tangle on her old mattress cover, 'being I've to go to Bury to buy fresh clothes for 'ee, and soap and turpentine and camphor and a deal else besides. 'Twould be much appreciated if you could all be up and washed before I return. I daresay you would like to shave your heads for greater cleanliness, so I have set a jug and razor by the pump. Our gardener has a good bonfire going.'

Mr Abbott got out of the bed at once and wrapped his feet

and put on his collection of coats, which were the only articles he'd taken off the night before and went humbly out of the door. "Twill all be done as you say, ma'am,' he promised. 'Thank 'ee kindly.'

But Mrs Abbott stayed where she was. 'I en't a-shavin' my head, ma'am,' she said, when her husband was out of earshot. 'No not for you nor for the Reverend nor for anyone. Tha's my crowning glory that is, an' a pleasure to my Jack, an' tha's a-stayin' where 'tis.'

"Twould be a deal more glorious if 'twere clean,' Annie observed drily. 'Howsomever, I cannot force you. On your own head be it.' And she went off downstairs considerably annoyed.

'The woman is a slut,' she said angrily to Harriet, 'and means to infect the house. Well, we shall see about that. I am off to Bury now, but I promise you I shall be there and back as quick as a wink. I ain't having my dear boys made lousy, and there's an end on't.'

And even though Harriet felt extremely sorry for the Abbotts and especially the children, poor little things, she had to admit that Annie was right to protect her own.

By the end of the day Mr Abbott and his three children had been transformed. Scrubbed under the pump until their skin was bright pink, their heads shaven as close as sheep, adequately shod, and dressed in quite presentable clothes, they looked like different people as they sat down to their second dinner in the kitchen. But Mrs Abbott was still belligerently dirty.

'Tomorrow morning,' Annie said, when she and Harriet and Pollyanna were escorting the boys up the west stairs to their nursery, 'we will scrub the study and make all clean, ready for James to write his sermon.'

'Why Mrs Hopkins, ma'am,' Pollyanna said, settling little Beau more comfortably on her hip as she climbed, 'it ain't Saturday come round again already, surely to goodness.'

Saturday, Harriet thought. I have been here nearly a week.

And then she remembered other things too. 'Your brother comes here tomorrow,' she said.

'Aye, so he does,' Annie said. 'But the work must go on notwithstanding.'

In fact he paid no attention to all the cleaning and scrubbing the following afternoon, beyond sniffing the air vaguely when he first stepped inside the house. He was far more concerned to see how Harriet was, and to give her the latest news of her parents. And when she came quietly out of the kitchen door, he was so pleased at the sight of her that Annie could have scrubbed him down as well as the study and he wouldn't have noticed. How very much better she looked! Why, her bruises were almost gone and the cut on her lip was quite healed.

'I am glad to see you well,' he said.

'There is a basket of washing to be taken down to Mrs Barley in the six cottages,' Annie said to Harriet.

'We will carry it between us,' John offered at once. It was just the right sort of opportunity for them to talk alone. As Annie knew very well.

So the basket was fetched and he and Harriet walked out of the garden, carrying it between them like a chaperone, past the holm oak that marked the entrance to the rectory and the massive yew that stood sentinel beside the church. They left the churchyard by the lower church gate, which pleased him because it meant he could take the basket and hold her arm as he helped her through. There was an ancient timbered house beside the lower gate, tall as a man o' war and full of chattering children who tumbled out of the door and sat on the steps and tottered about the vegetable garden, and on the other side of the street a crowd of listless farmhands stood about in front of the smithy. Too public yet, John thought, as they set off downhill.

They walked in companionable silence past Bruges Cottage, where the smith lived, and Willow Cottage, where the wise woman sat knitting in the sun. They followed the path that led out of the village, and presently they found themselves at the meeting of the four footpaths which led to Woolpit, Stowmarket and Felsham.

'We could sit here for a while,' he said hopefully, 'could we not? It is a warm afternoon and there is no need for us to hurry.'

So they put their basket down beside the signpost and sat on the grass at the top of the little mound, both intensely aware of one another.

'You are well?' he said, admiring that apricot blush. Why, she was quite herself again!

'Quite well, thank 'ee kindly. Have you news of my parents, Mr Easter?' How very handsome he looked in the sunshine and how very brown his eyes were. Like pansies.

'Mr Teshmaker has written to suggest that they come up to London at the end of the month for a meeting with me and my mother and our lawyers.' If only we were engaged, I could lean forward and kiss her. There being no one here to see us.

'Have they agreed to it?' How kind he is to take such pains. And so gentle. Look how he helped to carry the basket.

'We await their letter. In the meantime the lawyers have asked me to ask you...' Would it seem impertinent to be asking her age? Oh, he mustn't upset her. Not now when she was recovering so well.

'To ask me what, Mr Easter?' How dear he is to be so worried about me. I know how worried he is, for he squints with worry. Oh I love him when he squints with worry.

'How old you are, Miss Sowerby.' Please don't take offence, dear Harriet. I have to ask you.

'I was sixteen in January.' Is that the right answer? Oh yes, it must be, for the squint is going.

'Thank 'ee kindly.' Sixteen! Sixteen! What good fortune. Too old for child-stealing and just right for marriage. He was smiling at her rapturously. He couldn't help it.

'Should we deliver the washing now, Mr Easter? Or is there anything else you have to ask me?'

Oh there was. There was. So much. But it could wait. There would be a time for it, when the Sowerbys were settled.

He stood up and offered her his hand to help her to her feet. 'Tell me what has been happening in Rattlesden,' he said. 'Who were those bald-headed children in the garden?'

'They are Mr Abbott's children,' she told him, adding with some pride, 'he has no work and nowhere to live and we are looking after them all.'

CHAPTER 14

M atilda Honeywood was dressing for a very important occasion. Her mother and father were under the impression that they were hosting a rather ordinary supper party with dancing afterwards, but Matilda knew better. For this was going to be the evening when Billy Easter would propose to her for the very first time.

She didn't particularly want to marry him, or at least she didn't think she did. She didn't particularly want to marry anybody really. She wanted to be loved because she knew from her friend Tabby, who had tried it, that it was the most exquisite pleasure in the world. But apart from that she didn't really know what she wanted. Her moods changed from day to day. And sometimes from minute to minute.

She knew it was her business in life to catch a suitable husband. Both her parents had made that perfectly clear to her, warning her away from young men who 'wouldn't suit' and singing the praises of those who would, like Billy, and Jeremiah Ottenshaw, who was actually in love with her cousin, and a truly awful man called Scatchard, whom no girl in her right mind would even want to speak to, leave alone marry. Billy was certainly the best of the bunch so far, and very good looking. She would probably marry him in the end, so it wouldn't hurt him to propose. She would tease him into several more declarations before she finally agreed to accept him, but this was going to be the first. So naturally she was taking great care to be as beautiful as possible.

The hairdresser had spent a miserable afternoon, trying to arrange her hair in exactly the way she wanted it, and having hot curling tongs flung at him for his pains, and now Lizzie Moffat and her cousins were being abused for being clumsy as they hooked her into her new gown.

'Now look what you've made me do!' she shrieked at Sophie. 'If that hem gets trod, I shall never forgive you.'

'It ain't trod, Tilda,' Sophie said, wincing. 'I held it up most particular, didn't I, Lizzie?'

'Weally high,' Lizzie said, nodding her head so violently that her lank curls swayed before her eyes.

'Which you could see for yourself if you spent less time shouting,' Maria said tartly.

'Oh, Maria,' Matilda said, smoothing her new skirt and instantly remorseful, 'I don't mean to shout, truly I don't. But if I ain't at my very very best and he don't propose I truly think my heart will break.'

'You look lovely,' Sophie said earnestly. 'I don't see how he could help but propose.'

'Do you truly think so?' Matilda said, gazing at her reflection in the long mirror. Oh yes, yes, she did look lovely, with her skin powdered so white and smooth, and her lips so pink, and her grey eyes so big and innocent, and her hair in such nice thick bunches of glossy ringlets dangling on either side of her face, no thanks to that fool hairdresser. Her gown was exquisite, too, with all those little pink rosebuds embroidered all over it and those three deep flounces making the hem froth like a tumbling wave and the décolletage cut so very low that if she leant forward, she could see her pretty pink nipples. How could he resist her? He couldn't, surely!

'You are the dearest cousins anyone could ever have,' she said to Sophie and Maria, and feeling she ought to make amends for her ill-humour, 'and I love you dearly so I do, and if you like I will hide you where you can actually hear him propose. How would that be?'

'What sport!' Sophie said. 'Do you think he really will?'

'Thwilling,' Lizzie agreed. 'Shall you get him to say widiculous things, Tilda dear? I should like to hear a man say widiculous things.'

'Personally,' Maria said, 'I shall be surprised if he says anything at all. But I will hide with the others if you wish it.'

'The carriages have started to arrive,' Claude said, putting his head round the door, without knocking. 'Ain't you ready yet Sis?'

The sight of him brought back his sister's irritation in such a rush that her cheeks burned scarlet with it. Little brother Claude who could do no wrong, who was spoilt and pampered and treated like a god, who didn't bother to knock, who would inherit all Papa's land and most of Papa's money without having to do anything to earn it, while she would only get her dowry if she caught a suitable husband. She fanned her hot cheeks furiously, pouting at her reflection. Life was quite horribly unfair. Oh, why couldn't she have been born a boy? Boys had all the fun. Well, Billy Easter had better look out, that was all. She would tease him ragged.

'I will coax him into the green parlour,' she said to Lizzie as they walked downstairs side by side. 'Nobody ever goes in there and you can hide quite easily behind the curtains.'

But first there were arrivals for her to greet, standing prettily beside her parents and remembering to say the right things, and plenty of partners to tease and Billy to bewitch, before there was supper to eat, which seemed to take for ever because the servants were being really beastly slow.

But at last the long boring meal was done and the guests had left the supper room and were drifting back to the drawing room to dance, or to the card room to gamble, and Matilda was able to signal to Lizzie and her cousins that it was time for them to slip away to the green parlour while she went in search of Billy. She felt like a cat flexing her claws, full of power and ready for the hunt. Watch out Mr Billy Easter, she said to herself, for I mean to have your heart before the evening is out, so I do. Oh 'twould be fine sport to see a man propose.

She found him in the drawing room standing beside the punch table talking to Jeremiah Ottenshaw, who was looking for her cousin Maria, and that long-legged idiot Ebenezer Millhouse who was looking drunk.

'La, Mr Billy Easter,' she said, giving him the full force of her grey eyes and attacking at once, 'if you ain't the most provoking creature.'

'Why, Miss Honeywood, what have I done?' Billy said, feigning alarm. 'I'm sure it ain't intentional. Never provoke a lady, would I, Jerry?' He'd learnt the rules of her teasing game now and could play it to perfection.

'Never,' Jerry agreed easily. He was far too full of supper to argue.

'Where have you been?' she asked, catching Billy by the arm because she simply had to touch him. 'You promised to escort me in to supper and you did no such thing, you bad boy. I declare I feel quite neglected.'

It was a little hard, since she'd deliberately walked in to supper with her father and Billy had seen her do it, but although he blushed he was too gentlemanly to argue. And besides you never knew with Matilda. Sometimes she was teasing and sometimes she seemed to mean things, so he often found it difficult to know how to answer her. If only she'd be serious.

'Ain't a feller to spend any time with his friends, damnit?' Eb Millhouse protested. 'Deuce take it, Miss Honeywood, you do rag a feller.'

'Oh well,' Matilda said, pouting with mock resignation, 'if I'm to compete with your friends...' And she started to drift away, but slowly, of course, so that he could catch at her hand and pull her back.

Which he did, 'Yours to command, Miss Honeywood,' he said, bowing to her with excessive gallantry.

'That's all very well, Mr Easter,' she pouted, 'since you don't mean a word of it. You gentlemen are all the same.'

'Put me to the test,' he challenged, squaring his shoulders and standing tall before her. 'You'll find I mean every word I say, so you will.'

She was very aware of how handsome he was and growing handsomer by the second. Why those side whiskers and that thick sandy hair of his were positively bushing.

'I've a secret to tell 'ee,' she said confidentially, leaning towards him so that the others couldn't hear her and she could touch his chest with her fingertips. 'But you shan't hear it 'till you've caught me. If you can!' And she ran off at once, tripping through the crowds and not looking back.

He charged off after her, running awkwardly through the crush of dancers who were now rapidly filling the room, and was just in time to see her cross the hall and dart through the door into the green parlour.

He caught at her hand as she reached the fireplace. 'Now tell,' he urged breathlessly. 'What's the secret?'

'Well as to that...' she said, glancing at the curtains. Were they all in place? The long velvet was very still.

'It's a sell,' he said with bristling triumph, still holding her hand. 'There ain't a secret, is there, Tilda? Confess.'

'Oh yes there is,' she said, daring him with her eyes. And she leant towards him and reaching up, fluttered her eyelashes against his cheek. ''Tis called a butterfly kiss,' she murmured. 'Would 'ee like another?'

The teasing, gentle touch triggered his desire so strongly that he was quite dizzy with the pleasure of it. 'Tilda,' he groaned. 'My love!'

She stepped back so as to get a good view of his face, delighted by the effect she was having.

'Am I your love, Mr Easter? Am I truly? I'm sure I don't recall any words being spoke upon the subject, nor no hints gi —'

But the sight of his face stopped her in mid-sentence, for it was blazing with such open affection that he was quite transformed by it, his mouth so soft and his eyes so dark and tender, and that fair hair gilded by firelight into a bronze mane about his temples, a carved helmet, a halo.

'Oh Tilda,' he said, shivering with emotion, 'I adore you. You must know that. I always have, from the very first moment I saw you. Always. Oh Tilda, Tilda, my dear, dear love!'

She had no words to answer him. This wasn't what she'd expected to provoke at all. This was overwhelming. She put her hand to her mouth instinctively, her eyes wide with surprise, forgetting herself, her scheme, her envied brother, even her listening friends behind the curtain. And her face grew soft with wonder, losing the mocking brightness that until this moment had put him on his guard and forbidden the truth. It was as if the blaze of his affection had melted all the barriers between them.

And then she was in his arms and he was kissing her mouth with such urgency it took her breath away. And his hands were stroking her arms and her shoulders, touching her nipples, sliding down her spine, gripping her buttocks, pulling her closer and closer until it felt as though they were fused together. And his every touch was magical, trailing a hot, tingling pleasure through her flesh. 'Oh Billy, Billy!'

'Say you love me,' he urged between kisses. 'Oh you do love me, Tilda. Say you love me!' His face was only inches away from her eyes, blazing, blazing, and his eyes were enormous.

'Yes, yes,' she said, as those magical hands trailed pleasure down her spine again. 'I do. I do. Oh Billy I do love 'ee. Kiss me again. I do love 'ee.'

He kissed her again, and again, and again, until they were both panting. And just as he lifted his mouth away from hers to catch his breath a little, a coal fell in the grate and split in two with a fizzing eruption of sudden flame. The sound restored her to momentary memory. How unkind she was being, putting him on display like this. 'Not here, Billy,' she whispered. 'Somebody might come in and find us.'

'Where then?' he said, still glowing with that last kiss, holding her locked against his body.

For answer she took his hand and led him to the hidden servants' door, opening it quietly and slipping through into the musty chill of the unheated corridor behind it. 'Quick, quick, quick,' she said.

Behind the curtain, Sophie and Lizzie were in tears, and even Maria was gulping.

'That was the most romantic thing I ever heard,' Sophie said rapturously. 'Oh Maria, oh Lizzie, to be spoken to like that. What bliss!'

'I shall never be spoken to like that,' Lizzie said sadly. 'I know. I'm a deal too plain to be spoken to like that. Oh Sophie, the womance of it!'

'Do 'ee think she means it?' Maria wondered. 'Does she truly love him?'

'Oh yes,' her sister said. 'How could 'ee doubt it, after that?'

'Where do 'ee think they've gone?'

'To Heaven,' Lizzie breathed.

Actually they'd gone to her bedroom, scampering up the steep servants' stairs with their arms about each other, stopping to kiss again and again, running arm in arm and thigh to thigh like a three-legged race, along the upper gallery, tumbling back into warmth through yet another servants' door, falling together into her welcoming bed, with no one to see them and nothing to stop them. Not that either of them could have stopped anyway, with desire burning so strongly in them both. For now the pleasure they were rousing in each other was too intense to be denied. Her hair was in her eyes and her gown was crushed about her waist and there was warm bare flesh under her hands and that marvellous tingling pleasure had gathered into one place, growing better and better and better like an arrow pointing him the way, pointing her the way, up and up and up until it exploded into such exquisite feeling that she gasped and cried aloud.

Lizzie was right. It was the nearest thing to heaven that either of them had ever experienced.

Afterwards as sensation dimmed and sense gradually seeped back to them, they were both a little confused by what they had done. It had been so quick and so overwhelming, and so pleasurable and so right, but now they wondered.

'Should we have?' she questioned. Was that why girls were chaperoned so closely?

He wasn't sure himself but he answered stoutly so as to comfort her. 'Of course. We've only done what we would have done when we were married.' That sounded highly ungrammatical, so he tried again. 'When we are married, we shall make love every night and no one will worry about it then, will they?'

That was a delicious thought. Every night!

'We will marry, will we not?' Billy said, stroking the side of her face. He had laid claim to her now. She was his, wasn't she?

'Yes,' she said. 'Oh yes, Billy.' Of course they would marry. It was the natural thing to do. Now.

'Soon?'

'Yes, very soon.'

'I shall speak to your papa?'

'Tonight?'

'If you think so.'

She thought about it, snuggling into his neck. 'He will agree,' she said easily. 'He considers you suitable.'

'Did he tell you so?' He was surprised that his courtship had been taken so seriously.

'Oh yes. You must not be angry, my dearest Billy. He and Mama discuss everybody. They are always on the lookout for a match for me. 'Tis all they ever think about, marrying me off. *He* will suit, *he* won't. 'Tis their manner.'

'And you?' he asked anxiously. 'Is that your manner top?'

'Until tonight,' she said with total honesty, 'I did not think of love at all, or marriage, only of teasing, playing games.' And scoring little victories, which now seemed horribly petty. 'Oh how badly I treated you, Billy my love, playing such games. What must you have thought of me?'

'It ain't a game now, is it my lovely Tilda?'

Oh no. It wasn't a game now. It certainly wasn't a game now. 'How quickly everything changes,' she said.

Down below them the musicians were playing a gallop. They could hear the fiddle scraping and dancers' feet thumping and thudding. 'We must go down again,' Matilda said, 'or they will miss us.'

'Yes,' he agreed. But he lay where he was.

'Get up,' she said, sitting up beside him and brushing the feathers from his jacket. And was kissed for her care of him, and still insisted.

'Oh very well,' he said, sitting on the edge of the bed and rearranging his cravat, which had untied itself and was trailing about his shoulders like a scarf.

'You must go down first,' she said. ''Twill be safe enough by the main stairs if we ain't together. I will follow presently.'

So he made himself presentable, kissed her goodbye, and did as he was told. 'I will speak to your father as soon as ever I can,' he promised as he left her. 'And you must dance with me when you come down. You will, will you not?'

'Yes,' she said 'I promise. Now go, before they come searching.'

But first she wanted to see if she looked any different.

It was almost a disappointment that her face in the mirror looked exactly the same: soft and pretty as it often did by candlelight, but unchanged. She gazed at it with great satisfaction for several minutes, the face of a loved woman, a woman in love, a woman engaged to be married — oh she had every right to look pretty! Then she decided that perhaps it was just as well nobody could see any different in her otherwise her mother would notice and know what she'd been doing, and she certainly didn't want that. Her hair was horribly tangled, which was hardly to be wondered at, but that could soon be put right.

She set to work with brush and comb, smiling at her reflection as she wound the unruly ringlets round her fingers. Then she stood up to inspect her gown in the long pier glass and was horrified to see that there was a stain on the back of her skirt. It was a long smear of sticky stuff, with two little streaks of blood in it. She would have to get that cleaned off before anyone saw it or her secret would certainly be out.

It was very difficult to struggle out of her dress unaided for all the fastenings were at the back, but eventually it was done, and the stain was put to soak in her basin, while she examined her wardrobe for a suitable replacement. It would have to be white with a pink trim so as not to attract too much comment, and so that she could wear the same ribbons and slippers. Oh quick, quick, she scolded herself, or he will wonder what has happened. But even though she dressed as quickly as she could, it was more than twenty minutes before she crept back down the servants' stairs into the green parlour.

And as bad luck would have it, the first person to see her as she walked into the drawing room was her mother.

'Ah, there you are, child,' she said. 'We were wondering what had become of you. You have changed your gown, I see.'

'La, Mama,' Matilda said, just a shade too artlessly, 'somebody spilt wine all down the back of the other. I have put it to soak.'

'No harm done then, I trust,' her mother said, narrowing her eyes in speculation. This deliberate insouciance of Tilda's was rather suspicious. She and young Billy Easter had been missing for rather a long time and she'd just seen Billy sneaking back into the room looking decidedly shamefaced.

But Matilda was already skipping across the room to join her lover.

After the third dance she was waylaid by Lizzie and Sophie and Maria, who were eager to know what had happened. But by then she had recovered her composure and her high spirits.

'I am engaged to be married,' she told them coolly. 'I decided to accept him because I couldn't bear to see him suffer. Ain't that so, Billy?'

Fortunately Billy didn't have a chance to feel embarrassed and he didn't have to think of any reply either because all three girls were squealing with pleasure and very busy with congratulations. But it meant he would have to ask her father that very night before somebody else told him the news, and that was rather daunting.

But when the moment came, it was easier than he expected.

'I have the honour sir,' he said, using the well-worn formula, 'to ask for your daughter's hand in marriage.'

'Is she agreeable to it, eh? That's what we need to know,' Mr Honeywood said, looking quite anxious about it. He was very warm after so much dancing, being a well-rounded gentleman, and now he was busy mopping his forehead with a spotted handkerchief.

'Oh yes, sir,' Billy said happily, 'Perfectly agreeable, I do assure you.'

'You've asked her, eh?' peering round the edge of the handkerchief.

Oh lor! Billy thought. Now I'm for it. He'll be bound to say I should have seen him first. But he admitted that he had.

'Done the right thing me boy, damned if you ain't,' Mr Honeywood said, pocketing the handkerchief and shaking him by the hand. 'Now I'll tell 'ee what we propose. Mrs Honeywood and I will meet your mother and discuss settlements and so forth. Deal with all the boring details, eh, while you two young things go off and enjoy yourselves. How would that be, eh?'

'Deeply grateful to you sir. Deeply grateful.'

'I shall tell Mrs Honeywood directly,' Mr Honeywood said, hoping she would be as agreeable as her daughter.

It was quite a relief to him that she made no objections to the match at all.

'Just in the nick of time if you ask for my opinion, Mr Honeywood,' she said, pursing her lips. 'She is grown unconscionably flighty in the last few months. Marriage will settle her. Write you to Mrs Easter directly. The sooner the wedding is fixed the better.'

'You do not think we should have waited for a better match, perhaps?'

'No, Mr Honeywood, I do not. 'Tis my opinion we have made the best match possible. In fact I would go so far as to say that we have discharged our duties towards our daughter quite admirably. Mr Easter is related to Sir Osmond Easter, don't 'ee forget, and the Easter empire is a force to be reckoned with.'

So two days later, Nan Easter received two letters by the same post, one rapturously incoherent from her holidaying son, the other politely formal from Mr Honeywood. She wrote back at once, telling Billy it was no more nor less than she expected and sending her love to her 'new daughter', and accepting Mr Honeywood's invitation to dinner the following Saturday.

'That's like to be an uncommon fine occasion,' she said to Cosmo Teshmaker. 'Don't 'ee think?' But first there were the Sowerbys to be attended to, and the Sowerbys were coming to London on Friday.

CHAPTER 15

It was three o'clock in the morning and Annie Hopkins, Harriet Sowerby and Pollyanna Thistlethwaite were all hard at work in the front parlour of the rectory. They had kept up a good fire and were working by the extravagant light of ten candles, because the job they were doing had got to be done before morning and without a single error or omission. When they began it Annie had been in floods of tears, and now they were all red-eyed with fatigue, but they worked on doggedly, backs bent, neatly capped heads lowered, small-toothed combs flashing in the firelight. For Jimmy and Beau had been infested with head-lice.

The two little boys were asleep where they sat, Beau propped against Pollyanna's cushiony bosom, Jimmy slumped against Harriet's knees, and both of them smelling pungently of the turpentine with which their heads had been washed that afternoon. From time to time when the harsh comb scratched their scalps too fiercely, or a nit was pulled too roughly from its sticky attachment to their hair, they woke to whimper and were hushed back to sleep by their mother. It had been a long, uncomfortable night.

'I reckon 'e's clear now, Mrs Hopkins ma'am,' Pollyanna said, running her fingers against the lie of Beau's soft, fair hair. 'Can't see another one.'

'No more can I, praise be,' Annie agreed, examining closely too. 'You can take him up to bed now, Pollyanna, and get some rest yourself, my dear. I'm uncommon grateful to 'ee. Harriet and I will finish Jimmy.' There was still a lot of picking off to be done on his poor little head.

'Perhaps we should have shaved them after all,' she said to Harriet when Pollyanna had carried the sleeping baby upstairs.

'And lose all their pretty hair?' Harriet said. 'Oh no, Mrs Hopkins, we could never have done that. Think how upset they would have been, and all through no fault of their own.'

'It's made a deal of work for you and Pollyanna, I fear,' Annie apologised, combing carefully.

'I am only too glad to be able to help,' Harriet said, glancing up to smile at this dear new friend of hers, 'after all that you and Mr Hopkins have done for me.'

'That slut shall leave this house tomorrow morning,' Annie said fiercely, sliding two nits carefully along a hair.

Harriet wondered whether the Reverend Hopkins would agree and thought it unlikely, but she didn't comment. She had never seen Annie so fierce and determined, or so angry, so perhaps it was possible.

'A fine thing,' Annie grumbled on, 'if Johnnie comes down here to propose to 'ee Saturday and you have to send him away for fear of infection.'

The word made Harriet's heart leap in her chest. 'Propose?' she said. 'Is he like to propose?'

'Well I should hope so,' Annie said, fingers busy. 'Mama sees your parents a' Friday does she not? Well then... Turn his head a little to one side, my dear. That's it! Oh what a dreadful collection, poor little man.'

They worked in silence for a few minutes till the dreadful

collection had been cleared and was burning in the fire and they began on another one.

Then Annie continued, 'You will say yes, my dear, won't you.'

'Well...,' Harriet murmured, embarrassed by the directness of the question. 'If he asks me. He hasn't said... We have not talked of ...'

'He always was secretive,' Annie confided, 'even as a little boy no bigger than Jimmy. No one ever knew what he was thinking. Mama used to call him a changeling, I remember. Billy was a harum-scarum, a-rushing into everything without stopping to think for so much as a second, but Johnnie was different. He thought about everything, did our Johnnie, on and on and on until he was quite sure. If he ain't spoken yet, my dear, 'tis only because he is still a-thinking.'

'Maybe we should not speak of — of these things either,' Harriet tried. It was very difficult to know what to say without seeming critical or ungrateful.

'You love him, do you not?' Annie asked abruptly, tugging at another nit.

'Yes,' Harriet admitted, answering truthfully because she was so taken aback. 'I believe I do.' He was a good, kind-hearted man, and he'd rescued her from her parents, and was protecting her from their anger even now. How could she help loving him?

'Then you will marry and we shall be sisters,' Annie said, as if the whole matter had been decided, 'and I tell 'ee I couldn't want for a nicer one.'

It was a delightful compliment and given so easily that it moved the exhausted Harriet to tears.

'You are so good,' she said, looking up tremulously. To have been accepted into this family so easily and lovingly was a greater good fortune than she could ever have imagined. But would Mr Easter really propose to her? She did hope so, for she loved him truly. What if the lawyers made her go back to her parents, as they very well might? The thought made her chest contract with distress. Oh, she thought, I couldn't bear it. Not after this happy time with Annie and Mr Hopkins and the boys. Mama will be so angry. If I have to go back, she will beat me as sure as fate. 'I think he's done,' she said, changing the subject to give herself something else to occupy her mind. 'Those were the last.'

'What a night this has been,' Annie said wearily, putting her comb back in the basin of water. 'I shall speak to Mr Hopkins as soon as he wakes in the morning.'

'About me and Mr John?' Harriet said alarmed. 'Oh pray, Mrs Hopkins, I beg you…'

'No, no,' Annie said yawning. 'About that slut. We'll keep the boys in their room until the matter is settled.'

IT WAS SETTLED IMMEDIATELY after breakfast, and in such an easy, amicable manner that Harriet was quite amazed by it.

The Abbotts were in the kitchen, and that was where James and Annie went to talk to them. They left the door open and so Harriet and Pollyanna, who were helping Molly clear the breakfast table, heard every word.

At first Harriet was ashamed to be eavesdropping. 'Do 'ee think we ought?' she whispered to Pollyanna.

Pollyanna was quite phlegmatic about it. 'Now whyever not?' she said. 'I hears every mortal thing what's said in this house. They don't mind, for if they did, they be a-whisperin'.'

'It is only right to tell you,' Mr Hopkins was saying, in his light voice, 'that we cannot keep you here for very much longer. There is a Hampden Club formed in the village, so I am told, and it is only right that I allow them the use of a room for their meetings, which they are most likely to request.'

Mr Abbott's answer was a subdued growl. 'Aye sir, I knows. My brother he's a one on 'em. He's all fer reform is my brother, sir, though I tell 'ee, sir, I can't for the life of me see what good'll come of un.'

'A man of much good sense, your brother,' Mr Hopkins said, adding delicately, 'Have you managed to find...?'

'No, sir, there en't a job a' work nowhere, an' that's a fact.'

'You tell un, Jack,' Mrs Abbott said, in her usual belligerent tone.

'It is a bad time,' Mr Hopkins said. 'There is no work for anyone. Your brother is right, Mr Abbott, reform is a most urgent necessity.'

"'Tis they machines, sir. Tha's what 'tis.'

'I would it were otherwise, howsomever...'

'You see how 'tis, do you not, Mr Abbot?' Annie said. 'You cannot stay with us for ever.'

'Yes, Ma'am,' Mr Abbott growled again. 'I see how 'tis, ma'am. We mussen be a burden. 'Tis uncommon kind of 'ee to have borne with us so long. If 'twern't for the babes we could walk to Norwich, ma'am, for a labourin' job or some such. But 'tis mortal long way for babes, ma'am. My brother could take 'em in after November when his youngest gel goes into service, ma'am, but 'tis a mortal long time to November.'

'Well now,' Mr Hopkins said, 'as to that, I am sure my wife would be agreeable to the children staying on here for a week or two, would you not, Mrs Hopkins?'

'They could stay till the end of November,' Annie said unexpectedly, 'if 'twould help 'ee. I'm sure I've no desire to turn your children out in the cold. We could manage to keep 'em till then, could we not, Mr Hopkins?'

'Well!' Harriet whispered.

'That's the way they always go on,' Pollyanna said. "'Tis called a compermise, so they say. That's what 'tis. A compermise. Meetin' halfway so Mrs Hopkins says.'

A compromise, Harriet thought, meeting halfway, giving something to each other, neither getting exactly what they wanted but both achieving something. It was admirable and what she ought to have expected from such a pair. And as the easy talk went on, she knew with a tightening of foreboding that her parents would never compromise about anything. They would either get their own way on Friday or they would be defeated. And she said a silent, treacherous prayer for their defeat.

Nevertheless anxiety kept her awake all Thursday night.

MR AND MRS SOWERBY had prepared themselves for their meeting with the infamous Mrs Easter by a week of prayer and righteous indignation. Unlike their daughter, they slept well on Thursday night and now, dressed in their Sunday-go-to-meeting black, they were in good time to catch the coach.

'Whatever else,' Mr Sowerby told his wife as he locked up the house, 'whatever else we will stand by our principles. Mr Easter has done us a grievous wrong, but I tell 'ee, Mother, he need not think he will prevail. When we open this door tomorrow, Harriet will be returned to us.'

'Amen!' Mrs Sowerby said fiercely. They'd had a very difficult time of it during the past few weeks, with their neighbours so obviously inquisitive about where Harriet had gone and the congregation asking pointed questions, and even though they'd answered with truth that she was working as companion to the wife of a clergyman, there was no doubt in anybody's mind that she ought to be at home, where she belonged.

IN NAN'S headquarters in the Strand, John Easter was making his last appeal to Mr Brougham and Cosmo Teshmaker. 'It is understood that Miss Sowerby is not to be returned to her parents,' he urged. He too had passed a sleepless night worrying about the interview, and he was dreading the moment when his adversaries would arrive.

He and Nan and their two lawyers had been watching out for them, standing at the window of her luxurious office with her splendid fire crackling behind them, both lawyers professionally noncommittal, Nan warm with mischief, John apprehensive. Outside it was blowing a gale and the wind was rattling the windowpanes.

'It is quite understood, Mr John,' Cosmo said. 'You need not concern yourself I do assure you. Mr Brougham is here.'

'I still maintain that I should be present, Mama,' John said, 'if not to participate, then at least to hear what is said.'

'Aye, so you say,' his mother said coolly. 'Howsomever, Mr Brougham thinks otherwise. Do you not, Mr Brougham?'

'Given the circumstances,' Mr Brougham said easily, 'I do believe your absence would be advisable.'

'He en't to be here,' Nan said. 'Come now Johnnie, you know 'tis for the best. You may sit behind the partition in the inner office if you've a mind to. Then you could hear every word.'

He was horrified at such a suggestion. 'I could not possibly stoop to such a thing, Mama,' he protested. How could an Easter play such a hole-in-the-corner trick? It would be terribly undignified.

'Then you must stay in your office and wait 'til we call 'ee,' Nan said. 'Don't 'ee fret. 'Twill all go well, take my word for it.'

'They are bullies,' he warned.

'We shall be a match for 'em,' she said, 'whenever they come.'

The Sowerbys appeared, just as the church clock of St Clements' Danes was striking four. They were dressed in their uncompromising black and stalked along the crowded Strand as stiff as broomsticks, looking neither left nor right, and set apart from everybody else in the street by their lack of colour and their rigidity. There was an extravagance of movement and excitement all around them, horses trotting, whips flicking, carriages jolting and swaying, pedestrians scurrying against the wind, greatcoats swirling, or stopping to greet a friend with much arm waving and head nodding and clutching of hats. Outside the Exeter 'Change the usual excited crowds were rushing to see the menagerie, pointing up at the brightly coloured pictures of monsters and wild beasts that decorated its walls and urged on by the doormen who were dressed up as Yeomen of the Guard and stood yelling at the entrance. Buskers turned wind-tossed somersaults; hawkers offered wind-dusted pies. But the Sowerbys were impervious to it all. Others might bend to the elements if they wished, they progressed.

'Yes,' John said, his heart sinking at the sight of them. 'That is Mrs Sowerby, I'm sure of it.'

'So we may safely assume that the gentleman beside her is her husband,' Cosmo observed.

'Unless she has taken a lover,' Mr Brougham laughed.

'Which don't seem likely,' Nan said wickedly, 'given the face she's got on her. My heart alive! Who'd be enamoured of that?'

And John laughed with the others, cheered by her irreverent humour, despite his apprehension.

'Hasten you down, Mr Jones,' she said, turning to the clerk who was standing behind her waiting for his orders. 'Honoured guests, remember. Don't 'ee forget to bow and scrape. And bring in the sherry after five minutes.'

Mr Jones touched his forelock and grinned back at her, enjoying the charade, before he strutted off to do her bidding.

And John left too, his anxiety gathering about him like a storm cloud as he paced along the corridor towards his own solitary office, with the wind howling at him through the windows. This should have been an honest confrontation, he brooded. Something could have been settled by an honest confrontation. But this meeting his mother had arranged was theatrical and false. It would achieve nothing. If only I could have been present, he thought. I should have insisted. They are terrible cruel people and they should be told the truth about themselves.

And certainly the Sowerbys looked as theatrical in their black clothes as the setting prepared for them. Their rage was real, though, and there was no disguising that. It pinched their long noses and hardened their eyes and reduced their mouths to gashes.

'I cannot wish a good afternoon to you, ma'am,' Mr Sowerby said brusquely in answer to Nan's greeting, 'since we are not here to exchange pleasantries. We are here to take possession of our daughter.'

'Pray do be seated,' Mr Brougham interposed smoothly, rising from behind Nan's desk to greet them. 'Your concern for your daughter does you much credit, Mr Sowerby. Pray allow me to introduce myself. Brougham, barrister-at-law, and at your service.'

They were impressed, although they tried not to show it. Mrs Sowerby's eyes grew quite bright. 'Well sir,' she said, ''tis a relief to see that *someone* appreciates our position.'

'Oh entirely, ma'am,' he said, indicating the chair she should occupy by the merest motion of his hand. 'You must be most distressed. How could it be otherwise given the great love that exists between mother and child?'

'Very true,' Mrs Sowerby said, seating herself with some satisfaction and glancing at her husband to show him that he should sit in the chair beside her. 'You have no idea of the anguish we have suffered.'

The sherry arrived, was offered and indignantly refused.

'Now dear lady,' Mr Brougham continued, 'we must decide what is to be done about this, must we not?'

'Our daughter is to be returned to us forthwith!' Mr Sowerby said angrily, determined to get his own way as quickly as possible.

'Indeed. Indeed,' Mr Brougham soothed. 'There should be no

difficulty with that, Mr Sowerby. The child is under-age I presume?'

'Under-age?' Mrs Sowerby said.

'Why yes, of course. 'Tis a mere formality to enquire, howsomever these small details must be cleared from our path, as I am sure you appreciate. She is not yet sixteen?'

'She is just sixteen, sir,' Mrs Sowerby admitted readily. 'A mere child and stolen away from her mother.'

'Ah!' Mr Brougham said calmly, dipping a pen in the inkpot and handing it across to Cosmo Teshmaker who was sitting at his left hand.

'And when was this?'

'In January, sir. You see how young she is. How much she needs our protection.'

'And could we have the exact date, if you would be so good.'

'The thirty-first.'

It was recorded. 'Thank 'ee kindly,' Mr Brougham said. 'And she has lived with you all her life, I presume.'

'Of course.'

'Of course. And she left your house...?'

'She was stolen from our house on September the sixth,' Mr Sowerby said. But he was speaking with less venom now, soothed, despite his resolve, by the warm fire, the comfortable armchairs and the barrister's obvious calm and helpfulness.

'Quite, quite —' waiting while that answer was recorded too. 'So naturally you wish her to be returned to you. That is so is it not?'

Vigorous nodding. And triumphant looks darted at Nan, thoughtful in her own chair beside the fire.

'At this point,' Mr Brougham said, turning towards Cosmo, 'it might be advantageous to ascertain the young lady's opinion in the matter, always supposing that she has one and that it is known. Is it known, Mr Teshmaker?'

'Yes, Mr Brougham,' Cosmo said blandly. 'Miss Sowerby has

communicated her opinions to us. She does not wish to return home.'

'*Nonsense!*' Mrs Sowerby said crossly. 'She is a stupid, foolish girl let me tell 'ee. No one should take any notice of what she says.'

'Quite possibly,' Mr Brougham said, in tones which implied that given a choice he would certainly agree with her sentiments, 'howsomever, should the matter come to court, which you have given me to understand might well be the case, the law would require her opinions to be sought and taken into account. Since she is over sixteen, you understand, dear lady, she is accountable by law.'

'Do you mean to tell me, sir,' Mr Sowerby said, 'that a magistrate would take the word of a child — a mere child — a runaway child — against the word of her parents? I cannot believe it.'

'It is the law nevertheless,' Mr Brougham apologised calmly. 'Howsomever many other matters would also be taken into consideration as you will appreciate. The young person would have to prove to the magistrates that she is competent to earn a living, and that she has some acceptable place of domicile, which since she is a runaway will hardly obtain in this case, I imagine.' And he glanced at Mr Teshmaker, raising his eyebrows slightly.

Cosmo took his cue. 'With respect, Mr Brougham,' he said, 'I believe the young person could satisfy the magistrate as to both these conditions.'

'Indeed? Well you do surprise me.'

'She has found employment with a clergyman and his wife,' Cosmo said, 'as nursemaid and companion. They are very well pleased with her services and say that they would be — ah —' He pretended to consult a letter — 'loathe to let her go.'

'Ah! I see!' Mr Brougham said, assuming a serious expression. 'Well now, Mr and Mrs Sowerby, I should tell 'ee that this puts quite a different complexion upon the matter. A clergyman you said, Mr Teshmaker? Yes indeed, quite a different complexion.'

'Complexion or no,' Mr Sowerby said, 'we mean to have satisfaction. There's a law against child-stealing.'

'Indeed there is, sir,' Mr Brougham agreed, 'but I feel I should point out to you that it only applies if the child is younger than sixteen years which, on your own admission, your child is not.'

Now and too late Mr Sowerby realised that this unassuming man sitting so quietly behind his expensive desk was actually in charge of everybody in the room, that his smooth talk wasn't helpful at all, quite the reverse in fact, and that he was a devilish kind of advocate.

'Well well,' he said tetchily, 'that's as may be, sir. We shall see when we come to court, sir.'

'So you are prepared to take the matter to court?'

'Indeed we are, sir! If 'tis the last thing we ever do.'

'And are prepared for the costs you will incur, doubtless?'

'Indeed.' But a flicker of concern passed across his narrow face.

'It is truly quite scandalous,' Mr Brougham said mildly, 'how costs do accrue in these cases. Is it not, Mr Teshmaker?'

'Indeed it is, Mr Brougham.'

'I should estimate that costs in this case would be some-what in the region of, say, one thousand pounds for both parties,' Mr Brougham said with splendid aplomb. 'For which you would undoubtedly be prepared Mrs Easter, would you not?'

'Undoubtedly,' Nan agreed, smiling horribly sweetly at Mr and Mrs Sowerby. 'They are the sort of costs a company like Easter's could most certainly withstand. Especially in a good cause.'

Mrs Sowerby exploded into temper. 'Oh I see how 'tis,' she shouted. 'Our daughter is to be ruined and we made fools of because we cannot pay your fancy fees. What sort of law is that I ask you?'

'The law of the land, ma'am,' Cosmo said.

'A fig to the law of the land!' Mrs Sowerby screeched. 'I don't give *that* for the law of the land. The law of the land is a villainous law, I tell 'ee, if it allows my poor dear daughter to be ruined and we powerless to prevent it. What is to become of her, once she *is* ruined, eh? You tell me that, sir! If she en't ruined already.'

Mr Brougham remained magnificently calm before her onslaught. 'Is your daughter ruined, ma'am?' he said mildly. 'I do not recall any mention of ruin before this moment.'

'If she en't ruined, sir,' Mr Sowerby shouted, catching his wife's hysteria, 'then she very soon will be, sir, being in the hands of a young rake, sir. We all know very well what young rakes are. What else is like to happen I ask you?'

'Nobody gives a thought to the suffering of our poor Harriet,' Mrs Sowerby said, now heavy with self-pity. 'She is to be stolen away it seems and used and *ruined* and we powerless to prevent it. *Powerless.* And when he's had his way with her and ruined her and she comes running home to us what will become of her then, sir? Who will marry her then? Soiled goods, sir!'

'Am I to understand that your purpose in this matter is to ensure a suitable marriage for the young lady?' Mr Brougham enquired.

'What else would concern *any* mother, Mr Brougham?'

'Quite so,' he said, smiling at her again. 'Well then, dear lady, I do believe we have a possible solution to all our difficulties. I am safe to assume, am I not, that a suitable husband would be a satisfactory solution to you, Mrs Sowerby?'

She was still stuck in her complaint. 'Who would have her then? Soiled goods!'

But her husband saw the advantage they were being offered. 'Did 'ee have a particular husband in mind, Mr Brougham?' he asked, reassuming his usual meek expression. 'If such is the case, sir, we would be pleased to hear of it.' And he scowled at his wife to warn her to desist.

'There is a young gentleman,' Mr Brougham admitted cautiously. 'Howsomever I do not know whether his family would empower me to tell you his name. And, of course, he would be in no position to marry your daughter unless you were happy to give your consent.'

By now Mrs Sowerby was interested too. 'Well now, sir,' she said, 'as to that, we would need to be certain that the person was quite suitable, as you will appreciate. He would need to be of good family.'

'I can assure you, ma'am,' Mr Brougham said, 'that the person is of quite excellent parentage.'

'And would marry her if we gave our consent?'

'Indeed.'

'How may we be sure?' Mrs Sowerby said cunningly. 'We all know what young men are like. They may give their word one day and withdraw it the next, and what sort of surety is that for a young girl?'

'The young gentleman is my son, Mrs Sowerby,' Nan said, 'and I can tell 'ee the young fool would marry her tomorrow so he would, were I to give permission. Which I don't, there being no need for him to marry the girl.' She was playing her part to perfection, looking angry and disdainful and every bit the disapproving parent.

'With respect, Mrs Easter,' Mr Brougham said, assuming an artful expression and making sure that Mrs Sowerby noticed by giving her the full benefit of it before he looked at Nan, 'it ain't your permission that is in question, since your son has come of age, has he not, and may therefore marry whom he pleases.'

Smug looks from the Sowerbys.

'No, no,' Mr Brougham continued. ''Tis Mr Sowerby's

permission that has to be sought in this particular matter, is it not, Mr Sowerby?'

'Mr Sowerby would not wish his daughter to marry my son,' Nan said tartly. 'That I do know. En't that right, Mr Sowerby?'

'He is prepared to marry her you say, Mr Brougham?' Mr Sowerby asked, and his face was quite peaked with artfulness.

'Without question.'

'Then we will permit it,' Mr Sowerby said. 'Will we not, Mother? 'Tis the right and proper thing for him to do, when all's said and done, seeing 'twas he that stole her away in the first place.'

'I am most happy to hear it,' Mr Brougham said. 'And if I may advise you, I should suggest that you put your consent in writing just as soon as ever you can.' And he gave a meaningful look at Nan.

'I would do it now if I had a pen.'

'I am sure Mr Teshmaker could provide a pen.'

'I could do better than that, sir,' Cosmo said. 'By a lucky chance I just happen to have a letter of consent in this drawer. One which I drew up for another party yesterday, but which I am sure would serve.' And he pulled it from the drawer and handed it to Mr Brougham, who glanced at it and pronounced it excellent and handed it across to Mr Sowerby.

'Do 'ee think this wise?' Nan said, scowling at her adversaries to encourage them with discouragement.

'Wise or not, ma'am,' Mrs Sowerby said with ugly triumph. ''Twill be done! Make no mistake about it.'

They signed at great speed and in high fury, one after the other, the pen spurting and scratching beneath their anger.

'We wish 'ee good day, ma'am,' Mr Sowerby said to Nan when the paper was returned to Mr Brougham. 'Good has triumphed over evil you see. You need not think you can ever force us, ma'am. Good has triumphed.'

'Aye,' Nan said coolly, as they made a dramatic exit, ramrod stiff, 'so I see.'

But she didn't laugh or crow until their footsteps had died away down the corridor. Then she threw her arms in the air and squealed with pleasure. 'Oh 'twas better than a play,' she said. 'Did 'ee see the face on 'em, Cosmo? "Good has triumphed." Oh my heart alive!' And she rushed at her happy colleague to kiss him warmly on both cheeks. ''Twas downright magnificent,' she said, her wide mouth spread wider than he'd ever seen it, so huge was her delight.

'Most happy to have been of service,' Cosmo said.

But she'd already turned to kiss Mr Brougham, first on one cheek and then on the other, with her arms about his neck. And Mr Brougham caught at her flying hands as she turned and began to spin away from him, still chortling, and, leaning down towards her, kissed her in his turn, first on one cheek and then on the other, pulling her to him so that they were eye to eye in their happiness.

It was a moment, no more, but she was suddenly and dizzyingly aware of him, breathing in the scent of his flesh, glimpsing rather more than mere regard in those close, smiling grey eyes.

And then she was off again, running to the door on tiptoe, skipping down the corridor to tell John, calling to Mr Jones as she ran that he was to 'hasten to the sorting room and fetch Mr William'.

They could hear her voice quite clearly even above the noise of the wind. 'Johnnie, my dear! We've won! We've won!'

'What an amazing lady she is, Mr Brougham,' Cosmo said admiringly.

'She is without equal, Mr Teshmaker,' Frederick Brougham agreed.

CHAPTER 16

The gale blew all that night, bringing rain with it, howling down the chimneys and flailing the tall trees and spitting out roof tiles like broken teeth. Harriet Sowerby lay awake all night listening to it. Not that she would have slept very much had the night been peaceful. She had too much to think about.

If only she knew what Mrs Easter's lawyers had arranged! Would they send her back to her parents or let her stay here with Mrs Hopkins? And would her dear Mr Easter really propose to her? Oh if only he would! By the time the first green edge of dawn lightened her eastern window and the tumult finally died down, she was so full of nervous energy she couldn't stay in bed a minute longer.

She got up and washed herself carefully, shivering under the impact of water cold from the ewer, and dressed in silence, while the dawn chorus began to pipe and carol most joyfully in the garden below her. Then she crept down the dark stairs and, taking her black cloak from its hook behind the kitchen door, lifted the latch and stepped out into the pale light of early morning.

The rain had stopped but the garden was awash with moisture, the long grass swishing wet underfoot and the branches of
the yew dropping raindrops upon her as thick as a shower. She
picked her way past the holm oak and through the wet gate into
the open churchyard where the high stone flanks of St
Nicholas's church rose above her, damp and dark against the
grey sky. The village was still sleeping in its hollow, black-
thatched by rain and spouting water from every shabby gutter,
but the birds were now in full song, thrushes and blackbirds
calling clear, a robin shrill and sweet, hedge sparrows a-twitter,
magpies clattering like wooden rattles.

She walked round the side of the church and arrived at the
south porch, where she paused for a second with her hand
resting on the rough flints, looking down at the village. Then
she took her uncertainties into the church.

The peace and silence of the place surrounded her like a
benediction, calming her and giving her strength. She walked
quietly past the font, touching its odd carved faces with gentle
reverence, and up the aisle past the box pews towards the
communion table, its cloth as green as glass in the dawn light,
and there she stopped before the altar rails. The bottom half of
the east window was still in darkness, but the figure of her
gentle Christ was glowingly visible, His hands upraised. And in
the peaceful light of that early morning it seemed to Harriet that
He was looking down with total understanding, straight into
her eyes.

She dropped to her knees before Him and began to pray,
speaking aloud in the urgency of her dilemma.

'Oh dear God, please don't make me go back to my parents,
for I couldn't bear it. If I have to go back to them, I will die. I
don't love them, Lord, and they don't love me. I love my dear
Mr and Mrs Hopkins and little Jimmy, who was so patient when
we had to clean his head, and dear little Beau and his pretty

ways, and Miss Pettie who is always so kind, and dear Mr Easter.'

The face above her looked down with unflinching compassion.

'I do believe I love Mr Easter more than anyone, Lord,' she said. 'He is the kindest man I ever met, to rescue me and bring me here, when I am nothing to him. I think of him every day and pray for him. And I dream of him too, Lord. I dream of him every night. Oh if I could marry Mr Easter and be part of his dear good family for ever and ever! I cannot tell him, because that would not be proper, but I do love him, Lord. Oh indeed I do. I love him with all my heart.'

There was a slight sound behind her, a suspiration of breath, or the last sigh of the wind, and she turned, startled, clutching her cloak about her, and Mr Easter was standing in the aisle.

'Oh my own dear, darling Harriet!' he said. 'I love you so very much.' And then she was in his arms and he was kissing her tenderly, tenderly, in the gentle light.

'Oh Mr Easter,' Harriet whispered, when the kiss was done. She couldn't believe this was truly happening, even though her lips were still tingling from his kiss. 'How do you come to be here so early in the morning?'

'I travelled on the overnight coach to bring you the news as soon as I could. I saw the church door open.'

But she was too stunned to realise what he was saying. 'I am dreaming,' she said, resting her head against his shoulder.

'No, no. You are here, my little love. And you will marry me, will you not? You said you would.'

'I should not have spoken so,' she said, looking up at him and blushing at the memory. 'How forward I must seem to you, Mr Easter. I would not have spoken so, indeed I would not, had I known you were there to hear me. Oh dear, oh dear!' And that lower lip was bitten by those two dear little crooked teeth.

'You must call me John now,' he said, holding her lightly about the waist, admiring her blush and thinking how very dark her blue eyes were in the half-light. 'And you must say you will marry me. You will, will you not?'

'Yes, John. If I am allowed to.'

'Why my dear love, what is to stop you now?'

'My mother and father, sir.'

'Your parents have given their consent to it,' he said, speaking calmly even though he wanted to crow in triumph.

She was so surprised that her mouth fell open. He could see her tongue, tremulously pink, behind those charming crooked teeth. 'They forbade me to see you or write to you,' she said incredulously. 'However did you manage to persuade them?'

'It was all Mr Brougham's doing,' he said, and told her the full story. 'A fine man, Mr Brougham. We are lucky to have him as an ally.'

'Have I to go home?' Oh the anxiety crumpling that pale forehead.

'No,' he told her triumphantly. 'That is settled too. You are to stay here until we marry, and I am to ask James to marry us. What do 'ee think of that?'

'If we — when we marry would you wish to live in Bury?'

'No,' he reassured, understanding her anxiety. 'We shall live in London, where I work. You need never go to Bury or see your parents ever again, if that is what you wish. Does that content you?'

'Oh yes, dear John.'

'We shall be so happy,' he promised.

'I think I am dreaming,' she said.

And was kissed again, to prove otherwise, and for a great deal longer this time.

. . .

'So we shall have two weddings, Sophie,' Nan said to her old friend the next Monday afternoon, when she'd told her the tale. 'What sport!' The two of them were taking tea in the drawing room at Bedford Square, and Sophie had greatly enjoyed the story of the Sowerbys' discomfiture.

'I do enjoy a good wedding,' Sophie said, accepting her dish of tea and sipping it happily. 'When is the first to be?'

''Twill be Johnnie's in April in Rattlesden with our dear Mr Hopkins to officiate. They have fixed the date already and I shall send out invitations within the week. Billy and Matilda are like to marry in June in St George's in Bloomsbury, according to Mr Honeywood. The family are coming to London in a week or two, ready for the season and mean to plan it all then. You are invited to both, of course, and will get two invitations accordingly.'

'I should be aggrieved if 'twere otherwise,' Sophie said. 'Shall you invite any of the Easters?' reaching out her plump hand to pick up a morsel of tea cake.

'The cousins at Ippark,' Nan said, 'since they always write to me and have been true friends over all these years.'

'Is that wise?' Sophie demurred. 'Remembering what happened last time.'

John had been furious to see two members of the Easter family included in his sister's wedding party, and there had been a rather nasty row about it.

'He was young then,' Nan said, 'and thought every Easter the devil incarnate, simply because his poor father's parents were so unkind to me. Now he has better sense. 'Tis all forgiven and forgotten long since.'

'Let us pray so,' Sophie said, smoothing the crumbs from her ample lap, 'for your sake, my dear. Howsomever, 'tis my experience that a wedding too often serves to bring out the very worst in any family.'

John's certainly brought an extraordinary answer from the ladies in Ippark.

My dearest Nan, Thomasina wrote.

We are delighted to accept your most kind invitation to John's wedding, and in April too when the weather will be more clement, which is always to the good. It seems but yesterday that we attended your dear daughter's wedding which we enjoyed so much and remember so well. Such a pretty bride and now a mother with two young boys.

It is quite possible, although by no means certain, it would be wrong of us to pretend otherwise, not having quite all the information we would wish, howsomever we cannot complain of that since Osmond may not know all he would wish to know himself, nor the lady either for that matter, that we may have to face a change in our circumstances. Howsomever we shall be certain to attend the wedding, you may depend upon it and remain,

Your most devoted cousins,
  Thomasina and Evelina.

'What are they talking about?' Nan said, handing the letter across the breakfast table to Johnnie.

He read it carefully, squinting with effort. 'If you ask me,' he said, after some thought, 'the precious Sir Osmond plans to marry again and they are fearful of the consequences.'

'Aye, 'tis possible,' she said, re-reading the letter. 'There's a lady in the case sure enough, but why should that change their circumstances?'

'Perhaps he don't mean to support 'em, or the new wife wants 'em thrown out of the house.'

'He couldn't be so cruel,' Nan said. 'How could they live without his support, poor souls?'

'You have a touching faith in your relations, Mama,' John said, calmly returning to his haddock. 'When did they ever show any concern for their kith and kin? They were quick enough to show you the door when you were young and widowed and penniless, don't forget. There is mischief afoot, you may depend upon it.'

'I shall write back, directly,' his mother said, 'and ask them what 'tis. We don't want any unpleasantness at your wedding.'

But although she didn't know it, unpleasantness was gathering like a carbuncle in the pretty bosom of her other future daughter-in-law.

WHEN MATILDA HEARD that John's wedding had been arranged, she was very pleased, delighted to think that Billy's younger brother was getting married before she was. It would allow her to follow with a much grander and more spectacular ceremony should she so wish. And of course she would wish. That was only natural and would be most agreeable. And goodness knows she needed some agreeable moments in her life just at the moment, for ever since the rapturous night at their party her mother had kept her so tightly chaperoned that she and Billy had rarely had the chance even to kiss. This was just the third time they'd been left in a room alone together and she knew that they would only have privacy for a matter of minutes until the carriage arrived to take the entire family to the opera. She was miserable with frustration and he was wasting their opportunity by preening in the looking glass.

'Miss Harriet Sowerby,' she said idly. 'Do we know her, Billy?'

'Don't we just!' Billy said, admiring his reflection in the mirror above the fireplace. 'She was the gel we rescued. Don't you remember? Me and Johnnie and Eb and Claude.'

'But she is a servant!' Matilda said, outraged, frustration

erupting into anger. 'He ain't a-marryin' a servant, Billy. Never tell me that, because I won't believe it.'

'She ain't a servant, Tilda,' Billy said mildly, still more occupied with his appearance than her annoyance. 'Her father is a clerk or somesuch. She's a deuced pretty girl. You will like her.'

'I shall not!' Matilda said, with furious determination. 'Oh Billy, how could you even suggest such a thing?'

Alerted at last by the anger in her voice, Billy turned from the mirror to cuddle her into a better frame of mind. And was punched in the chest for his pains. 'Oh come now, Tilda,' he complained. 'Where's the fuss? This ain't like you, upon me word.'

'People like us don't go marrying servants,' she said. 'Whatever is your brother thinking of? 'Tis a scandal, so 'tis.'

'He loves her,' Billy tried to explain.

And was hooted at. 'And so I've to be related to a servant,' she said. Her cheeks were flushed and her eyes shining with passion. She wanted him so much and she couldn't even kiss him because her horrid brother would be back in the room at any minute. 'How could you demean me so?'

'I don't demean you.'

'My sister-in-law a servant! The shame of it! You must talk him out of it,' she ordered.

'It can't be done,' Billy said, amazed by her vehemence. 'Nor should it. 'Tis his choice, not ours. Come now, Tilda, there is no harm in it.'

Her fury flared like a burnt coal. 'You do not love me,' she cried, 'else you could not say such things.'

'I do love you,' he said, surprised by the sudden turn this trivial conversation had taken. 'You know right well I do. Ain't I proved it?' And he made another attempt to put his arms around her.

She shook herself out of his grasp. 'If you do not persuade him, Mr William Easter, then I declare I will… I will…'

He was touched by her furious inability to find a suitable threat. 'Oh what will you do, you beautiful creature?' he said, teasing her with laughter. It was a great mistake.

'I will not marry you,' she said stamping her foot.

'Tilda!' he implored. 'I beg you!'

But Claude was opening the door and he and Mrs Honeywood were bustling into the room and their argument was abruptly curtailed.

Matilda turned her body away from him, walking across to her mother, and for the rest of the evening she kept herself aloof, sitting as far away from him as she could, talking to other people and never to him and, finally, when the carriage came to collect them all at the end of the performance, saying goodbye as though he were the slightest acquaintance.

'You will recall what I vowed, I daresay,' she said coolly, 'and what is to be done if we are to resume our friendship.'

'Tilda!' he begged. 'You don't mean it.'

'Oh indeed I do,' she said, and swept into the carriage, straight-spined with determination.

He was awake all night worrying about it. And when a letter was delivered early the next morning just after he arrived home from the stamping and sorting, his heart gave the most uncomfortable lurch at the sight of her furious handwriting. How had they come to such a pass, so suddenly and just at the very moment when he thought their futures settled and assured?

I hope you have reconsidered your decision to talk to your brother,' she wrote. 'I do not wish to hurt you, dearest Billy. I have lain wakeful all night considering how I hurt you. I love you to distraction. Howsomever I do have a position to keep up. Please talk to your brother. Is that truly so much for your loving Tilda to ask?

Put like that it seemed reasonable, if impossible. He wrote back to her at once.

I will do as you ask my love, this evening as ever is.

Your own devoted Billy.

PS I love you to distraction and beyond. I would do anything for you. You are my heart and soul.

But doing this particular thing was going to be extraordinarily difficult.

He worried about it all through the day, making several uncharacteristic mistakes at the sorting, and growing steadily more and more irritable. By mid-afternoon, his underlings were glad to see the back of him.

He made it his business to travel home in the same carriage as his brother, but John was so withdrawn and thoughtful he wasn't even able to start a conversation with him, leave alone an argument, and he was still in this quiet mood when Nan came home, in a great rush as always, picking up the letters that had been left on the hall table for her attention, and ripping them open as she ran upstairs. One was from Annie, two were bills and the fourth was from Thomasina Callbeck.

'You were right, Johnnie,' she said as she strode into the parlour, still reading. 'Sir Osmond is engaged, and they don't like the lady. "Her name is Jane Bellingham, daughter to a manufacturer and prodigious rich." '

'Then she should suit,' Billy said.

'Oh come now, Billy,' his brother laughed. 'Daughter to a manufacturer? That's a deal too common for our precious Easters.'

'Then what would they think of your intended?' Billy asked, seizing his opportunity.

'Fortunately, they do not need to think of her at all, it being none of their affair.'

'You are wrong as to that, Johnnie,' Nan said, 'since Thomasina and Evelina are invited to your wedding.'

'The Easter cousins?'

'Indeed.'

'Mama!' he said, enraged. 'How could you when you know my feelings on the matter?' Nothing had changed. He might be her manager of sales but she still gave no thought to his feelings at all. She didn't even bother to consult him.

'I thought you'd ha' grown to more sense,' she said, riled by his anger.

'But they are Easters!' Deuce take it, after all this time you'd have thought she'd have understood that.

'So are you.'

'I won't have it,' he said furiously. 'You should have more pride.'

'They are invited.'

'Then you must write back and tell 'em they ain't welcome.'

'I will do no such thing,' she said. 'Have a care, boy! Remember who I am! 'Ten't for you to tell me who I'm to invite.'

'I am not a child, Mama! I mean what I say.'

'And so do I, Johnnie. So do I.'

'I will not have an Easter at my wedding.'

'They are Callbecks, you ridiculous boy,' glancing at Billy in the hope that he could say something witty to diffuse their temper.

'They are cousins to the Easters,' John insisted.

'And your Miss Sowerby is the daughter of a clerk,' Billy pointed out, taking the chance his mother had offered but not in the way she'd intended. 'Had you thought of that?'

'No,' John said turning to him coldly. 'Why should I? Her parentage is of no consequence.'

'It may not be of any consequence to you Johnnoh,' Billy said, 'but 'tis a deuced nuisance to me and Matilda, I can tell 'ee.'

Now what? Nan thought. Is there no end to temper this evening? What is the matter with Billy?

'It is none of your affair,' John said crossly, transferring his anger to his brother. 'And if that stupid Matilda of yours —'

'She ain't stupid! She's a fine girl. With a position to keep up.' Bristling.

'Oh ho! I see what 'tis. She looks down on my Harriet, is that it?'

'She could hardly help it,' Billy defended, 'seeing your Harriet is only one step above a servant.'

'And your Tilda one step above a fool. Devil take it, Billy, you shan't speak of my —'

'I'll speak as I please. The truth hurts don't it, Johnnie? One step above a ser —'

'Be quiet! Be quiet or I'll not be answerable for — '

They were like two fighting cocks, Nan thought, jumping at each other, shrieking defiance, hackles rising, hair bristling, red-faced and staring-eyed, her two dear boys, who'd always been so close.

'Boys! Boys!' she cried. 'Have done!'

But they were too far into their anger to hear her.

'Your precious Matilda is a nasty little snob, let me tell 'ee.'

'Your precious Miss Sowerby is a skivvy.'

There'll be fisticuffs, Nan thought, watching them with alarm and admiration. 'If you continue,' she shouted. 'You shall dine elsewhere, so you shall. Stop it at once! D'ye hear?'

But they went on screaming abuse at one another. 'Deuce take it,' she said, as much to herself as to them, 'I can't abide much more of this. Are we to scream our way through dinner, you poor fools? Is this the sort of behaviour I'm to expect from my sons?'

'Snob!'

'Skivvy!'

Nan picked up her letters and left them to fight it out. Short of lifting them up and carrying them out of the room, which was obviously and totally beyond her powers, there was nothing else she could do. There was no sense in either of them, and if they were going to break the furniture or crack one another's skulls she would rather not be there to see it. Blamed fools! She would go and dine with Mr Brougham, that's what she'd do. Dear, calm, cultivated, civilised Mr Brougham.

CHAPTER 17

I t was a fine October evening, which was just as well, for Nan had stormed out of the house in too much of a temper to wait for the carriage, although she'd snatched up her muff and crammed her bonnet on her head, before she slammed the door. She strode through Bedford Square, scowling with fury, her russet coat as bright as the plane leaves in the gardens, her black button-boots swishing against each other like scythes.

Above the shadowy shops of Holborn, the sky pulsed with colour, blood red, russet, orange and purple, smudged and veiled by the grey-brown smoke from the city's busy chimneys, but the streets below were dark and as yet unlit. She pushed through the crowds and crossed into Chancery Lane, walking more steadily now, eased by her exertions. And presently she came to the entrance to Lincoln's Inn, a great, competent, reassuring, red-brick gateway, built like a fortress with an impressive coat of arms carved above the cornerstone and twin towers on either side of the arch, judicially balanced the one against the other. The gas lights on either side of the arch were already lit, pale gold blooms against the sombre red brick, and the oak doors still stood open, but the archway to justice was as black as a coalmine.

She ran through it quickly into the garden. It was a beautifully kept garden and well laid out, with plenty of thick shrubbery, neat gravel paths, a long avenue of black poplars, and overlooking Lincoln's Inn Fields, an elevated terrace walk, dark and shadowy now but still peaceful and decidedly rural. A sweet, green, country place right in the middle of the city. It restored her to good humour just to look at it.

The court itself was surrounded on three sides by tessellated towers and ancient Gothic windows, and it was lighter here than it had been in Chancery Lane, for lamps were lit both inside and outside the buildings. She could see the pale face of a clerk who was busily writing beside one of the windows immediately above her, and the brass plates were glowingly legible beside the entrances. She drew her hand out of her muff and ran her fingers down the brazen lists until she found the name she wanted: 'Appleby, Brougham & Furnival'. Yes, she had done the right thing to come here.

Mr Frederick Brougham had just returned from court and was still wigged, gowned and weary when his servant came quietly into the room to announce that 'a Mrs Nan Easter has arrived to see you sir, *without* appointment, sir'.

'This is a lady who could never be constrained by appointments, Brandyman,' he said, smiling happily. 'Show her up at once.'

She walked into his chambers like the leader of an invading army, disturbing the smell of ancient dust and old leather with a pungent combination of newsprint, horse-sweat and new warm wool. 'My dear,' he said, holding out his hands in greeting. 'To what do I owe this unexpected pleasure?'

'My family's gone lunatic,' she said, beaming at him, brown eyes glistening with mischief, dark eyebrows arching like wings in flight, dark curls springing about her forehead as though they were growing before his eyes.

What vitality she has, he thought, removing his wig. 'Well now, I'm sorry to hear that,' he said. 'How may I be of service?'

'You may feed me. I've left home in a temper and not eaten.'

'It shall be done at once, if you will allow me to send Brandyman out on a few errands.' He'd been invited to dine with one of his colleagues that evening, so he would have to send excuses. 'Would pigeon pie and porter serve?'

''Twould be capital.'

And so it was, tasty and peaceful, sitting at his little round table beside the window, among his learned tomes and his neat papers, as the dusk rolled in from the gardens and somebody below them swept the courtyard, swish, swish, swish.

When the meal was done and Brandyman had removed the dishes and made up the fire, they sat one on each side of the hearth and talked, like an old country couple.

He said he was glad to see her in better humour.

'Aye,' she agreed, 'so I am. That's the difference food makes.'

'And company too, I trust?' he teased.

'It could be said. I've a deal too much company at home and that's a fact. A deal too much company and a deal too many troubles.'

'A trouble shared?' he suggested, taking a taper from its pot on the mantelpiece and leaning forward to light it at the fire.

It was a new experience for Nan Easter to be offered help and advice. She was usually the one who gave both, being the undoubted head of family and business. She looked at him thoughtfully, weighing the situation. If he gave advice 'twas like to be sound, and he would put no pressure on her to accept it. 'My sons fight like Kilkenny cats,' she said, deciding to confide in him, 'my daughter is afraid her husband will be arrested for supporting rioters, if you ever heard of anything so ridiculous, and my cousins are like to be homeless in a month or two, if what they say is to be believed. And if that en't enough, trade is down for the fourth month in succession.'

'Trouble enough in all conscience,' he said, lighting his pipe. 'Which' — puff — 'is the most serious' — puff — 'would 'ee say?'

She lifted her muff from the back of the chair where she'd flung it when she first came in and took Annie's letter out of the pocket. 'If my son-in-law is like to be arrested then this is the matter of most urgency,' she said, handing it across to him. ''Tis from my daughter, Annie. Pray read it. She says there is a Hampden Club meets at the rectory every Thursday, and now some of 'em mean to fire a barn, and James, her husband, knows of it and cannot dissuade 'em.'

He read attentively. 'Write back and advise her that giving house-room to such meetings is perfectly legal. It may not remain so should the present administration alter the statutes, but for the present there is no harm in it. Howsomever the matter of firing barns would be construed as riot, and your daughter and her husband would both be well advised to have no cognisance of it, however much they might sympathise with the perpetrators.'

'The papers are full of riots,' Nan said. 'Scarce a day goes by without a machine being broke or a rick fired or somesuch. But 'tis no wonder they break the law when 'tis the law keeps the price of corn so high. What else is there for them to do?'

'We shall have that particular law repealed eventually,' he promised, 'when my cousin and his colleagues prevail. Meantime I would strongly advise you to write some sort of warning to your daughter.'

''Twill be done,' she said. ''Tis sound advice.'

He nodded, puffing his pipe. 'There are other problems which concern you, are there not?'

But sitting there in his comfortable armchair with good food to sustain her and a good fire to warm her, she had been quietly solving some of those for herself. 'I know what is to be done about the homeless relations,' she said.

'And your warring sons?'

'As to them,' she said, 'they will have cooled by now.'

'Why do they fight?' he asked mildly.

'Because they are in love and not married, I daresay.'

'So 'twill amend with time and opportunity.'

How worldly wise he is, she thought. 'Aye,' she smiled.

'I would the same might be said of my own case.'

'How so?' she asked, noticing the affection of his smile and wondering.

'You are an uncommon difficult lady to pay court to, my dear. I might almost say impossible.'

'How so?' she asked again, pleased by the turn their conversation had taken. 'I do not discourage you, I think.'

He puffed at his pipe for a few seconds before he answered, drawing in smoke and thoughts together. ''Tis your situation which presents the difficulty,' he confessed. 'Were you not who you are, I could court you, if not with any particular hope of success, then at least without fear of misinterpretation. But since you are a woman of power and wealth, and renowned power and wealth I may say, then I fear there are many who would condemn me as a fortune hunter were I to advance but one step in your direction.'

'Correct me if I misremember,' she said, grinning at him, 'but was it not once your opinion that you and I were to be above such things?'

'Aye so 'twas,' he said, rather ruefully, 'howsomever if I were to propose marriage to a lady in your position...'

'Or even to me,' she laughed, 'or en't that within the realms of supposition?'

'Or even to you, my dear,' he agreed. 'Well then, what

follows? Should you return my affection and agree to marry me, which would be a great happiness to me, I need hardly tell 'ee, I should then become the legal custodian of all your wealth and influence, and on the very day, what's more, when I should be bestowing all *my* worldly goods on *you*. And that, I need hardly tell 'ee, would be a very considerable unhappiness to me, for 'twould not be any part of my intention.'

She understood this situation very well, for hadn't her sons warned her about it when she was wondering whether or not to marry Calverley Leigh? 'Aye,' she said. 'I know it.'

'So, like your sons, for whom I have considerable fellow feeling, I may say, I too love and do not marry.'

'There are those,' she said, smiling encouragement at him, 'who would find another way. 'Tis not one I would recommend to my children, you understand...'

'Yes,' he said. 'That solution had suggested itself to me, I must confess, but since it is less honourable than the first, I have hesitated to suggest it until now, for fear of total and deserved rebuff.'

She looked at him for a very long time, while he sucked his pipe and smiled at her. 'I will consider it,' she said eventually, and smiled at him, thinking, that's your cue to kiss me, Frederick Brougham.

But he made no move towards her at all, and his face was far too calm. 'If I do accept you,' she warned, disappointed by his lack of response, ''twill be on my terms.'

'Agreed,' he said, watching her quietly in the flickering light of the fire.

'Whatever they are?'

'Since they are your terms, they are like to be sound and sensible, and that being so, acceptable.'

'I should continue to maintain my own home,' she said. 'I should not live with 'ee.'

'Agreed,' he said, 'with one proviso.'

'Name it,' she said, and it occurred to her that they were discussing this matter as though they were arguing over business terms, and she wasn't sure whether she was pleased or annoyed by the knowledge.

'That you will host my dinner parties and use my home as though it were your own, which it would be, were things other than they are.'

'Agreed.'

'Then perhaps I may hope for an early reply?'

'If you seal our bargain with a kiss,' she said lightly, 'you may have your answer now.'

'Do you tease for kisses, Mrs Easter?'

'No, nor beg for 'em neither.'

'I am glad to hear it,' he said, 'since this is not a matter to be rushed or entered upon lightly. I think too highly of you for that.'

'You play the lawyer even in this, I see,' she teased.

'Particularly in this,' he said seriously, 'since it is a matter of greatest import to us both.'

His extreme care touched her, despite her irritation at his lack of response. 'It grows late,' she said, 'so you may have your answer now. 'Tis time for you to escort me home, I think, and as I don't intend to go back to John and Billy and their squit, you'd best escort me to Bedford Row, had you not? And if we are both still of the same mind by tomorrow morning you shall take me to the play at Drury Lane, a' Thursday. Sophie tells me 'tis an excellent comedy.'

'I should warn you,' he said, 'I have to travel to Lewes tomorrow afternoon for the quarter sessions. We shall have very little time together.'

'Then we'd best not waste a minute,' she grinned at him.

'I am yours to command,' he said and he put down his pipe and kissed her at last.

And very pleasant it was, being soft and leisurely and with just the right amount of ardour. And he apologised for it. 'I am out of practice, I fear.'

'I'm uncommon glad to hear it,' she said, 'for I would not welcome competition.'

'My peerless Nan,' he said, holding her handsome face between his hands. 'Then perhaps you will allow me to put the old adage to the proof.'

'Which old adage, pray?'

'That practice makes perfect.'

JOHN WAS UP and out of the house the next morning long before Frederick drove her home, and the place was blessedly quiet. She was in such an excellent humour that the previous evening's squabble seemed petty and ridiculous. To be loved again and loved so skilfully was not only unexpected but uncommon rewarding. He was a man of surprising talents, this third love of hers. Who would have thought there would be so much passion hidden under such apparent reserve?

Billy came down to join her at breakfast with an obvious hangover. He was bleary eyed and unshaven and humbly apologetic for the scene he had made.

'You're a blamed fool,' she told him cheerfully.

''Tis Tilda,' he confessed. 'She says she won't marry me if Johnnie marries Miss Sowerby.'

'Young girls say such things,' she said calmly. 'They don't mean it. You'll see.'

He was comforted but doubtful. 'She's uncommon angry. She said Miss Sowerby was a servant.'

'Then you tell her she en't.'

'I did,' he said, sighing heavily. ''Tweren't a bit of use.'

'We will give a grand party and invite her to it and see if we can change her mind.'

That sounded possible, for there was nothing Tilda enjoyed so much as a grand party. 'If they meet and talk at a party that might… Yes. Oh yes. 'Tis a fine idea. Thank 'ee, Mama.'

'Think yourself lucky I'm such a good mother to 'ee,' she said.

And he agreed that she was and went off to work forgiven if not restored.

But it was John she really wanted to see, and John was keeping out of everybody's way. He contrived to be visiting shops in Essex all through the day and he dined out that evening and was gone in the morning before she was awake. She didn't see him until Thursday evening when she was waiting for Mr Brougham to collect her in his carriage, and then they met by accident.

She was in the study checking the day's figures when he suddenly opened the door.

'Ah!' he said, embarrassed to have found her there. 'I — um — I…'

'You were absolutely right about that wretch Sir Osmond,' she said, closing her account book at once and plunging straight into the conversation. ''Tis a cruel crittur as you knew, did 'ee not?'

She could see he was pleased although he was keeping his expression well under control. 'I did, Mama.'

'He means to marry again, as we suspected,' Nan said, 'and, what's a deal worse, he means to throw his two poor old cousins out into the street, just to make room for his new in-laws, if you ever heard of anything so scandalous.'

'I told you so,' he said, with considerable satisfaction, and then, since she was watching him and obviously expected him to say something else, 'What will become of 'em?' It was possible to feel a flicker of compassion for the poor old things, for they were harmless enough in all conscience, even if they *were* Easters.

'I shall see to it that he gives 'em an adequate annuity and then I shall advise 'em how to set up in business, so I shall.'

That made him smile. 'What possible business could it be, Mama? Two timid old ladies like that. They ain't Nan Easters, neither one of 'em.'

'They can take in lodgers,' she said.

'Will they want to?' he asked, amused at her determination.

'I don't see why not,' she said. 'With a good cook and sufficient maids, what could be simpler? Ah, there's Mr Brougham.' For she could hear the carriage drawing up outside.

'I am sorry I was so churlish,' John said. 'I did not mean to offend you.'

'All is forgiven,' she told him, picking up her gloves. 'I've a mind to ask the two ladies to visit here for a day or two, as Sir Osmond treats them so unkindly. They might care to see how another kinder branch of the Easter family can behave. We could give a party and your Harriet could come. How would that be, think 'ee?'

'It might well be a good idea,' he said, cautiously. As they were victims, just as his mother had been, it might be possible to accept them, Easters or no. And if their visit proved difficult, he could always go to Rattlesden and see Harriet.

'I will write tomorrow,' she said, dusting her gloved hands against each other, swish, swish. And she went happily off to meet her lover.

FIVE DAYS LATER, Mr and Mrs Honeywood arrived at Bedford Square to call upon Mrs Easter. They were considerably agitated, for their dear daughter Matilda had hinted that there might not be a wedding after all.

'A lovers' tiff,' Nan said practically, when she'd served them tea. 'My Annie was just the same. She will come round to a different view in a day or two, depend upon 't.'

'She ain't changed her tune for more than a week, Mrs Easter,' Mr Honeywood said, shaking his jowls. 'There's no sense in the girl. She'll snap off your head as soon as look at you.'

"Tis hard to know what is to be done for the best,' Mrs Honeywood worried. 'Is William of the same mind, think 'ee?'

'William would marry tomorrow,' Nan assured them. 'I never saw a young man so enamoured. You need have no fear from that quarter.'

'Then what should we do?' Mrs Honeywood said. 'Is a wedding to be arranged or ain't it? That's what I need to know.'

'I've a mind to hold a party in November, a rout on Guy Fawkes' Day, with fireworks and such,' Nan said. "Twould be principally for my sons and their friends, you understand, howsomever two of Sir Osmond's cousins are coming to London to stay with us, and Mr Frederick Brougham is to attend. He is cousin to Lord Brougham, as I daresay you know, and a most cultivated gentleman. I do hope you will be able to bring Matilda to it. 'Twould be a chance for her to meet the Easter cousins and others of our friends, and she would doubtless enjoy the rout.'

The mention of the Easter cousins and Frederick Brougham's aristocratic connections appeased them and, Nan hoped, would appease their daughter too. 'Tis all snobbery with this family, she thought, so that is what I shall work upon. I will dress young Harriet in the latest style and persuade Mr Brougham to make much of her and then we shall see. It was high time Matilda saw sense and her two foolish sons settled their unnecessary differences.

But her plans were wrecked, and by Annie of all people.

We would dearly love to come to London and attend the rout,' she wrote, 'but we have promised to care for Mr Abbott's children until the end of the month, which takes a deal of work as you can *understand, which being so, we could hardly leave them for poor Mrs Chiddum, when she has such very bad rheumatics. Harriet begs to be excused too and I would be loath to urge her to attend since she is uncommon helpful in a house so full of children. Please give my kind regards to Cousin Thomasina and Cousin Evelina and pray tell them we look forward to seeing them at Johnnie's wedding.*

With fondest love to you and Billy and Johnnie.

IT WAS UNCOMMON AGGRAVATING, particularly as all her other guests had accepted her invitation almost by return of post, and the two Miss Callbecks had written to say they would be most happy to attend.

'People are uncommon difficult,' she complained to Frederick as they set out to the Theatre Royal that evening.

'Indeed they are, I am very glad to say,' he said, handing her into his carriage, 'since the practice of law depends upon it.'

'You will come to my party, will you not?'

'I give you my word. When do your cousins arrive?'

'Tomorrow.'

'Then I wish you success in your endeavours,' he said, 'although I could wish that you had fewer people in your house to demand your time and attention.'

NAN WAS surprised by how much the two Miss Callbecks had aged in the six years since Annie's wedding. They looked like little old ladies, in their old-fashioned faded gowns and those odd day-caps they would wear, and very worried ladies at that. But she made them welcome and settled them into their rooms and assured them that she had found a solution to their present troubles and would tell them of it when everything was arranged and that in the meantime they were to forget Sir Osmond and simply enjoy the party, which they promised they would do.

And despite his uncompromising view of the Easter family, John was actually quite kind to them. In fact at breakfast the next morning, when Thomasina took a pair of spectacles from her reticule in order to read Annie's letter, Nan caught him looking at his aunt with a transparent, almost tender, pity. And no bad thing, she thought, for pity brought out the best side of his character.

So the first evening's dinner went well, even without Annie and James and Harriet. The aunts made a good meal and Frederick Brougham made an excellent host; Ebenezer Millhouse cracked jokes for the table and walnuts for Mrs Fuseli; John sat as far away from Lizzie Moffat as he could and Jerry Ottenshaw as close to Maria; and Billy and Matilda seemed to be in high good humour and spent the meal slapping one another and laughing at everything and everybody.

But it hadn't solved the problem it had been organised to deal with.

'Daughters-in-law,' Nan said to Sophie as they walked slowly upstairs to the drawing room after the meal, 'are a deal more bother than they're worth. How am I to bring my two together when one won't see reason and the other won't travel?'

'The two you should bring together, my dear,' Sophie said sagely, 'are Matilda and Billy, for if ever I saw a couple starved for love…'

'You think that too?' Nan said, giving her old friend a shrewd look.

'They are lovers already, if I am any judge,' Sophie said, 'and they lack opportunity. All eyes and hands, my dear. She slaps him for every other word, and that's a sure sign of desire thwarted.'

'So I should play pander?' Nan laughed. 'Is that what you suggest? Shame upon you, Sophie!'

''Twould do no harm,' Sophie said easily, 'discreetly done.'

'Times change,' Nan said. 'Folk don't take lovers so free as they did when we were young.'

'Aye,' Sophie said. 'We grow Puritanical, more's the pity. How is that charming Mr Brougham of yours?'

'I will consider what you say,' Nan said, grinning at her friend as they reached the drawing room door.

'In which case, pray?'

'Ah! That would be telling.'

IT WAS EASILY DONE, for the pretty Miss Honeywood had a bedroom to herself and only needed a key to achieve complete privacy. It was delivered later that evening as Matilda's maid was preparing her young mistress for bed.

'With a house so full of people,' Nan said casually as she handed it over, 'you may find the need to be alone from time to time.'

Matilda's grey eyes widened in amazement. 'Why, thank 'ee, Mrs Easter ma'am,' she said. ''Tis uncommon kind.'

Nan grinned at her. 'The Misses Callbeck tell me they mean to lock 'emselves away and sleep for an hour or two every afternoon, that being their custom. I have promised they will not be disturbed, for I like my guests to be comfortable. Good night to 'ee, my dear. Sleep well.'

And she went off to her own room at once, well pleased with her manoeuvre.

'Do 'ee think she meant for us to spend the night together?' Matilda asked when she'd dismissed her maid and she and Billy had come tiptoeing back to her room.

'I daresay,' he said amorously, between kisses.

'Mama would take a fit if she knew of it.'

'Why are we talking?'

Why indeed. 'Oh!' she asked. 'Kiss me, do. I starve for kisses.'

AND SO THE house party continued and was adjudged a great success by all the participants, even though Frederick declined Nan's invitation to stay the night, saying that he would not wish to embarrass her before her guests. John and Billy went off to work in the small hours as usual, but they both made a point of returning for breakfast, which rapidly became a noisy family meal. By the fifth and penultimate morning the two Miss Callbecks were declaring that they hadn't spent such a happy time in anybody's company for years and years.

'Not that there is ever very much company at Ippark,' Evelina said. 'We tend to be rather — well — lonely there.'

'I mean to travel to Bury on Saturday,' John told them, 'to see my future wife, who is staying with Annie and Mr Hopkins.' And he added unexpectedly, 'Perhaps you would care to accompany me, there being no need for you to return to Ippark just yet awhile?'

Well, well, well, Nan thought. What acquaintance can achieve! But she shot a quick look in Billy's direction, just in case the news had annoyed him. He was happily feeding Matilda with the choicest cuts of steak from his own plate, and to his mother's delight he offered no resistance or comment. And what was more, and better, neither did Matilda.

'A capital idea,' Nan said to John.

'Is it not?' Evelina said. 'I would so like to meet your young lady, John my dear. We both would, now that we have met our dear Matilda, whose wedding is to be in June so she tells us. Is that not so, Matilda?'

And it appeared that it was. Praise love for it!

'Then we must find a home for you as soon as we can,' Nan said. 'Johnnie favours a house in Fitzroy Square, I know. Where would you prefer, my dear?'

'There are some capital houses a-being built in a brand-new square just north of here,' Matilda said happily. ''Tis to be called Torrington Square I believe, ain't it, Billy?'

Billy agreed that it was and seemed amiably content to live there.

'We will inspect them this very afternoon,' Nan said.

'I HAVE ACHIEVED a great deal in a short time,' Nan said to Frederick Brougham during one of the less raucous moments of the rout.

'Are all your troubles over?' he asked, sidestepping away from a swirling couple.

'I would never make so bold as to claim that,' she laughed. 'Howsomever we move in the right direction. The weddings are arranged and the invitations sent, and I shall take out a lease on a house in Fitzroy Square for Johnnie and Harriet, and Billy and Matilda are to choose one of the new houses in Torrington Square, providing 'tis built in time for the wedding, and Johnnie is to find a property in Bury for the cousins, so that they can earn their keep a-taking in lodgers, which they've agreed to do. We move in the right direction.'

'I am glad to hear it,' he said, 'for perhaps when your children are all married and settled you will have a little time for me.'

'Fie upon you!' she teased, taking his arm. 'When I have danced three whole measures with you this very evening.'

'Ah, indeed you have. I am greatly honoured. Notwithstanding that, we must spend another night apart, must we not?'

'I fear so,' she said. 'Would it were otherwise. But we are busy people, you and I. 'Twill be all the sweeter for waiting.'

'Do you promise me?' he teased.

'Indeed I do.'

'I have to be in Aylesbury on Thursday. How if you were to accompany me there?

''Tis an uncommon good idea, so 'tis, I could start negotiations for a shop and reading room.'

He laughed aloud. 'And I was fool enough to think that the pleasure of my company would be sufficient to tempt you to the town. Hey ho!'

CHAPTER 18

John was none too pleased when he heard that his mother had gone haring off to Aylesbury to open a shop and a reading room. He'd been planning to open up all the routes to Birmingham as soon as he'd finished work on the Oxford road, and now he would have to take time away from what he was doing to organise delivery to this solitary venture of hers.

''Twill mean a special run,' he said to her, rather crossly. 'There ain't another shop on the route.'

'Something you'll amend before long, I daresay,' she said unabashed, dusting the palms of her hands against each other in that infuriating way of hers. 'I'm off home, my dear. Shall I see you at dinner?'

'Tis all very well for her, John thought, as she swished out of his office. She don't have the job of arranging deliveries to all these unconnected shops she will keep buying.

Nevertheless, despite his mother's unpredictability and Matilda's snobbery and Billy's occasional and incomprehensible bad temper, John Henry Easter was happier than he'd ever been. For the first time in his life he had found another human being

243

with whom he felt perfectly at ease. Physically it was tantalising, of course, painfully tantalising sometimes, that had to be admitted, but there were such rewards: the pleasure of her quiet company on Sundays, the secret delights they shared whenever they were alone, her daily letters when he was in London, but best of all, oh much the best of all, the knowledge that he was loved, and loved without reservation. Not providing he worked well and said the right things and behaved himself and hid his deeper feelings, but totally and openly, just as he was. It was the sort of love he had ached for all his life and now, just when he'd least expected it and he wasn't trying to earn it, it was being given to him freely and in abundance. The old, insecure, teased Johnnie was gone. Now he was Harriet's John and full of confidence.

'You are so good, dear John!' Harriet would say, every time they parted. 'So good and so kind. You cannot imagine how much it means to me to be loved by you.'

And he would answer, 'Oh I can. I can. It is the same for me, my own dearest girl.'

They were blessed. That was how it was. Miraculously and abundantly blessed, so that difficulties could be weathered like the trivial matters they were, and everything else could be turned to their advantage. Even the fact that they were courting in winter.

From that very first morning in the church, the new responsible John Easter had made it quite clear both to her, and more importantly to himself, that his courtship would be completely proper. They would walk arm in well-clothed arm, and hold gloved hands, and from time to time, when passion was running very strongly, they would kiss, but he would go no further until they were man and wife. It was a difficult promise to keep, for the more frequently he saw her the more ardent his desire for her became, but on his third visit to Rattlesden he found a teasing game that made their self-imposed abstinence not only possible but rewarding.

They had walked out to the six cottages, well wrapped against the chill of the wind, he in beaver hat, greatcoat and muffler, she in heavy bonnet, pelisse and long black cloak. Despite the cold, they continued their walk along the track until they were out of sight of the rectory and the village and had reached a thick holm oak where they stopped to kiss and murmur.

'If we were married,' he said longingly, 'do you know what I would do?'

'No, John dear, what would you do?'

'I would unfasten the top three buttons on your pelisse and kiss your throat.'

To hear such a thing made her breathless with anticipated pleasure.

'Would you?'

'I would. I would.'

'Oh how I wish we were married!'

'So do I!' he said, emboldened by her tremulous response, 'And then I would unfasten the next button and kiss you here.' Touching her breast most delicately with the tip of one finger. 'Would you allow it?'

'Oh yes,' she said breathlessly, 'for 'twould not be a sin, would it, dear John, not if we were married.'

'No, my dearest. Nothing that married people do is ever a sin. We shall be snug and warm in our own bed and may do as we please. Oh if only April weren't quite so far away.'

BUT IN THE MEANTIME, they could at least imagine their forbidden pleasures, and imagine them they did, in greater and more lingering detail, sometimes from the mouth down and sometimes from the ankle up, but always until they were aching with desire. It was a delicious game, a 'way round' that Harriet understood and entirely approved of, marvellously pleasurable and yet without risk, and with an opening gambit that either of them could use whenever they wished and had the privacy for it. 'If we were married what would you do?' It sustained them all through the long, dark months of the winter, when they 'walked out' in sleet and hail, and biting wind, and the occasional flurry of snow. And the cold was their guardian angel, putting several very necessary layers of cloth between their ardent bodies and making it quite impossible for any of it to be removed.

In the middle of December the lease of their house in Fitzroy Square was finally purchased and the place was vacated and ready for their inspection and possession. Nan sent a letter to Harriet telling her all about it and inviting her to Bedford Square for Christmas.

I will inspect the house on Wednesday next, she wrote, *and then you and John shall see it so soon as you arrive. After Christmas we will choose carpets and curtains and suchlike. 'Tis an uncommon fine house.*

Harriet didn't doubt it, and the thought that she was going to choose 'carpets and curtains and suchlike' thrilled her but alarmed her a little too. It would be marvellous to be able to furnish a house entirely to her liking, but what if she chose the wrong things? And how was she going to run a large London house? She knew nothing about such matters. Still at least she would be travelling to the capital for the first time with Annie and Pollyanna and the children, and Annie would be sure to help her.

It was a long cold journey and London was every bit as noisy and crowded as she'd imagined, with its narrow streets thronged with carts and cabs and coaches and pungent with trodden horse-dung, and people rushing about and running between the wheels, or standing weighed down with baskets and trays, or lurking behind rickety stalls and trestles selling things — combs and dog-collars and nutmeg graters, oysters and spices and baked potatoes, tracts and pamphlets and song-sheets — and huddled at every corner hordes of the most tattered and evil-smelling beggars shivering and shouting. Her heart contracted with pity for them. How dreadful it must be to be so poor and so terribly needy. But before she could find a coin to give them, Annie had hired a cab and they were all climbing into it.

'Travel is always wearisome,' Annie said comfortingly when they were settled. 'But we are nearly there.'

And how impressive 'there' was. The Easter house in Bury was a fine building, but this one in Bedford Square was like a palace, with its fluted columns and that imposing pediment and rows and rows of tall windows facing the public gardens. It made Harriet feel gauche and awkward simply to step inside. There were so many rooms and all of them sumptuously carpeted and furnished in the latest style and warmed by great coal fires, and so many servants to carry their luggage and bring them hot water and warm towels and scented soap so that they could wash after their journey, and pervading everything the most mouth-watering smell of roast beef and roast potatoes drifting up from the kitchens. She was overwhelmed by it.

'I had not realised such houses existed,' she whispered to John when she had washed and tidied and had crept downstairs to tiptoe shyly into the front parlour where he was waiting for her. 'Is our house to be as big as this? I do hope not.'

'Our house,' he said, 'is modest and proper, just like us.' He couldn't wait for her to see it. Their own home. Their very own home. 'The carriage is ordered for ten o'clock tomorrow morning, as soon as I get back from the stamping.'

'But tomorrow is Christmas Eve.'

'Yes,' he said happily.

'Do you work on Christmas Eve?'

'I work virtually every day of the year,' he said proudly, 'since papers are printed virtually every day of the year. Our honeymoon week will be the longest I have stayed away from work since I first began and that was more than ten years ago, when I was thirteen. Oh yes, I work every day of the year.'

'But not on Sundays,' she said. 'You are in Rattlesden on Sundays. You do not work then.'

'That is because I come to Rattlesden to see you, my love. If I were in London on Sundays I should work then.'

'Ah, there you are!' Nan said, brisking into the room. 'Are you settled in, my dear? Good! Dinner will be served in three minutes.'

It will be a very different sort of life here in this city, Harriet thought, as she followed her dear John to the dining room. I do hope he doesn't really mean he'll be working all hours the way he says.

But at least he took time away from his office to drive her to see her future home the next afternoon. And she was delighted with it, for Fitzroy Square was considerably smaller and neater than the great wooded park that faced Nan Easter's palace, and the house was considerably more homely. It stood in the centre of a long, straight, quiet terrace, and was stuccoed a pleasant creamy-white like all the others, three neat storeys high with its roof discreetly hidden behind a parapet, and its front door unobtrusive below a quiet semi-circular fanlight that exactly matched the curves of the two venetian windows alongside it. A house that would simply contain them, she thought, without wanting to impress anybody. He had made a good choice, her dear John.

Even so it was bigger than anything she'd ever been used to. She inspected the basement kitchen and the housekeeper's parlour and the butler's pantry, and walked up the beautiful oak staircase, and admired the drawing room with its decorated ceiling and the dining room with its marble fireplace, and trembled in the master bedroom that overlooked the square and was awed because the dressing room attached to it was bigger than her parents' parlour.

'What do 'ee think?' John asked.

'I think it is beautiful,' she said. 'How well this room would look with red curtains and a red counterpane.' At present the walls were white and white walls reminded her of the cold little cell she'd slept in at Bury.

'When Christmas is over,' he promised, 'we will hire a housekeeper and have the decorators in. You shall have your red room as soon as it can be arranged.'

'Our red room,' she corrected rapturously.

'Our red room,' he agreed, and kissed her to prove it.

In the meantime there were Christmas celebrations to enjoy. And they started as soon as she and John got back to Bedford Square. That evening they all went to the play with a gentleman called Mr Brougham who seemed to know John and Billy uncommon well and said he was charmed to make her acquaintance. And the next morning they were up early to go to church and when they got back the household was busy with arrivals, as the family and their friends gathered for Christmas dinner.

Miss Pettie was the first to arrive, flushed and dishevelled with Jane fussily attentive. She had no sooner been settled when Billy came home in the Honeywood carriage with Matilda, who was sporting a magnificent red coat, heavily trimmed in thick dark fur with a large fur bonnet on her head and an equally large fur muff laid across her lap like an otter. Her arrival caused a stir, as she'd fully intended it should because if she was going to share a Christmas party with that low-born Harriet Sowerby she meant to be the cynosure of all eyes there.

And then just before the meal was due to be served, and it was already quite dark, the two Miss Callbecks drove quietly up to the door and James arrived in a flyer and was greeted with much excitement by his family. By the time they were all finally seated there was so much rapid talk about the table that it made Harriet's head spin to hear it.

Nan and John described the new house in Fitzroy Square while Billy carved the goose and the vegetables were being passed and served, and then Matilda made it her business to entertain them all with a witty tale about how slow and infuriating the builders were being over *her* house in Torrington Square and, not to be outdone, Miss Pettie, now flushed with port wine, embarked upon a lurid story about a riot in Gedding where a threshing machine and a mole plough had been 'smashed to fragments, my dears, to positive fragments', and four rioters had had their heads broken 'like eggs'. And Annie said it was all quite true and perfectly dreadful but what else could they do, poor things?

'Smashing machines won't make work for 'em, surely?' Matilda said, tossing her curls at Billy.

'According to their logic it will, Miss Honeywood,' James explained. 'Without a machine, you see, threshing requires a deal of labour. And work is precisely what these men lack.'

'They are so poor, Matilda, that they starve,' Annie said, defending her husband's parishioners stoutly. 'I cannot see what is to become of them. Last year's harvest was so bad that the farmers in Rattlesden were laying off labourers even before it was over. We give out loaves and soup of a Friday evening and for some it is the only dependable meal they have all week long.'

'Do they imagine that the farmer won't repair his machine, foolish creatures that they are?' Matilda said. 'They cannot un-invent 'em, though I daresay they'd like to. The servant class are all the same. They want everything done for 'em.' She was parroting her father's views as she usually did, and without much thought, flirting her grey eyes at Billy.

'How if I were to tell 'ee that I was a servant once?' Nan Easter said.

It would have been hard to tell which of her two future daughters-in-law was the more surprised.

'I'd not believe it,' Matilda said, her eyes like saucers. A servant? Not the great Nan Easter, surely.

Her discomfiture was so obvious that Nan laughed out loud at her. ''Tis true,' she said. 'I started work as a scullery maid when I was nine years old. There en't a thing goes on below stairs what I don't know about from personal experience.'

What an extraordinary woman she is, Harriet thought, lost in admiration at such a revelation, to have come so far and from so very little.

'Why then you must have been an uncommon servant, that's all I can say,' Matilda said, recovering a little, and trying a hesitant and placatory smile. 'A most uncommon servant.'

'Aye,' Billy said, grinning at his mother, 'so she was. And an uncommon mother. And an uncommon boss.'

'I think so too, Nanna,' little Jimmy said, gazing at his grandmother earnestly with his spoon halfway to his mouth.

'What do 'ee think too, lambkin?' Nan said.

'That you are an uncommon Nanna.'

'Quite right,' Nan approved. 'Have some more goose.'

AFTER THE MEAL they all retired to the drawing room together since this seemed to be the established custom, and a wooden box full of bright parcels was carried into the room by the two grooms, who were then released to their own Christmas dinner below stairs. And the ceremony of the presents began, with Jimmy and Beau acting as postmen, with a little encouragement from their mother.

Harriet had never been given a Christmas present in her life, so this was a revelation. There were gifts for everybody. 'She must have spent a fortune,' she whispered to John, who was sitting beside her on one of the four sofas.

'She always does,' he whispered back. 'She loves it. Christmas wouldn't be Christmas if she didn't give us all a present.'

And Harriet's was a gold cross set with seed pearls. 'Which would look well with a wedding dress, my dear, don't 'ee think?'

'I don't know how to thank you,' Harriet said, feeling spoilt and honoured. What an amazing family this was! And how freely they spent their money.

'Now then, Beau,' Nan said to her toddling grandson, 'this is for Matilda. Carry it carefully.'

And it was another cross, this time set with square-cut amethysts which were considerably more expensive than seed pearls and very fashionable. It was a fitting gift for the modish Miss Honeywood, and as it made a perfect foil for the lilac gown she was wearing, she insisted that Billy fasten it about her neck immediately, which he did with lingering attention.

Uncommon clever, John thought, for his mother had given each girl exactly the right sort of jewel to fit her nature.

'You are *so* generous Mrs Easter,' Matilda said, kissing Nan. ''Tis the prettiest cross I ever saw. I shall wear it on my honeymoon, which is like to prove a deal longer than a month. Oh yes, indeed, a great deal longer. Papa has promised to send us upon a tour of the Continent.'

It was said with splendidly casual aplomb and of course it had an immediate and dramatic effect, just as she'd intended it to.

'But my dear!' Miss Pettie said, clutching both sets of curls with amazement. 'How thrilling!'

And Thomasina asked, 'How long will you be away?'

And Evelina, 'Where will you go?'

And Billy tried to reassure his mother that he wouldn't go anywhere unless he could be spared.

'Go and enjoy it,' Nan said, grinning at him. 'You'll not get another such chance.'

So Matilda was able to tell them all about it, which she did in happy detail. 'We shall be away until November,' she said, 'for we mean to visit France, and there is a deal to see in France, Paris and Versailles of course, and the antiquities of the south, and then we shall travel through Switzerland to see the mountains, which are supposed to be sublime, and then on into Italy to see Rome and Turin, and then on to Venice, I believe, by way of Milan, Bergamo, Brescia, Verona' — checking them off on her fingers — 'and Vicenza, to see the works of Palladio, which Papa says we must not miss, and Florence, if we have time. Oh 'twill be a wondrous tour.'

John was rather annoyed by her display. She is trying to put our noses out of joint with all this, he thought, glancing at Harriet, and Billy should stop her. But Billy was looking like a cat that had stolen the cream and everybody else except his mother was cooing and exclaiming with wonder. And Harriet looked stunned. Her lips were parted and her eyes quite round, like they'd been when Mama told them all she'd started off as a servant. While all attention was focused on Matilda, he reached for her hand and held it to comfort her. But news of such a splendid honeymoon had made him feel that he ought to have planned something similar and the feeling intensified when Evelina turned towards him and asked where he and Harriet were going on their wedding trip.

'Ah well, Cousin Evelina,' he said stiffly. 'As to that, 'tis a secret, so it is.' And he was annoyed to feel himself blushing.

''Twill be romantic, I'm sure, wherever it is,' Miss Pettie said, trying to be helpful. And failing, for he blushed more than ever.

'And what have we here?' Nan said, plunging her arm into the box to retrieve another present, and rescue them. 'Why I do believe 'tis a present for you, Beau. Open it carefully, lambkin. Let Mama untie the string.'

After the presents had all been distributed, and Pollyanna had taken the boys off to bed, the card tables were set up and the company discreetly divided, James and Annie and John and

Harriet at one table, Nan and Miss Pettie at a second, and the two aunts with Billy and Matilda at the third. And so the rest of the evening passed pleasantly enough, with plentiful supplies of port wine and brandy.

By the time the clock struck midnight they were all in a very cheerful mood and made their way up Nan's splendid staircase stumbling together, Miss Pettie and the two Miss Callbecks giggling and Billy and Matilda amorously arm in arm. Then there was considerable noise and activity as servants were rung for and warming pans were removed from beds and fires were dampened and clothes folded away.

Harriet was rather embarrassed to be the recipient of so much attention and sent her particular maid away as soon as she'd been helped out of her gown, but that turned out to be a foolish decision, for the unaccustomed wine had made her extremely thirsty and she'd forgotten to ask for any drinking water. She knew that Miss Pettie was in the room at the end of the landing, so she picked up her carafe and crept out of her firelit room into the darkness to tiptoe down and ask her whether she would be kind enough to let her have a glassful.

And there was a lighted candle approaching her, held by a man's hand, a strong hand, covered in fine fair hairs. She could see them quite plainly from where she stood. She shrank back into her doorway at once, but she went on watching, fascinated and fearful, wanting to see who it was and where he was going. And as her eyes grew accustomed to the darkness, she recognised that it was Billy and that he was walking boldly into Matilda's bedroom. And Matilda's plump white arms came snaking out of the door and wound themselves around his neck and drew him into the room. And Matilda's voice was murmuring endearments and the door was being locked behind them. Locked!

Harriet was so shocked she forgot all about her need for water. They are lovers, she thought. Here in this house, and before they are married. How dreadful! She crept back into her room and climbed into bed as more uncomfortable questions niggled into her mind. Did Mrs Easter know what was going on? And if she didn't should she be told? What would her dear John think about it? Ought she to mention it to him? Perhaps not, for it would be a difficult thing to talk about, even to him. Oh dear, oh dear. What a dreadful thing to have seen!

She slept fitfully, plagued by thirst and waking from time to time to ponder the questions all over again, but when morning came and a servant brought her a cup of hot chocolate 'to revive her' she was still no nearer any solutions. And Billy and Matilda were both as bold as brass at breakfast. There wasn't the slightest sign of shame in either of them. These Easters truly were extraordinary people.

She worried about it all through the morning, while Nan and her sons were out at their work and finally, she plucked up courage to tell Annie what she had seen. They were taking the two boys for an afternoon promenade around the gardens and were well away from any possibility of being overheard. To her amazement Annie wasn't even surprised.

'Yes,' she said, 'I rather imagined that was how things were. The signs are all there.'

This was intriguing. What signs? Harriet wondered, and wished she were brave enough to ask. Were there marks upon you afterwards when you behaved like that? She was quite glad John had arranged for that secret honeymoon, even if it wasn't a tour of the Continent. 'Does Mrs Easter know?' she said.

'I daresay she does,' Annie said. 'There is little occurs in this house that she does not know about.'

'Then she will stop it, will she not?' It was a relief to know that it wouldn't be necessary to tell her.

'I don't think so, Harriet.'

'But it is sinful, surely?'

'In our eyes,' Annie said, 'yes, it is. Howsomever Mama has a different view of such things.'

Now, and a little late in the conversation, Harriet remembered that Mrs Easter had had a lover, and the memory of them driving about Bury in their fine carriage suddenly filled her mind, complete in every detail, so that she blushed and dropped her head, feeling confused. But what Annie said next was even more disturbing.

'I must say, 'tis easy to understand why she should, my dear, for of all the sins this is the least harmful, surely.'

The idea of a sin being praised was so extraordinary it made Harriet's mouth fall open. 'But a sin...' she said.

''Twas the sin our dear Lord forgave most readily,' Annie said, 'and I cannot help thinking that must have been because He knew how often it is due to simple human weakness, and how often it springs from love, the self-same love that is blessed in marriage. "Let him who is without sin amongst you cast the first stone," He said, and that shows, does it not, that He expected the same love and the same sin to be present in all His hearers that day.'

'But that was the story of the woman taken in adultery,' Harriet faltered. 'Surely you do not condone adultery, Annie.'

'No,' Annie said seriously, 'but I endeavour to understand it. Mama had a lover for many years, you know, and try as I might I could never see any wrong in it. He was a charming man and uncommon kind to me and the boys. And now she has Mr Brougham, and a better man you couldn't find anywhere, you must admit. Come now, my dear, Billy and Tilda will be married in a few months and no real harm done. That you'll allow, I'm sure.'

But Harriet wasn't sure. 'She was so grand in her red coat,' she said, 'with her talk of a Continental tour and how stupid the poor are, and yet she behaves like the woman taken in adultery. What am I supposed to think?'

'Think kindly, my dear,' Annie advised. ''Tis always the best way. And if you can't think kindly, why, then don't think of it at all.'

It was sound advice and in the weeks that followed Harriet took it and acted upon it, although to start with she was being sensible as much by default as by anything else. The truth was she was too busy planning the decoration of her new home to have time to think about Matilda, buying new furniture, and matching curtains and carpets, and stocking her new kitchen with everything it could possibly need, from the first jar of salt to the last wooden spoon. She and John walked to Fitzroy Square every day, and every day brought a new pleasure, their bedroom a-glow, with red curtains at the window and a huge fire in the grate, their dining room completely furnished, very cool and elegant with its blue and white striped wallpaper and eight fine chairs set against the walls and the table polished until they could see their faces in it.

'We shall be so happy here,' she said, as they stood beside the drawing room window looking down at the quiet square below them.

'Soon,' he said, kissing her. 'Oh very soon now.'

CHAPTER 19

On John Easter's wedding day ominous notices appeared all over Bury St Edmunds. Nan saw one when she first looked out of her window that morning. It was pinned to the carved corner post of the chemist's shop on the corner of Abbeygate Street. When breakfast was over, she and Frederick walked across the square to see what it was.

April 29th Notice, it said,

> *Whereas disorderly assemblages of persons have taken place, and outrages have been committed in some parts of the division of Bury St Edmunds, the magistrates present at the above session do hereby signify their determination to take prompt and effectual measures and to bring to justice all persons who are found offending against the peace.*

> *And the magistrates will in their respective districts take such measures for strengthening the hands of civil power as shall seem necessary to preserve the peace therein.*

> *By order.*

'And what's the meaning of that?' she said

'They mean to call out the military to the next demonstration hereabouts,' Frederick told her. 'That is what it means.'

'In that case,' she said, 'let us hope they have no cause, at any rate not today or until after Johnnie's wedding.'

'Your sympathy for strikers is somewhat limited this morning, my dear,' Frederick teased. 'Correct me if I misremember, but do I not recall that you once expressed the sentiment that they had every right to protest?'

'I don't care what they do,' she said, 'nor where they do it, as you know right well, providing they don't go upsetting my family.' And she stamped her foot when he laughed at her. 'Especially with the weather so fine.'

And so it was: a beautiful spring day, with white clouds billowing like sails in the blue sky above the abbey walls and the smell of warm earth and green corn rising into the town from the surrounding fields.

'HAPPY THE BRIDE the sun shines on,' Annie said as she and Harriet walked out of the rectory on their way to church. The sunlight dappled down upon them between the branches of the yew so that Harriet's new blond gown and Annie's re-trimmed yellow one were spangled with shining discs of brightness. So slim and trim they were in their long straight gowns, and as pale and pretty as two spring flowers, with huge poke bonnets framing their faces like jonquils, and little green slippers already dew-stained on their feet and dark green stockings on ankles as slim as stems, holding their posies of spring flowers waist high so that the green ribbons they trailed lifted and winnowed in the morning breeze, like Annie's fringe of fair hair and the one straight silver tress that had flown free from the restraints of Harriet's modest topknot.

'I shall not disgrace him, shall I, Annie?' Harriet asked,

clutching her posy of flowers so nervously that the jonquils trembled above her fingers.

'You will be the dearest wife to him,' Annie comforted, 'and make him uncommon happy.'

But now that the moment had arrived, Harriet was anxious. What if her parents had found out about the wedding? They could be sitting in the church at this very minute, just waiting for her to appear. And what would happen then? Oh dear, oh dear, she thought, as they arrived at the south porch. Suddenly she couldn't be sure of anything. What if she was doing the wrong thing to marry him, after all?

But then they were inside the dear peaceful church and the world and the sunshine were left behind and Mr Teshmaker was waiting to walk her down the aisle. The light from the great east window was diffused and gently coloured, and in the midst of it her compassionate Christ gazed down upon her and upon her dear, dear John, who was standing at the altar rail glancing back over his shoulder to see if she'd arrived.

And all her worries melted away like the foolish things they were, and she walked happily down the little aisle towards her new life, with Mr Teshmaker gliding beside her. She was vaguely aware of Mrs Easter's fine clothes and of the children gazing at her in round-eyed awe. And then there was only John's face relaxing into a smile at the sight of her, and Mr Hopkins reaching down to take their hands.

'Dearly beloved, we are gathered together here in the sight of God, and in the face of this congregation, to join together this Man and this Woman in holy Matrimony; which is an honourable estate…

BACK IN BURY two hundred men were congregating in South-gate Street. Some of them carried sharpened sticks, and their leaders bore a red and white flag on which the legend 'Bread or

Blood' had been painted in letters every bit as ominous as the wording on the posters. They had marched in protest to the house of Mr Wales the hosier, who had bought one of the new spinning jennys and laid off most of his workforce in consequence, and now, as more and more men arrived to pack the narrow street, they were listening to Mr Henry Abbott of Rattlesden, who had organised the march.

'We got right on our side, don' 'ee forget, no matter how many men o' the militia them ol' mawthers do call out for to stop us,' he was saying. 'We don' ask for nothin' but what's our nat'rul birthright, when all's said an' done. Our nat'rul birthright to work for a livin'. Tha's all 'tis.'

They were mild sentiments, and reasonably expressed, but the growl of agreement that rose from the packed masses around him was terrible to hear.

In Manchester Mr Caleb Rawson was saying much the same thing to a meeting of Salford weavers. 'I say we should go to London, friends, as many on us as can mek the journey. We've the right to do it. We should go to London and sign t' petition, and gi' our support to Mr Hunt at t' meeting in the Spa Fields and show t' bosses we mean business.'

'What if t' bosses ignore us, Caleb?' another weaver asked. 'What then, eh?'

'Why, then we should march on Parliament, wi' pikestaffs if need be, and mek our meaning so plain to 'em they must tek it whether they will or no.'

'Eh lad, tha'rt a rare 'un,' the other weaver said.

Mr and Mrs John Henry Easter, having breakfasted with their friends and relations, drove to their honeymoon through the green cornfields, past woods hazy with bluebells and hedgerows blossoming with white cow parsley and purple vetch. Above their heads horse chestnuts carried their heavy blossom like carved candles, creamy-white against the luscious new green. It was nearly May Day.

'Where are we going, dear John?' Harriet asked, as the horses trotted the Easter carriage easily along the road to Scole. 'Shall you tell me now, or have I to wait until we arrive?'

''Tis a hidden place that no one has ever heard of,' he said, tucking her hand inside the crook of his arm.

'Is it far?'

It was a very long way, five coach journeys, in fact, and uncommon long journeys at that, even with loving talk and fine weather to sustain them. The afternoon was still balmy as they drove through the Vale of St Albans, but by the time they reached Oxford, where they stopped to dine, it was beginning to grow chill; the western sky was already more grey than blue and the ancient colleges looked stony and forbidding. But the meal refreshed them and the last lap of their journey, to a village called Witney, hardly took any time at all.

'There will be a carriage waiting for us somewhere here-abouts,' John said, as he helped her down from the coach outside the Crossed Keys Inn. But there was no sign of it and once the stage had gone trundling away taking its lanterns with it, the road was dark and empty. He was very annoyed, as she could see from the way he was squinting. But he remained calm and courteous, escorting her into the inn and ordering brandy and hot water for her, 'to keep you warm while you wait, my love, which I promise you will not be for long,' and then he went striding off along the dark street to find their promised vehicle.

It took him half an hour and considerable suppressed temper, which was not improved when he discovered that the groom he'd hired had driven the carriage to the far end of the village green and was waiting in the shadows beside the church.

'What possessed 'ee to wait in such an out-of-the-way place?' he asked in weary exasperation.

'I allus waits 'ere,' the boy said, looking very puzzled by the gentleman's annoyance. 'I thought you'd ha' know'd, sir. I allus waits 'ere. Right 'ere, right on this werry spot. I meant fer the best, sir.'

There is nothing to be served by getting angry with him, John told himself, for he is plainly a dolt who knows no better, and the longer we argue the longer my Harriet will have to wait. But it marred the journey for all that, and he'd planned it so meticulously, wanting it to be perfect for her. Sighing, he climbed into the little vehicle and ordered the dolt to drive him to the Crossed Keys, 'If you know where that is.'

And so the honeymooners arrived at last in their hidden village, but by now it was so dark that they could hardly see anything of it: a vague huddle of low cottages, a blackness of trees soughing and sighing, three candlelit windows among the sloping timbers of an inn. The night air was redolent with wood-smoke and farm manure and two owls were whooping to each other in the darkness.

There is a mill stream hard by, Harriet thought, as the boy held up his lantern to light her down from the carriage. She could hear the creak of great wheels and the water murmuring and splashing in unmistakable rhythm. I wonder where we are.

'Welcome to Minster Lovell, Mr Easter sir, Mrs Easter ma'am,' the landlord said, rolling darkly out of the candlelight to greet them. 'Thomas will take tha' luggage sir. I hopes 'ee made a pleasant journey.' And they were ushered into the inn.

They were in a wide, warm room with oak beams above their heads and rushes under their feet. There was a settle drawn up beside the huge log fire all ready for them to sit upon, with cushions for their backs and stools for their heels, and two pewter mugs steaming on the hob.

'Hot punch,' their landlord explained, 'for to send 'ee warm to tha' slumber, sir and madam, after such a long journey. Now whatsomever else you may require, sir and madam, say the word, that's all tha's to do and 'twill be in tha' hand soon as mentioned.' He was a very short man and extremely stout with a round red face, sparse sandy hair and very pale eyes, but what he lacked in stature he more than made up for in hospitality.

Although they would have preferred to go straight to their room, they drank their punch and toasted their toes and spent as long in the landlord's company as John deemed polite, while Thomas clumped their luggage upstairs and two maids ran after him with brass bed warmers. But at long long last etiquette was satisfied and they were allowed to open the oak door and climb the spiral staircase behind it to their bedroom, preceded by their landlord with a broad smile and a triple candlestick.

It was an old-fashioned panelled room, which reminded them both of the hall in the rectory at Rattlesden, hung with tapestries and warmed by a log fire in the old stone hearth. There were two small shuttered windows set in the eaves, a carved oak linen-chest in one corner, a sheepskin on the boards before the hearth, and the bed was a huge four-poster, heavily curtained as they were both glad to see. The servants' door was set directly in the corner of the room, but there was a key protruding from the lock and as soon as the maids had departed John closed the door after them and locked it firmly. They were on their own at last.

'Now we are married, my own dear love,' he said, 'I shall undo the top three buttons of your gown and kiss your neck. Like this. And this. And this.'

He was rather surprised that instead of standing still to receive his caress, as he'd hoped and expected, she ducked away from his hands and sped across the room to open their carpet-bag, which had been left on a wooden stand beside the bed. He watched with growing amazement as she took a large towel out of the bag, turned back the covers of the bed, very neatly and deftly he noticed, and spread the towel across the under-sheet.

'What are you doing?' he asked, walking towards her. She had made him feel rather aggrieved running away like that, and just at the very moment when he was feeling most loving.

'Annie told me to,' she said, pulling the towel smooth.

'Do you always do as you are told?' he asked, his sense of grievance melting as he began to tease.

She answered him seriously. 'Oh yes. Always.'

'Then come here and let me kiss you.'

Oh that was easy to obey! And so were all the other commands that followed. 'Come back to the fire, my love, where it is warm' ... 'Unpin your lovely hair and let it fall' ... 'Put your arms about my neck, my dearest'... 'Hold me close, close, closer still!' ... 'If I undo this lace, so, your chemise will fall, so, and you can step out of it, can you not?' Oh she could, she could, shivering naked, her feet white against the yellow fleece, her mind shivering too, in case this was sinful, but reassured almost at once because his face was blazing love, his eyes lustrous as water and quite quite black in the leaping firelight.

'Oh Harriet, my own dear darling,' he said. 'You are so beautiful.' Standing before him, pearl-white and blue-eyed, like a goddess, with that straight pale hair framing her face and shimmering over her shoulders, and her limbs so slender and her belly so tenderly rounded and those pretty breasts casting pale blue shadows on her white skin. And he knelt at her feet, nuzzling her belly, kissing her breasts, and whispering, 'I adore you. Adore you. Adore you,' over and over again between kisses.

She had not expected to be worshipped. Kissed and caressed and held close certainly, but not worshipped. Whatever we do when we are married, he had said, is right and proper and cannot be a sin. But to be worshipped? The confusion of it made her feel dizzy, so that she swayed and put out her hand to steady herself against his shoulder.

The touch broke what little control he had left. In one movement he was on his feet and had lifted her in his arms. Two strides took them to the bed. Or was it even two? Neither of them could tell. Then time and movement blurred as kisses led them pleasurably on, swimming through emotion and sensation, warm and moist and vibrant, on and on until the moment of entry. 'Yes, yes, yes,' he said, thrusting in triumph, 'you are mine, mine, mine.'

And he hurt her. A sharp stinging pain as though he were pressing her with thorns. Neither the sensation nor the knowledge of it was any surprise to her. She had always suspected that she had been born for pain, so why should this supreme moment be any different? Even so, it was hard to bear in silence, and after a while she caught her breath, despite herself, and gave a little involuntary groan.

He stopped moving at once. 'What is it, Harriet my darling? Have I hurt you?'

'It is nothing,' she said, trying to reassure him.

He was still panting and aching with desire, but he couldn't go on. Not now. 'I have hurt you,' he said miserably. 'Oh my beautiful, lovely Harriet, I am so sorry.' Tears were already blocking his throat and stinging his eyes. How could he have done such a thing? 'I am so sorry!'

'It is nothing,' she repeated softly. 'It always happens. Annie said so. You have taken my maidenhead.' And it was odd how proud it made her feel to say it. She had been sacrificed on the altar of love, like all wives since the beginning of time. 'It always happens.'

Then she realised that his eyes were full of tears and she was torn with pity for him. 'Oh my dear, John, you mustn't mind, for I'm sure I don't.'

'I love you and I have hurt you,' he said, lifting his body away from her and sitting up. 'You are all the world to me and I hurt you. I shall never forgive myself for it.'

'There is nothing to forgive,' she said, putting her arms round his neck and kissing him. 'It is God's will, my dear, and quite natural. Consider that.'

'Then I do not understand His purpose.'

'Perhaps he means to teach us that there is always pain in love.'

'I love you more than I have ever loved anyone in the whole of my life,' he said. 'Without you my life would be unbearable. You are everything to me. I would never, ever hurt you, not willingly. You must believe me.'

Why, what a child he is to be so upset! she thought. And she felt wonderfully responsible for him. 'You will not hurt me next time, I promise you,' she said. 'it is only the first. Annie said so.'

'Devil take her,' he said with sudden fury. 'She had no cause to speak of it at all.' *He* hadn't discussed these things with Billy, even though he'd wanted to, so why had she been talking to Annie about them?

'Hush, hush, my love,' she said, smoothing his hair from those angry eyes. 'Do not speak so.'

He got out of the bed and found his nightshirt and put it on, controlling himself, wrapping calm and reason about him with the folds of linen. They must talk of other matters, to take their attention from this terrible failure. Other matters, he thought. And he remembered his notebooks.

He unpacked her nightgown and handed it to her, trying to smile, and while she was putting it on, sitting with her feet hidden among the tumbled sheets like a mermaid in white weed, he found the books, closed the bed-curtains and climbed back into the bed beside her.

'Now that we are married,' he said, and how matter of fact the old phrase sounded now, 'I have great plans for the business. With you to help me, I shall expand our trade clear across the country.'

The realisation that he could turn from love to business so

abruptly made her want to laugh, but she controlled the urge and sat up in the bed beside him ready to hear what he had to say.

'Look 'ee here,' he said, opening the largest book.

It was a map of the British Isles, yellow in the candlelight, and threading through it, like veins through the body politic, were the red lines of Mr Chaplin's coach routes. 'I enter each new one as it is opened,' he said with pride, 'and here, do you see, are the shops that Easter's own already, marked in black ink, and here are the ones I intend to open, marked in pencil. It is all planned.'

'Is this your work, John?' she asked, feeling she ought to show an interest. The candles were beginning to gutter and the shadows they cast flickered across the page.

'Indeed it is,' he said. 'Billy may be a manager too, but he does nothing more than keep the warehouse in order and supervise the sorting. I am the one who builds up sales. And the key to building up sales lies here in Birmingham — He put his finger on a black circle in the middle of the map. 'As soon as we are back in London, Harriet, I mean to travel to Birmingham and open as many shops as I can, and a sorting house, for once our papers are established there, they can be sent out to every point of the globe. It is a huge centre, and a growing one.'

The first candle went out, with a gust of strong-smelling black smoke. Almost absent-mindedly he picked up the snuffers and put out the rest, talking all the time. 'Mama is a magnificent businesswoman, but she has no method. She buys shops in fits and starts, you see my dear, and there is no profit in that. Howsomever, one day she will retire, or stand down, and then I tell you, Harriet, I mean to take over the business. This must be our secret, my love, for there ain't another single living soul knows what I intend. But I shall do it, you may depend upon it. I understand the business so entirely, you see. Growth has to be deliberate and planned, moving from one town to the next, so that supplies are always moved easily, I might almost say inevitably…'

Half lying, half sitting against the warmth of his body, Harriet began to feel drowsy. She slid down into the bed again as he went on talking into the darkness. 'There is so little strong news these days, that is one problem. What we require is something important to happen, something influential or unexpected or dramatic that everyone will want to read about. Then you will see our sales increase I can promise you…'

They were the last words she heard as she fell asleep.

WHEN SHE WOKE, it was early morning, the bed-curtains had been drawn and sunshine was knifing in through the opened shutters. John was already up and dressed. He was standing beside the washstand, in his shirt and trousers, stooping forward for a better view in the little shaving mirror, the lower half of his face bearded with white soap, wielding a formidable cut-throat razor. She watched his long hands working steadily and was lost in admiration for him. Then he caught sight of her face in the mirror and they smiled at one another through the glass, he rather sheepishly, she with open affection.

'Good morning,' he said, very polite and formal. 'Shall I ring for tea?'

'Is it late?' she said, suddenly anxious at the thought that she might have overslept and annoyed him.

'No,' he reassured her, holding up his nose with his left forefinger and scraping underneath it very delicately, 'but it would not matter if it were. We are here to rest and be waited upon.'

So tea was ordered, and 'hot water for the lady', and when the maid had disappeared through the servants' door to fetch them, John walked across to the opposite corner of the room and opened another low door, with the air of a conjuror producing a rabbit from a hat, for neither of them had noticed it on the previous evening. It gave out to a little low dressing room with its own washstand and towels and soap all neatly ready.

'Uncommon convenient, eh?' he said, well pleased with it and with himself for finding it.

'Oh yes, dear John, it is,' she agreed, very much relieved to see it. To be naked before him by firelight was one thing, when passion was running strong in both of them and they were contained in their own half-lit, private world, but to be washing and dressing before him in broad daylight would have been altogether too bold, and especially now with that painful love-making between them.

So she waited quietly while he finished his shave, and when the tea had been delivered and enjoyed, she slipped from the bed, gathered her clothes and scurried into the dressing room, shutting the door behind her. When she emerged again, she was clean and clothed and perfectly contained, her long hair pinned into its modest topknot, her face calm, her daytime self-resumed.

'We could take a walk in the village before breakfast,' he suggested.

And very agreeable and proper and idle it was, to stroll along the single street between the low stone cottages they'd glimpsed the night before, their thatches steaming in the early morning sun, and their inhabitants already hard at work, scrubbing and sweeping or feeding pigs or hoeing cabbage patches. They passed a small child in a blue holland pinafore waddling a gaggle of geese down to the millpond, and a red-chapped milkmaid swaying towards the inn under the weight of her two full churns. And the pale sun shone on them all.

At the top of the village the path grew steeper as it approached the church of St Kenelm, which was built of the same yellow-grey stone as the rest of the village. Its square tower was turreted and the grey tiles upon its roofs were old and gnarled and discoloured like discarded oyster shells, but what was even better about it was that it stood at the gateway to a mystery. To the left of the porch they could see the round roof of a very old dove cote and towering behind the church were the broken walls of a huge ruined castle.

'Did you know of this, dear John?' Harriet asked, gazing at it in some awe.

'Indeed I did,' he said, 'and thought it uncommon romantic.'

'Yes,' she said, 'so it is. Uncommon romantic.'

They explored the ruin, arm in arm, walking through the dank porch and standing in the remains of a stone hall, so tall and impressive that it could have been a cathedral, and presently they found themselves entirely alone in a green water meadow facing the stream.

'I am so very sorry I hurt you,' he said.

She flung herself into his arms. 'It was nothing,' she said. 'Nothing. Such a little pain. It is forgotten already.'

She has suffered so much, he thought, remembering her swollen face on the night he rescued her. And he yearned to make amends to her. 'You shall never be hurt again, my dearest,' he said. 'I give you my word.'

She was remembering that beating too. 'When we have children,' she said, 'we will not beat them, will we John?'

The very idea was abhorrent. 'Never!' he said passionately. 'Never ever. We shall love them most dearly, I promise you.'

She knew it but it was wonderful to hear it said. All hurt and pain was behind her now.

'Oh how happy we shall be,' she said, and put up her face to be kissed.

AND SO THEIR HONEYMOON CONTINUED, with modest promenades by day and the most tender lovemaking by night. And

Annie was proved right. The second time wasn't painful, the third was faintly pleasurable, the fourth was delightful.

'Oh,' she said, as he lay panting and triumphant beside her afterwards, 'how I do love you, my dear, dear John.'

'You are my life,' he said passionately. 'I could not live without you.'

CHAPTER 20

The Sowerbys were furious when they read an account of their own daughter's wedding in *The Times.*

'And we not even *invited,*' Mrs Sowerby snorted.

'Impoliteness, that's what 'tis,' Mr Sowerby said, 'which is a greater sin than either you or I would ever allow ourselves to be guilty of.' And he assumed his superior expression.

''Tis not to be endured,' Mrs Sowerby said, and she put on her bonnet and went straight round to the Easter's fine house on Angel Hill to protest.

'And I don't even get over the doorstep!' she reported furiously to Mr Sowerby when he returned from work that evening. 'Oh I know that Mrs Thistlethwaite of theirs. I've got her mark, don't you worry. All smiles and friendly-like and "Yes Mrs Sowerby" and "No Mrs Sowerby" and she en't told me a *thing.* Not *one single thing.* The young masters are travelling abroad, so she *says.* She don't have the least idea when either the one of 'em will be in Bury, so she *says.* Oh she don't fool me! The effrontery of it. But one thing I *did* get out of her. They invited that Miss Pettie to the wedding *if* you please. Oh, they have no sense of propriety. No sense of propriety at all.' It was very galling.

''Tis all that dreadful Mrs Easter's doing,' Mr Sowerby said darkly. 'An immoral woman a-gallivanting about town with her lover. Oh I remember! We must visit our dear Harriet and remind her of her Christian duty. 'Twould be plain sinfulness to sit idly by and say nothing and allow her to be contaminated.'

But as they didn't know where she was, there wasn't a lot they could do except sit idly by.

Miss Pettie didn't know where the newly-weds were, either, although she was very forthcoming about the wedding, which she described in great detail to every member of the congregation who enquired about it. Such very great detail indeed that the Sowerbys wondered, privately and bitterly, whether her interest in it wasn't so perverse as to be verging on the sinful.

''Twas *our* wedding, when all's said and done,' Mrs Sowerby complained, 'and *we* are the ones who ought to have attended and reported upon it.'

'That Mrs Easter will have a deal to answer for at the Day of Judgement,' Mr Sowerby said grimly.

But 'that Mrs Easter' didn't give the Sowerbys a thought. And neither did the new Mrs John Easter. It was a very wet summer and the autumn that followed was chill and damp but she didn't notice that either because she was so fully occupied completing the decoration of her new home in Fitzroy Square, filling each room in turn with the brightest colour she could find, duck-egg green and gold for the drawing room, rose madder and china blue for the parlour, pale pink and yellow for the nursery, ready for the children who would be loved so much and never beaten.

She soon discovered that being the mistress of the house was considerably easier than being the maid-of-all-work to two intemperate parents. After a little initial nervousness, she and her housekeeper, Mrs Toxteth, grew to like and respect each other, Harriet because Mrs Toxteth was plump and motherly and kept the house in highly polished order, Mrs Toxteth because her mistress was young and inexperienced and quite touchingly in love with her husband. They had a butler, called Paulson, who had been a footman in Nan's house and took his promotion most seriously. And Harriet's personal maid, who was called Peg Mullins and was even younger than she was herself, rapidly became a friend.

Despite the unseasonable weather the new Mr and Mrs John Henry Easter were sunnily happy together in their beautiful house. What did it matter to them that Billy and Matilda had married like two of the gentry, wearing costly clothes and dining upon expensive foods? What did they care now that Matilda was on her extravagant continental tour? Let the third Mrs Easter go where she will, Harriet thought, as she mended her husband's shirt, it was all one to the second.

On John's first trip to 'check upon the London shops' she was allowed to ride with him and sit quietly beside him and watch while he negotiated rents or renewed leases, checked sales, and hired managers and shop assistants. She was full of admiration for him, impressed by the ease with which he handled so many different people, John Henry Easter, her husband, and undeniably his formidable mother's son.

He spent two or three days every other week travelling the country renting properties, and, on the night he returned, they would enter his newly acquired premises on that complicated map of his. Gradually as the months passed his plan began to take shape.

'Do you see Harriet?' he would say excitedly as the new shops clustered along their chosen route. 'Do you see?'

And she did see. It was like watching blossom unfold on a bare winter bough. Soon she understood his plan well enough to be able to predict the next town he would visit, and that pleased her, even though she missed him sorely when he was away.

In November, when he was in Rugby negotiating for a reading room, the London papers were full of news about bread riots 'all over East Anglia' and secret meetings in London 'planning insurrection', and on the very day he came back posters appeared announcing a reform meeting to be held in Spa Fields, just around the corner from their quiet square.

'Is it like to prove violent, think 'ee?' Harriet asked. 'Mrs Toxteth says there will be a riot. All the shop windows are to be shuttered and the constables called out.' There were so many beggars in London, that was the trouble, hundreds and hundreds of them, and all so poorly dressed and so dirty, with unkempt hair and sullen faces. She was used to the country poor who met in Mr Hopkins's study to talk about reform, people like the two Mr Abbotts. They would never slit anybody's throat, whereas the men and women who pushed and thronged in the streets of the city looked capable of anything.

'Corn is a guinea a bushel in Yorkshire,' John told her, 'and after those bread riots in East Anglia anything could happen.'

'There was no trouble in Rugby, was there, dear John?'

'No, my dear. The riots were in Birmingham, this time.'

'What a terrible world we live in,' Harriet said, as they walked upstairs together. But she felt so happy now that he was home with her again.

'It is all news,' he said, patting her hand, 'and good or bad, news makes profits for the Easter family, don't forget.'

THIS PARTICULAR NEWS increased sales quite dramatically, because the ten thousand citizens who gathered in Spa Fields on that dark November day, having been given a rousing address by the famous orator Mr Henry Hunt, decided to petition the Regent for reform, and delegated Mr Hunt and Nan's friend Sir

Francis Burdett to deliver the petition on their behalf. It was a daring move and the papers made much of it.

'I will stay in London for a week or two,' John decided, 'and see what transpires.'

Four days later Nan told them at dinner that her friend, Sir Francis, had withdrawn his support for the petition, saying he had no desire to be a catchpaw. 'There's dirty work afoot,' she told her sons, 'or my name en't Nan Easter. We en't seen the end of this affair, not by a long chalk.'

'What dirty work do you suspect, Mama?' John asked coolly.

'Government spies, I shouldn't wonder.'

'Government spies?' Harriet echoed, shocked at the very idea. 'Oh surely not, Mrs Easter. Surely not.'

''Twont be the first time,' Nan said. 'Nor the last. Put a few spies into a meeting and you can guarantee 'twill get out of hand.'

'But surely the government would not wish a meeting to get out of hand,' Harriet said, bemused.

'I am afraid they would, my dear,' John explained, 'for then the constables have a good reason to arrest the ringleaders. That is why it is done.'

'But that is dishonest,' Harriet protested. 'They could not do such a thing, surely.'

'Well,' her mother-in-law said, touched by her innocence, 'we shall see.'

And sure enough two weeks later, on 2nd December, there was another meeting at the Spa Fields and this one did get out of hand and the ringleaders were arrested. But the Easters were all too happily busy to notice it.

Billy and Matilda had come home from their long trip on the continent, looking very plump and well, and bearing gifts for every single member of the family, even Harriet, which Nan was pleased to see, and Billy was delighted about. He hadn't been at all sure how Tilda would take it when he first suggested including their sister-in-law, but his dear girl had agreed at once.

'We are all married now,' she'd said easily, as if that settled it. So there was French brandy for James, and French perfume for Annie, a wooden hobby horse for Jimmy and a jointed doll for Beau. John was given a copy of Dante's 'Inferno' and Harriet a fringed shawl from Sicily, and as the final and most valuable gift of all, there were two fine watercolours of the ruins of Pompeii for Nan. What riches!

And Nan's welcoming dinner was very lavish too, with jugged hare and roast pheasant and so many tarts and pastries there was barely room for them all on the table.

'How well we live,' Harriet said, as she and John were driving home afterwards. 'I feel extravagant to be eating so much when there are so many poor people in London with nothing to eat at all.'

'You couldn't help them,' he said reasonably, 'even if you were to give away every single dish on Mama's table tonight. They are too many and our resources are too small.' But he was touched by her concern. 'Now that you are an Easter you must grow accustomed to riches, you know.'

'And Billy and Matilda bringing us all such presents! Wasn't that kind?'

'I have invited them to dinner on Friday,' he said.

'What should I serve them?' she asked, thinking how hard it would be to follow Nan's splendid meal.

'Nothing fancy,' he said, giving her the lopsided grin that she now recognised as the sign that he was going to tease. 'A dish of larks' tongues, perhaps, or dolphin stew, or roast swan.'

She kissed him lovingly. 'Roast beef,' she said, 'with horse-radish sauce.'

. . .

THANKS TO NAN'S association with Frederick Brougham, the Easter family were moving up in society. They weren't quite in the swan-eating ranks, but they were invited to routs and balls in various houses in Bloomsbury, and Nan and Frederick were frequent guests at Holly Hall.

In the spring of the following year they had a most particular invitation.

'There are two other guests to be included in the party,' Frederick said, 'both of whom I particularly wish to introduce to you.' He was so deliberately calm about it she knew it was important.

'Ah,' she said, teasing him, 'but shall I wish to meet them?'

'Oh I think so,' he said easily. But he didn't tell her who they were.

HOLLY HALL WAS ALWAYS an agreeable house to visit, but it was at its best in spring, when crocuses burgeoned into bright colour under the elms and the banks were a flutter of wild daffodils.

But their host was in very ill-humour. Spotted fever had broken out in the low streets behind their London house, and Lady Barnesworthy had overridden all his instructions and instantly despatched all fourteen of their noisy, energetic children to the quiet and safety of his country seat.

'Two hours till dinner, dammit,' he said to Nan and Frederick when they arrived, 'and children all over the place. 'Tis a cruel world. Leave the dog alone, Sebastian, or I shall tell him to bite you, dammit.'

Sebastian, who was a determined six-year-old, went on tugging the spaniel's ears. 'We shall none of us survive,' his father said lugubriously. 'Mark my words. What's to be done with 'em?'

Nan stood by his semi-circular window and looked out at

the tumult on the lawn, remembering the games her own children had played when they were young. 'How if we were to run races?' she said.

So races were run. A bruising three-legged, a marvellously messy egg-and-spoon, and an obstacle race that went on and on because the winner of each round was entitled to add a further and more devilish hurdle to the course.

Frederick Brougham ran with the best of them and submitted to having his long elegant legs pinioned to Sebastian's short stubby ones, and then cheated so efficiently, swinging the child completely off his feet and running with him spread-eagled in the air, that they won a resounding and derided victory.

Nan was happily occupied all afternoon. She didn't notice the arrival of the two most important guests, although the two most important guests certainly noticed her and were highly entertained by what was going on. When she came panting into the house to dress for dinner, they were standing beside the drawing room window.

Frederick introduced her before she could catch her breath. 'Mrs Easter, pray allow me to present my most esteemed friend the Earl of Harrowby and my cousin, Lord Brougham.'

Well, well, well she thought as she wiped her dirty hands on her kerchief and smiled at the two gentlemen, I've arrived in society now, and no mistake. Then she touched the two gloved fingers that Lord Brougham was holding in her direction and had her entire hand engulfed in the warm grip of the noble earl, who was tall and grey haired and leaned upon a gold-topped cane.

'You run a circus, ma'am, I see,' he said, and his expression was amused and faintly mocking but not unkind. ''Tis not at all what I was led to expect of 'ee, upon me word. They told me you were a queen in the world of news sheets and newspapers and suchlike, and I find you running races, upon me life.'

'She could turn her hand to most trades had she a mind,' Frederick said with easy affection.

'I can well believe it,' the Earl said and he swayed his stiff spine towards their hostess. 'I trust this lady and I are seated together, Lady Barnesworthy. There is nothing more aggravating than to make interesting acquaintances and then lose sight of 'em all through dinner.'

'It shall be as you wish, my dear Lord Harrowby,' Lady Barnesworthy said smoothly.

'If it don't inconvenience you, dear lady.'

''Tain't the slightest inconvenience,' the dear lady said at once, thinking what a dratted nuisance he was being. Now she would have to rearrange her entire table and all her friends would know that Mrs Easter had been taken up by the Earl. Really, men had no judgement in these matters! He will invite her to dine at Grosvenor Square, she thought rather crossly as she excused herself from their company. And then it will be as we feared: all doors will be open to her. I should never have allowed my dear Frederick to persuade me to invite her here in the first place. I was doubtful of the sense of it at the time. Howsomever, at least he has had the good sense not to marry her, which is some consolation. And whatever else might be said about the lady, she was entertaining company at dinner and would keep the Earl of Harrowby amused. The gentlemen were so tetchy these days what with bread-rioters and machine-breakers causing a nuisance and that dreadful penny press fairly screaming for universal suffrage and parliamentary reform, as if either would do any good at all.

IT WAS a sentiment expressed with some force by several of her guests that evening.

'Give 'em the vote?' Sir Joshua mocked. 'Whoever heard such impudence? And allow pig-ignorance to outvote the likes of you and me? I should just think not! What say you, milord? Folly ain't it?' He had quite recovered his humour now that his exhausted infants had been retired to the nursery.

'If suffrage were to be extended,' Lord Harrowby said diplomatically, 'and the necessity for such reform is arguable, I will agree 'twould need to be done by degrees.'

'Meantime the mob is vociferous,' Lord Brougham pointed out. ''Tis my opinion that we ignore their demands at our peril.'

He is very like his cousin, Nan thought, tall and elegant and grey-eyed, with his hair greying at the temples in exactly the same way and in exactly the same place, but he is rangy and nervous and loud where Frederick is quiet and contained. And the thought made her feel very fond of her Frederick.

'Put a few of the beggars in jail,' Sir Joshua advised. 'That 'ud soon stop their noise.'

'The jails are already crammed to bursting,' Frederick Brougham said mildly. 'Even the new penitentiary at Millbank is rapidly filling, so the courts are advised.'

'Then send the beggars abroad,' Sir Joshua said, unabashed by such difficulties. 'Get rid of 'em. That's what I say. Can't send 'em to America, more's the pity, not since those damned settlers stole the place, but there's always Van Dieman's Land.'

'On what grounds would you transport 'em, pray?' Frederick asked.

'On the grounds that they're a damn nuisance,' Sir Joshua said trenchantly. 'On the grounds that they've took pot-shots at the Regent, dammit. Have we to wait until they assassinate the man?' There had been wild rumours in January that somebody had fired a gun at the Prince Regent as he was returning to Carlton House in the state coach.

The Earl of Harrowby was watching him with a faintly amused expression on his face. 'An assassination attempt is likely enough in all conscience,' the noble gentleman said lightly. 'He ain't the most popular monarch we've seen. Howsomever, there are other means of dealing with the situation. Our Mrs Easter would put him to running races, I don't doubt.'

'If I had a mind to I might,' Nan agreed, laughing with the rest of the company. 'But I'd rather sell him a newspaper.'

It was a splendid summer, just as Lady Barnesworthy had feared. Nan and Frederick were invited to Grosvenor Square no fewer than six times, and each occasion was more successful than the last. Soon they were among the most popular guests at Lord Harrowby's table. And when the autumn began, Billy and Matilda set the seal on the season by bringing Nan a rather special piece of news.

Frederick Brougham was away in York preparing for the quarter sessions, so it was only John and Billy and their wives who had joined her for dinner that evening at Bedford Square. Nan's cook had prepared them a special Michaelmas meal of broiled chicken with oysters, followed by roast plover and a dish of sturgeon, so they had dined well and soon they would all be going on to the Michaelmas Masque at the Vauxhall Gardens.

'What would you say,' Billy said, beaming across the table at her, 'if I were I to tell 'ee you're to be a grandmama in the spring?'

'I'd drink a health to the baby and I'd say' — pretending to consider her words — 'about time too.'

'When is it to be?' John asked soberly, gathering his last mouthful of blackberry and apple tart.

'In April,' Matilda said, blushing prettily.

'Ain't she a corker?' the proud father-to-be wanted to know, patting his wife's plump arm.

'We are very happy for you,' Harriet said, but secretly she was wishing that she could have been the first to make such an announcement. She and John had been married for nearly eighteen months and there was still no sign of a baby.

'I have something to say too, Mama,' John said, giving Harriet his lopsided grin. What on earth was it? 'And mighty opportune, given Matilda's present condition. Our new sorting office in Birmingham is primed and ready for action. The very next piece of important news can be sent there by express coach to catch the inland mails, which are all prepared to accept it I may say, and then I promise you, 'twill be spread all over the North West on the very day of printing. If you can contrive to have your baby before the papers go to print, Matilda, they shall know of it in Manchester and Liverpool before it's a day old.'

'Quite right too,' Matilda said, not the least bit put out by his teasing, 'when you consider he will be the first of a new generation of Easters.'

'You are decided upon a boy, then?' Nan said, teasing too.

'Oh indeed,' Matilda said, preening herself. 'I am sure of it.'

'Well, here's to the baby, whatever sex it may be,' Nan said, raising her glass. 'You are in good company, Matilda.'

'Yes, indeed,' Billy said, drinking the toast. ''Tis a year for babies in all conscience.' For Princess Charlotte, the heir to the throne, was expecting her first baby too and there was a great deal of interest in it. The birth was due in little more than a month, so the papers were running daily bulletins about the Princess's health, and there was much speculation as to what the child would be called, especially if it turned out to be a boy.

'Time for brandy,' Nan told her butler, who had come into the room in answer to the bell. 'The best, if you please. We've a new Easter to celebrate.'

Matilda was enjoying her pregnancy. She was the centre of attention at the masque, declaring that she was too fatigued to sit through the first half and then insisting that she had the most powerful desire for caraway comfits.

'I *must* have them, Billy my dearest,' she said, pouting prettily. ''Tis a *craving*, you see, my love, and heaven only knows what would happen were we to ignore it. There could be the direst consequence for our precious baby, the direst, I do not doubt.'

So poor Billy had to miss the second half of the performance while he took a carriage to the nearest confectioner. And then she only ate two of the comfits and complained that she was feeling sick.

'Your poor brother,' Harriet said to John as they prepared for bed later that night. 'She had him fetching and carrying all evening.'

'He enjoys it,' he said, pulling his shirt over his head. 'Wouldn't do it if he didn't. Don't you worry your pretty head about Billy. I never knew him do anything he didn't want to.'

'Will she truly announce the baby's birth in *The Times?*'

'I daresay.'

'You won't send it by express, will you John?'

'No, my dear,' he said, grinning at her. 'I shall reserve that distinction for such events as the birth of the new Heir Apparent.'

'What a joy that will be,' she said, unpinning her hair.

BUT SHE WAS WRONG. There was no joy in the news at all, for the infant Prince was stillborn. On Thursday 6th November *The Times* printed the sad news between black borders, and John Easter, who had been waiting for it in Easter House all through that long cold night, had it dispatched right across the country before the day was out, just as he'd promised.

The following morning the news was even worse. Mrs Toxteth brought a copy of *The Times* up to the dining room where Harriet was eating alone, Mr Easter having remained in the Strand yet again, and one glimpse at her housekeeper's face told Harriet that the news was very grave indeed.

'What is it, Mrs Toxteth?' she said, biting her bottom lip with concern.

'Read it, my dear,' Mrs Toxteth said, 'an' tell me if it ain't the saddest thing you ever heard.' And she tiptoed from the room with her apron at her eyes.

The Times leader was headed *Friday, 7th November 1817*, and it made harrowing reading:

> *It is our painful and unexpected duty this day to give an account of as melancholy an event as occurs in the annals of hereditary monarchies,'* it said, *'the death of the only two presumptive heirs to the Crown in direct succession, the mother and her child. We have lost a Prince just before he saw the light and a Princess in the prime of her youth.*

The Princess was dead too.

For the next four days *The Times* was printed with a black border and was full of angry correspondence. Harriet read every word and agreed with most of them. The Prince Regent had no business being away in Suffolk when his poor dear daughter was dying. And hunting with the Hertfords too. It was scandalous. He thought of nothing but his pleasures. And why hadn't he allowed her mother to come home and see her, just once? But no, the poor lady was still banned from the country. While as to that other dreadful man, Sir Richard Croft, the obstetrician, he should be put on trial for his life, so he should, for allowing the Princess to die. It was all due to his carelessness. He should never have gone to bed and left the poor lady alone. What was he thinking of?

On the fifth day *The Times* seemed to have returned to its normal self. But John brought a copy home at breakfast time and read it closely.

'Would you care to see the paper?' he asked folding it and preparing to hand it across the table to her. He was looking rather pleased with himself, she thought, and wondered what it was he wanted her to read.

It was an advertisement, right in the middle of the front page, and set within its own panel so that it caught the eye immediately.

The Times published on Friday the 7th inst. at half past eight o'clock in the morning, was forwarded, by special express, to Birmingham, where it arrived in time for the inland mails, by which the subscribers to the above paper in Birmingham, Liverpool, Chester, Warrington, Manchester, Rochdale, Preston, Lancaster obtained their papers fourteen hours before the arrival of the London mail. The above express was sent by A Easter & Sons, newspaper agents, Easter House, Strand, London. It is the intention of A Easter & Sons, to continue to forward The Times by express whenever there is any important news or when parliamentary debates prevent an early publication. J H Easter, Easter House, The Strand.

'John!' she said, appalled.

He misunderstood her. 'Well done, is it not?' he said. 'We have given our first demonstration of the speed by which news may be spread through the midlands. If we were not a name in the land before this, we shall certainly be one now.'

She looked up at his face, at the glint of his dark eyes and the glow of satisfaction on his cheeks and forehead. 'The news you spread was of the death of a young woman,' she said, and now there was no mistaking her abhorrence. 'A terrible death, John, in agony and in the prime of her life. How could you make a newspaper advertisement of *that*? How could you?'

He straightened his spine and sat stiff-necked. She was right. His instincts had recognised that immediately she spoke. But he had no intention of admitting it to her, for this was business. 'In the matter of selling the news,' he said coldly, 'you must allow me to know rather more than you do, Harriet.'

She was confused and upset by his coldness and began to stammer apologies, for she knew very well that a wife should never criticise her husband's calling. 'I am sorry John. I didn't mean… it was not my intention…'

'We will say no more of it,' he said coldly. 'I have to return to the office.' And he was gone before she could think of anything to placate him.

How dreadful to have upset him so, she thought. I should have considered before I spoke, that much is very plain. I grow careless because I am so happy, that's what it is. And she bit her bottom lip with agitation. It wasn't as if she didn't know the likely outcome of thoughtless speech. She had been chided about it often enough. And yet, and yet, the death of the Princess was the most heartrending thing she'd ever heard, and she knew that it should never have been used as the subject of an advertisement, business or no.

Oh, how I wish there were someone I could talk to, she sighed to herself. But there was no one except Peg, and you couldn't discuss your husband with a servant. The great Mrs Easter was quite out of the question for she was too much in awe of her, and Annie was too far away.

She put on her thick pelisse and its matching bonnet and set off for Smithfield Market to choose the meat for dinner that night. The walk would clear her head and, besides, the sooner she got on with her household duties this morning the better. It was a brisk clear morning, spiced with smoke but not overcast, and the streets were full of busy women off to market, baskets swinging. An oddly cheerful day when all flags were flying at half-mast and so many front doors were swathed in black crepe.

In High Holborn there were black ribbons everywhere, tied to door knockers, plaited into horses' tails, trimming hats and fluttering quite gaily at window frames. After a while the sight of so many marks of mourning began to oppress her and she averted her eyes, seeking some other colour that would remind her of something else. And her attention was caught by the display in one of the Easter shops, of all places.

There was a green baize counter in the window and set in the middle of the counter was a pretty fan-shape composed entirely of quill pens and containing within its centre a loyal address of sympathy to the Royal Family, neatly penned on a black-edged card, and quite easily avoided. Six large bottles of ink stood sentinel behind it and to the right and left there were stacks of writing paper tied with purple and white ribbons and piles of account books with red marbled bindings. It was a very pretty display. She was quite charmed by it and resolved to tell John so at dinner that very evening. But then she saw that placed in a neat row in front of the quill fan were half a dozen sturdy books bound in the same marbled red and marked by a plain white card which bore the legend, 'Suitable for notebooks, recipe books, diaries, etc, etc'. And she recognised at once that here was the answer to her dilemma. A diary. Of course. It was the very thing. A silent confidante, a listener who could always be depended upon to keep counsel, an ear without a mouth. She went into the shop and bought one at once.

That afternoon, when she had made sure that preparations for dinner were progressing satisfactorily, she went quietly upstairs to her bedroom and took up her pen to write to her diary for the very first time. It was like making a friend.

> *Monday 10th November 1817,* she wrote.
>
> *Dear Diary, there is so much I want to tell you I hardly know where to begin. Such a tragedy has occurred. The Princess Charlotte is dead and my husband John has put such a dreadful advertisement in The Times, but I must not criticise him. I will tell you all about it...*

She felt so much better when her complaint had been written and delighted to think that it had all been done while John was out of the house. And of course writing a diary was perfectly proper. Plenty of great ladies did it. There was no question of intending to deceive. Now she could say exactly what she liked and no harm done. It was an admirable solution. Quite admirable. She hid the book under the mattress and rang the bell for Peg to come and help her dress for dinner.

By the time John came back to the house that evening, worrying about how he could mend their quarrel, she was quite herself again. They dined happily, and she encouraged him to talk of the day's affairs, although they were both very careful not to mention the advertisement. When they retired to bed, they walked upstairs arm in arm as if there had never been any argument, as if their customary mode of behaviour had never varied. Which apart from that sudden uncharacteristic row, it never had. And so they made their peace without a word of explanation or apology, and the subject of the Princess Charlotte and her untimely death was never discussed between them again.

Although Harriet talked about it at length with Annie and Matilda. But that was at Christmas time and for another reason.

CHAPTER 21

The Easter family were celebrating Christmas at Bury that year, so that Annie and James could be together at the Christmas dinner. It was the first time that John and Harriet had been back to the town since the day they were married, and, rather to her surprise, Harriet was actually quite pleased to be there.

It was pleasant to see the pale frontage of the Athenaeum again shining on the north side of the square, and the carved post of the chemist's on the corner, and the long winter shadows darkening the cobbles before the Angel Inn as the coach clanked and clattered into the yard. But it was the smell of the place that made her realise how much she had missed it, the dank familiar earth and the hedgerows full of winter dust and the warm rank reek of stabled horses steaming from behind Mr Kent's long flint wall. Oh it was lovely to be back. And besides, she had something rather important to talk to Annie about.

However it was the sort of Christmas she had come to expect from her new family, being noisy, cheerful, extravagant and very crowded. So it wasn't until the afternoon of the third day that she finally got a chance to talk to Annie alone.

Jimmy and Beau had both had colds and fevers that winter and they were still pale and easily tired, so when dinner was done Annie settled them for a nap on the chaise longue before the parlour fire, and she and Harriet took their sewing into the room and sat with them. Nan and Mr Brougham were out riding, Thiss and John and Mr Teshmaker were busy examining the books in the office, James had driven over to Rattlesden, and Billy and Matilda were out visiting their friends. Suddenly the house was blessedly quiet.

'We have so much to talk about,' Annie said, beaming at Harriet as they settled themselves on either side of the fire. 'I am so glad they have left us alone. I am breeding again, my dear, and I wanted to tell 'ee myself.'

'Oh Annie!' Harriet said, with transparent delight. 'When is it to be?'

'June, I think,' Annie said. 'I shall know more when I've quickened. 'Tis three months now, if I am any judge. I have seen nothing since before the poor Princess died.'

'Nor I since the very day,' Harriet confessed, just as she'd planned to. 'But I do not dare to hope yet.'

'Oh my dear, whyever not?' Annie said, leaning forward to take her hand. 'When was the last time? Tell me, do.'

So notes were compared, and symptoms discussed, and after a most informative half-hour, Annie announced herself convinced that she and her sister-in-law were 'carrying together'.

'Have you told John?' she asked.

'I thought I would wait until three months were past.'

'Uncommon good sense,' Annie approved, 'and just what I would have expected of 'ee. Won't Matilda be *peeved.* We shall steal her thunder.'

'But she means to have a boy,' Harriet said wryly. 'The first of a new line of Easters. Oh Annie, you cannot imagine how glad I am that you will keep me company. I could not face such a trial alone.'

And at that moment Matilda herself strode into the room, bringing a stream of cold air in with her and sharp with curiosity.

'What trial is this?' she said at once. 'Do tell, Harriet, for I love a scandal.' And she settled herself beside the fire, her plump face eager.

Annie and Harriet looked at one another quickly, both asking the same question with their eyes. Then Annie decided to answer it.

'You ain't the only one a-breeding this season,' she said. 'Harriet and I are both...'

'But my dears,' Matilda said, clapping her hands. 'How thrilling! Three new Easters at once. What could be better?' And to Harriet's surprise, she kissed them both most warmly. 'Now I know what trial it is you speak of, Harriet. If the heir to the throne can die giving birth, what help is there for such as us? Ain't that so? I read every single word about it, and I tell 'ee I was fairly sick with fear.'

Harriet was most surprised to hear such things, for she'd never imagined that her light-hearted sister-in-law would ever be afraid of anything.

'We are all in God's hands,' Annie said gently. 'Remember that. From the highest princess in the land to the poorest beggar at the gate.'

'But who will He help?' Matilda said. 'That's the great question. It ain't a bit of use you saying that when the Princess Charlotte was allowed to die.'

'And is now in heaven,' Annie said mildly. 'She and her infant son. And what greater joy could there be for them than that?'

'Why to be alive and well,' Matilda said, opening her grey

eyes wide. 'And safely delivered. That is the greatest joy I could imagine.'

Harriet tried to think of the compassionate God in the church at Rattlesden, but the image of the God of retribution she'd worshipped for so long in Churchgate Street frowned into her mind too, ugly and unbidden. Oh please, she prayed, whichever God You are, be kind to me and Annie and Matilda. You've had one awful death. Be satisfied with that. 'Are *you* not afraid?' she said to Annie.

'I was the first time,' Annie admitted, glancing at the chaise longue to make sure her two boys were still asleep. 'But not now. Not now I know how 'tis done.'

'Is there much pain, Annie?' Matilda asked. 'Tell us true, for we need to know.'

'Yes,' Annie said honestly. 'There is. But it soon passes. You forget it the moment you hold your own dear baby in your arms. Think of that. Your own dear baby. That is what makes it all worthwhile.'

'Oh I do hope so,' Harriet said. But fear was still scratching away inside her.

'I'll tell 'ee what, my dears,' Matilda said. 'I mean to enjoy every single day of this pregnancy, just in case. And I'd advise you to do the same.'

So that's why she makes Billy pet her so, Harriet thought, and she suddenly felt quite fond of her. 'I'm so glad we carry together,' she said.

That night she recorded the entire conversation in her diary, almost word for word.

I never thought I should like Matilda so much, she wrote.
She is not at all as I first thought her. Annie is so dear to me, so dear to us both. Better than any sister could ever be, I do believe. Pray God she is proved right in what she says and that we shall all come

safely through together. Should I tell John now, I wonder, or wait as I planned?

She told him two days later, when they were back in their nice red bedroom in Fitzroy Square, and to her delight he began to make preparations for the child as soon as the news was out of her mouth.

'We must hire another cook,' he said, 'for you will need special foods now, will you not? And a new carriage with better springing. Our present one is far too uncomfortable for a mother with child. A mother with child, my dearest! Oh how happy you make me! What else will you need? You have only to say the word and you shall have it at once.'

'With you to love me, I have everything I could possibly need,' she said, kissing him.

'A nursemaid,' he said. 'We will need a nursemaid.'

She remembered Rosie who worked in the laundry in Churchgate Street, fat, comfortable, dependable, loving Rosie, who came from the same part of the town as she did, and was as poor as she'd been, and was so easy to get along with. 'Yes,' she said, 'and I know just the person, if she'll agree to it.'

If he was surprised by her choice, he didn't say so. 'I will write to her this very evening,' he said. 'And at the same time I shall write to Mr Thistlethwaite. His young Tom can run your errands.' Tom and Rosie had worked together once before on the night of the rescue. What could be more appropriate?

Young Tom Thistlethwaite said he was 'chucked all of a heap' to be asked to enter Mr John Easter's service. 'Who'd ha' thought it? he said over and over again on the day John's letter arrived. 'Who'd ha' thought it? 'Tis the first step to becomin' a gentleman's gentleman, ain't it, Ma?'

He was still grinning with delight several months later on the morning of his departure. 'Who'd ha' thought it, Ma?'

'Never mind "who'd ha' thought it",' Bessie said, brushing his blue jacket with the stiff clothes brush, 'you jest do as you're a-told an' no larkin' about. I know the way you go on.'

'If 'e grins any wider,' Thiss said, grinning himself, "e'll bust 'is chops.'

'There's yer bag all packed and yer coat all lovely,' Bessie said, putting the clothes brush back on its rack. 'All nice time fer the coach. Give yer ol' ma a kiss then.' And was seized in a bear hug and kissed until she protested she couldn't breathe.

'Onny one thing,' Tom complained. 'I can't see why they 'ad ter go an' take that ol' Rosie from the laundry an' all.' The two of them were to travel to London together and he felt rather aggrieved to be put in charge of her.

'Now come on, Tom,' Bessie said. 'There's no harm in ol' Rosie. She's jest a bit simple, that's all. She's a good gel.'

'Gel, Ma!' Tom said, eyebrows raised. 'She's no gel. Why she's thirty if she's a day. Thirty an' enough ter drive a saint wild the way she will keep on repeatin' every word you say. I can't see what they wants 'er for.'

'She won't be no trouble, son,' Thiss said. 'Pick up yer bag. It's time you was off, as the guillotine said ter the ol' king's 'ead.'

'Oh Thiss,' Bessie rebuked, 'the things you say!' Now that the time had come to say goodbye to this tall son of hers, she was very close to tears, so her husband's awful joke was something of a relief to her. Letting Pollyanna go to service had been bad enough, and she'd only travelled a few miles up the road to Miss Annie's but letting Tom go was worse. Oh much, much worse. London was such a very long way away, that was the trouble, and Mr John rarely came up to Bury these days, and besides, now that her Tom was twelve and nearly fully grown, he reminded her so much of Thiss when he was young, because he was skinny and slender-necked and quick-moving, and his dark hair was never tidy, and his brown eyes were full of devilment, and his grin was like a slice of melon, and he was always so gentle and kind and full of jokes. It made parting with him uncommon painful. 'The things you say!'

'I was there,' Thiss said, brown eyes glinting at the memory. 'I seen it.'

'You never!' his son said, thrilled at the idea.

'Straight up! Me an' Mrs Easter, we both seen it. That ol' guillotine come a-whistlin' down, an' whosh! That was the end a' the king. Pick up yer bag, son, an' you shall 'ave all the gory details on the way across the square.'

'What a picture ter leave in a boy's mind!' Bessie scolded mildly. 'Shame on yer, Thiss.'

'None better, Goosie,' her husband said. 'They were great days. Liberty, Equality an' Fraternity, they was, which the Prince Regent would do well ter remember when 'e's a-feedin' 'is fat face at our expense. Him an' them great fat overpaid brothers of 'is. Oh yes, they was great days! If they 'adn't gone a-killin' one another afterwards. Come on, Tom, an' I'll tell you all about it.'

Rosie was waiting in the coach yard of the Angel Inn, sitting in a plump sagging heap on top of her bundle, with all four laundry maids standing about her ready to give her 'a good send-off'. When she saw Tom she began to grin.

'Ready fer the off?' Tom asked, grinning back, for he could see that it wouldn't be long before the coach was ready to start.

'Ready fer the off,' she echoed happily, wriggling until her little stumpy legs were touching the ground. 'Fer the off. Yes. I'm a-goin' to look after the babba, Tom. Look after the babba. Yes.'

And all the laundry maids kissed her and bounced her and told her to be sure to be a good gel, and Miss Pettie, who was walking past the Angel Inn on her way to visit her dear friends, the two Miss Callbecks in Whiting Street, ducked her head in at the entrance to wish her Godspeed. Oh it *was* exciting!

And Mr Easter welcomed them both so warmly when they finally got to Fitzroy Square.

This is the life, Ma, Tom wrote to Bessie two days later.
   A capital job in a Capital place. Rosie ain't so dusty, even if she do poll-parrot. She's uncommon fond of Mrs Harriet, who is in the pink, as you said I was to tell you.

Pregnancy suited Harriet Easter, and with Rosie to wait upon her and John to dote upon her the months passed pleasantly enough. And the few worries that surfaced from time to time could be written away into her diary.

In April she recorded the safe arrival of Matilda's infant, which, despite the services of two midwives and an accoucheur, turned out to be a girl, and a very odd-looking one, as Harriet reported secretly, 'with such a big head, such an odd shape, and such a deal of scruffy-looking hair, neither fair nor dark, and little piggy eyes quite sunk into her face, poor child. I do hope my baby is prettier than that. Matilda says she is the dearest baby alive and positively dotes upon her and John says beauty is in the eye of the beholder. The most important thing is that she is safely delivered. Praise God.'

In June, when the roses were in full bloom and the weather was unseasonably cold, Mr Hopkins wrote to tell them that Annie had been safely delivered, too, of a little girl who was to be called Margaret and was every bit as pretty as her brothers. Although she was now heavily pregnant and John was anxious about her travelling at such a time, Harriet insisted on driving to Rattlesden to see the baby for herself. And she was a delicious little creature, with a fluff of fair hair and big blue eyes.

'If I could have one even half as pretty,' Harriet confided, 'I should be the happiest woman alive.'

'You will, my dear,' Annie promised, smiling at her from the pillows. 'You will see.'

But Harriet's pregnancy was growing at an alarming rate, and now that Annie and Matilda were safely through theirs and into the contentment of motherhood, she felt alone and vulnerable. She wrote in her diary every day, of her present aches and discomforts, of the agony to come, and of the terrifying thought that she might not be alive in another six weeks' time. 'How shall I support the anguish,' she wrote, 'when I am such a coward? Oh dear, oh dear.'

She was rather surprised when her labour began just after dawn one morning right at the end of July, which was earlier than she'd estimated, and with pains no worse than those she'd endured without comment every month. John had already left the house to go to the post office for the stamping, so she was all on her own. She got up and put on the loose gown, which was all that would fit her, and began to pace up and down the room. If I am quick, she thought, I could have this baby born before dinner this evening. I will make an excuse that I cannot come down to breakfast because I am fatigued or sleeping or somesuch, and I will wait until he has returned to the Strand before I send for Mrs Young, and then he need know nothing about it. If this is all there is to the pain, I may endure it easily. She was quite light-headed with relief.

'I do believe I shall have this baby safely after all,' she said to the midwife, as the bells of nearby Holy Trinity struck midday.

'I should hope so,' that lady said trenchantly, 'with a good breakfast inside 'ee and me to attend to 'ee. Come let's have 'ee in this bed now 'tis all ready.'

And even when the pains took hold and gripped her most cruelly, Harriet was still sustained by her odd, unexpected euphoria. 'I am nearly there, am I not?' she asked, over and over again.

And Mrs Young said, yes, she was, very, very nearly, and a fine good girl she was being.

And the afternoon was squeezed away, minute by heaving minute. 'I am nearly there, am I not? I am a good girl?'

Four o'clock sounded, half-past, three-quarters. But the child wasn't born. 'Oh!' Harriet grieved between the massive pressure of these long, long pains. 'Why — is it — so — slow?' And Mrs Young's rosy face loomed into her line of vision, 'Nearly there! What a good girl! Nearly there!'

At five o'clock she heard the bells as though they were a long way away, somewhere behind the pain, and she had a moment's panic at the thought that John would return home and find her with the child unborn and the house uncared for. And what would she say to him then? 'I must —' she tried to say, struggling to sit up, 'I must —' But she was beyond speech now, and sitting up was impossible. The very next pain gave her such an uncontrollable urge to push that it simply had to be obeyed, and from then on, she was out of touch with everything and everybody.

John came home and knocked timidly on the door to beg for information, which was given in urgent whispers, but she didn't hear him; Mrs Toxteth brought tea in an invalid cup, but she could barely pause to moisten her lips with it. It was true that when Mrs Young gave her instructions, she obeyed them instinctively, but her senses were concentrated on the great effort she had to make and her eyes were shut tight against all distractions.

And at long long last the child's head was born. On the very next push she could feel its slippery body sliding between her legs and its little hands scrabbling against her thighs, and she opened her eyes to see what it was. And fell in love.

Mrs Young had lifted the baby up between her hands so that he was dangling just above Harriet's belly, trailing his long dark grey cord, with his little fists tucked beneath his chin and his little legs curved towards his chest, pink and entire and perfect and male. And as Harriet gazed at him, spellbound, he opened his eyes and looked at her, a long, profound intelligent look, for all the world as if he'd known her all his life.

'Oh!' she cried. 'Give him to me, do! I must hold him. I must.' And Mrs Young flung a hand towel about the baby's shoulders and lowered him into Harriet's arms. It was a moment of total bliss. A timeless moment. Afterwards she had no idea how long she held her baby, examining those miniature fingers with their fragile shell-pink nails, and kissing the soft skin of his face, very very gently, and ruffling the soft fair down on his tender head, very very gently, breathing in the delicious new scent of him, watching the pulse that throbbed just beneath the skin on that little vulnerable skull, and loving him so very much and so very responsibly.

John arrived in the room and kissed her most lovingly and admired his son, and said he hoped they would call him William after his grandfather. Being shut outside the door while this inexorable process continued, listening to the sobs and groans of his poor dear Harriet and knowing that *he* had been the cause of all her pain had upset him terribly. But he was too weak with relief to share her happiness just yet. 'Was it as bad as you feared, my love?' he asked, dreading the answer.

She had quite forgotten her fear. 'Why no,' she said, 'it wasn't bad. No, indeed. I would not call it bad.' Oh no, bad was quite the wrong word. Giving birth was the most natural thing in the world. A good thing. Almost entirely good. 'Isn't he the prettiest baby you ever saw? Have you told your mother?'

'She is waiting below,' he said. 'Perhaps she could see him?'

'In the morning,' the midwife said firmly. 'There's been enough excitement for one night, I'm thinking. Mrs Easter should sleep now.'

And she is right, Harriet thought, I am very sleepy. 'Should I tell *my* parents?' she asked, half closing her eyes. She felt quite amazingly benevolent towards them.

How could he answer? At a time like this? He didn't want to

tell them anything at all, but he could hardly admit that. Not now.

'I ought to let them know,' she said, resting her cheek against the baby's soft head. Contentment was lapping her into sleep, easily, easily, a long slow pulse of satisfied endeavour. 'He *is* their grandchild, John. I ought to write.'

'You must do as you think fit, my love,' he said, adjusting the blankets so that she and the baby were hooded with wool. 'But not now. Not tonight. Now you must do as Mrs Young says and sleep.'

'Um,' she said. Her eyes were closed now, their lids blue-shadowed. 'I will write tomorrow.'

I do hope you won't, John thought. And as he watched her sleeping, he tried to think of a gentle way to dissuade her.

But he needn't have worried, for he had a powerful ally in his newborn son.

Young Will was a very pretty baby and a very demanding one. He kept his newly enraptured mother so busy that for the next two months she barely had time to think of anything or anybody else, even if she'd wanted to, which she most certainly did not. John himself was frequently ignored, but he endured it happily because it was natural and because his dreadful in-laws seemed to have been forgotten altogether. The promised letter wasn't sent, the child was christened and they weren't invited, he grew and smiled and learned to clap his hands and crow with pleasure and they weren't even mentioned.

And as an additional delight during those long warm days, London society was entertained by the unedifying spectacle of three elderly royal dukes a-courting. The Easter family enjoyed that very much.

The death of the Princess Charlotte and her newborn son had caused something of a constitutional crisis, for the Prince Regent had no other children and, what was worse, no likelihood of any, since he had long ago banned his lawful wife from bed, palace and kingdom, in that order, and now spent his time with a succession of elderly grandmothers long past childbearing. His royal brothers hadn't done much better either for, although they'd produced plenty of illegitimate children, none of them had married. But, fortunately, they were all head-over-ears in debt, so when Lord Liverpool, the Prime Minister, offered to pay off their creditors on condition that they married some suitable German princess or other and managed to father a child to continue the royal line, they began wife-hunting at once.

The royal stud was much derided. The cartoonists were scathing, depicting the fat dukes leaping and cavorting with their possible fiancées, vast bellies well to the fore. And, of course, reports of these elderly courtships sold newspapers in their thousands, as did the accounts of the two royal weddings which took place soon after, when the Duke of Clarence, aged fifty-three, left his ten illegitimate children to fend for themselves and married Princess Adelaide of Saxe-Meiningen, and the Duke of Kent, aged fifty-two, left his elderly mistress, Madame St Laurent, to marry Victoria Mary Louisa of Leiningen.

'Scandalous!' Matilda said when she and Billy were dining with John and Harriet. 'Just think of the hideous babies they'll have. Not like our pretty dears.'

'But then our pretty dears are Easters,' John said, giving her his lopsided grin, 'and Easters are beautiful by definition.'

'Quite right,' Billy said, beaming at Harriet and Matilda. 'Ain't we got wives to prove it?'

'What fun we shall have at Christmas,' Harriet said, 'with three babies at table.'

AND FUN IT CERTAINLY WAS. The three new babies sat in three highchairs and were fed their very first slops and made a dreadful mess of their hands and faces in the process and were cheered and kissed and tossed in the air and passed from aunt to uncle until they were rosy with handling. And Jimmy and Beau distributed the presents and were told they were the best-behaved children anyone had ever seen.

Nan and Mr Brougham took the entire party to the playhouse at the Market Cross to see an uncommon foolish play about a man who could grant wishes. James preached the sermon in the church of St Mary and did it exceedingly well. And Annie and Matilda and Harriet spent their afternoons together, playing with their babies and talking of everyone and everything.

'You must bring Will to Rattlesden for a week or two in the summer,' Annie said to Harriet. 'In June, perhaps, when Billy and Matilda are visiting Bury. They will be nearly a twelve-month by then and old enough to play together. What sport we shall have with three babies crawling and beginning to walk. Just think of it!'

It was a lively summer and the three babies kept them all very fully occupied, for Meg and Matty were toddling about and into everything, and Will took his first few staggering steps on the rectory lawn on the last day of their holiday.

'A terrible trio,' Nan said, watching with affection, as Jimmy and Beau gave the two little girls piggyback rides. 'I shall buy them all hobby horses the next time I'm in town.'

How our lives revolve around these children, John thought, as Will climbed onto his lap and laid his little fair head against his father's shoulder to rest for a while. He was growing more like Harriet every day, with that soft hair as pale as flax and his cheeks the same apricot pink and his eyes a quite startling blue. So pretty and so loving, just like his mother. It is a good life, John reflected, holding his son tenderly and smiling across at Harriet where she sat among the cushions under the holm oak. A good life and long may it continue.

CHAPTER 22

Nan Easter was chairing the quarterly meeting of her regional managers, and a very sticky meeting it had turned out to be. Sales of writing paper, pens, blotters, inks and sealing wax were all high and steadily rising, while newspaper sales had never been better. So she'd come to the meeting expecting it to be cheerful and congratulatory, and hoping that it would be quickly over, because she was planning to visit Harding and Howell's cloth emporium in Pall Mall with Sophie Fuseli later that afternoon to choose material for an evening gown to wear at the Earl of Harrowby's soirée in ten days' time. It was a great surprise to her, and a considerable disappointment, that the meeting was actually quite acrimonious.

It started with a general grumbling of the kind she'd met before and found easy to deal with. Mr Burns of Cambridgeshire was dissatisfied.

'We had not envisaged such an enormous increase in the sale of stationery, Mrs Easter,' he said, 'and that is the truth of it. Our shop assistants cannot keep pace with it.'

'When there is an item of news like the marriage of the Royal Dukes last year,' Mr Elphick from Bath declared, 'or more recently the birth of the new Princess Victoria in May, which it has to be admitted sold in prodigious numbers, nevertheless it gives our shopkeepers such a mort of work to do and all at once, if you take my meaning, ma'am, they are hard put to it to attend to all the custom that presents itself.'

'Do others have the same experience?' Nan asked, looking round the table to assess the strength of feeling.

It appeared that they did. In fact Thiss said the East Anglian shops often had so much trade 'they could do with bein' four-'anded'.

'Then hire more assistants,' Nan said, making up her mind to it at once. 'The solution is plain. Appoint more shop hands, two where you have one, three where there are two, five where there are three, and so on accordingly. We cannot lose trade on account of our success. That would be plain folly.'

'But how would such a thing be done?' Mr Burns asked, his brow wrinkled with concern at the enormity of the task. 'I have asked Mr John to attend to three new appointments already and he says we must wait.'

'Is this so, John?' Nan asked.

'There is considerable pressure for new appointments,' John said, taking his notebook from his pocket. 'I have twenty-four in all to attend to. There is bound to be some delay, I fear.'

'No there en't' his mother said cheerfully. "Tis grown too big for one man, that's plain. Very well then, you managers must appoint for yourselves. You know enough about the business to make good choices by now I should hope. Offer two-thirds the going rate for newcomers, three-quarters for experience.' And she dusted her hands against each other, swish, swish. She would probably have to get a bank loan to cover the first two- or three-weeks' wages for such a sudden increase in staff, but after that, if there really was as much trade as her managers were claiming, the new assistants would pay their way.

The managers were all rather flattered by her decision, for it gave them considerably more power than they'd enjoyed until that afternoon and was a bold and public demonstration of the confidence she was placing in them.

But John was *not* pleased. To have one of his most cherished tasks casually taken away from him and then given to every single local manager, whether or not he was capable of doing it, seemed to him an undeniable folly, to say nothing as to whether the firm could afford so many new staff. But he remained deliberately calm and made no comment, for that would have been a second and even greater folly. He would talk to her about her decision when the meeting was over and he and Billy and Cosmo remained behind. There might be some way he could mitigate against the worst results of her impetuosity then. But really her thoughtlessness was impossible. Oh, if only he could be the director of the firm, as he surely should be now that he had a son and heir to follow on after him! He would make a much better job of it.

Unfortunately Billy wanted to talk to his mother too, and as soon as the managers had left the boardroom and while Nan was opening the windows to let in some fresh air, for the afternoon was excessively hot, he started up his own conversation, speaking before John could open his mouth.

'And how of me, Mama?' he said, giving Nan his affectionate grin.

'How of you?' she said, busy at the windows.

'You've made a deal of work for me and my department, too, with all that stationery.'

'Then hire more men. The answer's simple.' Lifting the last window.

'And what of the extra work I have to do? Don't I deserve some recompense?'

Oh I see how it is, Nan thought, looking at the hopeful expression on that open face of his. Matilda wants a new carriage or new furniture or some other expensive purchase.

'Aye,' she said, 'I daresay you've earned it. When the new appointments are all made, I will consider it.'

'Not before?'

'No.' She grinned at him. 'The firm en't made of money.'

'I do have a family to support now, Mama.'

'So does your brother, but you don't hear him asking for anything, you notice.'

'He'd take it if 'twere offered though, wouldn't 'ee John?' Billy asked, turning to his brother.

'I would depend upon Mama to be fair,' John said, 'And I would not expect extra remuneration unless the firm could afford it.' How annoying Billy was to bring money into the discussion. Now, if he tried to talk about the way the appointments should be handled, she might think he was simply making an argument for higher wages.

'Is there any other business, Cosmo?' Nan asked. And on being told that there wasn't, 'We can decide upon your wages some other time, Billy. If my sons are to be given a rise, then the local managers should have something too, I daresay, considering all the extra work I've just put upon 'em. Perhaps you could produce some estimates for me, Cosmo. I shall need to know how much all these extra assistants will cost. Assume that three-quarters of 'em will be paid at the two-thirds rate.'

She was on her feet. Cosmo was agreeing that this could be done. The moment was passing. With a lurch of irritation, John realised that if he wanted to make any sort of protest about her decision he would have to speak now.

'Mama,' he said, 'were we entirely wise to hand over the appointment of new staff to the local managers?'

'Yes,' she said briskly. 'Entirely wise.'

'Mr Burns could certainly do it,' he persisted, 'and Thiss, of course, and Cosmo, but how of Mr Tadcaster? He will hardly know how to begin.' Mr Tadcaster had only been the Yorkshire manager for a few short months, and in John's view had by no means proved his worth.

She had an answer immediately. 'Then you shall travel back with him and show him how 'tis done,' she said, completely unabashed. 'He and then any others who need help, which I leave to your discretion. I may depend upon you to be tactful and unobtrusive I am sure. They'll expect you to oversee 'em, I daresay. Now I'm off to meet Mrs Fuseli, or she will think I've taken a fit I'm so late.' And that was the end of the discussion. It was extremely irritating.

Now I shall have to travel the country supervising appointments I don't actually make, he thought irritably, and just at the very moment when I most want to be at home with Harriet and my dear little Will. For Will was one year old now and at his most bewitching. She don't take my feelings into account at all. Billy may beg for more money and complain about the amount of work he has to do, and she smiles at him. While I say nothing, ask for nothing, never complain, and she puts more burdens upon me. And all the old feelings of isolation and rejection returned to sting him. He decided to go home to Harriet and Will at once and be comforted.

HARRIET AND WILL had spent the afternoon in Fitzroy Square.

It was very hot, even for August, and the afternoons were dusty and breathless although all the windows in the house were flung wide open to glean as much air as possible. Will was so uncomfortable indoors that Harriet took him out into the square every afternoon for a walk in the circular gardens among her promenading neighbours. With a straw hat to shade his pretty blue eyes from the sun, a silk coat to protect his little white arms and soft leather shoes on his stumbling feet, he was the prettiest thing in the square.

By now he had learned to say 'Dadda' and 'Mama' and 'yook!'

and there was a great deal to 'yook' at in their enclosed garden: stray dogs sniffing trees and superior cats sleeping under bushes, sparrows as shrill as flutes and pigeons strutting like aldermen. To say nothing of their neighbours, who stopped to pass the time of day or to deplore the continuing heat or to compliment Harriet upon the beauty of her baby and his admirable behaviour.

That afternoon they'd been talking to Mrs Mannering, from next door but one, and Mrs Mannering had given her favourite baby a sugar stick.

'Such a delightful child,' she said, watching him as he ate it with the solemn concentration he reserved for food. 'Mrs Easter fairly dotes upon him, does she not? I saw her lifting him into her carriage only yesterday. Such a pretty sight! How he must please your parents, my dear.'

My parents, Harriet thought. Why, I've forgotten all about them! But she could hardly tell Mrs Mannering that. 'He pleases everybody,' she said diplomatically. And she made up her mind then and there that she really would write to her parents and tell them about this child. It was high time for, after all, she'd vowed to write on the day he was born. How very remiss she'd been.

It took her quite a long time to compose a letter that was suitable, for there were so many things she couldn't say, and she felt obliged to apologise for not writing sooner, and she was trying hard not to brag too much about Will. But by now her conscience was stinging her, so before John's chaise came trotting home from the Strand, the letter was written and sealed and taken to the Post by Tom Thistlethwaite.

He was none too pleased to hear about it. 'Whatever did you do that for?' he said crossly. 'I thought you had decided against it.'

'They are my parents, John,' she said. 'And Will is their

grandson. Surely they should be allowed to see him just once in a while?'

'It's deuced inconvenient,' he said, squinting with annoyance. 'I have to visit York in two days' time, and heaven only knows when I'll be back.' And he told her about the meeting and his mother's thoughtless decision.

'If she has told you to go to York and assist Mr Tadcaster.' Harriet said reasonably, 'then I daresay you must. You need not worry on my account. I'm sure I can deal with my parents well enough by now.'

But he worried just the same. Harriet seemed to have forgotten her beating, but he could not. Before he left, he gave detailed instructions to Paulson that he was to watch out for the arrival of a strange man and woman who would, most probably, be dressed in black, and refuse them entrance if he possibly could. 'Tell 'em your mistress is out of town,' he said. 'Put 'em off.'

'Quite so, sir. I understand,' Paulson said. 'Leave it to me, sir.'

But he had underestimated the cunning of the Sowerbys who arrived five days later, dressed in their best black as John had predicted, and full of righteous indignation.

Paulson opened the door to them and looked down on them in every sense of the word as they stood on the bottom step, with their black hats silhouetted against the wilting plane trees in the square.

'Is your mistress at home?' Mr Sowerby asked, as his wife walked confidently up the steps.

Paulson moved to bar her way into the house.

'I regret Mrs Easter is out of town,' he said smoothly.

That was disconcerting. 'Indeed? You surprise me,' Mr Sowerby said. 'Being she invited us to call upon her.'

'When will she be back?' Mrs Sowerby asked.

'I'm sure I couldn't say,' Paulson replied.

'You must know, man!' Mr Sowerby eyed the butler suspiciously. He was young to be holding such a position and was not as confident as he seemed. 'Very well then,' he said. 'We have travelled a great distance to no purpose. My wife would like a rest and some sustenance before we return. I am sure you can arrange that, can you not?'

This was becoming tricky, 'I'm afraid that will not be possible, sir,' Paulson said. 'I've the most strict instructions to admit no one.'

'Ridiculous!' Mr Sowerby said, now sure the butler was lying. 'We are Mrs Easter's parents, you understand.'

'That's as may be, sir,' Paulson said, visibly digging in his heels. 'But orders are orders.'

'Kindly stand aside!' Mrs Sowerby said, taking her cue from her husband. 'I wish to enter.'

'I don't doubt you do, ma'am,' Paulson said doggedly. 'Can't be done.'

Mrs Sowerby scowled at him for several seconds without speaking. She was now determined to gain entrance to the house for, like her husband, she was convinced the butler was lying. His dignified mask had dropped and he looked uncertain and confused. It was uncommon aggravating to be denied admission in this heartless way. What was Harriet thinking of to write to them after all this time and invite them here and then to leave instructions such as that? 'Twas quite singularly ill-mannered. She decided to try another tack.

'Oh,' she said loudly, 'I see how 'tis. We are to be *spurned*! I see how 'tis, Father. She has forgotten all the rites due to loving parents. We are to be *publicly spurned.*' And she turned up her eyes and began to groan.

'Ingratitude!' Mr Sowerby said. 'Downright, filial ingratitude! Ooh, sharper than a serpent's tooth!'

'You love 'em,' Mrs Sowerby said, 'and what do 'ee get? *Rejection*! That's what you get! Oh, oh, oh, the agony of it!'

'My wife is ill!' Mr Sowerby cried dramatically, throwing his arms into the air like an Old Testament prophet. And as if to prove him right, Mrs Sowerby gave a terrible combination of shriek and groan and threw herself backwards onto the pavement. 'Aaah! Aaah! Have pity on a poor, suffering women, you heartless wretch!'

The heartless wretch was so nonplussed he didn't know what to do, but by now Mrs Sowerby was making such a noise that Harriet heard her upstairs in the drawing room and, recognising her voice, came down at once to see what was going on. But this time Mrs Sowerby was rolling about on the pavement, and windows on all three sides of the square were full of faces, pale aristocratic faces under lace bonnets, wide-eyed with curiosity, round red faces giggling and gossiping under servants' caps.

'Get up I beg you, Mama!' Harriet said. 'You make us a laughing-stock.'

But her mother was well into her fit, rolling from side to side, and beating the ground with her fists, and groaning and howling louder than ever.

'You see what you have done,' Mr Sowerby spat at his daughter. 'I bring this to *your* door, my gel. To *your* door. I hope you have the grace to feel ashamed.'

She was certainly feeling very embarrassed. Whatever had brought this on? Somebody must have annoyed her mother to make her throw a fit like this. I must get her inside, she thought. A public exhibition of this kind would do them no good at all.

'Would you be so good as to fetch a chair, Paulson,' she said. 'The lady will have to be carried into the house.'

It was surprising how quickly the lady recovered once the chair had been set down inside Harriet's parlour, and even more surprising what a prodigious quantity of tea and cakes and white bread and butter she managed to consume. Her fit seemed to have given her an appetite.

'Very well, Harriet,' she said, pleasantly enough when all the food had been eaten. 'Time for us to see our grandson, I believe.'

So Will was sent for and escorted into the room by Rosie, who was very put out to see the Sowerbys again and dropped her chin on her chest and tried to look fierce. Will, on the other hand, was his usual friendly self.

'Yook!' he said, pointing at them with cheerful interest.

'How grossly ill-mannered!' Mrs Sowerby said, bristling away from him. 'I see you have not taught him how to behave.'

'He is only one year old, Mama,' Harriet said, springing to his defence. 'At his age...'

'At *his* age,' Mrs Sowerby said sternly, '*you* had been taught to speak when you were spoken to. But I daresay that is a result of his being entered into the *wrong church*.'

Harriet was taken off balance by this sudden attack. 'He has not been entered into the wrong church, Mama,' she said. 'He was christened...'

'The *wrong church*,' Mrs Sowerby repeated. 'Why of course 'tis the wrong church. Has childbirth addled your brains that you cannot understand what I am saying? It was bad enough to be informed that you had been so immeasurably foolish as to marry in the wrong church. And I might say, *being informed* instead of being invited, was a *great hardship* to us. How could you treat your own parents with such discourtesy? Well, well, we will not talk of it now. You may be thankful that your father and I are of a forgiving disposition and are resolved to forget your poor behaviour. Howsomever, our grandson must be baptised again and this time he must be baptised correctly. Make no mistake about that.'

Harriet's heart was beginning to throb just as it used to do when she was a girl living at home and with no escape from them. Why on earth did I invite them here? she thought. And why do they imagine they may still bully me now, in my own home? I have only to ring the bell and Paulson will show them to the door.

'The child has been christened according to the rites of the Church of England, Mama,' she said, trying to be reasonable. And she was horrified to hear that her voice was quavering.

'Humph!' her mother snorted. 'We'll soon see about that. That's Mrs Easter's doing, I don't doubt. Is the child's mother to have no say in the matter? You must exert yourself. Take a stand. You are a mother now and must fight for your child's immortal soul. Bestir yourself. Satan is all about you. Oh, what a blessing I have found out where you live, you feckless girl. I shall come here every month, no matter what the cost. *Every single month!* You may depend upon it. It is my God-given duty, en't it, Father?'

'Indubitably,' Mr Sowerby said.

But Harriet had rung the bell to be rescued and there were footsteps scuffling up *the* stairs towards them. More than one pair by the sound of it. Two? Three? The door was opened without ceremony and the room was full of people. Mrs Easter, who had just arrived and been told all about the visit by Paulson, Paulson himself behind her and Peg Mullins, who'd been eavesdropping in the hall, stomping in behind him, and Tom Thistlethwaite, who had heard the commotion and didn't want to be left out, bringing up the rear. Oh, what a relief to see them!

'Why, Mrs Sowerby,' Nan said briskly. 'Just on your way out, I see. Pray allow me to escort you to the door.'

'No,' Mrs Sowerby began to argue, 'I was not...'

'Oh 'tis no trouble,' Nan said, holding her adversary's arm in a surprisingly firm grip and propelling her towards the door. 'No trouble at all.' They were on the landing already. 'I trust I find you well.' Jogging her down the stairs, with Mr Sowerby trailing behind them.

'I have no desire to...' Mrs Sowerby said, trying in vain to pull her elbow out of Nan's grip. 'No desire...'

'I'm sure on't,' Nan said affably. 'And here's Paulson with your umbrella. I trust you have a pleasant journey home. Good afternoon to you both.'

THE MINUTE the door closed behind them poor Harriet burst into tears. Oh, how could she have been so foolish as to invite them into her home? John was right. She should have left things as they were. But she'd forgotten how terribly they upset her when they began to bully. Whatever should she do? They would visit whenever they felt like it, now that they'd established how easily it could be done.

'Come now,' Nan said, striding back into the room. 'Get your bonnet. We're off to have supper upon the river. You'll look after our Will, won't you Rosie?'

How quickly she restores things to normal, Harriet thought, tying on her bonnet. And she was glad to have such a mother-in-law. But she was still worried about what John would say when he heard.

Much to her relief, when he finally came home five days later, John was not cross with her or his butler, nor surprised at the behaviour of his in-laws.

'I blame myself for leaving you without protection,' he said seriously. 'I had the gravest doubts about the wisdom of going to York, but I could not avoid it!'

'Perhaps they will not come here again,' Harriet hoped, but they both knew she didn't think it likely.

'If they do, you must refuse to let them in.'

'If she throws another fit,' Harriet confessed, very near to tears, 'I should be forced to let her in. I could not allow her to shame us before our neighbours. And besides, she makes me feel so feeble. I can't think how she does it, but she does.'

'Does she often throw such fits?' John asked, beginning to feel very suspicious about the whole affair.

'Well yes,' Harriet had to admit. 'I fear she does. From time to time, when things are particularly bad.'

'Or when she can't think of any other means to get her own way.'

'Yes. That is so.'

He looked at her lovingly, moved by the misery on her pale face. 'I must go to Manchester next week,' he said. 'I cannot leave you and little Will behind to be tormented. There is only one answer. You must come to Manchester with me.'

CHAPTER 23

'How if you were to travel with me?' Frederick Brougham asked. 'Three months in France and Italy, eh? Our own Grand Tour.'

Nan was still in London even though it was the middle of August when she was usually in Bury. She and Frederick had been to the Theatre Royal that evening to see a new play called *Teasing Made Easy.* They had returned to Bedford Square, still laughing at the folly of it, to dine well and love at leisure. Now they were talking in that easy desultory way that follows love and precedes sleep, and he had broached the subject he'd been considering all through the evening. 'My cousin and I have been given a rather unusual commission, d'ye see, which we've to start in a week's time.'

'Um?'

'We are to travel to France and Italy, to find the Princess of Wales and there make discreet inquiries as to how she might envisage her position were the Regent to become King.'

'As he will when the old King dies.'

'Indeed. How if you were to travel with me and spend the summer upon the Continent instead of in Bury St Edmunds?'

'And leave the firm for three months?' Nan said, opening her eyes. 'My heart alive! That en't the way of things at all. 'Twould be mortal folly, so 'twould, and we expanding into Scotland.'

He grimaced at her, lying beside him among the pillows in her curtained bed. 'You might ha' done me the courtesy of considering it,' he said. 'Or made some pretence of considering it, at the very least. Here you've been telling me how your son has taken his wife to Manchester with him and roundly approving such action I believe, and yet you deny me a similar privilege.'

'Harriet travels with John, my dear, because they can't abide to be parted and he thinks she needs protecting from those dratted Sowerbys. I got a job to do.'

'So we must part,' he said, sighing. ''Tis a disappointment to me that you take the news with such equanimity, my dear. A tear or two would not have gone amiss.'

'Had you needed such tricks,' she said sleepily, 'you'd ha' taken up with a milliner or some such. 'Ten't in my nature to dissemble.'

More's the pity, he thought wryly, for there were times when a little feminine flattery would have been balm to his spirit, dishonest or no. He would be celebrating his fiftieth birthday while he was on his travels, and the thought of how short his life was becoming was making him melancholy. 'You will not miss me, I fear,' he said, fishing for reassurance. ''Twill be out of sight, out of mind.'

She had closed her eyes, drifting towards sleep again. 'That's all squit, so 'tis,' she said kindly. 'You know better than that, Mr Frederick Brougham. En't there another saying concerning absence? Makes the heart grow fonder, I'm told.'

'Amen to that,' he said. But it would have been better to have had her company for he knew he would miss her sorely, headstrong creature that she was.

But the headstrong creature was already asleep.

. . .

IN AN UNFAMILIAR BEDROOM in the Swan with Two Necks at Leicester, Harriet Easter was writing her diary. John had fallen asleep within minutes of getting into bed, but she was too wakeful to settle and after a while, when she was quite sure she could move without disturbing him, she had crept from the bed, unpacked her diary from its hiding place among Will's small clothes and taking her candle to the table, had begun to write, licking her pencil from time to time in the earnestness of composition.

To see so much of this countryside is a great pleasure and the more so to see it in John's company, which I must confess I have not done today, being as I travelled inside the coach with Will and Rosie and Peg and he travelled outside, which I daresay is the reason he is so quiet. He said very little at dinner, perhaps because he is fatigued, but I hope and believe that he enjoys our journey together. We stopped for refreshment at an inn called the Saracen's Head at a place called Newport Pagnell. We have travelled ninety-eight miles today, in fine weather and without mishap. Tomorrow we ride on to Manchester. Little Will has been an absolute saint making no fuss and sleeping for a good deal of the journey. Such a good boy. What will tomorrow bring, I wonder?

It brought a lovely summer day and a late start and John quieter than ever. He said good morning to her when she woke, but then lapsed into complete silence, watching as she fed little Will, shaving himself ruminatively, and dressing without a word. It worried her that he was so withdrawn, for he could hardly be fatigued first thing in the morning, but she busied herself with the baby and tried to persuade herself that he had a great deal to think about with all the business he had to do, and that his silence was to be expected.

But the brooding expression on his face was the sign of a conflict which he hadn't expected and which was making him feel so ashamed that he couldn't talk to her about it. To be at home with her and Will in their beautiful house was unalloyed pleasure. But now, after one day travelling *en familie*, he had to admit that he did not welcome her presence on this journey.

She was too eager to talk, that was the trouble, and too busy with Will, and there were altogether too many people fussing around them. In the three years since their wedding, he had grown used to travelling quietly and alone, busy with his thoughts and his plans for business. So he had been short with her during the previous day, and too tired to make much conversation at dinner, and now he was irritable with himself, and sorry for her.

Fortunately, the Swan with Two Necks was already crowded when they came downstairs, for the Saturday market was under way, and the coffee room was full of farmers drinking ale and enjoying one another's raucous company, and farmers' dogs gnawing chop bones and enjoying a little idleness. The coach-yard was crowded, too, with two coaches ready to leave and their own awaiting a new team, which had still to be led out.

'What's amiss, Horace?' John asked the coachman, glad to be back in the easily familiar world of men and horses.

'Two gone lame, so they say, Mr Easter sir,' Horace said, spitting a long stream of chewed tobacco onto the cobbles. 'Deuce tek it. We're five minutes late all-a-ready.'

He knows every coachman on the road, Harriet thought admiringly, as the two men continued their complaint, and she was glad that her dear John seemed more himself again. It did not concern her at all that they were five minutes late. Will had made a good breakfast and was chirruping with contentment on Rosie's broad shoulder, and it was pleasant out in the courtyard, with the morning sun warm on her shoulders and the place full of unusual people. There were several local women wrapped in shawls and wearing black bonnets over their caps selling stockings from huge wicker baskets carried on their hips. Perhaps there would be time for her to go and look at them. They seemed uncommon pretty.

'Should we settle Will inside do 'ee think, John dear?' she asked, when he finally came back to stand beside her. 'Or do I have time to go and look at the stockings?'

'Look by all means, my dear,' he said. 'We shall be a good many minutes yet. You might find a pair or two you would care to purchase.' A present would make amends for his neglect. 'Choose two pairs.'

So while the new team was backed into position, and the travellers gathered about the coach ready to board, she picked two pairs of fine white hose, and an excellent bargain they were, being embroidered from mid-calf to ankle and only sixpence a pair. For a moment, as John handed over the shilling, she even wondered whether it might not be an economy to buy another pair, but then the ostler sang out 'All set!' and the passengers surged forward and the stocking seller was pushed aside.

And then the whole place was caught up in the noise and excitement of departure, with dogs barking and leaping, and hooves clopping against the cobbles and pole chains clinking, and voices calling goodbye.

'Yook! Yook!' Will said to her happily as Peg passed him to Rosie, who was already in the coach, and John offered his arm to his wife to help her climb aloft to her outside seat, and she was so happy to be on the road again that her spirits lifted like a bird taking flight. And then, just as the coachman was gathering the reins, there was a further excitement as a gentleman came running out of the coffee room into the yard, yelling 'hold hard!' and scrambled aloft to sit beside her.

'Just in time!' he said cheerfully. 'Lord, what a rush!'

He was a most affable gentleman, and a very good looking one, being at least six-foot-tall and with a most open and honest expression on his face. A man you could hardly help noticing, she thought, noticing him, for he had thick fair hair beneath his blue top hat and yet his moustache was almost ginger. How curious. He wore a blue cloth coat to match his hat and his gloves were made of chevre leather and even his boots and breeches were quite spotless. A very noticeable gentleman.

Then she realised that he was looking at her and she dropped her eyes in confusion, embarrassed to have been caught staring.

'It is a fine morning, sir,' the gentleman said, addressing his remarks to John in the correct manner. 'Do you travel far?'

'To Manchester, sir,' John said, speaking shortly and without expression as he always did when addressed by a stranger. He had no intention of making unnecessary conversation, not if he could help it.

But this stranger wasn't at all put down by coldness. 'Why so do I, sir,' he said cheerfully. 'So do I. What a fine thing to have company. Travel can be wearisome, can it not, when one is alone?'

'That depends entirely upon one's cast of mind.'

'Oh indeed,' the stranger said. 'My opinion entirely. Entirely my opinion.' And he smiled at them both.

Harriet smiled back because he really was such a nice friendly man and it would have been discourteous to have ignored him even though John *was* cool.

'You travel with your family, I believe, ma'am,' the stranger said. ''Twas your baby I saw you kiss, was it not? A pretty baby, ma'am, if you will permit me to say so. Uncommon like her mother.'

'He is a boy, sir,' Harriet said. 'William.'

'A find child, ma'am. You must be very proud of him.'

'Oh I am,' Harriet said and she proceeded to explain how much. And so their new companion complimented his way into conversation. By the time they reached Loughborough, where the church bells were ringing with uncommon sweetness, John had unbent sufficiently to exchange names, and the stranger, who said he was called Mr Richards, pronounced himself honoured to have met one of the sons of the great firm of A Easter and Sons, 'it being quite the most dependable of any I have ever encountered, sir, if I may make so bold as to say so.'

So Harriet told him about the shop in the Strand, 'where all the work is done', since John still seemed disinclined to talk and she didn't like to appear rude to such a friendly man. And he seemed very interested.

At Derby, at an old black and white inn called the Dolphin, they changed teams in less than three minutes, which, so Mr Richards said, was 'an uncommon impressive feat'. Consequently they arrived at the Green Man and Black's Head in Ashbourne just as the parish church was striking midday.

'Best church in the whole of the Peak District, ma'am,' Mr Richards said, admiring the great spire that dominated the little town. 'They call it the Cathedral of the Peaks, did 'ee know that? Now you will see some scenery, I'll warrant, for we're to take the high road to Buxton so I'm told. But you must sample a piece of the famous Ashbourne gingerbread before we leave this place, must she not Mr Easter? Made from a secret recipe passed on to the local people here by French prisoners during the war against Napoleon. Did 'ee know that?' He was a veritable encyclopaedia of information, a fact that made John dislike him even more heartily, particularly as Harriet found him entertaining.

And of course he was right about the gingerbread, which was hot and spicy and very filling, and the scenery, which was breath-taking.

Harriet was deeply impressed by it, for she had never seen mountains before and the sight of these high peaks ranged one upon the other was wonderfully romantic, all those wild slopes covered in green scrub and patched with dark pine forests, and the distant heights so far away that they were little more than mauve and ochre mist, and all those higgledy-piggledy dry-stone walls dividing the rocky fields, and the low clouds fairly scudding overhead and casting long swathes of moving shadow over everything beneath them.

'How beautiful it is!' she said to John as the coach rocked them along. 'What a joy to be travelling here.'

'Yes,' he said, and he bent his head so that his mouth touched her ear. 'I would enjoy it a deal more,' he whispered, 'if we could have the place to ourselves.'

'I too,' she said, smiling at him. And she was glad that he seemed more himself.

It was past three o'clock when they reached Whaley Bridge, and by then the sky was beginning to cloud over.

'It will rain now, you may depend upon it,' Mr Richards said. 'It always rains in Manchester. In fact, the poets would say that Nature herself is weeping against the iniquity of the place.'

'I do not doubt they would,' John said to him coldly. 'Poets being free with such foolish sayings.'

'Oh, my own view entirely,' Mr Richards hastened to agree. 'Entirely my own view.'

'Is it a bad place, John?' Harriet asked, quite anxiously. But even as she spoke, they reached the top of the incline and she saw the city for herself. Or to be more accurate, she saw the smoke cloud under which the city lay, a huge, grey-brown, amorphous mass of shifting vapour, several miles across in every direction, heaving and swelling like some vast stranded sea monster.

For a few startled seconds she thought the countryside was on fire, for she could see the occasional glimpse of red flame glimmering under the murk, or a streak of yellow light, lurid and unearthly, but then she realised that the fires were merely lighted windows and that the oily black smoke that was coiling upwards out of the mass was rising from the tops of equally oily black chimneys.

''Tis a city of seventy thousand souls,' Mr Richards said, 'if souls they can be called, not one of whom has the right to cast a vote, and not one of whom has elected any member to the present Parliament to represent his views, since Manchester does not have the right to return a member to Parliament, which many would consider a scandal when Old Sarum returns two with an electorate that number merely eleven.'

'John,' Harriet said, 'why is it so smoky?'

'It is a manufacturing town,' he told her. 'And you cannot have manufacture without smoke, or soot or machinery. That is the way things are, I fear.'

'My opinion entirely,' Mr Richards said. 'Entirely my opinion.'

And so they rocked downhill into the city and no more was said. After a mile they could smell the soot and taste the oil in the air. After two they could hear the noise of the mills, a steady unremitting reverberation like distant thunder. It made Harriet feel uneasy, despite her attempts to be reasonable.

And seven miles later they were trundling along an unkempt road between the mills, tall, square-set, uncompromising build-ings, bearing their owners' tall, square-set, uncompromising names. Here machines crunched and clashed with such power that the whole place juddered under their impact and the windows rattled in their frames. Here huge black pistons punched and pounded with monotonous and terrible regularity, like chastening rods in huge iron fists. And everything was grimed. The red brick of the factory buildings was smeared with soot and encrusted with oily black grease; a warehouse with small barred windows had green lichen stains all down its walls as though someone had thrown green slime over it. And above all these damp, dour, formidable buildings the sky was totally empty; there was no colour, no cloud, no movement, no summer, just a vast dirty grey blankness.

'Oh John,' Harriet whispered,' 'tis an ugly place.'

'We shall only stay for as long as is necessary,' he promised, warmed to be able to comfort her.

The coach toiled up the steep winding alley that was Market Street and stopped outside a black and white inn so ancient and ramshackle it looked as though it had been cobbled together from the remnants of six or seven other buildings. They had arrived.

'I trust I shall meet with you again,' Mr Richards said, bounding down into the coach yard. And was gone before he could hear John's reply. Which was just as well, since the disgruntled Mr Easter's answer was, 'I very much hope not.'

They settled into their rooms at the Royal Hotel. The next day was Sunday, so they went to church in a fine new church dedicated to St Ann which formed one side of a new tree-lined square, to which they returned later that afternoon to dine with Mr Clarke, who kept a bookshop in the market place and said he was 'proud to be a friend to Mr Easter, yes indeed, and delighted to have the opportunity to meet his charming wife'.

The guests about the table that evening were all concerned with books and newspapers in one way or another, being book-sellers, and newspaper sellers and the editors of two local papers, so the conversation was easy and relaxed and familiar. But presently they began to tell their two visitors from London all about a great radical meeting that had been called for the following morning. Mr Taylor, who wrote articles for the local papers and was short and dark-haired and full of energy, had a poster advertising the meeting, which he passed about the table to Harriet's considerable interest.

It was signed by Mr Henry Hunt, the orator, and was addressed to the *Inhabitants of Manchester and Neighbourhood.*

Fellow Countrymen, it said:

You will meet on Monday next, my friends, and by your steady, firm and temperate deportment you will convince all your enemies that you have an important and imperious public duty to perform.

The eyes of all England, nay, of all Europe, are fixed upon you: and every friend of real Reform and of rational Liberty, is tremblingly alive to the result of your Meeting on Monday next.

It sounded very important. ''Twill be a big meeting, I don't doubt,' John said.

'Very big,' Mr Taylor agreed. 'They do say there will be sixty thousand people there. 'Twill be a magnificent sight to see. There are to be bands and banners, and reporters from all the London papers.'

'Are you to be there, Mr Taylor?' Harriet asked.

'Indeed I am,' Mr Taylor said. 'I would not miss it for the world.'

'Ain't there like to be a riot with such a large gathering?' John asked, mindful of the safety of his wife and child.

'No indeed, Mr Easter,' Mr Taylor reassured at once. 'That is the entire point of issuing this notification. The marchers are all pledged to keep themselves in perfect control. Each and every one of them. They are all quite splendidly prepared and totally calm, despite the presence of government spies and suchlike who would like to provoke them. Indeed, that is one purpose of the meeting: to demonstrate their calm in the face of provocation.'

That sounded reasonable, Harriet thought, despite the excitable tone of the notice. Sometimes, as she knew from the preachers of her childhood, it was necessary to show your enemies how resolute and calm you could be. In fact, calm was one acknowledged way of defeating the devil. 'An admirable purpose,' she said.

'The other and more important purpose, however,' another

guest pointed out, 'is to ask for reform of our present parliamentary system, which is manifestly rotten and agreed to be so by all reasonable men.'

'Sixty thousand people,' Mr Taylor said, 'gathered together peaceably to ask for their rights as citizens. What could be more proper or well-controlled than that?'

'Nothing will come of it,' Mr Clarke said, 'for 'tis all folly. Howsomever 'tis like to be a moment of history and my wife and I will be there to see it. I have a friend with lodgings in Windmill Street, d'ye see. His rooms overlook the very field itself, so we shall have the best of possible views. How if you were to accompany me there, Mr Easter? You and your charming wife, of course. I'm sure he would be agreeable to it.'

'I have work to do tomorrow,' John said, 'thank 'ee all the same. But Mrs Easter might care to accept your offer.' She was looking quite animated about this meeting, and if she were with Mr and Mrs Clarke, and inside a house she would be quite safe, even if the crowds *did* get a little boisterous. It would keep her occupied and make up to her for his neglect.

She considered the offer thoughtfully for a moment or two, her neat head bowed. 'Yes,' she said at last, 'thank 'ee, Mr Clarke, I do believe I should like to see this meeting, for it sounds as though 'twill be a great occasion. There is only one thing...'

'What is that, my dear?' Mr Clarke encouraged.

'May I bring my baby and his nursemaid too, an't please you? I should not care to be parted from him for too long in a strange city.'

So it was agreed. And the next morning, when John set off for Salford and the office of the solicitors who were handling the rent of another Easter shop, Harriet put on her pretty new embroidered stockings, and promised John that she would stay inside the building until the meeting was over and disbanded, and then she and Rosie and baby Will took a threesome carriage to Windmill Street to see history being made.

CHAPTER 24

A bove the smoke haze it was a lovely summer's day, and even below it the air was warm and the motes that swirled within it gilded like tiny fireflies. As the threesome carriage joggled Harriet and Rosie and baby Will out of the narrow crush of Market Street, sunshine was visibly filtering through the cloud.

They were in a wide street lined on either side by fine town houses, which the coachman told Harriet was 'Moseley Street, ma'am, where the nobs live hereabouts'. But it wasn't the nobs who were promenading that morning. The street was completely filled with working people, all going in the same direction and all of them on the march, men in felt caps and leather breeches and rough brown fustian jackets, women in summer cottons and Sunday-go-to-meeting bonnets, children in brown holland pinafores, toddlers riding pig-a-back, babes in arms. There was a fife band playing 'St Patrick's Day in the Morning' some distance ahead of them, and two of the marchers were carrying an enormous silk banner, bracing their backs against the weight of it because it was billowing in the breeze like a great sail. It was made of green silk and bore the painted legend, 'Taxation without representation is unjust and tyrannical.'

Harriet looked at the faces all around her and knew that there was no need for any anxiety about this meeting at all. These people were not rioters. They were decent, working people, quiet and orderly. They smiled up at her with cheerful friendliness, and one or two waved as the carriage trotted alongside them.

'We'll see thee at Peter's Field,' one young woman called. And Harriet called back. 'Yes. Yes indeed.' And was glad to be included in her company.

It took a long time to negotiate the half-mile between Market Street and the chosen assembly place because all the approaches were full of marchers, but eventually the threesome inched past the classical portico of St Peter's church and was able to trot along the relative emptiness of Lower Moseley Street. It came to a halt before a dense mass of people who were streaming into a narrow pathway immediately to their left.

'That opening there is Windmill Street, missus,' the coachman said, pointing at the pathway with his whip. 'You'll need to walk t' last step I'm thinkin', for there'll be no teking this horse through such a scrimmage.' Which was true enough. ''Tis nobbut a step.'

And that was true, too, although their steps were very much jostled and they were both quite glad to see Mr Clarke looking out for them on a doorstep a little further along the path, for Windmill Street turned out to be a single terrace of very plain houses facing an open field.

'Come in, come in,' he said. 'We've been quite worried for you in this crush. Did you ever see such a turnout? Come upstairs, pray do. 'Tis a fine room and a quite excellent view. Just wait until you see it. Mr Murgatroyd expects you.'

Mr Murgatroyd was a gangly young man with very thin limbs and very sparse hair and moist protruding eyes like a rabbit. He greeted them at the top of the first flight of stairs, shaking Harriet's hand most warmly and then ushering her into his 'sitting room', which was very sparsely furnished but had two windows overlooking the field. There he offered a stool to Rosie and the baby and a rather battered armchair to Harriet, arranging it next to 'Mrs Clarke's chair', right beside one of the windows.

'What a day this is!' he said excitedly. 'Do you not think so, Mrs Easter? What a day! We shall have tea and cakes presently. The landlady is to bring them up for us. I trust that will suit. What a day! Did you ever imagine we should see so many turn out, particularly when Mr Nadin and the magistrates expressly forbade it a week ago? Oh they must agree to reform now, surely, in the face of such numbers.'

'You support the reformists, Mr Murgatroyd?' Harriet asked.

'Indeed I do,' her host said ardently. ''Tis a truth I hold to be self-evident.'

'Self-evident nonsense,' Mr Clarke said cheerfully, looking out of the window at the gathering crowd. 'What would the likes of them know of voting and elections, eh? Tell me that.'

'With education...' Mr Murgatroyd offered.

'Education, sir?' Mr Clarke said. 'Hotheads the lot of 'em. And hotheads get their skulls cracked. That's all there is to be said about hotheads. Our Deputy Constable, Mr Nadin, has called out the Manchester Yeomanry.'

'Manchester Yeomanry,' Rosie echoed admiringly.

'Then he is a fool,' Mrs Clarke said, tickling Will under the chin. ''Tis a peaceable crowd and will stay so left to its own devices.'

'Own devices, yes,' Rosie said.

'The Yeomanry are a pretty poor set of hotheads, too,' Mr Murgatroyd said, smiling amiably at Rosie. 'Local tradesmen, Mrs Easter, cheesemongers and ironmongers and suchlike, who fancy themselves as gentry. Ain't accustomed to horseback, though, not like the old squires. Hard put to it to keep their seats at the best of times.'

'They'll be more hard put to it than usual this morning,' Mr Clarke said, 'if the gossip is anything to go by.'

'How so?' his wife asked. 'What gossip?'

'Gossip?' Rosie said hopefully.

'Our Deputy Constable, Mr Nadin, has had 'em in the alehouse since eight o'clock this morning,' Mr Clarke informed them. 'So they'll be rolling drunk by now, I shouldn't wonder.'

'Shouldn't wonder,' Rosie agreed.

In the field outside the window another marching column had arrived with yet another band, and the squeal of pipes and the thudding of drums set Will bouncing on Rosie's ample lap.

'Will you look at that child!' Mrs Clarke exclaimed. 'Such strength on those legs, me dear. A fine boy!'

Harriet was looking down at the crowd. The field was already thronged and yet still more people were marching into it, their arrival marked by bands and banners but soon becoming nothing more than a ribbon of white faces swirling forward into the mass. There were so many faces, thousands and thousands of them, and all so pale and pressed so close together, and all of them turned towards the house because the hustings had been erected directly in front of it: round white faces topped with dark caps and dotted with dark eyes; round gentle faces, Harriet thought, like a meadow full of daisies. And all those flags and banners fluttering above them were like flowers too, huge, brightly coloured flowers, hollyhocks, perhaps, or lilies, red and gold, green and scarlet, yellow and orange and black and white, their poles topped with bright red caps of liberty. She was pleased by the image she'd found because it was peaceful and homely, and well suited to this meeting in a green field that could have been a garden.

On the opposite side of the field there were several fine oak trees with a pile of loose timber and logs left beside them. A group of women and children had climbed up onto the logs to get a better view, and now they sat in the sunshine as though they were at a picnic. The large plain building behind them belonged to the Quakers. Harriet could see the words 'Friends' Meeting House' painted on the front of it in tall, clear letters. And immediately to her right there was a beautiful walled garden, full of roses and honeysuckles and ivies. It looked very green and welcoming after the harshness of all that unrelieved red brick in the centre of the town, and it was another indication of how peaceful the place was.

By now Will had bounced himself red in the face and Mr Murgatroyd's landlady had arrived with a pot of tea and a plate full of honey cakes, which Mr Murgatroyd urged on his guests. It was well after one o'clock before the refreshments had been eaten and Will had been rocked to sleep on Rosie's lap, and by then the field was full and several men who seemed to be officials of some kind were gathering the banners onto the hustings.

Harriet and Mrs Clarke stood at the open window to read what was written upon them. 'Universal Suffrage', they said, 'Hunt and Liberty', 'Unite and be Free', 'Vote by Ballot', and on one very splendid red and green banner, which proclaimed that it belonged to the 'Female Union of Royden' were the ringing and inappropriate words, 'Let us Die like Men and not be Sold as Slaves'.

'Why look, Mrs Easter my dear,' Mrs Clarke said, 'there's Mr Taylor, I do believe. Look! Look there! Beside the gentleman in the red hat.'

And sure enough, when Harriet looked, there *was* Mr Taylor, striding into the crowd in his smart blue jacket, talking in a most animated way to the gentleman beside him. And standing directly behind him, watching the crowd, was the man who had travelled with her from Leicester, Mr Richards of the fair hair and the ginger whiskers. Well, fancy that!

But there wasn't time to tell her companions about him because the crowd had begun to stir. Hands were foresting upwards to point and wave. She could hear a band playing somewhere close at hand, and a rolling cheer began on the left side of the crowd and spread like a wave all across the field. It was obvious that something was about to happen.

'There they are!' Mr Murgatroyd shouted. And the crowd to the left of the hustings parted to make way for a barouche. It was full of passengers and bristling with blue and white flags and it was being drawn not by a team of horses but by the people themselves.

'There's Mr Hunt,' Mr Murgatroyd said. 'The man standing up, in the white top hat, d'ye see? He always wears a white top hat. And there's Mr Carlisle from London, who sells the penny press so cunningly when he ain't supposed to. And Mr Saxton of the Manchester *Observer*. Oh, how splendid!'

And splendid it certainly was, for Mr Henry Hunt was an imposing looking man and when the coach reached the hustings he sprang up onto the canvas in the most athletic and dramatic way, like a prize-fighter, turning to the crowd to wave and bow. And the crowd gave him a long full-throated cheer and waved back. 'Good old Hunt!' 'Hunt and Liberty!' 'Hooray! Hooray!'

Then a band began to play the National Anthem and Mr Hunt took off his fine white top hat and held it before his chest respectfully and sang in a deep booming voice that Harriet could hear quite clearly from her window. And the men in the crowd doffed their caps, too, and the movement of their action was like the wind rippling a field of corn. How respectful they all are, Harriet thought, as they stood to attention and sang. And the sunshine gleamed on Mr Hunt's white hat as he returned it to his head and began to speak.

'Friends and brothers,' he said, and his voice rang out across the field, 'we are gathered here this morning, in St Peter's Place, not to break the law, for that we would not do, nor to cause an affray, for that we would not do either, but to consider the propriety of adopting the most *legal* and *effectual* means of obtaining reform of the Commons House of Parliament. To this end we have come, unarmed and in good faith...'

There was a movement on the edge of the crowd, an alarming movement, quick and fluttery, that made Harriet and Mrs Clarke look away from the hustings to see what it was. A woman's voice called out, 'Soldiers! Soldiers!' on a high-pitched panicky note and the next minute a troop of cavalry, all very bright and smart in their blue and white uniforms, trotted round the corner by the beautiful walled garden, sabres in hand, and reined up in a line against the garden wall. At the same time half a dozen well-dressed men emerged from the house beside them and began to walk importantly through the crowd towards the hustings. Now Harriet noticed that there was a double line of constables keeping a way open for their importance and she looked back at Mr Murgatroyd to see if he knew what was going on.

'Those are the magistrates,' he explained. 'They've been waiting in Mr Buxton's house, I do believe, for that is where they came from. The gentleman in front is Mr Nadin, the Deputy Constable.'

'He means to arrest Mr Hunt,' Mr Clarke said, rubbing his hands together. 'Now we shall see some sport. Those fellows in blue and white are the Manchester Yeomanry. Didn't I tell 'ee?'

'Stand firm, my friends,' Mr Hunt boomed at the crowd as those nearest to the soldiers glanced fearfully over their shoulders at those flashing sabres. 'This is a trick. Give them three cheers.'

And to Harriet's amazement three cheers were given.

The last was dying away as the magistrates reached the hustings. And then a great many things happened all at once and in great confusion. One of the magistrates made a grab for the nearest banner and snapped the pole in two across his knee, and then there were several seconds' confused argument. Punches were thrown, voices raised, and the people nearest the hustings surged forward, waving their arms in the air and shouting. The platform party were jostled down onto the ground, arguing violently.

And then without any warning the Manchester Yeomanry galloped into the crowd, slashing as they went. Their onrush was so sudden and precipitate, nobody had any time to get out of their way. People yelled warnings and screamed in terror, and many fell and were trodden underfoot, but the Yeomanry pushed forward, red-faced with excitement, using their spurs cruelly, sabres flashing in the sunshine as they cut to right and left, at pleading hands and unprotected heads, with a crunching of bone and blood spurting into the air and running red and terrible down white arms and white dresses and white, white faces.

The watchers in Mr Murgatroyd's dingy sitting room were so shocked they couldn't believe what they saw. Harriet was frozen to the spot and Mr Murgatroyd was galvanised into frantic and useless movement, running from window to window, wringing his hands and moaning.

'Good God alive!' Mr Clarke said, pulling his wife backwards from the sight. 'They can't do this! Stop it, d'ye hear? This is England, damnit. We don't do things like this in England. Stop it!'

Rosie ambled to the window, with Will still asleep in her arms. 'Stop it,' she echoed.

And Mrs Clarke burst into tears and covered her face with her hands. 'They cannot do this. They mustn't! Oh somebody make it stop!'

But the terrible screams went on and on and on. At the edge of the crowd people were running away in every direction, scattering like mercury, but in the centre, they were still too close-packed to be able to move at all. And there were more soldiers arriving. Oh, please God not more! Make it stop! Make it stop! Horses stamped and snorted right underneath the window and a contingent of Hussars waited for orders in front of Mr Buxton's house, their colonel looking up to the first floor where a stern face watched and didn't speak. Some of the Yeomanry had reached the hustings and were slashing at the banners, screaming abuse. Others were marooned among the crowd. One or two had been disarmed and were taking a beating from the fists below them.

And then the horror intensified as the Hussars plunged into the crowd. There was so much movement and so much noise and such clouds of dust it was impossible to take it all in. Voices yelled, 'Break! Break They are killing us! Break!' And then sound and sight took on the kaleidoscopic quality of nightmare as images of horror emerged from the dust with brief and terrible clarity. Two small hands streaked with blood clinging to the shawl of a woman running like a deer. A wound gaping like a red mouth in the shocking whiteness of a living, moving skull. A man falling backwards from the hustings with blood pumping out of a great bloody hole where his nose had been.

'Oh stop it!' Harriet begged, 'for pity's sake!' It was impossible to look away and the sight of all those sabres rising and falling, hacking and cutting, in such steady, remorseless rhythm was paining her with a familiar pain that she recognised but could not remember. It was as if the long blue blades were cutting into her own chest, over and over again. 'They are children,' she wept. 'They have done no wrong. They are innocent children. You are killing innocent children!' But in the turmoil of screams and neighs and the blur of terrified movement and the nightmare roar of hooves and feet, nobody could hear her. She saw that Will was awake and crying and she took him in her arms and held him close, knowing she ought to comfort him. But she was shivering with terror and pity and she only made him worse.

'Take him away from the window,' she said to Rosie, putting her mouth close to her ear to be sure of being heard. 'Hide him if you can. Oh Mr Murgatroyd, is there anywhere he can be hidden? Is there anywhere anyone can be hidden?' The tears were streaming down her cheeks. And the mass below her was loosed at last and the people scattered and ran, pell-mell, torn hair flying, babies screaming, without hats or shoes or hope, pursued by those enormous horses and those terrible, blood-stained, hissing blades.

And suddenly it was all over. The crowd was gone and the field was empty and so silent that Harriet could hear her own heart beating. She realised that she was hanging on to the curtain, and that she'd been hiding her face in its folds. Mr Murgatroyd was leaning on the windowsill, panting as though he'd been running a race, the Clarkes were in the furthest corner of the room clinging to one another and weeping, and Rosie and little Will were nowhere to be seen. 'In the bedroom,' Mr Murgatroyd explained seeing that she was looking for them, but then he went on gazing at the field.

'Oh my dear God, the place is full of dead bodies.'

I must look, Harriet thought. It is cowardice to look away. Terrible though this is, I must look.

The rough grass of the field was littered with fallen bodies, some hideously and totally still, some trying to crawl away, or sitting head in hand in the swirling dust too stunned to move, or gasping and grey-faced and calling for help, and some heaped together in an ungainly pile as though they were of no more account than rubbish. Around them the ground was strewn with debris of every kind: broken drums and shredded banners, hundreds of hats and caps and bonnets trampled filthy, blood-stained shoes, some pathetically small torn clothing, smeared scarlet and brown. And at the edge of the field the Yeomanry were calmly easing girths and adjusting accoutrements and — oh most horrible! — wiping the blood from their sabres, and all just a few feet away from the men and women they'd killed and injured. It was a battlefield.

And in an instant the sight of it brought all Harriet's beliefs and fears into sharp inescapable focus. Every Sunday of her childhood the preacher had hectored her about good and evil and the dangers of sin, and she had listened obediently but without understanding. Now she knew what he'd been talking about. *This* was evil. Totally, incontrovertibly, hatefully evil. To take a sword and kill unarmed men and women and children was evil. To inflict pain and terror and injury on anyone smaller or younger or less powerful than you were was evil. And evil had to be opposed, with all your strength and all your wit. That was the simple duty of a Christian. That was why God had brought her to this place.

'I must go and help them,' she said.

Mr Murgatroyd was horrified. 'Out there?' he said, his voice squeaking with disbelief. 'With soldiers on the rampage? You can't! What would Mr Easter say?'

But she was already at the door. 'Look after little Will,' she said. She was perfectly calm, as though she were going for a promenade.

'They won't let you,' he called after her as she ran down the stairs.

There was a constable on guard just outside the house. He turned as she opened the front door and put out an arm as though to prevent her, but she was too calm and too quick for him.

'I am going to attend to the wounded,' she said and walked straight past him into the field, while he was still estimating her social position and considering what he ought to say.

There were people moaning all about her. So many men and women lying hurt. Where should she start among so many? Then she saw that there was a man walking from group to group. He seemed to be examining wounds and he was urging those who could stand to get up and walk away from the field. Four hands are better than two, she thought, and went to help him.

He was kneeling beside a young man who had been cut through the shoulder and was lying on the ground grey-faced and shivering with his head in the lap of a girl who was rocking to and fro, moaning 'Oh God! Oh God!' over and over and over again. The boy was bleeding profusely, his fustian jacket dark and damp with blood and a red pool of it on the grass beneath him.

'It's Caleb Rawson, Tommy,' the man said. 'Canst sit up, lad?'

'Caleb is it?' the boy said, opening his eyes.

Harriet knelt beside them on the scrubby grass. 'How can I help?' she asked.

The man called Caleb wasted no time in introductions. 'Hold that arm,' he instructed, 'while I ease t' sleeve away. Hold on, lad, an' we'll staunch tha' wound. Tek his head, Molly lass, he's in mortal pain.'

Between them they eased the sodden cloth away from the cut, which was long and angry but less deep than Harriet had feared. The girl was still rocking.

'If I'd a bandage I could bind this clean,' Caleb said.

Harriet was tearing a strip from her petticoat before he'd finished speaking. 'Bind away,' she said. "Tis good clean linen, I assure you. Use it and welcome.'

JOHN EASTER HAD INSPECTED the property and decided upon it and was discussing terms with the solicitor in Salford when the clerk ran into the room bolt-eyed with his exciting news. 'There's been a riot, across t' river, sir. Hundreds and hundreds killed. They say St Peter's Field is full o' corpses.'

The shock was so profound that for a few seconds John could hardly breathe or think. But although the colour drained from his face, he kept control of himself. 'I fear this matter must be deferred until tomorrow,' he said, and was proud of himself to be speaking calmly. 'My wife is visiting in St Peter's Field. I must return to Manchester immediately.'

The solicitor said he quite understood and sent his clerk off at once to find a flyer, which he did after an interminable time. But the driver was none too happy about his commission. 'I'll tek thee as far as t' old bridge at Blackfriars,' he said, 'but no further. Nobbut a fool would go further with t' Yeomanry afield.'

'You shall have twice the fare,' John offered.

But it was refused. 'T' Blackfriars' Bridge. No further.'

So to Blackfriars' Bridge it had to be, because he didn't have the strength to argue in his present state of anxiety. And then a long, fraught walk between the old timbered houses of Deansgate, which was alarming empty and made him feel worse with every step he took, particularly when he saw three mounted men galloping down a side turning brandishing swords. By the time he reached Windmill Street his heart was beating so violently it was shaking his jacket.

He took one glance at the littered field and the shattered flagpoles sticking up out of the hustings and the ominous bundles lying on the ground and ran to Mr Murgatroyd's lodgings. There was no sign of any bloodshed there, thank God. But Mr Murgatroyd's first words sent him spinning off into panic again.

'She ain't here, Mr Easter sir,' the young man said, waving both skinny arms in the air in his agitation.

'Not here?' But she'd promised to stay inside the building.

'She went off to help the wounded,' Mr Murgatroyd explained. 'Mr and Mrs Clarke took your servant back to the hotel with the baby just so soon as ever the coast was clear, but Mrs Easter, she's been in and out of the house for water and suchlike all afternoon, and in and out of the field, too. Couldn't persuade her otherwise, sir, upon me life.'

John was so furiously anxious he couldn't find words. What was she thinking of to run such risks? With people lying dead in the field and cabbies too much afraid to venture into the city and the Yeomanry galloping the streets sword in hand — and after she'd given her promise, too.

'Where is she now?'

'I couldn't say, sir.'

SHE WAS in the infirmary holding the hands of a young woman called Mary who was having the terrible gash in her skull cleaned with milk and water, and murmuring encouragement, 'Soon be done, my dear. Only a little more I promise.' She was tired and bloodstained and very, very dirty and her hair had come unpinned and was trailing over her shoulder like a gipsy's. Her petticoat was gone and so were her new stockings, which she'd used to bind up a fearful head wound, but she was doing the right thing and she knew it, right through to her weary, weary bones.

'How shall we mek out?' the girl said, between groans. 'I shall lose my job, miss, an' then how shall we mek out, with Joe hurt an' all? The littleuns'll starve. We're the breadwinners, me an' Joe. The littleuns'll starve if I lose my job.'

'You are lucky not to have lost your life,' Harriet tried to soothe. 'And so is your brother. You must use your energies to mend and try not to fret about your work. There will be people who will help you, depend upon it.'

But the girl moaned and wasn't comforted. 'Will there? Will there?'

'There will,' Harriet said, holding her hands firmly. 'I shall make it my business to find them. You have my word.'

'Where is Mr Rawson?'

'Gone with Joe. He'll be back directly.' Her brother had fallen and been trampled on and was likely to be kept in the infirmary for some time, but there was no need to tell the poor girl that.

It was growing dark. One of the orderlies had arrived with a basket full of candles, which he was lighting methodically one after the other, setting them neatly in their sconces about the bare walls. It must be getting late, Harriet thought, but it was of little consequence. In a vague, faraway part of her mind she knew she ought to be concerned about John and dear little Will, but that was of no consequence either. There was a job to do and she could not stop until it was done.

She and Caleb Rawson had worked all afternoon, binding wounds as well as they could to stop the worst of the bleeding, fetching water from Mr Murgatroyd's house, struggling to support the walking wounded at least part of the way home, pushing the most badly injured here to the infirmary in an old cart they'd found beneath the oak trees, soothing and reassuring, lifting and carrying, spattered with blood and vomit, for so many of the injured were sick when they were moved, working on and on and on, beyond fatigue and beyond imagination, numb with horror and effort. She was aware that other people were helping too. Mr Taylor was there and the man from the Manchester *Gazette,* and the field was gradually being cleared, but she was aware without understanding.

There was nothing real in the world beyond their four hard-working hands, hers narrow and white and quick, with blood-caked nails, his broad and brown and competent, with black hairs growing from his knuckles and the joints of his fingers. She knew his face by heart, as if it had been printed on her memory by the emotion of the afternoon: the short, broad forehead under dark, ill-cut hair, the blunt broken nose, the two missing teeth she could see when he spoke, the blue scar on his right cheek; and she could read his every expression, too, instantly and with ease, as though she'd known him all her life, the wince of compassion so quickly suppressed, the square jaw set before physical effort, the long, dark, tender lashes sweeping down over his grey eyes to brush away fatigue. An ugly, lovely man. And standing beside her now, warning her with his eyes that Joe was very ill but that his sister was not to know.

'You're to stay here overnight,' he said. 'You and Joe both. T' surgeon thinks it for the best. I'll be back in t' mornin' to see how you do.'

'You are in good hands,' Harriet said.

'Aye,' the girl said, dull with pain and confusion. 'Thank 'ee.'

The last candle was lit, the girl's wound bandaged.

'We must leave,' Caleb said, signalling to Harriet with his eyes that she was to begin to walk away.

'Aye.'

'We will see you tomorrow,' Harriet promised, walking obediently.

But when she had followed him along the corridor and out through the portico into the darkening light of Lever's Row, she was overcome with lethargy, her feet leaden and her mind empty, all emotion drained away. She had no desire to go back to the hotel or to see John or even to find out how her baby was. She simply wanted to stay where she was. And what was even more peculiar, her odd behaviour didn't surprise her or worry her.

Fortunately he was still full of energy. 'I'll see thee to tha door,' he said, smiling and showing those missing teeth. 'If that'll tell me where 'tis.'

It was the first time she'd seen him smile. 'We have been too busy for such things,' she said. 'I am Harriet Easter. My mother-in-law is Easters the newsagents.'

He did not comment on the information. 'Where shall I tek thee?' he said.

'To St Peter's Field, I suppose,' she said. She couldn't think of anywhere else she wanted to go.

So he collected the cart and they set off through the eerily empty streets, keeping a careful watch for the Yeomanry. The dusk was gathering quite quickly now and the sky above the soot-smeared houses was a gentle lilac.

'Is Joe very ill?' she asked, as they cut through the narrow alleys between Market Street and St Peter's.

'He'll not work for a long while,' he said dourly, 'if at all. His ribs are cracked, they say. He can barely breathe.'

'What will become of the family if neither of them works? Mary told me there are six little ones and she and Joe are the only breadwinners.'

'They will starve,' he said shortly. 'That is t' way of it. That is how t' poor live and die.'

'Something must be done about it,' she said. 'A fund must be started. I will see Mrs Easter about it. She has powerful friends.'

'Tha'rt a good woman, Harriet Easter,' he said.

'We must all do what we can, must we not?' she answered. 'After this.'

JOHN EASTER WAS PROWLING the streets around St Peter's Field. He'd been walking for over an hour and he was frantic with worry. He'd been to Market Street and back three times in case she'd returned to the Royal Hotel and he'd seen Rosie and little Will, who'd been driven home by Mr Clarke. But there was no sign of Harriet.

Anything could have happened to her, he thought, and his mind pushed all sorts of horrible images at him: Harriet struck down with a sabre, trodden under flying hooves, lying in an inert bundle like the bodies in the field. Even though they'd all been taken away they still haunted him. What on earth had possessed her to go out into such danger? Harriet, Harriet, he mourned, come back to me, my darling, for I cannot live without you.

And yet, when he finally saw her walking towards Mr Murgatroyd's lodgings for a few seconds he didn't recognise her. He thought she was a whore, walking along with that scruffy-looking workman, with no hat on her head and no shawl and no stockings and all that dirty hair tangled about her face. A whore with a passing resemblance to his Harriet. It gave him a palpable shock when she turned towards him and he realised who she was.

He ran to her at once. 'Harriet, my dear, where have you been?'

'Come to no harm, Mr Easter sir,' the workman said.

'Thank you, my man,' John said, stiff and awkward with suppressed emotion. 'Much obliged to 'ee I'm sure.' Oh go away, do, he thought. I need to be alone with my wife and you are in the way. 'If you care to call at the Royal Hotel tomorrow morning, I will see to it that you are rewarded.'

Caleb Rawson straightened his spine with anger. 'I dunna work for reward, sir,' he said furiously. 'I shall be at the infirmary tomorrow morning, Mrs Easter.' And he turned on his heel and marched away before Harriet could stop him.

Not that John gave her any chance to do or say anything. He seized her by the elbow, dragged her into Mr Murgatroyd's house and lugged her up the stairs to where their host was dithering on the landing. 'She is back, Mr Murgatroyd. Praise God!'

'So glad!' Mr Murgatroyd said. 'Such a relief. No harm done I trust. Such a relief!'

'Could I prevail upon you to find us a carriage of some kind?' John asked, struggling to be calm and polite. 'A closed carriage, if at all possible. We must return to the hotel as soon as may be and my wife can hardly walk through the streets in this condition.'

'Pleasure!' Mr Murgatroyd said, and went at once.

'I walked here through the streets,' Harriet pointed out. After the terrible events of the afternoon she found his concern rather ridiculous. 'I was safe with Mr Rawson, who is a fine, good man and should never have been insulted the way you insulted him.'

'We will wait in this room,' John said, ignoring her remark. He was shaking with anger now and needed to be away from prying eyes.

She followed him into the room and sat down wearily in her chair by the window.

And to his horror he realised that the sight of her was rousing desire in him so strongly that it was almost painful. Slumped inelegantly in that grubby chair, with blood under her fingernails and her hair wild about her face and her dress clinging to her legs and revealing her breasts as clearly as if she were naked before him, she was attracting him more strongly than she had ever done. It was immodest, improper.

'How could you, Harriet?' he said, his eyes strained with fear and anger and this terrible desire. 'I've been worried half out of my mind. Where have you been?'

'At the infirmary attending to the wounded,' she said, her eyes half closed.

'Why didn't you leave a message?' he said, anger and desire still growing at a dizzying rate. 'You might have known I would worry with all this going on.'

'There was no time, John.'

'No time?' he shouted. 'No time? You should have made time. I am your husband. You should have thought what you were doing. Or did you want to upset me? Was that what it was? Am I nothing to you? How could you do this to me, when I love you so much? Harriet, Harriet!'

'They were hurt,' she explained calmly. 'I had to help them. You would have done the same had you been here.'

'I would not!' he shouted at her. 'I would not. I would have had more sense. I would have stayed where I was and not gone wandering about the streets with common workmen covered in

348

filth and blood and heaven knows what else. How could you worry me so? I didn't know where you were. I thought you were dead. Do I mean nothing to you that you treat me so?' He was talking wildly, saying things that shouldn't be said, but his control was gone. 'You behaved disgracefully! You made an exhibition of yourself. How could you?' He was shaking with emotion. 'Oh, I can't bear it!'

She got up slowly and wearily and walked to him and put her arms about his neck. 'John! John!' she said. 'Don't speak so!'

And at that he began to tremble with fury, and he seized hold of her roughly and held her so tightly that he hurt her. 'I thought you were dead! I thought you were dead! Oh Harriet, my dear dear darling. I thought you were dead.'

She hushed him like a baby, stroking his hair with her blood-stained hands, understanding his fear. She had so little energy left and it was draining her to respond to him. 'Hush! Hush!'

They stood together for a long time, and she held him and kissed him and soothed him with her hands, using the same movements she'd been using all afternoon. And finally he regained control of himself. And not a minute too soon, for they could hear a carriage pulling up in front of the house.

'We will go back to the hotel,' he said, making a supreme effort to speak normally. 'Tomorrow we will return to London, I promise. This is no place for us now.'

'Oh no,' she said. 'We must stay here for a day or two, John. I have given my word to visit the infirmary tomorrow morning.'

It was such a surprise to hear her arguing against any decision of his that for a moment he didn't know what to say to her. 'But it is all over now, surely,' he tried.

'Oh no,' she said. 'It certainly isn't over. It has only just begun.'

CHAPTER 25

The next morning Harriet was awake at cockcrow and, once she'd assured herself that Will had eaten sufficient breakfast to sustain him for the morning, she set off for the infirmary. It was another beautiful day.

There was already a crowd of visitors waiting for admission in the portico, and among them she found Mr Taylor looking very angry.

'They've arrested Mr Tyas,' he said, '*The Times* correspondent. Did you ever hear the like? I've written up my own account to send 'em, for they'll never know what's what with their man in jail.'

But Harriet was more interested in Mr Rawson's whereabouts.

'Gone inside already,' Mr Taylor told her. 'Him and three others. That's all they would allow for the present. We're to wait here. A good man, our Caleb.'

She agreed with him.

'His wife and child died of the smallpox three years back,' Mr Taylor told her, 'and ever since he's been a tower of strength to the Manchester and Salford weavers. There ain't a thing he wouldn't do to help 'em, you know.'

She was sure of it.

'Being a weaver himself, you see, he knows the score,' Mr Taylor went on. 'And a powerful speaker. You'd not think it to look at him, but he could rival the great Mr Hunt if he had a mind.'

She could believe that, too.

'Gates is open,' an orderly shouted. 'One at a time, if you please, ladies and gentlemen.'

It was a great pleasure to stand beside Mr Rawson again, even though he paid no attention to her at all, being far too busy reassuring his injured friends that he would look after their children. 'I'll see to 'em this very day,' he promised. 'Dunna tek on. I'll see to 'em.' And she listened and admired him and decided that she would visit these poor children too and take as much food to them as she could carry.

So that afternoon she packed three huge baskets full of loaves and pots of butter and mutton chops and potatoes and fish and potted meats, and she and Peg and Rosie set off in a carriage to visit the sick, taking Will with them wrapped in a shawl like a gypsy. It was a sobering experience, for she had never seen people living in such abject poverty before. But it made her more determined than ever that she must do everything she could to help them, even if it did alarm her dear John. The situation was simply too dreadful and too urgent to be ignored.

John was finding this new active Harriet very difficult to contend with, rushing off to the infirmary, or travelling who knew where with enough food to feed a regiment and no sense of danger at all. It was extremely worrying. It took him two whole days before he could persuade her to come home to London, and then she went haring out of the house again almost as soon as she'd set foot in it. And to visit his mother, of all people! It was as if she was bewitched.

Nan was most surprised to see her. She and Sophie Fuseli were taking their usual Thursday afternoon tea together, cosy and gossipy and comfortable, like the old friends they were, when the parlour maid arrived in the garden to announce that Mrs John Easter was asking to see her.

'Well show her through, do,' Nan said, and, when the maid had gone, ''Twill be that Mrs Sowerby again as sure as Fate. Poor Harriet.'

But one look at her daughter-in-law's excited face changed her mind. 'How now,' she said, intrigued, 'what's afoot?'

'We must start a fund for the people who were wounded at St Peter's Field,' Harriet said without preliminary. 'What happened there was an iniquity and we must do something about it.'

'Must we indeed?' Nan laughed. 'Tell me why, pray.' And was highly impressed when Harriet did just that, describing the good order of the meeting, the fury of the attack, the horror of the wounds and the poverty of the wounded. 'Now they have nothing,' she ended. 'No work, no hope, no food, especially when the chief breadwinner is in prison. Some of them are drilling and making pikes out of old spades and forks and suchlike. There is such desperation, Mrs Easter. They are down further than any human creature has the right to be.'

'How our old friend Mr Paine would have applauded!' Sophie said when the tale was told. 'Did he not always maintain that the French cry for liberty and equality would spread into England sooner or later? And now here it is, if I ain't mistook.'

Nan looked at the warm flush on Harriet's ardent face and grinned at her. There is fire in her after all, she thought. 'Tis an admirable passion. 'The matter is already in hand, so it is,' she said. 'Sir Francis Burdett has formed a committee for the relief of sufferers at the Manchester meeting, and there are others forming, I believe.'

'Praise God for it,' Harriet said. 'I will help them in any way I can, if you will tell them so.'

'Well now,' Nan said, 'as to that, how if you were to attend their next meeting and tell them all you saw at St Peter's Field?'

'Oh willingly. Most willingly.'

'Then we will take another dish of tea together,' Nan said, 'and Sophie and I will drive you round to Charing Cross Road to see our old friend Mr Place. He knows where all the meetings are being held and will be only too happy to advise, you may depend upon it.' And she rang the little handbell that stood beside her plate.

'I always knew we should live to see a revolution,' Sophie said. 'Heinrich will be cock-a-hoop to hear all this.'

'If Frederick don't look slippy,' Nan said, 'he'll still be hossin' about Europe and miss it all.'

Later that afternoon, when she'd visited Mr Place in his book-crowded shop in the Charing Cross Road and agreed to speak at four meetings in the next six days, Harriet confided to her diary:

I have kept my promise to Mr Rawson. Mr Place was full of sympathy and understood at once how terribly and undeservedly the weavers and spinners have suffered. He is a fine man and will do everything in his power to help. But we must be speedy or those poor children will starve. Perhaps these meetings will lead to a change of heart in the government. I do hope so.

She was so warm with enthusiasm for the new work she'd undertaken that she didn't stop to think where it might lead her.

In fact it was to take her straight back to Bury St Edmunds. But by way of Sir Francis Burdett's gloomy house in Park Place, Lady Mauleverer's expensive blue and gold drawing room in

Grosvenor Square, the huge hall of the Crown and Anchor tavern in the Strand, Mr Penray's crowded untidy house in Tyler Street in Carnaby Market, and a certain Mr Whittle's well-filled orderly sitting room in West Street in Spitalfields, where she made her first speech just two days after offering to help.

She was husky with nerves and so pale that the colour had even drained from her lips, but her audience listened with rapt attention and, to her embarrassment and delight, applauded when her tale was told.

'Who'd ha' thought it?' Nan said to Sophie, watching as an apricot blush began to warm her daughter-in-law's cheek. 'Our quiet Harriet become a firebrand!'

'Still waters, my dear,' Sophie said, fingering her curls, 'invariably run deep. Ain't I always said so? Consider my Heinrich, so neat and quiet and abstemious and yet he paints nightmares that are enough to curl your hair. He has one upon the easel now that I cannot bear to look upon.'

'Just so. And Harriet talks of this nightmare and makes us all look upon it.'

'What will John think of it, I wonder?' Sophie said, still twisting her curls.

John was none too sure what he thought of it. Sometimes, when his colleagues in Easter House spoke with abhorrence of the massacre and declared that the victims should be helped and the Yeomanry punished for what they'd done, he was proud that his wife was speaking at political meetings to urge people to do just that. But on other occasions, when he listened to lawyers reasoning the need for stronger laws to improve public order, or when he stood in newspaper offices while editors spoke passionately of 'the danger of the mob' which 'will lead directly to an armed insurrection if the government don't act', he was afraid of her involvement, just as he'd been on the field of Peterloo, and he wished she would stay safely at home with him, quietly and obediently as she'd done before.

But it was undeniable that this new determined Harriet was far more attractive than the quiet obedient one had been. She might be preoccupied sometimes and she certainly spent far too much time out of the house and far too much answering letters, for these days she had almost as much correspondence as he did, but she was more passionate than he'd ever known her. They made love so frequently and pleasurably that for most of his time he lived in a glow of such well-satisfied desire that all other considerations were trivial.

And then there was the way she'd answered her mother's letter.

It had arrived on the morning after her speech in Tyler Street. She read it calmly and then set it aside without comment to return to her breakfast and the conversation its arrival had interrupted. And that evening, while they were dressing for dinner at Billy's, she showed him her answer.

My dear mother, she had written.

Thank you for your letter. I quite understand that you would like to visit my dear Will who, as you rightly say, is your grandson, on Thursday week. Howsomever I feel it only right to tell you that I shall not be at home on that day, nor on many other days during that week and the others following. I have work to be done which it is right and proper I do, since I truly believe I have been called by God to do it, which is a call that none may deny, as I am sure you agree.

Therefore I beg you, do not distress yourself by a wasted journey. I will come to Bury just so soon as ever I may and then I will bring Will to see you, which is the better way about, for half an hour one morning or afternoon, whichever is available.

I am, your obedient daughter,
Harriet Easter.

It wasn't quite the flea in the ear that Nan Easter advocated, but it was certainly a very firm refusal. How much she had changed!

Mrs Sowerby was infuriated by it. '"Called by God"!' she snorted. 'Did you ever hear such blasphemy?'

'That,' Mr Sowerby said, 'is what comes of worshipping in the wrong church.'

'She don't tell us what this precious work of hers *is*, you notice,' Mrs Sowerby snorted. That was the most annoying thing about the letter, for without such knowledge she didn't know whether she could brag about it to the congregation or whether she ought to avoid mentioning it.

And to make matters worse Miss Pettie knew everything about it and started to tell people the moment chapel was over.

'Speaking at meetings, my dears,' she said. 'Fancy that! Our Harriet speaking at meetings!'

'By *particular invitation!*' Mrs Sowerby told them, wresting their attention from Miss Pettie with a scowl and a very loud voice. 'They think so *highly* of her, you see.'

'What does she speak about, Mrs Sowerby?' Miss Susan Brown inquired.

Oh how aggravating! What an impossible question! 'All manner of things, Miss Brown,' she said loftily. 'All manner of things.'

'She was at the Peterloo Massacre,' Miss Pettie explained, tugging her curls with excitement. 'She gave succour to the wounded, so she did, the dear girl, and now the Corresponding Societies and suchlike are all agog to hear what she has to say about it. Such excitement!'

'Fancy that!' Miss Brown said, very much impressed.

'Well I don't know about you,' Mrs Sowerby said, extricating herself from the conversation before anyone could ask her any more unnecessary questions, 'but I have a dinner to attend it. I must go home at once or I simply can't think what will happen.'

And she walked down the hill towards her cottage with as much dignity as she could command in her present state of irritation.

'Thoughtless to the last,' she said to Mr Sowerby when they were safely inside their own front door, 'Miss Pettie may be told, you notice, but not her own mother.'

'Oh what a deal we shall have to say to her when she makes her precious visit,' Mr Sowerby said.

His wife snorted. 'I'll believe *that*, Mr Sowerby, when I see it.'

She was to see it a great deal sooner than any of them imagined.

AT THE BEGINNING OF OCTOBER, when John was planning what he hoped would be his last trip to open up the Scottish routes, and Harriet had only one more speaking engagement and was looking forward to a rest and the chance to spend more time with Will, Nan Easter received a letter from Miss Pettie asking her if she and Harriet would attend 'the opening meeting of a Bury St Edmunds relief fund for the victims of Peterloo', and wondering whether Harriet would consider being their first speaker.

'What think 'ee?' Nan said to Harriet when they met over dinner later that day. 'I'm game for it, if you are. We could stay in the town for a day or two and visit with Annie.'

'I shall visit my parents whilst I am there,' Harriet said, and John was pleased to see that she wasn't at all anxious about it. 'Then they will have no cause to complain of neglect. Half an hour should suffice, would you not think so?'

'Half an hour would be plenty,' Nan grinned.

So the two women made their plans. They would travel together, taking Will with them, and Nan's maid, Tess, and Peg and Rosie to attend on them.

When John left to catch the early morning coach to Edinburgh, Harriet was happily packing.

'I do not think there will be any disturbances in Bury whilst you are there,' he said, reassuring himself. One positive result of the massacre was that it seemed to have put paid to riots, at least for the time being. There were plenty of meetings and marches but they were all peaceful. 'You will take my advice this time, won't you my love, and stay within doors if there is any sign of trouble.'

'There is no cause for you to worry, John dear.' She smiled at him. Ever since Peterloo she felt she was living a charmed life. 'Go now, my dear, or you will miss the coach. I have your mother to protect me.'

'Yes,' he said, 'you do. That is true.' And it was a relief to him to know it.

He would have been most upset if he'd been at home in Fitzroy Square that afternoon, for at four o'clock a message was sent round from Bedford Square to say that Nan would not be travelling to Bury after all.

Mr Brougham is returned from Italy, sick of a raging fever with vomiting and colic. I have sent for a surgeon. He en't in no fit state to be left, my dear, so I fear I cannot journey with 'ee tomorrow. Shall you travel alone? The boy will wait your answer.

Your loving Nan.

The old timid Harriet would have cancelled her journey; the new public spirited one wrote back at once to say that she would travel as planned, 'for I cannot disappoint the meeting'. But it was a surprise to her that the great Nan Easter was prepared to stay at home and nurse her sick lover, for all the world as if he were her husband. She is tender-hearted after all, she thought, under that fierce manner. How much I have learnt about her in the last few months.

Then she turned her attention to her journey.

It went remarkably smoothly, for it was a fine day and the roads were in quite good condition, there having been just enough rain in the previous week to keep down the dust without making mud. They made good time and were welcomed in Angel Hill by an excellent dinner and a well-warmed cradle for Will, who was exhausted after his long imprisonment in the coach. Then there was just enough time for Peg to dress her mistress in her plain 'meeting gown', before Miss Pettie came knocking on the door to escort her to the Athenaeum. She put on her bonnet and her blue redingote and walked briskly across the square. This was to be her thirteenth speech in support of the victims of Peterloo.

It was a blue October evening and the moon above Angel Hill was the colour of clotted cream. Candles bloomed in every un-shuttered window of the Angel Inn, and across the square the carriages arriving at the Athenaeum were black swaying shapes tossing their lanterns like yellow will-o'-the-wisps.

I am tonight's speaker, she thought with pride. I have come a very long way since I lived at Churchgate Street.

It was an excellent meeting and produced a rich subscription. Her former neighbours listened with shocked compassion when she described the sights she'd seen on the famous field of Peterloo, and sighed when she told them the story of Mary and Joe and the littluns who depended upon them and would starve because they were both too gravely injured to work.

And afterwards the newly formed committee served wine to their guests and gathered about their young speaker with congratulations and offers of assistance. And to her delight and gratification, there among the crush were the two Miss Callbecks, beautifully dressed in their finest silk gowns, their long rabbity faces smiling benignly between the old-fashioned lappets of their brown silk caps.

'My dear,' Evelina said, 'how brave you were to go out upon

that fearful field. It made my heart quite sink merely to hear of it.'

'I could do no other,' Harriet said, blushing. 'How d'ee do, Cousin Thomasina, Cousin Evelina. I trust I see you well.'

The aunts darted a quick anxious look at one another, like rabbits waiting for the signal to bolt. Then Evelina decided to confide in their cousin's courageous wife.

'We have lost two of our lodgers,' she said, 'and if we cannot find another by word of mouth, I fear we may have to advertise.' It had been difficult enough to agree to Nan's suggestion that they might take in lodgers in the first place, although of course they'd been in no position to refuse it, but if they had to stoop so low as to advertise like tradesmen...

While Harriet was trying to think of something to say that would be helpful or comforting, a man with a ginger moustache suddenly bristled into the conversation.

'I do hope you will forgive this intrusion, dear ladies,' he said, 'but I could not help overhearing and truly I do believe this is the most fortunate thing.' And he looked at Harriet, as though he were waiting for an introduction. It was Mr Richards, her travelling companion from Manchester. What an extraordinary coincidence.

Although she was surprised, she made the introduction easily. 'Cousins, allow me to present Mr Richards, who travelled to Manchester with John and me, and was present at Peterloo, just as I was. Mr Richards, my husband's two cousin, the Misses Callbeck.'

'A terrible tragedy, Mr Richards,' Thomasina said, as she shook his hand.

'Entirely my opinion, dear lady,' Mr Richards said. 'A terrible tragedy. We must all try to assist the injured and bring succour to the poor. That is the very reason I am here in Bury St Edmunds.'

'Indeed?' Evelina said, much impressed, and wondering what

he intended to do.

'Indeed,' he said, but he didn't enlighten her. 'We must all do what we can, must we not?'

There was a murmur of agreement throughout the group.

'Our dear Harriet has done more than any of *us* would ever have *dared*,' Susan Brown said, misty-eyed with admiration. 'Were you never afraid, Harriet?'

'There was no time to be afraid,' Harriet said truthfully.

Mr Richards took the two Miss Callbecks by the elbow and steered them deftly to a quiet corner beside the fireplace. 'I do hope you will not think me impolite if I ask you a question, dear ladies,' he said, gazing at them earnestly, 'but so very, very much depends upon your answer. So very, very much.'

'Tell us what it is you wish to know, Mr Richards,' Evelina said, charmed by his earnest manner.

'Do you truly have accommodation in your home for a paying guest, Miss Callbeck? There now, perhaps it *is* impolite of me to ask, but I do so hope that you have for between ourselves I am quite desperate to find accommodation in this town. But then, of course, I do realise that I might not suit, for I can see that your requirements would be admirably high. I would be prepared to pay whatever was agreeable to you.'

'If you would care to visit us in Whiting Street tomorrow morning,' Thomasina said, smiling at him kindly, 'I do believe we might arrange matters to our mutual satisfaction.' Why the man was a Godsend!

So there was quite a flurry of visiting in Bury St Edmunds the following morning. Members of the Relief Committee called at Angel Hill one after the other to congratulate Miss Pettie; Mr Richards put on his best jacket and his new top hat and walked to Whiting Street whistling cheerfully; and Harriet went to visit her mother in Churchgate Street. She would get that over with first and then she could spend the rest of her time with Annie.

CHAPTER 26

Annie Hopkins was waiting at the study window enjoying the warmth of the October sunshine on her rounded forehead. She had baby Meg in her arms and Jimmy and Beau kneeling on the windowsill beside her and Pollyanna was bobbing about behind them, but the minute the two bays snorted into the drive they all came scrambling out of the study together and tumbled to the front door singing, 'Here she is! Here she is!'

'Come right in, my dear, do,' Annie said, flinging the door wide. 'I've such a lot to tell 'ee, I hardly know where to begin. But you must settle into your room first —' leading the way upstairs. ''Tis all a-ready for 'ee. You must be fatigued after your journey. Did your speech go well? You are quite a celebrity, you know. How was Mr Brougham when you left London? I had a letter from Mama this very morning. What a condition he was in when he returned! Such a miserable thing to be ill and forced to travel! Did you visit *your* mama, my dear? You must tell me all about it. Does little Will need a drink? We've a dish of junket for his supper. Oh, how good it is to see you!'

It was a lovely welcome.

While Peg and Rosie were unpacking, Annie and Harriet took their children into the drawing room and settled them on the carpet with games to play and picture books to read. Then they settled themselves among the cushions on the settee and began to gossip.

Harriet's speech was relived and admired, and her brief, formal visit to her parents described and applauded. 'Quite right too, my dear,' Annie said. 'If you don't give 'em the chance to talk then they can't scold.' Then they discussed Mr Brougham's illness and the cutting of Meg's latest teeth and Will's sunny personality. And finally John and James were considered and declared to be well and the dearest of men.

'Mr Weatherstone means to retire after Christmas,' Annie said, 'and how my dear James will make out with a new curate after all these years with that kind old man I simply do not know.'

'You will miss him sorely,' Harriet agreed. 'Will, my lambkin, give Meggie back her rattle, there's a good boy.'

'Between you and me, I think 'tis all on account of that Jack Abbott coming back to Rattlesden. Things have never been quite the same since the day he turned up here again. His wife died in Norwich, you know, of the spotted fever, and the youngest child with her. After that he said there was nothing to keep him there. He left the two boys apprenticed to a cooper and came back here.'

'Poor Mr Abbott,' Harriet said. 'How terrible!' Despite the bugs and the dirt he'd seemed such a nice quiet man. 'He was always so gentle.'

'He ain't gentle now, my dear,' Annie said surprisingly. 'He's quite a firebrand these days. He spends all his time tramping from village to village hereabouts, urging people to work for parliamentary reform and to join the Hampden Clubs, and telling 'em of meetings and such. We have a club meets here every week, with forty members all a-traipsing in and out of the study, if you can imagine such a thing, and a fine old mess they make with their pipes and their papers, to say nothing of the mud they bring in. There is a meeting tonight so you will see for yourself.'

'I daresay they do make a mess, Annie,' Harriet said, 'but 'tis excellent work they do. If reform is to come about, 'twill be because of the Hampden Clubs. And after Peterloo, reform *must* come about. I am sure of it.'

'We have a man coming to speak to the meeting this evening,' Annie remembered. 'He is to stay the night here as there is no room for him in the village. He was present on the field of Peterloo, so they say. You might have seen him there.'

'I doubt it,' Harriet laughed. 'There were more than sixty thousand people on the field that day. But' — seeing Annie's face fall — 'I should be happy to attend the meeting and hear what he has to say.'

'We will attend it together,' Annie said happily. 'We won't go in until they've finished all their tedious business, though, for 'tis all points of order and such and mighty boring. He ain't due till nine o'clock. He's a-coming in from Ipswich. Jack Abbott is to fetch him in the farm cart and Henry Abbott is to chair the meeting. Oh 'tis all Abbotts in Rattlesden these days.'

'They won't mind our presence, will they, Annie?'

'Mind?' Annie said. 'Why, they won't even notice there will be such a crush.'

Which was certainly true, for when the two women opened the door into James's study later that evening, they could barely squeeze into the room.

The speaker had arrived, as they could tell from the welcoming noises that were being made somewhere near the fireplace, but they couldn't see him because there were so many villagers packed into that little panelled room that it was impossible for them to see anything except the broad back and the thick moleskins of the man directly in front of them. Swirls of blue tobacco smoke patterned the air above their heads and the place was pungent with the smell of sweat and farmyard.

But presently they heard James's mild voice suggesting that 'it might be better if some of us were to sit upon the carpet' and gradually the crush eased as, one after the other, his parishioners lowered themselves to the floor where they squatted in a tangle of rough boots and patched knees, black-rimmed fingers and tousled heads. And now Annie and Harriet could see Jack Abbott, resplendent in a green corduroy jacket, standing beside the speaker who was a small dark-haired man in brown fustian.

'It is a great pleasure to me to introduce our speaker,' James was saying, 'for not only was he present in St Peter's Field on the day of the massacre, but in addition to that he attended to the wounds of no fewer than thirty-two of the injured.'

'Why good heavens!' Harriet said. 'It is...'

'Mr Rawson from Manchester,' the Reverend Hopkins introduced.

He looked smaller and uglier than Harriet remembered him, but he was undeniably the same man, standing awkwardly before them with his back to the blaze of the fire, listening to dear old James. Then, to her total amazement, she saw that Mr Richards had come to this meeting, too. He was sitting in James's chair tucked into the corner beside James's desk. His black notebook was open in his hand and he was watching Mr Rawson with complete concentration. What a coincidence!

She turned to Annie to tell her all about it, but Annie had her finger to her lips, because Mr Rawson was clearing his throat ready to start his speech.

'Ladies and gentlemen,' he said, 'first I must thank thee for all t' help and comfort tha's been a-sendin' to t' victims of t' massacre at Peterloo. 'Tis sorely needed and uncommon kindly. Thank 'ee. Next, I must tell thee t' battle is only just begun.'

How extraordinary to hear his voice again, Harriet thought, and she had a sudden powerful vision of his blunt hands tenderly bandaging a wound, and for a few brief seconds she was back on St Peter's field among the moans and the dust and the terrible injuries. Then she realised that the parishioners of Rattlesden were listening to this man with attention and admiration and she remembered Mr Taylor telling her what a fine speaker he was, and she began to listen to him too and was surprised that there was so much passion in him, for he'd been so restrained and quiet among the wounded.

He spoke of the weavers and their wages, 'seven shillings a week, and I don't need to tell thee what that means. If tha pays t' rent, there's no money for food, if tha buys food, like as not tha'lt be out on t' street wi'out a roof over tha head'; of the mill-owners who kept dogs to guard them, 'uncommon well-fed, their dogs, a deal fatter than t' weavers I can tell thee'; and finally he told his audience he was going to ask them a question.

'What must be done to persuade t' masters to pay a proper wage to t' likes of thee an' me?'

'Hold shotgun to 'is head,' Jack Abbott growled. 'Try how a little lead would change the beggar's opinion. Uncommon persuasive, a little lead.'

James looked decidedly uncomfortable at this, but a murmur of approval rolled around the room and Mr Richards was scribbling furiously in his notebook.

'Lead may work fast, I'll grant thee,' Caleb said, 'but 'tis my opinion t' vote is better. Why? I'll tell thee why. 'Tis because it is bloodless and indisputable. I'd rather work for universal suffrage, my friends, than for armed uprising, though after Peterloo we might have to settle for both. We just might.'

And that was approved of too, with a deep-throated growling. And noted down.

'What of tyranny then?' Henry Abbott asked. 'En't we to oppose the tyrant, eh? What's your opinion o' that, Mr Rawson?'

'If we've no'but an ounce of compassion in our natures, we must rise against tyranny wherever we see it, and speak out against it an' all, no matter what t' cost. Being human we can do no other. What right-thinking man could stand by and watch his neighbour cut to t' brains and do nowt?'

'Aye!' his audience growled. 'Tha's true. Tha' uncommon true.'

'But to vote, my friends, to vote is t' key to lasting power. If every man grown were given t' vote, and vote by ballot what's more what can't be coerced, and parliaments elected annually to mek 'em answerable to t' people, why then every manufacturer would need to consider his workers, for they would be voters just exactly t' same as himself, with equal civic power. I doubt we'd have so much talk of seven shillings a week being sufficient if t' weavers were voters.'

'No, indeed!' the listeners said. 'Tha's true! You got the essence of un there. Them ol' mawthers'll have to change their ways, when we gets the vote.'

Harriet was uplifted by such talk. It was all so exciting and so true, and, what was even better, she was a part of it. When the eleven dead of Peterloo were praised as martyrs, her eyes filled with tears at the memory of those pathetic bundles left like so much rubbish on that bloodstained field, but she rejoiced even as the tears gathered at the thought that their deaths would not be in vain. Now, surely, the government must listen to the voice of the people, just as Mr Hunt said then and Mr Rawson was saying now. Surely, oh surely, the time for universal suffrage had come.

The evening ended on a burst of spontaneous cheering, and for once in her life she dared to join in, shouting hurrah with the best. Oh, what they were doing was right and honourable! What a blessing to be part of it!

And then the meeting was breaking up and men were struggling to their feet and beginning to amble out of the door into the hall. She could see Mr Richards striding across the room towards the two Abbotts and greeting them as though they were old friends, which was odd. But then Annie grabbed her by the hand and leapt through the mass of bodies, dragging her along behind.

'Come along my dear,' she said, 'We must ask James to introduce us to the speaker.'

'Annie, I...' Harriet tried to explain, but the crush was still too great for Annie to hear her, and in any case, they were already beside the fireplace and the introductions were being made.

'Mrs Easter was at Peterloo, too,' Annie said proudly.

'We met,' Harriet said, smiling at him and feeling suddenly quite shy to be meeting him again like this. He was such a wonderful man, giving all his time and energy to help his neighbours, and she admired him so much. But to her disappointment his face remained politely blank and he did not respond to her at all.

He does not recognise me, she thought, and she realised that it distressed her to have been forgotten.

But he hadn't forgotten her. It was just that her appearance was so unexpected. The woman he remembered was a creature from a legend, wild as a gypsy, in rags and tatters, her petticoat torn for bandages and her beautiful stockings stripped from her feet, an angel of mercy with a dirty face and pale flowing hair and bloodstained hands. The person who stood before him now was a lady of society, beautifully dressed in the latest fashion, in a blue and green striped gown with elaborate sleeves and fine frills at the hem, with her pale hair hidden under a fine lace cap, and pearls at her throat. He could find no words with which to address her.

But they were rescued by their common concern. 'Is Mary recovered?' she asked. 'And her brother, Joe? I think of them often.'

'He was in t' infirmary six weeks,' he told her, 'and no better now he's out, I fear.'

'Is he able to work?'

'No, ma'am. He still has trouble breathing, d'ye see.'

'You must deliver part of the Bury subscription to him and his family,' Harriet said at once. 'Do you return soon?'

'Not till I've spoke at Thetford,' he told her. 'I've a deal to do afore I see Manchester again.'

'If you will tell me your address,' she said, 'I will see that the money is dispatched straight to you.'

'You're uncommon kind,' he said, smiling at her.

'We have a little supper laid on for 'ee in the dining room,' Annie said. 'If you care to walk through…'

And so the four of them walked into the dining room where the cloth was set with tankards of ale and half a dozen meat pies and two dishes of Annie's famous lemon pickle, and where their two maids were waiting to serve them. And now that the first awkwardness was gone they all made an excellent meal together, although Harriet noticed that her Mr Rawson was ill at ease when it came to eating the pie and handled his knife and fork awkwardly, and that made her feel more sympathetic towards him than ever, for a little weakness in a man so strong was rather touching.

But the talk about the table was as uplifting as the meeting had been, and ranged over so many subjects, not just parliamentary reform and universal suffrage, but the proper care of the sick, the rights of man, the necessity and rewards of doing God's will. It absorbed them all so thoroughly that they were still talking when the grandfather clock struck midnight in the hall behind them.

'We are keeping you from your rest, Mr Rawson,' Annie said, making a little grimace of apology. 'If you are to be up and ready for Mr Abbott by six of the clock tomorrow morning…'

And so the evening had to end. And although Harriet was so excited, she hardly slept at all that night, she was up early in the morning ready to wave goodbye to her hero. She and Annie and

James took lanterns and walked down to the gate with him when the farm cart arrived.

He shook them all warmly by the hand, holding Harriet's just a little longer than the others, then he took a paper out of his pocket and gave it to her before he climbed into the cart. 'The address you wanted,' he said.

'Why, yes indeed,' she said. 'Thank 'ee kindly. I will see that funds are sent as soon as may be.'

'Happen when we next meet, t' government will have made some decisions,' he said, smiling at them all in the flickering light.

'Let us pray so,' James replied, as the cart went joggling down the lane. 'Let us pray so.'

'They must have some plans, must they not?' Harriet asked as she and Annie walked back into the house.

'Who?' Annie asked vaguely, her thoughts already directed towards her children's breakfast.

'Why the government, Annie dear, the government. When they return to London in the autumn, they will have to bring in a reform bill, will they not?'

BUT WHEN LORD Sidmouth and his cabinet returned to the House of Commons, they had no intention of bringing in a reform bill. The mob had risen and the mob were to be put down, or the English aristocracy would suffer the same fate as the French had suffered thirty years ago. To that end they had two simple purposes: one was to prevent any further demonstrations of any kind, the other was to make it impossible for anyone to voice any criticism of the government.

Their plans were put into operation in December, and highly repressive they were. They took the form of six Acts, couched in vague terms designed to be as helpful as possible to the magistrates, and making it perfectly clear that despite the dead and injured of Peterloo, the reformers' petitions were to be totally ignored.

The first Act prohibited drilling, military training and marches; the second gave magistrates the right to enter and search any house, without a warrant 'on suspicion of there being arms therein'; the third prohibited any meetings of more than fifty people without authorisation from the magistrates; the fourth, as Nan had suspected, increased the stamp duty on newspapers and periodicals, raising their cost to sixpence or more; and the fifth and sixth gave increased powers to the authorities to deal with sedition and libel.

'We are gagged and forbidden,' Caleb told Harriet, when he wrote to thank her for the third donation she'd had sent to his weavers.

We may not march or meet together or speak or write, and moreover our homes may be entered and searched whenever it takes a magistrate's fancy so to do. When you consider who the magistrates are, and whose rights and properties they protect, you will see there is little hope for any of us to escape persecution. Many here are in despair. These are miserable times and for the moment it is hard to see how they may be opposed.

Mary is still unwell, suffering dizzy turns and loss of memory which she finds uncommon distressing. Howsomever Joe says he means to return to the mill come what may. They send their particular thanks for the monies you sent and wish you to know 'twas all spent upon food for the little ones.

Kindest regards from your despondent friend,
  Caleb Rawson.

Harriet was rather thrilled to be receiving these letters, for the more she knew about him the more Mr Rawson was becoming her hero. It was an honour to be written to by such a man and it made her feel important to know that she was part of the great struggle for reform.

'I cannot imagine what may be done now,' she wrote back, answering by return of post as she always did.

> In the light of such legislation, how may any of us even make our wishes known? It is a desperate situation, I agree. Mrs Easter is very angry that the stamp duty has been increased again. She is of the opinion that if the price of newspapers is forced any higher by this wretched tax, nobody will buy them. And then how will anybody know what is going on? It is all very distressing.
>
> I am glad to hear that Joe is better. Pray give my kind regards to Mary.
>
> Kindest regards to yourself.
>
> Your friend, who only wishes she knew what could be done at this unhappy time,
> Harriet Easter.

But Mr Richards, of the affable smile and the ginger whiskers, who was still lodging most comfortably with the two Miss Callbecks, Mr Richards knew exactly what should be done. There was a plan to outwit 'these monstrous men of government', he said, and at the very moment that Harriet was signing her letter to Caleb Rawson, he was sitting in the snug of the White Hart at Scole pouring that plan into the willing ears of Henry and Jack Abbott.

'There are men gathering in London now,' he said, 'who mean to fight these intemperate laws. I can tell you two gentlemen the secret of their whereabouts, where I wouldn't tell another living soul, you understand, because I know you would never give them away. That is so, is it not?'

'Indeed, 'tis, sir,' Jack Abbott said rather drunkenly, for Mr

Richards had bought them a great deal of ale. 'You may depend on us sir. Tha's a fac'.'

'I have two tickets here in my pocket,' Mr Richards confided, producing them, 'for the night mail to London from this very inn, this very evening, as ever is; two tickets that would take you to the very meeting house of these brave men, and here is the address, d'ye see, and a letter to their leader, and a map to guide 'ee to the very spot. Two tickets, one letter, one address, one map —' setting them on the table before him like a winning hand at cards. 'I would be happy to give 'em to 'ee, so I should, were you prepared to take 'em and use 'em. Are you game? Now don't say you ain't, because I won't believe a word of it.'

It was late in the evening and they were out of work and full of beer and bravado, and besides Mr Richards was uncommon persuasive.

'With my Nell gone and the boys 'prenticed,' Jack Abbott said, 'I've nought to lose.'

'And a deal to gain,' Mr Richards urged.

So they were persuaded, and took the tickets and the address, and caught the night mail, which by great good fortune, so Mr Richards said, just happened to be ready for the off in the yard outside.

CHAPTER 27

'Harriet and John grow uncommon dull these days,' Matilda said. ''Tis all work with John and all politics with Harriet. I declare they ain't fit for polite society, neither the one of 'em.'

She and her friends were at a party at the Ottenshaw's London house in Henrietta Street. They had retired from the ballroom temporarily and were drinking wine in a vain attempt to cool themselves after a particularly energetic mazurka.

'Oh come now, Tilda,' Billy said, 'that's a bit hard. She does uncommon good work for the poor.'

'And where's the fun in that?' Matilda said, pouting at him prettily. She was pregnant again and blooming. 'Lectures and meetings night after night. It wouldn't do for me I can tell you. 'Tis enough to turn the stomach. Oh no, Billy my love, she should have come here tonight, so she should. 'Twould have done her some good. It ain't every day of the week we get a new king, now is it?'

'He ain't exactly a new king though, is he Tilda?' Jerry Ottenshaw said reasonably. ''Tis only the Prince Regent with a new name.' The poor old mad king, George III, had finally slipped away from his painful, puzzled existence and the Regent was proclaimed George IV. Nobody could pretend the news was surprising, but it was a good excuse for parties.

'La, I'm dry,' Maria said, flirting her eyes at Mr Ottenshaw. 'Is there any fruit cup, Jerry?'

'Time we were dancing, my charmer,' Billy said, as the first notes of the waltz drifted out into the alcove. And he seized Matilda about the waist and walked off with her, moving in time to the music and with such a marked rhythm that her skirt swung like a bell.

'She'll be the only woman sitting at home tonight,' Matilda said, as she skipped along beside him, 'in the whole of London.'

'Who will, my beauty?' Billy said, grinning sideways at her.

'Fie on you, Billy Easter,' she said, pretending to scold. 'You don't listen to a word I say. I shall refuse my favours, so I shall, if you don't pay me more attention.' Her face was bright with affection, encouraging him.

So he kissed her.

NAN AND FREDERICK were at a party too that night, and a very grand one. They were the guests of the Earl of Harrowby and among the many others there were more than half the members of the Cabinet. It was such prestigious company that she and Frederick found themselves sitting well below the salt at dinner, right at the far end of the table, in fact, and with the Barnesworthys for company. They were presided over by Lady Harrowby, it was true, but they were well out of the way of the excitement at the centre of the table.

Something was going on, Nan thought, that was plain, for the atmosphere in the room was extremely tense, and Lady Harrowby was brittle with nervousness which was most unlike her, and servants arrived every five minutes with messages for Lord Sidmouth or their host or both of them together. And the butler had obviously been detailed to keep a watch for somebody or something, because he went to the far window as soon as one messenger departed and watched there until the next arrived. It vexed Nan Easter not to know what it was all about. If she'd been a little nearer the centre, she could have listened to what Lord Sidmouth and Lord Harrowby were saying, but at her present distance it was impossible.

And to make matters worse, Sir Joshua was more than half drunk and horribly irascible, holding forth about everything and anything. Now he was blundering on about Sidmouth's spy system.

'Spies,' he declared, as the fish course was cleared, 'are a damned fine thing. Where would we be without 'em? I'll tell you, where we'd be, my friends? In the dark. That's where we'd be.'

'They have their value,' his neighbour agreed. 'Howsomever 'tis my opinion they are best when they are used with discretion. As agents provocateurs I sometimes wonder if they ain't a good deal worse than the mob we pay 'em to control. They provoke riots a-plenty, I'll grant you that, but it don't lead to a hanging, and a hanging is what we need to deter the sort of mob we see in this country today.'

'Quite right,' Sir Joshua said. 'Ain't had a good hanging for years. Used to enjoy 'em, so I did.'

'How of our own two special government spies?' Lady Harrowby said urbanely, smiling at Frederick in the hope that he would help her to ease the conversation. 'I believe you found our roving Princess when you were on your travels last autumn, did you not?'

'We did, ma'am,' Frederick said.

'And did you discover her intentions too?'

'I fear we may have done.'

'She means to return,' Lady Harrowby said, understanding

him. 'Dear me. That won't please the new King. Can he do ought to prevent her, think 'ee?'

'I doubt it, ma'am.'

'They say he will divorce her rather than allow her to be Queen.'

''Twould seem likely.'

'She is hardly a fit person to be Queen of England,' Lady Barnesworth said. 'Flaunting her lovers and dancing in the streets and wearing indecent clothing. 'Tain't seemly.'

'The King takes lovers,' Nan pointed out, grinning at her, 'and we forgive him for it. One law for the goose and another for the gander, I'm thinking.'

Another message had arrived and Lord Harrowby was looking uncommon serious.

'And what of her lover, Count Bergami?' another lady asked. 'Did you meet with him? They say in the *Gazette* that he is a commoner and a fortune hunter.'

'As to that, dear lady,' Frederick said, "tis an impossibility to believe all that one reads in the press since no two news sheets ever agree.'

'The government should put paid to the damn press, once and for all,' Sir Joshua said, filling his mouth with buttered parsnips. 'That's what they should do. All this pussyfooting around with stamp acts and agreements and such. 'Tain't a bit of use. Oh I know what you'll say to that, Mrs Easter, but upon me soul I never read such unmitigated balderdash as you see in *The Times* nowadays. I used to think it fair-minded, but upon me soul...' And he slopped more wine in his glass to show his ill-humour.

The butler was standing at the window shaking his head at his master, which seemed to be the correct signal for the noble Earl was smiling in answer. Now what was going on?

'Hang the lot of 'em,' Sir Joshua said, drinking his wine noisily. 'That's what I say.'

Frederick gave him a disparaging look. 'A very charitable sentiment,' he said.

A FEW HUNDRED YARDS AWAY, on the north side of Oxford Street, a group of excited men were waiting for a signal. There were about twenty of them, crowded together in a darkened attic above a stable at one end of a narrow alley called Cato Street, guns primed, swords sharpened, last instructions given. And among them were Jack and Henry Abbott, both in a state of frantic excitement, Jack prowling, Henry cracking his fingers like a fusillade, crick, crick, crick, over and over again.

Voices in the stable below them. The signal at last. Standing, gathering their weapons together, breathing fast with excitement. The trap door flung aside with a thud, a head protruding through the opening. But not the head they expected. Dear God! This one wore the stovepipe hat of a constable.

'Hellfire boys! We are done for!' somebody shouted. Then the candles were kicked out and the room was full of struggling bodies. Somebody fired a pistol with a flash of red flame, acrid smoke, deafening reverberations. Somebody was duelling, blades hissing. Impossible to tell friend from foe in the noise and darkness. Then Henry saw one of the windows opening and a man squeezing through headfirst, kicking as he fell, and he seized his cousin by the hand and followed, landing jarred but feet first in a street full of excited people.

Two men fighting for a cutlass, rolling over and over in the midden beside the door, constables rushing madly into the stable, conspirators struggling even more madly to get out, and scores of spectators herding into the road through the archway, alerted by gunfire and all agog for blood, running and shouting.

'Come you on,' Henry said, and he picked himself up, turned and backed into the oncoming crowd. 'Through the arch, bor!' And then they were in John Street and running like madmen, with no idea where they were going, wild with fear to get away, and with half a dozen men roaring after them, shrieking, 'Stop thief!' and 'Treason!' They ran and ran, until their lungs felt as though they were bursting, continuing long after their pursuers had tired and given up the chase, and when they finally stopped it was because they had no breath or strength left at all.

They were in a quiet garden in the middle of one of the new fashionable squares, having thrown themselves bodily over the railings and crawled on their hands and knees to the cover of a thick holly.

'What — shall — do now?' Henry panted.

Although he could barely speak, Jack knew the answer. 'Go — Fitzroy Square,' he gulped. 'Mrs Easter.'

HARRIET EASTER WAS SPENDING a quiet evening at home, exactly as Matilda had predicted. John was out dining with Mr Walters of *The Times*, as he did every two months with his customary regularity, and she had been writing letters in the study downstairs, sitting peaceably beside the fire with her feet on the little velvet stool and the ticking of the grandfather clock for company. Two letters were written and ready for the early morning post, one very long and voluble to her dear Annie and the other short and restrained to her mother and father, and now she was earnestly composing a third in answer to a request for a speaker. She had hardly begun it when there was an urgent rapping at the front door. Whoever can that be at this hour of the night? she wondered, putting down her pen, and she listened while Paulson brisk-footed into the hall.

Muffled voices. '— Mrs Easter — could 'ee? — d'ye see, sir?'

And Paulson's solemn answer: 'If you will wait, I will make enquiries.'

She had recognised one voice before Paulson came in to

announce its owner. 'Two *persons* of the name of Abbott, so they say, ma'am.'

'Show them in, Paulson. They come from Rattlesden. Mrs Hopkins told me they were working in London and might be calling.'

But not at this hour of the night, Paulson's expression said. However, he did as he was told.

'Welcome to my house,' she said as the two men shuffled into the study. 'Pray, do sit down.' But then she saw that they were both bolt-eyed and red in the face with effort. 'Why, what is the matter?'

'We've a pack of constables at our heels,' Jack Abbott said. 'Tha's the truth of it, mum. We'm on the run an' we don't know which way for to turn. Could you hide us an hour or two, mum? If it en't too much to ask.'

'What have you done?' Harriet asked, thrilled to think that they had turned to her for help. It was almost as though she were the great Nan Easter. Or even Mr Rawson. 'Was there a meeting?'

'Not in the general sense of a meeting,' Jack admitted sheepishly.

'Well what, then?'

'Well now, mum, 'tis like this here,' Henry said, perching on the edge of the chair. His tone was decidedly artful, but she was too excited to notice. 'We been a-keepin' stables over the other side of town, since we come to London. Your friend Mr Richards sent us to it, for which we'm good an' grateful, en't we Jack?'

'Yes,' she said. 'Mrs Hopkins told me of it. 'Twas at Cato Street, was it not?'

They seemed loathe to admit it, and she did notice that, but thought it no more than odd.

'Well yes, mum,' Henry said after a long pause. 'So 'twas.'

'What we wasn't to know, mum,' Jack went on, 'was that

them he sent us to is a parlous bad lot, mum, wanted by the constabulary so they are. And now we'm a-wanted along of 'em. Bein' they'm on the run, mum, we've had to run too, d'ye see. And bein' they'm a-wanted, we'm a-wanted along of 'em.'

'Do you mean that the constables are chasing you?' she asked. 'Actually on foot and chasing you? Now? Tonight?' How dreadful and how exciting!

'Yes, mum,' Henry Abbott said. 'Got away by the skin of our teeth, mum, so to speak.'

'But you have done nothing wrong? You assure me of that?'

'Oh no, mum. Nothing at all.'

BUT THIS WAS TERRIBLE. Something would have to be done to protect them and done at once. 'Wait there,' she said, happily taking command of them. 'I will return to 'ee presently.' And she went off to order the pony cart, planning as she went. She would send them out of London on the first available coach, well out of harm's way, somewhere where the constables would never think of looking for them. The price of the tickets could be added to the Easter account, so that would present no problem. John would be sure to agree to it, as it would be an act of simple Christian charity, no more, no less. Now where could she send them? And the answer to that was in her mind almost as soon as she'd asked herself the question. Why to Caleb Rawson, of course! He would know exactly what ought to be done with men on the run from the constables. Had he not dealt with hundreds such after the massacre of Peterloo? She could write him a little note explaining the matter and throwing them all on his mercy. What a thrilling business, it was!

The pony cart was ready in half an hour with Tom Thistlethwaite to drive it and Peg Mullins to accompany her for propriety's sake, for it wouldn't have done at all to be seen driving about London at night in the sole company of two rough-looking men and a boy. And it was just as well she had such foresight, for it took over an hour and a half to find a coach to Manchester with two vacant seats aboard. But at last it was done, and the two Abbotts were dispatched with their letter of introduction. It was striking the first quarter past midnight when she and Peg and Tom finally arrived back in Fitzroy Square.

John had been home for half an hour. 'Wherever have you been, my love?' he asked mildly. 'Paulson tells me you took two *persons* to the midnight coach. Was that truly so? He does not approve of such goings-on at all.'

'A most extraordinary thing,' she said. 'Do you remember Mr Abbott from Rattlesden? Well...'

'You have a tender heart, my dear,' he said when the tale was told.

'It was right to help them, was it not?'

'Let us hope so,' he said, even though he wasn't at all sure, for it sounded very suspicious. But he was too tired to worry about it now.

However, the next morning his suspicions were confirmed as soon as he arrived at Easter House and saw the morning papers. He went home early for breakfast, taking a copy of each one.

'You had best read this,' he said to Harriet, handing over a copy of the *Chronicle,* as she met him in the hall. 'From what you told me last night, I am afraid you may have harboured two desperate criminals.'

No, she thought, as she walked through into the dining room paper in hand. The Abbots are not criminals, surely not. It is a mistake. He can't mean criminals. But the words in the paper were unequivocal.

Thursday Feb 24th 1820, they said. *DREADFUL RIOT AND MURDER.*

Yesterday evening the West-end of the town was thrown into the utmost confusion, the streets lined with soldiers and spectators, and the greatest alarm prevailed in consequence of the following circumstances. Information having been received at Bow Street, that a meeting of persons armed was to be held at a house in Cato Street Marylebone, the magistrates, fearing something serious would be the result, forwarded a formidable body of their officers to the place.

A desperate affray took place. An officer by the name of Westcot received three shots through his hat, and Smythers, an active officer, received a stab in his right side, and he was carried away, quite dead. The officers endeavoured to enter the place, and secure nine of the offenders, who had received much injury; one of them, a butcher, had a desperate black eye, and his hands were much cut. Several others escaped and are being sought by the officers. Captain Fitzclarence arrived on the spot with a party of the Guards, and the prisoners were escorted to Bow Street by a strong body of soldiers, who surrounded the coaches.

The person, whose stab proved fatal to Smythers, has escaped. This person was stated at Bow Street to be Arthur Thistlewood.

Government is understood to have had previous information of this extraordinary meeting.

Harriet was so shocked she felt quite sick. Carried away quite dead! But that was murder! What were they doing with guns? They must have been planning an insurrection. Were the Abbotts conspirators?

'Oh, John!' she said. 'Cato Street was where they worked. They told me so last night. These must be the very people they worked for. How *awful*! How *absolutely awful*!' The implications were terrifying. Had she helped two conspirators to escape from justice? Or two murderers? That was even worse. Oh surely not! Dear God, please don't let this be true, she prayed. I meant no harm by it. You must know that, Lord, for you know the secrets of all hearts. I thought I was helping the afflicted, not two men who were privy to murder. Please don't let it be true. 'They swore they had done nothing wrong,' she said.

'Oh Harriet, my dear,' he reproved, 'and you believed them?'

'I saw no reason not,' she pleaded. *He* had been quite sanguine about them too, last night. 'I thought they were telling the truth.'

'You'd best read the *Advertiser* too,' he said, handing it across to her. 'There is more and worse.'

The *Advertiser* told the same story but at greater length, adding a final fearful paragraph:

> *It is believed that the object of this conspiracy was to attack the London home of the Earl of Harrowby, where last night were assembled nearly half the members of the Cabinet and their distinguished friends, and there to massacre each and every one, guns and firearms having been purchased especially for the purpose. Fortunately the government had been appraised of the situation throughout and neither the noble Earl nor his guests received any harm whatsoever. Howsomever, in different circumstances who knows what might have occurred.*

'But your mother was at Lord Harrowby's dinner,' Harriet said, her eyes bolting. She could have been party to the murder of her own mother-in-law.

'She was,' he said grimly.

'Oh John. I did not know they were conspirators. I swear it.'

He was squinting with distress. 'Why did you have anything to do with them?' he said. "Twas total folly and you should have known it.'

'You did not say such things to me last night,' she said.

'I thought them,' he said grimly, 'although I did not say them. I was tired. I hoped it would be nothing. I hoped we should have no cause to fear.'

'Do we have cause to fear?' He was making her feel worse and worse.

'The wife of one of the managers of A Easter and Sons gives aid to two criminals escaping from justice and you ask if we have anything to fear?'

She was weak with shame. 'Oh John, whatever shall we do?'

'The cousins shall give notice to Mr Richards, for a start,' he said angrily. 'I shall write to them at once. You should never have introduced them to such a man in the first place.'

Being rebuked so sternly made the tears gather in her eyes, and John realised it was no use pursuing the matter. It was distressing her too much and served no purpose.

'Don't cry, Harriet,' he said, trying to be kinder. 'We will take legal advice. I will send a message round to Cosmo Teshmaker straight away. Let us see what he has to say.'

Cosmo Teshmaker had lived on the edge of the ebullient Easter family for more than twenty years, but he was first and foremost a solicitor, so when John's message arrived, asking for his advice and marked 'URGENT' in letters an inch high, he put on his best hat, took up his new gold-tipped cane, and went gliding off to Fitzroy Square at once to attend to it.

He was almost disappointed to find that the matter was so easy to deal with.

'I do not think you need to be unduly alarmed, Mrs Easter,' he said. 'For as I see it neither you nor Mr John could have known that the two farm labourers you assisted were employed by conspirators, which is your opinion, Mrs Easter, I believe, nor that they were part of the conspiracy themselves, which is your opinion, is it not, Mr John? They did not carry arms, you say?'

'Oh no, no,' Harriet assured him.

'And they removed themselves from the scene of the commotion at the very first opportunity?'

'Yes.'

'And are now out of London?'

'Yes. I sent them to Manchester, to a friend of — ours.'

'He would be a business acquaintance of some sort, I daresay?'

Harriet looked anxiously at John, who was squinting at the carpet, his face dark. What was she to say now? Must she admit the full story of her involvement with this man? Mr Teshmaker would be sure to agree with John and see him as a dangerous insurgent and not the sort of person with whom the wife to Mr John Easter should associate. Whatever else she did or said, she must try not to harm her dear John any further, particularly now when he was being so understanding and she had been so foolish.

'We met him when were in Manchester on business,' John rescued. 'Yes, indeed.' Oh how very good you are, dear, dear John, to protect me so!

'He would be trustworthy?'

'Entirely, in my opinion.'

'Then my advice to you, dear lady, would be to lie low, keep mum and wait for the matter to blow over, as it most certainly will. If the two labourers were merely servants, as you believe, they will not wish to do or say anything that would associate them with this conspiracy, and if they were conspirators their desire to stay hidden and silent will be even more imperative. It will blow over.'

'Yes,' Harriet said. But he could see she didn't believe him.

CHAPTER 28

Caleb Rawson was a man who drove himself hard, nature having given him the strength and disposition to do it. He was one of those people who can exist on very little sleep and his energy was legendary. 'Tek it to Caleb,' his fellow weavers would say, for they knew that whatever hour of the day or night they brought him their problems he would deal with them.

So when the Abbotts came knocking at his attic door that February morning in the dank, early hours, he put on his breeches, lit the remains of his candle, shook the sleep from his head like a dog shaking himself free of water, and went to attend to them, wide awake and in full command of his situation and his senses.

'What's amiss?' he asked as he opened the door. 'Come in.'

They handed him Harriet's note, and began to tell their tale. But when they started to make the same excuses that won favour with Harriet, he stopped them in mid-sentence.

'Nay,' he said, 'best to speak t' truth, if I'm to aid thee. I'd not think ill of thee, if tha'd'st broke into t' party and shot the lot of 'em, every man jack from Harrowby down.'

'It en't the Cabinet what's dead, sir,' Jack Abbott said, 'least-ways not accordin' to the papers. 'Tis a constable, so they do say. We'm hunted men sir.' And in the flickering light of Caleb's candle, they certainly looked it.

'Tha must quit t' country,' Caleb said. 'I'll get one of t' barges to tek thee to Liverpool. Then tha must tek ship there to the Indies or America or some such. The further the better!' He was already on his way out of the door.

They followed him meekly, accepting exile as they'd accepted Harriet's help twenty-eight hours ago, quietly and without protest because they were still numb with shock. There was nothing in their heads except the ambush in Cato Street and the fear they still carried with them. They began to tell the story of it all over again as soon as they reached the street.

'Nay,' Caleb said, holding up one blunt hand to prevent them. 'If tha means to survive, lads, tha'd best leave such talk in England. Not a word of it from now on. Tell ought and tha's dead men.'

Their folly annoyed him, but he was used to folly among his fellow insurrectionists. Few of them seemed capable of the detachment and determination that he saw as the prerequisite for success. Their plans were inadequate and their tempers uncertain, and both were great weaknesses in them. He knew it but he didn't criticise them for it. When all was said and done, he could hardly expect them to have quite the same urgent motivation as he did.

Ever since his wife and son had died of the smallpox, he had been a man dedicated to change and reform. It was the only way he could contain the driving anger their unnecessary suffering had left in his personality. He knew from the bitterness of that experience that pain and suffering were the direct result of poverty, and he was convinced that poverty would only be alleviated when the poor were given the vote. It was obvious, simple and urgent. Now every step he took was one step nearer reform.

As he watched the barge inch through the oily murk of the Manchester Ship Canal with its extra cargo hidden under the tarpaulins, he felt he had struck one more blow in the struggle for liberty and he was glad of it.

Then he set off to Mr Mulliner's mill, where he was employed to weave black crepe for the funeral trade, and quietly got on with the rest of his day.

BACK IN FITZROY SQUARE, Harriet was still anxious. Even her diary was little consolation to her now. She confided her fears to it, of course, explaining that she only meant to help, that she had known nothing of the conspiracy, that she was truly, truly sorry for her folly, but it wasn't until Caleb's laconic letter arrived two days later that she was able to relax even a little.

'The cargo you sent,' he wrote, 'is on its way to the Indies. You will hear no more of it.'

But there was still the trial of the conspirators to face, and that was reported in terrible detail in all the newspapers. Harriet read them with fearful fascination. By the second morning it was clear to her that these wild, foolish men had almost certainly been provoked by government agents, but they'd been too simple and too much inflamed by their own passions to realise it.

And by the final day when the jury pronounced their inescapable verdict, she was torn with pity for them, even though she knew they were parlous sinners and would have committed murder if they hadn't been prevented. She read the words of the judgement, trembling with compassion:

That you, and each of you, be taken from hence to the gaol from
whence you came, and from thence be hanged by the neck until dead,

and that afterwards your heads shall be severed from your bodies; and your bodies be divided into four quarters, to be disposed of as his Majesty shall think fit. And may God of His infinite goodness have mercy upon your souls.

She was quite horrified when she went to dine with Nan and Mr Brougham later that week to discover that the others around the table took the matter so lightly.

'I wonder how much a seat at the execution will cost this time,' Sophie Fuseli said, mounding food onto her fork. 'There ain't been a public hanging these many months, so 'twill be a pretty penny. But then it ain't every day of the week you get to see a dozen men a-dancing at the rope's end.'

'I should like to see it,' Matilda said, her eyes shining. 'Would you buy me a ticket, Billy dear?' She was sparkling at him, teasing him, touching his cheek with lingering fingers.

''Ten't such a fine thing to see, I can tell 'ee,' Nan said brusquely. 'I was in Paris during the revolution, on the very day they put the old King to the guillotine, and I saw it all, a-hackin' and a-choppin' and blood in all directions. That's a fearsome sight.'

'I should like to see it, fearsome or not,' Matilda said, pouting at Billy and smoothing the folds of her muslin gown luxuriously across her belly.

'Well you shan't,' Billy said, amiably but firmly. And he turned to his mother. 'Now she's breeding again, Mama, she must stay at home, must she not?'

'If 'tis to be my sixth grandchild or a hanging,' Nan said, grinning at Matilda, 'why then, I favour the grandchild.'

'Amen to that,' Sophie Fuseli said. 'There will always be other hangings. I daresay Mr Brougham could arrange one for 'ee if you asked him prettily.'

'I cannot offer you my present client,' Frederick Brougham

said urbanely, 'the man is a mere bankrupt you see, my dear, and insolvency ain't a hanging matter.'

'Now if I've took a craving for the sight of hanging men?' Matilda teased, giving Billy the full benefit of her fine grey eyes and her pretty plump cheeks. 'You couldn't deny a craving in a breeding woman, now could you, my love?'

'Cravings are for food,' Billy said, sparkling back at her, 'as you know right well, you impossible creature.'

'No they ain't,' she said, shaking her curls. 'You can take a craving for the smell of sea air, or a coal fire, or any number of things. Ain't that so, Mrs Fuseli?'

'So we hear,' Sophie allowed.

'Very well then,' Matilda said, looking at Billy imperiously, 'if I ain't to see the hanging you can rent me a house in Bury ready for the summer. I've a right to that, in all conscience. A family house, for us and our two children.' And now she was looking at Nan questioningly.

'I see no reason why not,' Nan said coolly. 'Your Billy can afford it, or if he can't, I daresay I could arrange a loan.'

And what of me? John thought. You do not even consider whether Harriet and I might care for a country house too. But he said nothing, for if she couldn't offer it of her own accord, it would be demoralising to ask for it. Always Billy, he thought, never me, and I work twice as hard as he does. And then he was ashamed of himself for being so jealous.

Harriet was watching Billy and Matilda too, but she was making a great effort not to envy them. How happy they are, she thought, and how very well they look. For Billy was every bit as plump as his Matilda, as though they were breeding together. And she glanced at her dear, slender John, squinting at the table, and she wished she could make him happy like his brother, instead of distressing him so. This trial had upset him as much as it had upset her. Oh how she wished she'd never been involved in it.

But at last the whole horrible episode was over. The five principal conspirators, Thistlewood, Brunt, Ings, Davidson and Tidd, were publicly hanged, the lesser six quietly transported to Australia and the Easter family turned their attention to Matilda's new baby, who was born at the end of April in her new house in Bury and was a boy called Edward Percival.

And now, perhaps, Harriet told her diary, *I may take up my ordinary life again. My dear John is still unhappy and works so hard. I would I could tease him into laughter as Matilda does Billy.*

MAY BEGAN TENDERLY and tentatively but with an unmistakable balm in the air and the promise of gentleness and warmth and colour. It would be Will's second birthday this summer.

'He should have a birthday party with all his cousins,' John said, looking down at him as he slept moist-skinned and red-mouthed in his little truckle bed. 'I've a mind to rent a house in Bury for the summer, like Billy and Matilda.' His brother's new establishment behind the Athenaeum in Chequer Square was extremely fine and had renewed all his old shameful feelings of jealousy and rejection. They were invited there for the christening, of course, in six weeks' time, so it would be pleasant to have a country seat of his own before then. 'How if we were to rent a house in Bury?'

'I would rather spend the summer in Rattlesden with Annie,' Harriet ventured, adding hastily, 'But only if you were agreeable to it, of course.' If they were to live in Bury all summer, she would have to visit her parents at least once a week, and once a week would be far too difficult and far too often.

'I have to visit Norwich this Thursday,' he told her. 'I will call in at Rattlesden on my way back and see what may be done.' Were there houses in the village large enough to contain his household and, even more important, impressive enough to equal Matilda's obvious style? For himself he would be happy in a cottage, but he could not bear to think that his choice might leave poor Harriet open to criticism.

But he was in luck. There was a sizeable house standing empty no more than a hundred yards away from the rectory. It had belonged to a cousin of the manor.

'We buried her last Thursday,' Annie told him cheerfully. 'Eighty-two she was. Imagine that! 'Tis a good age. And now they need a new tenant. Would it suit, think 'ee?'

'Only one way to find out, Sis,' he said. 'When could I see it?'

It was a long, low rambling building, facing the sunshine, in a garden framed by burgeoning white lilac and fragrant with tawny wallflowers, its pink-washed walls warm and welcoming. He liked it at once. And when he discovered that it had its own pump inside the kitchen and an indoor privy, and that there were five bedrooms and a well-panelled dining room and a little pale blue parlour that seemed designed to suit his quiet Harriet, he rented it on the spot.

Afterwards as the 'Phenomena' rattled off along the road to London, he was surprised at himself. To have made such a quick decision was really rather extraordinary. More like Billy or his mother. But it felt so right. And it was a beautiful house.

Which exactly what Harriet said, when she came down to Rattlesden four weeks later to take possession of her new country home and attend the christening of Edward Percival Easter.

'Oh John!' she said, throwing her arms about his neck. "Tis a lovely house. And so near to Annie. Why the children will be able to run from garden to garden all summer long. It couldn't be better. How clever you are to have found it!'

'That was Annie's doing,' he said, basking in her approval. It had been a long time since she'd kissed him so lovingly. And unasked, what was more. It was a most rewarding moment.

And so they settled down to enjoy the summer. Billy and Matilda gave a grand party in their grand house for all their local friends and relations, at which Billy's friend Jeremiah Ottenshaw at long last plucked up the courage to propose to Matilda's cousin Maria and was accepted, to nobody's surprise except his own; John spent as much time in Rattlesden as he could, given the vast amount of work there was for him to do in London; and Annie and Matilda and Harriet played in the sunshine with their children, and dined with one another every other day and were ridiculously happy together; and Nan and Frederick Brougham decided to spend their entire summer in Bury, for, as Nan said, in her trenchant way, 'If we en't earned ourselves a rest, my dear, I should like to know who has!'

And then, just as they were all enjoying their holiday, Queen Caroline, the long-estranged wife of their newly proclaimed king, decided to return to England and claim her right to the throne.

The papers were full of stories about her. Her progress was followed hour by hour and her clothes described in lavish detail; 'A rich twilled sarcenet pelisse of a puce colour lined with ermine, and a white willow hat similar in shape to the fashionable leghorn hats' for her arrival in Dover; 'a black twilled sarcenet gown, a fur tippet and ruff, and a black satin hat and feathers' for her progress to Canterbury. Her horses were taken from the shafts of her barouche and 'the people themselves' drew the great lumbering vehicle wherever she went. There were festivals and fireworks, a hundred men carrying flambeaux at the entrance to Canterbury, flags and banners and cheering crowds all along the road to London, and a royal fair at Blackheath. It was a triumph.

To Nan's considerable annoyance, Frederick Brougham was recalled to London by his cousin for a conference.

'There is like to be a trial of some kind,' he said, 'for the King will never accept her as consort. He made that abundantly clear to us even before we went to Italy to discover her opinion in the matter. If she persists in courting the favour of the crowd, as she does at present, there will be nothing for it but legal action. 'Tis my opinion he will seek a divorce.'

'And you will act for him?'

'Why no, indeed. Henry and I are already spoken for upon the other side.'

'To defend the Queen?' She was very surprised.

'Why not, pray?' he teased.

'When you know she's took lovers?'

'You and I are hardly in any position to cast blame upon her on that account, poor lady. The King has amassed some formidable evidence against her and will find more if he can, so she will need a strong defence. He offered her fifty thousand pounds a year for life, you know, if only she would renounce her title and stay abroad. Her refusal put him into a parlous rage and now we are all to feel the edge of it.'

Meantime there was a ball at the Athenaeum to enjoy before his departure. And an uncommon lively ball it turned out, for the town was a-buzz with gossip and there wasn't a woman in the place who didn't have an opinion to express. Matilda thought it was romantic and was unequivocally on the side of the woman she called 'our poor, wronged Queen', even though the impending court case was keeping her Billy in the Strand for far too long each week waiting for news to break; Miss Pettie clutched her curls and declared that she didn't know what the world was coming to and it certainly wasn't like that in the days of Good King George; and Cousin Evelina said she wasn't at all sure whether a woman of such flagrant immorality truly had the right to sit upon the throne of England, adding, in an admirable attempt to be fair, 'if what is said about her is to be believed, which of course we cannot know as yet.'

'They will all know soon enough, I fear,' Frederick said as he waltzed with Nan.

And he was proved right. Four days after his return to London news broke that the Queen was to be tried by the House of Peers. 'Their Lordships are to bring in a bill of Pains and Penalties,' *The Times* said, 'which will deprive the Queen of all rights and titles and dissolve her marriage to the King at one and the same time. The trial is to be delayed until August 17th because the King needs more time to find his necessary witnesses.'

John had travelled straight to the Strand on the day the Queen set out from Calais, and now that there was to be a trial he decided to stay where he was. Important news like this would be sure to sell in vast quantities and it had broken at just the right time for A Easters and Sons. It pained him to be apart from his family, but this was business and had to be attended to. The North Wales route was open and ready for rapid delivery. Now it would be tested.

By now, Harriet was well used to his sudden departures and, although they still upset her, she had learned how to cope with them. She and Will and Rosie stood at the gate and waved goodbye to him until his carriage disappeared round the curve in the road, then they went back indoors to eat their breakfast. It was necessary to find something immediate to do so as to fill the emptiness his sudden absence left behind him, and feeding young Will was one of the best things she knew. But this morning there was something else to distract her. As she sat down at the dining room table, she was told that the new curate, Mr John Jones, had come to call.

'Show him in,' She told the maid.

Mr Jones was terribly embarrassed to be disturbing her at breakfast for, being new to the parish, he was anxious to do the right thing. But Mrs Easter smiled at him calmly as though she saw no wrong in it.

'You could take a dish of tea, perhaps,' she said to him. 'Pray do sit down. Tell cook we are ready, and bring another cup,' she said to the maid, and then turned back to Mr Jones. 'To what do I owe the pleasure of this visit?'

'I believe,' he said, sitting himself gingerly on one of her delicate chairs, 'that you were actually present on the field of Peterloo.'

'Yes,' she said calmly, not knowing whether to be pleased or distressed.

'I came to Mr Hopkins from Norwich, Mrs Easter,' he said earnestly, 'as I daresay you know. While I was there, I was secretary of one of the local corresponding societies.' Pollyanna had told him it was safe to tell her that. Pollyanna was so helpful to him. 'We do not call ourselves a corresponding society now, Mrs Easter, for it seems that such an organisation is outside the law, but the members still meet — as a choir, if you take my meaning. It would be much appreciated if you would join us one evening and tell us what you saw on that fateful day.'

'Would I need to join the choir, Mr Jones?' she asked, perfectly straight-faced. 'I should tell 'ee I have but a poor ear for music.'

He gave her a smile of sudden and unexpected sweetness. 'Pollyanna told me you would agree,' he said.

Have I agreed? she wondered. But she supposed she had. What harm could come of such a meeting now, when the world and his wife were fully occupied following the affairs of the poor Queen? It wasn't as if she would be helping insurrectionaries.

But just to be on the safe side, she decided to write to Mr Rawson for some advice. She couldn't ask John, because she wasn't at all sure whether the subject would be acceptable to him and in any case, John probably wouldn't know the answer, whereas Mr Rawson would and would tell her the truth, whatever it was.

It is hard to know what is for the best, these days, she wrote.

I would not wish to disappoint Mr Jones, who is a most well-meaning man and uncommon fond of Mr Hopkins, as who could not be? On the other hand I would not wish to do anything against the law, but as the government keeps changing the law it is sometimes difficult to know how to act. I hope you do not mind me writing to ask your advice, but it occurred to me that you were just the very person to know what it would be best for me to do?

He didn't mind her writing at all. Quite the reverse, in fact, for he took it as a sign that she was ripe for conquest. One of the unexpected and private results of his fame as an orator was the fact that whenever he spoke at a public meeting there would always be women who would seek him out afterwards, ready and eager to share his bed. At first their compliance had surprised him, but now he was used to it, and expected it, and took his pick of the prettiest, feeling that the pleasure they gave him was a right and fitting reward for all the work he did for the cause. But he had never enjoyed a society lady and until he met Harriet had never imagined he would. Now she had given him hope of it.

Attend the choir meeting, he wrote back.

There's nought illegal in it, and good may come of it. Any road, government will have its work cut out for it in the months ahead, for now the people have found a cause and we shall see what will come of it. None may prevent them from demonstrating patriotic affection for their Queen, that's plain, so they'll appear upon streets in their thousands, I guarantee. If it weren't for the fact that I have a deal of work these days and am like to get more, I should beg a lift to London and join crowds myself. Let me know how tha makes out at the meeting.

That would provoke another letter, and if he continued their correspondence, sooner or later she would be his. He knew it.

'Should you decide to do such a thing,' she wrote in her next letter, 'and John and I are in London at the time, pray do come and visit us in Fitzroy Square.' It was only right and proper to invite him after his kindness in helping the Abbotts. And in any case, she would be in Rattlesden all summer so there was no real likelihood of such a visit actually being made.

But although she didn't know it as she wrote, she was to be in London sooner than she imagined.

ON 2ND AUGUST, a matter of days before Frederick Brougham had to return to the capital again to begin work on his cousin's brief, and a week after Harriet had addressed the choir, the new Regent's Canal was due to be opened with full ceremonial.

'Let the Queen and the Lords do what they will,' Nan said, when she read of it. 'I shall return to London with 'ee, Frederick, and keep 'ee company, so I shall. And as I see there's to be some merriment on account of this canal, I shall hire a barge and join in the procession and throw a great party afterwards. I'm a-weary of trials and suchlike. We've all been dull and work-a-day quite long enough.'

Sophie Fuseli, who said she'd been languishing in London without her dear old friend, thought it an excellent idea. 'Let us join forces, my dear,' she said. 'I would so love a party and Heinrich will be sure to agree if 'tis at your suggestion.'

And so the two of them made preparations. They hired the biggest barge they could find and furnished it with gilt chairs and trestle tables, several hundred yards of bunting and a string band. They ordered enough food and drink to provision an army and an army of waiters resplendent in Nan's green and gold livery to serve it. Sophie invited all her gossipy friends, and Heinrich all his ardent students from the Royal Academy, where he had just embarked upon another series of lectures. Frederick Brougham was prevailed upon to leave the Inns of Court, 'just for the day,' and Cosmo Teshmaker was teased away from Easter House, and Nan hired a coach to bring all her relations down from Bury.

They arrived late in the afternoon of the previous day, baby Edward fast asleep on his mother's bosom, all three toddlers sticky and fractious and glad to be released from their long ride, Beau and Jimmy pale and patient beside their father, Miss Pettie and the two Callbeck cousins giggly, having been plied with champagne 'by your naughty Billy, and all the way here, my dear', as they explained to Nan amidst drunken blushes. Bessie and Thiss had packed a picnic basket for the children and had spent their journey nursing one or another of them so that they were both as crumbed and crumpled as a pair of tablecloths. But they were delighted to be travelling with Tom and Pollyanna and their dear Miss Pettie. It was a very good-humoured company that came tumbling down from the bulging sides of the coach that afternoon, and the dinner that followed their arrival was a very jolly affair.

The next morning they woke to find that they had a marvellous day for their jaunt. The sky was a cloudless blue and it was already pleasantly warm at eight o'clock when the Easter carriages began to gather in Bedford Square, and as Matilda's stylish Briska came trotting round the corner, they could hear the murmur of the crowds gathering around the new Grand Basin somewhere to the east.

'There'll be some sport today,' Nan said happily to Frederick. 'I can feel it in my bones.'

Her grandchildren were as excited as she was, although the three toddlers looked angelic in their white petticoats and neatly starched cotton sunbonnets. 'How long that'll last I wouldn't care to gamble,' Pollyanna said as she settled Meg on her lap. Jimmy and Beau had new suits for the occasion, narrow trousers of blue nankeen with short-waisted jackets to match and 'brass buttons like real sailors' as Beau told everybody who was listening. Annie had sewn red tassels to their caps and provided them with streamers to throw, and now they couldn't wait to get upon the water.

'Are we really to go in a boat, Nanna?' Beau asked. 'A really truly boat?'

'A really truly boat,' she said, hugging him. 'Look sharp all of you. There en't a minute to loose.'

And they all clambered into their carriages again in a flutter of fine cottons, sky blue and snow white, sugar pink and apple green, creamy yellow and toffee brown, the women as light as butterflies and the men as jolly as cockchafers in their tight light trousers and their fine frock coats. Matilda was wearing a blue and grey gauze gown with a poke-bonnet to match from Paris, of course, and very stylish, and Annie and Harriet had decorated their leghorn hats with so many ribbons that it was a wonder they could keep them on their heads.

Only John was quiet and sober, wearing his old buff jacket and his gabardine trousers and his second-best hat, and sitting beside his pretty Harriet in their sober carriage, stern-faced and stiff-necked. Soon he would be thrown into close proximity with crowds of yelling, sweating, overexcited people, and the thought was torture to him, especially as he knew there would be no escape until late in the afternoon.

'Deuce take the boy. What ails him?' Nan said to Frederick as his coachman drove them out of the square. 'He looks like a dying duck in a thunderstorm.'

"Tain't to his taste, I fear,' Frederick said. 'It pains him.'

'Squit!' she said, laughing the idea away. 'What could there possibly be in a day like this to cause pain to anybody?'

'Well as to that, my dear,' Frederick said wryly, 'I'm sure I couldn't say. But pain him it does. That much is very clear. So all the more honour to him for joining us.'

The barges were drawn up and ready at the Horsfall Basin in Pentonville when they arrived, most of them full of people and all of them decorated with flags and streamers and loud with competing bands. Sophie and Heinrich Fuseli were aboard the Easter barge, sitting like royalty in two of the gilt chairs, with his students buzzing attendance about them and their band playing frantically behind them. Sophie was very elegant in red and white striped silk and the artists all wore red and yellow turbans like Bad Lord Byron so they made a dashing picture against the blue and white suits of the boatmen.

'Coo-ee!' Sophie called. 'We've broke open the champagne!'

'Are they cheering us, Nanna?' Jimmy asked as they balanced along the gangplank.

'Us and the day and the pretty flags and the new canal and I don't know what else besides,' Nan told him, holding his hand tightly. 'Wait till the procession starts. You'll hear some cheering then.'

And what a great roar there was as the State barge of the City was swung away from its moorings to lead the cavalcade out of the basin. The bands played the National Anthem, more or less together, and the crowds sang and cheered with such abandon that it didn't matter whether they were together or not, and Nan's barge followed all the others and went gliding slowly into the great Islington tunnel, where the music echoed and re-echoed round and round and round until there was such a cacophony all about them they felt as though they were swimming in sound.

And then out they came, pop! into the fresh air again, and the artists gave three cheers for daylight, and presently they came to the Grand basin in the City-road, where a salute of guns was fired, which made Sophie shriek and the children jump and even woke baby Edward. The crowds here were packed shoulder to shoulder and the cheers were deafening. By now Will was beginning to get hungry. He pulled at Harriet's sleeve, reminding her: 'Eatin, Mama. Eatin.' And Nan said he was a fine boy and should eat a leg of chicken as soon as they got to Limehouse.

It was a sumptuous meal and a very drunken one. There were flat pies and raised pies, mustards and pickles, cold diced potatoes and every kind of salad, melons and apricots, gooseberries and quinces, comfits and pastries, honey cakes and crystallised violets. And, according to Bessie, enough champagne 'ter float one of these 'ere barges'. Evelina Callbeck declared she'd downed more champagne in one afternoon than she had 'in the whole of the rest of my life put together', and Mr Teshmaker, who had made it his business to keep her glass replenished throughout the proceedings, said he was sure ''twas the best thing that had ever happened to him'. And Nan confided to Frederick that she'd never thought she would live to see the day when old Cosmo got tipsy.

And when they were too full to eat another mouthful, the races began. Several of the Paddington barges were lined up ready to compete for the honour of being the first to land a barrel of beer on the new wharf at the new Grand Basin. They set off, side against wooden side, with the procession following, and lo and behold, the prize was won by a barge called 'The William', so Will was the hero of the hour and Rosie made him a little crown out of three streamers plaited together.

It was a splendid day.

CHAPTER 29

It was eight o'clock in the evening and beginning to grow dark before the Easter carriages carried their dishevelled passengers back into Bedford Square. The children were sent off to bed at once with their various nursemaids to attend them, Jimmy and Beau and little Meg to the nursery in Bedford Square, the others to their own houses nearby, but the adults retired to the drawing room, which was cool and clean after the heat and clamour of the day, and tea was made and brandy served to those who needed it.

The person who needed it most, and received it last, was John. Harriet carried his brandy glass to him and put it tenderly into his hands. I know how very well you have earned it, her expression said.

'Thank 'ee,' he said, smiling into her eyes, and his expression said, Yes, I *have* done well today.

'Such colour everywhere,' Aunt Thomasina was saying. 'The bunting they must have used!'

'Did you see the advertisements?' Nan said, swirling her brandy.

'Everywhere you looked,' Thiss said. 'Colman's mustard. Pennyquick's Patent Thingumajig. Never seen so many.'

'I'll tell 'ee what, Thiss,' Nan said. 'They've given me an idea.'

Oh no, John thought. His mother's ideas invariably meant work and difficulties.

'I've a mind to sell space for advertisements in the Easter shops and reading rooms,' she said.

'Capital idea,' Cosmo said. 'A money-spinner.'

'What do 'ee think of that, Billy?' Nan asked.

'Makes no odds to me one way or t'other,' Billy said lazily. 'Just so long as it don't make more work in the warehouse.'

Just what he would say, John thought, bone-idle creature. And what of my opinion? I wonder. Is that to be sounded too? A day of rigid self-control had left him feeling very touchy.

'What do you say to it, John?'

I must choose my words with care, John thought, for the idea of offering space in the Easter shops for advertisements was making him shudder, but if he opposed her too violently, she was quite capable of going her own way out of simple waywardness. 'I feel we should consider what the feelings and opinions of our customers might be,' he said, walking across the room to sit beside her and speaking slowly and carefully. 'There are those who would consider advertisements rather a vulgarity.'

'As you would, eh?'

'No, no' he said hurriedly, caught out by that quick shrewd wit of hers. 'Not at all...'

'Then you would approve?'

What could he say? She outwitted him at every turn. 'If we wish to improve the profits of our firm,' he said, hoping she would notice that 'our', 'one possible and creditable method would be to open up the Irish trade.'

'Which is what you would suggest, eh?'

'Indeed.'

'Well, why not?' she said expansively. 'The time's ripe for it. Any more brandy anyone?'

He was delighted to think that he had won his victory so easily. 'Then we need not consider advertisements?' he asked.

She was full of food and wine and well-being. And she'd recognised his anxious disapproval. 'Well, not for the moment,' she allowed. 'Let's see how you fare in the Emerald Isle.'

'I SHALL GO to Dublin as soon as I can book a ticket,' he said to Harriet as they were undressing much later that evening. 'I can't allow Mama to take advertisements. That would be too degrading.'

She had feared it. That conversation with his mother had been much too fraught. But she made an effort to gainsay it. 'Could it not be delayed until the autumn?' she asked. 'Will and I have seen so little of you this summer, and with the Queen's trial coming you are like to be in London a good deal come the end of the month.'

'It is my job,' he said patiently. 'It is what I must do if I am ever to take over from my mother and run this firm as it ought to be run.'

'Yes,' she said sadly, biting her bottom lip.

The little gesture roused his pity and his affection. 'This will be the last area to be opened, I promise you,' he said putting his arms round her shoulders. 'After that, Easter's will sell the news the length and breadth of the kingdom, Mama will be well pleased, and I shall be able to spend as much time at home with you and Will as you could possibly want. Why,' he teased, 'you'll grow tired of my company, I shall be in the house so much.'

'Oh no, no,' she said passionately, turning in his embrace to throw her arms about his neck. 'That I never could, my dear, dear John. Never, never, never.'

And after that, words were superfluous, as action and sensation led them pleasurably away from the misery of argument.

BUT HE HAD MADE his decision just the same, and the next morning she still knew it wasn't the one she'd wanted.

He went to Dublin ten days later, but he had to travel back again after a little more than a week so as to be in time for the start of Queen Caroline's trial, and as his visit hadn't achieved a single shop or reading room he was in a very bad humour.

'The Irish are so slow,' he said to Harriet. 'You'd have thought they'd have leapt at such a chance. But no, they need a month to think about it, so they say. A month!' His mother could have colonised an entire nation in less time.

But at least she hadn't sold any advertising space whilst he'd been away, and that was some consolation. 'I shall go back to Dublin in four weeks' time,' he told Harriet, 'or when the Queen's trial is over, whichever is the first.'

It was his four weeks, for the trial of poor Queen Caroline was a very long-drawn-out affair. And a singularly mucky one.

There were so many Italian witnesses who were called one after the other to give evidence first in their own language and then, through various interpreters, in lengthy and much-disputed translation, and the gist of their evidence was extremely unsavoury, for they were questioned about sleeping arrangements, about stains on sheets, and even about the contents of chamber pots. And every word was reported and repeated and sold the length and breadth of the country.

Harriet went back to Rattlesden and refused to read it. Nan thought it disgusting and said so trenchantly. And Frederick commented upon it as infrequently as he could, and the longer the trial dragged on, the less he contrived to say. But thanks to the popular papers, there was widespread support for the Queen.

In October when Harriet and Matilda returned to London with their families for the Season, they were both amazed to see how passionately and protectively the London crowds were escorting their Queen to and from Westminster Hall.

'They turn out every single day,' Harriet said, when she and John played host to Billy and Matilda on the first Friday after their return.

'And such an ugly little woman, for all her fine clothes,' Matilda said. 'I know for a fact her hair was never born that colour. 'Tis altogether too black, and besides her eyebrows are made of moleskin. You can see.'

'But she makes news for Easter's, my charmer,' Billy said happily. 'Profits are up no end.'

'I shall be glad for her sake when 'tis over and done with,' John said. 'Yesterday she said that nobody cared for her at all in this business. Mr Brougham told Mama.'

'She has her wits about her then, in all conscience,' Billy said. 'For that's true enough. The King will divorce her no matter what the Lords decide, and, so far as I can see, the politicians spend all their time nowadays scoring points off one another. Half of 'em have forgot why they were called.'

But at last, on the tenth day of November, while John Easter was on his way to Dublin again, the third reading of the Bill of Pains and Penalties was defeated, and despite the odds and the evidence, Queen Caroline appeared to have won. A fortnight later, she went to St Paul's to offer thanks for her deliverance, cheered by an immense flag-waving mob. And standing amongst them, cheering with the rest, was Mr Caleb Rawson.

Trade was so slack he'd been without work for nearly ten days, so when some friends of his offered him a seat on an old farm buggy they were driving down to London for the occasion, he packed up his loom, counted out the remains of his money and went with them. Come and visit me, she had said. Well now was the time to put her invitation to the test. It could be an interesting conquest.

IT WAS AN UNPLEASANT AFTERNOON, dark and cold and wintry. Harriet was giving Rosie particular instructions that she was to dress little Will in his warmest clothes because the weather was so bad. They were going to Bedford Square to have tea with Nan and Sophie Fuseli, as they often did these days when John was away, because she missed him dreadfully and visiting helped to pass the time.

'His thick grey worsted coat, Rosie,' she said.

'Worsted coat,' Rosie agreed, nodding the information into her head.

'I will wait here by the fire until he's ready.'

''Till he's ready, yes,' Rosie said. 'Come along, lambkin.' And she took the child away to dress him.

But Harriet didn't wait by the fire. She walked to the window and stood beside the curtain with one hand on the soft damask, gazing idly down into the square. It was completely empty and completely grey, as though November had drained all colour from the world: grey cobbles, grey pavements, grey grass, grey boughs, blank grey skies. If only John would come home, she thought. For life without him was as grey as the square.

And a man came striding round the corner, a thickset brightly coloured man, in a wine-red greatcoat and a coachman's broad black hat, an energetic fast-walking man, who wore black boots and no gloves and had arrived so suddenly it was as though he'd been blown into the quiet square by some great gale, an interesting, lively-looking man who was walking straight up the steps towards her own front door. Good gracious!

She was still in a flutter when Paulson announced him. 'Mr

Caleb Rawson to see you, ma'am.' Mr Rawson! Good gracious! And he took the room by storm too.

He seemed so much bigger than she remembered him, so broad-shouldered and stocky, and so brightly coloured, for his jacket was wine-red too and his shirt buff and his trousers a sturdy tweed, to say nothing of soot-black hair and cheeks as red as apples and those missing teeth most noticeable against the white gleam of the rest. Caleb Rawson.

'I kept my word,' he said, beaming at her as they shook hands. 'Visit, tha said, and here I am.'

It took her an effort of will to play hostess. 'Pray do sit down, Mr Rawson.' The touch of his hand had sent her senses into alarm.

He sat in John's chair beside the fire, planting those black boots on the hearthrug, splaying those broad hands on his knees, for all the world as if he were the master of the house and belonged there.

'What brings you to London, Mr Rawson?' she asked, and her calm pleased her because it had been difficult to achieve.

'Why, t' Queen,' he said, as though she should have known it. 'I've been to St Paul's this very morning to give t' poor lady a cheer as she passed. Me and twenty thousand others, at a rough estimate, and not a soul to prevent us.'

She'd paid little attention to the Queen's Thanksgiving Service. It was enough that the trial was over. But she listened to his cheerful account of it. 'There must be something in your nature that attracts crowds, Mr Rawson,' she said lightly, 'for I don't believe I have ever seen you when you were not surrounded by hundreds of people.'

'Till now,' he said. And he smiled straight into her eyes.

It was such an intimate smile it made her heart jump alarming her and thrilling her and spinning her into confusion all over again. She really shouldn't be feeling like this. Not for Mr Rawson. It wasn't right.

'I fear that I cannot invite you to take tea with me, Mr Rawson,' she said, trying to defend herself. 'Will and I are expected in Bedford Square in half an hour, you see.'

'Nay, Mrs Easter,' he said warmly. 'I've not come to tek tea. I've come for t' sight of tha good kind face. I've come to see my angel of mercy again.'

'Angel of mercy?' she said. Oh this was getting worse and worse. It was almost as if he were making some sort of declaration.

'Angel of mercy,' he repeated firmly. 'That's how we think of thee in Manchester. Dunna tha know it?'

'Why no, no,' she said, biting her bottom lip. How embarrassing to be considered an angel. 'I can see I'd best beware of you, Mr Rawson, or I shall be canonised before I get to heaven.'

He roared with laughter at her, showing those missing teeth. 'Eh! That's rich!'

And then they were rescued by Rosie, which was just as well. She came straight into the room without knocking as she always did, leading Will by the hand and announcing, 'All ready, mum. Shipshape an' orderly. Ain't he the swell?'

At that Mr Rawson stood up and said he'd have to be going and could he call again tomorrow? 'We start back at dawn on Wednesday,' he said, and his expression pleaded, Say yes.

Afterwards she was annoyed at herself for giving way to the suggestion. But give way she did. 'Then you must take tea with me tomorrow.'

'Your servant, ma'am,' he said, grey eyes shining at her. 'At what hour should I call?'

THAT NIGHT SHE LAY WAKEFUL, thinking and thinking. Oh if only John had been home. Everything would have been so easy if John had been home. Ireland was much worse than anywhere else he'd travelled. It took him away from her so often and for such a long time, weeks and weeks, what with travelling there and travelling back. And when he *was* home, he spent most of his time at work, struggling to 'catch up'. It would have been better to let his mother take those advertisements, it would indeed. Not that she would ever tell him so, for that would be disloyal. But no, he had to go chasing off to Ireland, thousands and thousands of miles away, leaving her at the mercy of her own treacherous emotions.

She had spent a miserable hour before she went to bed, sitting by the fire in the bedroom writing to her diary, trying to make sense of what she was feeling.

Caleb Rawson is a good man, she had written.

He is kind and ugly and honest and I do not love him. I love my own dear John who is my husband and my lover and my knight in shining armour and a good deal else besides which I have written of again and again which being so, why did my heart leap when Mr Rawson looked at me? Why did I tremble? It was an act of disloyalty. My mother would call it a sin, I don't doubt. But it could not be a sin because I did not will it. It occurred despite my better intentions, despite me, as though I had no control upon my feelings at all. How could it have happened? I do not understand it.

However, at least she'd had the good sense to arrange for a chaperone to be present tomorrow afternoon. Sophie Fuseli had accepted her invitation to tea at once. 'There ain't a thing I enjoy more these days than a dish of good tea,' she'd said, twirling her curls.

And Nan laughed. 'If it en't a glass of good brandy!'

Oh dear, oh dear. If only John was at home. But then if he *were* at home, she would have to tell him what had happened. And how could she possibly tell him what had happened? Not that anything *had* happened. Oh dear, oh dear!

. . .

OVER IN HIS small back bedroom in the Bull and Mouth in Aldersgate Street, Caleb Rawson was reliving the afternoon too. She was his for the taking. He'd lay money on it. The way she'd blushed when he took her hand, the pretty confusion of her, the way she'd invited him tomorrow. Her husband's a fool to leave her alone so much, he thought, for it was plain the man was away. If she were mine, I'd not leave her for a minute. Well more fool he. And he fell asleep grinning with pleasure at the thought that he would see her again so soon.

He was disappointed when he arrived at Fitzroy Square the following afternoon to find that he was sharing her company with her little son Will and a fat woman who was wife to some artist or other, but on reflection he saw the wisdom of it and admired her discretion. To entertain a gentleman alone twice in two days might cause gossip, and even though their affair would be bound to cause a bit of gossip sooner or later, 'twas as well to start clean.

'I'll write to thee,' he promised them both as he took leave. 'I've no'but told thee half of all I meant to.'

'Had you done so,' she smiled at him, 'we'd have been talking here till midnight.' For he'd entertained them both with stories of the Queen's procession all through their tea and well beyond.

'I will write,' he said again, and on a sudden romantic impulse, lifted her hand to his lips and kissed it, pleased by the little start it gave her.

That night Harriet wrote at length in her diary:

I live in three different worlds, first as a wife to my dear John, when I must try to understand his business matters, because they are so important to him, and try to support him in every way I can because he does work so hard, second as a mother to Will, which is quite the easiest of the three because he is so loving and so pretty and I am so happy when I am with him, and third as a friend to Mr Rawson and supporter of the cause, which I consider an honour,

indeed I do, but which I may have to forego if he continues to act as
he does. He is a fine man, and orator and a leader, and yet I cannot
help feeling that there is danger in this. Oh dear, oh dear. What
should I do?

But in the event, she had no need to do anything, for the weeks passed and no letters arrived. Despite her misgivings she was disappointed to have been forgotten, but she persuaded herself that such a very great man would have other things to do than write to her, and in any case, there were plenty of matters to occupy her.

In January Jimmy was ten years old and ready to go to school. So at Easter she went with Annie to visit the grammar school in Bury to see if it was suitable, two opinions being better than one in such matters. And little Will would be three in July and by the time the summer began he was such a chatterbox that she seemed to spend all her days answering his questions.

'Why do the moon shine, Mama?'

'Why *does* the moon shine. I'm sure I couldn't say, lambkin.'

'Why mus' I wash, Mama?'

'Because you would be dirty otherwise and nice children aren't dirty.'

'This ant has six legs, Mama. Why do an ant have six legs?'

'Why *does* an ant, lambkin. To help it to run faster I suppose.'

'Where is Papa?'

'In Scotland, lambkin.' 'In Birmingham.' 'In Ireland.' And oh so rarely at home.

But he promised he would stay in London for the King's coronation, which was fixed for 19th July and was to be a spectacular affair. The King was to progress from Westminster Hall to Westminster Abbey along a covered walk specially built for the occasion, twenty-five feet wide and fully carpeted. It had a triumphal arch thirty feet high at its northern end and raked galleries on either side for his more wealthy spectators. Naturally enough, Nan bought seats on the gallery for all her family.

'That's a sight we shouldn't miss, eh?' she said. 'And we'll have a coronation party in the evening. What do 'ee say to that?'

Harriet said yes to it, of course, just like everybody else, and agreed to come back from Rattlesden for the occasion, for Nan's parties were always lively and well-fed and besides she could travel down with Annie and James and their children. But secretly she was anxious in case Caleb Rawson came to London to see the coronation too. If he did, he would be bound to call on her. Even though he hadn't written. And if he called on her, what would she say? What would she do? And even more worrying, what would he say? What would he do? Oh dear, oh dear. It had been eight months since she'd last seen him, but you never knew what might happen.

In the end she gave Paulson the most dishonest instructions that if Mr Rawson were to call while she was watching the procession or out at Mrs Easter's party, he was to say that she was 'away'.

But it upset her that she was being dishonest. Even if she wasn't actually lying, she was certainly hinting at an untruth and that was a sin every bit as bad as an outright lie. While the rest of the family enjoyed the King's procession, she bit her lip and worried.

And John watched her and wondered. She was often oddly distant these days, as if she'd retreated from him into some private world where he couldn't reach her. She always welcomed him most lovingly when he returned from his travels and she treated young Will with the utmost tenderness and kept the house in splendid order and seemed content when they were talking together, but there was a change in her just the same, and it didn't seem to be anything he could influence or alter. Where are you, my dearest? he yearned, watching her pale, pensive face as the procession passed by.

He would have been most upset to know that at that very moment she was wondering where Caleb Rawson was.

THERE WAS a good reason for Caleb's lack of correspondence.

When he and his friends had come trundling back to Manchester in their borrowed farm cart, they had found their mill closed for lack of work, and all through the winter they'd been hard put to it to find enough employment to keep them in food. Caleb accepted any job that offered, labouring, street-cleaning, even sweeping out the mill where he'd once been a skilled weaver. The springtime was no better, and although the early summer brought an increase in orders for cloth because of the Coronation, very little of the work came Mr Rawson's way. It was demoralising because it kept him at labouring jobs that took all his time and drained all his energy and rarely paid him enough to cover the cost of food and rent.

So he was grateful and relieved when he met a man in a Salford tavern who said he knew of a place where skilled weavers were in demand. It was a mild evening in May, and the gentleman was as mild-mannered as the weather, even though he was really rather extraordinary to look at, having fine fair hair and ginger whiskers. He said his name was Mr Richards and claimed to be a friend of the great Easter family, 'I lodge with cousins of theirs in Bury St Edmunds, damn if I don't' and a supporter of universal suffrage, what's more 'I was here at the time of Peterloo, so I was. A parlous business!'

'You were saying you knew where weavers were in demand,' Caleb prompted.

'Aye, so I do. I've a friend there crying out for skilled men.'

'Might I ask where, sir?'

'Why Norwich, sir. Do 'ee have a loom?'

'Aye.'

'Then permit me to give you the address,' the gentleman said. 'By great good fortune I have it here in my pocket.'

So Caleb went to Norwich and found to his considerable relief that the amiable Mr Richards had spoken the truth. There was a job for a cotton weaver and lodgings to go with it. He accepted both at once, even though they were in one of the many weavers' houses in King Street, right in the path of all the stinks and smells from the breweries to the north and the dyeworks by the river and the tanneries and slaughterhouses in Ber Street. It was a long, narrow, dirty street that ran parallel to the River Wensum and well below the castle, and the houses in it were mostly ancient and rickety, their roofs patched and pan tiled, their walls rough-plastered and their attic rooms through-lit by long weavers' windows.

Caleb's room contained a bed with a straw mattress, a battered table, one cane-bottomed chair and a chipped jug and basin. It had one small shuttered window which gave out onto the discoloured walls of the house opposite, a miserably small fireplace with an adequate coalhole beside it. And it was verminous. He started to do battle against his unwanted companions with turpentine and camphor on the day he arrived, but the weather was too warm and he knew they would breed faster than he could kill them. No matter, he thought, flinging himself down on his rough bed at the end of his first long day at work. He'd clear them all out once the cold weather set in. He'd make sure to light no fires until they were all dead and gone and swept away. For although he could endure most hardships willingly enough, bedbugs were an abomination to him.

Nevertheless there were blessings to count. His loom arrived safe and sound thanks to Mr Pickford's new delivery service, there was plenty of work and, although it was badly paid, something could be done about that too. He would set about the task of organising his fellow weavers as soon as he could. I'll achieve summat in this city, he promised himself, higher wages or better conditions, or both. One way or t'other, I'll better t' lives of t' workers in this town.

But first there was the summer to live through.

In Norwich, in summer, the River Wensum smelt like an open sewer, which to all intents and purposes it was, being sluggish and evil coloured and full of bobbing garbage, offal reeking from the shambles, straw foul from the stables, and the filth from countless privies. It could be smelt all over the city, for there was no breeze to carry the stink elsewhere, and down in King Street Caleb and his fellow workers had to sleep with closed shutters.

As always in foul weather, the weavers grew more and more discontented with their lot, working long hours in their stifling attics by day, bug-bitten by night, eating rancid food and paid a pittance on Saturdays. But although Caleb and his new friends from the Norwich Hampden Clubs argued that they should take to the streets and protest, they grumbled and did nothing. It wasn't until 6th July when their employers suddenly cut their wages, that they finally took action, and then things happened very quickly and with unexpected power.

Wages were docked on Saturday evening and that night the streets were full of angry men and women protesting to one another and saying something ought to be done. The next morning Caleb and his friends went from door to door in King Street knocking up their neighbours and calling them to a meeting in the local inn.

A hundred and fifty turned up, angry and hot and frustrated, and decided almost at once that they should start their campaign by petitioning against the reduction of their wages.

'Ask reasonable,' one man said. ''Tis always the best way.'

But who should carry the petition and to whom?

'To Mr Robbards,' Caleb suggested. ''Tis true he's nobbut t' deputy chairman of t' manufacturers' committee, but he's like to be t' most amenable.'

'Will you deliver un for us, Caleb Rawson?'

'With t' greatest of pleasure.'

So he was deputised at once. And when he pointed out that their petition would have more force if it came from even more people and suggested that two men from the meeting should go to each parish in the city to call out all the weavers and spinners to a grand meeting on Mousehold Heath the following day, the suggestion was passed on a roar.

Monday was hotter than ever, but for the first time since Caleb's arrival the looms were silent as the weavers and spinners of Norwich walked out of their houses and up to the great heath outside the city, crossing the Bishop's Bridge in a vast, determined crowd. The time for action had indisputably arrived.

It was an enormous gathering. Speeches were shouted through homemade megaphones, and cheered whether they were heard or not, and the weavers and spinners sat in the sun as their petition was signed and gathered, and the written sheets mounted on Caleb's trestle table until the pile was bigger than a book. And the upshot of it all was that Caleb and eleven others were deputised to deliver that book to the meeting of the manufacturers' committee that was going to be held at the Guildhall on the following day.

By Tuesday afternoon, when the meeting at the Guildhall began, the heat was intense and passions were running very high. The marketplace was packed with people, who booed or cheered as the manufacturers or their delegates struggled up the steps into the building. One of the manufacturers, a certain Mr Arthur Beloe, made a speech on the steps and said he thought the reduction of wages had been 'ill advised', which earned him a special roar of approval. But inside the building, once the weavers' delegates had left and so could not be privy to what was being said, negotiations were fraught and ill-tempered and went on far too long.

By four o'clock tempers in the marketplace were frayed to breaking point. A chant began, 'Return our wages! Return our wages!' Hastily painted banners appeared and were waved defiantly. And finally one of the manufacturers was attacked.

He'd arrived late and had been jostled as he went up the steps, and when he fell it was as if his vulnerability was a signal for violence to erupt. He was kicked and beaten and tossed from hand to furious hand, and as he struggled to get away, his hat and coat and shoes were pulled from him and thrown into the air. Caleb and the other delegates tried to force their way through the crowd to calm things, but they were too tightly packed in to move more than a foot or two. Somebody called out that the troops were coming, but the rage continued and the chanting grew louder, and neither abated until their victim had managed to escape and Mr Beloe appeared on the balcony with a paper in his hand.

'The committee have agreed,' he called down to them. 'We are to return to the old wages. Your petition is granted.'

Then what a roar went up! Mr Beloe was called down from the balcony and carried off in triumph on the shoulders of two strong weavers, and a procession formed behind them and a band arrived and the great crowd streamed out into Castle Meadow singing and dancing and quite restored to humour, with dogs yelping at their feet and the sun bright on their banners. 'Victory!' they yelled to one another. 'Victory!'

But Caleb and the eleven deputies were not in the procession. At the very moment the march moved out of the square they had been arrested. The constables had arrived so quietly and seized them all so quickly there was no time for struggle or argument. And the next day when they came up for trial before the local magistrates, there was no time for justice either. It took twenty minutes for the magistrates to find them all guilty of common assault and causing an affray. The eleven were sentenced to eighteen months imprisonment. Caleb, as 'the acknowledged leader' was given three years.

As the new King George progressed beneath his triumphal arch and Harriet wondered where her hero was, he was sitting on a bench in a stone cell in the dungeons under Norwich Castle, picking oakum, dirty and ill-fed and not thinking of her at all.

CHAPTER 30

'I can't say I think very much of your Cousin Thomasina's lodger,' Matilda Easter said, unlacing her chemise.

Billy was already in his nightshirt and waiting ardently for the moment when the chemise would be pulled over her head and thrown aside, but he realised from the expression on her face that he would have to make some conversation first. 'Mr Richards?' he said. 'Why, what's up with him?'

'He's got a deal too much side,' Matilda said, 'that's what's up with him. I passed him in the Buttermarket this morning, and he stopped and *talked* to me, if you please, for all the world as if we were acquaintances.'

'Well then, I daresay you put him down fast enough,' Billy said easily, enjoying the sight of her plump bosom.

'That ain't the point, Billoh. The man's an upstart and a rogue. Anyone with half an eye can see that. Why do your cousins endure him? They should send him packing.'

'John was of the same opinion once I remember,' Billy said, remembering vaguely. 'Something to do with that Cato Street business. Mr Richards knew someone involved in it, or somesuch. I don't recall the details, but at any rate John thought he should be told to leave. The cousins wouldn't have it.'

'They're a deal too kindly, that's their trouble,' Matilda said sagely. 'What does he do?'

'Do? Why he's a gentleman, I suppose.'

'Tosh!' Matilda said. 'If he's a gentleman, I'm Chinese.'

'He writes a good deal, I believe.'

'Well there you are then. That proves it. Writers are rogues to a man.'

'Are you ever coming to bed?' Billy said plaintively.

'Ooh! Is *that* how 'tis?' she teased. 'Is my Billoh getting impatient?'

'Yes,' he said, and he stood up to show her exactly how impatient.

She threw the chemise over her head in her lovely abandoned way, chuckling in her throat, Mr Richards forgotten. 'How could I keep 'ee waiting so?'

'Delectable creature!' he said, gathering her lovely plump nakedness towards him. Waiting was one of the delights of the game, and now that she'd lost interest in the objectionable Mr Richards, he could enjoy it to the full.

IN HIS QUIET front bedroom in the Misses Callbecks' house in Whiting Street the objectionable Mr Richards was writing a letter. It was addressed to Lord Sidmouth, who was his employer and mentor, and it was full of information.

The Hampden Club in Cambridge is much diminished. It has not met for more than six weeks to my certain knowledge, and the secretary informs me that 'tis his opinion 'twill soon be disbanded. He has no plans for any activities whatsoever.

The weavers' riot in Norwich has been successfully put down. Caleb

Rawson has been jailed for three years by the magistrates and his eleven associates with him, having stirred up trouble among the hand-weavers, as I predicted to you in my last letter. I therefore claim bounty for his arrest, but not for the eleven others since their leadership emerged during the course of the riot. I will keep careful watch upon all twelve when they are released from their present incarceration, you may be sure.

In Thetford John Owens, Obediah Mullins and John Patrickson are...

JOHN EASTER WAS in his mother's private dining room in Easter House, in the middle of a blazing row and suffering violent indigestion. The quarterly meeting had gone on until long past dinner time, so they had dined at their workplace, and now they were fighting over the decision she had announced at the meeting.

'You gave me your word,' he was saying, trembling with fury. 'You promised me that if I opened up the Irish trade you would not sell space for advertisements.'

'Squit!' Nan said, brown eyes flashing. 'I did no such thing. I said I would reconsider. Well I've reconsidered and the space is to be sold. Have some brandy and cool your passion.'

He ignored the brandy. 'By your own admission we sell more papers now than we've ever done. What were last year's figures? Nearly a million copies of the *Advertiser and* a million of the *Morning Chronicle*, one and half million *Couriers*, two and a half million *Times*. What more do you want? Why should we degrade ourselves by taking in advertisements? We might as well take in washing.'

'What we will take, Johnnie, is any opportunity that offers. That's the way to do business, I tell 'ee.' That determined chin of hers was jutting ominously but he was too far gone to heed it.

'No, no, no,' he cried. 'That's the way to lose business. We shall appear common, don't you see, mucky, catch-penny. We shall lose all our good custom.'

'Allow me to be the judge of that,' she said, coldly. 'I think I know my own business better than you do.'

My own business, he thought bitterly. Am I never to inherit, never to take command? Very well then, if this is how she means to go on, I will fight her. I will go round to all the shopkeepers in one of our areas and ask them what *they* think about it, tactfully of course, for it would be wrong to put pressure upon them. And of course the area he would choose would be Norfolk, for then he could stay with Harriet and Will while the work was being done. It was an admirable solution.

'WHAT A WONDERFUL SURPRISE!' Harriet said, tripping out of the rectory, arms outstretched to greet him and kiss him. 'I didn't think to see you for days and days and now here you are. Oh my dear, dear John! Will is in the kitchen with Pollyanna. Annie thinks she and Mr Jones are a-courting. Oh I've so much to tell you.'

Even if I find no evidence to support me, John thought, holding her happily against his side as they walked into the rectory together, I shall not care. It is enough to be with her again.

But the evidence was forthcoming. It was quite gratifying to note how many of his shopkeepers disapproved of advertisements, 'nasty untidy looking things' and clearly didn't want them in their shops. ''Twould mean more work for someone, Mr Easter sir, what I hopes en't me, if you takes my meaning.' For the next three weeks he travelled from town to town, writing every comment in a notebook neatly labelled 'Opinions'. By the end of October he had collected thirty-four disapprovals to nine approvals, and all from one region alone. Surely that would be evidence enough.

It wasn't.

'Yes, I daresay,' Nan said, when he finally showed her his notebook at their next business meeting. ''Tis as I'd expect. They know nothing of the benefits so they oppose the idea out of hand. What of it? They'll learn better sense when the advertisements are in the shops and trade improves.'

'With respect,' John said, keeping his temper with considerable effort, 'none of us may know for certain what the effect will be. Only time will tell us that.'

'Squit!' Nan said. 'What do you think, Billy?'

'Don't ask me,' Billy said affably. He didn't want to take sides. Let them fight it out between them. He was comfortable in his leather armchair.

'Cosmo?'

'Well,' Cosmo said diplomatically, 'since we are in the realms of conjecture and opinion, it is difficult, you must admit, to form any very clear policy upon the matter. The subscription list for the new reading room does seem to bear out your contention, ma'am, that advertisements will not deter trade; howsomever it might prove otherwise out in the provinces where opinions are always a good twenty years behind those in the capital.'

'I doubt it,' Nan said forcefully.

'But we cannot be sure,' Cosmo insisted. 'That is so, is it not?'

'If we always waited until we were sure,' Nan said, 'no business would ever get done, let me tell 'ee.'

'True,' Cosmo agreed. 'Very true. But it does not solve our present difficulty.'

'There is no difficulty,' John said stiffly. 'The shopkeepers do not want advertisements. Surely that much should be plain and obvious even to the most foolhardy. In my opinion 'twould be folly to insist.'

But his mother had an answer for him and a very fierce one. 'In my opinion 'twould be folly not to.'

'We shall lose trade.'

'On the contrary, Johnnie, we shall gain it.'

'I *know* we shall lose it.'

'You know nothing,' she shouted at him, sharp with fury. 'Deuce take it, am I to be told my business by my own son?'

He jumped to his feet, his control breaking under the combination of her fury and his own impotence before it. 'Yes, you are,' he shouted back. 'You are. I know as much about this firm as you do, every bit as much, oh yes, for I work every bit as hard. And if I can't tell you you're wrong, then who can? See sense, Mama!'

She stood up too and took a deep breath, eyes glittering while Cosmo winced and dropped his eyes, and John stood facing her, white-faced at his own presumption. And Billy spoke into the pause.

'Can't see what all the fuss is about, damn if I can,' he said mildly. 'Why don't you both do what you want and have done with it?'

Nan turned to vent some of her fury on him, and Cosmo looked at him, face peaked with anxiety, but he went on before any of them could speak. 'Seems quite simple to me. Let those who want advertisements have 'em, and those who don't, can go without. Run it for a year or two. See what happens.'

Surprise stopped Nan before she could roar. She considered it, thinking fast, eyes narrowed. 'Deuce take it, Billy,' she said, grinning with delight at him, 'you've a-given us the answer, so you have.'

The fight was over as quickly as it had begun and the decision made.

'Thank God for that,' Billy said, easing himself out of his chair. 'Now I can go home to Tilda.'

. . .

'I HAVE a year in which to prove my point,' John told Harriet later that night. 'Maybe two. But a year certainly. I shall need to travel a great deal, to check upon sales in all the shops that matter, to urge them on and encourage them to refuse, if that is what they wish to do. You know the sort of thing.'

She knew only too well. He would barely be in the house. But she didn't comment.

'I *must* show Mama what a difference there will be,' he said, his eyes strained with the urgency of it. 'It is a terrible thing to have to do, but I must prove her wrong. You understand that, don't you, Harriet?'

'Yes, John.' Oh, if only he didn't take it so seriously. What if he were the one to be proved wrong? She would never have admitted it to him, of course, because that would have been disloyal and unkind, but in her opinion, Nan was far more likely to be right than he was. Once a few shops started taking advertisements, sooner or later they all would.

'I shall start straight away,' he said.

'Now John? With the winter coming on?' Oh surely not.

'Yes indeed. I cannot allow bad weather to hinder me. This is far too important.'

IT WAS A LONG, cruel winter but he travelled, even in the worst of the weather, when coaches foundered in snow and horses fell, and passengers ran fevers all about him. He even continued his journey on one occasion when an old man died in the seat beside him. Bad weather always took a heavy toll of old men, he explained to Harriet, and there was work to be done.

It was a danger to babies too. 'Take care of yourself, my dear,' Harriet wrote to Annie, 'and look after Jimmy and Beau and dear little Meg. I will return in the spring.' For Annie's fourth baby was due in March, and by then the cold weather must surely be over.

But if anything March was the worst month of the lot. It started badly and got progressively worse. On the fifth day a south-west gale blew into London with such extraordinary violence that it actually stopped the tide on the River Thames.

Naturally enough, Nan took Matilda and Harriet and their children and their nursemaids straight down to London Bridge to see it. It was a most peculiar sight.

The river should have been in flood at one o'clock in the morning but at ten o'clock, when they arrived on the bank, the tide was still ebbing as though it had been bewitched, more than half the riverbed was exposed and there were scores of boats lying aground right in the middle of the Pool of London where they should have been riding at anchor. To the children's delight, the water disappeared as they watched, and although they were wind-buffeted and cold they were too excited to care. After an hour it was so low that they could see the riverbed even in the middle and two boatmen set off to see if they could wade across. And to cheers and catcalls discovered that they could! It was amazing.

After that all sorts of people strode into the shallows and soon, they were picking up treasures from the slime, old plates, chipped cups, ancient boots, coins, combs, even a necklace, held aloft in the air to drip greenish-black mud and rapturously declared to be 'Pure gold!'

'Come on!' Nan said, taking Will and Mattie by the hand. 'Let's go see what we can find, eh?'

And despite Matilda's protestations, off they went with Rosie squealing behind them. It was marvellous fun.

By midday all four of them were spattered in slime from their toes to their waists and Will had found a golden sovereign, no less, and was tense with the excitement of it. But then the wind changed abruptly and the tide suddenly turned and within seconds it was flowing back and running with such speed and strength that they were in real danger of being knocked over.

Matilda yelled a warning, but Nan was already taking action. She scooped up a child under each arm and ran to shore, bent double but determined, with Rosie trailing after her, squealing and yelling and kicking mud in all directions. And not a moment too soon. Within twenty minutes the river was in full and violent flood and the anchored boats were being thrown together like corks, with a most dramatic rending and splintering of wood. Mattie and Will and Rosie were thrilled by it.

Matilda was not. 'How she imagines we are ever to get these children clean again,' she complained to Harriet, tucking baby Edward into his shawl and returning him to his nursemaid, 'I do not know. Look at the state of your Rosie. Why does she encourage her? It's so childish. Running off into all that filth. Oh I know she's a great businesswoman and all that, but really…!'

Harriet made sympathetic noises and then turned her attention to her excited son. Secretly, she'd been watching her mother-in-law with admiration, envying her energy and vitality, and wishing she could share her extraordinary sense of fun.

She is the sort of woman I would dearly like to be, she wrote in her diary that night, after a full account of the events of the morning.

I feel pale and insignificant beside her, as I fear I am.

The next morning it was time to pack for her journey to Rattlesden.

'Must we, Mama?' Will wanted to know.

'Oh yes, lambkin, indeed we must,' Harriet said, unfastening the carpetbag. 'Your Aunt Annie is going to have another baby, and when ladies have babies, they are very weak and we have to look after them.'

'Couldn't Jimmy and Beau look after her? Then we could stay here an' paddle in the mud again with Nanna an' find another sov'reign an' see some more boats gettin' smashed.'

'The very idea,' Harriet said, lining the bag with clean paper. 'Do you like seeing boats smashed, you dreadful child?'

She didn't sound cross or reproving, only affectionate, so he told her the truth, 'Yes, Mama, very much.'

'Well,' she said, packing his nightshirt, 'I daresay you'll see a good many things broken in your lifetime. Humanity is uncommon destructive. But for the present we must go to Rattlesden and see your new cousin.'

So although he would much have preferred mud to a baby, to Rattlesden he went. And the baby wasn't there when they arrived. It appeared three days later and it was very small and uninteresting and spent all its time fast asleep. And Aunt Annie was as fit as a flea; she said so. So it was really rather a sell. The christening was quite fun because they had honey cakes afterwards and the baby, who was called Dorothy, kept its eyes open for once and looked at him. But it would have been much more sensible to stay in London and play in the river.

And then after all that they had to stay on in Rattlesden for another four weeks because Pollyanna was getting married to Mr Jones, the curate, and old Bessie said they'd got to give them 'a proper send-off'.

A proper send-off turned out to be a very big party, with more food than the guests could possibly eat and wine flowing like water and dancing into the small hours, and children allowed to sit up until well after supper time.

Nan and Frederick came up to Bury for the occasion and Annie was flushed with pleasure at the great success of her matchmaking and the obvious happiness of her nursemaid. 'Although how *we* shall make out, I do not know,' she said cheerfully to Harriet, as the party chuckled about them. 'We mustn't expect her to be at our beck and call all the time, not now she's a wife. That wouldn't do at all, would it, my dear?'

'If I know Pollyanna,' Harriet said, 'she'll not leave your baby unattended, wife or no.'

'Oh I know it,' Annie said, smiling lovingly at the bride as she danced by on her new husband's arm. 'I know it. We are greatly blessed in our Pollyanna.'

'I do wish John could have been here,' Harriet said sadly. She was the only married woman in the rectory that evening who didn't have her husband to escort her. He'd gone straight back to London after the ceremony. 'He works *so* hard; I rarely see him these days.'

'Would you like me to speak to him about it?' Annie offered, smiling her sympathy.

'Oh no, no, no,' Harriet said at once. That wouldn't do at all. It would upset him terribly if he thought she was complaining about him. 'If there is work to be done, he must do it. I know that. I am being selfish even to speak of it. He will soon be home again.'

''Tis my opinion,' his sister said trenchantly, 'that he is being uncommon foolish to waste so much of the time he ought to be enjoying with you. Work comes to us every day, but a wedding is a rarity, and we only live once. But I will not speak of it, my dear, since you do not wish it. Ah, here comes my dear James to claim the waltz.'

But it was an unhappiness to Harriet to be so much alone, hide it as she might. In fact if it hadn't been for Matilda's cheerful company, she would have been very lonely indeed that year. Nan was hard at work introducing advertisements to one shop after another, and John was equally busy travelling the country in an increasingly vain attempt to prevent her, and Annie was preoccupied with Beau, who was nine years old now and had followed his brother to school at St Edmund's Grammar in Bury and needed 'a deal of attention'.

'I drift from one day to the next without my dear John,' Harriet told her diary. *'I need occupation.'*

And rather to everybody's surprise, that summer she found it.

. . .

JUNE THAT YEAR was as hot and humid as March had been cold and stormy. Harriet and Matilda evacuated their families out of the city as soon as the hot spell began, for heat brought fevers, and none of their children was old enough to withstand a city fever. But even in Rattlesden the corn was as dry as bone, Harriet's roses burned as they bloomed and the trees in the garden could only cast a sticky shade.

Annie kept baby Dot indoors away from the sun and dressed her in silk to keep her cool. And Harriet paid particular care to marketing, searching out the freshest meat she could find, and walking to the farm gate every morning for fresh churned butter and milk straight from the cow, because food turned bad so quickly in the stifling air.

Beau was very impressed with his new life as a scholar. 'We have such fights, Aunt Harriet,' he said, blue eyes wide.

Harriet didn't want to hear about fights. 'What are you learning?' she said. 'What do they teach you?' She was sitting in the rectory garden with Annie and Matilda, and soon it would be time for tea.

'Oh history and geography and arithmetic and such,' Beau said airily. 'Some boys have to be taught to read; imagine that! Such dunces. Me and Jimmy don't, of course. I should say not!'

'Meg'll have to be taught to read when she goes to school though,' Jimmy said, watching his sister as she and Will and Matty climbed into their treehouse in the holm oak.

'Can't she read?' Harriet asked Annie.

'Well no,' Annie confessed. 'I haven't had time to teach her, poor child. Not with a new baby in the house.'

'I haven't taught Matty either,' Matilda confessed. 'Do you think I ought?' It hadn't occurred to her that her daughter might need educating.

Harriet had already begun to teach Will his letters, because

433

he was nearly five years old and wanted to learn. Now she looked into the oak tree where he was pulling Matty up by one arm and her pigtails, and a splendid idea came to her. 'Then I will teach them,' she said. 'I will run a little school, out in the garden when it is fine, and at home in my blue parlour when it is wet or cold. I will teach all three of them if you and Matilda are agreeable to it. How would that be?'

'It would be admirable,' Annie said at once.

Matilda thought it was an excellent idea too. 'You could teach Edward as well if you'd a mind to,' she said. 'But I suppose as he's only three he's a mite too young.'

So Edward was left in the nursery in Bury a little longer, Matty was driven over to Rattlesden each day and, although at first the trio was none too keen to be sitting still when they could have been running in fields, after a day or two teacher and taught began to enjoy themselves. There were rewards to this new life, out in the sun with their slates and pencils. 'Well done!' Harriet would call as a new letter was mastered and a new word learned. 'Well done! We must find a sugar stick for such a clever child.'

'You have a talent for it, my dear,' Cousin Thomasina said, when she and Evelina came to visit.

'I enjoy it,' Harriet said, looking at the three fair heads bent over their slates. ''Tis a real pleasure to see them learning so well. Will and Matty are reading little sentences already, aren't you my lambkins? And Meg draws such lovely pictures and nearly knows sixteen letters. What a clever girl! I make up little rhymes to help them, you see, and we draw pictures to fit them. Oh, I enjoy it.' And she held up her latest, a card on which she had written: 'O is for OAK on which we can climb, P is for PASTRY with jam every time.' 'When they can read the letter and the word,' she explained, 'they may climb the tree and eat the tart.'

'I can see why they enjoy your lessons,' Thomasina said. 'What shall you do when you reach Z?'

'Why, I shall have to take them to the Strand, and they shall see a real live zebra in the Exeter 'Change.'

'There is a menagerie comes to Norwich about this time of year,' Evelina said, 'but I believe they only have lions.'

'Lions would do,' Will said, looking at his mother hopefully.

'Well, well,' she laughed. 'We will see about lions when we get back to L again.'

Somehow or other they got back to L again a fortnight later, and the next day Harriet and her three excited pupils took the pony cart to Stowmarket and there caught the morning coach to the Bell in Norwich.

It was a fine August day, slow and warm and rather autumnal, with just sufficient breeze to cleanse the narrow streets and carry away the worst of the summer smells, although down below the castle the air was still rank with the smell of that morning's beast market. Castle Meadow was thronged with people in holiday mood, a-nod with bonnets and fine cottons, light-hearted in pale toppers and buff trousers and summer jackets and surrounded by street sellers, pie men and apple women, boot-blackers and ballad-mongers, cheap-jacks of every kind. There were three coaches in front of the Bell, two arrived and one ready for the off, and the ostlers in their smeared green aprons were hard at work attending the teams.

'What's that?' Will asked, looking up at the old castle towering above them, square and solid and imposing on its grassy mound.

'That,' Harriet told him, 'is the dungeon, where they lock people up, poor things.'

'What for?'

'For being thieves and vagabonds and suchlike.'

'What's a wag-a-bond?'

'Where are the lions?' Matty said, her round cheeks red with excitement. 'Aunt Harriet, you promised us to see the lions.'

'So you shall,' Harriet said, taking the two girls by the hand and walking them off up the hill. 'Come along.'

Mr Wombwell's menagerie was enclosed behind a hastily erected wattle fence on the open ground below the castle that usually served as the horse fair. There was a low gate in the middle of the fence, where Mr Wombwell stood to collect their entrance fees, and as they approached, they could hear the strange cries of the beasts.

'Come on! Come on!' Matty cried, penny in hand. 'Run!'

So they ran.

Inside the fence the animals were enclosed in pens, one beside the other, and the smell of them was so strong it made Harriet's eyes water.

Will said the first animal they came to was a sell, because it was just a sheep and you could see a sheep any day of the week, and where were the lions?

But the next two were deer with slender legs and mournful eyes, which was better, and the pen after that contained an odd-looking thing like a brown pig with a long snout caked in mud. Then there were three miserable heaps of black and white quills that the notice proclaimed to be 'Porky pines', and after that, and at last, they came to the lions, two of them in a pen only slightly bigger than that allotted to the porky pines, lying together, panting in the heat, their brown manes tangled and their tawny coats smeared with grime.

'Aren't they *big*!' Will said, his eyes round with awe.

But Harriet thought how sad they looked and how awful it was that they should be so dirty. They lay in indolent heaps, with their great paws as soft and still as cushions and only their tawny tails flicking from time to time to remove the flies that buzzed and plagued all about them. Such beautiful eyes, she thought, as yellow as honey, and so sad. Almost as if they knew they were prisoners. And she thought of the men locked away in the dungeons underneath her feet and remembered her own imprisonment in that cramped cell in Churchgate Street. 'I can't bear to think of anyone being locked up,' she said. 'It seems to me the greatest unkindness.'

'They're very smelly,' Meg observed, wrinkling her nose.

Then to Will's delight, one of the animals rose to his feet, shook his tangled mane and padded to the side of the pen, where he flopped down again just a few inches away from where they were standing.

'Why he's close enough to touch,' he said, enraptured. 'Could I touch him, Mama?'

Mr Wombwell was beside them in an instant. 'No you could not,' he said firmly. 'That there is Nero and the last little boy what touched our Nero got his head bit clean off.'

Will looked at Nero with increased respect. 'Clean off?' he said.

'Clean off.'

Nero yawned, exposing a vast expanse of pink tongue and formidable yellow teeth, at which Will gazed with admiration. 'Did he eat it?' he asked.

'I think we've seen enough for one afternoon,' Harriet said. 'Time we were off to the fish market. I promised your Aunt Annie to buy fish for supper.'

So they went to market and bought the fish and afterwards they had coffee and honey cakes at an inn called the Tiger in a street called Fishergate, which Will thought very appropriate. It was a splendid outing, even if they did come home as grubby as chimney sweeps.

It was a great disappointment to Harriet to have to leave her little school at the end of that season.

'I will buy you reading books,' she promised the two girls as she left, 'and I will come back next June, I give 'ee my word.'

It was a quiet winter and it seemed to go on for ever, for the next summer, being much anticipated, was a long time coming. But at last it was June again and Harriet and Will could return to their garden in Rattlesden, where the roses were blooming in profusion, and to the rectory garden next door. There were four slates waiting for pupils, for Edward was four now and according to his sister 'quite old enough'.

'Where shall we start?' Harriet asked her class on their first morning.

'L is for LION!' they chorused.

CHAPTER 31

I n London it was hot and sticky, and despite hot and sticky argument, the House of Commons had given the third and final reading to the repeal of the controversial Combination Act. Proposed by Sir Francis Burdett, supported by Mr Francis Place and his tireless petitions, and by the hundreds who had gathered signatures, the repeal had at last become law and the Combination Act was to be removed from the statute books. From 5th June 1824 it would once again be legal for working men and women to meet together to discuss the conditions under which they had to labour.

Frederick Brougham went to the House at the end of that historic week to meet his noble cousin, partly to take him off for a celebratory drink or two, and partly to see whether he had news of any government position on offer. The two of them had been manoeuvring for preferment for him for more than a year now and just before the third reading Lord Brougham had hinted that something might be decided upon soon. It would be a fine time to join the House, Frederick thought, just as the tide was turning in favour of greater freedom.

So he was rather put down by his cousin's greeting, as they walked towards one another through the lobby.

'What think 'ee of Tobago in the West Indies?'

''Tis a parlous distance to travel,' Frederick said, diplomatic despite his disappointment.

'But an uncommon good post,' Lord Brougham urged. 'Governor, no less. Think on it, Frederick.' He was turning back ready to walk to the coffee room.

It *was* an uncommon good post. There was no doubt of that. But not the one he wanted. 'Thank 'ee kindly, Henry,' he said. 'When do 'ee require an answer?'

'I should prefer one now,' his cousin said. 'Alacrity being the clearest indication of willing acceptance. Howsomever, should you need to think on it, we could take a week I daresay.'

I should accept, Frederick thought. It was the best offer he was likely to get at this juncture and if he refused, he might well be jeopardising his chances of a parliamentary career sometime in the future. Even so, the West Indies…

And somebody suddenly came up behind them. Somebody breathing hard as though he'd been running and smelling strongly of sweat.

Frederick turned to see who it was, moving slowly and easily because he was more curious than alarmed, and found that he was staring straight into the eyes of a wild, unkempt man with a horsewhip in his hand. He was muttering thickly, 'You have betrayed me, sir. I'll make you attend your duty.' And when Lord Brougham turned too, saying, 'Who are you, sir?' he raised the whip and struck the noble lord about the head and shoulders, shouting, 'You know me well! You know me well! You have betrayed me, sir!'

'Walk on!' Frederick said. The sooner they removed their bodies from the onslaught the better.

And Lord Brougham walked on, as well as he could under

the frantic blows, shielding his head with his arms. 'Never seen the feller before in my life,' he said to Frederick.

Feet were running towards them from the direction of the chamber. Two other MPs had arrived, Mr Littleton and Sir George Robbinson, weren't they? And a constable. They were struggling with the man, pulling him away, and the constable had pinioned his arms and they were half leading, half dragging him away. Frederick realised that his heart was pounding most uncomfortably. It had all been rather alarming.

'Brandy, I think,' Lord Brougham said. He was still wonderfully cool, but Frederick noticed that his forehead was filmed with sweat.

So they went off to drink a little brandy together and recover. And for a while at least the Governorship of Tobago was forgotten.

'AND YOU WANT to be a Member of Parliament?' Nan teased when he told her about the attack. 'I'd rather sell newspapers any day of the week. What was the matter with the man? Was he mad?'

'As a hatter,' Frederick said. 'And as to wanting to be a Member of Parliament...'

It was past two o'clock in the morning. They had dined well, loved long, and now they were lying side by side in his bed, talking in the easy fashion of long-established lovers. Perhaps this was the right moment to tell her about Tobago.

'I have the offer of a government post,' he said. He had intended to tell her casually, as though the matter were of little consequence, but despite all his efforts the words sounded forced and stilted.

She turned in his arms to grin her delight at him. 'At last!' she said. 'What did I tell 'ee? A man of such worth! Well? Well? What is it?'

He paused before he told her and, slight though it was, his hesitation alerted her.

'To be Governor of Tobago. In the West Indies.'

'You'll not take it, surely,' she said. It was impossible to read his face in the half-light, but she could see enough to realise that he was keeping his expression under tight control, and that made her heart sink palpably.

''Tis the best offer I am like to obtain,' he said, stroking her shoulder, half in affection, half to placate.

She shook his hand away and sat up to look at him more closely. 'I thought you asked to be made a Member of Parliament.'

'I did,' he admitted. 'But this is a better offer, Nan. And would assure me of a seat when I returned.'

'How long would you be there?'

There would be no avoiding it now. He must tell her. 'Six years.'

'Six years?' she yelled. 'Have you took leave of your senses, Frederick Brougham? Six years? You lie there calmly telling me we're to be six years apart?'

'You could come with me,' he tried. 'We need not be apart.'

She ignored that as being too preposterous for comment. 'I thought you loved me.'

'I do. I do.' Oh this was worse than he'd feared. ''Tain't a matter of love. 'Tis a matter of employment. I am fifty-five, Nan. I get no younger. I must progress. I cannot stay in the doldrums for ever.' But every word he said was taking him further away from her.

She scrambled out of her bed and put on her nightgown, pulling it violently over her head. 'Go where you please, then,' she said, snatching up her clothes. ''Tis all one to me, since you do not love me, nor never have so far as I can see.'

'Nan! Nan!' he said. 'I thought you knew me better than to say such things.'

'I thought I knew you better,' she answered, putting on her slippers. 'But it seems I don't. If you really loved me you wouldn't leave me for six whole years, no matter what. Oh no, you don't love me.'

'At the start of our affair,' he said, trying to be reasonable, 'we agreed that we should both continue with our work, neither interfering nor competing with the other. We were to be partners, if you remember. 'Twas my particular concern that my presence in your life should not harm you in any way. So how you can possibly accuse me of not loving you is quite beyond me. Everything that has happened between us during the last seven years should have given you proof otherwise.'

'It en't the last seven years what concern me now,' she said, ''tis the next six.'

'Nan!' he implored. 'Don't, I beg 'ee. What is six years? 'Twill soon pass and then I will return. We shall look upon it as nothing. No time at all.' But he was wasting his breath. She was already at the door.

'I shall sleep in the blue room,' she said. 'You'll not miss me. The night will soon pass. You'll look upon it as nothing. But don't 'ee look for *me* in the morning.' And she stamped her feet, glared and marched from the room, slamming the door behind her.

It was a very long night and took for ever to pass. Several times he got up and paced to the door thinking he might go down to the blue room and ask her forgiveness, but pride deflected him. Several times he drifted into sleep, to wake seconds later with the hope that she'd returned, but he was alone. And at last, when the dawn chorus began and the first grey smudges of dawn lightened the sky, he got up and overcame his pride and tiptoed down the corridor to see her.

The blue room was empty. She was up and gone.

Never mind, he comforted himself. I will take some breakfast and then I will call in at Easter House on my way to Chancery Lane and make all right between us.

But at Easter House Mr Teshmaker told him she had caught the early morning stage to Bury. 'She's gone for the summer, so she says,' he reported. 'Did you not know, Mr Brougham sir?'

'A creature of sudden whim, our Mrs Easter,' he said, trying to make light of it. But the news made his heart sink.

It would have sunk even further had he been able to see the foul mood she was in when she arrived in Bury.

When Bessie came to the door to greet her and see to her luggage and inquire after her journey, she was alerted by the brittle speed of her. 'You work too hard, me dear,' she said sympathetically, as Nan brisked up the stairs, skirts swishing.

'No, Bessie,' she said, as she went, 'if you ask me, I don't work hard enough. There'd be a deal less heartache if I had a deal less time.' And although she sounded her usual friendly self that was an odd thing to say.

Bessie followed her, but more slowly, trying another tack as she climbed. 'Is our Mr Brougham a-followin' 'ee down?'

'Don't speak to me about Mr Brougham,' Nan said, turning to face her old servant, her face dark with fury, 'for I can't abide it. Dratted man! Where's Thiss? I need to see the books.'

'Never know'd her in such a humour,' Bessie said to her daughter when she came visiting the next afternoon. 'Snap yer 'ead off soon as look at yer. And yer pa said she was that quick with the books he barely 'ad time to open the pages. Not that she 'ad nothink ter find fault with. You know yer pa, everythink shipshape an' orderly. An' now she's off out, all on 'er own in the pony cart, an' drivin' the poor animal that hard you'd never believe. That ain't like our Nan Easter, drivin' without company. An' no sign a' Mr Brougham.'

'Then 'tis a lovers' quarrel,' Pollyanna said sagely. 'You mark my words. An' the sooner 'tis mended the better.' And she went back to Rattlesden to report it all to Mrs Hopkins and Mrs Harriet.

'Mr Brougham will write to her,' Annie said when she heard. 'Or visit. 'Twill pass. These things always do. Is she to visit us, do 'ee think Pollyanna? Did she tell 'ee?'

'Tomorrow, ma'am,' Pollyanna said. 'I was to be sure to tell 'ee, and here's me forgetting.'

'He'll write,' Annie said. 'And if she's at all melancholy the children will cheer her.'

BUT FOUR FRAUGHT weeks went by and no letters from Mr Brougham arrived and Cosmo Teshmaker reported there was a rumour that he had accepted a position as Governor to some West Indian island. Nan was still in a most peculiar mood, which was hardly to be wondered at if the rumour were true, so her children decided they would have to take action. They met in Annie's parlour one Saturday evening after their own children were in bed to decide what should be done.

''Tis my opinion Cosmo has the right of it.' Billy said. 'Never known him wrong when it comes to rumour, damn if I have.'

'Poor Mama,' Annie said. 'How she'll miss him. Is he to be gone long?'

But nobody knew the answer to that. 'It could be for ever,' John said lugubriously, 'and how we shall cope with her then I cannot think.'

'She only seems happy when she's with the children,' Matilda said. 'I don't understand it, indeed I don't. I've never seen her like this before.'

'Neither have we,' Annie said, 'which is why something must be done.'

'She don't laugh,' John said. Her lack of laughter worried him more than anything else.

'She don't come to town,' Billy said. 'She sends letters but she don't come to town. That ain't like her either.'

'Perhaps,' Matilda offered, 'one of us should try to talk to her about it.'

'You can talk to her if you like,' her loving husband said. 'Just so long as you don't ask me.'

'No,' Annie said. 'I don't think that would do at all. She don't take kindly to us knowing her affairs at the best of times.'

'And this ain't the best of times,' Billy pointed out needlessly.

'Perhaps,' Harriet tried, 'we ought to write to Mr Brougham and tell him how she is.'

But John and James thought not. 'It is not for us to interfere between man and wife,' James said. 'Even those who are man and wife without benefit of clergy.' But he couldn't think of anything else that could be done instead. It was very difficult.

'The children are our greatest hope,' Annie said at last, when they'd all brooded in silence for several minutes. 'At least she is happy when she's with the children. How if we throw a party for her and the children? At least that might cheer her.'

So although they knew a party wouldn't solve the real problem, they set to and planned one. For, as Billy said, what else could they do?

Bessie tried to help her mistress by cooking special meals and making sure that the house was always full of flowers, but although Nan thanked her, that didn't solve the problem either.

'Never mind, Goosie,' Thiss said. 'You keep on. Water on a stone, eh?'

So she kept on. And three days later when she was arranging a bowl of roses in the drawing room window, she looked up and there was Mr Brougham striding across the square in his fine blue coat and that nice grey hat of his.

'Mrs Easter!' she called, running from the room to warn her mistress. 'It's Mr Brougham come at last.'

Nan was writing letters in her study. 'Humph!' she snorted as she put down her pen. 'He has, has he? Well then you'd better show him up.'

It didn't sound very encouraging.

But when Mr Brougham had been shown into the study, her mistress grinned at him, and that was more hopeful.

'Well?' she said, when Bessie was gone. 'All packed and ready for the Indies, are you?'

He had come to Bury intending to talk sense to her, to argue the case for this governorship sensibly and logically and reasonably, as befitted a barrister-at-law, but the sight of her bright face, there, looking up at him, rousing him, her bright, intelligent, loving face, drove all sense and logic and reason straight out of his mind. She was so quick and alert and full of vitality, brown eyes gleaming, wide mouth spread, dark curls springing from her forehead as if they had life of their own, and those two tender wings of white hair on either side of her temples to remind him that they were both ageing and that life was short, oh maddeningly short. And in the moment, he knew without doubt what he had suspected all along: that no matter what post he was offered, he simply couldn't leave her. She was more precious to him than any promotion and she made his ambition look the paltry thing it was.

He sat down in the armchair beside the window. 'No,' he said mildly. 'I am not.'

'Indeed?'

'Indeed.'

'And why not, pray? You'd best look slippy or you'll not be ready in time.'

'I'm afraid, my dear,' he said drily, 'this is one journey I shall have to forgo.'

'You mean to turn it down?' she said her voice rising with hope and relief.

'I've turned it down.' Smiling at her, loving her, holding out his arms to her. 'You are an impossible creature, my dearest, but I love you dearly and I cannot leave you.'

She ran to him at once and smothered his face with kisses. 'That's — the best — day's work — you've — ever — done.'

'I've to be in Exeter in two days' time,' he said, when he could get in a word between kisses. 'I hoped that you might accompany me there.'

'Bessie!' she yelled. 'Pack my bag. I'm off to Exeter with Mr Brougham. We will travel after the party,' she told him. 'We've a children's party in Rattlesden tomorrow. What fun!'

That night Harriet wrote at length to her diary, while John was over in the rectory with James.

I am so glad of this return, she confessed, when she'd described it in detail, *which is a great surprise to me, for I never thought I would rejoice at the resumption of a love affair, which I was always taught to consider a grievous sin.*

And yet I do. I do indeed. It is such happiness to see them together again. They love one another so dearly. They were arm in arm all afternoon I declare and looking so happy with one another.

Perhaps it is love itself which is important and not the outer forms and ceremonies. The important thing to them is that they are together again, husband and wife without benefit of clergy as dear James said a few days ago. How I have changed to be saying such things! I hope it is for the good. I think it is for the good.

This is an extraordinary family. You never know what is going to happen in it next. We shall have some sport at the party.

And it was. Great sport. For Nan was quite herself again, running races, and organising a blancmange-throwing competition, full of her old intoxicating, happy energy. And when they were all exhausted, the maids served tea and they all sat down among the cushions under the shade of the holm oak to enjoy it.

And the gate gave a sudden click and there was Caleb Rawson walking up the path.

Harriet was so amazed to see him after all this time that she didn't know what to say, but James was on his feet at once, with his hand outstretched in greeting. 'Why Mr Rawson,' he said, 'how splendid to see you again. Come in, come in and join the party. Allow me to introduce my mother-in-law, Mrs Easter, and Mr Brougham. Mr Rawson came here some years ago to address the local Hampden Club. You spoke of Peterloo as I remember.'

'Aye. I did that,' Caleb agreed as he shook hands.

'Do you still live in Manchester?' James went on, for the man certainly looked as though he'd been travelling.

'Nay,' Caleb said, smiling, 'I left Manchester more than three years since.'

'Then where have you come from?'

'I've come from Norwich Jail,' Caleb said. 'They let me out this morning.'

The news had a stunning effect on all his listeners. James and Annie were instantly full of pity, Nan and Frederick were intrigued, John and Billy interested, Matilda thrilled, and the children, having glanced at their elders to see which way the information ought to be received, were impressed.

But Harriet was torn with such a conflict of emotions that she still couldn't speak. To see him again like this, in stained, torn clothes, with the pallor of jail on his skin and the smell of jail still cloying about him, made her pity him as she had never done before, but the knowledge that he was a hero and a martyr, that he'd been jailed for the cause — for he must have been jailed for the cause, just like Mr Hunt — roused the most passionate admiration too. And the admiration increased when he told them all of the weavers' strike, and his arrest, and the way he and his companions had whiled away the time in their dungeons under the castle planning the next stage in the

449

campaign for reform, and how he'd come out of jail and gone straight back to his loom, 'where t' job were kept for me, by great good fortune, and my room an' all.'

'You are not deterred then,' she said, when he stopped speaking.

He looked straight at her and smiled, and the smile was greeting, affection, memory and something else she couldn't define. 'No,' he said. 'I am not.' And the expression on his face was so strong and so demanding she couldn't face it and she glanced down at his capable hands, resting among the cushions, to give herself something else to look at. And she was instantly taken back to that terrible afternoon on the field of Peterloo, and the dust and blood and suffering and companionship, and she heard the sabres swishing down again and the screams and the thunder of horses and saw blood spurt and the wounded crumple and fall.

'How did you get here, Mr Rawson?' James was asking.

'By carter's van to Stowmarket,' he said, 'then I took shanks' pony.'

'In that case you must stay the night with us, before you go on your way,' James said. 'Mrs Easter and Mr Brougham dine with us this evening, as we with them tomorrow in our neighbourly manner, you see, so we shall be a goodly company.'

So Caleb stayed to dinner and talked about reform to Frederick Brougham, and was told about the state of farming in Rattlesden, and news-selling in London, and the number of new Easter children who'd arrived since they'd last talked together. And Harriet watched him and listened to him and admired him, wondering at his strength of purpose, to have been in prison for three whole years and yet stayed so entirely himself. I could never have endured so long, she thought. Oh he is a very great man. A very great man indeed.

The next morning he went to church with Annie and the children and after the service they all walked with him as far as the path to Buxhall, James and Annie and Jimmy and Beau and little Meg, and Harriet and Rosie and Will. It was a fine day and Annie said the walk would do them all good, and that pleased Harriet because it meant she would be able to avoid any likelihood of being on her own with him.

On the homeward journey, Meg and Will grew tired and had to be given piggybacks because they said their legs were worn out. Their mothers were the willing horses, of course, and the slower pace at which the two of them were now obliged to walk gave Harriet the chance she'd been waiting for.

'It gave me quite a shock to see Mr Rawson again,' she confessed. 'I hoped he had forgotten all about me.'

'Did you so?' Annie asked, instantly curious. 'Why was that, my dear? Don't clutch my neck so Meg, there's a good girl. I thought you were one of his staunchest allies.'

'Yes,' Harriet said. 'I was. I still am. It's just...' And ducking her head for shame, she told her dear Annie all about that last visit in Fitzroy Square. 'I may have read more into his words than he intended,' she said.

'I think not,' Annie said, shrewdly. 'If I am any judge of it, your instincts told you otherwise, and instincts are invariably right. James has asked him to visit again.' Then she burst out laughing. 'Life grows more complicated by the minute, I do declare,' she said. 'The dear man sees no harm in it, you see.'

'No more do I, truly,' Harriet said, ashamed to have been criticising her hero. 'Mr Rawson is a good man, Annie.'

'Aye, so you say,' Annie said. 'But a man notwithstanding. So we must take care.'

They trudged on without speaking for several minutes, while two yellowhammers piped their one-line melody at them from the hedgerows.

'Leave it to me, my dear,' Annie said. 'I'll protect 'ee, depend on it.'

CHAPTER 32

That summer turned out to be the most delightful that Harriet had ever known. John spent far more time in Rattlesden for a start. The trio learned how to add and subtract and were uncommon pleased with themselves, and little Edward was the most attentive pupil of them all. Caleb came to visit nearly every Saturday evening and stayed with James and Annie all through Sunday, attending church and then making himself useful in the house or the garden. And never saying a word out of place. Not that Annie gave him the opportunity, for somehow or other she always contrived to be close at hand whenever it looked as though he and Harriet were going to be left alone together, and the conversation was quickly taken over and steered with delicate determination to the safest of safe topics.

The children enjoyed his company without reservation. Soon he was Uncle Caleb to them all, and master of the revels, the man to ask when you needed a skipping rope turned, or a book read, or a broken toy put together again, or a bruise wrapped in vinegar and brown paper.

When September came and it was time for Jimmy and Beau

to go back to school, they had an end-of-holiday party and Uncle Caleb was the guest of honour, which he said was 'a rare old feather in his cap'. Sitting about the trestle tables in the rectory garden, they ate end-of-holiday cake and drank end-of-holiday lemonade and toasted the new term. 'Good luck to us all, whatever the future may bring!'

What it brought was more terrible than any of them could have foreseen, even in their most anguished nightmares.

THE PONY CART brought Jimmy Hopkins home from school on that awful November afternoon just as it always did, but he was flushed and shivering and obviously ill. Beau was out of the cart and running into the house before their groom could climb down from the driver's seat.

'Stay there, Dickon,' he called. 'We shall need the cart again. Ma! Ma! Come quick! Jimmy's took a fever!'

Annie was hard at work in the laundry, scouring the copper while her two twice-monthly laundry maids mopped the floor, for it was washday and because nothing would dry out of doors it had taken them all day and much steam to complete the wash. The little stone-flagged room was hung with sheets and towels and small clothes, all dripping dismally from their racks in the ceiling, and the green walls were rivered with moisture.

'What now?' Annie said, wiping the sweat from her forehead with the back of her hand, and she went off wearily to find out, moving slowly and feeling rather hard done by. She was bone tired and she needed a rest, not another demand on her flagging spirits.

But one glance at Jimmy's putty-pale face changed her at once, re-charging her with terrified energy.

'Run for your father,' she said to Beau. 'Make haste. He's in the vestry with Mr Jones. Hot bricks,' she said to Pollyanna.

'More blankets. Jug of warm water. You'll need to finish the wash without me,' she said to the laundry maids. 'I'll be down to 'ee when I can. Drive in to Bury and fetch a surgeon,' she said to Dickon. 'Fast as the pony will go. Mr Chalmers if you can get him, otherwise Mr Brownjohn.' And all the time she was giving orders she was easing Jimmy out of the cart, with one arm to support his back and the other for him to lean on, 'That's it, my lambkin, easy does it. You'll be all right now. Just another step. You're home with me, lambkin. Easy does it.'

He was so ill it took him several minutes to tremble out of the cart and by that time Beau had come back with his father. James took one look at the boy and lifted him in his arms, big as he was, and carried him into the house.

'Keep everyone away,' he whispered to Annie as they climbed the east stairs together. 'Don't let the girls near. Nor Beau.'

'No, no,' Annie whispered back. 'I know. I can see that.' But she didn't ask him what he thought it was, because his answer might have been too terrible to face. It was sudden and it was serious and she was so afraid that she was finding it hard to breath.

She removed the child's boots and his jacket and trousers and held the chamber pot for him while he was horribly sick, and then she sponged his forehead, letting him rest a little before she finished undressing him and got him into his night-shirt. He was burning with fever, and there was a round red patch of unnatural colour in the centre of each cheek.

'I do feel bad, Ma,' he said.

'Yes, my lambkin,' she soothed. 'I know you do.'

'My back hurts.'

'Yes, my poor lamb. Never mind, we'll soon have you nice and comfy in your nice warm bed. Here's Pollyanna with a hot brick for your feet.'

But James wouldn't let Pollyanna walk into the room. 'Stay there,' he said to her. 'I'll come and get it.'

'Is 'e very bad sir?' Pollyanna asked as she handed over brick and blankets.

'Yes, I fear so,' James whispered. 'Is the surgeon returned?'

'No, not yet. I'll bring the hot water up presently.'

'Thank you.'

It was nearly an hour before the pony cart came clopping back, and by then Jimmy was delirious and groaning, and his parents were taut with fear.

Mr Brownjohn was short, stout, dapper and proficient. He felt the boy's forehead, took his pulse and examined his wrists, without saying a word. Then he led Annie and James out of the room.

'Does he vomit, Mrs Hopkins?' he asked, when they were all standing on the landing.

'Yes. But 'tis the fever, surely.' Oh say 'tis only a fever. Promise we shall soon have him well.

'Yes, yes. Maybe,' he said, shrewd eyes narrowed. 'Are there any other symptoms?'

'Pain in his back,' Annie offered. 'Perhaps he's taken a fall, Mr Brownjohn. What do 'ee think?' Yes, that's it. A fall. Tell me 'tis a fall. 'Children run fevers when they fall, do they not?'

'Aye, they do. Sometimes. But I must tell 'ee this don't look like a fall to me.'

James asked the question poor Annie was avoiding. 'What does it look like, Mr Brownjohn?'

'I'm sorry to have to say this to 'ee, Reverend Hopkins. It looks like the smallpox. There's rather a deal of smallpox in Bury at present.'

Annie put her face in her hands and groaned. 'Oh no, no, no. Not that.'

'You must keep all other children away,' Mr Brownjohn said. 'They should not enter the room for any reason whatsoever. Nor should they go to school to mix with other children. But I need hardly tell 'ee that. Keep the boy warm, give him plenty to drink. He don't want food with such a fever. 'Twould only serve to make him vomit. I will return on the third day, when the papules will appear if it is as we fear. I trust for all your sakes that we may be mistaken.'

But they were not. On the third day the tell-tale red spots began to cluster on Jimmy's forehead and by the time Mr Brownjohn arrived in the afternoon, they had become the familiar, terrible, raised papules and were spreading fast along his arms and his chest, and had erupted in such profusion on his wrists that his skin flamed with them.

Annie's face was frozen with the need to cry and the even more pressing need to control her emotions so as not to frighten her poor, stricken child.

'Is there anything we can do to help him?' she asked, when they had tiptoed out onto the landing. But she knew the answer even before he gave it.

'No, Mrs Hopkins, nothing at all, I fear. The illness must run its course. Keep him warm, keep him isolated, wash him gently, say your prayers. What of your other children? Are they well and out of the way?'

'They sleep in the two west rooms,' Annie said, 'on the other side of the house. I could send them to my sister-in-law, if you thought it necessary, I suppose. She is in Bury for the hunt ball.'

'No, not to Bury. We have an epidemic there, I fear,' Mr Brownjohn said. 'I have seen twenty cases in the last twelve days, and many from the grammar school. On no account allow your other children to Bury until we are notified that the danger is past.'

'What shall we do?' Annie said to James when the doctor had gone and he crept into Jimmy's bedroom to join her at the bedside. She rarely left her patient now, even when he was sleeping, as he was at the moment. 'Should we ask Mama, think 'ee?'

'Would she have the time? It is the quarterly meeting about now, surely.'

It was, Annie admitted. In her distress she had forgotten.

'No, no,' he said. 'Not your Mama, I think. Or at least, not yet. How if we were to ask Harriet?'

So while her poor boy was still asleep, Annie wrote to Harriet.

My dear sister,

I have such terrible news to tell you. My poor dear darling Jimmy has taken the smallpox, and Mr Brownjohn says we should send the other children away from the infection. I am at my wits' end. Could you possibly take them to London, my dear, and have them stay with you 'til 'tis safe for them to return?

Oh what a deal I ask of you. I know it. I shall think no less of you if you refuse.

I am so afraid for my babies. So very very afraid. Jimmy is so very ill. It would grieve you to see him. Pray for us, my dear.

You ever loving and most fearful,
Annie.

THE LETTER WAS DELIVERED to Fitzroy Square the following morning, just after John had left for work. He had set off earlier than usual because it was the day of the quarterly managers' meeting and he had a deal of work to complete before the afternoon. But even without him Harriet knew what her decision must be and she made it immediately.

'I am going up to Bury,' she told Mrs Toxteth. 'I shall take the first available seat on the first available coach, and I shall probably stay the night in Rattlesden and return tomorrow or the next day with Beau and Meg and little Dotty. Jimmy is ill and they cannot stay in the rectory. Could a room be made ready for them?'

It could.

'Thank 'ee kindly, Mrs Toxteth. And now send Peg to me, pray. I need to pack in a hurry.'

By twelve o'clock she was packed and ready, and Peg was carrying her carpetbag down to the carriage. She kissed Will and told him to be sure and be a good boy while she was away and do everything Papa and Rosie told him to. Then she wrote a quick note of explanation to John and gave it to Mrs Toxteth with instructions that it was to be handed over to the master 'the minute he sets foot inside the door'. By mid-afternoon she was on the road. Whatever the risk, Annie's children had to be taken away from that awful, awful disease.

DECISIONS WERE BEING MADE QUICKLY in the Easter boardroom, too, that afternoon.

'I've spent a deal of time a-courting the manufacturers for advertisements,' Nan announced to her managers, 'but I must tell 'ee the results are patchy to say the least. In London, Manchester, Birmingham, Leeds and Liverpool 'tis an established custom now, and mutually profitable, as I predicted. Howsomever, elsewhere 'tis largely a waste of effort. The manufacturers en't keen and the shopkeepers en't willing. That being so, I don't propose to waste any more time upon it. We shall take advertisements in the cities and discontinue 'em elsewhere. Will you all be so good as to tell your shopkeepers according?'

I've won, John thought. After all this time and all this effort, she's accepted Billy's compromise. If she hadn't been so headstrong, she could have accepted it long since. I always knew I was right. But he was surprised by how little relief he felt. It was such a small triumph. A small triumph in an unnecessary struggle.

Nevertheless at the end of the meeting he went back to Fitzroy Square at the gallop, for now, at last, he could spend more of his time at home with Harriet and Will instead of travelling the country so much.

It was a great disappointment to him that Harriet wasn't there.

'To Rattlesden?' he said to Mrs Toxteth when that lady had explained her absence. 'Do you know why, Mrs Toxteth?'

'She left a note, sir. 'Twas all done in a great rush.'

He read the note quickly, squinting with anxiety. Smallpox! Dear God! Of all the illnesses that was quite the most dreadful. Poor little Jimmy! Poor Annie! Poor Will! He must be kept right away from the infection. I will move him onto the third floor first thing tomorrow morning and he shall stay there with Rosie until all danger is past. 'We must rearrange the house,' he said, 'and then I must go and tell my brother and my mother. Wait dinner for me, Mrs Toxteth. This could take some time.'

NAN SAID she would go down to Rattlesden the very next day, as soon as she'd left instructions with Mr Teshmaker.

But Billy already knew the bad news. 'I had a letter from Tilda this afternoon,' he said, his blue eyes bolting with anxiety. 'I shall travel overnight, so I shall, and bring 'em all straight back here on the first coach out. They shan't stay there a minute longer than they need. Not with the smallpox raging. Harriet comes home tomorrow, too, you say? Well then, we will all travel together. How glad Annie will be to see her.'

'MY DEAR, MY DEAR,' Annie said running into Harriet's arms as soon as she tiptoed into Jimmy's darkened bedroom. 'You are so good to come here so quickly.'

'How is he?' Harriet whispered. It was unpleasantly hot and

airless in the little room, for the curtains were drawn and there was a great fire blazing in the hearth and the whole place was cloyed with the sickly-sweet smell of the illness.

'My poor, poor boy,' Annie said. 'Just look.'

The child lay on his back in his little white bed, asleep but tossing with fever, his nightshirt stained with sweat. His face and hands were completely covered with the huge raised blebs of the pox, some so close to one another that there wasn't a hair's breadth between them, and all of them pitted with hideous dark craters. His lips were cracked and his eyelids so swollen that his lashes had all but disappeared. He was so distorted by the disease it was pitiful to see him.

'I never leave him,' Annie said, speaking very quietly for fear he should wake and understand what she was saying, 'for there's worse to come, so Mr Brownjohn says. The eighth day is the worse. The eighth to the twelfth. Oh Harriet, I'm so afraid.' In the bronze light from fire and candle she looked haggard and hollow-eyed. 'I can't think what to do for the best.'

'I have taken four seats upon the eight o'clock coach from Bury tomorrow,' Harriet whispered, feeling she would have to take charge. 'Have you told Beau and the girls what is to be done?'

'No, not yet.'

'Could Pollyanna sit with Jimmy while you do?'

So it was arranged, and Pollyanna came to sit quietly at the door with her sewing. 'They're all in the nursery, ma'am,' she said to Annie. 'Dotty's having her little nap and the other two are a-reading of their books.'

But that wasn't quite accurate, as Annie soon discovered when they'd run quickly through the house to the west wing to reach the nursery. Dotty was fast asleep in her cot in the corner, rosy with health and with one fat thumb in her mouth, and Meg was sitting in her little low chair reading her picture book with happy concentration, but Beau wasn't in the room.

'Here's your Aunt Harriet come to see you,' Annie said. 'Where's Beau?'

Meg looked up distantly from her book. 'Gone to lie down, Mama,' she said.

'When was this?' Harriet asked Meg.

'Just this minute,' Meg said seriously. 'We was reading, Aunt Harriet, and he said, "Oh dear" and then he went to lie down.'

'Stay there like a good girl,' Annie instructed, 'while we go and see where he is.'

He was lying on the rug before the fire in his bedroom. His face was flushed and his eyes were closed, but when he heard his mother's voice, he opened them wearily and tried to focus them. 'Ma?' he said, 'I do feel ill.' But he added with touching pride, 'I got clear away from the girls, Ma.'

'Oh, dear God!' Annie said faintly to Harriet. 'Not another.' But she was already in action, sweeping forward into the room to kneel beside her poor Beau and feel his forehead.

'I'll send Dickon for the surgeon,' Harriet whispered, smothering her fear in action.

'Help me get him into bed first,' Annie said. 'Could you fill the warming pan?'

The two of them worked together quietly and gently, easing, smoothing, lifting slowly and finally tucking the child under well-warmed blankets. He had such a very high fever he was only partially aware of what they were doing.

'Shall I tell James?' Harriet asked, when he was settled.

'After evensong,' Annie said. 'No need to worry him unnecessarily. You might feel better by then, mightn't you, lambkin?'

But Beau couldn't answer and they both knew there was very little hope.

Although Dickon took horse to Bury as soon as he was bidden, it was long past evensong before a weary Mr Brownjohn arrived, and by then Beau's fever was even higher, he'd been sick, and he was complaining of pain in his back and his

461

neck. There was no doubt in anybody's mind that he had the smallpox too.

'Yes,' Annie said sadly. 'I know what it is I have to do. Is my Jimmy any better, think 'ee?'

But it was too soon to tell.

'Call me again when the blebs become purulent,' the surgeon said. 'Are the other children gone?'

THAT NIGHT ANNIE sat up with Beau in the west wing and James kept vigil over Jimmy in the east, and Harriet, who was far too worried and upset to sleep, lay on a truckle bed in the girl's room and said long and earnest prayers, pleading that Jimmy should be brought safely through the eighth day of his illness, that he should not take a secondary fever from the toxins, that he should be permitted to recover, urging that poor Beau should be spared the worst horrors of the disease. 'If he must have it, Lord, let him have it mildly. And help my poor Annie and her dear, dear James. They suffer so, to see their boys so ill. And protect my dear Will and Meg and Dotty, because we are all at risk.' For all she knew, they might be carrying the infection with them when they travelled to London in the morning. 'Protect us all,' she prayed, adding, because it was the correct thing to say, even though she knew in her innermost and honest heart that she could not mean it, 'Nevertheless not my will but Thine be done, oh lord.'

I've a ticket to spare now, she thought, as she lay wakeful and afraid, listening to the creak and tick of the ancient timbers as they cooled and contracted about her. Oh, would I had not! Poor little Beau! And although she fell into a light sleep some time towards dawn, she was harassed by such dreadful nightmares, she was glad to wake again.

She got up, washed, dressed and crept downstairs to start

cooking the breakfast. Pollyanna was in the kitchen before her, baking the bread and making flapjacks.

'They'll need a good meal in their bellies afore they go, poor little mites,' she said, 'an' it ain't time for Mrs Chiddum to come in yet. You've not slept much neither, 'ave yer? The Reverend's gone off ter say matins, him an' my John together, dear good souls that they are, so I thought I might as well come over and make myself useful.'

Harriet stoked the fire and began to slice the bacon. Chores eased the mind on such occasions, as she knew from her childhood. She was cooking the flapjacks on the griddle when Pollyanna gave a little shriek and ran to the window.

'Why it's Pa,' she said. 'Look 'ee there. It's Pa.'

And so it was, driving Matilda's smart blue Briska into the yard, with Edward tucked inside a travelling rug on the seat behind him.

They ran from the kitchen at once, not even stopping to snatch a cloak from the peg behind the door.

'What is it?' Harriet said, as Thiss reined in the two greys.

'There you are, Master Edward,' Thiss said to the child. 'Didn't I say we'd catch 'em. You got another visitor Mrs Harriet, if you'll be so kind. Young Master Edward here 'ud like ter come ter London along of his cousins.'

'Who is it?' Harriet asked, understanding at once.

'Matty,' he said, still speaking with deliberate cheerfulness so as not to alarm the boy. 'Third day yesterday evenin' if you takes my meanin'. I got a note for yer. Hello, Polly gel. Goin' on all right, are yer?'

Pollyanna was already scurrying Edward into the house, for it was bitterly cold and morning mist was still rolling off the fields in long chill swathes. 'Right as ninepence, Pa,' she called back to him. 'Come on in.'

'How is Mrs Matilda?' Harriet asked as she followed them.

'Wild with worry, poor soul,' Thiss said. 'Mr Billy come down first thing an' sez 'e'll stay with 'er. That's 'is note you got.'

And then they were all in the kitchen and Edward was sitting by the fire and Annie was reading the note and Pollyanna had gone upstairs to wake the girls.

There is no end to this nightmare, Harriet thought, standing with her hand against the kitchen table to steady herself. Who will be next? And she began to make the tea to give herself something to do.

It was the most peculiar breakfast. Thiss went upstairs to sit with the patients. 'Seein' I'm in no harm, you just make use of me all you can,' he said to Annie. 'I had the smallpox when I was a lad, so I did. Well, you've only ter look at my physog ter see that. 'An' the one good thing about it is you can't take it twice.'

The three women were brisk and cheerful despite the anxiety that was crushing them all so cruelly, and the three children ate as much as they could partly because they knew it was expected of them and partly because it was the only way they could placate the tension all around them. Then Pollyanna fetched the bags and carried them out to the Briska and Thiss appeared again and leapt into the driving seat, and the children were wrapped in rugs and settled together on the long seat behind him with hot bricks at their feet to keep them warm, and Harriet kissed Annie goodbye before she climbed in.

'I will write to you every day,' she promised. 'Every day in time for the night mail.'

'You are so good,' Annie said, kissing her. 'Oh, you will look after my little ones, won't you? Oh yes, yes, I know you will. You are so good.'

'All set?' Thiss said. 'Then off we go. What a lark, eh, littluns?'

'Every day?' Annie implored, as the greys walked away.

'Every day,' Harriet promised.

· · ·

AND SHE KEPT HER WORD, writing two letters every afternoon, one to Annie and the other to Matilda, and both as reassuring as she could make them.

> *They are all well, and although they miss you, they are not distressed. I keep them occupied with lessons and stories and suchlike, but we do not stir from the drawing room, which is now our abode, for fear of the infection.*

But she said nothing about how much she missed seeing her own dear little Will, nor about the little homemade calendar she kept on the last page of her diary, nor of the fluctuating hopes and fears it encouraged. She knew it would be fourteen days before she could be sure that none of her three charges had taken the infection, and fourteen days would not be completed until 11th December, which she had ringed in red ink, but which seemed an eternity away. Every single day was now interminable with anxiety and the nights were hideous, particularly as John was away on his travels.

Matilda and Annie wrote back, if not quite every day, at least as often as they could: 'Mama Easter arrived yesterday afternoon, for which we were all very thankful. Matty is covered with spots, her face so swollen poor soul, but do not tell Edward.' 'I believe Beau a little better since the blebs came out. Mama says she will stay with us until all three children are well again. Would that her determination could make it so.'

Four days after Harriet took the three children to London Annie wrote to say that Jimmy was very ill. The blebs were full of pus and he had high fever again, just as Mr Brownjohn had predicted. 'It is like to last another four days, poor child,' she wrote. 'Pray for us, Harriet my dear. We were never so much in need of prayer. Pray God to give him the strength to live through this dreadful time.'

And two days after that it was little Matty's turn. 'I cannot comfort her,' Matilda wrote, 'nor recognise her, I fear. Pray for us, Harriet. You are so good. Thiss is such a help to us, having no fear. I don't know how we should manage without him.'

John returned to London that afternoon with the news that the smallpox was in Oxford and Canterbury, and that doctors were saying that the outbreak was worse than any of the three great epidemics of the previous century. But he didn't tell her that nearly a third of all patients admitted to the smallpox hospitals were dying. Time enough for that when the danger was past.

'It could break out in London too,' Harriet said. '*The Times* says it is raging in Paris.'

'And in Sweden,' John said.

'So many deaths,' Harriet mourned, 'and no way of preventing any of them. It is a terrible thing.' And she said her constant, secret prayer, yet again: dear Lord, please don't let any of our children die.

Two afternoons later Annie wrote to say that Beau had reached the eighth day. 'He is very ill,' she said, 'but not as bad as his brother, who does seem to be improving a little, so we are a little more hopeful now.'

That night when she'd answered Annie's letter, Harriet crossed off the eleventh day of her long fortnight.

Only three more days to go, she told her diary, *and then we shall be safe. Caleb wrote me such a kind letter today. His wife died of smallpox and so did his little boy, so he says he knows what we are all suffering. It is a dreadful disease. But we are all so nearly clear of it. Thank the Good Lord.*

IT WAS BITTERLY cold in Rattlesden. Annie had moved Beau's bed into Jimmy's room as soon as the girls were gone, and now she and James kept the fire going there by night and day. It was the first thing Annie attended to, after she'd given her two patients a drink of water and sponged their swollen hands and faces.

On that thirteenth morning, she woke with a start, wondering why the fire was making such an odd wheezing noise. A piece of slate among the coal, she thought, straightening her spine and rubbing the sleep out of her eyes, for she'd fallen asleep in her chair, as she so often did on these long fraught nights. Then, with a shock that squeezed her heart most painfully, she realised that the noise was coming from Beau's little bed, and she jumped up and ran to his side. He was struggling for air, but lying so still, as if he were paralysed, his swollen face distorted and his eyes shut tight.

'Mama!' she called. 'James! Come quickly, do.' But they were on the other side of the house, and, although they both heard her, it took them several seconds to run to the room. By the time they reached her, the struggle was over and her dear, dear Beau was dead, lying quietly in her arms, still warm, but irrevocably without breath or life.

'Oh my dear, my dear,' Nan said, torn with pity for her daughter. And she and James fell to their knees beside the bed and held poor Annie as well as they could and wept with her. And for the first time since he fell ill, Jimmy actually sat up in his bed, and caught their grief and wept too, with tears running over his terrible black scabs and into his mouth, until Nanna came and sat beside him and put her arms round him, scabs and all, and told him he was her own dear boy and she would love him for ever and ever.

'On the very day my poor Jimmy is getting better!' Annie cried. 'Oh James, I can't bear it.'

And poor James, who was haggard with fatigue and sorrow, tried to find words of comfort, and for the first time in his life, couldn't think of any, and put his head in his hands and cried like a baby.

'Is Beau dead, Nanna?' Jimmy whispered as his parents wept.

'Yes, my love, I'm afraid he is.'

'Shall I die too, Nanna?'

'No,' she said fiercely. 'No, you shan't. Your Nanna won't let you.'

IT WAS a simple funeral and one of three that day, so violently was the smallpox raging. John and Harriet left the children in London with Rosie and young Tom and Mrs Toxteth, because it would never have done to bring them back into infection, and they travelled on the overnight stage so as to arrive in plenty of time to comfort poor Annie and James. But by then Annie had reached the first calm of grieving and James had mourned sufficiently to take the ceremony himself.

He spoke most movingly at the little graveside, reminding them of the great joy his dear Beau had brought to them all. 'A child of peace,' he said 'and always concerned for others. But it must be said with just enough mischief to bring us laughter. And daring, too, to provoke fear and admiration in us. We shall miss him most terribly.

'In pleasant times it is easy to bow ourselves to the will of God. When a child is born to bring love into the world, how readily we say, "Thy Will be done". At times like these it is hard for us.' And the drawn expression on his face showed how very hard it was. 'Nevertheless, death is Thy will too, like every opposite, beauty and ugliness, night and day, sickness and health, birth and death. When we say Thy prayer, Oh Lord, as we shall do presently, send us grace, we beseech Thee, that we may mean the words we say … Our Father, which art in heaven, hallowed be Thy name. Thy kingdom come. Thy Will be done, in earth as it is in heaven…'

. . .

HE IS A VERY GREAT MAN, Harriet wrote to Caleb, when she was home in London again. It was so easy to write to Caleb these days, for he had become such a friend, and understood so well what they were all suffering. *I could not accept the way he does, that I know. I would rail and rail against the injustice of such a death.*

He wrote back to her almost by return of post.

My dearest Harriet,

Tha's right. Tha shouldst never accept injustice. Never. Tha shouldst rail and rail and rail against it. And fight against it an' all. Acceptance is folly. Only by struggle will us common folk ever improve our lot. 'Tis a great cause and a great struggle. Tha's a fine woman to have joined us in it.

By now the fourteen days should be up and your worries over and done with, of which I'm uncommon glad.

We are well here, but work is scanty.

Your friend in love and admiration,
Caleb Rawson.

It was a comforting letter and she tucked it into her diary so that she could read it and enjoy it again when she wasn't quite so busy. But her worries weren't done with. They were beginning all over again.

CHAPTER 33

Bury St Edmunds was a forlorn town that winter. Horses stood idle in the stables and the streets grew dusty with lack of use. The two great inns were blank-windowed and empty, for there were very few visitors and the inhabitants kept within doors as much as they could, scurrying to market for such food as they needed and greeting their neighbours from a distance. The theatre closed and so did the Athenaeum, the courts sat twice and in great haste, and the churches were half empty. It was a town holding its breath, a town whispering, dressed in black, waiting for the next victim.

Like so many other landladies, the two Miss Callbecks lost their lodgers as soon as the infection started. The couple from Grimsby, who had occupied the two back bedrooms and sold tickets at the theatre, packed their bags on the day the theatre closed, and Mr Richards, who had been their mainstay for so long, wrote to cancel his tenancy saying he would be staying in London 'for the foreseeable future'.

'We must not despair, sister,' Thomasina said. 'The scourge will pass in time. Other lodgers will arrive.'

'Let us pray so,' Evelina said.

'Depend upon't,' Thomasina assured her. 'Meantime, you will stay indoors and I will go to market. There is no sense in both of us being exposed to infection and though you are younger you are weaker than I.'

'Should we not take turns?' Evelina asked. They had always taken turns. Always. In all their chores.

'No,' Thomasina said sternly. 'Not in this. This is too serious. My mind is made up.'

'Should we visit poor Billy and Matilda?' It seemed heartless to be skulking indoors when poor little Matty was fighting for her life. 'And Annie and James and Jimmy?'

'No,' her sister said again. 'I will post a letter from time to time on my way to market. There is nothing we can do to help, even if we were to visit. We should only be a nuisance. No, we must protect ourselves, Evelina. In any case, if I am any judge of character, Nan will remain in Bury until both the children are well and she will be sure to keep us informed.'

And sure enough, two days after Beau's funeral, Nan wrote to John to say that she and Billy would be staying in Bury until they were quite certain that Jimmy and Matty had recovered, and that Annie and James had been nursed through the worst of their grief.

'Tis like to be the middle of January afore we are back, so you must run the company without us, which I have perfect confidence you will do uncommon well. Pray give my love to Harriet and all the dear children. We put great burdens upon you both I fear.

So John ran the company single-handed. He was busier than he had ever been in his life, and even though he was torn with pity for his poor sister, and anxious in case the smallpox broke out in London, he was secretly well pleased with the way he was dealing with the firm's affairs. Billy came down to London once or twice to 'keep an eye on the warehouse', and Nan wrote daily letters, but they weren't necessary. Everything ran like clockwork. It was most satisfactory and proved that he could control the firm with ease for as long as his mother would allow and, what was more, that he could take it over entirely if she would only give him the chance.

In the freezing cold of early January many of the provincial coaches didn't run, and others were cancelled at the last minute because their drivers had fallen sick, but it was a matter of great pride to him that his carefully corrected timetables were equal to any demand that weather and epidemic could put upon them. As the weather worsened, he carried them about with him wherever he went, a bulky package in the lower pocket of his greatcoat, so if one coach failed, he knew at once how it could be replaced. It meant a great deal of work, of course, for he updated every timetable every night, often continuing into the small hours, sitting in his panelled office on the top floor of the house with two candlesticks to light his way and a purring sense of satisfaction to keep him wakeful until the job was done. And although he would never have admitted it to anybody, not even Harriet, because it was really rather improper, if it hadn't been for the smallpox it would have been one of the happiest times of his life.

Until the night he took a chill.

It had been a most unpleasant day, dark and cold and with a constant pervasive drizzle, and as he'd been out in it most of the afternoon, visiting the newspaper proprietors and checking the departure of the evening stages, he wasn't surprised when after he'd been working on the timetables for an hour or two, his throat began to prickle and his nose to run. He left his office with his brain still comfortably occupied with calculations, took up his candle and tiptoed downstairs to his bedroom on the floor below to find a clean handkerchief.

Harriet was sleeping, white as a statue in their high bed, lying on her side with the scarlet coverlet tucked underneath her chin and her pale hair trailing across the pillow. In the pool of golden light from his candle, she looked like a saint in a stained-glass window, so still and untroubled and pure of profile, and for a few seconds he stood beside the bed, simply enjoying the sight of her. My dearest, he thought. She is such a good woman, so quietly, comfortingly good, taking all these children into her home and looking after them so well. My dearest Harriet.

But then his nose needed attention and he had to find a handkerchief quite quickly. They were in a pile in the top drawer of the dressing table, beautifully clean and ordered. Dear Harriet. But as he shut the drawer, easing it slowly so as not to wake her, a white paper fell from the dressing table and fluttered to the floor. Neatness and order were disturbed. So naturally he bent down at once to retrieve it.

It was a letter, lying face upwards on the rug, its heavy handwriting spider-black, unfamiliar, foreign. He was reading it as he picked it up, his senses prickling because it had no place in their peaceful, gentle bedroom.

My dearest Harriet, Tha's right...

What presumption was this? Thee/ Tha? The familiarity of it was like a blow to his stomach, making him wince. But he read on, holding the little page close to the candle, for now that he had begun there was no turning back. He had to know it all, every single word, no matter how painful, and particularly the name of the man who had written them. For it had to be a man. It was too like a love-letter for any other possibility.

Your friend in love and admiration,
  Caleb Rawson.

473

ok‎ll

Of course, he thought, putting the letter back in exactly the same place from which it had fallen. Caleb Rawson. Of course. I might have known it. That ugly common man, with his low forehead and his coarse hands and his rough speech. Caleb Rawson. And he remembered the way the wretched man came visiting at Rattlesden, as if he belonged there and, worst of all, the way Harriet had walked through St Peter's Fields on the day of the massacre with her clothes torn and her hair tumbled about her face, looking so very unlike herself that he'd thought she was a whore. Dear God! He'd thought she was a whore.

She was still sleeping peacefully, as if nothing had happened, breathing softly into the pillow and looking more beautiful than ever. How could you? he thought, staring down at her. How could you do this to me when I love you so much?

But then reason returned. *Had* she done anything? There was a letter written certainly, and a most compromising letter, but it hadn't been written by her. She had merely received it. She might have answered it with the proper rebuke it deserved. But then if that were the case, she would surely have told him all about it, and she had said nothing. But then again, perhaps it had only just arrived. Perhaps she hadn't had time to consider what to do about it. I must not misjudge her, he told himself. I must not be precipitate. I must wait. Perhaps she will speak of it in the morning.

And the thought made him yearn to speak to her, then, at that moment, and desire rose in him so strongly that if he hadn't known how tired she was and how much she needed her sleep, he would have been tempted to wake her and make love to her. He needed to feel loved, to know that she was his, and his alone, to be comforted with kisses, lifted by passion, eased by ecstasy. But that would be selfishness, he told himself. I must not be selfish. I must wait till the morning. All this could be resolved so easily in the morning. He would get undressed, quietly, and go to sleep. That was much the best way. There was no need to be precipitate.

And truly, lying beside her sleeping warmth in the familiar ferny mustiness of their high bed, he felt more and more certain that there would be some perfectly proper explanation of that awful letter. It would all be resolved by love. In the morning.

When he woke, she was smiling at him, her eyes a mere three inches away from his own. He kissed her at once, before consciousness and memory returned, savouring the soft pressure of her lips, her white breast lifting, her belly rounding against his, desire growing slowly and pleasurably as it always did. He kissed her again and again and again.

'Dear, dear John,' she said, stroking the dark hair at his temples. 'How I do love you —' sinuous against him. 'Yes, yes, yes,' rolling onto her back, welcoming him.

And at the very moment of their sharpest ecstasy, as they rocked together, nearly nearly there, he suddenly remembered the letter, spider-black and foreign and insulting. All his desire was lost in an instant. He was weak and wilted. He couldn't continue. The ignominy of it was overwhelming.

'What is it?' she asked, holding him about the waist. 'Oh John, my dear, what is it?'

'Nothing,' he said, rolling away from her, turning his back on her, confused and embarrassed.

'John, my dear?' she said, putting her arm round his neck.

He shook her hand away almost angrily and got out of the bed.

'It is nothing,' he said brusquely. And he found a clean handkerchief and blew his nose loudly. 'Nothing I tell 'ee. Time I was dressed. I shall be late for the sorting.' And he rang the bell for young Tom.

She was very upset, but she decided not to say anything because he was squinting with misery. 'I will go and see how the children are,' she said, and she smiled at him to show that she loved him and that it was of no consequence. But he was putting on his dressing gown and didn't look at her.

I ought to tell her about the letter, he thought, watching her walk out of the door. I ought to ask her. But his courage had failed him too. No, no. Better to wait until the next one arrived. He would make it his business to stay at home until the post had been delivered. Today and tomorrow and tomorrow until a letter *did* arrive. Then he would see.

But although that morning's post brought two letters, neither was from Caleb Rawson. His was from his mother, saying she was returning to London that afternoon, and instructing him to have the books ready for her inspection at four o'clock, and Harriet's was from Annie.

Jimmy is now quite recovered, she wrote, *even from the stiffness in his poor hands, which has eased at last.*

Oh Harriet my dear, I cannot bear to be parted from my dear girls for another moment, and we are all out of quarantine now. Mama is bringing Jimmy and me back to London with her tomorrow, which will be today as you read this letter. She says we may stay at Bedford Square for a day or two, but I would so much rather be with you and John. Could we seek refuge with 'ee too, my dear? You must say no if it is too much. I would not wish to be a burden. James will stay in Rattlesden, of course, to be with his parishioners, since so many have lost children or relations in the outbreak. Three died in one cottage. It has been the most terrible time. I cannot tell you how terrible. The worst of it is that nobody can tell when it will be over. Your Mr Rawson wrote us such a fine letter. His little boy died of the smallpox too. Did you know? Oh how much I want to see you again!

'Yes,' John said, when he had read the letter too. 'Of course she shall stay here and for as long as she likes.' He wasn't sure whether he was pleased to hear of Mr Rawson's letter or not. It seemed to have comforted Annie, and it showed that the

476

wretched man wrote to everybody, but even so 'your Mr Rawson' was a deal too familiar.

And so Annie was welcomed and settled into the house and her poor scarred Jimmy was reunited with his sisters and cousins. Will examined the scars with intense interest and after they were both sent to bed that evening, demanded to be told 'all about the smallpox, and cousin Beau's death and the journey down and everything'. And was. Apart from the more lurid and personal details, which were too painful to contemplate.

He was most impressed. 'What a thing to have seen an epidemic,' he said, gazing at his cousin with blue-eyed admiration. 'We missed it all down here in London, you know.'

'You were jolly lucky,' Jimmy said. 'You just go on missing it, that's my advice.'

It was Harriet's most fervent hope, and the theme of every prayer she uttered for the next anxious fortnight. Although she was glad to see her dear Annie again, and although she did everything she could to comfort her and make her life easy, it still seemed the cruellest irony that in order to be kind and charitable to Annie she had to subject herself to the daily ordeal of another secret quarantine. For what if they'd brought the infection with them, after all? She drew another little calendar at the back of her diary, and crossed off the days, yet again, just as she'd done before and with exactly the same mixture of hope and foreboding.

On the third day Billy and Matilda came home, calling on their way to Torrington Square to collect Edward and thank Harriet with tears in their eyes for her 'uncommon kindness'. On the fifth, Nan arrived to take them all to the Vauxhall Gardens to see a firework display, which she said was just the thing to cheer them and which Harriet enjoyed although she hadn't expected to. And John went about his work as though nothing were the matter, except that he never made love to her once, so she knew he was secretly as worried as she was. Despite the fireworks, it was a difficult time.

But the fortnight passed eventually and John recovered from his cold and there was no sickness in anyone else. And James wrote to Annie to say that the epidemic was dying down. 'We only had two new cases in the parish last week,' he wrote, 'and that is a very good sign. Soon we shall all be together again, my darling, and what a joy that will be.' And a letter arrived from Caleb late one afternoon which was full of comfort and hope and pleased both women very much. 'All bad things pass,' he said. 'I reckon 'tis like a great wheel a-turning. But we must give t' wheel a shove now and then, else it 'ud crush us down instead a' carrying us on.'

'How very true that is,' Harriet confided to her diary. 'All bad things *do* pass. Even this dreadful epidemic cannot last for ever. Soon it must end, and then we shall stop feeling afraid and my dear John will love me again, just as he used to. It distresses him to be unable. That is why he makes no attempt. I am sure of it. For if that were not the cause, it would mean he did not love me, and I could not bear to think that. Oh, if only I could make all right for him. Pleasure would be so healing. I must hold on to Caleb's certain truth. All bad things pass.'

But this particular bad time was not quite over. There was another victim falling ill of the smallpox even as she wrote. And this time death came swiftly and most terribly.

Four days later, Nan received a letter from Evelina Callbeck.

This I am most sorrowful to say, my dear Nan, is to tell 'ee that my poor dear sister Thomasina is dead. Only three days ago she was out to market. I cannot believe it. She would not allow me to venture from the house because of the smallpox, and now you see how it is. Well, well. She was always so kind and loving to me. How I shall manage now I cannot think, but you are not to worry yourself on my account.

I shall think of something. Thomasina always said we would think of something.

Howsomever the funeral is arranged. It was so very quick, Nan dear. I cannot believe nor understand it. Mr Thistlethwaite came in every day. He said it was because the spots would not come out. They never did you see, my dear Nan, and she suffered so much. It is at three of the clock on Thursday. Pray on no account allow any of the family to attend. There is no end to the danger in this town. I am quite able to attend a funeral on my own, even the funeral of my own dear sister.

Nan wrote back at once:

I shall be in Whiting Street at two of the clock. You will most certainly not attend a funeral on your own. I never heard of such a thing.

And at two of the clock, there she was, with Bessie and Thiss beside her and Mr Cosmo Teshmaker behind them. So Evelina was well supported, after all, standing between Thiss and Cosmo and weeping quietly with her head on the lawyer's shoulder. Afterwards when the little gathering drove back to her house in the comfortable privacy of Nan's closed carriage, she wept again and told them all, between tears, how very grateful she was to them, and how much she valued their friendship.

'Squit!' Nan said, fretting her cold hands with loving fierceness. 'What are friends for? And you en't to worry about the future neither, for I'll take care of 'ee, so I shall.'

They stayed with her for over an hour, telling her what a fine woman Thomasina had been and drinking her tea, until she was over the worst of her tears and seemed more settled. It was growing dark when they climbed into the carriage for the return trot to Angel Hill.

And halfway across the square, Cosmo suddenly surprised

them all by announcing that he seemed to have left his gloves behind at Whiting Street.

''Ten't like you to be forgetful,' Nan said.

'No, indeed.'

'Then you'd best make tracks and retrieve 'em, had you not?' Shall we turn the coach about?'

'No, no' he said. 'A stop would be sufficient. I can walk.'

'Well, well, well,' Nan said, when they'd stopped and let him out. 'He's in a mortal hurry for a pair of gloves.'

'If it weren't fer that gammy leg,' Bessie said, watching him from the window, 'I swear you'd say he was running.'

And so he was, traversing the square in a series of long gliding hops, his greatcoat flapping behind him in the wind. He was on his way back to Miss Evelina Callbeck. He was forty-eight years of age, he'd been a bachelor all his life, and he had a club foot which he'd always considered a barrier to any possibility of courtship, but now her great need had overcome his timidity. He was going to propose to her.

THEY WERE married six weeks later, very quietly of course, in the church of St Clements' Danes in the Strand, on the day that Bury St Edmunds was finally declared to be free of the smallpox. Nan Easter and Frederick Brougham were witnesses and the new Mr and Mrs Teshmaker gave a private dinner party afterwards in the groom's modest house in Tavistock Street.

The bride declared she was glad of a quiet wedding, and vowed she was the most fortunate woman alive, 'to be rescued so and made so happy.'

But the groom said that the fortune was all his. 'I account myself most blessed. Most blessed.'

. . .

'ALL'S WELL THAT ENDS WELL,' Nan said, when she and Frederick were back in her drawing room at Bedford Square. 'And the smallpox over too, praise be. Now perhaps we may take up our lives again and enjoy ourselves a little. Bessie tells me she is to be a grandmother in the summer. Pollyanna is breeding.'

'I have a piece of good news too,' Frederick said, and he spoke so casually she knew at once that it was important.

'And what might that be?' Grinning at him as he lay sprawled in her easy chair.

'I have the offer of a seat in the Commons. I'm to be elected on the fourth of May.'

'At last!' she said, rushing to kiss him. 'Where is it?'

'Lostwithiel in Cornwall,' he said. 'A rotten borough I fear, but I assure you I will work to change such practices once I am a Member.'

'I'm sure on it,' she said. 'How fine 'twill be to see your speeches in the papers. Mr Frederick Brougham, MP speaking in the House today… Which reminds me, I en't set eyes upon a paper all day long, and that won't do.'

'Have you not?' he said, knowing quite well that she hadn't, because he had hidden them away himself. There was an item in *The Times* that he thought it better she didn't see. It would have spoilt all her enjoyment in the wedding.

'I shall read 'em all now, so I shall,' she said, 'while we have one last brandy. Where've they been put?'

So he had to produce them for her, and drink brandy with apparent calm while she went through them, one after the other. *The Times* was the third in the pile, but the news didn't disturb her in the least. 'Why sithee here,' she said, 'Mr Fuseli is dead. Fancy that! Died in Putney, it says, suddenly while visiting friends. Aged eighty-three. Well, well, well! I shall go and see Sophie in the morning.'

'Must you, my dear?' he protested mildly.

'Indeed I must. Can you give me one reason why I shouldn't?'

'You have comforted so many mourners in the last few months. One more might prove too much. Even for you.'

'My heart alive!' she laughed. 'You don't know Sophie, nor the life they've been leading, apart for all these years. She won't mourn. I can tell 'ee.'

CHAPTER 34

I n all the years she'd known her old friend Sophie Fuseli, Nan Easter had only visited her at home on three occasions, and the last had been more than twenty years ago when they were both in love with that old rogue Calverley Leigh. It was really rather odd to be driving towards the house now, with Mr Fuseli dead.

'The missus is in the garden,' the maid said. 'She said you might visit. You've to go through, if you please.'

In the garden? Nan thought. On such a blustery day? What's she doing in the garden?

She was standing in the middle of the vegetable patch beside a bonfire nearly as tall as she was, feeding it with large pieces of paper. She was wrapped in her blue and red velvet cloak, which flapped and swirled about her in the wind, curving and uncoiling in the sort of sinuous swelling shapes that her husband had painted so often and so well. There were neat red boots on her feet and her grey hair was covered by a bright red Parisian bonnet trimmed with ostrich feathers. She looked delectable and perfectly happy.

'What *are* you doing?' Nan said, joining her in front of the blaze.

'Cleansing the stables,' Sophie said, tossing two more papers on to the fire. 'I'm so glad to see you, my dear. They bring his body home tomorrow and all these must be burnt before they arrive.' And she waved her red gloved hand at a sack that lay at her feet.

Nan bent and pulled a handful of papers out of the sack. They were pencil drawings, the top one a sketch of two naked men playing leapfrog. Fuseli's drawings. 'Sophie!' she said in astonishment. 'You en't burning his drawings, surely.'

'Indeed I am,' Sophie said, burning three more. 'Throw them in. Nasty, mucky things.'

'But they belong to the nation. His great art, *The Times* said.'

'Take a closer look.' Sophie said, pausing in her work. 'You ain't seen what you're a-holding.'

So Nan looked again and got a shock. 'My heart alive!' she said staring. 'My dear heart alive!'

'And that's one of the milder variety,' Sophie said, glancing at it. 'Into the fire with 'em. 'Tis all they're fit for.'

The worked until the sky darkened and every single painting and drawing had been reduced to ashes. All that was left of the great artist's pornographic horde were half a dozen scraps of well-burnt paper floating soft, fragile and crinkled, like pale grey silk amongst the scarlet sparks.

'Well that's that,' Sophie said with great satisfaction. 'Where shall we dine?'

They went to Mr Babcock's in the Strand and made an excellent meal together, and neither of them mentioned Heinrich Fuseli's death nor his widow's future until they reached the brandy.

'How will you manage now he's gone?' Nan asked. 'Are you provided for?'

'Well now as to that,' Sophie said roguishly. 'I've made provision for myself. I've a pretty penny saved over the years and now I mean to buy an inn on one of the great roads out of London and become "mine host". Mine host in petticoats. What do 'ee think?'

'A capital idea,' Nan said. 'I'll be your first customer.'

And although she wasn't the first, for there were rather a lot of other things to attend to before she could go visiting, she was certainly the most honoured.

In May, Frederick was duly elected as Member of Parliament for Lostwithiel and gave a prestigious party to celebrate. In June, Matilda and Harriet took their children back to Bury for the summer and were relieved to see how well the place had recovered, even though many people were in mourning and many of the faces they saw were terribly scarred. At the end of the month Pollyanna's baby was born, a girl, christened Hannah by her doting father, and the apple of Bessie's eye. The newspaper trade went into a slight decline, which John took very seriously, of course, setting off on a tour of the midlands to see what could be done, but it was such a happy time that Nan paid little attention to such a minor setback.

Sophie took over her coaching inn at the beginning of July. 'A fine season for it,' she wrote on her 'particular invitation' to Nan and Frederick. 'I shall serve roast fowl to 'ee and green peas, and every fruit in season. The strawberries are quite excellent hereabouts, so I expect to see you both *very soon*. Given at the sign of the "Queen's Head", Islington. Hooray!'

So naturally they accepted her invitation, and it was a splendid meal, just as she'd promised, although the inn was very crowded and horribly noisy.

'What trade you do!' Nan said with admiration. 'How many coaches do you serve?'

'Twenty or more every single day, as ever is,' Sophie said with great satisfaction. 'I begin to know their names now,' and she rattled some of them off; 'the "York Highflyer", the "Leeds

Union", the "Stamford Regent", the "Rockingham", the "Truth and Daylight". Those three gentlemen in the corner came in on the "Truth and Daylight".

'Highly apposite,' Frederick said, 'since, if I am not mistaken, the one in the middle is a government spy.'

Both women turned at once to look at him.

'Fancy!' Sophie said. 'Now that's what my barman told me and I wouldn't believe him.'

But Nan said, 'Why, I know who he is. 'Tis Mr Richards, poor Thomasina's one-time lodger. Are you sure he's a spy?'

'If he is not, then there are two men hereabouts with fair hair and red moustaches and wearing identical clothes what's more. He works for Lord Sidmouth. They make no secret of it.'

'If he's a spy he pays uncommon well,' Sophie said.

'He would,' Frederick told her. 'Spying is lucrative employment.'

'Who does he spy upon?' Nan wanted to know.

'That I couldn't say for certain,' Frederick admitted. 'But I could hazard a guess. There's a move afoot to reintroduce the Combination Act, so a legal meeting that could be turned into a riot would be rather opportune, would it not?'

'That old trick!' Nan said. 'Who are his companions?'

'Never seen 'em before,' Sophie said. 'But I shall know 'em again if they mean to make a riot. I'll not have an affray in *my* inn, and there's an end on it.'

'Matilda will be pleased to know all this,' Nan said returning to her strawberries. 'She never did like him.'

MATILDA HAD QUITE RECOVERED from the horrors of the winter. It was such a happy summer and there were so many pleasures in it: balls at the Athenaeum, which Miss Pettie came out of her long hibernation to attend, picnics and parties and a splendid midsummer fair, which even cheered poor little Matty who'd been rather withdrawn since the smallpox, and no wonder when you considered how badly she was scarred. She and Jimmy were constant companions nowadays. They called themselves the gargoyles, which Matilda thought a joke in rather poor taste, but which Billy applauded.

'Plucky little devils!' he said admirably, when Matilda protested. 'I'd ha' done the same myself, so I would.'

''Tis Mr Thistlethwaite's doing I'll be bound,' Matilda said, not placated.

'Aye. Very likely,' Billy said. 'We've a deal to thank old Thiss for.'

The two children would have said exactly the same thing had their opinions been asked. They spent as much time with old Thiss as they could that summer, asking him endless questions and taking comfort from him at every opportunity.

'Sit in the sun all yer can,' he advised. 'That'll smooth them ol' scars out a treat, you see if it don't.'

'They'll never go away though, will they, Thiss?' Jimmy would say. He knew they wouldn't, but he needed the reassurance of hearing it said as though it were of no consequence.

'No,' Thiss said, ruffling the boy's fair hair. 'That don't matter though, do it? Handsome is as 'andsome does. My ol' woman don't think any worse a' me on account a' me physog. Fact, between you an' me an' the gatepost, I reckon I gets more love than most because of it.'

'Am I very ugly, Thiss?' Matty would ask, touching the worst of the pits on her cheeks with apprehensive fingers.

And he would swing her into the air and kiss her soundly.

'Prettiest gel I ever did see,' he told her. 'And quite the nicest. Give yer ol' Thiss a great big kiss.'

Oh, he was a great comfort.

. . .

ANNIE SPENT a quiet summer that year. She needed time to sit and remember, time to think and dream, and in his wisdom and affection James made sure she got it. The birth of Pollyanna's baby was a mixed pleasure, because it reminded her too painfully of the time her dear Beau had been born. But the child was a joy, there was no doubt of that, and Meg and Dotty were thrilled with her. And Harriet was the dearest of sisters, teaching all the little ones every morning, and staying with her in the garden nearly every afternoon when they weren't off on a picnic or to a fair or somesuch, and letting her talk and talk, and never wearying.

Actually Harriet found Annie's company extremely comforting, although she couldn't tell her so because that would have meant talking about John and seeming to criticise him, and that was unthinkable. Despite fine weather and healthy children and no further advertisements to upset him, he was still quite unable to make love, and now she was beginning to wonder fearfully whether it was her fault.

He had tried on two most unhappy occasions, his face tense with the anxiety of possible failure even when his body was ardent, but although she held him and kissed him as closely and lovingly as she could, nothing had happened, and it had upset him so dreadfully that she was almost glad now he had given up trying. But the knowledge of it, and the lack of love it caused, were private torments to both of them. John solved his misery by working harder than ever, travelling as much as he'd done when he was trying to prevent those awful advertisements and sitting up until two and three in the morning poring over his timetables. The less he slept the less sleep he seemed to need. And Harriet confided all her misery to her diary and took refuge in helping Annie, having discovered that helping somebody else through their unhappiness was quite the best way of taking her mind off her own. However, Caleb's letters were a difficulty of another kind.

The last one to arrive in Fitzroy Square had provoked an outburst of extraordinary bad temper. John had been calmly eating his ham and eggs, and reading *The Times* in his usual quiet way, when Mrs Toxteth brought in the post on its familiar silver platter. He gathered the envelopes into their usual neat pile beside his plate, and began to slit them open, one after the other as he always did. And suddenly he gave a roar and threw one of them straight across the table.

'Have we to endure this?' he shouted.

'What is it, John dear? Whatever is it?'

'I forbid these letters,' he said, his face dark with anger. 'Do you understand me, Harriet? I positively forbid them!'

She picked up the letter, her hand trembling, wondering what horror it might contain. 'Why 'tis from Mr Rawson,' she said, trying to stay calm and be reasonable. 'There is no harm in a letter from Mr Rawson, surely. He writes so kindly to us all and is uncommon fond of the children.'

'I forbid it,' he shouted. 'You ain't to receive 'em.'

'But I could hardly tell Mr Rawson not to write. That would be unmannerly.'

'If you don't, I will. Is that understood?'

She gave in to him at once. It wasn't important enough to argue about. It was only a letter. 'Very well,' she said. 'Yes, I understand.' But her voice was cold.

'I forbid it! Forbid it! Forbid it!' he cried, the words pecking the air. And he flung down his napkin, snatched up *The Times* and ran from the room, leaving his anger pulsing behind him.

Harriet sat where she was with the letter still in her hand. She was stunned by his violence. It was so unlike him. And all over such a thing as a letter. Had she really to write to Caleb and end their correspondence? It seemed uncommon hard, especially when his letters were such a comfort to her. And in any case, he would go on writing to Annie, for *she* wouldn't forbid him, so the situation could easily become ridiculous. My poor dear John, she thought. He suffers so much and says so little. Perhaps that is why he is so angry over a letter. What other reason could there be? Meantime what should she do about it? She had almost given her word not to receive any more letters. Almost, but not quite. She would have to think about it carefully. There was no need to make a decision yet. Poor, poor John.

It wasn't until later the next afternoon that she decided what to do, and then she was surprised by the ease of the solution. It was the sight of the letter that had roused her poor John to such passion, not the contents. Very well then, the answer was simple. She must arrange for the letters to be left in the post office for her to collect, then Caleb need not be upset or insulted by being told not to write to her, and John need not be upset or angered by seeing things he didn't want to see.

She wrote to Caleb that afternoon before John came home:

Would it be possible for you to address your letters to me Post Restante at Bury? When I am in Rattlesden it would be more convenient for me to collect my letters myself instead of having them collected for me. I travel to Rattlesden tomorrow and will answer your next letter from there.

Your true friend,
Harriet Easter.

Caleb was more pleased by that letter than by all the others she'd sent him since they first started to correspond. She means to keep my letters hidden, he thought, grinning to himself, an' if she means to keep my letters hidden, 'tis ten to one they're to be hidden from her husband. It's all a-falling out just as I foresaw. He's beginning to lose her. Well serve him right, poor fool. He don't value her sufficient.

The only trouble was that there was so much extra work available that summer and he really felt beholden to accept it.

There was a shortage of cheap gauze for shrouds, and there'd been a run on black bombazine too because of the epidemic. In one way this was all to the good, because it meant he could increase his earnings, in another it was an annoyance because he felt himself so close to success and could not travel to Rattlesden and take what he was sure was his. However, time was on his side, and there were plenty of other obliging women.

So the summer dreamed past, warm and easy and kept sweet by strong breezes. And Harriet collected her letters from the post office in Bury on her once-weekly trips into town and John knew nothing of it, because she was so careful and because he was so rarely at home. And August was nearly over when Matilda came to take tea with them all, in a new gown and full of excitement.

'You will never guess what I've just heard,' she said, when she and Harriet and Annie were settled on their cushions under the holm oak in the rectory gardens.

'No,' Annie agreed, laughing at her excitement. 'I don't suppose we shall, so you must tell us, must you not?'

'That lodger of Cousin Thomasina — you remember the one — is a government spy!' Matilda said triumphantly. 'What do 'ee think of that?'

Annie was interested at once. 'Mr Richards, do you mean?'

'The same.'

'You don't surprise me,' Annie said. 'How did you find out?'

Harriet was so shattered by the news she couldn't say anything. While Matilda told the tale, with happy embellishments, she sat perfectly still as though she were listening, her face controlled and her emotions in turmoil. A government spy, she thought, shivering. How dreadful. But of course. I should have known it. He knew so much about so many people and he turned up wherever there was trouble, wherever there was a political meeting, at the field of Peterloo, here at the Hampden Club that night, sending Caleb to Norwich and the

Abbotts to Cato Street. A government spy! I ought to have realised.

'I always knew he was a wrong 'un,' Matilda was saying with great satisfaction. 'He had a deal too much side, addressing people of quality as though he were their equal. Well now we know all about *him*. Ain't it a caution?'

Caution, Harriet thought, catching the word in its other meaning. Oh yes, we shall all have to proceed with caution now. If Mr Richards is a government spy, he mustn't be told anything more about any of us. How wise John was not to trust him. I must warn Caleb. I will write to him tonight, and tomorrow morning I will take the pony cart into Bury and pay my duty visit to Mama and post my letter and see if he has written to me. The sun was casting dappled patterns through the branches of the oak tree onto the soft flowered cotton of her skirt and she could hear the voices of the children lilting and piping as bright as birds somewhere behind the house. Such a beautiful day, she thought, and yet there is danger all around us. First the smallpox and now this.

The next day was easy with sunshine too. Will said he didn't mind being left with Rosie at all. She and Aunt Annie and Pollyanna and Peg Mullins had a picnic planned and he would rather go on a picnic than visit grandmother Sowerby, if Mama said he could. So Harriet set off on her errands alone, with Tom to drive the pony cart.

Her mother treated her to her usual mixture of gossip and complaint, which she endured for the statuary hour as patiently as she could. Then she walked briskly back to, the post office and the waiting pony cart. There *was* a letter for her, just as she'd hoped. She stood in the post office, to one side of the counter, and opened it and read it.

My dear Harriet,
    There's been a deal happened since I wrote thee last. News came on

Thursday that Parliament means for to foist another Combination Act upon us after all our good work to the contrary. Meetings are to be rendered illegal again and on t' quiet-like so we must watch out. 'Tis a scandal and not to be endured. We began to put our minds to it straight away to find means to oppose it.

By great good fortune we heard last night that we've a first-rate opportunity served up to us in this very town. Tha friend Mr Richards were here in Norwich yesternight to tell us that Lord Harrowby comes here 26th August to visit his friend, Lord Suffield, a man much respected hereabouts on account of his views concerning land reform. If 'twere up to him t' land would be restored to those who labour on it. A fine man, I can tell thee, and one who works for reform.

With Mr Richards's help we have devised us a plan. We are to gather before the Guildhall (where the two lords will be dining according to Mr Richards) with banners on t' Tuesday evening, there to petition him for his help in t' matter and t' help of his friend Lord Harrowby.

I will write again when more is known or to tell thee of our success.

Thy loving friend in every endeavour,
Caleb Rawson.

He mustn't do it, she thought. 'Twill be another trap as sure as fate. And she looked around her for pen and ink so that she could add a warning postscript to her letter before she sealed it. And her eye noticed the date in its oak case beneath the clock: 'Tuesday 26th August 1825.' But it's today, she thought. Today. There was no time to send a letter. If Caleb and his friends were to be warned in time she would have to go to Norwich and tell them herself.

She put both letters into her reticule and ran out to the pony cart.

'I have to go to Norwich,' she said to an astonished Tom.

'Take the cart home, if you please. I will catch the night coach back home. Peg is not to sit up. 'Twill suffice if she leaves the door upon the latch for me.'

And she was gone, tripping off downhill towards Angel Square and the early afternoon coach to Scole and Norwich.

It was well past six o'clock when she arrived in Castle Meadow. There wasn't a minute to lose.

CHAPTER 35

Preparations for that evening's march to the Guildhall were well under way. The banners were stitched and the petition forms ruled and as soon as work was over for the day and the weavers had snatched a bite to eat, they would begin to gather in the Market Square. Caleb had worked all day with his head full of plans and counterplans, so he was very surprised when left his loom and came down the stairs from the attic to find Harriet waiting for him on the landing. She was the last person he expected to see in Norwich that day.

But surprise immediately gave way to pleasure. 'Harriet!' he said, beaming at her. 'My dear Harriet, what brings thee up to Norwich? Hast tha come for t' meeting?'

'In a manner of speaking, yes, I suppose I have,' she said, and then he noticed that she was looking anxious and biting her bottom lip.

'Come in, come in,' he said, opening the door to his room and standing aside to let her enter first. 'I'm about to send out for a bit o' supper. Happen tha'll join me?'

She stood hesitantly just outside the door, looking round at the whitewashed walls covered with prints and posters, and the

495

fire red in a polished grate, and the bright curtains, and the heavy woven bedspread on his single bed, noticing how house-proud he was and how well he kept the room. I am alone in a gentleman's bedroom, she thought, alone and unchaperoned, and she knew it wasn't at all proper, and that she really shouldn't be there, and she couldn't think what to say.

But Caleb was perfectly at ease. 'Come now,' he said, 'I'll mek thee a dish of tea, and tha shall tell me why tha's come to see me. Sit down, sit down.' Normally he would have supped ale with his chop but in her honour, it should be tea. And he pulled his two cane chairs closer to the table by the window and held one out for her.

She hung her bonnet and shawl on the hook behind the door, put her reticule on the table and sat down nervously, watching while he filled an old black kettle from the covered jug on the dresser, and set it to boil on the hob. It was very warm in the room, for the fire had been burning since five o'clock, ready for cooking. 'You mustn't go to the meeting tonight,' she said abruptly.

'Must I not?' he said, putting two cups on the table.

'No indeed,' she said earnestly. 'You are betrayed, Caleb. Mr Richards is a spy.'

He understood everything so quickly, standing beside her chair, so close to her and so powerful, those blunt hands inches away from her eyes, the dark hairs on his fingers bristling. 'Who told thee?'

'Nan Easter told Matilda and Matilda told me. There's no doubt of it, Caleb. Nan had it from Mr Brougham. Matilda said it was no secret. The government would like a riot to prove the need for another Combination Act.'

He considered what she was saying, looking down at her, but far too calmly, and smiling at her as though the matter were amusing. 'Aye, 'tis likely. That's the way they work. Allus have done.'

His calm agitated her. 'Oh you mustn't go to the meeting,' she cried. 'You would be walking into a trap, don't you see?'

He had his arms about her and was lifting her from the chair before she realised what was happening. 'Caleb!' she said, but he was kissing her, smothering the word back into her throat. And kissing with such passion, so hard and strong and demanding, his eyes blazing and his hands holding her waist and shoulders so that she was locked against him.

'We mustn't.' she said breathlessly when the kiss stopped at last. 'Caleb, it's not right.'

'Tha loves me,' he said. 'Why else wouldst tha've come all this way with tha warning? Tha loves me, as I love thee.' And before she could answer, or even think of an answer, he kissed her again so pleasurably that despite herself she began to kiss him back.

This can't be happening, she thought, as the kiss went on, and she could feel his member huge and hard against her belly even through the cloth of their clothes. We must stop. I must make him stop. It's not right. I must... But sensation was making thought difficult, fractured, impossible, non-existent. Oh, to be kissed again, after all this time!

'I've loved thee for years an' years,' he said, stroking her back. 'Years an' years an' years.' How red his mouth was and how oddly he smelt. Like a gluepot. 'I allus knew 'twould be so.' Kissing her so long and so hard. 'Harriet, my own dear love.'

He was making her feel dizzy. 'We mustn't...' she cried, struggling to put her hands against his chest to push him away. But he was so strong and so urgent, lifting her off her feet, kissing her as he carried her backwards towards the bed. It is wrong, she thought. I must stop him. But, how could she? What words would she use? There were no words left in her head. Only sensation and confusion and everything happening too quickly for her to cope with it. She knew in a vague way that it would humiliate him to be denied, and that she admired him too much to want to humiliate him, a *good* man, enduring prison, working so hard for the cause, so brave and dependable. And yet. And yet. Should such a man be acting as he was? No, surely not. It is wrong. I must stop him, she thought again, as she landed on the rough weave of the coverlet. But part of her didn't want to stop him and she knew that too, although she was too confused to feel ashamed, and aroused too little to feel justified. Oh what did she want? She didn't even know that. If only he would stop and give her the chance to think. But they had already gone too far, too quickly. He was pushing up her gown, bunching it about her waist, he was on top of her, so hard and close she could barely breathe, the cloth of his waistcoat scratching her cheek, he was inside her, thrusting hard. It was too late to stop him. Too late to say anything. Too late.

It was all over so quickly. Even in her present state of confusion she was amazed at how quick he was and how easily he recovered, sitting up almost at once, straightening her skirt, adjusting his trousers, ambling off across the room to attend to the kettle. He made her feel more guilty than ever. She couldn't look at him, she simply couldn't. She turned her burning face to the wall and covered her eyes with her hands.

He was busying himself at the fire, riddling ash and splitting a coal with the poker, crick-crack, clacking the lid of the kettle, whistling to himself. Then his boots clomped cross the floor and she heard the door open and close. Then silence. He hasn't left me, surely, she thought. But the silence went on, except for the crackle of the fire, and presently she turned her head cautiously to see where he was. The room was empty.

She was almost as surprised by his abrupt departure as she'd been by his precipitate lovemaking. But at least it gave her the chance to recover herself. She got up and straightened her gown and found her cap which had fallen off her head onto the floor. Then she smoothed the creases out of the coverlet and tiptoed across the room to the little looking glass hanging from its nail beside the dresser and did her best to tidy her hair. I must make myself look respectable, she thought. But the thought was ridiculous. I am not respectable, she told herself. Not any longer. I am the most grievous sinner. I have committed adultery. But none of these things had any meaning. It was as if she'd moved beyond meaning, beyond sensation, beyond thought, into the most extraordinary calm, so that 'I am the most grievous sinner' and 'now I will make the tea' had exactly the same validity.

And while she was standing before the mirror wondering at her lack of emotion, he came back into the room. 'I've bought us a fine pair of chump chops,' he told her, 'and for thee, lass...' He pulled a peach from the pocket of his jacket and laid it tenderly before her.

She was touched, despite her guilt and her confusion and that odd overriding calm, for he certainly couldn't afford such an extravagant fruit, and the affection on his face was unmistakable. 'Thank 'ee,' she said. 'You are very kind. Shall I make the tea?'

So she made the tea while he cooked the chops in a battered frying pan set on top of the coals, and they sat down to their rough meal together at the table beside the window. And Harriet discovered that she was hungry and was glad of the food he'd provided and enjoyed every mouthful, but distantly, as though it were being eaten by somebody else. And they talked of the price of cloth and the children's health and the progress of her little school. It was all a little unreal.

'Now,' he said, when the meal was done, 'we must make haste. 'Tis no'but twenty minutes till t' start of t' meeting.'

'The meeting?' she said, bemused. 'Surely you don't intend to go to the meeting now. Not after — all this.' And she looked at the bed and then blushed at her indelicacy, for she hadn't meant to imply that she'd allowed him to make love to her simply to stop him from going to the meeting. Had she?

'My word's been given,' he said. 'There's nought for it. I must go.'

'But you will be arrested again.'

'I think not,' he said easily. 'And if I am, what o' that? 'Tis all within t' law.'

'Please,' she said, feeling that she must make an effort to stop him. 'I came all this way to stop you. You mustn't go. Mr Richards has laid a trap for you.'

'Aye,' he said. 'Happen he has, but I must go, all t' same. 'Twere on my persuasion t' meeting were called. I'm duty bound to attend, d'ye see? 'Tis a matter of principle. I'll not let t'others down. They depend upon me to be there.' And from the noise of trudging feet outside on the landing and the growl of voices in the street below them the others were already gathering, pulling him by their presence.

A matter of principle, she thought, weary resignation and her odd passivity pulling her down. He will go. I cannot prevent him. 'Yes,' she said. 'Yes, I see that. Then I will come with you.'

He was disappointed. 'I thought tha'd stay here,' he said. 'Be here when I get back, like.'

'No,' she said, taking her shawl from the hook and wrapping it about her shoulders. 'I shall come with you. I mean to see justice done.' And she put on her bonnet, as though no more need be said.

'Eh!' he said, following her out of the door. 'What a grand lass tha'art, my Harriet.'

The street was full of people, men in their working clothes, women in linen bonnets and heavy shawls, all milling about in the dusk, too excited to stand still. Two men had a homemade banner coiled between them and a third was standing beside the door firing a bundle of about twenty rush lights that were to be carried as torches. The blaze of them took away all other light from the doorway, so that Caleb stepped through darkness to join his friends. And what a cheer they gave him. 'Good old Caleb! Tha's our Caleb!'

'All set?' he asked.

And the crowd bubbled about him, eyes glinting. 'En't we jest!' 'We'll show them ol' mawthers a thing or two.' 'Jest you lead on, bor!' And somehow or other, for no orders were given, they formed themselves into a column, a long column of dark heads and smoking lights, and went marching up King Street, singing as they went, with Caleb at their head, and Harriet tagging along beside him, running a little from time to time to keep with them all, so brisk was the pace they set.

The erupted out of Davey Place into the Market Square just as the clocks were striking eight. Darkness was setting in, but there were so many torches already in the square that it was possible to see quite clearly from one side to the other. Over by the Guildhall a husting had been erected, with an awning above it, all green and white stripes like a sugar stick. 'That's where I've to be,' Caleb said, looking over his shoulder at Harriet. 'Stay here by the alley. Happen they'll provoke us, and I'd not like to see thee hurt.'

She hesitated for just a second, uncertain whether to obey him or not, and the march surged forward, carrying him on towards the hustings and leaving her behind. Perhaps it was for the best, she thought. There seemed to be an inevitability about everything that was happening on this peculiar day, and this calm of hers made acceptance easy. Perhaps it was meant to be.

It was very noisy in the square and very crowded as more marchers arrived to flock between the deserted stalls, and mass in the space before the old Guildhall, their banners floating illegibly in and out of the light and their torches bobbing like buoys on rough water. Caleb had reached the hustings and was climbing up the steps, urged on by a flurry of hands, and five other men were climbing behind him. One carried a bundle of petition forms which he waved at the crowd. It all looked cheerful enough, and there was no sign of troops or constables.

Then the crowd hushed itself, and gradually grew still to hear what the first speaker had to say. He was a sturdy-looking man and he had a strong voice. Harriet could hear him from where she stood.

'Friends,' he said, 'we've come here this night, for to send a message to the two noble gentlemen, the Earl of Harrowby and Lord Suffield, who are here to dine in the Guildhall behind us. Let's give 'em a cheer since there en't more than six inches o' stone wall here atween us.'

And a cheer was given. Hurrah! Hurray!

Why it's just like Peterloo, Harriet thought. Mr Hunt asked that crowd to cheer when the constables arrived. And the memory struck chill. But the man went on speaking, less clearly now and at greater length, and there was still no sign of the constables. And then another man spoke, and another, and nothing untoward happened. Perhaps it was simply going to be a quiet meeting after all. She couldn't hear what any of them was saying, partly because they spoke too quickly and partly because the people all around her were talking to one another, but when the third speaker stopped, he waved his hand towards Caleb and was plainly introducing him, and then the crowd shushed silent again. 'Mr Caleb Rawson.'

He stood at the edge of the hustings, holding up his right hand, waiting as the torches steadied and the banners were set down and ranks of white faces turned towards him out of the darkness. He could see his Harriet pale as a statue on the corner of Davey Place, her shawl a dark cross against the pale cotton of her gown, and he was glad she had obeyed him and stayed in a safe place. 'Friends,' he said.

There was a rush of bodies behind him. He glanced over his shoulder to see what it was. Four constables were clambering up the back of the hustings. The awning was being torn down.

More dark figures were climbing. He could see a pistol, two, three. Constables were swarming towards him from every direction.

'What's this?' he said, turning to face them. There was a burly constable standing right in front of him.

'Riotous assembly,' the man said, leering. The light from the torches below them made his face look like a mask, with huge black nostrils flaring, and black pits for eyes and a down-turned menacing mouth. 'Riotous assembly.'

'Nay,' Caleb said, with some pride. ''Tis a peaceful meeting. We've no riot here.'

'Try this for riot then, bor,' the man said, and punched Caleb in the stomach.

The blow was so sudden and unexpected it winded him. For a few seconds he staggered backwards, gasping for breath, as bodies rushed and hurled all round him, shouting and swearing. Then he recovered a little and saw that his friends were punching back, attacking the constables, and he knew he had to do something to stop them. 'Nay!' he said again, putting out an arm to restrain his nearest ally. 'Think on't, Amos. Think how 'twill look in court.'

'You think on it, bor,' his tormentor said, seizing his arm and twisting it behind his back. 'Since you'm all a-being' arrested. Here's an end to your fine ol' tricks, bor.'

Thoughts plummeted into Caleb's brain too quickly to become words. He simply knew them. She was right. They were all in danger. He must warn the others. He struggled with all his might against the strength of his captor, pulling the man with him to the edge of the platform. 'Disperse!' he yelled at the crowd. 'We are betrayed. Mr Richards is a spy. Disperse. They will call out t' troops.'

Then two more constables joined the struggle and he was pulled from the hustings and thrown to the ground and kicked. And then they were marching him away. But he'd heard his voice echoing across the square, he'd seen understanding in the faces below him, the warnings had been given.

Harriet was still entirely calm. She watched the whole thing as though she were at a play. There you see, he's being arrested. I knew he would be. I *did* try to warn him. She wasn't even shocked by her lack of emotion. When the crowd obeyed him and began to run out of the square, she turned and went with them, walking sedately among their flying feet and outstretched hands.

The night coach was standing outside the Bell Inn, its inside passengers peering from the windows at the rush. She produced her ticket from her reticule, showed it to the coachman without word or expression and climbed to an outside seat. Now she would go home. She would drive away from this nightmare and go home to her nice quiet house in sensible Rattlesden. To dear Will and dear Annie and dear James. Home.

She was the only passenger on the cold outside seats and that pleased her, for conversation would have been impossible. She felt as though all words had been frozen inside her head. She watched the ostlers and post-boys at work as though they were in another world and when the coachmen told his team to 'walk on' she sat back in her seat and began to count the lighted windows as they flickered past. And in this odd detached state she travelled through the countryside.

There was a full moon that night, clear and ice-white, whenever she could see it, but it gave the most fitful light, because it was obscured by a fast-moving torrent of blue-black clouds, some no more than a trail of blue gauze, others dense and black as ink. Sometimes she saw the road below her quite clearly and sometimes she was rocked forward in total darkness. It is like my life, she thought, as the hooves drummed on, sometimes so clear and easy, sometimes obscured by sin. But the thought was distant, too, as though she were thinking of someone else, and after a few more miles her mind emptied altogether and she wasn't thinking at all. Nothing was real now. Nothing was happening. The hours and miles rolled past together.

They passed the White Hart at Scole and made a brief stop at Stowmarket while she sat where she was and waited quietly, thinking of nothing. Then they were off again. 'If you would be so kind as to put me off at Woolpit, sir,' she said to the coachman as he gathered the reins.

Which he did, and she climbed down, moving slowly and carefully, thinking of nothing, but remembering to thank him.

She watched until the lights of the coach swayed towards the bend of the road, flickered and were gone, all at once as if they'd both been doused together. Then she set off to walk the rest of the way home, following the farm path south through the fields, walking automatically, thinking of nothing.

And there was her house, its pale pink walls pure white in the light of the moon. The door was on the latch, and there were candle and tinder box set on the window ledge ready to light her way. But she climbed the stairs in darkness, following the curve of the walls with her hands, and at long, long last, she was home, in her own room, falling face downwards onto her own bed, the bed she shared with her own dear John, home and safe. And her grief broke into anguished weeping and she put her face into the pillows to stifle the sound, for it would never have done to wake Will. Thought returned hot and cruel like pincers in her brain, and she cried and cried and cried, weeping for her dear, dear John, because she'd been unfaithful to him, and he was so good and kind and he didn't deserve it, and for Caleb because he'd been arrested and she'd tried to warn him and she didn't know what they would do to him, and for her own terrible, unpardonable sin. Thou shalt not commit adultery. Adultery. Adultery. She had broken her marriage vows and there was no health in her. 'Oh!' she moaned into the pillow. 'What shall I do? Whatever shall I do?'

It was dawn before the crying stopped and by then she was

totally exhausted and fell asleep where she was, face down on the pillows and still fully dressed in all her clothes. Which was how Peg Mullins found her, when she came in at seven o'clock with her mistress's early morning tea.

'Lawks a' mussy, Mrs Easter,' she said. 'Why didn'tcher call me, when you come in instead a' goin' off like that? Your feet'll be all swole up. Let's have them boots off quick.'

And they were swollen, so that the tops of her boots were cutting into her flesh. A bowl of cold water had to be fetched and cold compresses applied at once, and Will came into the bedroom wakened by all the fuss and was most concerned when he saw his mother's ankles and insisted on rubbing them to make them better. And then Rosie arrived and held the tea for her to drink as if she were a baby, even though she protested weakly, 'I can manage, Rosie.'

'Manage, yes,' Rosie said holding the cup firmly beneath her chin. 'Manage.' And the word was not an agreement but an instruction for the tea to be drunk at once without argument.

They are all so kind to me, Harriet reflected as she sipped the tea. So kind and so dear. How can I possibly tell them how evil I have been? And as the taste of the tea soothed her mouth, and Will's small busy hands soothed her feet, the words of old Cosmo Teshmaker came back into her mind: 'Lie low, keep mum and wait for the matter to blow over.' Would that be possible? Oh please, Lord, let it be possible! I did not mean to sin. Truly I didn't. Let it be possible. And then she felt ashamed of herself for pleading with God. I must take the consequences of this sin, she thought, whatever they are. But not yet. Not just yet.

'We've got ducks' eggs for breakfast,' Will said happily. 'Aunt Annie brought them over yesterday. Are you better, now Mama?'

'Yes,' she said, smiling at him because he was being so loving. 'How silly of me to fall asleep in my clothes.'

'That's what comes a' midnight coaches, mum,' Peg said, removing the compresses.

'Did you travel on the midnight coach, Mama?' Will said. 'Was it dark?'

'Very dark.'

'Were you stopped by highwaymen?'

'Why, bless the boy,' Peg laughed. 'Would she be here if she had?'

'If she had,' Rosie echoed, laughing too.

I will take each moment as it comes, Harriet decided. That's what I'll do. There's no sense in provoking trouble. I will wait. There is no need to say anything yet. 'I think I'd better dress and start the day,' she said.

'You got a letter from Mr Easter, mum,' Peg told her as they all left the room. 'Come yesterday.'

He was in Cambridge and would travel on to Rattlesden in four days' time.

Mama has some wild scheme to take us all off to Stockton, to ride in a carriage drawn by puffing billy, if you ever heard of such a thing. It will please the children, I suppose, but I could do without such jaunts. These locomotives are mere toys and like to remain so. I cannot see how they will ever carry passengers as coaches do. In my opinion we should not bother with them. Howsomever, she comes to Bury in a week's time and proposes to tell us all about it then. You are much missed, my dear love,

Your own,
John.

There is always something happening in this family, Harriet thought. And for once in her life she was very glad of it.

CHAPTER 36

'I s that *it*, Nanna?' Will asked.

'That's it,' Nan said. 'That's a locomotive. The wonder of the age, so they say. What do 'ee think of it?'

Will considered the wonder of the age for several seconds, concentrating as well as he could for the pressure and noise of the crowd all around them. 'It looks like a water tank on wheels,' he said. 'A round one, with valves and things all over it and a box of coal up behind it.'

His father laughed out loud. 'A capital answer, Will,' he said. 'I'm blessed if I ever heard better. A water tank on wheels, eh Mama?'

'With the power of thirty horses, don't 'ee forget,' Nan said, grinning at them both.

The grand opening of the Stockton and Darlington Railway had attracted an even bigger crowd than the organisers had hoped. Hundreds of people had arrived from Middlesbrough and Darlington, of course. That was to be expected. But there were coachloads from York and Leeds and Harrogate too, and it was even rumoured among the locals that there were visitors who had travelled there from as far afield as London and Manchester. It was a great occasion, and the local street sellers did a roaring trade in hot pies and baked potatoes, shrimps and cockles, books and ballads and balloons. In fact there were so many people standing along the banks of the Tee that afternoon or ambling up and down on rather startled horses, and so many carts and carriages lined up on the rough track behind them that a casual observer could have been forgiven for supposing that he had stumbled upon a royal progress.

The focus of all their attention perched on two narrow rails between the crowd and the river, occasionally blowing a small round cloud of steam from the long stovepipe that stuck into the air where the horse's head would have been if it had truly been a carriage. It didn't look capable of moving, leave alone pulling all the open carriages that were attached behind it.

'Will it really roll along those little rails, Nanna?' Meg wanted to know.

'So they say.'

'It smells horrid,' Matty said wrinkling her nose.

'How will the driver see where he's going with that great pipe sticking up in front of him?' Jimmy said. He'd been feeling concerned for the driver ever since they arrived. This locomotive looked a rackety old thing when you got up close to it, and he was sure it wasn't safe to be balanced on rails like that.

The three seven-year-olds stood in a group together right at the front of the crowd where Nan had pushed them, with Jimmy closely protective behind them. But Dotty and Edward hung back, clinging to their grandmother's hands, nervous in such a vast crowd, and a little afraid of the great iron machine they were all supposed to be admiring.

'It won't come off the rails will it?' Edward asked. It would squash them all if it did.

But Nan didn't have time to reassure him because one of the officials was beaming towards her. 'This way, Mrs Easter ma'am, this way. If you and your party would be so good as to take your seats, ma'am. You are in the second carriage.'

The second carriage was a crude open cart with wooden seats set all around the sides. It was extremely uncomfortable but it gave them a fine view of the crowds agog with excitement on their right-hand side, and the river peacefully minding its own business on the left, and the wonder of the age before them now busily puffing more steam through its tall stovepipe.

They were a large party, so they had the carriage to themselves, Nan and John and Billy sitting on the left-hand side, Harriet and Matilda on the right, with the six children distributed between them. People were climbing up into the carriages all along the track. And the wind was freshening.

'If it rains,' Matilda said, 'we shall all be absolutely soaked.' She had joined this silly jaunt on sufferance and because Billy had begged her to, but really, all this way just to sit in a cart!

'There's a man on horseback in the middle of the track,' Jimmy said. Now that was better. A horse was dependable. You knew where you were with a horse.

'He's come to lead us to Darlington,' Nan said.

'Why is he carrying a red flag?' Will wanted to know.

'To let people know we're on the move.'

'But we're not,' Meg said.

The locomotive gave a sudden sharp shriek as if it was surprised and began to glide along the rails, slowly at first so that the movement was barely perceptible, but then gradually picking up speed. And the crowds cheered and a shower of black smut fell backwards out of the stovepipe all over the illustrious guests in the first carriage.

'Well if that's how it's going to go on,' Matilda said crossly, 'I shall put up my umbrella.' Which she did. 'I see no reason why we should be covered in filth for our pains.'

But Harriet endured and said nothing, just as she'd been doing ever since that shameful night. She lived in a daily nightmare, outwardly running the household and going to market and teaching the children and trying to answer Will's endless questions, but inwardly anguished by shame and remorse, and terrified in case somebody had seen her in King Street, or Caleb wrote to the house, or her parents got to hear of it. Four days after her return she'd taken the pony cart into Bury and blushingly asked for letters at the post office. To her great relief he'd remembered to be discreet, but the letter he sent crushed her chest with a new fear.

There are seven of us kept here and t' cell is a right foul hole, wi' rotten vittles and foul air. But no matter. They've set trial for the Quarter Sessions at the start of October, so we've to endure a month of it, wi' good consciences for company. That is all they'll keep us, be sure of that, being we've committed no crime.

Thine own, imprisoned or free,
  Caleb.

I will write to him the moment he is free, she told her diary when she'd burnt the letter.

However painful it might be to him he must be told that I mean to stay faithful to my dear John from henceforth. But I cannot send such a letter to him now. That would be too cruel. Time enough when the trial is over and he is free again. It will be easier for him to accept such tidings then.

The decision eased her, making her feel that she was beginning to right the great wrong she'd done, and that all might yet be well despite of it. But then, as the days passed and the nightmares receded, she began to suspect that there was another and even more terrible price to pay for her transgression. For the last two weeks she'd been smothering a secret so dreadful that travelling in an open cart or being showered with soot was trivial by comparison. She had 'seen' nothing since a fortnight before that terrible evening in Norwich, and now with every new unstained day she grew more and more afraid that she was pregnant.

She did her best to stay calm and keep cheerful, but the suspicion weighed upon her so heavily she was perpetually dragged by it, no matter what she did to occupy herself. She wrote to her diary every afternoon, before John came home from work, reporting *'No change'*, or trying to persuade herself that she had miscalculated, or hoping that she might just have missed a month, but the writing didn't help her at all, and afterwards as she hid the book underneath the mattress, she was miserably aware that if she *was* pregnant, it was a secret she wouldn't be able to hide for ever. Sooner or later everybody would know, and John would be the first.

It was a relief to her to be involved in this expedition. It gave her plenty to do and quite a lot to think about and it took her far away from Norwich at the time of the trial, which could have been distressing as it was bound to be reported in detail and that would recall all the events of that evening. It was much better for her to be away. Now she could simply hear the good news of their acquittal when she returned, and meantime she was in Nan's cheerful company, with plenty to see and plenty to do and plenty of children to keep her busy.

But now, as the locomotive picked up speed and the crowds were left behind, she suddenly found herself peculiarly alone. Everybody else was occupied: Jimmy and Matty talking to Matilda, huddled together under her umbrella, Will questioning Nan, Edward and Billy in deep conversation, John nursing Dotty and holding Meg's hand. And her thoughts went sliding back to their incessant preoccupation. She couldn't stop them.

'We shall soon be there,' Nan said.

John smiled at her. 'You may say what you like about this

locomotive, Mama,' he said, 'but I tell 'ee 'twill never replace the stagecoach. Never in a million years.'

And Matty was suddenly and violently sick all over her father's new trousers.

'Ugh!' Meg said and began to retch in sympathy.

'Over the side of the carriage, if you please,' John said, turning her body adroitly and not a moment too soon.

'Oh dear!' Harriet said, for the smell of vomit was turning her stomach. 'Oh dear!' And then she was hanging over the side of the carriage too.

'My heart alive,' Nan said. 'What weak stomachs you've got the lot of you.'

'If you ask me,' Matilda said, withdrawing her skirts from the mess, 'Annie and James had the best idea, staying at home.'

'Cheer up, Tilda,' Billy said, cheerfully giving his trousers a shake, 'it ain't your clothes she's ruined and we're in sight of Darlington.'

'And not a minute before time,' Matilda said. 'The sooner this thing stops the better. I never was so uncomfortable in my life. You come with me, Harriet my dear. Billy can look after the littluns.'

She was full of tender concern, helping Harriet out of the carriage the minute their journey was over and the chocks were in place, holding her arm as they walked towards the inn, settling her into the most comfortable chair she could find and then rushing off to order soap and warm water and clean towels. 'I've told 'em to brew a nice dish of raspberry tea,' she said confidentially. ''Tis the best thing I know for your kind of sickness, depend upon it.'

'Thank 'ee,' Harriet said weakly. She still felt nauseous and raspberry tea would be calming. 'You are so good to me, Matilda.'

'And so I should think,' Matilda said stoutly, 'after all you did for us when our Matty was ill. Are you restored just a little my dear? Now tell me, do.'

'Oh yes,' Harriet assured her. 'I am quite myself again.'

''Tis always the same when one carries,' Matilda said carelessly. 'I was sick every single day, I remember. You do breed, do you not?'

She knows, Harriet thought. Oh dear God, not yet! Not so soon! And what little colour she had drained from her face. 'I cannot tell,' she stammered. 'I do not think so.'

'I'm sure on it,' Matilda said confidently. 'You wouldn't be so sick otherwise. Won't your John be pleased? And Mrs Easter, too.'

'Where *is* John?' Harriet said, trying to change the conversation.

'Gone off with his mother and that Mr Chaplin,' Matilda said, 'and all talking like ninepence.'

That was a surprise. 'Mr Chaplin? The coach king? Why whatever is he doing here? Surely he didn't ride on a locomotive?'

Her mother-in-law was saying much the same thing. 'I must confess I never thought to see *you* here, upon me life.'

'Reconnoitring the enemy position, Mrs Easter,' Mr Chaplin said cheerfully. 'If this is to be the new way to travel, I mean to know about it.'

'And *is* it to be the new way to travel, sir?' John asked. 'I found it mighty uncomfortable and a deal slower than a pair of horses.'

'Only time will tell us that,' Mr Chaplin said. 'On balance I think it as likely as not. Meantime I have taken shares in the Stockton and Darlington Company, and would advise you to do the same.'

'Have you so?' Nan said, her eyes shrewd. 'Then I declare I will take your advice.'

She would, John thought.

'We must travel back to London together,' she said, 'and you must tell me more.'

In the Guildhall at Norwich the Quarter Sessions were under way. The seven accused had been brought across from their squalid cells in the castle prison and shuffled into fresh air and daylight for the first time in more than a month.

'By t' end of this day,' Caleb whispered to his friends as they trudged up Guildhall Hill, 'we shall be free men again.'

'Aye,' his nearest neighbour whispered back, as they passed Mr Rossi's goldsmith's shop, and the brisk winds of early October buffeted downhill against their faces. 'God willin'!'

But it wasn't God's judgement they had to face that day. It was Justice Ormorod's. And Justice Ormorod was a personal friend to Lord Sidmouth.

He sat in legal glory on the high dais, a handsome man in his heavy wig and his rich red gown, and impressive too with a fine embonpoint and a resonant voice.

'A legal mind,' the clerk to the court approved to his junior as he wrote up the gentleman's judgement after the first case that morning: 'Mr Joseph Wiggins, driver of the 'Phenomena', fined £90 for having in his possession 36 head of partridge. I likes a judge with a legal mind. He'll know what to do with rioters, upon me life he will.'

Proceedings opened calmly, with an admirable statement from Justice Ormorod, assuring 'this court, the defendants and whomsoever else may be concerned with the outcome of this trial, that matters here this morning will be decided strictly according to the letter of the law and with no other considerations of any kind whatsoever being either permissible or possible.'

Caleb was much heartened by his words. 'Aye,' he muttered, 'a fair trial. 'Tis all we ask.'

And at first, as evidence was given in the slow pace and ponderous language of the judiciary, it all felt extremely fair. The seven weavers listened as witnesses were questioned with interminable patience as to the estimated number of people present, and the estimated number of torches the said people took with them, the direction in which the said people had been seen to be walking, or not walking, or marching as the case may be, whether or not banners were carried by the said people and what words were written upon the said banners. The court-room smelt of polished wood, new leather and ancient parchment, and a spiral of golden motes nudged and gentled in a visible beam of sunshine, falling slowly and delicately, to disappear into the grandeur of the judge's robes. The clerk to the court nodded off beside his table, and up in the public gallery the newspaper reporters were yawning like frogs.

But they sat up when judgement was given. 'On the first count of unlawful assembly,' Justice Ormorod opined, 'the facts as I see them are as follows: since the repeal of the Act of Combination, assemblies entered into for the purpose of discussion as to matters of trade are legal. Howsomever, this particular assembly was not called by the defendants to discuss trade. This assembly was called in order to express the defendants' displeasure at the proposed re-enactment of the Act of Combination, and as such was plainly unlawful. To my mind this was a riotous assembly and a riotous assembly of the worst possible kind. Consequently I find this charge proven.'

We are lost, Caleb thought, fear crushing his chest for the first time since his arrest. He means to find against us no matter what. We are lost. But the judge was speaking again, rolling onwards with the weight and implacability of a treadmill.

'On the second count of common assault, the evidence given by the constables, who were plainly punched and manhandled in the most grievous manner (and incidentally deserve the commendation of the court for the splendid manner in which they executed their duties in an uncommon difficult situation), this evidence, as I say, is sufficient to remove all doubt from my mind. I find this charge proven also.

'I shall therefore proceed to judgement and I shall give judgement upon each of the defendants in turn. Caleb Rawson will please to stand.'

Caleb stood, angered to discover that his legs were trembling. 'Are we not to say a word in our own defence?' he asked. 'We been waiting all morning to be called to give evidence.'

'What word could you say, sir?' the judge inquired, raising his eyebrows in an almost perceptible sneer.

'I could tell 'ee t' truth, sir. T' constables lied to 'ee, we could all tell 'ee that. T' first blow was struck by t' man over yonder. He struck me, sir, as he knows full well. Not another blow were struck 'til that moment, I give thee my word.'

The judge snorted. 'Am I to take the word of a common criminal against the word of one of His Majesty's constables, duly sworn?' he asked.

'I am a weaver, sir,' Caleb said, 'not a common criminal.'

'You are a common criminal, sir,' the judge replied coolly. 'You have a record. I sentence you to seven years penal servitude, to be served in His Majesty's penal colony in Van Dieman's Land. Jonathon Murdoch will please to stand.'

He sentenced them one after the other, seven years, five years, four years, but the number of years was meaningless. They were banished for life and they all knew it. I spent every minute I wasn't at t' loom, working to better t' lot of my fellow weavers, Caleb thought, shaking with anger at the injustice of it, and now I'm to be transported on t' word of a lying constable. 'What sort of justice is this?' he cried when the sentences were all given and the great book closed.

'British justice, sir,' the judge told him sternly. 'The best in the world, sir.'

The news was in all the London papers by the following morning.

Nan saw it as she was eating dinner at six o'clock that evening with her travelling family all around her. They were on their homeward journey now and had got as far as Stamford.

'Why look 'ee here, John,' she said. 'Norwich rioters to be transported. Caleb Rawson — en't that our Uncle Caleb?'

John took the paper calmly and read the news aloud so that they could all hear it. 'Yes,' he said. 'That's the man. It seems a little harsh, don't 'ee think, even if he did cause a riot.' He kept his face expressionless but inwardly he was smiling with triumph, even though he knew that triumph at such a time was really rather ugly. He'll do no more harm to us now, he was thinking. Not in Van Dieman's Land. We are free of him. And there'll be no more letters either.

Harriet was so shocked by the news she couldn't say anything. Transportation! How terrible! How unfair! When he was such a fine, good man, helping the injured at Peterloo, working for the weavers in Norwich. They'd only met to protest about this stupid law. Oh, if only he hadn't gone! If only none of them had gone! They'd never harmed anybody, and he'd always put other people's interests before his own. Except for that one humiliating time in Norwich, of course. But that was...

And then it occurred to her with a shameful lightening of heart, that he wouldn't be able to see her again, after all. She was free of that, at least. And for all her admiration of him, and her sorrow at his undeserved punishment, she knew that the emotion she was feeling was relief. And then she was more ashamed of herself than ever, for being selfish and thinking of her own situation rather than his when he was being transported. What could be worse than that? To be sent away from your friends and your family to live with savages on the other side of the world. Poor, poor Caleb. What a terrible punishment!

The conversation around the table had moved on. Billy was telling Will and Edward how a steam engine worked. John was brooding, and Nan and Matilda were planning their journeys for the following day.

'If you're to be up in the morning in time for the eight o'clock coach, young Edward,' Matilda told her younger offspring, 'then 'tis high time you were a-bed. Say goodnight to your father. I doubt you'll see him in the morning.'

'Not at the pace your grandmother keeps,' Billy said, grimacing. 'We've to be up at six in the morning, damn if we ain't. 'Tis an ungodly hour.' He and John were to travel to London with Nan while their wives took the road to Bury via Peterborough and Ely.

'Yes,' Harriet said, remembering her duties. 'Time you were a-bed, Will. The girls are half asleep already.' And so they were, their eyelids swollen with the need for rest.

I will clean the house, she thought, as she escorted the children upstairs to their rooms, and I will put flowers in all the rooms, and I will get Mrs Chiddum to help me cook a special meal for him on the day he gets back, and when he is as rested and easy as I can make him, I will confess. I *am* pregnant. There is no doubt about it. Caleb has been most cruelly punished and I still hide my sin. It is time to be honest.

It was so good to be back in Rattlesden again, with Annie and James and Pollyanna close by, and dear old Rosie in their quiet house. The high woods blazed with autumn colour, gold and purple and berry-red, and the fields had been ploughed brown while she'd been away. I belong here, she thought, hanging her washing over the bushes in her garden. It is so beautiful here and so peaceful. But the confession had to be made, nevertheless. She had made up her mind to it now and she would do it. It *had* to be done.

John came home a week later. He brought Will a mechanical toy, which he'd found in a tiny shop in Hatfield, and until Rosie took the boy to bed, the two of them played with it, sitting on the rug before the fire in the parlour, while Harriet set the table for her special meal.

But when her good food had been eaten, quietly and with hardly a word said, and the cloth had been removed, and the moment had finally arrived, her nerve failed her. She couldn't confess here, in the house. 'Should we take a turn through the village?' she said. ''Tis a fine evening.' And among the hedgerows it would be a private one.

'Yes,' he said, 'if you wish.' But he didn't smile or encourage her or say anything else. Oh, how difficult this was! It was almost as if he knew what she was going to say.

Dusk was clouding the sky with lilac as they walked to the holm oak at the crossroads, where they'd stopped so often to kiss and talk in their courting days. Now perhaps it would be possible.

'I have something to tell 'ee, John,' she said.

'Whatever it is,' he said, 'it must wait, for I can't abide it. Not tonight.' His shoulders were drooping with more than fatigue and his eyes were limpid in the half-light, almost as if he were about to burst into tears.'

'Why, John?' she said, torn with sympathy for him. 'What is the matter?'

'I'm a failure,' he said. 'A failure.'

'No, no,' she cried. 'You are not. Oh John, my dear, you are not. You must not say such things.'

'If locomotives prove popular,' he said, stony-faced with distress, 'and more railways are built, Mama means to transfer all our trade from coaches to railways. I have argued and argued against such folly, but there is no talking to her. Oh Harriet, I have spent my entire life perfecting the coach lines and now she means to undo all my work for a whim.'

'The railway is an oddity,' she said. 'It can only run where there are rails to run upon and I have only seen one set of rails.

Why, it is hardly more than a toy. I do not think you need to fear it.'

'Mr Chaplin has bought shares in four different railways, ' he said. 'And Mama has too. It is the end of everything, I know.'

'Even so,' Harriet tried to comfort. 'The coaches run everywhere and with great success. Oh my dear, dear John, you mustn't be dismayed.'

'I started planning how to send papers along the coach routes when I was little more than a boy. Fourteen years ago, it was. I was nineteen, Harriet, and I've spent every working minute since then perfecting the system. And now she means to wreck it all and she won't listen to me.'

His face and his voice were both so anguished that she put out her arms instinctively to hold him close, pulling his head down onto her shoulder, kissing his cheek, murmuring comfort to him as though he were an injured child, her confession forgotten.

It was the first time they had touched for many, many months, and the sudden sensation of being loved and held dissolved his misery like a charm.

'Oh Harriet, my love,' he said, 'you and Will are the only good things in my life. The only good things.'

'Hush, hush,' she said. 'The railways will fail. You'll see. Your mother will be proved wrong. I know it.'

'The only good things.'

'My dear, dear love.'

And he raised his head to look at her, and they were mouth to mouth in a kiss so sweet and long and full of pleasure that it took their breath away.

'Harriet! Harriet!' he said, holding her about the waist. 'Oh my dear, I love you so much.'

And she kissed him back, lost in the old familiar sensation of being loved, and she kissed him and kissed him, straining against him and loving him with all her might, kissing away his sorrow and her shame and all the long empty nights of their abstinence. Now, oh now, they would not fail.

They walked back to the house thigh to thigh in a deliberate unison that kept them as close as they could possibly be. And they kissed on every step as they climbed the stairs. And when they reached their bedroom and had locked the door safely behind them, he began to play their old, old game, slowly and with exquisite pleasure, as though they were courting, which, in a way, they were. 'If we were married, I would…'

'Yes, yes' — breathless with pleasure — 'what would you do?'

And so, moment by delicious moment, they moved nearer and nearer to ecstasy. And they were both strong in their passion for each other. And this time he didn't fail.

Afterwards, as he slept, oh so peacefully, beside her, his arm still flung about her waist, she remembered her plans. But they were unimportant. She had her own dear John back in her arms again. The confession could wait.

It waited all through the rapturous days and nights of that October and November. And it was still waiting when Christmas came, and the family gathered in Bedford Square for Nan's elaborate celebration. By now John was busily making plans to switch trade to the railways after all. For now that they were lovers again, somehow or other the certainty of change no longer looked like a defeat. On the contrary, it had become a challenge and one that he could meet with ease. He was so sure of himself again that Harriet simply couldn't bring herself to spoil things by introducing such sour news. She was happy in her pregnancy now, and when the baby quickened right in the middle of the Christmas Service, she was happier than ever. It seemed appropriate somehow. As though the child were approved of, despite the sin of its conception.

And in the end, it was John who spoke first.

He'd been watching her as she dressed for Christmas dinner,

easing the buttons of her bodice together because it was very tight on her now.

'Are you breeding, Harriet?' he asked, and the question was such a touching blend of curiosity, disbelief and hope, that she simply told him that she was.

'Oh, my dear love,' he said, looking at her with affection. 'A child from our reunion. What could be better?'

I should tell him now, she thought, as he held her and kissed her. But she couldn't do it. It would have hurt him too terribly.

So although she confessed her cowardice to her diary, the pregnancy continued unexplained and was accepted by every-body in the family with immense pleasure and unstinted congratulation. Everybody in the family, that is, except the Sowerbys. For Harriet could not bring herself to tell her parents. They might mock or lecture. Time enough to let them know of it when the child was born. By the spring her condition was very obvious, and the baby was kicking healthily, to John's delight and Will's very considerable interest, but she still said nothing to her parents. It had become a superstitious necessity. If they knew nothing of it, all might yet be well.

After Easter, she wrote to Annie to tell her that she and Will would be coming up to Rattlesden rather earlier that year, prob-ably at the end of May. The reason she gave was that she wanted to visit the grammar school, since Will ought to attend school soon and it might be sensible to send him with his cousin. But the real reason was that John thought the birth would be at the end of July, and she knew that the latest she could actually hope for was the beginning of June. An 'early' birth out in the country might just seem possible to him.

But it is folly, she confessed to her diary.

I know it is folly. When the child is born, the secret will be out in the world too.

If only she could stay pregnant for ever, never to change, never to see the tell-tale face of this child she carried, never to hurt her dear John or cause pain to anyone else, but simply to be held in this easy languorous expectation for ever and ever, like a fly made beautiful by being caught in amber, with John and Annie and Matilda and Nan all happily looking forward to a child they would never see, and her mother and father perpetually unaware of it, and John most loving and the sun always shining.

CHAPTER 37

'I hear you are to be made grandparents again,' Miss Pettie said, blinking as she stepped from the darkness of the Unitarian Church into the bright May sunshine of Churchgate Street. 'What a joy that must be to 'ee!'

Mr Sowerby was surprised and looked it, but his wife recovered quickly, frowning at him to alter his expression. 'Why yes indeed,' she said smoothly, 'although I wonder *you* have heard of it, Miss Pettie. We gave our word it would be kept *secret,* you see. Her father and I have known for…' she was going to say months but thought better of it in case the pregnancy had only just begun… 'as long as our dear Harriet, of course.'

'Of course,' Miss Pettie agreed, but she narrowed her eyes, and looked positively sharp.

Really, Mrs Sowerby thought, if I weren't an excessively charitable woman, I would think Miss Pettie was going out of her way to make mischief.

'Does she keep well?' the old lady asked artlessly.

'Oh yes, indeed.' Wretched girl. Why couldn't she have warned us?

'How you must be longing to see her again,' Miss Pettie went on, patting her curls. 'Miss Turnkey and I were so pleased to hear of her return. We were just remarking what a very long time it has been since we last saw her in town. But I daresay she has visited *you* already.'

'No, no,' Mrs Sowerby said, adopting a carefree expression and a rather vague tone. 'We've been uncommon busy these last few days, have we not, Father?'

'Oh yes indeed,' Mr Sowerby said, glad to be able to make amends for his initial mistake by supporting her now. 'Uncommon busy! So many commitments, you know, dear Miss Pettie.'

'Well, well,' Miss Pettie said, stepping towards her carriage. 'Pray give her my fond regards when she *does* arrive to visit you. Are you travelling my way, Miss Turnkey?'

Mrs Sowerby extricated herself from the rest of the congregation and went stomping off downhill with Mr Sowerby straight-faced and stiff-legged beside her.

'Wretched creature!' she said.

'Yes indeed,' her husband agreed, although he wasn't sure which of the two troublesome women she was castigating.

'She should have told us.'

Ah! It was Harriet. 'She should indeed.'

'I shall write to her directly after supper.'

But her letter, furious and immediate though it was, brought no response other than the usual vague greetings they'd been receiving ever since her last visit to them, which as Mrs Sowerby had pointed out in her opening attack, she knew *only too well* was as *long ago* as *last August*. There was no mention of a further visit.

We are all well, Harriet wrote, *and have been here for a little less than a week. Will is most attentive to his lessons, which I give him every morning, you will be pleased to hear. John will join us here in a day or two, having been in the Midlands to attend to business there. It will be a great joy to have him home again. I will visit you as soon as may be; I do assure you.*

Yr obednt daughter,
   Harriet.

'Obedient, my eye!' her mother shouted. 'Not a word about the baby, you notice. Is this the sort of letter a mother should expect? I ask you, Mr Sowerby, as a man of great good heart and Christian charity.'

'Very definitely not!' Mr Sowerby said stoutly, seeing that an answer was expected of him.

'Very well,' Mrs Sowerby said with tight-lipped determination. 'If the mountain will not go to Mahomet, Mahomet shall go to the mountain. That is all there is to that. We will hire a carriage — from Mr Kent, perhaps — he en't too costly — and we will set out first thing on Monday and *we* will go and see *her*. High time this was *out!*'

'A capital idea, Mother,' Mr Sowerby said, but adding, because he was a man of great good heart and Christian charity, 'Providing we don't anger Mr Easter, or old Mrs Easter, being she's such a dreadful woman.'

'I am so *vexed*, Mr Sowerby, I declare I don't care *who* I anger. Are we to endure *neglect* and say nothing? Are we to be *ignored* and not protest? Ho, no! That en't the size of it at all. Give me my umbrella, pray. I mean to hire the carriage here and now, so I do. Our daughter has gone to the bad, Mr Sowerby. We must seek her out at once and work upon her until she can see the error of her ways.'

And so the carriage was hired and the crusade undertaken.

Harriet was in the kitchen making apple comfits for dinner that night. She had planned a celebratory meal to greet John's homecoming, and apple comfits were his favourite dish. Her pregnancy was very far advanced now and she was slow and cumbersome and easily wearied, but she worked on doggedly, encouraging herself by thinking how delighted he would be when the comfits were served.

When Rosie came into the kitchen to tell her there were 'a lady and gent'mum in the hall', she tucked the last three comfits into their little dish before she wiped her hands and went off to attend to her visitors. Whoever they might be, they weren't as important as John's special dinner.

They filled the hall with their blackness, her father's stern trousers so long and his jacket so wide and dust-smeared, her mother's formidable black bonnet touching the beams. And their faces as black as their clothes. Harriet's heart contracted at the sight of them.

'Well, miss,' her mother said, snorting like a horse, 'we would appear to be just in time. Another day, Father, and this child would have been born and we *none the wiser* that it was even on the way. Not that I judge you, Harriet. No, no, I am too full of Christian charity to judge *anybody*. If you wish to keep your *very own parents* in the darkness of ignorance then that is your affair. You must consult your conscience about it. *I* cannot advise you, nor would I presume to do so. Although it is only right to tell 'ee that I *do* mark that Miss Pettie is informed of *all* your doings. I *do* mark it.'

'Would you care to step into the parlour, Mama?' Harriet said, opening the door. Her face was calm but her thoughts were seething. The child was *not* due to be born so soon. She would hold on to it for another *week*, at least. Another week and it could be born in June. Another week and it could be John's child. Oh, how could they come here, today of all days, saying such things?

'We have half an hour,' Mr Sowerby said, as he sat down stiffly in John's easy chair, 'so if you mean to serve us tea, miss, I suggest you set about it.'

'Rosie shall bring the kettle,' Harriet said, ringing the bell.

Then she opened the cabinet and began to set the tea things on the side table, swaying between the chairs, uncomfortably aware of the size of her belly. 'I trust I see you well,' she said, using the old formula automatically because she couldn't think of anything else to say to the two disapproving faces before her.

'And a lot *you* care of that,' Mr Sowerby said, 'when you leave us unvisited.'

'I have only just arrived here, Papa,' Harriet said.

'Not according to Miss Pettie you en't,' her father said, pursing his lips. 'But I see how it is Mother. *We* don't count. *We* are only her *parents*.'

'Yes, mum?' Rosie said, wandering in without knocking.

'Could we have a kettle of new-boiled water, Rosie.'

'New-boiled water,' Rosie agreed and wandered out again.

'Really!' Mrs Sowerby sneered. 'I wonder you still endure that foolish creature. I should have sent her packing long since. Great lummox!'

'Rosie is a good and faithful servant,' Harriet said, stung to her defence, 'and as kind as anyone I have ever known. A deal kinder than some.'

'A great lummox!' her mother insisted. 'Howsomever we en't come here to talk of fools.'

'No, indeed,' Mr Sowerby said, glaring at his daughter. 'We've more important matters in mind, en't we Mother?'

'It is our *sad* duty,' Mrs Sowerby said with immense satisfaction, 'to have to hire a carriage — at *great* expense I might say — and travel *all this way* to remind you of your simple Christian duty, which you appear to have forgotten.'

'No, Mama,' Harriet said, 'I do not believe I have.'

'Pardon *me*!' her mother said massively. 'Pardon *me*. You must allow me to be the judge of that. And if I say you have, then you *have indeed*, depend upon it. You may think that being married to an Easter puts you above all moral considerations. You may think that your wrong-doing is hidden and will remain so, if you are an Easter. But let me tell you, your sins are scarlet to a mother's eye!'

'We know all about your wicked ways, my gel,' Mr Sowerby said, taking advantage of his wife's pause for breath. 'There en't a thing hid from us. Not a thing. We know about your heartless decision, which you thought to keep hid from us, foolish creature that you are. Oh we know right enough. Don't 'ee think we don't.'

Heaven help me, Harriet thought, as their hateful words stabbed into her mind. Do they know about Norwich? Oh surely not! How could they know? And fear of them was a strong pain gripping her low in the belly. What can I say? Her mind was spinning with panic. Found out! Found out!

'You may think that refusing to visit *your own mother* was some kind of *protection*,' her mother went on. 'But now you know otherwise. Be sure your sins will find you out, Harriet. Oh yes! Be sure your sins will find you out.'

'I meant no ill Mama,' Harriet said, frozen-faced with distress. Found out! 'You must believe that of me. I meant no ill.' And she dropped her head because she couldn't bear to see the ferocity on her mother's face. How could she possibly explain?

'Good intentions are worthless without good actions,' Mrs Sowerby said sternly. 'Good *intentions* don't count. When you meet your Maker, my gel, and who can tell when *that* will be? — it could be *far sooner* than you think — you will be judged by the things you *did*. Depend upon it. Or the things you did *not* do.' And she gave Mr Sowerby a satisfied look. Now she knows, the wretched creature.

Pain stabbed again, gripping Harriet most cruelly.

'How right we were, my dear,' Mr Sowerby said to his wife, 'to come here and face her with her faults. We have been lenient with her. Too lenient altogether. I trust you now see the error of your ways, my gel.'

But Harriet was hanging on to the back of her chair, drooping forward and panting with pain.

'Come now,' her father said. 'None of that. Time for apologies I think, not play-acting.'

The pain held, too strong for speech, and too familiar to be denied. Even sight was impossible. It was the child. Coming now. Coming too soon. Coming on the very day her mother was here and she would tell John all about it. She closed her eyes, panting and counting, vaguely aware that her father was clicking his teeth with displeasure and that her mother was snorting. But neither of them were of any consequence now. The child would soon be born and the child would tell its own story. She could not escape her punishment any longer. Her mother was right. Her sin would find her out. Then she heard the rough stomping of Rosie's feet and the pain receded at last.

'What's this, my lamb?' Rosie was saying, bent forward in a clumsy attempt to see her mistress's face. 'What's this eh?'

'The baby, Rosie,' Harriet said. 'I fear 'tis the baby.'

'The babba,' Rosie said with awe and delight. 'Oh yes, to be sure, the babba,' And she turned to Mr and Mrs Sowerby. 'Hassen you off out of it, you two,' she said cheerfully. 'We got a babba to 'tend to.'

'So it would appear,' Mrs Sowerby said. How very annoying to be stopped in mid-flow like this. How inopportune. 'Well you just mark my words, Harriet. Baby or no, your sins will find you out.'

'Get Mrs Easter,' Harriet said, leaning on the chair again and closing her eyes as the next pain began to bite. 'Please, Rosie. Quick as you can. Get Nan Easter.'

CHAPTER 38

Nan had spent the afternoon at the rectory, building a treehouse for Jimmy and the girls. When Rosie came panting into the garden to say the babba was coming, she left all three children with Pollyanna, who was sitting in the porch with her baby, and walked straight to Harriet's house. She was just in time to see Mr Kent's carriage trotting off towards Bury with its two disagreeable occupants.

'Been here hours, mum,' Rosie explained. 'Upset Miss Harriet somethin' cruel they have! Somethin' cruel.'

'I don't doubt it,' Nan said. 'Well good riddance to 'em. Where is she?'

Peg Mullins had put her to bed and dispatched will to Bruges Cottage to fetch old Mrs Babcock, who besides being the village wise woman also acted as sick nurse and midwife when those services were needed. As they certainly were now.

Harriet was already flushed and pain racked, groaning as each new contraction took hold.

'Well now,' Mrs Babcock said, sidling into the room with her willow basket. 'I brought 'ee concoction o' motherwort, me dear. You try a-sippin' this. Brings a birth on lovely, does motherwort.'

But Harriet didn't want to bring the birth on lovely. She wanted to stop it or at least delay it and she fought it with all her might. So, despite its strong start, it progressed slowly.

Will spent the evening with his cousins in the rectory and to his surprise and delight was allowed to sleep there. And John came home to wait and worry as he'd done when Will was born.

'Is she well?' he asked anxiously whenever anyone came down from the bedroom.

But the answer was always the same and always unsatisfactory. 'As well as you'd expect.'

At midnight Frederick Brougham arrived in his barouche to see why Nan hadn't come back to Bury. They walked in the garden together for a few minutes, for Nan said she needed cool air.

'I shall be home by morning,' she promised, as the night breeze swished the branches all around them and owls hooted in the high woods. 'The child should be born by then.'

'We will breakfast together,' he said. 'I've to be in Norwich by ten.' He had a case, in sessions there.

'Depend upon it,' she promised, kissing him.

And so they went their separate ways, he to sleep and she to watch. But they didn't have breakfast together.

'She don't push,' Mrs Babcock complained when Nan returned to the bedside. 'I don't understand it. She should ha' been pushing long since. Why don't she push?'

But Harriet was still fighting the birth, even in this last and most powerful stage. 'Sinner,' she panted, her voice slurred with effort. 'Grievous sinner. Wages a' sin. Oh I mustn't. I mustn't.'

'Delirious,' Nan said, 'that's what 'tis.' And she turned all her attention to her daughter-in-law. 'Come you on, my dear,' she said, 'hold my hand. You shan't do nothing you don't want. You got my word.'

'Promise?' Harriet panted, opening her eyes.

'Promise.'

'I am a grievous sinner...'

'No you en't. You're a dear good girl and my John loves 'ee.'

'John...'

'Arrived, my dear. Down below. Don't 'ee fret about John. Come on now, give a good push. You'll come to no harm; I promise.'

And at last, and to Mrs Babcock's relief, Harriet relaxed and began to push. Forty minutes later the baby was born. It was a fine eight-pound girl, an exact replica of her mother but with a shock of black hair.

'Oh,' Harriet said, weeping freely. 'She's just like me. Just like me.' She was so relieved she paid no attention to the afterbirth which Mrs Babcock was pressing out of her belly. But the midwife did. She paid very particular attention to it.

'Just like me. Oh you dear little thing. Just like me.'

'With her father's dark hair,' Nan said. 'Shall he come in and see her?'

'Her father?' Harriet asked bemused. Was Caleb here then? No surely not. He was transported.

'Her father, your husband,' Nan said, grinning at her confusion. 'Have 'ee forgot the poor man?'

'Yes,' Harriet said. 'No. I mean...' Oh she couldn't face John with this child. Not yet. What would he say?

But Nan was already letting him in. And he said all the right things. Dear, dear John. 'A daughter, Harriet. What could be better? Now we have a pigeon pair. Are you well, my dearest?' Kissing her so tenderly, seeming to accept. Dear, dear John. 'What shall we call her?'

'Could we call her Caroline? After the poor Queen?'

So Caroline it was, and as soon as she was named the baby opened her big blue eyes and looked solemnly at them both. Caroline Easter.

'Now you must rest,' Mrs Babcock said, joining them at the head of the bed. 'Just drink another concoction for me, will you dear?'

'You must need your sleep too, Mrs Babcock,' John said when the baby had been settled in her cradle and Harriet had been tucked up for what was left of the night. He and Nan and the midwife were standing on the landing together looking at the first lightening in the dawn sky outside the window.

Her answer was rather alarming. 'No, no,' she said. 'I shall stay with her till morning, sir. The afterbirth en't all come away. Not just yet. I shall stay with her till morning.'

The words struck chill into both her listeners.

'We should send for a surgeon,' Nan said. ''Ten't a matter to be left. Tom shall ride into Bury directly.'

'Is there danger in it?' John asked, looking from one woman to the other. 'You must tell me the truth.'

'Mortal danger,' Nan said. 'And the sooner dealt with the better.'

'Motherwort should bring it away,' Mrs Babcock said, trying to soothe him. 'Howsomever, a surgeon would be wise precaution.'

So Tom was sent.

When Harriet woke the next morning, for a moment or two she couldn't remember where she was or what had happened the night before, although she knew in a vague sort of way that it was important and that she was happy about it. Then she realised that she was bleeding and she remembered her daughter and tried to sit up to see her. The rush of blood her movement caused was really quite shocking. Surely, she hadn't bled so heavily when Will was born? 'Mrs Babcock!' she called. 'Mrs Babcock!' Then she started to shake.

The midwife had been snoozing in the armchair beside the embers of the fire. Now she woke at once. 'I'm a-coming,' she said. 'Don't 'ee fret. I'm a-coming.'

The rigour lasted for nearly an hour and by the end of it Harriet was completely exhausted. 'What is it?' she asked. 'What is the matter?'

Mrs Babcock made professional light of it. ''Tis nothing, my dear. Many a mother has the shakes. That's the loss of the baby from your body as does it, that's all 'tis.'

But when Mr Brownjohn arrived half an hour later, he examined her belly for so long, prodding and peering and muttering to himself, and all with such an anxious expression on his face that she couldn't believe it was truly nothing. 'What is it?' she asked again, and now there was fear in her voice.

'Has your baby fed?' he asked.

'Why yes. Twice.' As she remembered very well because it had been surprisingly painful.

'I think we should wake her and you should feed her again.'

So the baby was woken and put to the breast, which didn't please her at all because she'd been sleeping very peacefully and wasn't ready for more food. Nevertheless Mrs Babcock insisted and after a fit of irritated coughing and sneezing, the little creature obliged them and began to suckle.

'La, but she makes my womb pull so,' Harriet said, holding the baby's finger. 'She's so strong. And just like me, aren't you my precious?'

But her two attendants were down at the other end of the bed, pressing on her belly. 'You hurt me,' she said. 'Must you hurt me so?' She tried to roll her belly away from them but she didn't have the strength to do it. I am very weak, she thought, and that worried her. 'Please don't hurt me so.'

'We have to hurt you, I fear,' Mr Brownjohn said. And told her what was the matter.

She surprised herself by how calm she was at the news. 'Then I might die,' she said. 'That is so, is it not?'

'We will do everything in our endeavour,' Mr Brownjohn said.

'Yes,' she said politely. 'I know you will, Mr Brownjohn.' And she began to shake again. 'Oh take the baby, pray do take the baby. I cannot hold her.'

They took the baby right out of the room, and they put hot bricks at her feet and a warm compress on her head and they packed her about with blankets, but none of it did any good. The fit went on and on and on. And when it finally stopped, she was too weary to lift her hand from the coverlet. 'Oh dear,' she said. Then she lost consciousness.

Downstairs, John was frantic with anxiety. 'What news?' he asked, rushing into the hall whenever he heard footsteps on the stairs. But they were too busy to tell him and their lack of response frightened him even further.

It wasn't until Nan came down that he managed to get an answer.

'She'll not die, will she, Mama?' he asked, when she walked rather wearily into the parlour and sat down beside the window. 'Oh please say she'll not die. They will save her, won't they?'

Tired as she was, she told him the truth. There was no point in dissembling. 'Mr Brownjohn says he thinks all the afterbirth is clear but he en't sure, and either way there's a likelihood of blood poisoning.'

'But what is he doing?' John said, bolt-eyed with distress. 'Surely he should be helping her!'

'There is little he can do, my dear,' Nan said, closing her eyes against his anguish because she couldn't bear to see it. 'If poison is in her blood, she must fight it herself. There en't a medicine known to man that's proof against this sort of fever.'

'She will not die,' he said flatly and he thought, she is too young and too precious and I love her too much, but these were things he couldn't say aloud. 'We will hire another surgeon.'

So another medical opinion was sought and arrived that afternoon and had to admit 'with uncommon sadness, Mr

Easter sir' that he agreed with his colleague Mr Brownjohn 'in every particular'.

'The testing time is the third day,' he told John. 'That is the point at which the fever will recede or take hold. If it recedes, we may nurse her to health again, with caution and good food and so forth.'

'But if it takes hold?' John said, his heart thudding most painfully.

'If it takes hold Mr Easter, sir, the prognosis is not good.'

'You mean she will be very ill.' Oh give me this little hope, at least.

'She will certainly be very ill, Mr Easter, sir. In fact she will be very ill indeed.'

'But we shall recover her...' John started to say.

But the surgeon was pressing on, telling him the worse, while his courage was sufficiently high for him to do it. 'In fact, Mr Easter sir, she might die.'

'No!' John said, and the sound he made was more like a howl than a word. 'No! No! No! She won't die. You are not to allow it.'

'John, my dear,' Nan tried, putting her hand on his arm. But he shook her voice and her touch away.

'It is in God's hands, Mr Easter sir, not mine,' the surgeon said, wincing to be the cause of such distress.

But even the sight of the poor man's face was more than John could bear now. 'You are dismissed, sir,' he said. 'Pray send me your account in the morning.'

Then he went upstairs to prove to himself that she was still alive and was fighting her sickness, that she would survive and become herself again and prove all their foolish predictions wrong.

SHE WAS HALF LYING half sitting, propped up among the pillows with her long hair combed over her shoulders, as straight and fair as flax. The curtains had been drawn to keep out the sunlight in case it disturbed her, and there was a candle burning night and day on the table beside her bed. It cast long, ominous shadows across her face, deepening the hollows under her eyes into terrifying pits, making her nose appear sharp and giving her skin an unhealthy pallor. She looked more than half dead already. He simply had to wake her.

He sat beside the bed and took her hand and gave it a little shake. 'Oh Harriet, my dear love,' he said, 'wake up. Look at me.'

She opened her eyes, very slowly, and focused with an effort, like a child puzzled by unfamiliar circumstances. 'Have I to see another surgeon?' she asked. The last one had hurt her poor tender belly so very much.

'No,' he assured her. 'Only Mr Brownjohn.'

'Ah!' she said and seemed to sleep a little.

He sat beside her, holding her limp hands and listening to the muffled sounds of the day outside the curtain. He felt so strong and so desperate and so utterly useless. If only he could find a way to transmit his strength into her weakness, down his fingers and through the palm of her hand, like new, strong, warm blood straight from his heart to hers.

She opened her eyes again. 'Am I very ill, John?'

'No,' he lied stoutly. 'You are weak after the birth. That is all.'

They both knew he was lying, he with anguish, she with the most tender affection. 'You are so good to me,' she said. And slept again.

'I'm off back to Bury for an hour or two,' Nan said, tiptoeing into the room to stand beside him. 'I shall be back at first light tomorrow.'

'Should Will come home, do 'ee think?' he asked. He was suddenly exhausted, incapable of making any more decisions.

'If I were you,' she said gently, 'I would leave him where he is for the time being. Let the third day pass.'

'Yes,' he said, looking at her thankfully. 'Yes that is best.' Let the third day pass. It would be cruel to let the child see his mother in such a state.

But as they were both to discover, even though he was only eight years old, Will had a mind of his own. That evening he decided he had stayed with Aunt Annie quite long enough. Despite the usual welcoming atmosphere in the rectory, he had caught a sense that there was something the matter at his house, a whispered conversation stifled when he entered the room, anxious glances flickered from Aunt Annie to Uncle James across the dining table, furtive comings and goings at the kitchen door. So that evening, when dinner was over and the cloth cleared, he told Uncle James that he was going back home, announcing his intention in tones so firm and irrevocable that he could have been his grandmother speaking.

Ten minutes later he was in his mother's bedroom.

He took everything very calmly, being curious rather than alarmed. 'Why is she ill?' he asked his father, looking down at his mother's flushed sleeping face. 'Is it the smallpox?' And when he was assured that it wasn't, 'Shall we catch it too, Papa?' And being assured about that too, 'When will she get better?'

'I cannot say,' John told him sadly. Then, in an attempt to persuade his solemn child out of the room, 'Would you like to see your new sister?'

'Not very much,' Will said. 'She's a baby, ain't she? I don't much care for babies.'

So Rosie was called for to put him to bed. He kissed his mother's clammy forehead and stroked her long hair with his fingertips. 'She will be better by morning,' he said. And he sounded so determined about it that his father quite took hope from him.

But the next morning was the beginning of the third day and Harriet was very much worse, with high fever and pain in her limbs and her belly so horribly distended she couldn't bear to be touched. And to add to her misery she had no milk and the baby had found her appetite, crying for food with lusty insistence, 'A-la, a-la, a-la,' on and on and on, no matter what the midwife did to placate her.

John was so distressed by it all he retreated into the parlour and covered his ears with his hands in a vain attempt to shut out the noise. Which was how Nan found him when, true to her promise, she came back to Rattlesden at a little after seven o'clock.

'Leave this to me,' she said at once. Getting a baby fed could be dealt with. And she went upstairs to deal with it.

'She needs a wet nurse,' she said to Mrs Babcock.

'Early days yet, Mrs Easter, mum,' the midwife said. ''Tis a matter of a-waiting for the milk to come in. Tha's all 'tis.'

'Waiting be blowed,' Nan said. 'Do 'ee know of a woman suitable?'

'Not hereabouts,' Mrs Babcock said firmly. Really the way this woman behaved you'd think she owned the earth and not just a newsagent. 'No, I don't.'

'Then I will find one,' Nan said equally firmly, dusting the palms of her hands against each other. Annie would be sure to know of someone somewhere.

Annie was in the rectory kitchen, helping Pollyanna and Mrs Chiddum with the breakfast. 'Mrs Barnes maybe…' she said.

'Or me, mum,' Pollyanna offered. 'I've milk a-plenty an' 'tis high time my Hannah was weaned. I could take the poor little mite for a day or two.'

'It could be for a deal more than a day or two,' Nan warned. 'You could be taking her 'til *she's* weaned too.'

'Is Mrs Harriet as bad as that, poor lady?' Pollyanna said.

'I fear so. And getting worse.'

'I'll ask my John,' Pollyanna said, 'If he's agreeable to it, I'll take her, no matter how long.'

And being as warm-hearted as his wife, he was agreeable to it, so the matter was settled. Baby Caroline was bundled into shawls and carried across to Mr Jones's house to be fed with such abundance that she slept for five hours afterwards, her little belly as round as a drum.

But helping her mother was a great deal more difficult. Towards noon Matilda and Bessie arrived, shocked by the news that a second surgeon had been called for and bearing a basket of dainties, calves' foot jelly, a baked egg custard and little cakes made of honey and almonds, because they were the only things they could think of to show their concern.

Ill though she was, Harriet was touched by their affection and did her best to eat a little of the custard, but after two mouthfuls she felt so sick she had to stop.

'I am sorry,' she said weakly to Matilda, 'when you are so good to me.'

'Hush, hush, my dear,' Matilda said, patting her hot hand. 'You ain't obliged to eat it, for pity's sake.'

'Where is baby?' Harriet worried.

'With Pollyanna being nursed. And you ain't to go a-fretting yourself. She's fine and fair and full of health.' Oh, if only you were too, poor Harriet.

'Yes,' Harriet said, glad of the information. 'Thank 'ee. Thank 'ee kindly.'

Matilda and Bessie and Annie and Nan took it in turns to sit with her from then on, sponging her face and hands when she stirred from sleep, offering her sips of water or the juice of lemons or raspberry leaf tea, standing aside when Mr Brownjohn made his daily visit, and all of them anguished by the fear that whatever they did to try to help her, she was gradually slipping away from them.

Now that the baby was gone and the room was peaceful, John sat by the bedside, too, and watched with haggard eyes, and said nothing. What was there to say?

And Rosie brought Will in twice a day to see his mother. 'There she is poor soul. Yes. There she is.'

And James administered the last rites and prayed with her and for her until she slept again.

And fifty-nine hours toiled past.

Towards evening on the fifth day of her fever, Harriet struggled out from a confusion of pain and foul dreams and knew where she was. Rattlesden, of course, dear gentle Rattlesden, where she belonged. Here in her bedroom, with the curtains drawn and the candles lit and dear John beside her, asleep in his chair. I must wake him, she thought, and tell him how much I love him. For she remembered that James had given her the last rites and she knew she was dying. Her mother had predicted it, here in this house. 'The wager of sin is death.' she'd said. Harriet could still hear her voice, but it was a distant sound now, and drained of all malice and all power to harm.

Death is painful, she thought. Pray God it may get no worse. But that was a foolish prayer, as she realised even while she was thinking it. Whatever was to come, she could not avoid it. It would have to be endured, whether she would or no. And she offered up another prayer more suitable even if it was only half formed: for the grace to endure. Then a merciful sleep washed her away from all thought into blackness.

When she woke for a second time the candles had burnt a great deal lower and John was gone. There was a quiet figure in his place writing in a black notebook set close to the candles. For a few seconds she couldn't think who it was. Her mind was stuck, unmoving and incapable of thought. Then with a sudden rush she knew a great many things and all at once. That the figure was Nan, that her diary was still under the mattress, that it would have to be destroyed, and quickly before it was too late.

'Nan! she said and the word was almost too hard to speak, her lips and tongue were so swollen. 'Nan!'

'What is it, lovey?' Brown eyes very close to her, full of tender concern.

'Under...mattress...' Then words so slurred and inadequate. Her right hand fumbling the sheet.

'Do 'ee want to sit up?'

'No, no.' Shaking her head.

'Do the bedclothes trouble 'ee?'

'No, no.' Clawing at the mattress.

'Under here? Is that it?'

Nodding.

And the mattress being lifted. How hard it is! Like a plank of wood.

'Is this what you want, lovey?' The diary, mottled red as though it were streaked with blood, and heavy as sin, held in the candlelight before her eyes.

Nodding. Struggling for words again. 'Burn it...please burn... John...not... John mustn't see it...please.'

Complete understanding in those brown eyes. 'Yes, my dear. Don't 'ee fret. John shan't see it. I give 'ee my word. I'll burn it directly if that's what 'ee wish.'

Hot tears, scalding her cheeks. Dear, quick, loving Nan. Does she know why? Doesn't matter now. Little matters now. John is protected. 'John?' she said.

'I'll fetch him for 'ee. He'll not be far, depend on it.'

Feet thudding like drums. Why is everything so loud? The door clicking. Feet on the stairs. Slipping into blackness again. Ah! Ah! I must stay awake for him. More feet drumming, drumming. Or is it my heart? Drumming. Drumming.

AFTER SHE'D CALLED John from the parlour, Nan took the red notebook down to the kitchen to burn it as she'd promised. The kitchen fire was little more than a pile of glowing embers, and certainly too low to burn through such a thickness of paper, so she would have to tear it to pieces first. She opened it idly, glancing at the first page before she stripped it from the book, and was intrigued by what she saw.

Monday 10th November 1817.
   Dear Diary...

Well of course, a diary. That would account for why she wanted it burnt.

There is so much I want to tell you I hardly know where to begin. Such a tragedy has occurred. The Princess Charlotte is dead and my husband John has put such a dreadful advertisement in The Times, but I must not criticise him. I will tell you about it.

En't that just our Harriet all over, she thought, dropping the loose sheet into the embers. She was afraid of her own shadow in those days, so she was. You should have told him straight out, my dear. I know I would have done. It don't help to hide things.

And she wondered what else her pale, quiet daughter-in-law had been hiding, and read on as she pulled the pages from the spine one after the other and fed them into the flames. It wasn't long before she came to the trip to Manchester and Caleb Rawson appeared on the pages. Then she realised why the diary had to be hidden from John, for it would never have done for him to know that his wife had been paying so much unnecessary attention to another man. What folly, she thought. And yet there's more good than folly in our Harriet. Her heart's in the right place, even if she do make mistakes. And she pulled three more pages from the book and decided to read no further. If this was the matter the poor girl wanted hidden, then so be it.

But the very next page she revealed was so smudged and tear-stained and full of corrections she read it despite her vow. And it was the story of John's sudden impotence and Harriet's bewildered pity for him, which she found so upsetting that she read on, until she reached the account of Caleb's seduction.

'My heart alive!' she said under her breath. 'Then the child en't John's.' And she wondered what he would do about it, and read on again, through Caleb's arrest and the daily anguish of Harriet's guilt to the sudden and rapturous account of her reunion with John and her decision to renounce her lover:

The moment he is free. However painful it might be to him, he must be told that I mean to stay faithful to my dear John from henceforth. But I cannot send such a letter to him now. That would be too cruel. Time enough when the trial is over and he is free again. It will be easier for him to accept such tidings then.

And how will it be for my John to accept your bastard child? Nan thought angrily. You en't thought of that. But then she remembered where she was and what was happening in that darkened room above her, and she was ashamed of her anger and ashamed of her curiosity and wished she had the power to 'put all right', as poor Harriet had yearned to do so often.

The book was dismantled now and most of it burnt and gone. Only the red marbled cover was left in her hands. She turned it over, looking at it sadly. And a small, much-folded sheet of paper fell out of it into her lap. It was a letter, written in a dark scrawling hand. Even before she read it, she knew it was from Caleb Rawson.

My dearest Harriet,

I am sentenced to transportation for seven years. This in great haste for we've no'but an hour afore they take us to t' hulks, and we've paper for one letter apiece, no more.

Be of good cheer. Come what may, I'll not heed it. I shall serve out term, and come back to England, depend on it. Then we'll make light of all and our enemies shall be confounded.

Thine, who will return,
   Caleb.

God help us all, what a tangled web! Nan thought, burning the letter and the cover together. And as she stirred the mound of grey ashes with the poker, a terrible wailing pierced the silence of the house, an unearthly endless shriek that made her heart pound and the hair stand on the nape of her neck.

She threw the poker into the hearth, snatched up her candle and ran to see what it was.

Feet were pattering along the landing above her head and as she climbed the stairs, she could see the flicker of carried candles darting like will-o'-the wisps ahead of her. She arrived in Harriet's room immediately after Will and Rosie, who stood in the darkness just inside the door with Tom and Peg Mullins behind them, gazing round-eyed and open-mouthed at the candlelit bed. It was John who was howling, kneeling at the side of the bed with his head in Harriet's lap and his hands clutching her waist. 'Oh, my darling, darling,' he cried. 'Come back to me. You mustn't die. How can I live without you?'

But Harriet could not answer him. Her struggle was over and now she lay still and peaceful, her face marble-pale, her blue eyes glazed and one dead hand still resting on his hair.

CHAPTER 39

They buried Harriet Easter in Rattlesden churchyard on an idyllic summer afternoon, while the young corn ruffled like green fur in the fields below the village and skylarks rose in rapturous spirals of song into the clear blue sky above their heads.

To Nan's surprise Matilda had taken full charge of the event, inviting their friends and relations, organising a supper, arranging flowers and even dealing with Mrs Babcock and the undertakers. ''Tis little enough for me to do in all conscience,' she said to Nan, 'and it helps make amends, so it does. I was uncommon cruel to her once, to tell 'ee true, when we were all first wed, and I regret it sorely now.'

So Nan handed over the entire affair and was thankful to do it. After that first terrible sorrow had kept them all awake and weeping until long after daybreak, and frightened poor little Will so much that he'd been sleeping in her bed ever since, she'd been torn with concern for her poor John.

His grief was so extreme it made all the others she'd ever seen or experienced seem mild by contrast. He had sat by Harriet's bedside for more than twenty-four hours, weeping and groaning and refusing to be comforted, with the curtains drawn and the candles lit and the smell of death growing steadily more and more oppressive all around him. Annie had tried to talk to him, and so had Nan and Bessie, but in the end, it was Matilda who had persuaded him out of the room.

'Come along, my dear,' she said, speaking to him as though he were no older than Matty or Will. 'Take my arm. There now. That's the way. No one will blame 'ee for taking a rest. I'm sure she wouldn't, when she loved 'ee so. Why you're so fatigued you can barely stand.' Which was true enough for he tottered as he walked, like an old man.

But although he allowed himself to be led to the spare room and, for all they knew, slept there for an hour or two, his grief was still extreme. From then on, he stayed locked in the room, neither eating nor speaking, but simply sitting beside the window, staring out at the village as though he were a stranger and lost. Which in many ways he was, for her death was a gaping void that had removed all feeling from his heart, all power from his limbs and all thoughts from his head, save one, and that was too unbearable to think, even though it filled his entire being. Oh, how could he live without his own dear love? What was the point of life now she was gone?

On the day of the funeral he got up and washed himself and put on the black clothes that Matilda had laid out for him, and followed the bier, his face expressionless with control. And when everybody else was weeping at the graveside he was silent, although Annie and Matilda sobbed aloud in one another's arms, Will burrowed his head into Nan's black skirt, Bessie covered her face with her kerchief, and Cosmo and Evelina stood hand in hand with the tears running down their faces. Mr and Mrs Sowerby made much of their grief, of course, dabbing at their eyes with two most ostentatious black-rimmed handkerchiefs. But John had no tears left to shed. His life was over. She was dead and buried and there was nothing left.

After the, service, Matilda's coaches carried them all off to Bury and her quiet supper in Chequer Square, which, as she explained to Nan, 'will take us all out of it, don't 'ee think?' But John was still silent.

'What shall 'ee do now?' Annie asked him gently, when the supper had been picked at and the Sowerbys were holding forth to the Teshmakers, and Matilda had removed Miss Pettie to the garden, because she had embarked on a long upsetting tale about how she made the match between John and Harriet. 'Billy goes back to London in the morning. Shall you travel with him?'

But it was a question impossible to answer. He had no idea what he would do. There was no point in doing anything as far as he could see. 'I cannot see,' he said dully.

'Perhaps you would rather stay with me for a day or two?' Annie suggested.

'Perhaps,' he said, in the same dull tones. 'It is of no consequence since I have nothing left to live for.'

'Come now,' Nan said, trying to cheer him up, 'there's always things to live for, John. It don't always seem so at the time, but I give 'ee my word there is. I felt much the same when your father died but see how we've all got along since. You have a son, don't forget.'

He roused himself to accept what she was saying and to answer correctly. 'Yes,' he said. 'I have a son.' And after a visible effort, he added, 'And a daughter, too. I must care for them.'

What strength of character he has, this son of mine, Nan thought. 'I always knew I had three fine children,' she said, putting up her arms to hold him about the neck, 'but I tell 'ee, John, you are the best of the bunch, my dear.'

He looked down into the open affection on her face and knew at last and in the unfeeling calm of his grief, that she loved him every bit as much as she loved the others. And he knew that he ought to rejoice at such a discovery. But rejoicing was beyond him. The most he could do was to smile back at her bleakly. But then she said something else which gave him the first glimpse of hope since Harriet died.

'And besides,' she said, 'there is always work.'

Yes, he thought, that is true. There is always work. There is comfort in work well done.

'I shall stay here in Bury,' Nan said pressing home her advantage, 'and look after Will and keep an eye on baby. In all likelihood I shan't be back in London 'til the autumn, so you will have to run the firm on your own. I see no reason why you should not take over full responsibility for our affairs. 'Tis time you were in charge.'

'Yes,' he said, and there was just a little life on his face.

'Here's Miss Pettie back from the garden,' Annie warned. Really the old lady should have more sense than to be telling everybody about their meeting. It was wanting in tact, so it was, and yet she was still at it.

'Time we were all off to our own homes,' Nan decided briskly. 'Shall you stay here with Billy then, John my dear?' And seeing from his face that he would, she went off at once to organise departures.

Cosmo was quick and discreet, gliding from the room with Evelina tucked beside him, and all Billy's subdued friends trailing after. And Miss Pettie went quickly, too, finally aware that she had overstepped the mark with her romantic story. But the Sowerbys tried to delay.

'What is to become of the children, ma'am?' Mrs Sowerby asked, instead of saying goodbye. 'Are they to live with their father?'

'I couldn't say,' Nan said vaguely. 'Time enough for all that later. Now John should be resting. He is grievously upset.'

'We will visit you again,' Mr Sowerby threatened, 'when I trust suitable arrangements may be made.'

'Yes, yes,' Nan said, shepherding them to the door. Couldn't they see they weren't wanted, wretched critturs?

And at last they went, walking off into the evening sunshine, stiff and black and disapproving, using their umbrellas as walking sticks.

'And let's 'ope we seen the last of 'em,' Bessie said. 'Nasty horrible pair.'

But they hadn't.

JOHN AND BILLY caught the early morning coach back to London, with the rest of their family standing about in the clear sunshine to wish them God speed.

'Where am I to go, Nanna?' Will asked, when the coach had turned out of the square.

'Why, you're to stay with me, so you are,' Nan told him, holding his hand firmly. 'You and Peg Mullins and old Rosie. And a rare old time we shall have together, I can tell 'ee.'

'Papa won't die in London, will he?'

'No. He most certainly will not. He'll write us a letter this very evening. You'll see. 'Twill be beside my plate by tomorrow morning. You shall read some if it if 'ee've a mind to.'

But his anxieties persisted, making him pucker his forehead and bite his lip like a pale copy of his mother. 'You won't die, will you, Nanna?'

'No, lambkin. I en't the dying kind. I shall live to see you married, depend on 't. Now let us go back to the house and see what Bessie has cooked for our breakfast.'

The letter was delivered the very next morning, just as she'd predicted. It was a very long letter and full of facts and figures which Will found rather boring, although he didn't think he ought to say so, especially as Nanna was so pleased with it. And there was another the next day, and another the day after that, and they were full of facts and figures too and even longer than the first one, so he didn't bother to do more than glance at them, which Nanna said was very sensible.

And so his new life in Angel Hill began to establish a pattern, with visits to Matty and Edward and trips to market and a very grand church on Sundays. Aunt Annie came to visit twice a week too, sometimes with Jimmy and sometimes with the girls, but always with Pollyanna and little Hannah and the new baby, who never seemed to do anything except suck and sleep but grew bigger every time he saw her.

'Ain't she jest a little duck?' Bessie said.

And he agreed that she was, although secretly he much preferred his cousins, who could talk and shout and run about with him and play all sorts of games once they were out in Nanna's garden on their own.

It was only the nights that were unhappy now, and they were still full of nightmares and the most terrible yearning to see Mama again. But he knew he could walk across the landing into Nanna's room if he felt too unhappy, and climb into her bed, taking care not to wake Mr Brougham if he was there too, and be cuddled to sleep again.

'Oh Nanna,' he would say, as she gathered his head onto her shoulder. 'I *do* love you. I shan't have to leave you ever, will I?'

'No, my lambkin,' she would answer. 'You won't. Not ever. Now just 'ee close up those little eyes and go on back to sleep.'

IN FITZROY SQUARE, John was wakeful, as he was night after night. By day work kept him occupied and removed the need to think or feel, so he stayed on in the office for as long as he possibly could, dining at his desk and sending out for various drinks whenever he realised he needed them. But even when he stayed in the Strand until the early hours of the morning, there was still the rest of the night to be got through and got through alone.

The house was excessively quiet, for even by day the servants spoke in whispers whenever he was near them and crept about as though they were afraid of their own footfall, and in the long bleak watches of the night the silence was total. He took to wandering about the empty rooms, remembering how she had sat in that particular chair, or stood beside that window, or written letters at that desk. And it didn't seem possible that she would never do any of those things again.

At night he could weep unseen, and rage against the God who had allowed her to die so young and curse the world for continuing when she was gone. And when he had suffered to exhaustion he would slump to sleep in the nearest chair or fling himself down on *the* nearest bed, providing it wasn't his own, and there Tom Thistlethwaite would find him at six o'clock in the morning. He would cover his master with a blanket and leave him to sleep for as long as he could.

'Best thing, sleep,' he would say when he was back below stairs, reporting on the night's events to the rest of the household. 'I'll take up the cards presently and leave 'em for him when he wakes.' For every day brought a batch of calling cards and sympathetic messages from Harriet's friends and acquaintances, and Mr John was most particular about them, reading and answering every single one, for although it was painful to be made aware of how much she was missed and valued, there was comfort in the reminder.

But it was Sophie Fuseli's visit that was the most comforting. She arrived in the Strand late one afternoon when a soft rain was obscuring the view from John's office window.

'Oh my dear,' she said, kissing his cheek in greeting, 'what can I say to 'ee? How you must miss her.'

'Yes,' he said, choking back his emotion.

'Put her portrait where you will see it every day,' Sophie advised. 'There's a deal of comfort in a portrait.'

'I do not have a portrait, Mrs Fuseli,' he said gruffly. 'We never commissioned one.'

'Then you must do so at once,' Sophie said. 'And I know just the man. Shall I send him to 'ee? You've but to say the word.'

So the word was said and the painter sent. He turned out to be a quiet sympathetic man who lived just around the corner. He told John he had seen 'your pretty wife' at the opening of the Regent's Canal, 'besides a-coming and going hereabouts' and added that he would be only too happy to paint her portrait if Mr Easter would be so kind as to correct him when it came to 'the likeness'.

So a tailor's dummy was brought into the drawing room and adjusted for size and stance until it was as slender and straight as Harriet had been herself. Then it was dressed in her favourite blue and white gown and given a parasol to hold in one china hand and a glove to wear on the other and the artist set to work.

For three weeks he toiled and observed and remembered, taking such pains over every detail and working with such tender concern that his canvas soon became the focal point of the house. Now John came home every afternoon to see how it was progressing and to give his advice over the shape and colour of the emerging face, 'her nose a little longer, so,' 'her blush rather nearer to the colour of apricots I think.' 'Yes. Her hair was so fair, fairer than any I have ever seen.' Until one miraculous afternoon when he arrived home to find that the painted eye had been given light and life and that his beautiful Harriet was looking straight at him out of the greenish-grey shadows behind her.

It gave him a shock, but there was pleasure as well as pain in the emotions that raced through his mind and made his heart throb and his eyes sting with tears. 'Oh my darling,' he said. 'You are not gone for ever.' And then he had to sit down, because his legs were suddenly no support to him at all.

He hung the completed portrait in his bedroom, where it would be the first thing he would see when he woke in the morning and the last to ease his misery before he slept. The painted figure glowed like moonstone against the warm red of Harriet's chosen wallpaper and wherever he was in the room her loving eyes seemed to follow and watch over him. The comfort it brought him was quite extraordinary.

And then just as he was beginning to sleep without nightmares, a letter arrived from his mother to warn him that the Sowerbys were out to make trouble. She enclosed a letter from them in which they demanded to be told 'if any arrangements for the *upbringing* and *education* of Harriet's two children has been taken in hand, it being *imperative* that they should both know *as soon as possible* what plans are being made for them.'

He looked from their black underscoring to the pale patience of their poor dead daughter and made up his mind at once. Billy could care for the company for a day or two while he went to Bury to look after his children.

He took a seat on the next available coach and arrived in Angel Hill just as Will and Nan were eating their supper. 'We will see them,' he said, 'and settle all this for good and all.'

'Yes,' Nan said grimly. 'We'll all see 'em. Now then, Will, eat up sharpish. We've preparations to make. Grandpa and Grandma Sowerby are a-coming.'

'What for?' he asked fearfully.

'Well now, my dear, as to that, we shall see.'

POOR WILL WORRIED about it for the next two days. What if they were coming to take him away? Their letter had said, 'upbringing and education of Harriet's two children'. He knew because he'd looked. Did that mean they were going to bring him up? Oh he couldn't bear that. It would be terrible. But Nanna had promised he should stay with her for ever. And Nanna always kept her promises. So perhaps they weren't coming for him. Perhaps they only wanted the baby. And if that were the case, everything would be all right. They could have the baby and welcome. It wasn't a bit interesting. And it was only a baby.

Even so, when Thursday afternoon arrived bringing Pollyanna and Hannah *and* the baby, and he was sat on the low stool in the parlour, between Nan's blue chair and his father's black one to await his other grandparents, his heart was beating so violently it was making his jacket tremble.

'They're 'ere!' Bessie said, peering round the door. 'Bold as brass if you please. The nerve of 'em!'

'Show them up, Bessie,' Nanna said. 'Tell Pollyanna I'd be obliged if she'd bring baby down. Sit up nicely, there's a good boy, Will.'

He obeyed, taut with apprehension, sitting bolt upright on the stool, his pale hands spread like lilies against the grey cloth of his trousers. Grandma and Grandpa Sowerby! It chilled him to the marrow just to think of them.

They were in the doorway, smiling their horrible false smiles, expecting to be kissed. Grandma Sowerby's nose was longer than ever and there were three new bristles on her chin. Oh I can't go and live with her, Nanna. You mustn't let me!

'Well now,' Nanna was saying, 'I believe you wished to speak to me on the matter of the upbringing and education of these two children. That was the case, was it not?'

Papa was sitting very still in his black chair, not saying a word.

'Indeed it was, ma'am,' Mr Sowerby said, folding his hands across his waistcoat and considering them thoughtfully. 'High time, ma'am. High time. So many children go to the bad these days, ma'am. We must do all in our power to ensure that these two unfortunate little ones do not number among them, must we not?'

'The boy is already entered for the grammar school,' Nan said smoothly, 'as I daresay you know, since it was Harriet's doing. Did you have another establishment in mind?'

'No, no,' Mr Sowerby hastened to assure, glancing at Papa, who still didn't say anything. 'I am sure his *academic* education could quite safely be left in the hands of *that* establishment. It has an excellent reputation. Howsomever, his *moral* education is another matter. Oh yes, quite another matter indeed.'

'And into whose hands would 'ee suggest that we commit that?' Nan asked, smiling just a little too sweetly.

'Well now, ma'am,' Mrs Sowerby said, 'as to that, it would appear to me that we should endeavour to find *two persons* of the *highest* and most *Christian* sensibilities, who would make it their life work — I think I may safely say that — their life work to foster the very *highest moral tone* in both these unfortunate children.'

'Such as yourselves, for instance,' Nan smiled.

'Well,' Mrs Sowerby preened, 'if you say so. We *are* peculiarly well qualified in this regard.'

She can't mean it, Will thought, beginning to panic. She's not going to make me live with Grandma Sowerby. Not after her promise. And he tried to catch Nanna's eye and couldn't do it.

'Do tell me,' she was saying calmly, 'do 'ee have a moral code, Mr and Mrs Sowerby? A set of precepts, perhaps, by which you would ensure that no child in your care would ever go to the bad?'

'Ho, indeed we do,' Mr Sowerby said. 'Spare the rod and spoil the child you know.'

'So the children will be beaten if they are placed in your care?'

Oh no, no. Please, Nanna.

'Of course. Whenever it is necessary.'

'As you beat your daughter?' Papa said suddenly and his voice was as cold as ice.

Mr Sowerby showed a flicker of surprise at John's sudden intervention, but he answered stoutly, 'Chastisement is a necessary part of correction, sir. All children need chastisement.'

'You will lock these children in dark rooms, I daresay?' Papa went on.

'When they require such treatment.'

No, no.

'And feed them on a diet of bread and water?'

'When it is necessary, yes, indeed we would. Children have such tempestuous spirits. They are like wild horses, sir, like wild horses. They need a deal of taming.'

Papa please, look at me. I don't want to be tamed like a horse. Nanna, say something!

'As you tamed, Harriet?' Nan mused, looking at Mr Sowerby sharply.

'In *my* opinion,' Mrs Sowerby put in, sensing criticism, 'we were altogether too lenient with Harriet. We should have dealt with her with far greater severity.'

'That's as may be, my dear,' Mr Sowerby said, feeling that they were getting side-tracked and that he ought to change direction while he could. 'Howsomever, we did not come here this afternoon to discuss our Harriet. We came to settle the future of these two poor unfortunate little ones. But there you are, Mrs Sowerby, perhaps we are wasting our time. Perhaps Mrs Easter does not intend to allow us our rights in this matter.'

'On the contrary,' Nan said, grinning at him. 'I have every intention of allowing everybody's rights in the matter.'

They were both very surprised and looked at it.

'What 'ee both seem to have forgot,' Nan went on, 'is that others have opinions too.'

'Others?' Mrs Sowerby said.

'Others, ma'am. The children. Will and Caroline.'

'Caroline is a babe-in-arms, ma'am.'

'But Will has a mind of his own. Don't 'ee, my lambkin?'

'Yes, Nanna.'

'So Will shall tell us. Would 'ee like to go and live with Grandpa and Grandma Sowerby?'

'No, Nanna. I would not.'

'And what of your sister? Should we let her go, do 'ee think?'

Will looked across to where the baby was lying in Pollyanna's arms, holding onto her forefinger with its entire fist. She looked very small and soft and vulnerable. 'She is my sister,' he said, understanding what he meant as he was saying the words. 'No, Nanna. She mustn't go.' He couldn't allow her to be beaten and starved and locked in dark rooms. 'She is my sister and I love her.'

'Well that's settled then,' Nanna said, dusting the palms of her hands against each other, swish, swish. 'The children stay with me. I wish you good day, sir. Good day, ma'am.'

'If you imagine for *one* moment,' Mrs Sowerby said furiously, 'that we intend to allow this matter to be settled on the word of a *child*, you are very much mistaken. A *child*! I never heard of anything so preposterous. I shall take this to the highest court in the land.'

'Where you will be roundly defeated, ma'am. Good day to 'ee,' Nan said, holding open the door.

'We are well and away the best people to be entrusted with the care of these children,' Mr Sowerby said fiercely, 'as any magistrate would allow. When you consider how we brought up their mother...'

'Oh yes?' Nan said acidly. 'And how would 'ee describe her manner of upbringing, pray?'

To Will's amazement, Papa suddenly sprang up out of his chair and strode across the room. His face was so angry that for a few wonderful seconds Will thought he was going to pick Grandpa Sowerby up by the scruff of his neck and throw him out of the window.

'Short of killing her,' he said, 'I don't see how you could have treated my poor wife any worse than you did. Except that now I come to think of it, I'm not at all sure you haven't done something every bit as bad. You took away her will to live, dear gentle creature that she was, and that amounts to much the same thing. I don't forget your visit to her when this baby was being born, nor how badly you treated her then. And I certainly don't forget any of the dreadful things you did to her when she was a little more than a child. You beat her, sir. You starved her. You locked her in dark rooms. You ought to be ashamed of yourselves, the both of you, not strutting round here demanding another child to torment. You haven't an ounce of love in your natures.'

He was so splendid in his anger that Will was lost in admiration for him, for he knew now, and beyond any doubt, that his father would love him and protect him, always and always, and never let him go to anybody else, no matter what might happen.

Mrs Sowerby sucked in her breath with fury. 'Do 'ee accuse us of killing our own very own daughter?' she said, her voice rising in disbelief and anger.

'Have a care, sir,' Mr Sowerby blustered. 'We could take 'ee to court for such unseemly utterances.'

'And have your wrong-doing emblazoned in every newspaper in the land?' Papa mocked. 'Oh, I think not. You are not such fools as that.'

'Aaagh!' Mrs Sowerby shrieked, flinging herself backwards onto the carpet. 'Now I've took a fit! Look! Look! See how ill you make me!' And she began to writhe about, arching her back and groaning. 'Did I not tell 'ee t'would come to this?' she asked her husband.

'Now see what you've done!' Mr Sowerby said, with great satisfaction as the shrieking and frothing progressed.

'I'll soon have her cured of that,' Nan said. 'Don't 'ee fret.' And she stepped round the body and strode to the door. 'Rosie!' she yelled above the din. 'Rosie! Jug! Quick as you can!'

Rosie was so quick she must have been hiding just round the corner. She was in the room before Nan had stopped shouting, and she'd brought the jug, which was the biggest ewer in the house. It was full of water and so heavy it was making her stagger.

'Thank 'ee,' Nan said. And she took the jug and balanced it on her hip. 'You've played this trick for the last time, my lady,' she said, 'it might ha' worked with your poor Harriet, but it don't cut ice with me.' And she emptied the water all over Mrs Sowerby's writhing body, drenching her from head to knee.

The fit was cured at once. It was quite miraculous. The screaming stopped instantly. Mrs Sowerby gulped, sat up, and stared at her opponent with disbelief. 'I am soaking wet,' she said.

'And like to be even wetter,' Nan promised, 'if 'ee don't get up this minute and leave my house. Another jugful Rosie, if you please.'

'One for the lummox, eh Mrs Easter?' Rosie said happily. 'One for the great lummox, eh Mrs Sowerby?' And she went cheerfully off for fresh supplies.

'This is an outrage,' Mrs Sowerby said. But she stood up and tried to shake the water from her sleeves. 'Do something, Mr Sowerby. Or do 'ee mean to stand by like a post and see your wife insulted?'

But Nan didn't give him the chance to say or do anything.

'As to you, Mr Sowerby,' she said, standing right in front of him with her arms akimbo and the air of a woman who would knock him to the floor as soon as look at him, 'if you've any sense at all in that ugly head of yours, you'll be off out of this town on the very next stage. There en't a thing to keep 'ee here, either the one of 'ee, and I've took such a rare exception to 'ee both, I shan't be answerable for the consequences if you stay.'

'You cannot tell us where we are to go, ma'am,' Mr Sowerby began, but then Rosie came staggering back with the second ewer, and he decided it would be politic not to provoke. 'Howsomever...'

'You got two seconds to be out of my house,' Nan warned,

taking the jug from her grinning servant, 'or damn if I won't drown the pair of 'ee.'

'We leave under protest, ma'am,' Mr Sowerby said, but he was walking towards the door.

'You may leave how you please,' Nan said. ''Tis all one to me, so long as you leave. Show 'em the door, Rosie.'

But they knew where the door was and stalked through it, Mrs Sowerby dripping water as she went, and they paid no attention when it was shut after them. Their feet clumped down the stairs, the front door opened and shut. They were gone.

'Jolly good riddance!' Bessie said.

Will and Pollyanna ran to the window to watch them slink across the square, for now that the drama was nearly over and they were all quite safe, they could enjoy it to the full. Their rush woke baby Caroline, who opened her eyes and looked over Pollyanna's nice cushiony shoulder straight at Nan and Bessie and John.

'Pretty dear,' Nan said, admiring her. 'Just as if we'd let her go to be beaten and starved by those two varmints. The very idea!'

'How will she make out, I wonder,' Bessie said, stroking the baby's cheek, 'all on 'er own with no mammy?'

'How can you ask such a thing?' Nan said. 'With your Pollyanna to feed her and you and me and our dear John to bring her up and love her. We're survivors Bessie. She'll survive.'

SIXPENNY STALLS

BERYL KINGSTON

CHAPTER 1

'Mr Burdock looks just like Humpty Dumpty, don't you think so, Papa?' Caroline Easter said, grinning across the breakfast table at her father. 'All your dinner guests are jolly funny, aren't they, but Mr Burdock is the funniest. He's such a pompous ass.'

It was just after eight o'clock on a dark December morning two days before Christmas and the dining room was miserably cold, for snow had been falling steadily since two in the morning, and although the fire had been lit at six it was hardly giving out any heat at all. Their breath was clearly visible in the chill air, steaming before them with every word, and poor Papa looked positively grey. A little joke about one of his awful dinner guests would cheer him up.

But this one didn't. He sucked in his breath in that sharp, snorting way that showed he was cross. 'Caroline!' he rebuked. 'That is no way for you to talk about a gentleman.'

'Why not?' she said, fighting back at once. 'It's true.'

'It's unseemly,' her father said, two deep frown lines scoring his forehead. He was shocked to hear such words coming from a child, but he remained calm, because he was always calm. It was

567

important to him to be in total command of himself and his situation. He was renowned for it, Mr John Henry Easter, Managing Director of the great firm of A Easter and Sons – Newsagents, the man in command. 'Come now, I cannot allow you to say unseemly things at my breakfast table. You are ten years old, miss, not a baby. Make some effort to behave yourself properly, if you please.'

'I *always* behave myself properly,' Caroline said, determined not to be put down by his stern tone, 'I am an Easter.' She was very proud of being a member of the great Easter family, and now, sitting opposite her father on the other side of his fine oak table, she certainly looked it, for her face was bold with defiance.

'Then pray try to act like one,' her father said. 'You should know by now that you cannot say whatever you please. As an Easter you should exercise a little more decorum.' If only she could have been more like her dear dead mother; if only she could listen to him patiently now and then and admit her faults instead of arguing back all the time. These constant battles were very wearing.

'I *do* exercise decorum,' Caroline said. 'I do too.' Her voice rang sharp as cut-glass in the chill of the room. Really, Papa was being quite ridiculous to make such a fuss over a little joke. Her grandmother would have laughed out loud at it.

'It is neither decorous nor kind to describe any gentleman as a pompous ass,' her father said, frowning at her, 'and certainly not this particular gentleman. Mr Burdock owns some of the most popular newspapers ever published in this city. He puts a deal of trade the way of Easter & Sons. He ain't a man to be mocked.' And yet he *was* pompous. The child was right. As she so often was, in that alarmingly forthright way of hers. It made correcting her extremely difficult.

'I don't mock him, Papa,' Caroline said, sticking her chin into the air. It was such an abrupt, determined movement it made her dark ringlets bounce against her cheeks. 'He doesn't know what I said about him. Nobody heard me except you. So how could I be mocking him?'

'That is not the point,' John Easter said, maintaining his calm with considerable effort, because her defiance was so provocative. 'Nobody should have heard you at all. It isn't the sort of thing a well-bred young lady would ever say.'

Her answer was immediate and infuriating. 'Nan says it.' Nan was her grandmother, who had brought her up ever since she'd been a tiny baby. Dear Nan, who took her to fairs and pleasure gardens and water sports, and played all sorts of marvellous games with her, when she wasn't in London overlooking the business, and treated her to pretty clothes, and a pony all of her own to ride about town, and two shelves full of books to read whenever she wanted. She adored her grandmother and missed her passionately whenever they were required to spend time apart. In Nan's nice warm dining room in Bury they both said all sorts of things about all sorts of people and nobody ever said they were rude or indecorous. They only laughed. Sometimes Nan would say, 'My heart alive, you *bad* crittur!' but always in tones of pure affection and approval. So why couldn't Papa be the same? After all, he *was* Nan's son, so he ought to resemble her, in one or two things at the very least.

'Yes,' her father sighed. 'I daresay she does.' The great Nan Easter was always saying things that would have been better left unsaid. Sometimes he wondered whether it had been altogether wise to allow her to bring up his two children after Harriet died. It had seemed the obvious solution at the time and Will had flourished in her care, but Caroline was becoming increasingly and infuriatingly independent, pitting her will against his on every single visit. 'I daresay she does.'

'Then I don't see why I shouldn't,' the child persisted.

'Because you are a young girl and she is a very old lady,' he

569

explained, trying to be patient with her. 'Because she is your grandmother and the founder of the firm, and you are not. Because people make allowances for her, considering who she is, which they certainly wouldn't do for you. All of which you know perfectly well, so I wonder you argue about it.'

'I don't argue,' Caroline said defiantly, feeling rather put down by the weight of all this evidence. 'I made an observation, that's all. Miss Murphy says observation is the cornerstone of education.' Miss Murphy was her governess in Bury. 'Am I not to make an observation, Papa?' She looked straight at him across the table, grey eyes flashing, daring him to disagree with her.

'No, you are not,' he said, anger gathering in him despite his control. 'And especially in company.' When she defied him like this she looked like a goblin, indeed she did, dark and swart and glowering, despite her fashionable ringlets and that expensive woollen dress. That was his mother's doing too, he thought, scowling at it — rose-pink and cream checks overprinted with scarlet flowers for a ten-year-old! No wonder she gets above herself sometimes. 'If that's the sort of observation you intend to make, you had better remain silent.'

'How long for?' she asked, and the question was a challenge.

'For as long as I say,' he told her, ruffled despite himself.

'All day?'

'All day if need be.'

'Am I to remain silent when I come down to meet your dinner guests tonight?' the child asked. 'They'll think that *very* odd. I always talk to your dinner guests.'

She is deliberately provoking me, John thought, looking at her bold face. Why must she do it? There is no need to drag this quarrel into the evening. Why can't she accept that she is wrong, apologise, and have done with it?

'If you wish me to,' he said coldly, 'I will explain to them that you are in disgrace for ill-mannered behaviour and not allowed to speak to anyone in consequence. How would you like that?'

She wouldn't like it at all, and they both knew it, but she had no intention of admitting it and allowing him the victory. 'As you please,' she said calmly. ''Tis all one to me. I'll come down and sit mum as a statue if that's what you really truly want. But they'll all think it jolly peculiar, I can tell you.'

'Well,' her father said, trying to rescue them both from their impasse, 'we will see about that when the time comes.' She might be more amenable by eight o'clock in the evening. 'Come now, eat up your breakfast and let us have no more of this.'

Caroline put a forkful of bacon into her mouth and grimaced. 'It's gone cold,' she said.

'And whose fault is that?' he asked, speaking mildly and trying to tease her a little, in the hope that this time she could admit error and grow more reasonable.

It was a vain hope. 'Not mine,' she said coolly, looking him straight in the eye, daring him again. '*I* didn't start all this.' She had joined battle with him and there was no backing down. If he was going to insist on silence when she was supposed to be talking and everybody would expect her to be talking, then she would fight him to the end.

He was suddenly annoyed beyond patience. 'Enough!' he said, and now there was no mistaking the authority in his voice, nor the anger. 'I cannot endure any more of your rudeness, Caroline. You have been rude to Mr Burdock and now you are being rude to me. You will go to your room, miss, and stay there until you are in a better frame of mind and ready to apologise.'

'Very well, Papa!' she said calmly. And she folded her napkin very very slowly and with the most aggravating precision, laid it neatly beside her plate, glared at him and flounced from the room, red skirt swinging.

She even takes her punishment with a flourish, he thought, admiring her despite himself. She behaves as though *she* is punishing *me*. Which in a convoluted way she was. For despite her bad behaviour, he was excessively fond of her, even though he knew he would never have been able to tolerate her presence in his house all the time, and even though he looked forward to her visits with a mixture of pleasure and dread. She lightened the routine of a life that had become undeniably dull and unvaried since Harriet's death. And besides, she was a living reminder of her mother.

In repose she was very like Harriet, for she had the same heart-shaped face and her hair grew in the same attractive widow's peak in the centre of her forehead, but where her mother had been pale-skinned and gentle, with blue eyes and hair so fair as to be almost silver, Caroline was dark-skinned and turbulent, with eyes the colour of storm clouds and thick curly hair so very dark brown as to be almost black, and unlike her mother, she was very rarely in repose. She was a spring-time creature, that was the trouble, brightly coloured, strong tempered, quick and unpredictable, a creature of strong sunlight and sudden showers, and although the sunlight was warming, the showers could drench him with temper before he had a chance to prepare himself for them.

Sighing, he walked across to the fireplace to ring the bell for his man servant. She had taken away all his appetite, wretched child, he thought, as he positioned himself on the hearthrug with his back to the coals. Now he would have indigestion for the rest of the day. And the fire was giving out no heat at all. Even when he stood right in front of it with his heels on the fender and his coattails lifted high in the air he could barely feel any warmth at all.

'Ah, Tom,' he said to his valet, when the young man opened the door, 'I shall be leaving for the Strand in ten minutes. Is my greatcoat ready?' He was pleased to notice that his calm was almost entirely restored.

'Yes, sir,' Tom Thistlethwaite said, 'and yer gloves and yer muffler, what I've took the liberty a' laying out. And two rugs fer the carriage today, sir. Snowing like billy-oh it is. Sky's full of it. Can't be too careful, eh sir?'

'There's no heat in this room at all, Tom.'

'Leave that ter me, sir,' Tom said at once. 'I'll 'ave that fire going a treat by the time you gets back. Was there anythin' else, sir?'

'Ask the housekeeper if she would be so kind as to see me for a moment,' John said. There were last minute instructions for the dinner party to attend to before he could leave the house and set out for the comfort of his office in the Strand.

'She'll be with you in a jiffy, sir,' Tom promised, and went bustling out to make sure that she was.

Above his head, Caroline stood beside her bedroom window looking out at the falling snow and the white mound that was all that was left of the garden in the middle of Fitzroy Square. The bare trees were furred with whiteness and so were the railings, which looked coal-black through the curtain of falling flakes, and the cobbles below her were covered with such a thick layer of snow that they appeared quite smooth. She was shiveringly miserable at being treated so unfairly, and the cold air blowing in underneath the window and the depressing dowdiness of the bedroom were making her feel worse. I'm like a poor caged bird, she thought, a poor caged bird in a dirty cage.

There was nothing young and lively in the room except her and the fire. It had been a splendid room once, so people said, decorated in pink and gold and all ready for Will when he was born, but it hadn't been redecorated since, and Will was eighteen years old and up at Cambridge. Now the ceiling was ochre, and the once-pink fringes that edged the long curtains were an unpleasant dirty grey, and the wallpaper was faded to a dowdy monochrome, patterned here and there with a darker dirtier brown like old tobacco stains. It depressed her just to look at it.

Papa doesn't care about anything except his work, she thought

573

mutinously, watching him as he climbed into his carriage, stooping against the cold. He doesn't care about me or he wouldn't be so beastly. He doesn't understand how I feel, and he doesn't care. Only Nan understood, and Nan was miles away in Bury St Edmunds.

The thought of her grandmother brought a wave of home-sickness so intense it was like nausea. No, she thought, why should I stay here in this dull house and be shamed because I've spoken the truth? It's not fair. I was only trying to cheer him up. I'll go to Bury, that's what I'll do. I'll go to Bury this very minute. The snow was falling quite heavily now, the flakes swirling in such profusion she couldn't see the square, but it was only snow. She wasn't afraid of snow. She'd put on her warmest clothes and her embroidered mantle and her nice new boots and her fur bonnet and her fur muff and she'd go to Bury.

She was dressed in ten minutes and out in the square in twelve, having crept down the stairs while the servants were busy cleaning the dining room, and let herself out of the house so quietly that the front door gave the merest click. I am like a caged bird, she thought, thrilled by what she was doing, escaping from captivity and flying home to my nest. It was exciting and romantic.

But bitterly cold, for a sharp north-east wind was blowing straight at her across the square and the snow was falling so thickly that her mantle was studded with it in seconds. There was nobody else about, although she could hear the muffled sound of horses' hoofs and a carriage creaking somewhere just out of sight.

She tucked both hands into her muff and began to run, slith-ering a little where the snow had been flattened by earlier feet, but moving as quickly as she could, partly to keep warm and partly to get away from the house before somebody saw her. It was the first time she'd ever been out on her own in the London streets and she knew it was improper to be walking abroad unchaperoned and that her father wouldn't approve, and the excitement and release of it filled her with energy.

But she had barely reached the corner of Fitzroy Square and Grafton Street when she heard somebody calling her name. 'Miss Caroline! Miss Caroline Easter!'

She turned her head at once, fearful but ready to defend herself, and found that a two-horse chaise was scuffling to a halt behind her and that she was looking up through the snow into the eccentric countenance of one of their next-door-neighbours, old Mr Fazackerly, who claimed to be 'an illustrator, me dear' but according to Cook had never been seen drawing anything in all the time he'd lived in the square. He was sitting above her in the driving seat, wrapped in a dilapidated rug from his armpits to his knees, and wearing an ancient topper brimmed with snow. He looked even odder than usual, for his wild grey hair was so wet it was sticking to his forehead and his long nose was the colour of port wine and his horsy face was a peculiar greyish-yellow. But he turned out to be a friend in need.

'No weather to be out walking, me dear,' he said, taking out a large pocket handkerchief and wiping the end of his nose with a brisk movement to and fro as though it were a bell he was trying to ring. 'And all on your own too. Where are you off to? I'm on me way to the city to see about a commission so I am. Can I give you a lift?'

'I'm going to Ludgate Hill, to the Belle Sauvage,' she told him, 'to catch a coach to Bury.'

'To meet your father, doubtless,' he said. 'Bury for Christmas, eh.' And when she didn't deny it, 'Hop aboard. I'll have you there in a jiffy.'

Which he did, or if not in a jiffy, at least in commendable time given the state of the roads and the age of his horses. 'What luck I was passing, eh?' he said as they creaked along Tottenham Court Road. 'Pull that rug right up under your chin, me dear.'

And when they reached the entrance to the coach yard, he helped her down most gallantly, as though she were a princess, and wished her 'Bon voyage!' before he creaked off into the snow again.

Now *that* was the proper way to treat an Easter, Caroline thought, as her boots touched the snow. Dear Mr Fazackerly. He's an omen, that's what he is, a good omen, a sign that this will be a great adventure. And she went trotting off to the booking office, which was full of bulky passengers and loud with argument. The clerk, who was small and sharp, stood his ground behind the counter like a terrier before a herd of buffaloes, barking to right and left that he couldn't make the coaches run, not no how, not he, and that he only had one pair of hands *if* you please gent'men. And the buffaloes snorted and grumbled and shook the snow from their thick coats and stamped their feet in the puddles they were making.

Fortunately Caroline was used to dealing with irate gentlemen. She'd heard enough of them bellowing in her father's house at dinner time not to be afraid of their noise. She pushed herself through their greatcoats until she was standing in front of the counter. 'I want a seat on the next coach to Bury, if you please,' she said.

The clerk stopped barking and smiled at her. 'Well now, Miss Easter,' he said, 'that's something I *can* manage, Bury being a different matter altogether by reason of there being no proper hills thereabouts, you see, what *some* people don't seem capable of understanding. On your father's account was it, miss?'

'Yes please.'

'Leaves in eight minutes,' the clerk said as he wrote out her ticket. 'Just nice time.'

And sure enough the Bury coach was ready for the off, with ostlers at the horses' heads and most of the passengers already aboard. There were three people inside and two bundled in rugs aloft. But, as the coachman was explaining loudly to two gentlemen in green top hats, there was no possibility of making a start while the Oxford coach was still blocking his way. 'He don't think a' the rest of us, not he, not that one. Stay here all day, we can, for all he cares.'

The Oxford coachman stood beside his bulky vehicle as though he were guarding a gate. 'I ain't a-taking no coach through the Chilterns today,' he said stoutly. 'I done it once, an' once is enough. You ain't seen the state a' them hills. It's a wonder we wasn't killed comin' through them hills.' He'd been complaining about it ever since he'd eased his snow-laden coach into the yard at a little after six o'clock that morning. 'Them roads is treacherous.'

Although there was less snow falling here in the shelter of the courtyard, it was foul underfoot, for the cobbles were awash with brown slush, horse dung and dirty straw. Caroline clambered up into the Bury coach at once, holding her mantle close to her knees to keep it as clean as she could. There was dry straw on the floor of the coach and one narrow seat still available squashed beside a very fat lady in a very damp cloak, and opposite two lugubrious gentlemen, one dressed entirely in brown and the other entirely in green, and both steaming like kettles.

'Just in time,' the brown gentleman said kindly, as the post-boys folded up the steps and shut the door.

'If they ever pluck up enough courage to make a start,' the fat lady said, 'which don't seem at all likely to me, I must say, Mr Grinder.'

'They are doing their best, my love,' Mr Grinder said. 'You must allow that, Mrs Grinder. They are doing their best.'

'Such a fuss about a little bit of snow,' the fat lady said. 'Such babies.'

'In all fairness, my love,' her husband murmured, 'it ought to be admitted that it is quite difficult to control a coach and four in bad weather, and this bids fair to be very bad weather.'

'Babies,' the fat lady said contemptuously. 'Blethering babies the lot of 'em. Give me the reins, that's what I say, and you wouldn't hear so much about snow.' She gave a splendidly derisive sniff and turned her attention to Caroline. 'Where do you hope to travel, my dear?' she said. 'Always allowing that they actually manage to get this coach out of the yard.'

'To Bury, ma'am, to my grandmother.'

'Who lives in Bury, I daresay?'

'Yes, ma'am. On Angel Hill. She is Mrs Easter, the newsagent.'

Mrs Grinder was impressed, as people always were when Nan's name was mentioned. 'I know the lady,' she said. 'By sight, of course. Mr Grinder and I live in Bury too, you know. A very great lady I believe.'

'Yes, ma'am,' Caroline agreed happily, 'she is.'

'Do you travel alone, my dear?'

'Yes, ma'am.'

'All alone?' Mrs Grinder said, swivelling her face towards the child and opening her eyes wide, like a plump barn owl.

'Yes, ma'am, all alone.' How thrilling to be able to say such a thing.

'There you are you see, Mr Grinder,' the fat lady said with great satisfaction. 'You see how the world changes. It is 1836 now, my love, and not the Middle Ages. If Mrs Easter the newsagent, who is a very great lady, will allow her own grandchild to travel alone all the way from Ludgate Hill to Bury St Edmunds, why then whether is possible.'

There was a commotion in the yard.

'Now what?' the brown gentleman said.

Caroline took her hand out of her muff and cleaned a little porthole in the steamy window beside her. 'They're moving the Oxford coach,' she said.

'Are we off then?' the fat lady said.

And off they were, their great wheels lurching through the

slush, echoing under the arch, crunching over fresh-fallen snow in the street outside, past Mr Sparrow's, the tea dealer, and Mr Parry's the shawl manufacturer and the Italian warehouse, off on the road at last.

Now, Caroline thought triumphantly, as the pole-chains clinked and the coach rocked from side to side, my adventure is beginning.

If you sign up today, you'll get:

1. A free historical fiction novel from Agora Books

2. Exclusive insights into timless fiction, as well as the opportunity to get copies in advance of publication; and,

3. The chance to win exclusive prizes in regular competitions.

Interested?

It takes less than a minute to sign up.

You can get your free book and your first newsletter by visiting

**www.agorabooks.co/
timeless-fiction-newsletter**